THE FIRST TERRORIST ACT

THE FIRST TERRORIST ACT

BY

HAROLD THOMAS BECK

The First Terrorist Act
Published by Mountain Laurel Publishing Corporation
P.O. Box 28, Custer City, PA 16725 USA

Copyright@Harold Thomas Beck, 2002

Cover and book design: Jonathan Gullery: jg@midcity.net

This book is set in Janson Text and Univers Bold

ISBN 1-929382-02-2
Library of Congress Card Number: 2001097795

This novel is a work of fiction.

FIRST EDITION: FEBRUARY 2002

DEDICATION

This book is dedicated to my mother,
Susan Ruth Beck, who taught a young man to survive.

ACKNOWLEDGEMENTS

The First Terrorist Act is a novel. It should not be construed as anything but fiction. To do so would be an enormous mistake. While historical personages appear in this work and take on their true historical roles against actual historical events, the portrayal is dramatized and is fiction.

However, not withstanding the fictionalized account, battles that took place in the First Tet Offensive are historically accurate to the extent that units that participated were properly identified. *Vietnam Order of Battle* by Shelby L. Stanton, Captain, US Army, Retired, was used as a verifying reference.

Certain reference material and explanations concerning TWA Flight 800 were obtained from *The Downing of TWA Flight 800* by James Sanders (Zebra Books, 1997). I acknowledge the work of Mr. Sanders and the fact he made himself a target for taking a stance opposite to the position of the government.

The writings of Mr. Richard M. Ruiz, taken from the Internet, provided historical insight into the man, Ernesto "Che" Guevara. Mr. Ruiz at the time was 65 years old and knew El Che. He states: "The El Che that I knew was a man of conscience, a crusader against injustice, oppression and misery. Ernesto was a man concerned for the poor, not a demagogue. He was a symbol of rebellion against hypocrisy, injustice, human suffering and a society without soul."

The story makes a reference to a report by Andrade and Conboy on Laos and the violation of Laotian neutrality.

Mr. Andradé is a Vietnam War historian with the U.S. Army Center of Military History, where he is writing a book on combat operations from 1969 through 1973. He has written numerous articles on Vietnam War-era special operations and is the author of two books on the war: *Trial by Fire: The 1972 Easter Offensive, America's Last Vietnam Battle* (Hippocrene Books, 1994), and *Ashes to Ashes: The Phoenix Program and the Vietnam War* (Lexington Books, 1990). Formerly an analyst with the Washington-based Asian Studies Center,

Mr. Conboy is vice president of Lippo Group, a large financial services institution in Jakarta, Indonesia. He is the author of *Shadow War: The Secret War in Laos*, as well as several short studies on special operations, including *The War in Cambodia* (Osprey Books, 1988), *The War in Laos* (Osprey Books, 1989), and *Southeast Asian Special Forces* (Osprey Books, 1990).

A time line of events leading up to September 11th was referenced in the story and was reprinted with the permission of Michael C. Ruppert and From The Wilderness Publications, www.copvcia.com, P.O. Box 6061-350, Sherman Oaks, CA, 91413.818-788-8791. FTW is published monthly with annual subscriptions priced at $50 per year.

Beyond those people and those works, I gratefully acknowledge my wife, Sharyn Walter Beck, who was my editor, critic, confidant, and friend through the tedious task of writing this book. Without her encouragement the book in its final form would never have become a reality.

Edna L. Habicht of Buffalo, NY, one of my oldest friends and my first mentor as a writer, was there at the very beginning when I struggled getting the first words down on paper. It was her belief in a young man that gave me the idea that I could one day complete this work. I acknowledge her with the deepest respect and gratitude.

Also there are Brenda Mallams and her husband, Rod, who were some of my first fans going back to an earlier version in 1988.

I also acknowledge a person I met only once under the strangest of circumstances. On a Friday evening in August 1976 in Lilydale, NY I attended an assembly meeting hosted by a male psychic. I was an incidental attendee acting as an escort for a woman I knew who wanted to see what it was all about. Entering late and sitting in the back, the man had occasion to pick the two of us out of a crowd of several hundred other people. Finishing with her, he turned his attention to me.

"I see you sitting with a large stack of papers in a bright yellow chair," he said. He got my attention immediately as I was writing the beginnings of this book and I had yellow vinyl furniture. "You are writing a book," he said. "And it is hard and you want to give up." He was correct. I did want to give up. I knew I would never be a writer.

"Don't," he admonished me. "I know it's hard. What you are doing will not be easy. It will take a long time for you to finish what you've started. Believe me when I tell you, you will finish. It will take a long time and it will be difficult. You won't have everything you want while you are doing this, but you will have everything you need. And in the end when you are finally done, then you will have the reward you are looking for. Don't give up."

I never lost those words. I didn't give up and now it is finally done.

Finally, I acknowledge the men and women who served this nation during the Vietnam War in whatever capacity and wherever they were ordered to go. It was a time when serving in the military was looked down on and those who returned were believed to be tainted. I acknowledge all of those who served as true heroes, just as those who serve today are likewise just as heroic.

CHAPTER ONE

SAN FRANCISCO, CALIFORNIA
SEPTEMBER 11, 2001

Charley Hayes was asleep when the phone rang that morning. He was used to it. The phone always rang early. This was the price he paid for the privilege of living with Alicia Masters. The phone calls always were for her. He rolled over and looked at the clock. The digital read-out said it was 5:52 a.m. Pacific Daylight Time. He rolled over again and tried to ignore it.

But that morning and that particular phone call were different. He could hear her talking. He could hear the sound of her voice. There was a distressed urgency in it.

"What are you going to do?" she asked.

There was something about the way she asked the question. It made him bring himself out of his state of slumber.

"I love you, too," he heard her say.

Then she said, " Don't hang up. Stay on the line as long as you can and talk to me. I'm going into the bedroom and turn on the television."

Charley woke up. Why was she turning on the television at six in the morning and with whom was she talking? He sat up and watched her walk into the room.

"What's going on?" he asked.

She waved him off and kept talking to whoever it was on the other end. "I have CBS on," she said.

Charley looked at the television screen. A large building was on fire. He recognized it. It was the north tower of the World Trade Center. Then he realized whom it was she was speaking with on the telephone. It was her twin brother, Jerry. Jerry worked there for a bond company and had an office on the 101st floor.

"Yes," she said. "I see it now."

"How are you going to get out?" she asked.

She stopped and listened.

"Don't say that," she said. "They can get to you. They can reach you with helicopters. Isn't there a heliport on the roof? Can't you get up to the roof?"

As she asked the question, it was clear she didn't get an answer.

"Hello?" she asked. "Jerry? Are you still there?"

She waited staring at the television. Thick black smoke was pouring out of a hole in the side of the building. Somewhere above the hole was her brother. He was her twin brother. He was her twin baby brother by two minutes. Their parents were dead and there was no one else but him. He was all she had.

Then she turned to Charley who was sitting up in bed. She turned to him with a shocked look on her face, fighting back the tears.

"Jerry is in there," she said. "He said he couldn't get out. He said it was a jetliner that crashed into the building and the fire is burning up to where he is. He saw it from his office. He said it was an American Airlines jetliner. He could see the markings on its tail."

She walked over and sat on the edge of the bed, but couldn't take her eyes off the television. Charley looked at the clock. It was five minutes after six.

As they watched, the unthinkable happened. Another jetliner flew into the television picture and crashed directly into the other tower of the World Trade Center. Flames shot through the building and came out the other side. They couldn't believe what they were watching.

"My God," Charley said. "What is happening?"

That was just the beginning. The phone rang again. Alicia answered it on the first ring.

"Jerry?" she asked frantically.

Charley realized it wasn't Jerry.

"Yes," she said. "I know. I have it on. My brother Jerry is in the north tower on the 101st floor. He called me. He said he saw an American Airlines jet fly directly into his building below him. He said there was no way to get out and the heat was becoming unbearable. The fire was burning up to where he is. Then the phone went out. The fire must have burned the trunk line.

"Okay," she said.

Charley could tell she was taking directions. Alicia was the west coast correspondent for a national news organization and was their eyes and ears in San Francisco and the entire west coast.

"I'll see what's available and get back with you."

She hung up the phone and looked at Charley. "My God, what's happening?" she asked.

"I don't know," he answered.

"I'm scared. That was Washington. They said there are two to four other planes still in the air that have been hijacked. They are saying the two that hit the trade towers came out of Boston."

"What do they want you to do?" he asked.

"They want me in Washington to man the desk."

Charley was used to Alicia being gone. It was part of the package. As much as he didn't like it, it was something he had to live with.

In the next few minutes, events began to unfold.

At 9:18 Eastern Daylight Time the Federal Aviation Administration shut down all aircraft takeoffs nationwide and shut down all New York City airports.

At 9:22 President George W. Bush in Sarasota, Florida called the crashes "an apparent terrorist attack" and "national tragedy."

Also at 9:22 American Airlines acknowledged one of its flights, Flight 11, crashed into the World Trade Center.

Then at 9:32 the New York Stock Exchange was closed.

Alicia tried to put her brother out of her mind but couldn't. She began to run a shower and broke down in tears. Hearing her crying, Charley went to her and held her. She sobbed uncontrollably, repeating his name over and over again. Charley turned off the shower and took her back to bed.

"You need to take a few minutes and get hold of yourself," he said.

Four minutes after the Federal Aviation Authority grounded all domestic flights, halting all flight operations for the first time in U.S. history, American Airlines Flight 77, en route from Washington's Dulles International Airport to Los Angeles, crashed into the Pentagon between the 4th, 5th and 6th corridors. The Pentagon began a complete evacuation. The plane carried fifty-eight passengers, four flight attendants and two pilots. The picture of the burning Pentagon came on the television moments later.

The President left Florida on Air Force One at 9:57 a.m. and three minutes later, at exactly 10 o'clock, the south tower of World Trade Center collapsed. Five minutes later, the White House was evacuated.

While Charley was consoling and comforting Alicia, he had no idea that how what was happening would directly affect him.

At 10:10 a.m. United Airlines Flight 93 from Newark to San Francisco crashed eighty miles southeast of Pittsburgh. In route to its rural resting place, the airliner flew over the house Charley grew up in. The plane was carrying thirty-eight passengers, two pilots and five flight attendants.

Like the rest of the nation, Alicia and Charley watched in shock and amazement. The events continued to unfold as the minutes passed seeming like hours.

At 10:13 a.m. the United Nations evacuated 4,700 people from its headquarters.

At 10:22 a.m. the State Department, World Bank and Justice Department evacuated their offices.

At 10:25 a.m. all international flights were rerouted to Canada.

Then at 10:29 a.m. the second World Trade Center tower collapsed. It was then Alicia sobbed, knowing her brother was dead.

It might have been that realization or it might have been the fact she was a consummate professional. Either way, for whatever reason, a strange calm came over her. She got up and took her shower and began to get ready to do her job.

The phone rang and she answered it. She listened and took down a few notes.

"Okay," she said. "I'll get back to you. I'll see what is available. If the airlines are grounded, they will probably stop the trains and busses, too. I might have to drive. That will take at least two days. I can make reports from the road as I cross the country. You know, give an insight as to what is going on in America in the face of a national disaster."

Charley listened and noted the immediate change in her. He had seen it before. She pulled herself together and went about her work. Then at a later date, she collapsed. Until then, she would have little use for him. All he could do is stay out of her way.

"Is there anything I can do to help you?" he asked.

She walked across the room to him. She touched his face and kissed him.

"No," she said softly. "Just let me do what I do. I love you. I just have to do my job."

He understood. He got up and made coffee. He stayed out of her way while she packed. He went out in the garage and opened the trunk of his car. It was a new Cadillac. He took his golf clubs out and checked the back seat. He took out a jacket and then checked the gas. The tank was full. He went back into the house. She was drinking her coffee.

"Are you going to drive to Washington?" he asked.

"Yes," she said.

"Do you want me to go along with you?"

"How can you do that?" she asked. "You have a business to run."

"I will if you feel you want me to," he said. "The business will take care of itself."

He already knew what she would say. When she said she appreciated the offer but felt it was better she go by herself, he handed her the keys.

"If you are going to drive, take my car," he said. "It's more comfortable than yours and it's new. It will give you good mileage and I'll feel better about you driving across the country if you are in it rather than yours."

By noon Alicia was on the road heading east to Washington, D.C.

Like every other American, Charley Hayes watched his television and realized life, as he had known it, had changed for all time. He thought back. He thought of when it had changed for him the first time. It changed then and he had not even known it.

Just as Sunday, December 7, 1941 forever changed the lives of his parents, so did another date, an obscure date, forever change his.

Franklin Roosevelt called the first "a date which will live in infamy." The second would prove to be just as infamous. The only difference was the President of the United States never reported it. He didn't because he was the one who perpetrated it. The date was August 7, 1964.

That was the date Congress, after an urgent request from Lyndon Johnson, overwhelmingly approved the Gulf of Tonkin Resolution.

Congress gave the President a blank check, which converted the Vietnamese conflict from a civil war to what was to become a major international conflict. Immediately, an American army of 250,000 men quietly began to be deployed. Forever the lives of Charley and his generation would be changed. In addition, the view of the American dream would also change.

That August day Charley cut the grass at his home. His father was the Chief of Police in a small suburban bedroom community south of Pittsburgh. His mother, a housewife, made spaghetti and meatballs for supper. He reminded his mother he was pitching in the evening against Munhall. To accommodate him the family ate at five as soon as his father came home from work.

He was in his baseball uniform and ready to leave for the game when Walter Cronkite reported the actions of Congress that day. He didn't pay attention to the fact only two senators dissented. Charley was unconcerned with world events. All he worried about was his game.

The game was under the lights and started at 8:15. The first pitch was hit up the middle for a single. He walked the second and the third batters and the fourth hit a sound double to left. Three runs were in and Ernie Bonelli walked out to the mound to take him out. As he walked from the field, he had no way of knowing how much of his life had already changed. No, he didn't know and neither did several million others of his generation.

He began college in September. In March of the following year U.S. forces began the significant buildup, which would ultimately cost sixty thousand American lives. By the summer of 1966, Charley was in the service and wearing the uniform of his country.

Along with his basic military training, he also had a flair for spoken languages. He was fluent in Spanish and managed to learn Vietnamese in less than a month.

That was so long ago and all of it was so far behind him. He seldom spoke of it and even when Alicia pressed for more specifics, he would evade her questions and politely change the subject. Early on in their relationship she learned that part of his past was off limits. He preferred it that way.

For most of the day he stayed glued to the television. He wasn't any different than any other American. Around two p.m. he heard from Alicia. She called him from the road.

She was checking in and wondered if anything new had happened.

Aside from all the airlines being grounded, he didn't have much to tell her. She didn't speak about her brother. She only talked about her assignment. When she hung up, he walked to the bedroom and got lost in his thoughts.

Chuck Hayes was a mystery to most people. He kept to himself even though he owned a piano bar. He owned it for the last fifteen years.

It was just before his fortieth birthday when he decided to work for himself. He had been bartending in the bay area for sometime. One of his best customers was the vice president of a local bank. When the Minuteman Lounge was taken over by the bank, he suggested Charley negotiate for it. With some favorable financing and the idea to make it a piano lounge with couches and a quiet atmosphere, it was a success in no time. He worked hard and had some luck, too. The luck came when he looked for a piano player.

Charlotte Jenkins was a first-rate singer and an accomplished pianist. She came with a ready-made following and was packing them in four nights a week. The remaining three nights were filled by up-and-comers who were trying to make a name for themselves. Charley's Place was an immediate success.

At first he tended bar and did everything himself. It was fun, but as the business grew he took up managing full time and left the bar to the cute college girls he was able to hire. It was a profitable venture from the beginning.

Gradually he began attracting the after work crowd. He added help and additional entertainment. Charlotte was his headliner who worked the best nights, but he used a variety of others to fill the expanded hours. He had non-stop entertainment and it was paying off. While other clubs and bars were going under, his flourished.

Alicia was a Charlotte Jenkins fan. She came in one evening and Charlotte introduced her to Charley. Almost immediately her attention turned from the singer to the owner.

Alicia had not broken in nationally yet. She was doing the news for one of the local television stations and was making a name for herself. Ironically, Charley didn't know who she was. At first she thought he was kidding, but soon she realized he was genuine. That, she thought, was odd.

"I don't get a chance to watch the evening news," he explained. "I'm always here working."

She laughed and brushed it off. Nevertheless, she was very taken with the tall redheaded man with a beard. She became a regular, not so much for the entertainment, but for the man who was the owner.

At first she would drop in and if she didn't see him, would casually ask if he was around. This happened two or three times and on each occasion he did come out and join her. Then it became a regular thing. She called ahead and asked if they could have a drink together. He always said yes. Finally, she knew she had to break the ice with him. She wanted it to be more than a few drinks. She wanted a whole lot more.

Charley was not the kind of man who came right out and hit on women. Actually, he was sort of shy and standoffish around them. It was as if he was holding himself back or was afraid of being involved. Alicia realized this and took the first step. She invited him to dinner at her apartment.

"Sunday evening?" she asked.

"Sure," he said agreeing.

And that is how it all began.

She made meatballs and spaghetti and served an enormous salad.

He brought a large bottle of wine and before long they were in bed.

Over the next few months it became a regular thing. At first they were together every night. Soon Charley began staying at her apartment.

His association with the beautiful newswoman was good for his business. Charley's Place became the in place to go and celebrities, when they were in town, always dropped by. But as popular as the lounge was, Charley Hayes always took a backseat.

He was the perfect match for Alicia. As outgoing as she was and as much as she needed the attention and the spotlight, Charley did not. Actually, he shunned it as much as he could without insulting anyone. He was a great listener and seldom talked about himself. For this reason in a community full of egomaniacs, Charley Hayes became one of the most well liked and popular characters in spite of himself. He was everyone's friend.

Charley was a good businessman. He reinvested the profits from the piano bar into other businesses and in turn, each was a success. He oversaw a group of managers, watched his books, and within five years had built a very successful group of businesses. Life was good.

It was then he stumbled into another deal. This time it was a house. He was surprised when he mentioned the idea to Alicia how enthusiastic she became.

"Are you going to ask me to marry you, too?" she asked.

"If you want me to," he answered her.

It had always been a sore subject between them. For a time two years before, they broke up because Charley didn't want to get married. Faced with the subject once more, he was ready to give in.

"Sure," he said. "Why not. Let's get married and have kids. Let's have three of them. Two girls and a boy."

The mention of children made Alicia sit back. Married, yes. Children, she was not too sure about. She had her career. She still was looking to break in nationally. She did not press the issue of marriage after that. Instead, while he arranged the financing, she turned her attention to decorating the new house.

The next month he closed on the three-bedroom ranch house just across the bay in Oakland. It was convenient to the bar and his other businesses. It was also easy for Alicia to get to and from work.

And life got even better.

Six months after they moved into the house, she was offered the job she wanted. It was a national position, but it was all the way across the country in Washington, D.C. They wanted her to be the White

House correspondent.

"What do you think about it?" she asked him.

"It's what you want," he said. "It's what you've always wanted."

"What about us?" she asked.

"What about us?" he asked back.

He did not wait for her to answer. Instead, he explained himself.

"Time will tell about us. If we really love each other, we'll make it. I'm not going to tell you not to take the job. It is your decision. It has to be what you want or else you will end up hating me. If you turn it down, we can get married and have a family. I'd like that.

"If you want to take it, then that's another story. We will have to play that one by ear and see how things work out."

And that is the way things went.

Alicia Masters became the face people recognized reporting on the Clinton White House. She traveled with the media when the President traveled and she covered events of the world as they unfolded.

As far as her life with Charley Hayes, they managed when they could. Charley made a habit of flying to meet her when they had a chance to spend some time together. It was on one of those occasions Charley saw something he would later wish he had not.

CHAPTER TWO

JULY 17, 1996

He was going to meet Alicia in Providence, Rhode Island. She had been out of the country for his birthday and this was going to be a belated celebration. He had turned fifty.

She was covering a story and was going to be there for a week. She called the night before and said she missed him terribly and wanted to see him. Charley missed her, too. He tried to book a flight, but it was the heart of the summer season and the only way he could get to Providence was a roundabout way.

He had to fly from San Francisco to Dallas-Fort Worth on TWA. From there he flew to Charlotte on American. Finally, after a full day of traveling, he would fly from Charlotte to Providence on US Air. It was US Air 217.

The flight to Providence was not full. Charley was seated on the right side of the aircraft on the aisle next to a Chief Petty Officer in the Navy.

It was a nice flight. The two men exchanged pleasantries as they ordered several drinks and chatted about why they were traveling. The Chief was on his way to the naval base at Newport. He said he was an electronic warfare technician. Charley mentioned Alicia and the man immediately knew who she was.

As they spoke, the stewardess came on the public address speakers. "Ladies and gentlemen," she began. "We are beginning our descent for the final approach to Providence. Please bring your chairs into an upright position..."

As she was speaking, the Chief pointed out a plane that was close to them.

"Look at that," he said to Charley, drawing his attention to what appeared to be a private aircraft about five hundred feet below them off their wing. "He's pretty close."

Charley sat up and saw the plane.

"Yes, he is. He's very close," Charley agreed.

It was at that moment both of them saw a streak of light come up from the horizon.

"Look at that."

"Is that a flare?" Charley asked.

"It looks like an emergency flare," the Chief said.

As they watched, they saw it rise much higher than any flare ever would.

"Look at it go," Charley said. "What is it?"

"I don't know," the Chief said. "Could it be a missile?"

The object was moving through their line of sight from left to the right, south to north, and was moving faster than their jet. Neither man had any way of knowing they were passing through 21,000 feet and going 420 knots per hour. Moments later both men saw a large ball of fire.

"What the hell is that?" Charley asked.

Before the Chief could answer there was a second ball of fire. It was much larger and appeared to be heading downward.

The Chief turned around to the man behind him. "Did you see that?" he asked. "Did you just see what we saw?"

The man behind him said he did. He did not see the flare or missile, but he did see the explosion. He saw the explosion and said it was another jet.

"I was watching the cabin lights of another jet," he said. "I was watching and suddenly it became a fireball. There was an explosion and then another much large explosion."

"My God," Charley gasped.

"My God, and we saw it," the Chief said.

Fifteen minutes later they landed in Providence. The Chief wanted to call the news media and let them know what they saw. Charley Hayes wanted no part of it. He caught a cab to the hotel where he was to meet Alicia. When he arrived, she was already gone. He had missed her by minutes. A phone call sent her off to cover the story.

Charley stayed that night and returned to California the next day.

What the three men saw was TWA Flight 800. They had no way of knowing what they saw had been a missile, even though both Charley and the Chief had seen them before on active military duty.

John Hughes was in the Middle East anti-terrorism section of the Central Intelligence Agency. He was assigned to TWA FL 800 even though a full-scale FBI investigation was underway. His job was to find out what really happened.

There were rumors of missiles. There were rumors of friendly missiles and unfriendly missiles.

The National Security Agency listening post intercepted messages coming from Afghanistan earlier that month making reference to an Iranian weapon, which was adapted for use aboard a boat.

Armed with that information Hughes went forward looking for the weapon. It didn't take long. He chose the anti-aircraft missile most closely fitting the eyewitnesses' descriptions of flight characteristics and launch noises as well as the warhead lethality demonstrated in the incident, which is the Iranian AIM 54A Phoenix.

Sold to the Shah of Iran prior to 1979, it is 13 feet long, weighs 985 pounds with a long-burning solid fuel motor and a 135-pound expanding rod warhead. Updated models were still in operational use by the U.S. Navy's F14 Tomcat for long-range fleet defense. In the 70's it was considered for adoption as a point of defense missile for surface ships. It is almost a self-contained unit, carrying its own onboard terminal guidance radar. The AIM 54 is one of the most lethal anti-aircraft weapons ever developed, specifically designed to cut Soviet Bear bombers in half.

He decided with hardware from an Iranian F14 or a missile rail, etc., it would be easily adapted for surface launch and concealment aboard any ocean going boat or ship. Once airborne, Phoenix's flight trajectory appears rock solid unlike most small missiles. Because of this and its weight the Navy code name for Phoenix is Buffalo. It would steer to the center of maximum radar return, in this case the center wing tank on a 747, and detonate forty feet from whichever part of the target airframe it first encounters. On that particular night, it was the left wing tip, the number one engine or number two engine.

He realized if fired within visual range of the target on a bearing within its terminal guidance radar's search limits, the probability of kill would be very high against large non-maneuvering aircraft. This weapon used in the manner described would be deadly against any subsonic airliner at all altitudes, anywhere, anytime.

Hughes made an initial report to his superior officer pointing to the cause of the downing as an unfriendly missile attack. He wrote:

"We have access to 107 witnesses on four aircraft, nineteen on boats, and thirty-one locations ashore. They were located in a 360-degree circle around the missile engagement. Their live testimony alone will prove the aircraft was shot down. The FBI has failed to identify and interview seventeen of these people. Among these seventeen are witnesses on a boat who may have seen the escaping shooter."

That was his initial report. Later he would surmise the following:

"Less than ten minutes after sunset, two missiles were fired at TWA FL800 from a vessel lying in wait three nautical miles off shore.

"The missiles were fired with both an elevation and azimuth spread bracketing the target.

"Missile number one was initially fired almost vertically and tracked outbound about 180° and overtook FL800 from the north and west. People on the shore saw it maneuver hard left immediately prior to its warhead detonation.

"The second missile was fired at a lower climb angle with a longer lead more to the southeast. It corrected and engaged TWA FL800 from the east. That was the missile the two men watched aboard US Air 217.

"Missile number one at warhead detonation was heading 150° in a 20° climb, 70 to 100 feet from the forward left fuselage below and ahead of the left wingtip. The warhead's lateral blast immediately sheared a piece of left wing that landed 8,836 feet short of main left wing debris and a much bigger piece of left wing that landed 5,828 feet short of the same field.

"At detonation hundreds of pounds of forward missile body, everything located ahead of the warhead section, already moving over 2,000 feet per second were propelled to extremely high velocity. Fragments from this mass penetrated the forward left cargo compartment, left wing root, left side center wing tank, main landing gear wheel wells and left cabin side. These fragments struck the aircraft about 1/100 of a second after detonation, the powerful sonic over pressure wave striking 5/100's of a second later.

"A six inch diameter piece impacted a few feet aft of L2 door left side, passed through the cabin exiting a few feet above R2 door right side cutting a main longitudinal frame above the door. A similar fragment passing through aft of R2 assisted by cabin pressure and the slipstream caused the door and frame to break away almost immediately.

"Missile fragments both misted the center wing tank residual fuel and ignited a fuel/air burn in the tank that exploded with the arrival of the warhead shock wave.

"When the shock wave hit the left side of the fuselage, passengers not already hit by collateral fragmentation of aircraft parts from the missile impacts were showered with aircraft rivets. The one individual whose seat armrest was shattered and pieces projected as fragments into his chest was proof by itself of extremely high velocity events that can't be explained by a kerosene/air explosion well away from his seat.

"The warhead blast compromised the left side number two engine, which eventually impacted the ocean first 1.5nm down range in sixteen or more large pieces ahead of the other three engines.

"The combination of warhead overpressure, structural failure due to fragment penetrations, and the secondary explosion in the center wing tank caused the nose section to leave the aircraft.

"The final ballistic vector of the separated nose was imparted by hard left yaw induced by warhead over pressure effects on vertical stabilizer, left wing, engine pods one and two as well as left fuselage side.

"The loss of the forward fuselage gross tonnage immediately shifted the aircraft center of gravity radically aft toward the center of lift causing instantaneous dynamic instability.

"Within fractions of a second, the rotational force of the tail snapping down and the wing snapping up coupled with the large frontal parasite drag induced by the gaping hole forward imparted additional rotational moment, which then coupled with an overwhelming deceleration force when the flat plate area of the wing bottom went perpendicular to the relative wind at about 600 feet per second.

"The result was immediately fatal to passengers causing severe whiplash and universal cranial/cervical spine ligament separation. The aircraft pieces began to fall immediately. This force also probably broke the tail/rear fuselage section free, and broke open remaining wing tanks.

"Missile number two probably engaged the center fuselage/wing, right side clipping the 30-foot outer section of right wing. The result was the downing of Flight 800 and the loss of everyone on board."

Several hours after the downing of Flight 800, the Al Queda network headed by Osama bin Laden took credit for the attack. The Clinton Administration placed an immediate shield over that information and the FBI set out to discredit the idea the airliner had been shot down by a missile, even though several dozen witnesses would swear they saw one streaking toward the doomed 747.

John Hughes was complete in his report. He ran a background check on every witness. He interviewed the Navy Chief and it was then he realized three people had seen the explosion from Flight 217, not two as the FBI believed. He wondered why the third passenger didn't come forward. What could he be hiding?

It didn't take him long to find out the man seated next to the Navy Chief was someone named Charles Wilson Hayes.

He ran the usual checks on him. He had a California driver's license. He owned several businesses and paid his taxes. He lived with Alicia Masters, a well-known television journalist and initially Hughes believed it was the reason he chose to remain silent. And as much as any other investigator might have ended it there, John Hughes didn't. He went on.

When he ran his social security number, he found the discrepancy. Charles Wilson Hayes came up in the files of the Central Intelligence Agency as a former operative who died in Vietnam in March 1968. For whatever reason someone who appeared to be very successful was using his identity. John Hughes was going to find out why.

In the meantime, Alicia was involved with reporting on TWA Flight 800 for most of the month. They never did get to see one another until August. When she came home for an extended weekend, immediately she knew something was wrong.

"Is there someone else?" she asked.

"No," he said. "Nothing like that."

"Then it's because I'm never home any more. Isn't it?"

"No," he said again.

"You don't miss me?" she asked.

"Of course, I do," he said. "I miss you more than you realize. I don't like having you so far away from me. But I know this is what you want to do. I'm not going to stand in your way."

"Then what is it?" she asked.

"You haven't been the same since you flew to Providence. I'm sorry if I disappointed you," she said.

Charley dismissed it. "That isn't it," he said. "It isn't you. It's me. Maybe it's turning fifty. I don't know."

They went to bed and made love. Then they fell off to sleep.

He didn't sleep long. He had not been sleeping well. All he did was think. He thought back. He thought way back. As he did, he wished he could keep everything buried. He wished he could, but he knew he might not be able to do so. If that happened, he wondered what he would do. He wondered what would happen to him.

CHAPTER THREE

SEPTEMBER 11, 2001

John Hughes was at his desk when the first jet slammed into the north tower of the World Trade Center. Moments later his phone rang. There was an alert and he was to report to the situation room located in the deepest and most secure part of the complex of the head-quarters of the Central Intelligence Agency.

The corridors were buzzing as word spread from office to office. While the American people were watching and wondering what happened, the Agency hierarchy already knew it was a hijacked airliner and they were tracking three more. All division heads were ordered to secure areas. One of the airliners was in the Washington, D.C. vicinity.

While he was still making his way down to the situation room, the second airliner crashed into the south tower. He got to the high-speed elevator. It took him down twenty-seven stories to a location carved out of the bedrock deep below the Potomac River. Guards checked his identity and allowed him to proceed. He stepped onto a moving walk-way and went deeper into the secure area.

Finally at 9:15 a.m. as he passed through security with first a voice match, followed by a retina match, and then his own personal code, he entered the room to see both burning towers on the huge screen that usually showed a map of the world with various situations and locations of military units.

The normally quiet nature of the room was replaced by the sounds of phones and voices in various states of excitement. They were following a third and then a fourth airliner, both of which had turned around and were headed back toward Washington. At exactly 9:20 they gave the order to evacuate the above ground complex. At the same time, the order was given to seal the entrance from above. Giant steel doors rolled shut and the elevator shafts were closed in several places.

Less than a hundred key Agency personnel settled themselves into the security of the situation room.

While on the surface thousands of employees streamed out of the buildings making up the Langley complex of the CIA, the staff in the situation room guessed at the targets of the remaining two airliners. The White House was being evacuated as was the Senate and the House of Representatives. Then at 9:36 the third airliner crashed into the Pentagon. All that was left was the United Airlines flight.

As it was being tracked, the international eavesdropping network was on a heightened state of alert. They had been monitoring some unusual traffic between New York and Germany for several weeks and moments after the second jet hit the south tower, a single message was sent via e-mail. It read:

"We praise God, seek His help, and ask for His forgiveness.

"We seek refuge in God from the evils of our souls and our bad deeds.

"A person who is guided by God will never be misguided by anyone and a person who is misguided by God can never be guided by anyone.

"I bear witness that there is no God but Allah alone, Who has no partner.

"Allah's angels are triumphant."

The innocent sounding message traveled over the Internet to Hamburg, Germany. In a matter of moments following the receipt of the message, it was forwarded to Dhahran, Saudi Arabia. The exact location in Dhahran was the palace of Prince Al Mamlakah al Arabiyah al Suudiyah, a half brother of King and Prime Minister Fahd bin Abd al-Aziz Al Saud, himself, the supreme ruler of the Kingdom.

It did not stop there. Once again the message was forwarded. This time as it left Saudi Arabian Royalty, it went directly to Kandahar, the headquarters of the Taliban supreme leader Mullah Mohammad Omar, who at that moment was entertaining Osama bin Laden.

Eleven minutes elapsed from the time the message left New York City until it reached the hands of Osama bin Laden. And it appeared people along the way all were waiting for the message. There was no lag time, which is normal with e-mailed messages. Generally the receiving party is not waiting at their computer to send it along its way. That day and with that message, it was forwarded on with haste.

As the message was tracked and the fourth airliner crashed in rural Pennsylvania, the select group of men in the situation room began to spring into action.

While other agencies in the government are under the strict control of the Director, it is not the case with the Central Intelligence Agency. The Director is the figurehead. He is the public relations man. He gives the faceless government within the government a face. He provides the identity-less organization with an identity. In fact, the Department Heads and Section Chiefs who make decisions on a consensus basis rule the Central Intelligence Agency and set policy in motion. And it was from this room the order was given to move on the originators of the message which left New York at 9:07 a.m. Eastern Daylight Time.

While New York was in a state of panic and disbelief, five minutes before the south tower collapsed, an agency team of six operatives arrived at the Second Avenue apartment of Mohammed Abdullah. They kicked in the door and overcame the four men who were there watching the events unfold on television. Within moments of the collapse of the south tower, the four were in the back of two vans on their way to an unspecified location for questioning.

Another team took physical control of the apartment, seizing computers, cell phones, and various documents. They were thorough and were careful to take even the most innocent looking items. Nothing could be overlooked. By ten-thirty they were gone and the apartment was empty.

Once Mohammed Abdullah and the other three men were at a secure location for interrogation, a scrambled satellite link was established between the operatives and the situation room. The Section Chief, from his location in Langley, could supervise the interrogation.

While Abdullah claimed his rights as a Saudi citizen, no one was really concerned. There had been no warrant for either his arrest or the search and confiscation of what was in the apartment. There would be no concern for his rights and he was told that in no uncertain terms.

The four men were stripped naked and taped to chairs with duct tape. Then the questioning began. Questions were asked and no answers were given. That lasted for only a few minutes.

When it was obvious the four Arabs had no intention of cooperating, the man immediately to the right of Abdullah was summarily shot between the eyes with a 40-caliber automatic pistol. His brains and pieces of his head exploded outward covering Abdullah and the man on the other side.

Abdullah remained silent but the other two men were obviously shaken. One cried out for mercy. Immediately, Abdullah ordered him in Arabic to keep silent. As he did, the side of the chrome 40-caliber pistol was smashed across his mouth, knocking out several teeth.

Two of the operatives keyed in on the man who asked for mercy. They took him, still naked and taped to the chair, out of the holding area to a private room. There they asked him his name.

His identification said he was Ragib al Mostef, a Palestinian. He immediately told the operatives it was indeed his name. They played the obvious hunch that it wasn't his name and the documents were false. The butt end of a pistol slammed into his mouth, breaking teeth as it did. It didn't take a second blow to get him to admit he was Khamis al Mamlak, a twenty-six year old Saudi from the Al Bahah region of the Kingdom.

While he was being interrogated, the other man with Abdullah was taken into another room. Within minutes he identified himself as Ash Sharqiyah Asir, a twenty-five year old Saudi from the Al Bahah region, too. Both men, now that they were away from Abdullah and fearing for their survival, were more than willing to cooperate. Abdullah was another story. They did not want to waste time. They brought out the Sodium Pentothal.

The effects of Sodium Pentothal are simple. Drinking a glass of water with Sodium Pentothal depresses the central nervous system, slows the heart rate and lowers the blood pressure. All of those effects are the functions of any sedative.

Sodium Pentothal is commonly used as an anesthetic during surgery. The patient is unconscious within 30 to 60 seconds after the drug administration to the veins. The duration of the anesthesia is very short; it only causes a few minutes of sedation.

Veterinarians also use Sodium Pentothal. When an animal is injured and needs an examination, a quick dose of the drug by tranquilizer dart gives a few minutes to the veterinarian to do an examination. It can also be used to calm down a large animal that needs to be shipped from one place to another. Sodium Pentothal slows the metabolism and minimizes the stress and excitement. While all of this is true, this drug has another important property.

Psychiatrists, as a part of narcotherapy, also use Sodium Pentothal. This drug produces the state of full relaxation and makes patients more susceptible to suggestion, allowing the psychiatrists to uncover the repressed feelings or memories. With that in mind, the operatives administered it to Mohammed Abdullah.

As the next four hours passed and as Abdullah was administered dangerous amounts of the truth drug, the array of characters involved in the events of the morning was painted for the agency. In a very deliberate and very painstaking manner the operatives were careful to crosscheck what one man said with the other and then confirm it with a third. With Asir and Mamlek fearing for their lives and lulled into a sense of security if they cooperated and Abdullah under the influence of Sodium Pentothal, the network that carried out the attacks began to unfold.

From the secure location below the Potomac River, the Agency ordered twenty-two others to be taken into custody and interrogated. As was the case with the taking of Mohammed Abdullah, no warrants were ever issued. There was no question as to rights. As far as the Agency was concerned, these men had no rights. Wheels of machinery that had been put away for years began to turn once more.

While this was happening and as those wheels began to creek from the rust of non-use, and then as they turned, the unsuspecting and grieving American public was still glued to their televisions. Among them were three women who were sharing a common loss. They were Cindy Ganley, Tina Ganley, and Jerilyn Gardner Holt.

Chuck Ganley had been in the south tower of the World Trade Center above the floors the jet crashed into. Chuck was Cindy's son, Tina's husband, and Jerilyn's son-in-law. Immediately, they joined the thousands of relatives and loved ones who hoped against impossible odds the one they loved had somehow survived.

They all hoped for a miracle. And at the same time, they all realized there would be none.

And across the country Charley Hayes had no way of knowing how he would suddenly be tied to them. Now everything was coming back once more. It started that night he flew to Providence and it had stayed. As he sat, it was as if it was yesterday.

CHAPTER FOUR

VIETNAM
1968

Group A-545 MACV-SOG-CCN was deployed to northern
Quang Tri Province to seal a hole in the defenses north of Dong Ha
in the early days of the First Tet Offensive. They were just below the
Demilitarized Zone (DMZ) and took up their position at Lang Vei with
group A-101. Along with the South Vietnamese defenders they numbered nearly 350 armed troops.

On the sixth of February probing attacks began on their positions.

The following day they were attacked in force led by Russian
made tanks and several thousand infantry from the North Vietnamese
Regular Army. It started just after midnight with a barrage of Chinese
rockets and French mortar. For well over sixty minutes the pounding
drove them into holes for protection. Every part of their defenses was
hit and by the time the tanks appeared they had already lost half their
numbers.

At first the tanks sat out in the jungle and began to pound them
with their guns. They had no artillery and were unable to respond.
They called for air support, but none was available. The entire country was under attack at that moment.

The attack was so severe they didn't even have the opportunity to
withdraw. Any attempt at retreat would have been suicide. Staying in
place seemed no better. No one expected to survive the night. Then
the tanks began to move and with them came the infantry attack.

There were less than a hundred men when it began. They had
three M20 rocket launchers and one M67 recoilless rifle with which to
fight the tanks. Along with those the minefields were still in tact and
very much a shield for them, which the lead tank discovered all too late.

The left track was blown off and the vehicle came to a dead stop.

As it did a second tank hit a mine and exploded. A third tank had both tracks blown off and that halted the infantry and allowed the defenders to open up.

A fourth tank was hit by direct fire and exploded, but five more followed and made it into the center of the camp. Sergeant First Class Gene Ashley led a handful of men in an attack on the armored vehicles. It was around four in the morning, but it could have been noon. The bunkers were ablaze and the ammo bunker had taken a direct hit and burned like a small volcano. It seemed like daylight when it shouldn't have been.

Men were on top of tanks dropping grenades down the hatches. Machine gun fire from the tanks formed a defensive wall, but the men broke through and kept up the assault. Gene Ashley destroyed three tanks that way before he was machine gunned by the fourth tank. The M67 fired on that tank hitting it in the turret. It exploded. Before they could turn to the fifth tank, it fired on the M67 position and eliminated it. With its machine guns spitting death, it withdrew back through the minefield and rejoined the infantry that was unable to penetrate without the tanks to lead them.

They had no way of knowing how many other tanks were still in the jungle. They had no way of knowing there were eight of them out of commission. They dug in and waited. A second attack by the infantry would destroy all of them. They waited, but it never came.

Taking advantage of the lull in the fighting and with one more hour of darkness left, they slipped out and went to the safety of the hills to the west. Less than seventy survived and Gene Ashley would later be awarded the Congressional Medal of Honor posthumously.

With Lang Vei neutralized, the attacking enemy forces moved through Quang Tri and drove on the American-built highway QL-1 toward the city of Hue.

Hue was the ancient capital of Vietnam. Huge walls ten-feet high and six-feet thick surrounded it. Less than twenty kilometers from the sea to the east, it was surrounded by a thick growth of jungle and rain forest.

As Tet began, the Viet Cong had massed in the jungle where they stored a huge cache of arms. Well armed, they moved on the 1st and 5th Marine Regiments.

The attack took the Marines by surprise and threw them into disarray. They were scattered throughout the city and cut off from their command. The Viet Cong moved to surround them and kill them one at a time.

First Marine Headquarters at DaNang was under attack. The attack threw the entire coastal region of I-Corps into chaos. The American forces found it difficult to formulate a unified battle plan. At home the American people would never know the full extent of the damage our forces were sustaining, but in the field things were bad and everyone knew it.

The 1st and the 5th were ordered to hold the city. As they received their orders, the 324th Division of the North Vietnamese Army arrived. It was the morning of February 9th and the Battle of Hue was in its tenth day.

The North Vietnamese Command in Hanoi realized they had taken the Americans by surprise. The 304th Infantry Division occupied the port city of Dong Ha and controlled the Cua Viet River bridges, allowing reinforcements to pour into South Vietnam. Hue became their target and the 202nd Armor Group moved in to reinforce the 324th.

With the door open the 325th Infantry Division along with the 312th Infantry Division deployed and entered the battle on February 12th.

By this time the survivors of A-545 and A-101 came out of the hills. They were sent to Phong Dien to mop up with the 3rd Battalion of the 1st Air Cavalry. It was then the A Team received their orders from Colonel Ladd himself. They were to proceed immediately to Phu-vang where they were to assist the 2nd Battalion of the 101st Airborne in the relief of the Marines in Hue. The North Vietnamese Army had them surrounded and they were moving artillery into position to annihilate them.

The weather was not cooperating. Monsoons from the South China Sea gave the Americans less than an hour in the day to operate their aircraft. Ceilings and visibility remained below operational minimums. At the same time the Vietnamese tanks had moved up and taken positions to begin the assault on the city.

The 545th arrived at the headquarters of the 2nd Battalion on February 13th. Everywhere men and machines were being mobilized for the expedition into the city. The aircraft carrier Bon Home Richard sat off the coast like an impotent warrior as the first elements of the 101st engaged the 324th Infantry. Immediately, the 101st was stopped cold.

While the airborne battled on the road to Hue, A-545 waited to go into action. Charley was twenty-two.

As they waited, the battleship New Jersey with its 16-inch guns was steaming from Japan. It was scheduled to arrive off the coast on the fifteenth and the day before it arrived, a naval officer briefed Charley's unit.

They were to probe the NVA positions and direct the fire from the battleship. The New Jersey was going to cut a path so the 101st could advance and rescue the trapped Marines.

That day the 324th overran Marine Base Bravo and captured twenty M102 105mm Howitzers and thirty thousand live shells. Each Howitzer had a range of 12,000 meters and could be fired by two men. With those twenty pieces they could hit the American forces at will. They also proved to be very effective against the M48A3 tanks the Marines and the 101st were using to fight them back. The North Vietnamese made them operational immediately and that day ten M48's were lost.

As daylight broke on the morning of the fifteenth, the clouds were so low it seemed as if you could reach up and touch their bases. Nothing was flying because they were still below operational minimums. Visibility on the ground was measured in yards and made it virtually impossible for anyone to pinpoint where they were.

It was Charley's job to direct the fire from the battleship and had the other men realized he was guessing when he ordered the first attack, he might not have survived the day. His buddies out of self-preservation just might have shot him in the back.

They began their infiltration of the enemy positions the night before. He knew approximately where they would first encounter the enemy. They disposed of them and continued on. He was approximating each location and marking it on the map. When the gunnery officer first called his sign, Eagle Eye, their location and that of the first enemy gun emplacement was only an educated guess. Actually, it was a wild-assed guess. Charley called it a WAG.

As he gave the location, he silently took a deep breath and waited for the sound of the guns. He watched and he waited.

The sound never came.

Suddenly, a half a mile beyond the Howitzers, there was an enormous explosion and a flash they could see through the fog. The second round was long also, as was the third. Finally, the fourth volley found its mark and the gun was gone.

The North Vietnamese gunners had no way of knowing a battleship twenty miles out to sea was firing on them. They assumed the Americans had moved in more M102's so they fired back to answer. As they did, they gave away their positions. With the first gun as an accurate reference point, the Americans were able to take out ten more guns with fourteen volleys.

They were well behind the NVA lines and several thousand meters from the highway. The 16-inch guns had been silent for about an hour when the Captain told Charley to call in fire on the infantry between them and the 101st.

He called for three volleys in rapid succession. Within minutes a hole several thousand yards wide had been cut so the American forces could advance. In an attempt to counter the advance, the NVA guns fired once more.

Charley keyed in on them. Moments later they were silenced. By noon a single tank and thirty men joined with A-545 and became the spearhead of the force moving on the city.

Charley's locations became more refined and not one shot from the Navy guns was wasted. They were able to hit what they were shooting at and their advance was limited only by their own ability to move.

Command wanted them back on the highway and that proved to be a problem because they had to cut and fight across to it. Several thousand of the enemy was in their way. Before the afternoon ended, they were directing fire on the enemy positions.

It was a steady stream of death from the sea lasting twenty minutes. All Charley could do once it began was sit in total awe of the firepower he directed. Of the 5,100 confirmed enemy casualties suffered in the Battle of Hue, more than half occurred that afternoon as a result of naval fire.

Only the North Vietnamese knew for sure, but after that day the 324th Infantry Division of ten thousand men ceased to exist. Looking back years later, Charley realized there was no way to count the soldiers who were vaporized as the shells as large as compact cars exploded directly on them. To this day, those men remain the nameless missing in action.

Even though the major portion of the infantry had been eliminated, their advance on the road was stymied by mines and retreating enemy fire. However, by the eighteenth they were at the walls of the city and were ready to break through to the Marines.

The New Jersey was still out there on patrol.

At first, because of the historical significance of the city, her guns were silent. But as the enemy resistance mounted and the situation of the Marines became desperate, Charley once again was directing fire.

Entire sections of the ancient wall system were blown out and the advance progressed. On the twentieth the Marines were rescued and over the next six days the last of the NVA and the Viet Cong were driven off in full retreat.

The 101st maintained the pressure. They pursued them to Quang Tri City where another battle ensued. The 304th Infantry still occupied Dong Ha and were in a strong position to reinforce the retreating 325th. The 202nd Armor Group still controlled highway QL-1, but a sudden change in the weather allowed naval air strikes to destroy eighty-five tanks committed by the enemy.

By the end of February the North Vietnamese Army was driven back to Dong Ha and the Cua Viet River. Officially the Tet Offensive was over. However, as long as the regulars of the NVA were below the DMZ, I-Corps would not rest.

Command knew how lucky they were. They had averted disaster only through the sheer determination of the 1st and the 5th Marine Divisions. Now they directed the 1st to engage and defeat the NVA at Dong Ha.

As the coastal resistance collapsed, the NVA looked to the west and the highlands region.

Khe San was a stronghold of the Army in early 1966 and was later turned over to the Marines. It was the high ground and the American guns could rain death over a twenty square mile area. A presence was maintained so shipments of supplies to the Viet Cong in the south could be stopped. The 325th was committed to the defeat of the Marines at Khe San.

Fresh reinforcements were arriving daily. General Giap in Hanoi was looking for an embarrassing defeat to hang on the Americans. He had been close to it in Hue, but even he had not counted on the awesome use of naval firepower. Now he looked to Khe San and remembered Dien Bien Phu and the French.

His supply lines were safely hidden in the mountainous jungles of Laos. Men and materials poured down out of safe staging areas in the north and were immune to attack inside the neutral Laotian borders. The 325th was to be reinforced and the 324th rebuilt. He was determined to prevail at Khe San just as he had at Dien Bien Phu.

On February 29th Captain Van Name and Charley were called to DaNang.

Charley was only a Staff Sergeant and did not assume any special significance that he was traveling on special orders with his commanding officer. He didn't until they were directed to CCN Headquarters and Colonel Ladd, Special Forces Commander in Vietnam.

Major Beckwith did most of the talking. He spoke with West Point arrogance and an obvious disregard for their lives and safety. Colonel Ladd sat silently and allowed the Major to brief them as to the location of the enemy and his growing strength. It was at this meeting that Charley first head of the Ho Chi Minh Trail.

Beckwith explained to them the trail was actually many improved and unimproved routes into South Vietnam. Penetrations and cross-ings were made anywhere along the Laotian and Cambodian borders with South Viet Nam depending solely upon their ultimate destination. He explained each convoy was set up in central staging areas in Laos after they had been transported across North Vietnam from the City of Haiphong on the Gulf of Tonkin.

All arms, ammunition, rockets, mortars, and so on traveled this route. They were told Russian-made surface to air missiles (SAMS) protected Haiphong and the cross North Vietnam route. He explained the political ramifications of bombing the harbor while Russian and Chinese ships were unloading. He also told them of their mounting losses of aircraft to the improved SAMS. Then he told them about Operation Archangel.

As Beckwith turned over a page on a flip chart, Colonel Ladd interrupted. As he stood, Charley could not help but be reminded of John Wayne in The Green Berets. He smiled at the thought and Colonel Ladd looked directly at him and paused before he began.

Still looking at him he managed a smile and told them that Archangel was above Top Secret. Only a select group of people would be involved and like Operation Eagle Thrust the year before, when it was over, it never existed.

Charley was surprised to hear the name Operation Eagle Thrust. The mere mention of it made him nervous. Many of those who were associated with it were dying off at an alarming rate. Charley looked away when Colonel Ladd spoke of it.

"This will be a joint operation of the Army, Air Force, and the Central Intelligence Agency," he said.

"The unit designated A-545 MACV-SOG will operate under CIA authority.

"Fifth Special Forces Headquarters will issues orders designating you for mountain training in the Philippines, while you will be assigned elsewhere in an unspecified and secret area. Your authority comes from the President of the United States and your mission is to destroy the enemy supply lines and force him to the peace table."

Colonel Ladd sat back down and Beckwith took over once more.

"The 185th Bomb Wing is based in Guam," he began.

"Surface to air missiles currently used by the North Vietnamese, SAM-2, have a maximum altitude of 41,000 feet. B52 bombers flying at 45,000 feet will carry out nightly raids on the Ho Chi Minh Trail in Laos. You, the 545th Special Ops Group, will be the eyes of this mission on the ground.

"This is a ninety-day mission in which you will be re-supplied weekly inside of Laos. You will have the support of all intelligence gathering and have a chopper group available to transport you as needed.

"Your mission is to locate the enemy supply lines, contact the bombers who will already be in route, and talk them to the target. Your experience in the action at Hue makes you the best qualified unit for this mission," Beckwith said.

The meeting ended. They were given a codebook, a list of frequencies, call signs, and detailed maps of Laos. The frequencies and call signs were all in code and they matched the various maps and grid points with which they would direct the air attacks. With that, they returned to their base camp.

On March 2nd they were transported to the hills near Ban Cha La on the Noi River, placing them near a main staging area on the Ho Chi Minh Trail. From there they were to inflict major damage to the war effort of the Communist government in the north.

For one month, from March 2nd until the morning hours of April 3rd, 1968, twelve men, all members of A-545 MACV-SOG, all under special orders from Lyndon Baines Johnson and the Central Intelligence Agency, operated within Laos, outside of the resolution laid down by the United Nations and the Congress of the United States. They participated in a secret war that would result in the end of a Presidential administration, the betrayal of men on the ground, and bring both sides to Paris and the beginning of the peace talks. Charley had no idea how it all would ultimately impact his life.

CHAPTER FIVE

WASHINGTON, D.C.
MARCH 1,1968

Group A-545 MACV-SOG-CCN was John Hughes concern. It was a qualified Green Beret A Team. The men who made it up were very qualified. The only problem was their last mission. They survived it. Dong Ha was a suicide mission, yet somehow they all came back. These men were good.

When he reported the fact that they survived the attack of an armored division and then were placed in the front of the advancing forces at Hue and survived once more, his supervisor, Henry Townsend, told him he had a mission in store for them they could not survive.

"If those slimy little bastards don't get them, we can have our B-52's drop a load of bombs on them, by accident of course. Then our problem will be solved once and for all."

"Mr. President," the man spoke. "Operation Archangel is now in the process of being initiated.

"Raphael, Mr. Rusk, will be my contact to pass information to you. You will be known as Almighty."

Johnson smiled when Mr. Townsend referred to him as 'Almighty.'

"I will be known as Gabriel. The 545th on the ground will be Uriel, and the bomber wing will be referred to as Leviathan."

"When will we be operational?" the President asked.

"Tomorrow," Townsend answered. "Tomorrow will be in a few hours as they are on the other side of the International Dateline. They are near midnight right now."

The President rose and extended his hand to the CIA representative. "Thank you very much, Mr. Townsend. I am looking forward to a decisive victory over these Communists."

"Thank you, Mr. President," he said. "Mr. Rusk, thank you, too."

He shook Dean Rusk's hand and then left the Oval Office and returned to Langley.

The President turned to his Secretary of State. "What do you think?" he asked.

"Honestly, I don't know. We have to do something and at least this is aggressive warfare. If anything is going to work, this has the best chance. We have the bastards between a rock and a hard place. Everyone knows the supply lines run through Laos, but they adamantly deny it. So if they say they aren't there, they also can't say we are bombing them. Westmoreland finally gave us something we can use."

Johnson laughed. "You don't believe this came from Westmoreland, do you? I don't believe Westy is capable of independent thought. He's a yes man. I have him there because he does what he's told and doesn't give me any shit."

"Mac would have liked this move," Rusk said.

"Yes, he would have," Johnson agreed. "This is right up his alley. Destroy the enemy supply lines and you destroy the enemy. He just lost his balls, that's all."

"You're right," said the Secretary of State. "And we are in a sorry state now. Clifford isn't much of a replacement for Mac."

"I know," Johnson said. "Mac was an engineer. He was analytical and a problem-solver. Clark is a lawyer. He's a problem-maker and someone who can't be trusted. I owed a favor and he was payment in full. Next term, I'll find someone like us. I'll get us a Secretary of Defense we can trust.

"We can't trust him and there is no way we can allow him to know about Archangel. Too much of what he knows finds its way into the Washington Post," said Johnson.

"He won't find out from me.

"What do you think Hanoi will do when they realize what we are doing?" asked Rusk.

"They won't stop the war. I expect them to move SAMS in and I expect them to try to get our men on the ground. Their SAMS are 5,000 feet short of being able to hit us, and our boys on the ground are the best. We figure they have a 45-day window for success until they can find them. By then we'll have four other teams ready to replace them.

"We'll bomb them right through the election. As their supplies run out, the war will take care of itself on our terms. Maybe then all these assholes will get off our back," Johnson said with a frown.

"Did you see the Post today?" Dean asked.

"You know I don't read that garbage. What did they say this time?"

"They're trying to make a big thing out of Nantucket."

"Christ!" Johnson exploded. "That fucking Clifford! I know he leaked that memo."

What the President was talking about was several, actually ten of his top aides, went to a weekend party given by Ted Kennedy on Nantucket Island. Many of the more friendly women from Washington attended and at the end of the weekend they stayed on through the week with the Johnson aides, all of them calling in sick.

"This is an internal matter and now it is all over the fucking Washington Post. I'm sorry I'm stuck with that son-of-a-bitch. If I could, I'd fire his fucking ass."

INSIDE LAOS
MARCH 2, 1968

Just after midnight on Saturday morning they were on the top of a ridge overlooking a valley, which led to the border between Laos and South Vietnam. To the east they could hear the rumble of artillery and even see an occasional flash. Khe Sanh was less than twenty miles away. They had been on this position for several hours.

"Are they in the air yet?" Billy Campbell asked.

"They should be," Charley answered.

Everyone was nervous. This was the first mission.

"How long does it take to get here?" he asked.

"That's classified," Charley said joking with him.

Billy laughed.

"Four hours, I believe," he told the other man.

"That's enough," Captain Van Name said. "You were right the first time. It is classified and you don't need to be divulging that information."

Charley didn't say anything. He just looked at the officer. His attitude annoyed him and what he did next made it very clear how he felt.

"There are fifteen to twenty B-52's assigned to our target. Each one will be carrying sixty one thousand-pound bombs. This is the primary target area. If we have no activity, they will go to the secondary, which will be the hills south of Khe Sanh. That is a hit or miss target because otherwise they won't have enough fuel to return if they are still loaded," Charley said.

"That's enough, Sergeant," the Captain ordered.

"Is it, sir?" he asked.

"Shouldn't every man here have the right to know what we are doing? Every man here should know how to talk to these jokers just in case something happens to us."

Van Name thought a minute and then agreed. Actually, he was a pretty decent guy. Charley wrote it off to nervousness.

"What do you think?" he asked Charley. "Are we in the wrong position?"

"I don't think so," he answered. "Intelligence said this is the main route to Khe San. They need to get across the border at night and that's the road down there in the valley."

Tank, Master Sergeant John P. Tankersley, and Jesse Teague had gone down to the valley floor and confirmed there was a solid road that heavy trucks could travel. They found the location they were in, giving them a full view of a turn in the road. From there they could see any activity.

They waited and they watched. They listened and continued to wait.

The artillery fire to the east continued without letting up. Still they waited. They waited and they waited some more.

Finally, just after two the first truck came around the bend in the road.

"Bill," the Captain said. "You count vehicles and estimate the size of the movement."

"Yes, sir," Campbell answered.

The trucks were Mercedes and were towing what seemed to be 105mm Howitzers. After he counted twenty-five of the trucks, he asked the Captain what he thought was in them. As he did, Armored Personnel Carriers appeared. There were twenty of them. Jeep-type vehicles towing 50mm guns followed them and finally they were followed by large numbers of infantry.

"Does that answer your question?" Captain Van Name asked.

"We've hit the jackpot," Charley said.

The Captain agreed. "Yes, we have," he said.

"How long until they get here?" he asked.

"Forty-five minutes," Charley answered. "I think it's time to make contact. I don't think we want to be around here when they start."

"Go ahead," the Captain said.

Charley turned on the radio and began. "Michael," he said. "Michael, this is Uriel. Come in Michael."

He waited and then repeated his message.

As he did, the wing commander answered. "This is Michael. Go ahead, Uriel. Do you have a position for Leviathan?"

"That's affirmative, Michael. Are the Seraphim ready?"

"Affirmative. Transmit now."

Immediately he began giving the B-52's their targets. The Captain estimated how far along the road in the valley the enemy convoy would travel. They knew where the valley and the road began and ended. It was nearly fifteen miles long and the slow-moving convoy would not be out by the time the flight arrived. They wanted the beginning of the attack concentrated on what had just passed and then work back up the valley. That would inflict the maximum amount of damage.

"What is our target?" the commander of the flight asked.

"A convoy of trucks towing Howitzers, APC's, and infantry," he answered.

"How long until you are over the target zone?" Charley asked.

The officer paused before answering. "Seventeen minutes," he said. "I suggest you move out of the area muy pronto."

"Affirmative," Charley answered. "Uriel out."

"Let's move," the Captain said.

Even before he spoke, Charley was already breaking down the radio. As he finished, they moved across the ridge to the north. They were moving at a right angle to the target zone in order to place as much distance as possible between them and the valley.

Billy Campbell was timing them with a wrist-mounted stopwatch. They would find cover when they had between three and four minutes left.

The ridge ran almost a mile before it dropped down toward a river. As they started down, Billy alerted them it was time. There were no holes in which to hide. All they had was the jungle and the hill itself. The hill would shield them from the explosions. All they could do was sit down and wait. It didn't take long.

It was as dark as it was quiet. Then without any warning it turned into daylight and a rumble sounding like it was the end of the world broke the silence. Blast after blast, at first individual blasts and then one solid continuous blast, roared across the night. The sound was deafening and the ground shook and rocked as if they were at ground zero in an earthquake of enormous proportion. It seemed to continue forever.

Then as suddenly as it began, it also ended. The ground no longer shook and the glow from the other side of the hill gradually decreased in intensity. They rose and started back to do the damage assessment.

As they started back, twenty thousand Pennsylvania public school teachers went to the state capitol in Harrisburg to demonstrate for higher pay. The Associated Press released a wire photo of the control tower at the airfield in Khe Sanh that had been damaged in a rocket attack. New York Governor Nelson Rockefeller was waiting for a call from the Republican Party to ask him to run for President. U.S. Marines lost twenty-two and had eighty-seven wounded in a daylong battle at Dong Ha. Thirty-six members of the enemy forces were reported killed.

WASHINGTON, D.C.
MARCH 3, 1968

The President rose at seven. As was the custom, his manservant, Walter, woke him. He laid out the President's robe along with a folder containing situations and summaries of the events taking place while he slept. As Mr. Johnson sat in his stuffed chair by the window overlooking the south lawn, Walter poured a cup of black coffee and placed it on the table next to two cornbread muffins.

"Walter," the President said. "Is Mrs. Johnson awake?"

"I don't believe so, Mr. Lyndon. Would you like me to call up there and find out?"

"No," the President answered. "I'll read for awhile. Then we'll see."

"Yes, sir," Walter answered.

As the President scanned his papers he found a letter-sized brown envelope marked EYES ONLY. He took the envelope and opened it. It was a report from John Hughes to Henry Townsend and forwarded to the President of the United States.

"Uriel reported at 0500 Levi was destroyed. Along with destruction of the primary target, Uriel further reported that the position will be of no further use to Levi as it is now impassable. He believes this tactic will be an effective deterrent for the movement of materials on Area X."

A smile came over the President's face. He reached for the phone on the table next to the cornbread muffins and waited for someone to answer.

"This is the President," he said to the voice on the other end of the line. "Contact Henry Townsend at the CIA and have him in my office at 10:30 this morning."

HANOI

Lieutenant Colonel Gnu had been in an agitated state for most of the day. His phone began ringing at dawn. What was to be a day off with his wife and two daughters soon turned into a major crisis. A car was sent for him and upon his arrival at headquarters and he realized the seriousness of the situation.

"Have we had any contact?" he asked.

"No, sir," the aide replied.

"Exactly what units are missing?" he demanded.

"Nearly the entire 3rd Division," he was told. "The 1st Battalion, the 52nd Battalion, and the 141st Battalion. Along with them was the 54th Artillery from the 320th Division."

"This is absurd!" he exclaimed. "How can nearly four thousand men and all their machines, weapons, and ammunition disappear from the face of the earth!"

He walked to the window and looked out at People's Park. He remembered other days when the French were here and the war was only in the hills. He was a boy then and his mother used to take him to the park on Sundays. As he remembered his mother and the park, he came back to reality.

"Is it possible they have only lost communications?"

"Sir," his aide answered. "They should have arrived near Khe Sanh an hour ago. The area commander sent out patrols to look for them and they have found nothing. We don't believe they have ever re-entered the country."

"How can that be?" he questioned.

His aide did not answer.

He would have his answer, but it would not come until just before noon. It was then he was called to General Hap's office. The news was devastating.

"They are all gone," the small General told his staff.

"How can that be?" he quietly asked his aide.

The aide did not know.

"The area is totally destroyed," General Hap said.

"An atomic weapon?" someone asked.

"We don't know," the General answered. "It is a possibility that has to be explored. The Americans have atomic cannons capable of fir-

ing a nuclear projectile fifty miles. One shell can do the damage that
has been reported."

"What kind of damage are we talking about?" someone else asked.

"An entire valley for three miles is now a giant crater one hundred feet deep. The jungle on the surrounding hills is gone, burnt to
a smoldering cinder. An hour ago there were still fires burning and
there is no debris to indicate men and machines ever existed. The damage in the valley is so severe we will never be able to use that route
again."

The room fell silent. All of the officers understood what this
meant.

The 3rd Division was to link up with the elements of the 7th
Division and the 308th Division south of Khe Sanh. This was all to take
place by the fifth of March. At the same hour, forces around Saigon
would attack the Americans while the forces in the field would over-
run Khe Sanh, giving them control of all of Quang Tri Province and
the western half of Quang Nam Province. This move would leave
DaNang vulnerable to attack and capture. Now it appeared all of that
would change.

General Vinh, who was seated next to General Hap, spoke.

"We still have enough units positioned to carry out our offensive
against Khe Sanh. It is imperative we deal the Americans a devastating defeat. If we do that, they will end the war themselves. Their
Senators Fulbright and Eugene McCarthy are openly challenging
Lyndon Johnson. If we can destroy their Marines, we can destroy their
interest in our country."

The officers rose to their feet and began to cheer their General's
words. He raised his arms and everyone sat down.

"Now, back to work!"

General Hap moved to a map of Laos and western Vietnam.

"The 36th, the 88th, and the 102nd Battalions of the 7th Division
are here," he said pointing to Muang Ngoy. "The 84th and the 164th
artillery are with them. They will follow the Banghiang River and cross
near Tou-rout."

"The 141st, the 165th, the 209th, and the 205th infantry units are
here at Ban Katip. With them are the 572nd tank/artillery and the
675th artillery. They will move and cross at Ba-na. Then they will join
our forces here!" he said, pointing to the hills southwest of the Marines
base camp of Khe Sanh.

"Our forces must be in place by mid-day Monday. The attack
will begin at 0130 Tuesday."

Later Lieutenant Colonel Gnu sat alone in his office. He twirled a glass of cognac as he watched the sun set over People's Park. All of the orders were issued. The troops would begin to move in several hours. Everything was put in motion for the greatest offensive ever.

And while he waited, Lyndon Johnson was not wasting any time.

WASHINGTON, D.C.

Following a meeting with his Security Advisors, the President met promptly at 10:30 with Henry Townsend. Townsend was already in the President's office as Mr. Johnson entered.

"Good morning! Good morning!" the President said as he shook the other man's hand. "It looks to me as if we are winners!"

"Yes, sir. It was an overwhelming success."

"Great! What's next?"

"I'm glad you asked, Mr. President. We're not out of the woods yet. The cloud cover burnt off early today and our Ageus weather satellite took these pictures."

Townsend reached into his briefcase and produced two dozen glossy black and white photos already illustrated and enhanced.

"Ageus weather satellite?" the President asked.

"Yes, sir," the man from the CIA answered. "It's a multi-purpose satellite. All we did was add a few more lenses and a scrambler on a different frequency. The National Weather Service believes that it's sun spot interference. We can access it whenever we choose and we have perfect spy capabilities."

"My Lord!" the President exclaimed. "Look at the fucking detail! Here's a group of tanks parked side by side."

"Yes, sir," Townsend said. "We believe these units located outside of Muang Ngoy and these to the east of Ban Katip have massed to move on the Marines at Khe Sanh. We believe the North Vietnamese General Staff is looking for one devastating victory over us to embarrass your administration. We feel they have decided the American people, with the upcoming election, will lose heart and force your administration to withdraw American forces."

"The fucking bastards!" Johnson blurted out.

Townsend smiled at the President.

"Sir," he began. "We already have been in contact with Colonel Ladd in DaNang. We have moved the 545th into position along the Banghiang River. When we locate a precise position on what we have called Target A, we will unleash the B-52's. Starting at midnight local time they will be orbiting over the South China Sea only minutes from the target area. We have the 695th Refueling Wing airborne in case it takes longer than we expect.

"Once they hit target A, they will return to Guam to be refueled, rearmed, serviced and back in the air within twelve hours of the first strike."

"How will we move the 545th into position?" the President asked.

"We have choppers standing by. Even before the damage assessment is completed, our spotters will be moved into position near Ban Katip. We'll be moving so fast the Commie sons-of-bitches in Hanoi will believe an entire division is arrayed against them."

"Good," the President said. "I want an in-person report tomorrow at noon. Bring me more pictures like this."

"Can I keep these?" he asked almost like a little boy.

"Yes, sir," Townsend said. "We have more."

"Good," Johnson said. "Good. Very good."

CHAPTER SIX

As the meeting at the White House ended, thirty thousand Pennsylvania public school teachers held a rally on the steps of the capitol building in Harrisburg. Among them was Bob Robinson who taught at Washington High School in Washington, Pennsylvania.

Bob was hung over and cold. He wondered how he ever got involved with this mess. As he did, he immediately knew the answer. It was Vietnam.

There were deferments for teachers. There were none for farmers. As long as he taught, he could have his cake and eat it, too.

He lived on the farm. He raised his cattle and he taught school. While his fraternity brothers were in the army and even in Vietnam, he planned to teach school until the war was over. He had this one knocked!

Meanwhile, on the island of Guam forty-seven B-52's were loaded with thousand pound bombs. Lt. Col. Michael Stanton was leading this mission and General Shelby was conducting the briefing.

"This will be the largest bombing mission since the end of World War II," he began.

"Our targets over the next twenty-four hours are two North Vietnamese divisions in and around Khe Sanh, all poised to attack.

"Uriel will give you target parameters and you will bring everyone into the run and over the target."

Lt. Col. Stanton coolly accepted his orders and then joined his crew in the ready room.

"Top Secret again?" his co-pilot asked.

"Yes," he said nodding. "Enemy divisions of infantry and artillery."

"Live targets," the co-pilot said.

"They are all live targets," Stanton said to the co-pilot. "When we bomb, we kill. Tonight we kill by the thousands."

Colonel Tuong was the field commander of the 7th Division. A week ago he was in Hanoi with his family. He took command of the 7th just before it crossed into Laos near Napi. They traveled nearly four hundred kilometers in a week and now were preparing to go into battle against the Americans. He welcomed the opportunity.

Colonel Xuen was in command of the 308th Division. As he prepared to issue the order to move out, he couldn't help but sense disaster for himself and his men. War, he thought, was always a disaster.

MARCH 3, 1968

The 545th was in position along the Banghiang River before midnight. It was Sunday morning and once more they waited. None of them slept very much. There had not been very much time.

Once they did the damage assessment, they were ordered to a place on the map at 1200 hours. There two choppers ferried them to the position along the river.

The twelve of them were divided into four groups of three. They maintained contact by radio and Charley was set up to call in precise coordinates as soon as someone located the enemy.

They had been told they would not be responsible for damage assessment. They were going to be moved as soon as the mission was completed. Gabriel informed them they should expect to be back in action between twelve to twenty hours following the attack. They sensed something big was in the air.

Just like the night before they waited.

They were observing radio silence until the enemy was located. There were three possible approaches to the point where they expected them to cross into South Vietnam. Charley, the Captain, and Billy Campbell were on what they considered to be the most likely place.

As they sat there, none of them felt particularly heroic. Charley felt out of place. He was twenty-two years old and scared to death. He looked at the Captain and wondered if he felt the same way. As he did, the silence was broken.

"This is position two," Tankersley said in his Louisiana drawl.

"Go ahead position two," he answered.

"We have contact. We have trucks towing Howitzers traveling west to east. We have infantry on foot, armored personnel carriers and supply vehicles. This is a large concentration."

"Roger," he answered.

He looked at the Captain for instructions.

"Tell him to stay put. Tell him to observe and keep us posted."

He was in the middle of his instructions when Billy spotted another column at their crossing.

"Holy shit!" the Captain exclaimed.

Charley watched as Billy began to count. That group was comprised the same as the one spotted by Tankersley.

"Why would they use two different routes?" the Captain asked out loud.

"Maybe because there are so many of them," Campbell answered.

Charley looked up and agreed.

"This is position three," they heard. "We have movement here."

"Three routes," the Captain said. "This is unbelievable. We must have a whole Division."

"Captain," Charley said. "Bring them all in and let's get out of here before we get caught up in this."

They checked with the fourth group. They had no activity.

"Yes," the Captain agreed. "Tell them to meet us at the pre-arranged point."

Charley radioed everyone and called them all in. After giving them instructions, they moved, too. After a half an hour they stopped and Charley made contact with Michael.

"We have three targets," he informed him.

As Charley carefully gave him each location, he asked how close to the targets they were. Charley told him they were about a mile or so out of the area. The pilot reconfirmed their location by map reference and said the attack was about to begin immediately.

"This is one," Charley said as he radioed to the others. "Come in two, three, and four. Are you secure?"

One by one they confirmed that they were.

"Button up. This is going to be a big one," he said.

The attack began immediately.

They were south of the river that ran east to west. By their terms it was not much of a river. It was more like a creek. Men and equipment had little problem crossing. They crossed in the same manner people had crossed for centuries. Everyone got their feet wet. That night the river was the target.

Charley was looking up in the night sky as it began. Without any warning, the world seemed to end. There was no sound of falling bombs. Once the explosions began they did not end.

As the first sixty bombs fell from the lead ship, they illuminated the sky in such a way he could see the bombs raining out of the darkness. The light and the sounds of the explosions grew more intense as each B-52 emptied its bomb bay. The force of it all shook the earth, creating an artificial earthquake.

It was bone shaking to be so close to the attack. There was no adequate way to describe the experience. Charley tried to put his mind somewhere else and control his fear. The more he tried, the less he was able to do it. He found himself trembling. He found himself wanting to cry out.

And as he did, something happened.

Something was reaching out and touching him. It was not a touch like a human touch. It was as if something had touched his inner being and it was not a good feeling. He felt soiled and dirty.

As afraid as he was, he suddenly didn't care. He looked out at the destruction before him and he perceived man with all of his conquests and his inventions of destruction had finally devised a way to soil the very soul and essence of a human being. From his place he rose to his feet and faced the inferno.

A hot breeze blew in his face and he didn't turn away. He stood there facing the fires of hell, realizing how many lives were being consumed by the devastation. As the bombs fell on the three targets, the entire northern horizon lit up.

Colonel Tuong, field commander of the 7th Division, was in the main column along the river. He was riding in the armored personnel carrier he had taken for his own. He had it fashioned so it was like his home on wheels. He had a table and four chairs in the center and his bed on the wall behind the driver. Campaign maps hung on the opposite wall and a radio unit was anchored to a table across from his bed. A small bar was in place along with a refrigerator powered by the vehicle's batteries and engine.

Colonel Tuong was comfortable and secure in his position as commander. Then it all ended. Only the blackness of eternity remained for him.

It took ten full minutes for the B-52 Stratofortresses to drop 3,300 tons of explosives. As each bomber purged itself, the bomb bay doors closed and the pilot made a gentle turn to the south and assumed a heading of 190 degrees. They maintained the heading until they were over the Mekong Delta region and were out to sea. Then they turned to the east and returned to Guam.

The choppers were on the ground and waiting for the 545th when they arrived. The sky to the north was still aglow. There had been secondary explosions even after the B-52's stopped bombing.

The men wondered what they hit, but were afraid to ask. Secretly they all believed they had inadvertently bombed the city of Muang Ngoy along with the enemy. On that they were correct.

SAM emplacements protected Muang Ngoy. They were undetected by American intelligence. And as the attack began and the missiles were launched, several bombers turned their attention to the general location, which made the city a target. The devastation was enormous.

Henry Townsend worked late into the night preparing for his meeting with the President. The satellite photos showed a perfect strike. It appeared not one of the enemy could have possibly survived.

The B-52's were already back in Guam being rearmed and refueled. A message came in at the same time as the satellite photos stating the 545th was in place and had already located the enemy.

The SAM site in Muanng Ngoy was a bonus. He decided to give the 545th credit for finding it and what was actually an accident was to become aggressive reconnaissance by the fighting men in Vietnam.

The President had been asleep in his chair. He and Mrs. Johnson ate around seven and went into the plush living room for an after dinner drink and some conversation. After all the years and all the campaigns, they both realized they had little to say to one another.

Mrs. Johnson and the President differed over the war in Vietnam. She was his conscience. She was the one who reminded him this was not some game where pieces were moved around on a map. It was Mrs. Johnson who understood there were young American boys, who were far from those who loved them, dying alone. That night she questioned why they had to die at all and as she did, the President drank more than usual.

"Why do you have to do this to me?" he demanded of her as he poured a full glass of scotch over ice.

"Lyndon," she pleaded. "Someone has to tell you. My job at this late date doesn't depend on me telling you you're right all the time. You've done great things as President.

'You've finished what Abraham Lincoln started. The slaves are finally freed. Now it is up to them to make their own place in this country. That will take time.

"You've given poor children a hot meal program and you've given our old people health insurance.

"You've done so many great things and then there is this black rotting thing that is killing our young boys. Vietnam is a cancer on our country. Until we can cut it out and cleanse where it was, none of us will ever be the same."

"You don't understand!" the President insisted. "This is Communism trying to pick away at us!"

"Horse feathers!" she said.

"The only Communism we have to fear is that baloney coming out of Bobby Kennedy's mouth. He and his brother Ted are the only real Communists I've ever met."

That made the President smile.

Lady Bird never did like the Kennedys. She accused them of believing they were American royalty. "Just like that phony Nelson Rockefeller," she would say.

In a way, Lyndon knew his wife was right. She was right about the Kennedys, Rockefeller, and in all probability, the Vietnam War, too. He knew he was in it too deep. All he could do was fight. She did not understand that.

He admired her strength and goodness. He wished he could have half the strength. He would have been satisfied with that. He knew he could never have the goodness.

When he woke it was 2 a.m. He thought about Archangel and wondered how it was going. He had an urge to find Townsend and get a report. Instead, he poured himself another drink and sat alone in the darkness. He would wait until noon. His Cutty Sark would do until then.

CHAPTER SEVEN

PITTSBURGH, PA
SEPTEMBER 11, 2001

Cindy Ganley was in a state of shock. She had been trying to reach Tina but all the phone lines were busy.

It was just after the second jet crashed into the south tower when her phone rang. It was Chuck.

"Mother, are you aware of what has happened?" he asked.

"No," she answered. "What?"

"Turn on your television," he told her.

"Jets have crashed into both of the Trade Center Towers and both buildings are on fire. I am above the fire in the south tower. It's burning upward and everyone is in a state of panic. I'm doing the best I can to keep everyone calm, but this is bad. It really is."

"My God, what floor are you on?" she asked.

"The ninety-first floor," he answered.

Then she heard him yell at someone.

"Don't do that!" she heard him scream.

She heard glass breaking and heard him yell.

"No! No!"

"What's happening?" she asked.

"People are jumping, Mother. They are jumping out the windows!"

Cindy caught her breath.

"I love you, Mother," he said. "I'm not going to get out of this."

Cindy was looking at the television and the inferno that was below her son. She knew he couldn't get out. She knew he was going to die and she knew that he knew it also.

"Tell Tina that I love her and the children. Tell her for me. I tried to call her, but she must be shopping. Please, Mother, tell her for me.

And tell the girls I love them, too. Tell Julie I love her. She'll take this hard. Tell her not to. Tell her I was all right at the end."

"I will, honey," she said. "I will. I promise."

"And tell Jerilyn I'm sorry I hurt her."

Cindy promised she would. And as she did the phone went dead.

She stayed at the television and was watching as the building her son was in collapsed. As it did, something inside of her died.

She sat staring at the television. Then the phone rang. First it was Julie, then the other girls. Chuck was their brother and he was gone. She had to tell them their brother was gone.

Finally, at noon Jerilyn called. She was concerned.

"Cindy," she began. "Have you heard from Chuck? Is he okay? Have you heard from Tina?" she asked all at once.

"I haven't heard from Tina. I tried to call her, but I can't get through."

Then Cindy paused for a moment.

"He's gone," she said. She took a long breath and fought back the tears. "He called me. He was trapped on the ninety-first floor. People were jumping out of the windows."

"Oh, no!" Jerilyn said. She began to weep over the telephone and Cindy began to cry again, too.

"This can't be true," Jerilyn said. "This can't be true!"

Jerilyn began to cry uncontrollably and apologized.

"I'm sorry, Cindy," she said. "I have to call you back. I can't talk now." She hung up the phone.

Cindy wanted to take the phone off the hook, but she didn't because of her daughters and because of Tina. Tina might be able to get a phone call out of New York easier than she would be able to get one in. All she could do was wait, cry, and remember. At the same time, Jerilyn Gardner was doing the same thing.

CHICAGO, ILLINOIS
1992

It was one of those chilly Sunday afternoons. The day seemed to promise to warm up, but just before kickoff at Soldiers Field, the wind changed direction and began to blow in from the lake. It was then the city lived up to its well-earned reputation.

It was another sellout for the Bears and every neighborhood bar around the city was packed with the usual assortment of regulars wearing their ball caps and football jerseys. Everyone was supporting the home team. Jack O'Halloran's Pub on the north side was not any different. By game time the bar was full and the buck ninety-five breakfast special was over.

Jerilyn Gardner worked at the Pub. She had been a mainstay for quite awhile and was popular with the Sunday football crowd. While she didn't care to work on weekends, when she did, she did very well on Sundays. So, she made an exception during football season. O'Halloran was glad when she did. Business always was better.

She was a petite woman with long dark hair. Her eyes were gray with a shade of green through them. Very often she had the habit of looking upward and beyond the person to whom she was speaking. This gave the other person, usually a man, the feeling she probably was not very interested or at least distracted during their conversation. The impression was usually true.

Nature had been kind to Jerilyn. She was forty-four but could easily pass for a woman who might have just turned thirty. There was no trace of age in her face and her hair was still the same rich color it had been when she left her father's house. Her body, while always very attractive to men, was never abundant in the breasts or hips. For that reason, plus the fact she worked nearly every day, left her subject to none of the cruelty gravity imposed on the average American woman. On the contrary, Jerilyn Gardner's body was every bit as firm as it had been when she was twenty.

While she might have looked twenty or thirty, Jerilyn certainly was not feeling that way when Chuck Ganley walked into the bar just after five Sunday afternoon.

It was supposed to be her day off but Jessica called in sick and O'Halloran called her at the last minute. She wanted to tell him no, but she had been with him a long time and knew how they depended on her. Reluctantly, she agreed to work.

When Chuck left her that morning, everything was fine. Now he was there with another woman. It hurt her. He was already starting to act like his father.

Jerilyn caught herself. She had no way of knowing if what she suspected was true. Even though everything fit and the resemblance was uncanny, she had no proof. All she had was the way she felt. Every time she saw him she was that much more sure of her feelings. She couldn't get over seeing him then, or now.

It was on Thursday when Chuck first walked up to the bar and ordered a round of drinks. As he did, she couldn't help but feel the cold shock of a memory long since forced into the recesses of her mind. She thought she was seeing a ghost. She thought she was seeing Charley Reed.

It easily could have been him, even to the very shade of his hair and tone of his skin. It was as if he was frozen in time. She knew that couldn't be.

His voice carried the same nasal twang and his eyes seemed to move across her body the same way Charley's had so many times before. She was frozen as the young man ordered the drinks a second time, this time with a hint of laughter in his voice. It was uncanny. It had to be him, but she knew it was not. Charley Reed had been dead nearly twenty years.

A shiver brought her back into the present moment. She forced a smile, asked him to repeat the order a third time and never heard what he said because she was too intent on listening to the voice of a man long since gone. She apologized and after a fourth request, she finally gave him the three Buds he requested.

She watched as he walked away from the bar and couldn't believe her eyes. She was sure her memory was playing tricks on her.

How could this be?

Jerilyn could not believe it. She continued to work, very preoccupied by the young man in the corner with his two friends.

It wasn't a very busy night. There were the regulars in after work. They came in for one but wound up staying for the football game. Thursday night football was not the draw Monday night was, but Jerilyn didn't notice much of a difference in her tips. The Monday night fans were drinkers and grabbers. The tippers came in for Friday happy hour. Twenty years as a bartender, or barmaid as Charley called her, meant she knew them all.

She walked over to his table and the three men ordered another round. One of the young men made a comment about her as she walked away and she felt a flush come over her she hadn't felt in years.

She was blushing as she returned with the beers and felt her body respond as he looked directly into her eyes and smiled. His smile was identical to the same one Charley first used to seduce her mind, body, and soul. As uncomfortable as she was by this unexpected encounter, Jerilyn allowed her mind to escape into feeling the same way she had felt years ago. She felt like a girl.

He asked her to start a tab for them and winked at her. She smiled and went back to the bar with the empties and not ever thinking twice, wrote Charley's name on the top of the bar tab. She poured herself a coke and for the first time in many years thought of Charley Reed and what their life might have been like had they stayed together and had he not died.

Those were crazy years.

The Vietnam War had just ended and the country was being torn apart by one scandal after another. An entire nation was trying to find itself and in the midst of it all Charley Reed left his wife and took her and her three children out of North Carolina to Washington, D.C.

He needed her and she needed him.

She was a young mother with babies and found a world wanting to rape her soul. She was young, beautiful, and intelligent. She was the woman every man wanted for at least one night.

Charley was different. He didn't want anything from her except the chance to love her. Love was the one gift no man had ever given her. Charley gave it freely. Jerilyn remembered that love. It was fierce and consuming.

Just as he physically devoured her body in their lovemaking, his love enveloped her heart and soul. It was so intense and powerful, her chest would grow heavy and she would find it difficult to breathe.

His love was commanding and bound her to him in such a way she seemed to lose her own identity. It made her an extension of him and even after he was gone and she was with other men, she still felt it was holding onto her.

As the years dulled one memory after another, even a love as powerful as his weakened and was eventually forgotten. Now, she could feel its presence once more. What she believed was gone seemed to have returned.

She couldn't stop watching him. Her eyes stole one glance after another. She served them three more rounds of drinks, but wasn't able to start any sort of conversation. Jerilyn was uneasy with what she was feeling and thinking. He was young enough to be her son. He easily could have been the same age as her daughter, Tina.

She listened and caught pieces of their conversation as she served them. He was an attorney and had just gone out on his own. He was worried.

Brad, the dark one, was a doctor interning somewhere north of the city. Mark was teaching at Marquette and had driven down for the evening.

She still had not caught his name, but the sound of his voice was as chilling to her as it was warm.

During the third quarter of the game the bar got busy. The noise level increased and as one of the teams mounted an offensive drive and scored, it became impossible for her to pick up anything else from their conversation. Jerilyn was busy with a full house.

It was a good night for tips. Her regulars joked with her. It wasn't anything special. Just the usual comments about wanting to take her home and send her off to where she'd never been before. That was one thing that never changed.

Mark stood up to leave with only a few minutes remaining in the game. She walked over to their table to see if they needed anything else. Mark said he was going and insisted he settle up with the bar. They all walked over to the bar where Mark paid the bill. Then again, as if a hand reached out from the past, Mark said goodbye to Brad and Chuck.

Jerilyn's mouth dropped open. She turned away from them. Her stomach knotted and ached. As soon as he paid her, she walked to the ladies room and looked into the mirror at the face of the shocked woman staring back at her. Something happened to her and she began to cry.

How could this have happened?

Wiping the tears from her face, she returned to the bar. Chuck and Brad, along with all of her regulars needed drinks.

They were seated at the bar now and it was easy for her to listen to their conversation. It went from the game to women to Chuck's parents to Brad's wife who was not too pleased with Brad's friendship with Chuck. Jerilyn smiled and remembered her Charley's friend, Walker and how his women always had problems with Charley.

"Do you fellows live here in Chicago?" she asked them.

"Yes," they both answered.

"Is this your first time here?" she asked referring to the bar.

"Yes," they both answered again.

"I just rented a place around the corner," Chuck said. "We wanted to check out the neighborhood watering holes."

"Well, what's the verdict?" she asked.

Chuck smiled that electric smile. His entire face seemed to explode in warmth. His eyes drew her eyes to him as he answered.

"The pub is okay. The service is not only prompt, efficient and courteous, but absolutely gorgeous as well."

With his tender voice and soft, boyish face, she felt herself melting inside. He was magnetic and just like her Charley.

"Thank you," she said blushing. "It's nice to see new faces in this old place."

She got them each a beer on the house and then went down to see Harry, one of the regulars and insulted him. Harry laughed. Her insults were as expected as they were welcome. He had told her many times she reminded him of his ex-wife. Evidently he still loved the woman because the insults were worth at least five dollars every time he came in. Harry was a good tipper and never once hit on her. He was about sixty and Jerilyn figured with all the booze, nothing probably worked any way.

Chuck and Brad were laughing as she walked back to their end of the bar. Chuck was talking about his dad. She felt strange again as Chuck started to tell her what was so funny.

"He's a stiff, intolerant jerk. He's the mayor of Sunset, Utah and if he knew I was sitting here drinking beer with my friend and admiring you, he would probably try to thrash me and deliver me from the hands of Satan."

"He would probably want to thrash all three of us," Brad added, including Jerilyn in the conversation.

"No," Chuck said. "Not you two, only me. You see I'm one of the elect. I'm the flesh of my father, a saint on earth. You two he'd ignore."

Chuck began to laugh again.

"The only problem is the old saint seems to forget his younger days at Purdue when he met my mother. She was four months pregnant with me before God finally directed him to marry her. And that happened only after she agreed to repent and become a saint like the great Adam Ganley. But she failed miserably. No one can be a saint like Adam Ganley."

"Who in the world told you that?" Jerilyn asked.

"My Grandmother George in Pittsburgh."

Pittsburgh stopped Jerilyn cold. Pittsburgh was where Charley Reed was born and raised. How much farther would this likeness continue? Jerilyn was afraid to go on, but she was more afraid to stop.

She listened as the young man talked about his father and family. His parents were still married. There were four other children, all girls, ranging in ages from seventeen to twenty-three. Charley had just turned twenty-five and had gone to college at Brigham Young University and law school at Duquesne University. He was just out of law school and was on his own.

"Saint Adam wasn't very happy when I went to law school at a Catholic university, but as my old grandmother always says, the hell with him if he can't take a joke."

Jerilyn could not believe her eyes or ears. Here she was, a thousand miles and twenty years away and she was looking Charley Reed in the face and listening to him speak in the same voice and using identical sayings, even to the old grandmother routine.

"Saint Adam and I haven't spoken since then. My grandparents lent me the money for law school and I'm still paying them back, even though when Grandfather died, Grandmother George told me to stop. I made a deal and I'll live up to it."

Just before midnight Jack O'Halloran came in to collect the night's receipts. Like Jerilyn, he was surprised at the business they had done.

Chuck and Brad were still there when Jack told her to set up the bar with a round of Kamikazes. When Jack heard Brad was a doctor, he immediately tried getting free medical advice plus various prescriptions he could use.

Jerilyn sat on a stool behind the bar and studied the face of a now quiet Chuck Ganley. It was the same face taken from her years ago. She found herself drifting back to those times when he picked her up after work and they drove out of town and made love in his car. She remembered his hands on her body and his mouth on hers. She thought of his body, and then Jack demanded another round of Kamikazes.

"The Giants came through for me tonight," he bellowed. "Monday night killed me but now I'm even."

Jerilyn set up the round and clinked glasses with Chuck as they drank the shot. Chuck smiled at her and said he was certainly glad he came in.

"You should try happy hour tomorrow. All the single girls from the neighborhood come in after work. It's really quite a pickup spot," Jerilyn told him.

"I'm really not into that," he said.

"Why not?" she asked. "Did someone break your heart?"

"Sort of," he admitted. "I guess I'm over it by now."

"I'm not sure you ever get over something like that," she said.

The way she said it made it sound as if it was almost like a confession.

"I used to know someone who told me that every time you love someone, not just screw, but love them, you give away part of yourself to them. He used to say it was really, really important to get something back from them, otherwise before long there'd be nothing left of you."

Chuck thought for a minute. His eyes went far away. His voice was soft and his face sincere. "You must have loved him."

"Very much," she answered.

"What ever happened to him?" he asked.

"He loved me much more than I was able to return at the time," she said. "He left me and when he tried to come back, I wouldn't let him."

She stopped. She was thinking about what she had just said, as well as what she was about to say. Then she continued.

"Then he was killed in a car accident and I lost him."

She looked away.

"When that happens and there is unfinished business or unspoken love, I don't know you ever get over it."

He was silent. She looked across the bar and felt the loss of her Charley again and wondered why this was happening now.

At one o'clock Jack told her to take off. "I'll handle the lockup," he said.

Jerilyn knew Jack and his buddies would lockup and play cards all night. She happily obliged. She was tired and had been working since four.

When she walked outside, Chuck was standing next to a car talking to Brad. She got in her own car and started it up. She watched as Brad drove away and then backed her car out of its parking place. As she drove out of the lot, she passed Chuck walking down the street.

"Need a ride?" she asked.

"I just live down the street," he answered.

"I thought you might be afraid of the dark," she kidded.

He laughed. "I'd love a ride."

He only lived three blocks away in a two-story townhouse. When he asked her to come in, she very nearly accepted. Instead, she said she was tired.

"Maybe some other time," he said.

"You never know," she kidded. "Come in and see me tomorrow."

Twenty minutes later she was home. She couldn't get him out of her mind. As she showered, she remembered meeting him when she was the bartender at the Carolina Inn. She remembered letting him give her a ride that first night. It was raining and he had on an eight-track tape of Johnny Mathis as they rode in his new Cadillac.

She turned off the lights and got into bed. Tonight she did not mind going to bed alone with her memories and desires. The darkness surrounded her as she slowly ran her hands down her body.

She remembered them alone in an empty apartment and their first kiss. She turned into his arms and remembered how he hesitated and she kissed him. His hands had gone across her back and slipped under her blouse to touch her skin. His hands were gentle as they moved across her back and then beneath her bra and softly held her breasts.

Now her hands reached the center of her body and she began to caress herself, much as he had done to her that first night.

She could remember her clothes falling to the floor and his lips running down her neck to her breasts and finally to the very place she was touching now. The best thing that first night was when she placed him inside of her.

His body spoke to hers and she answered. They moved together in a way that made it seem they always had. She remembered the feeling of his explosion and how only her own surpassed it. And now as she remembered, she exploded again. She was as breathless as she had been then, and once more wave after wave swept through her body. She cried out in her bedroom as if he was there with her.

"Charley, I love you. You make me feel so good. I need you!"

She said it once more and then she slept.

CHAPTER EIGHT

Jerilyn slept well that night. Her dreams were about the bar and some of her regular customers. Sunlight flooding through the bedroom window was her alarm clock and even though it was a chilly November day outside, the sun warmed her bed as she slowly woke from the night of sleep.

It was Friday. She was scheduled to work. She knew it would be busy. Fridays always were and Jerilyn just stared at the ceiling trying to get in gear to begin the day. She rolled over and looked at the clock. It was just before ten. She thought about trying to sleep some more, but before she could make up her mind, the phone rang.

"Hello," she forced from her throat, her voice cracking in the process.

"Did I wake you?" he asked.

"No," she answered. "I was awake."

It was Bob and she was glad to hear from him.

"What were you doing?" he asked.

"Just laying here. I just woke up and was trying to decide whether to go back to sleep or not."

"What's the decision?" he asked.

"I haven't decided," she said in a playful voice.

"What are you wearing?"

"Right now?"

"Yes," he said.

"My blue cotton nightgown."

"Any underwear?"

"What?" she asked.

"You heard me," he teased.

"Well, I don't think that's any of your business," Jerilyn said feeling her face grow warm. "If you want to know so bad, come over and find out."

"Is that an invitation?" he asked.

"Sure," she said. "Why not."

"I can't make it until noon," he answered.

"That's fine," she said. "I can sleep some more."

Jerilyn hung up the phone and rolled over on her other side and looked out at the blue November sky.

It was this time of year she first met Bob Holt. It was when she started tending bar at the Marriott. Bob was one of the afternoon regulars and he was there on her first day.

She didn't want a day job. Jerilyn had always been a night person but days were all that was available. She needed a job so she took what they had, asking to be worked in at night when it became available. She found the tips during the day were not bad and when they offered her a cocktail waitress spot, she refused.

Bob was an attorney for one of the fancy Michigan Avenue law firms. She didn't realize he was a partner until someone ran into her car one day while she was on her way to work. She mentioned it to him and when he handed her his card, there he was. His name was one of the four in the firm's name with partner as his title. He offered her his services and when the insurance company began giving her the runaround, she asked if he was serious.

"I most certainly am," he said. "When can you come into my office?"

"Tomorrow," she told him. "It's my day off and I can be there any time you'd like."

"Come in at eleven and then we'll have lunch," he said.

She was there on time and a secretary took her back to his office. It was an enormous room looking out at Lake Michigan from the thirty-seventh floor. His walls were covered with diplomas and pictures of him with important people. She immediately recognized one of him with President Nixon. There was another with Ronald Regan. There was one on his desk of what seemed to be his wife and two teenage daughters. There was another that appeared to be his parents.

He offered her a seat and got right to business.

"What have they offered you?" he asked.

"Sixty-eight hundred dollars. The only problem is I owe over nine thousand on the car, plus I've had to have a rental car for over a week."

"Have you been to a doctor?" he asked.

"No," she answered.

"Good," he said. "From now on you don't talk to anyone about this accident except me. I'll get the car paid off and some money for you besides."

"How much will this cost me?" she asked. "I'm not sure I can afford you."

"You can't," he said smiling at her. "The insurance company can."

She remembered liking his confidence. He had a way about him that made her feel like she was safe now that he'd taken her case. Then they went to lunch.

Jerilyn was glad she wore a dress. Bob took her to the private club in the building. They had a table with flowers in the middle next to a window and a waiter instead of a waitress.

It was a polite lunch and never once did he try to hit on her. She remembered liking that. She remembered how it gave her even more confidence in him. After lunch he walked her to the elevator and shook her hand, promising to see her the next day.

During the following weeks, Bob came in every day she worked. They had plenty of time to talk and Bob told her about his situation at home and how it was tied to his work. She realized he was not happy and she tried to be there just to listen.

It was just before Christmas when he brought her a check for nearly fifteen thousand dollars. It was made out to her and signed by someone in his law firm. It was more than she ever expected to see.

"Our fee was four thousand six hundred," he said. "We've already taken it out. All of this is yours."

Jerilyn could not believe her eyes. She opened a bottle of champagne and toasted their success. He stayed until she got off at six and took her to dinner. From dinner they went back to her apartment and he stayed until nearly three.

That was the beginning.

During the next four years they had a torrid love affair that went hot and cold with the seasons. At first it lasted eight months, followed by a two-month breakup. Then they were friends for two months while Jerilyn dated a twenty-two year old bartender. When he dumped her, they became lovers again. And when they did, it changed.

It became a quiet love with the sex becoming gentle and caring. Bob needed her and she grew to depend on him. He took her to Las Vegas over Labor Day weekend and to Toronto at Thanksgiving.

His wife was always going away by herself or with their daughters so they had plenty of time to be together. Then about a year ago something happened between him and his wife. He stopped coming around and stopped calling. Jerilyn assumed it was over. She knew the day would come. It was then she left the Marriott and took the job at Jack O'Halloran's Pub.

She didn't hear from him until two months ago. When she did, she didn't ask any questions. She took him back and now it had become a regular and very different thing.

As she took a bath, she thought about the changes their relationship had gone through. She was sure he loved her, but things were different now. Their sex was just as good as it always had been. It was just that he wanted different things.

He seemed more of a pervert to her and she found she really didn't mind it. She didn't mind, but it was just that he wanted things he never wanted until now and that surprised her. It excited her, too.

Jerilyn wondered what he might expect when he arrived today. Drying herself, she walked out of the bathroom.

The sunlight flooded through her bedroom windows and warmed the carpeted floor. She was still naked when the doorbell rang. She went to pick up her robe from the chair in the corner of the room. As she picked it up, she paused to look at herself in the mirror. Her body was still perfect with small upright breasts and a small firm rear end. She smiled.

When she answered the door, Bob was standing there holding a bottle of wine. She began to laugh even though he hadn't said or done anything. That was one of the reasons she put up with him and was probably the reason she liked him.

"Hi, baby," she said to him. "Come on in."

"I brought some champagne," he said. "We can have mimosas."

"Great," she said. "That's a good way to start the day."

Bob walked into the kitchen and found two glasses and the orange juice. He opened the bottle of wine and made the drinks. He went over to the couch where she was sitting and offered her one.

Jerilyn took her glass and toasted. "Here's to us, baby. Today."

She knew Bob didn't understand, but she didn't care either.

"Where are your high heels?" he asked with a smile.

"In the bedroom closet," she answered.

"Go put them on."

"What else?" she asked.

"You don't need anything else. The heels are all you'll need."

Jerilyn smiled at him. She lit a cigarette and sipped some more of the champagne. She could see the bulge in his pants and knew he wanted her.

He probably had been thinking about her for the past two days.

He may have even tried to satisfy himself with Anne and it was probably either really bad or Anne wouldn't have anything to do with him. Bob told her about Anne's hormone imbalance and how she refused to take the prescription the doctor gave her. Jerilyn finished the glass of wine.

"Pour me another, baby. I'll be right back."

When she returned, he already had his pants off as well as his shoes and socks. His shirt was still on, but it was unbuttoned and his hand was holding his erection.

Jerilyn walked across the room wearing nothing but a pair of red spike heels. She watched him as he licked his lips and slowly stroked himself.

She had been with him before when he was like this. Each time it was the same and each time she wondered why she put up with it. But in a strange way, it excited her, too.

"Touch yourself for me," he said. "Come here and stand on the coffee table and touch yourself. I want to watch you."

She did as he asked.

His hand moved faster as she stood on the coffee table doing exactly what he wanted.

Reluctantly she found herself becoming turned on by the sight below her as well as her own familiar touching.

She stepped from the table to the couch and stood above him. Slowly and deliberately she lowered her body to him. Slowly she placed him inside her.

She caught him by surprise and he acted irritated by her action. He didn't want it that way. He raised her body from him and took her by the hair, forcing her head down and him into her mouth.

Something was really wrong. He wanted a whore. She knew it and accommodated him.

She began to do as he wanted and it didn't take long. He exploded almost immediately. Bob brought her face up to his and kissed her. He forced his tongue into her mouth, attempting to taste himself. The kiss lasted longer than usual.

After kissing her, Bob reached for his wine and began to drink.

Jerilyn lay back on the couch and looked at him. Still not satisfied, she ran her hand down between her legs. Her fingers found that spot. Bob continued to drink as he watched her touch herself. She wondered if he had any intention of joining her, but instead he poured more wine and began to stroke himself.

"Kiss me," she told him.

He just stared at her and kept on touching himself.

"Kiss me," she said again.

He ignored her and continued what he was doing to himself.

It was too late for her to stop even though she was angry with him. Watching her was making him excited again. She continued and then it was over for her. She lay there and watched as he brought himself to a second climax. As he did, he fell back exhausted.

The next few moments seemed to last forever. Then she broke the silence.

"Why don't you go?" she said angrily.

"What?" he asked.

"Go," she said. "You got what you wanted. You got off twice. Now you can go home to your fat wife and be bored until you get horny enough to call again."

"What's your problem today?" he asked.

Her answer came quickly and was one she did not think twice about.

"Selfish bastards like you are the only problems I've ever had.

"Just get dressed and leave and take what's left of your cheap champagne with you. You know as much about wine as you do sex."

She picked up her robe and went into her room, slamming the door as she entered. She didn't get dressed. Instead, she began to brush her long black hair, something else that hadn't changed over the years. When she heard the front door close, she left the bedroom, still naked. She made sure the door was locked.

The phone rang just as she finished dressing. It was Tina, her oldest daughter.

Tina was twenty-five and a graduate student at Northwestern. Jerilyn was really proud of her. She had put herself through four years of college and was now working on her master's degree.

"Hi, honey," she said.

"Hi. When are you going to work?" Tina asked.

"I don't go on until four, why?"

"I thought I'd come by and maybe we could do some shopping."

"I don't have all that much time to shop," Jerilyn said. "We could have a late lunch. I haven't eaten since yesterday."

"That'd be great, Mom," Tina said. "I'll pick you up."

"Okay. When?"

"Twenty minutes, if you're ready."

"I just finished. Honk and I'll be out," she said.

Jerilyn was ready and Tina took them to a north side restaurant and bar. She knew her mother would not eat unless she sat her down and let her smell the food. She didn't want her getting sick like she had five years ago.

"Order a dinner, Mom. I want you to eat before you go to work."

"Okay," Jerilyn said, ordering the fish dinner they had on special.

As she lit a cigarette, Tina frowned.

"I wish you would quit that," she said.

Jerilyn just ignored her and continued to smoke until the meal arrived.

After they ate, they sat and sipped coffee.

"What's up with you?" Jerilyn asked her daughter.

"I'm a little confused, I guess," Tina said. "Maybe disillusioned and disappointed, too."

"Why?" she asked.

"Terry," Tina answered. "He's married."

"Oh," her mother said understanding immediately.

"I find out now that he has a wife and two little kids and he's been seeing me for three months."

"How did you find out?"

"His wife called me."

Jerilyn just shook her head.

"You can imagine how I felt. I thought it was some joke at first, but it didn't take long to realize she was serious. I really felt low when she got through."

"What did Terry say about it all?"

"Nothing! He acted like a real jerk. He acted like there was nothing wrong and I should have known all along."

"They're all dogs," Jerilyn said.

"Daddy says we're all whores."

"Tina, don't pay attention to your father. He's an asshole. He was just like Terry when you were a baby and your sister was born. He had two going at once and I was home with you girls."

"Well, he's not that way now," Tina said. "I've been to his home and he seems very happy. He loves those kids and is really good to her."

Tina was careful not to mention his wife's name to her mother. The mere mention of it might send her into a rage. Jerilyn hated her.

"Is she pregnant again?" Jerilyn asked.

Tina laughed. "Oh, Mom, just because she was pregnant when Daddy married her you think she stays pregnant."

"Doesn't she? They have three already."

"Come on, Mom," Tina grinned.

"I'm serious," Jerilyn said.

"Maybe your father finally grew up. Don't expect me to be over-joyed if that's happened. He put me through too much and I can't be happy he's finally giving some other woman what he couldn't give me. In the end he'll probably revert. They all do! He's the biggest dog of them all."

"Are they all like Daddy and Terry?" Tina sighed.

"Sometimes I think so, baby. But then I remember some good men I've known, too. They were men that other women hurt more than I could ever repair."

"Who?" Tina asked.

"You know who," Jerilyn answered.

"Yes, but you never talk about him to me."

"That's because he's hard to talk about," Jerilyn said. "He was the one man who was different."

"I remember him, but I was only six and I just remember how he used to scold me."

"He used to love you, too," Jerilyn said, defending him. "He used to love you a lot. Your sister was his favorite though."

Tina laughed as she remembered. "She used to call him The Man," she said.

"That's right. Anne was afraid of everything. He'd get up and hold her at night for hours when she was scared of the dark. I used to get angry with him for babying her, but he just killed me one night with what he admitted.

"He said he was still afraid of the dark himself and understood how she felt."

"I remember him being so tall and strong and how he'd lift weights all the time. He drove really nice cars and had the prettiest shirts," Tina said.

"That was Charley Reed," Jerilyn said with a sad smile.

"He must have been some lover," Tina said.

Her mother never answered. Some things were better left to memory and not shared with anyone, even a daughter.

Happy hour began at four when Jerilyn got to work. It was typi-cal for a Friday. It was well under way by that time. By five-thirty the bar was packed and it was all she could do to keep the drinks poured. Chris helped out on Fridays and she was just as busy handling the ser-vice bar.

In the midst of the confusion, Jerilyn picked him out of the crowd.

As had happened the night before, the same cold chill swept over her. Even though she thought she was prepared, the shock of seeing him left her nearly speechless. She kept on working, but seldom took her eyes from him for very long.

The crowd thinned out about nine-thirty and Chris offered to take over the bar. It had been a good night for Jerilyn so she accepted the offer. After a quick trip to the ladies room she sat down at a stool and ordered a vodka and tonic. Chuck moved to join her.

"Off early tonight," he said trying to start a conversation.

"Yes," she sighed. "And I'm not upset one little bit. This has been some day."

"For me, too," he agreed.

At first they spoke very little. They had several drinks. Then they chatted about his day and a divorce case he was handling.

Jerilyn found she couldn't take her eyes away from his face.

As he spoke she touched his arm, and then she touched his hand as it lay on the bar. Finally she placed her hand on his leg just above the knee. Jerilyn knew this was not her Charley, but didn't care. She found herself wanting him.

Shaking her head to clear it, she got up and shot a game of pool with Mick, one of the regulars. She looked back at the bar and he was smiling at her. She began to imagine making love to him and remembering Charley Reed, she was easily confusing the two. She thought about him and just before midnight, she asked Chuck for a ride home.

The ride was reminiscent of a ride she took twenty years before, even with the music he had on the radio. She knew what was going to happen that night just as she expected would happen this night. Jerilyn thought it might be a little twisted, but it couldn't be any worse than her little skits with Bob.

Jerilyn didn't have to coax when she asked him to come in for a while. He locked the car and followed her up the steps to her front door. It was just starting to rain as they closed the door behind them.

"Beer, wine, or whiskey?" she asked as she took off her coat.

"Scotch?" he asked.

"Johnny Walker Black okay?"

"My brand," he answered.

"You only drink beer in the bar," she commented.

"I've only been there twice," he said, "and both times in jeans and those are my beer drinking clothes normally. I'd rather have scotch, but I try to control it. I don't want to go to eternal damnation all in one night."

She laughed remembering how he spoke about his father. At the

same time she found herself wondering how this fluke of nature could
have happened.

After pouring herself some wine and his scotch, she sat next to
him on the couch. Their legs touched and she felt the goose bumps
begin. She wondered what to say and then realized she didn't want to
say anything anyway. She wanted to kiss him.

She wondered how long it would take him to kiss her.

She wanted more than just to kiss him. She wanted to make love
to him. She wanted him inside her. She wanted to feel him and taste
him. Jerilyn needed him and she wasn't going to wait. She didn't care
about anything at that moment except having him make love to her.
She took the glass from his hand, placed it on the table and brought
his face to hers.

It had been a very long time since she became excited like this.

There was urgency in her kiss and her hands rubbed across his
chest and back and pulled him closer to her. Her mind was flooded by
feelings coming from memories out of her past. She felt herself growing hot and dizzy and he hadn't even touched her yet, other than their
kiss.

His hands went beneath her sweater and touched her skin.

The shock of his touch was too much and she knew she had to
stop him so they could get to the bedroom. She wanted to undress him
slowly and love his body. When she told him, he offered no argument
and followed her into the bedroom.

And they made love, and she loved him, and then he loved her.

He was Chuck, and not Charley, but it made no difference to her.
His body, the sight of it, the feel of it, the smell and taste of it, excited
her more than she had been in years.

There seemed to be no end to it, only beginnings. Each crescen-
do of pleasure was greater than the one before it. Her whole being was
in his control and he loved her body as a musician might love his music
and he played each note in perfect harmony with the note he played
before.

Jerilyn was overcome with pleasure and it seemed as if it would
never end. She knew she couldn't stop and wouldn't until he chose to
end.

She lost all sense of time and place. She lost herself in the moment
and gave herself over to the pleasure of it all.

When dawn finally came, she fell asleep with his head held close
to her breasts. They never stirred because when the phone woke her
just before three, they were still in the same position. The phone rang

many times before she finally woke. Her voice was rough and crackling as she answered.

"Did I wake you up, Mother?" Tina asked. "Don't you have to
work tonight?"

"Yes to both questions," Jerilyn answered, trying to clear her head.

Chuck stirred and his hand moved down her body and rested
between her legs, sending a shock through her body.

"Are you going to work? It's three o'clock."

"Yes, why did you call?" Jerilyn could only manage to say.

"I just wondered how you were."

"I'm fine, honey. Come in and see me tonight. I've got to go and
get ready for work now."

Jerilyn hung up the phone and turned to Chuck. He was ready to
make love again and Jerilyn forgot about being to work on time.

CHAPTER NINE

Jerilyn got to work an hour late. No one said a thing. Jerilyn was never late. Usually she was the one covering for the rest of the girls.

The evening dragged on for her. The Saturday afternoon football crowd was still there and in full swing. Notre Dame was playing USC. The game was rolling back and forth, drink after drink.

She found herself simply going through the motions, still preoccupied by Chuck, their lovemaking, and the memories of Charley Reed. Perhaps she was more preoccupied by the first Charley, Charley Reed. How was it possible for her to find him years after his death?

She thought about the lovemaking and how it was so similar. Actually, she thought it was the same. She had been with many men since Charley Reed, but none of them made her feel the same until that morning.

Her memory wandered through the year with Charley. She kept pouring drinks, smiling at the jokes she half listened to and thought of him. Jerilyn thought about making love with him in his car. He always drove a Cadillac and he would put the seat back. Then there was always the special feeling he gave her with their first kiss. She could remember anticipating it as they drove to some private place tucked away in the Carolina countryside.

She could still remember him touching her, undoing her clothes, and running his lips down across her stomach, kissing all of her. He not only made love to her, he made her feel he utterly adored her. He made her feel that way with his mouth and hands.

His body gave her his adoration. His mind joined with hers and took her where she had never been before.

She never once thought to question his love. He was hers and hers totally. He would give up anything for her. As they made love, she knew it. He would give her anything. All she would ever have to do is ask.

And he proved it to her. He left his wife and moved in with her and the children.

Then he tried to leave her, too, but their love was so strong and he came back. He came back in conflict, but he came back just the same.

It was then she began to adore him and join with him the way he did with her. She tried to give him what he gave her. She hoped her love for him was powerful enough to take away his guilt. For a while it worked, but it didn't last. It couldn't.

He was too good of a man to be able to just walk away. That was why she loved him as much as she did.

She could give him her children, but there was always something missing. Even then after all of those years she found herself wondering.

"Mother, how long do we have to wait for a drink?" she heard Tina ask.

Jerilyn looked up to see her daughter with her sister, Ruth.

"Hey!" she squealed at her sister. "How in the devil did you get out tonight?"

"The old man is down state hunting," Ruth said in a strong North Carolina twang. "He loves shooting those little deer more than shooting me. That's okay 'cause I'm out with my niece."

Jerilyn laughed at her sister. She never changed, which was what was nice about her.

"Who's taking care of the kids?" Jerilyn asked.

"I got Anne Marie and her latest over at the house. She jumped right on it. I guess she needed a place to bed down this new stud, and does he ever look like a stud!"

Jerilyn laughed again. There was never any stopping Ruth once she got started.

Anne Marie was Jerilyn's other daughter, four years younger than Tina and more like her father than anyone else. No, she thought, she was more like the man she used to call 'her daddy' than anyone else. Just like her mother, Ann Marie never forgot Charley Reed either. Anne Marie loved him.

"Mother!" Tina said, attempting to get Jerilyn's attention. "Where were you?"

"Lost in the past before you and your sister went to live with your dad," Jerilyn said. She walked away to make drinks.

Tina shook her head. "I have to meet this man."

"What man?" Ruth asked.

"You remember him," Tina answered. "Charley."

Ruth froze, her heart beating rapidly at the sound of his name.

"Charley? Charley Reed?"

"That's him," Tina laughed.

"Tina, Charley's dead!" Ruth exclaimed.

"Not this one," Tina said. "Mom has someone else who reminds her of him."

"What on earth do you mean?" Ruth asked.

She didn't have to wait for an answer because through the doorway Charley Reed, or his double, walked. Ruth was speechless.

Tina turned to see what her aunt was staring at with her mouth hanging open. They both watched as the man walked up to Jerilyn and gave her an affectionate kiss on the cheek.

"Gawd damn!" Ruth said. "It is him in the flesh!"

"Who?" Tina asked.

"Him! Charley Reed! It's him or his Gawd damn twin brother!"

"Or son?" Tina asked.

"Whatever," Ruth answered, shaking her head. "But it sure enough looks like his spittin' image."

"Really?" Tina asked becoming interested.

Her mind took her back as she watched him and vaguely remembered the man who taught her to swim when she was six.

"Does he really look like him?"

"Yes," her aunt answered, not adding anything more.

"Well," Tina said, "I have to meet this man."

She stood and walked down the bar where her mother was looking into Chuck's eyes. Her mother was holding his hand and mumbling something to him when Tina took each of their hands, broke them apart and demanded an introduction. Later, Jerilyn would never forget that moment.

Chuck just laughed and introduced himself. "And who might you be?" he asked.

"Maybe your illegitimate daughter!" she joked, waiting for her mother's reaction to begin. "But not likely," she finished with a laugh.

"Tina, stop!" Jerilyn said.

By now Ruth had followed her niece to the end of the bar.

"Charley?" she asked.

Chuck turned to her as if he knew her.

"Yes? Do I know you?"

"Gawd damn! You're dead!"

"Not hardly!" he answered.

"Well, if you aren't, I need a drink!" exclaimed Ruth.

"I'm not. Give her a drink on me, babe!" he said.

The name babe shook both Jerilyn and her sister. Ruth looked at Jerilyn in disbelief. Jerilyn knew what was going through her sister's mind. She wasn't sure she could get used to another Charley.

"Please introduce me?" he asked Jerilyn, looking at Ruth and Tina.

Before Jerilyn could begin, Ruth stuck out her hand, gave him a hardy handshake, and introduced herself. Tina laughed at the forwardness of her aunt.

"Hi," she said. "I'm Tina."

"Another sister?" he asked.

She shook her head never bothering to check her mother's reaction.

"Daughter," she said.

"That's hard to believe. She's kidding, isn't she?" he asked Jerilyn.

"No, she's not kidding," she answered.

Chuck shook his head. He could barely believe Jerilyn was old enough to have a daughter as old as Tina. It was written all over his face.

Jerilyn watched his eyes as they moved from Tina to her and then back to Tina. A smile came over his face and he winked at her. Finishing his beer, he asked for another.

Ruth cornered Chuck and started working on him for the story of his life. Tina sat with her aunt and listened.

Jerilyn watched her sister as she talked to Chuck and at one point whispered in her ear not to mention anything about Charley. She was afraid of what Ruth might say. Jerilyn wished she didn't have to work and could steer the conversation in a different direction.

They sat at the end of the bar. Tina pushed her stool slightly away from the bar at an angle between her aunt and Chuck. Ruth was entertaining the two of them with stories about Jerilyn and herself when they were growing up.

Jerilyn watched her daughter staring at Chuck and was jealous. She was jealous because her daughter was his age. She wished she could go back. Knowing she couldn't only made it worse.

She watched Ruth grab his hand and pat his arm as she talked. Jerilyn felt possessive. She forced her attention to the rest of the barroom and tried to ignore their innocent conversation.

Later in the evening the young doctor, Brad, came in with his wife and joined them. Ruth continued her joking with the men while Tina seemed to warm up to Brad's wife. It turned out they were the same age and their birthdays were a day apart.

Jerilyn laughed at herself, an incurable people-watcher, watching her own daughter. She was trying to figure out what was in her mind. If this Chuck was Charley's double, Jerilyn knew Tina was certainly hers. Watching the two of them together reminded her of when she was with Charley.

If Tina felt the least bit insecure around the attractive doctor's wife, it certainly didn't show. Her college graduate daughter was undoubtedly comfortable enough and on equal ground and every bit as delightful and interesting.

Jerilyn enjoyed watching Tina toss her hair as she laughed. It made Jerilyn feel proud to watch the three younger people listening intently to her daughter as she made a point about something to do with a current political event. Jerilyn's jealousy left and was replaced by motherly pride.

Meanwhile, Ruth was sitting at the other end of the bar with two strange men.

Jerilyn's attention turned to her sister who was drunk and could easily walk out the door and go off with both of them. Much to Jerilyn's relief, Tina noticed, too, and shortly after midnight took her aunt home.

Even though Chuck sat at the bar until closing, he wasn't falling down drunk. He was able to consume a large amount of alcohol and still stay standing and never get mean. Even when they reached her apartment he could still make love and satisfy her. Then he finally fell asleep snuggled in her arms.

While he slept, his breathing constant and comforting, Jerilyn's eyes wouldn't close. Had he been any other man, she would have gently wiggled out of the bed and left the bedroom to sit alone and stare out at the Chicago skyline. But this wasn't any other man. This was Chuck. This was her Charley.

Somehow, some way, it was Charley again. Maybe not her exact Charley, but she didn't care. He was young, innocent, and undamaged by life.

"I love you," she whispered.

Her eyes stayed open staring into the darkness of her bedroom. Charley had come back and he was in her arms once more. How and why had she been given this gift?

She didn't understand. And as she lay awake in the darkness, she questioned whether it was necessary to understand.

Jerilyn remembered Charley trying to find a hidden meaning from every facet of life. She remembered trying to make him accept life as it was and just live. She remembered being unsuccessful. Now, twenty years after his death, she found herself guilty of exactly what she felt was his greatest fault.

"The world is round, baby," he used to tell her.

"We get paid back every time, some how, some way. It doesn't make any difference if anyone else knows. We may appear one hundred percent in the eyes of the world. We may look that way, but we know. That is all that matters."

As she remembered his words, Jerilyn finally knew the meaning. In a way she even understood the dismay he had felt as he spoke them. She was finally able to place his guilt together with his imagined punishment and at last place a portion of their life together at rest. Now it had come full circle and what he had been compelled to feel guilty for, she finally did in her own life.

His steady warm breath caressed her breast. She was still wet from him. The darkness closed around her, a blanket protecting them from the rest of the world. She felt herself drifting as her body and mind finally began to relax.

Jerilyn wanted him again and caressed his body until he woke and responded to her loving. As she mounted him, he came to life until they climaxed together. Collapsing on top of him, a smile came over her face. She rolled over next to him and they both dropped off to sleep.

She slept for hours. She didn't dream. It was a sound sleep and when she finally woke Chuck was gone.

At first she didn't understand and began to cry. She tried to fight her tears, but the more she did the less she could control them. Finally her tears changed to full-fledged weeping. He had gone home. At that moment something inside her knew he was gone from her for good.

She wanted to call him, but resisted. It was Sunday morning and snowing outside. She didn't have to work, but knew they would probably call to ask her to help with the overflow after the Bears game. She decided she wouldn't be available. Something was wrong. She felt as if she was in mourning again.

Her apartment was warm as she walked through the living room still naked from the night before. She enjoyed being naked in the warm air. She stood at the window watching the snow falling and covering the city outside her window.

Jerilyn Gardner didn't exactly understand why she had to be paid back again and again, but knew there was a reason. And just before Tina rang the doorbell, she thought of Michael, her baby. As she opened the door to her daughter, she burst into tears. The realization of it all was more than she could handle.

Tina didn't understand why her mother was crying and imagined scenarios far from the truth. In tears, Jerilyn wasn't able to answer any of Tina's questions.

"No! No!" she cried and screamed.

"No!" she repeated hoping her daughter would believe her. "Nothing bad happened. I'm just sad. Let's talk about something else, anything else."

"Okay," Tina said.

Returning from the bedroom with a robe for her mother, Tina asked, "Tell me about Charley Reed."

"Charley Reed!" exclaimed Jerilyn.

She found she was immediately angry with Tina and she didn't know why. The pain was new again. It was new and her daughter was only six years old when it all started. She found herself angry, asking what right she had to even ask.

Jerilyn answered her own question. Tina had every right. She was part of this as it happened.

Jerilyn had seen the two of them together at the bar. She remembered herself with Charley the first time. She remembered the innocence, the gentleness, and the instant attraction. At the same time she remembered her own jealousy. Before she could answer her daughter, she had to remember the two men were separated by years as well as death, and remembered the vitality they both shared.

"Tell me about Charley Reed," Tina asked once more.

"Charley Reed has nothing to do with you," Jerilyn answered her daughter.

"That's not true," Tina replied. "Evidently he's back. He's in both of our lives this time and I want to know about him."

"Where in the world did you get that idea?" Jerilyn demanded of Tina.

"Aunt Ruth," she answered.

Disgustedly Jerilyn answered, "That figures."

"And what does that mean?" Tina asked.

"Just what I said," Jerilyn repeated. "Your Aunt Ruth can be a real moron sometimes. Right now is one of those times. Even your precious Charley Reed would agree with me."

"Mother!"

"Mother what?" Jerilyn snapped back.

"He was your Charley Reed, not mine."

"Then what is all this about?" Jerilyn asked.

"I don't understand what interest you have in a man I once loved, especially a man that's been dead for twenty years. What interest do you have in him? You only have bad memories of him," Jerilyn said.

"Bad memories! Who said that?

"I remember him. He taught me not to be afraid of the water and he taught Ann Marie not to be afraid of the dark. He was there for me when you weren't.

"I don't remember my father when I was little, but I remember him. I remember being sick and throwing up in my bed. I was six and thought I was some young lady. Here I was sick and lying in my own mess. I was crying for you, Mother, and there he was. It was summer. It was hot and he walked into my room in a pair of shorts.

"Ann Marie said, 'The man is here!' She was two. You weren't there but he was and he picked me up and held me to him in spite of the fact that I was covered in vomit.

"I was crying and he took me to the bathroom and started the bath water. He put me in the warm, clean water. I remember him telling me he loved me. My own father has never told me that.

"No man who has never wanted anything from me has ever told me that except for Charley Reed.

"Mother, I was six. How do you think I feel?" Tina stopped.

Jerilyn could not answer. She had nothing to say.

"Answer me!" Tina demanded. "Is this Charley, our Charley Reed?"

Jerilyn still did not answer. She was numb from her daughter's questions.

"Is he or isn't he?" Tina said. "Answer me!"

Jerilyn could only cry.

"I love you," Jerilyn blurted out. "I love you."

Tina was angry and confused.

"I'm sorry," her mother said to her. "You can't possibly understand, but I'm so, so sorry."

"Don't apologize to me," Tina said. "Just tell me the truth."

"The truth about what?"

"Charley Reed."

Jerilyn stared at her daughter and hesitated a moment. "He's dead," she said. "That's the truth about him."

"Mother," Tina demanded again. "I want the damn truth."

"The damn truth is that he's dead and I can never, ever have him back again.

"He's gone and I don't believe in life after death and neither did he. I loved him and he loved me. There will never, ever be another man like him. He did everything I ever wanted a man to do to me. He's gone and that's a fact."

Jerilyn paused a moment before she spoke again.

"I don't care who looks like who, but there will never be another Charley Reed. I loved Charley Reed and he's dead."

"Mother?" she questioned.

"I told you," Jerilyn insisted. "Charley Reed is dead. You, your sister, and your brother Michael and I went to his grave. Charley Reed is dead and buried. That's all you need to know about Charley Reed."

The mention of her brother Michael redirected Tina's anger. Michael was another battleground, an issue between mother and daughter that had never been resolved. Tina couldn't understand what Jerilyn hoped to accomplish by saying Michael's name and resurrecting an old battle. She didn't let the moment pass.

"Tell me about why you did it, Mother," Tina asked.

"We've been through that before," Jerilyn said to her daughter. "I explained where I was then. How many times do I have to apologize? I can't undo the past. What I did then is done and I can't take it back. It's done and I'm sorry.

"If Charley Reed hadn't died, I never would have done it. Charley loved Michael. He looked at Michael as if he were his own son. He wanted to adopt Michael."

"So when he died, why did you sell Michael?"

"For God's sake, I put Michael up for adoption!"

"You got $25,000 for Michael. You got money for my brother!"

"Your half brother!" Jerilyn screamed.

"Half, quarter, whole, he was my brother and you sold him!"

"I gave him up for adoption because I tried one more time to make a home for you and your sister with your father. You're father wouldn't have him. That's why I did what I did."

"Mother, don't lie to me. I know you. You left Anne Marie and me with Dad two months after you went back to him. You may be able to fool everyone else, but you'll never fool me. I remember what you were like when I was little.

"I remember you when I was growing up and I know you now. This Chuck guy is just some other stud you need to scratch your itch."

Jerilyn raised her hand slightly, wanting to slap her daughter, but caught herself.

What Tina was saying was basically true and maybe more than Jerilyn wanted to admit. Sometimes she tried so hard to make something that is true false, that it only made it so much truer. There was no defense to what her daughter said. Jerilyn could only keep silent.

"So what is the story about this kid Chuck?" Tina asked again.

CHAPTER TEN

Chuck woke early that morning. He always had an inner clock and was able to set it with a thought and manage to wake up at the right time. Jerilyn was sound asleep and hardly moved as he left the bed. He dressed quietly and left the apartment. His mother was in town and he had to spend the day with her.

He had begged off meeting her at the airport. He claimed he had to be in Wisconsin overnight with a case and wouldn't be back before noon. His mother, a daughter of management, understood the demands of a man's profession and didn't mind hiring a cab to deliver her to the Drake Hotel. She assumed he would meet her for lunch and spend the remainder of the day with her.

Chuck understood what his mother expected of him and vowed to behave properly and try to make his mother's visit peaceful and enjoyable.

There was only one time he ever really went against her. It was over law school and they didn't speak for nearly a year. He stuck to his guns and never gave in. In doing so he realized during that time he gained her respect as a man who had his own life to live.

His father was another story.

It was difficult for Chuck to understand his father. He was a brutish, self-righteous bully of a man who preached hell and damnation to both his mother and himself alike. He was gentle with his daughters, but always expected more from Chuck than he was ever able to give.

By eleven Chuck was showered and dressed and at precisely noon knocked on his mother's door at The Drake. He was surprised at the affectionate embrace he received when she opened the door.

"My son!" she said as she put her arms around him, kissing him on his cheek. "I've missed you so much."

He was unable to answer because he was quite shocked by the

show of open affection from his mother. His mother had always been a little distant.

It was his father who was in control. His father was stern and unforgiving and didn't allow his mother to interfere or baby him. His father called the shots in their home and she was no more than his slave. Unless Adam Ganley approved, it did not happen.

The first transgression was when Chuck went to a Catholic university in Pittsburgh for law school. It was at that point Chuck lost his father.

"Mother, I've missed you," he said.

"I've missed you, too," she said.

She was trying to hold back her tears of joy at seeing her son for the first time in nearly a year. "I've really missed you," she repeated.

"How are the girls?" he asked as his mother closed the door behind him.

"Was your trip okay? How are you feeling?" He had so many questions and found himself acting like he was six and wanting them all answered at once.

His mother laughed.

He was surprised. His mother laughed!

"Mother," he said. "You're beautiful."

Tears filled his eyes as he spoke and he realized how much he had missed her and how beautiful she was.

Her hair was still naturally blond and her skin as soft and creamy as he remembered her when he was a small boy. Her figure was still trim, even though she did not work out or pamper herself as other women did. His father hadn't given her the kindest life, but she was an incredible women and seemed to thrive where other women would have collapsed and decayed.

"Why, thank you," she said, becoming embarrassed at her son's compliment.

It was a compliment that stung as much as it warmed. It had been so long since anyone told her she was beautiful. The last man to say it was her father just before he died.

Adam Ganley never commented on how she looked, only on how much it appeared she spent on herself. For the first time in her life, she felt truly cheated.

"I love you, Mother," he said, embarrassing her again.

"I love you, too, Chuck," she said back.

Sitting next to one another on the sofa in the sitting area, he asked about his sisters.

"Honey, they're fine. They all miss you and told me to tell you how much they love you. Julie especially misses you and made me promise to tell you so."

Chuck laughed, feeling the warmth in his mother's voice as she told him about his sisters.

"And, honey," she said. "They're all so beautiful. Especially Julie, she is a living doll and really misses her big brother. She tells all her friends about how her brother is this big famous Chicago lawyer who protects oppressed people from an evil city government and a corrupt police force.

"She's so much like you, Chuck. I just want to laugh and cry at the things she says and brings home to me. She has no regard whatsoever about what her father feels. She loves him, but she does what she wants. You can't help but love her. You would be very proud of her."

Chuck beamed hearing about his baby sister. "I wish I could see her," he said.

"And how is Father?"

"You're father is your father. Don't ever expect him to change. He is what he is. He was trained to be what he is and it suits him very well."

"Mother!" Charley started.

Cindy stopped him. "No," she said sternly. "I won't hear it. Don't even begin."

"I'm sorry," he apologized, becoming the submissive son as he had so many times in the past.

"Are you well, son?" she asked changing the subject.

There would be no discussion of Adam Ganley unless she wanted it.

"I'm fine, Mother," he answered.

Once again Adam Ganley stood between them and there was nothing more to say. This was one of the few times they had been alone together and didn't have to hold back their affection or try to hide some of their silly happiness at just being together. But it came to a halt when he asked about his father. So beyond that, what was left but lunch?

Chuck noticed his mother's new clothes, including her lovely full-length fur coat.

"Mother," he said as he held it for her to put on. "This coat is magnificent. Did Father get this for you?"

"No," was all she answered.

"So are you holding out after all these years," he teased. "Is there another man?"

"No," she laughed, once more making him uncomfortable with the levity. "It was my father's money and I spent some of it coming to see my successful, wonderful son, who I really miss."

"And what did Father have to say about this?"

"Absolutely nothing," she said defiantly.

"It is my money and my money alone. Your father would have nothing to do with my parents or my sisters. It's all my money.

"This trip is not costing your father or the church one blessed penny. It's all my money and you better believe there were more than a few words when I didn't tithe to the church the expected ten percent.

"But your grandfather wouldn't have wanted that. And while I'm a good wife, I'm not a Mormon. I'm not a saint on earth. I am only a woman trying to see her children succeed and live in this world."

For the first time Chuck saw his mother rise up and become her own person instead of a reflection of Adam Ganley. He saw the same life and fire in her that he saw in Jerilyn Gardner. His mother's newly formed opinions and defiance also reminded him of Tina and suddenly he wanted to tell his mother about both of these women.

"Where are we going to lunch, son?" Cindy asked. She thought about what a nice day this would be for her.

Chuck began to feel guilt and love at the same time. He realized he missed his family, especially his mother. Without warning he confessed to his mother.

"To say I'm sorry for what I've done to you would only amount to a neat collection of words. I can say it. I'm sorry. But that's all it is, words.

"I want to make it up to you and pay you back somehow for what I've done. I'm truly sorry for hurting you by being the rebellious son and opposing you and father and your wishes. Seeing you today makes me realize how sorry I am for hurting you and how much I miss you. If you want me to come home, I will. I'll work there, where you and father think I should."

Cindy could not believe her ears. Here was her spirited, independent son, collapsing before her eyes. It was distantly reminiscent of another young man who collapsed before her, agreeing to be whatever she wanted.

This time it was her son and she liked it less now than she did then.

Her life's experiences had been a bitter tutor and its harshness made that of her husband's pale in comparison.

"What are you talking about?" she asked.

"Are you trying to break your baby sister's heart? What would she say to her friends if she ever realized you sold out to please your father?"

He started to answer, but his mother stopped him.

"Don't you dare give up what you believe," she said.

"I love you and I'm proud of you. You're my son and always will be no matter where you live or what you do. Don't you ever cave in to the demands and pressures from your father. I love you for the way you defy him. I'm so proud of you and so are all your sisters."

Tears sprang to Chuck's eyes. Never in his entire life had his mother ever spoken to him like this. Only his grandmother had encouraged him and now it was his mother, too.

"Thank you," he said crying. "I love you, Mother."

Chuck had never enjoyed his mother so much. At lunch he ordered champagne and his mother shared the bottle with him and told him stories about her father and mother. Never in his life had he ever had a drink in the presence of his mother. Also, never in his life, had he ever seen her take a drink. He never heard her talk about her parents this way. Once the girls were born they didn't see his mother's parents. His father did not approve of them.

Cindy laughed and enjoyed her son.

She found herself touching and holding his hand. She was moved by the power and the certainty in his voice as he spoke. At times she would shiver and get goose bumps at the sound of one simple statement. He made her forget her own life and for this time, for a few moments, she was young again.

The champagne made her giggle.

Chuck laughed aloud at his mother's happiness.

Cindy looked at her son even as she giggled. She liked what she saw. She compared him to Adam.

In physical stature, he had certainly surpassed him. He stood six feet tall to his father's five foot seven. He was nearly two hundred pounds with muscular shoulders and arms and powerful legs, while his father was an obese two hundred sixty pounds.

Cindy knew her son was a physical giant compared to her husband. Beyond that he surpassed him intellectually. It was then the other young man came into her mind. This time she did not resist the memory. How could she?

She found herself wondering about him. Then she clutched her son's arm and tried at the same time to erase remembering a man she had never understood. The champagne, the emptiness of the past twenty-five years as well as her son sitting next to her, brought him back to mind.

The idea of her son surrendering to Adam and what her son perceived to be her own wishes scared her. She would never allow her son to give in to society as she had. She would rather die first or even see him die. Either choice would be better than the one she had made.

Cynthia Ganley had no idea what was ahead of her that day.

Chuck ordered a second bottle of champagne and she talked about high school and her freshmen year in college. She told him about her sisters, and she talked about his two aunts that he hardly knew, Lisa and Andrea.

Chuck marveled at his mother's openness. This was a part of her he never knew.

A small part of him realized how much he had been cheated out of knowing as a young boy, but he was a kind person and accepted now what was being given. It was easy to forget the past.

It was this wonderful forgiving kindness that only made Cindy love her son that much more. That afternoon the years of holding back and silent withdrawal ended.

Cindy found herself telling stories, sharing memories of her own girlhood, and realized what was important at this moment was that she was no longer holding back. Instead of feeling guilty for those silent years, she felt unbridled love for her son. This was her son and what they had, finally, felt good. In her mind she wondered how she had ever denied it this long.

Meanwhile, it had not been a good day for Jerilyn.

She was angry with Tina for her boldness. At the same time she knew her daughter was justified in her harsh judgment. Jerilyn knew she had been lucky to escape judgment of any kind for so long. What Tina was putting on her was overdue and deserved.

Jerilyn answered the phone and agreed to come in to work.

The Bears were on a roll. Green Bay was down 35 to 3 by the half. The bar was full of customers and it had all the makings of another crazy day.

Jerilyn couldn't get the conversation with Tina out of her head. At the same time she thought about Charley. Tina had come along with her to the bar, but she was still angry. Jerilyn decided this just was not her day.

When Chuck walked into the bar with a beautiful blond woman in a full-length mink coat, Jerilyn was taken totally by surprise. Then when he introduced her as his mother, Jerilyn was speechless. The name Cindy was one she thought she should remember but couldn't.

When it finally came back to her, Jerilyn suddenly felt the whole world was well beyond her control. Jerilyn suddenly had questions.

Why was this woman here? Did she have any idea what was ahead? Did she know the past? What did she know?

Tina was sitting at the bar. Chuck sat his mother down next to her and introduced her as his mother, Cindy. Tina shook hands with his mother and asked about what kind of trip she had and where she had come from.

Of the two women, Jerilyn was more jealous of her own daughter than she was of Chuck's mother. She was jealous because Tina posed more of an immediate threat to what Jerilyn perceived to be hers.

And ironically at the same moment Cindy was perhaps Jerilyn's greatest ally. Cynthia Ganley had finally regained her son and within two hours there was a young, dark-haired woman who was probably going to challenge her for her own son's attention.

Chuck was oblivious to all of this. When Mark and Brad came in after the game, both Tina and Cindy took a backseat to his good friends and the talk about the football game.

Cindy Ganley was a very beautiful woman and certainly did not look forty-three years old. She looked more like she was thirty and Chuck could never be her son. If anything, he was her young lover. Chuck's friends immediately liked her.

"How are you supposed to hit on your best friend's mother?" Brad asked Mark in front of Cindy, teasing her.

"I sure don't know," Mark answered quickly. "You're married. Call your wife and ask her for help and tell me!

"Now as far as I am concerned, Mrs. Ganley, I am very free and very available," Mark added.

Cindy sat there and laughed. She found herself enjoying the attention from the young men.

Tina had been at the bar since arriving with Jerilyn and was feeling slightly drunk. She stood next to Chuck with her arm around him. At the same time she was talking to his mother about the final year of courses her daughter Elizabeth was taking and where she planned to go beyond that.

Cindy said Elizabeth would probably get married. Hearing this Chuck immediately became the protective brother.

"To whom," he asked.

"To Rick Howell," she answered.

"Him?" Chuck said, shocked.

"She's dated him since high school. Why not him?"

"He's a carbon copy of Father," Chuck said.

Jerilyn was at their end of the bar and overheard the conversation.

As Chuck said the word father, Cindy's and her eyes met. Their eyes held long enough for Cindy to realize they shared something that she did not understand. Somehow as she looked at Jerilyn, she knew they shared something she wished they didn't.

1966

The last time Cindy Ganley had been in a bar it was with Charley Reed.

It was in the fall and she was a sophomore in college. She had joined the very best sorority on campus and was dating Adam who was a senior and vice-president of the student council. Adam represented everything her parents had raised her to want. She knew nothing of the Mormon faith, but considered it admirable that he was not a big drinker and had nothing to do with drugs.

Then Charley Reed arrived on campus.

Charley had been her first lover. She was his first, too. When she met him, she seduced him and never looked back.

For Charley Reed it was different. Making love to Cindy was not something he took lightly. Making love to her was a lifetime commitment. In his boyish way, he wanted her to know it, too.

The night he called her at the sorority house he became the topic of the evening. The other girls buzzed when he came and picked her up.

They walked around the campus and talked. He held her hand and very quietly said he had always wanted to be with her and had always loved her.

Cindy didn't know what to say.

She was nominated for Homecoming Queen and was dating the vice president of the student council. Charley was out of college and on his way to the Army.

It was 1966 and it was the year of the major escalation in the Vietnam War. It was a war for sure; only no one recognized it was a war yet.

Charley held her and kissed her goodnight on the steps of the sorority house. He went back to Delta House and was already asleep when she called.

"Were you asleep?" she asked.

"Yes," he answered. "I'm a growing boy."

"Not much of a boy from what I saw tonight," she said.

He didn't know how to answer that.

"Will I see you tomorrow?" she asked.

"That's up to you, babe," he answered.

"Then I'll see you," she said.

"You tell me where and when. I'll be there."

"The sorority house at noon."

"See you then," he replied.

"I love you, too," she said just before hanging up.

The next day they met at noon. It should have been different from when he was fifteen and she was fourteen. Then they both were virgins and she led them through that experience. Five years later Cindy found nothing had really changed. She recognized it immediately.

Charley was still shy. It wasn't that he didn't want to make love to her. He did. It was just she was different now and he didn't know how to act. Once more she took the lead.

"Let's get a motel room," she said.

Cindy had no more experience than Charley, not really. But Charley didn't know how to go about letting her know what he wanted. For the second time she had to engineer their lovemaking. She started, but this time it was different.

The first time they had been kids. This time he was no kid. He was a man and he was beautiful. When he touched her, she felt beautiful and special.

He adored her body and caressed the parts of her that let her know she was someone special. He loved her. And he loved her again and again. They never left the Holiday Inn for three days.

He didn't want to leave. He wanted to marry her. He always wanted to marry her. All he wanted was to be with her.

He had already enlisted in the Army and now was sorry. He knew there was no getting out of it, so he tried to figure out something else. He begged her to trust him and wait. He promised it would all work out.

She wanted to believe him, but she was only nineteen. He left on Thursday and Adam was still the senior class vice president.

Charley never wrote or called and she found herself wondering where he was and what he was doing. And still, she was only nineteen, but they had sat together in the Holiday Inn bar and swore their love to one another. She never understood why he never called or wrote.

From that moment, Cindy George Ganley had never been in a bar again. She had no idea of the ultimate irony in that visit.

CHAPTER ELEVEN

CHICAGO, ILLINOIS
1992

Cindy was enjoying her Sunday with her son. She didn't remember when she felt so relaxed and at ease. It was a good feeling for her.

"This is a nice place," she said to her son.

"It's just a neighborhood bar," said Chuck.

"And are these people your friends?" she asked.

"Some of them."

"What about the woman behind the bar?" Cindy asked feeling uneasy about her.

"Yes," Chuck answered. "I'd say she's my friend."

"And Tina, is she your friend, too?"

"Yes," he answered.

"How good a friend?"

"Mother," he said. "What difference does it make? These are people I know. That's all. It's no major thing."

"It is with Jerilyn. I can see that. And it could be with Tina," she said not even trying to make it all out to be a joke. She was very serious.

"Jerilyn is Tina's mother," he said.

It made no difference to Cindy.

"Well, where do you fit in?" she asked.

Chuck held his mouth and didn't answer. His mother's question was enough.

Just then Mark and Brad jumped into the conversation and distracted her. Even though she was talking to the fellows, she never took her eye off Jerilyn. Chuck joked with Brad and had another beer. Cindy rested her hand on her son's arm and sipped a glass of wine.

She found herself enjoying the small talk and joking. The entire atmosphere was totally different from what she was used to. Chuck ordered drinks and asked Tina to join them at a table.

Cindy thought Tina was a charming young girl. She was certainly attractive and the picture of her mother. Cindy was pleasantly surprised to learn she was a graduate student and had a good idea about what she was going to do with the rest of her life. Cindy questioned Tina about a variety of things and Chuck was uncomfortable to the point he suggested they leave.

"I have a full day tomorrow," he said. "I should get you back to your hotel."

Chuck told everyone goodbye, but was back in forty minutes after seeing his mother to the hotel. In the time he was gone, Jerilyn had gone home.

Brad and Tina were still there and Chuck took up where he left off.

"Your mother is a nice lady," Tina said.

"Yes, she is," he agreed. "She's nice enough, but she's still a mother and I'll always be her little boy."

"That won't ever change," Tina commented.

"How long is your mother staying here?" Brad asked.

"She's leaving tomorrow. She's going to Pittsburgh to see her mother. She does this once a year now and it's a good excuse for her to check up on me."

"Did you pass?" Tina asked.

"With flying colors," he said. "So did you as a matter of fact. You were all she talked about when I took her back to the hotel."

Tina felt herself blush.

They stayed another hour or so until Chuck finally admitted he was tired. Tina agreed it was a long day and asked Chuck if he would walk out with her. He saw her safely to her car and squeezed her hand when he said goodbye.

The phone was ringing as he opened the door, but he managed to miss the call before they hung up. Just as he turned off the lights and got into bed, it rang again. It was Jerilyn and he could tell from the tone of her voice something was wrong.

"You hardly even spoke to me," she complained.

"Jerilyn, I was with a group of people, one of which was my mother whom I had not seen in a year and a half. What was I supposed to do? I didn't even know you were working. Wasn't this your day off?"

"That's besides the point," she said.

"Look, it's no big deal. You had a job to do and I had to entertain my mother."

"Well, she sure didn't act like she thought much of me," said
Jerilyn.

"She never said anything one way or the other," he lied.

"Did you tell her about me?"

"No, I didn't," he said. "I don't make a habit of telling my mother who I sleep with."

"Are you ashamed of me?"

"Jerilyn, that has nothing to do with anything. It isn't the type of
thing I discuss with her."

"Where is your mother from?" Jerilyn asked.

"Sunset, Utah," he answered.

"Originally, where was she from?"

"Cleveland and Pittsburgh," he said. "My grandmother still lives
in Pittsburgh."

"How old is she?" she asked.

"Forty-three," he answered. "Why all the questions?"

"I think I know someone she did," Jerilyn said coyly.

"Really, who would that be?"

"A man I knew a long, long time ago. His name was Charley
Reed."

"I'm taking her to the airport tomorrow. I'll ask her. How would
she have known him?"

"I think they went to high school or college together."

"I'm sorry," he apologized. "I had no way of knowing you might
have a friend in common. You should have said something."

"It's not important. I wouldn't even bother her," Jerilyn said,
knowing now he would.

"No, I'll make a point of it."

"I'm sorry I'm so bitchy," she said. "I guess I'm just tired. Sleep
tight and I'll talk to you tomorrow."

Cindy phoned her son early the next morning and was pleased
when he said he would take her to the airport. At exactly ten-thirty as
he promised, he was at her room to take down her bags. She admired
his punctuality and remembered stressing it as he grew up. The lesson
was learned and she smiled, feeling satisfied with herself.

Chuck had been an easy child to raise. He had a warm disposition
and always had the finest of manners. She didn't remember him ever
having an awkward or an ugly age. He was always a good student and
well liked by his classmates.

Looking back, she was glad for all their sakes that he was not prone to rebellion or defiance. Her husband was a difficult man and a son's rebellion would have been unpleasant for the entire family. In fact, Chuck never opposed their wishes until his senior year in college with his choice of law school. Until then, everything he did was acceptable, even to his choice of the young women he dated.

Melissa Fuller had been his serious college romance. They had gone to the same high school, but didn't date then. It was when they began traveling to and from college together for holidays and week-ends that they both became interested. They were engaged the summer before their senior year and it was just after that Chuck began to change.

As they rode the elevator to the lobby, Cindy couldn't help but admire how handsome and well groomed her son was. He had an easy elegance about him. Everything fit from his black shoes to the gray wool suit and charcoal overcoat. Her son, a lawyer, could very easily become a senator or federal judge. He had that way about him. And while she seldom questioned any decisions he made, she was very concerned about his eventual choice of a wife. A woman who might be well beneath him could easily hold this brilliant young man back.

He tipped the man at the hotel entrance for keeping an eye on his car. Attentively he held open the door for his mother as she entered the car and then placed her suitcase and bag in the trunk.

Their conversation was mostly about his law practice and the different cases he took. She was careful to avoid the two subjects she knew would upset him, his father and the Mormon Church.

"Mother," he said. "You went to high school in Pittsburgh, didn't you?"

"Yes," she answered. "Why?"

"The woman behind the bar last night asked me to find out if you knew someone by the name of Charley Reed."

Cindy felt her face become very warm. Her son's question was surely innocent enough, but no one had spoken his name to her in years.

"That was thirty years ago, honey. I knew a lot of people when I lived in Pittsburgh, but that name doesn't ring any bells with me," she lied.

"If your grandmother has my old yearbooks, I'll check if it's important," she said trying to find out what was on his mind.

"Oh, I wouldn't go to any trouble," he said. "I think she was just curious. I got the impression it was someone she knew once."

Cindy could hardly believe what she was hearing. Here she was in Chicago, Illinois and a bartender was having her son ask her questions about his real father. Cindy wondered who this woman was. She had seen her, but her face was not familiar.

Cindy wondered if Charley Reed might be living in Chicago and if he was, what he might be like. It certainly would be a cruel trick if he would meet his own son, face to face, and not know it.

The rest of the trip they both were rather quiet. Cindy was alone in her thoughts of Charley Reed while her son concentrated on getting her to the airport safely. She told him not to park and insisted he drop her off and let the airport valets take her bags. Moments later, he was driving away returning to the city and she still had her thoughts of Charley Reed.

When Charley left her that day years ago, he was going to the Army. He promised he would write. He said he would call. He didn't. That was the end of September. In October her period was late to the point of never arriving. When she missed November, too, she called his parents in Pittsburgh to find out how she could get in touch with him.

She was in her sophomore year at the time and between boyfriends. She had broken up with Adam several days before Charley Reed appeared and even though she did see Adam again after Charley left, she hadn't gone to bed with him.

Charley was at Ft. Benning, Georgia going through paratrooper training. His voice sounded shocked when he finally came to the phone.

She began by apologizing. She could still remember how warm his voice sounded and how easy it was for her to tell him. He was great. She could still remember him proposing to her over the phone, promising to make everything okay. He truly wanted her and all of a sudden she was not scared anymore.

Cindy sipped her coffee as she stared out the window of the jet. That was twenty-six years ago and the whole experience seemed like it was last week. She wondered what her life would have been like if she hadn't given in and listened to her mother.

She went home that Friday night and told her mother she was pregnant and she was going to leave school and marry Charley.

"Leave school, yes," her mother agreed. "But I can't see you marrying Charley. His father is just a policeman and he's already flunked out of college and is in the Army. How can be possibly support you and a baby?"

It was then her mother decided she should tell Adam Ganley the baby was his.

"He's a Mormon and Charley's a Catholic," Cindy said.

"Religion has nothing to do with this," her mother said. "The question is who will be able to provide for you the best?"

Her mother's rapid calculations confirmed Adam was as sound a candidate as Charley Reed and the idea of love never entered the conversation.

Charley called on Sunday, but he was told she was not in. Adam was already planning to marry her. When Charley called the following weekend, he was told Cindy was married.

As the jet landed at Greater Pittsburgh International Airport, Cindy had no real bitterness. Her mother was right. Adam had been a good provider and even though he probably suspected Chuck was not his son, he never once mentioned it. She had given him four daughters and had always been a dutiful wife and homemaker. She walked up the jetway into the terminal and saw her mother waiting for her.

After the usual greetings and hugs and they were in the car, Cindy decided to mention it to her mother.

"You'll never guess whom your grandson asked about when he was driving me to the airport," she said to her mother.

Not waiting for her to guess, she told her. "Charley Reed."

"Why on earth for?" her mother asked.

"A woman he knows, a bartender, asked him to find out if I knew Charley Reed."

"That's strange," her mother said.

"Do you think he's living in Chicago?" Cindy asked.

Mrs. George looked at her daughter, surprised.

"He's been dead a long, long time, Cindy. He was killed in an automobile accident years ago. I thought you knew."

A cold feeling swept over Cindy. Her mother's words shocked her.

"No," she said. "I never knew. How could I? I've been tucked away in Utah now for a long time."

Charley Reed's death came as a real shock to her. She had always fantasized meeting him again. She even dreamed of telling him of his son. Now that could never happen. She always imagined him in some distant future.

"I wonder why that woman asked about him?" she said.

When Cindy went to sleep in her mother's home, she dreamed of Charley Reed and their son. She was in delivery and Charley was with her, wiping her forehead and talking softly to her. She could hear his love for her in his voice. It was calm and soothing. His words gave her confidence and made her believe everything would be fine.

Then their son was born and Charley was telling her how beautiful she was and how proud she had made him. She could feel him stroking her hair. She could smell him and feel his closeness. She was nursing their baby and he had his arms around them both, keeping them secure.

And then he was gone and Adam was there, scowling at the two of them. Adam was holding his book of prayers and standing so stiff and upright accusing her. It was then she woke.

"Is he buried here in Pittsburgh?" she asked her mother the next morning.

"I don't know. I still see Jeannie McCarthy's mother. She might. You could call her."

"Mother, I think I'd like to find out about Charley Reed."

"Why, after all this time?" she asked her daughter.

"I just would, for myself, no one else. I've always wondered what might have happened if I married him. He was my first sweetheart and love."

"Well, call Mrs. McCarthy. If nothing else, she can aim you in the right direction."

The right direction was Gary Carmen. She called him at home in the evening and spoke with him for nearly a half an hour. The next day she and her mother drove out to the Queen of Heaven Cemetery.

"Why must we do this, Cindy?" her mother asked.

"Because," she said. "He's the father of your grandson. I think you and I both owe this small tribute to him."

The caretaker gave them directions to a distant point in the cemetery, not too far from the highway. It was December and the ground was frozen. There was no snow, but the turf crackled as they walked across to the grave.

When they finally reached the place, Cindy read the headstone aloud.

"Charles Reed
Beloved Son and Father
Hero in War"

She stood there silent. Neither she nor her mother spoke. There was no traffic on the highway and the air around them was completely still. A faded American flag on a small stick stood motionless in the ground just above his body.

When Cindy finally spoke, she turned to her mother and said, "Let's go."

Her mother said nothing. She turned and walked back to the car. It was not until they were on the highway returning home that she asked about the epitaph.

"Gary said he had a son, but was divorced when he died. He also said he was in the Army. Later he was in the Special Forces and won the Silver Star in Vietnam."

Cindy's mother had no response to the explanation. She kept driving and said nothing.

"Well?" Cindy asked.

"I have nothing to say," her mother replied. "If you're expecting me to feel guilty, I won't. He's been dead for twenty years and life has gone on without him. My grandson never knew him and he's none the worse for it. Don't expect me to start beating my breast and say how horrible it is he's dead. His death is nothing to me and certainly is nothing to you either."

Cindy tried to understand her mother's words. If anyone understood, it would be her. Of the three sisters, she was most like her mother, but even she had trouble grasping the cold attitude toward a man who could have easily been her son-in-law.

Cindy couldn't feel that way. What was more, she was having a difficult time accepting her mother's way of dismissing the entire matter. She didn't speak of it the rest of the time they were out, but she did decide to talk with Gary once more.

Gary had been one of Charley's closest friends during high school and college, right up to the time he left for the Army. Cindy met both Gary and his wife, Bobbi, when they began dating at fifteen. Now, he was a successful businessman and they had a family of four boys and a girl. When she called the second night, Bobbi invited her over to visit the next night.

She couldn't stop thinking about Charley. It wasn't until she found his picture in an old yearbook did she realize how much her son actually looked like him. She was amazed she had never allowed the thought to enter her mind until it jumped off the page right at her.

Bobbi Carmen was very pleasant. She made Cindy feel at home almost immediately. Gary offered her a drink and she accepted a glass of wine.

"I want to know about him," she said. "The last time I ever saw him was when he went off to the Army. After that I was married and pregnant."

Gary started to speak about Charley and his days in the Army. He told her about his days in Walter Reed Army Hospital and finally his marriage to Joanna.

"Joanna never remarried after they were divorced. Tommy is about nineteen or twenty now and they live in Washington, D.C."

"What was Joanna like?" she asked.

"Clean looking and quiet," Bobbi answered her. "They were already divorced when he was killed, but she really took it hard."

"After he was divorced was there anyone else?" asked Cindy.

"Oh, yes," Gary said. "There was the one Charley left Joanna for."

"Who was that," she asked fearing she already knew the answer.

"Some girl from North Carolina who had three children of her own. She was really beautiful and seemed to be taken with Charley. He was really in love with her. Anyone could see that," he said.

"She had a different name," Gary said trying to reach back into his memory. "I can't remember for the life of me."

And as he searched for the name, Cindy was almost afraid to speak. She was positive she already knew the answer, but had to be sure just the same.

"Jerilyn?"

"Yes!" Gary exclaimed. "That's it."

Cindy had a lot to think about. She went back to her mother's house that night and left for Utah the next day. Her mother never asked her what she found out and Cindy did not volunteer either.

CHAPTER TWELVE

Jerilyn didn't see Chuck all week. She expected him to stop in the bar Monday night and when he didn't show, she was sure she would see him Tuesday. Her shift was exceptionally slow on Tuesday and by midnight she realized he wasn't going to show up either.

She tried his office the next afternoon, but was told he was in court. She left a message, but he didn't call back. Jerilyn made a point of waiting for his call and finally called once more, leaving the same message with her number at work.

Wednesday night passed and Chuck neither called, nor came in. When she got home she called his apartment, but there was no answer. A sick, anxious feeling came over as she began to feel he was with someone else. It was a feeling she truly hated, but it wasn't a new one.

She thought of Charley Reed. She had felt the same sick feeling over Joanna and the airline stewardess. Joanna had been his wife, but the stewardess, Happy, had been her competition. Jerilyn never competed for a man until Charley. She never felt the need to compete for one since, until now.

For a young girl raised in the tobacco fields of North Carolina, the big city of Wilson was an adventure when her daddy took her to town on Saturday. Those Saturdays were far and few between and became the exception when her daddy was aware of the boys and men noticing her. But Wilson wasn't the only place she was noticed. Right there at home in Fountain the men had begun to tease with her.

She was fourteen when her sister Ellen came home with an infant son. He was only days old and still unnamed. Jerilyn could still remember her mother taking him from her sister and naming him David, after her own father. Ellen left the next day and David became her baby brother from that moment on.

She helped her mother with David. Jerilyn liked the feeling of caring for a baby. It made her feel grownup, like a woman. She also liked the attention the men gave her, especially Jonathan Mekings.

At fourteen she was fully developed. The boys her age were well behind her, both physically and mentally. It was natural her first crush would be the eighteen-year-old Mekings boy who drove his own red convertible.

Even though she was fourteen, she passed for eighteen with little problem. Johnny, as she called him, enjoyed having her sit next to him as they drove the Carolina back roads from one hangout to another.

Jerilyn loved the attention and soon realized if it was to continue, there were certain things he wanted and she would have to provide them. In her mind it was only being a woman. Her mother put up with her father so he would continue to provide for the family. Jerilyn recognized she had to tolerate certain things about Johnny if the fun times were to continue.

It was new for her. No one had ever touched her body that way. At first, she held him to just touching her breasts through her clothing, but soon it progressed to unbuttoning her blouse and bra. Each date they went farther and before long she was even touching him.

Jerilyn liked that part. Once she realized what eventually happened when she touched him, she understood this was a way to control him.

With her jeans and panties down at her knees, she slowed him down, claiming to be scared. Then she would bring him to a climax. While she really wasn't all that scared, she didn't want to end up like her sister Ellen. For the most part, Johnny was inexperienced and her pretend fear usually held him at bay as long as she agreed to take care of him.

Every single day in the south had its own measured pace and the steamy hot summers slowed things to a crawl, but on Sundays things nearly stopped. Sunday at Jerilyn's house was never a day to sleep late. Not even for Daddy who spent each Saturday night at the local roadhouse drinking whiskey. Everyone was up and dressed and in church by ten o'clock. That summer Jerilyn began sitting with Johnny and his family while her momma and Ruth took care of little David and her daddy dozed in the pew.

She liked Sundays. Everyone dressed for church and stayed that way for the rest of the day. After church the women made a big breakfast. Momma's widowed sister, Sadie, came over with her children and ate. Afterwards the kids would play and the adults would sit around in the shade of the front porch.

Sundays were always hot and there was always lemonade. The afternoons always smelled delicious from ribs or pork roast, or even barbeque cooking in the kitchen. Chicken was for holidays and beef when there was a wedding or a funeral. At five they had their big meal. Later the children did the dishes while Momma and Aunt Sadie went to late church to finish their day. Her daddy wandered back to the roadhouse and the children usually fell asleep from pure exhaustion.

On one Sunday night in early August Jerilyn had all the kids asleep in Ruth's big bed when Johnny came calling on her. She was still dressed for church in her new yellow cotton dress. Her hair, long and dark, hung over her shoulders as they drove toward Bethel. The top was down and the moon was just beginning to rise out of the pine trees. The air was warm and she could smell the dampness of the swamps creeping off the Tar River.

The night seemed special as they parked near a boat landing at the edge of the river. The rising moon was silver and reflected in the lazy waters. His touch was gentle and instead of touching him right away, Jerilyn lay back and allowed him to continue. He pushed her panties down to her knees and with no jeans to keep them on, this time they continued the rest of the way to the floor of the car. He touched her and she only stared up at the stars as he probed her body with his finger.

Ever so softly his finger moved inside her. Her breathing grew heavy and she found it hard to lie still. She made no effort to touch him, even as his finger withdrew. She was shocked when his mouth replaced his finger. He was kissing her in this special place. He had taken her by surprise. She heard his belt come undone and his zipper open. She felt him move as he took down his pants. Then, as his mouth left her, he moved up between her legs and for the first time she felt him forcing himself inside her.

As much as everything else felt good, this was bad. It hurt and she held onto him to keep from crying out. She didn't make a sound, but tears began to flow down her cheeks. And then he stopped. She felt the wetness inside her. He sat up and took out a handkerchief to wipe himself. When he was through, he offered it to her and it was then she discovered the blood. Now she was a woman.

Johnny Mekings was the first of a long line of disappointments in Jerilyn's life. All their dates were the same and she worried about getting pregnant all the time. She couldn't stand the constant worry and just after her birthday she stopped having sex with him. Within a few weeks Johnny began dating Maryann Whorton who became pregnant by Valentine's Day and married to him when school ended.

Jerilyn dated an assortment of boys the next two years. They were football or baseball players, all of whom she easily controlled. They all did exactly what she wanted, when she wanted them to do it.

During her senior year, she began to change. By this time she was tired of the boys her own age and along with her friend Debbie she began looking elsewhere. The best place to look was Jacksonville. That was where the Marines were.

Vietnam was just building up. Young men ages eighteen to twenty-five were at Camp LeJune taking advanced training in preparation for going overseas. Debbie had a car and they could be in Jacksonville in little over an hour.

Jacksonville was a wide-open town. The bars all catered to the Corps and no one ever questioned a lady's age. The more ladies, the more Marines, and that meant more cash to the bar. Jerilyn and Debbie thought they were in heaven. They soon forgot about their high school football games and spent every Friday and Saturday night in Jacksonville. Towards the middle of November Jerilyn met Bart Pittman.

Bart was the all-American boy. He was an officer, a second lieutenant, and twenty-two years old. He was from Bowling Green, Kentucky and played basketball at the University of Kentucky before flunking out and joining the Marines. He had six more weeks to go before getting his orders and in all probability would be sent to Vietnam. No one knew very much about Vietnam and Bart, believing he was part of the finest fighting force ever assembled, wasn't afraid. As she listened to him speak with such confidence, Jerilyn believed each and every word he said.

February seemed a long way off as December began. Jerilyn was in love for the first time in her life and found she really enjoyed their lovemaking. Bart drove up during the week and they would go out. They always made love and he was very careful to be sure she wouldn't get pregnant. He said he loved her and she believed him. He even said he wanted to marry her and for Christmas he gave her an engagement ring.

She would finish school and he would go off to war. He would be home in March of next year and then they would be married. He spoke of taking her back to Kentucky where they'd live. Jerilyn didn't care. She just wanted to be with him. Jerilyn promised to wait.

February did come and Bart shipped overseas to Vietnam. His letters came several at a time.

He told her about the men under him and how very much different it was from what he expected. He wrote of the enormous build up of Americans and how much he missed her. He was still very confident and while she was reading his April 3rd letter, his sister called from Bowling Green. She called to tell her Bart was dead.

"Bart wanted me to let you know if anything ever happened to him," his sister said.

She was crying and Jerilyn was crying.

"I'll call you back and tell you when the funeral is," she promised.

She never did and Jerilyn was devastated.

The next few months were hard. Jerilyn went to school about half the time. The other half she stayed in bed and cried. She took care of her little brother and even took a part time job in a drugstore in Farmville.

Debbie still went to Jacksonville every weekend, but Jerilyn wanted none of it. School ended and Debbie invited her to go to Morehead for a week. Her mother forced her to go, insisting the ocean would be good for her. As it turned out, her mother was right. Both she and Debbie liked it so much they decided to stay.

Fourth of July weekends on the North Carolina coast are wild. Even though Jerilyn imagined herself a young widow, the antics and the drinking were too much even for her. She remembered going to a party with Debbie and the guy she was dating, but after the tenth or eleventh beer, Jerilyn was lost. She stayed lost until the next morning when she woke up next to Sam Gardner.

There was always something about the smell of a man Jerilyn liked. As a little girl she liked to be held by her daddy when he came in hot and sweaty from the tobacco fields. She always enjoyed it when her older brother hugged her. Even when sex with men wasn't all that good, she tolerated it because she liked the way men smelled. Sam had a good smell to him and as she woke that morning, she found herself cuddling up to a body her nose found so appealing. Still in a half awake dreamy state, she was aware the other body cuddled back and its hands began to explore and touch her body in a way she found pleasing.

Still half asleep, the part of her body that was half awake responded like it never had before. It had been five months and perhaps the period of abstinence was the difference, but as he entered her she woke and in spite of the shock, did not give him up. On September 28th, nine days after her eighteenth birthday, she married Sam and became Jerilyn Gardner.

Like most available young men in North Carolina, Sam was a Marine. He was stationed at Cherry Point Naval Air Station and just completed a tour in Vietnam. Jerilyn took reassurance in the fact Sam never spoke of Vietnam. It became their truce; he didn't want to talk about it and she didn't want to hear about it.

She liked the way he smelled and she especially liked the way he made love to her. In no time at all, she was pregnant. Tina was born on July 4th, certainly an appropriate date. Two weeks later, Sam was discharged and instead of Kentucky, Jerilyn went with her husband to Champagne, Illinois.

Sam was eligible for the GI Bill to go to college. They got just about two hundred dollars a month while he was in school at the University of Illinois. She took a job as a waitress for the breakfast shift at the Holiday Inn in Urbana. With the GI Bill and her tips, they barely managed a two-bedroom trailer west of the city.

Jerilyn was a southern girl. North Carolina has cold weather and it even has snow sometimes. An Illinois winter was more than she was ready for. It was always cold and the cold was ten degrees and below. She was taken from the land of tobacco and cotton fields dead in a winter of fog, rain and cold dampness to Illinois with snow, ice, and wind. Jerilyn, a new mother, sick with strep throat and a baby with constant ear infections, went home. No man smelled that good.

Within a month Sam followed. He was flunking out of school again anyway. The University of Illinois was the wrong place for him. All his old friends were still around and now marijuana was the thing. Marijuana must have made the winters warmer for him because he stayed out while Jerilyn was home with Tina.

Jerilyn was home with her parents when he showed up at their front door. Tina was asleep and he begged Jerilyn to at least go out with him so they could talk. She refused and he cried. He had never cried before, so she agreed. The next morning when they returned, she packed and the three of them left for Morehead where they would be happy.

Debbie, Jerilyn's best friend, was still in Morehead. Now Debbie was managing the Pirate's Cove, the hottest bar on the beach. Easter was just around the corner and was the beginning of summer in the Carolinas.

They found a trailer a block from the beach. Sam got a job as a roofer and Jerilyn realized she was pregnant again. What could have been a fun summer soon became a long one.

There were problems from the beginning. They didn't have any insurance. Sam lost his job and soon was back to where he'd been when they lived in Illinois.

Jerilyn took a part time job in a grocery store, but had to quit working in early October. Sam left two weeks later and Anne Marie was born December 2nd. Two weeks later the new baby had open-heart surgery to repair a birth defect. Sam arrived at the hospital as the doctor came out to tell Jerilyn everything was okay. Sam stayed for Christmas and just after New Year's they went back to Illinois where he had a job as a bar manager.

Jerilyn was a young mother with two small babies. She didn't have many choices and was at the mercy of her husband's whims. She trusted he was basically a good man, even though he was wild. She tried to be a good wife, but he wouldn't stay home. In the middle of February, he left again. That was when she went to work at the Holiday Inn.

It was one of the coldest Illinois winters on record.

She was alone in a two-bedroom trailer and the wind blew every night and the furnace never stopped. She rose every morning at four-thirty to get herself ready for work and the babies ready to go off to the sitter's. She had to be there at five-thirty to set up for breakfast and stayed through lunch until two in the afternoon. By then the outside temperature might have risen to ten degrees.

Invariably the door to her trailer was frozen, forcing her to go to the office and get some hot water to pour on the handle so she could put in her key. This only added more moisture and once again the lock would freeze, causing her to repeat the action the following day. Finally, she stopped locking the door.

When he left, Sam said nothing. He just came home and packed his things and was gone. Jerilyn called his mother, but she either knew nothing or wouldn't tell her anything. Mrs. Gardner acted as if she was too busy to talk and never asked about her granddaughters.

February turned into March and by the end of the month, the weather began to warm up. Sam never called during March.

Jerilyn didn't mind working. Everyone liked her and she did well on her tips. The baby girls were really no problem. It was just the incredible loneliness and the hurt over Sam leaving the way he did that bothered her.

At the end of April she was offered a job as night bartender. It meant more money, but she would need a sitter in her home until two a.m. Fortunately for her, a neighbor down the street was available and Jerilyn accepted.

The neighbor girl was about Jerilyn's age and was married to a young man in the Air Force who was going to school at Chanute Air Force Base. He was a C shift student and was in school from six p.m. until midnight. He never was home until two-thirty so the baby-sitting was perfect. Maryanne was happy to have something to do and really did like the girls.

As bad as the winter was, the spring was just that nice. May seemed to slip by and Jerilyn really enjoyed tending bar. She worked Monday through Friday and had her weekends free. Maryanne and her husband Jack introduced her to Tom, a classmate of Jack's. He was in the Air Force, too. Jerilyn enjoyed the company and the attention. She began to forget about Sam's absence. Another month went by without any word from him.

Over the Memorial Day weekend Jerilyn arranged her schedule so she could go away with Tom. She never forgot she was still married to Sam, but she was fond of Tom who treated both her and the girls very well. They were going to Des Moines, Iowa to visit his parents. Jerilyn had her reservations, but Tom insisted everything would be all right. Tom was wrong.

Tom was the oldest son in a family of four boys. His father farmed the land his family owned for over a hundred years. His mother was a stern church-going woman. She was not happy about Jerilyn and the girls arriving with her son. The only bright spot the lady found was the fact that Jerilyn was still married and could not marry her son.

The weekend lasted forever. Tina was sick and Jerilyn had a miserable time. Tom wanted to sneak off and make love, but Jerilyn would have none of it. Tom pouted all day Saturday and Sunday, as well as most of the way home on Monday. When they stopped to eat in Springfield, they finally began to see the whole trip as almost being funny.

Tom apologized and told her he loved her. He asked her to go to North Dakota with him when he finished school in July. He was in Minuteman Missiles and would be there for the next three years. Jerilyn didn't answer him, but did hold his hand as they continued driving home. She held his hand until they arrived home where she saw Sam's car with a U-Haul trailer parked in front of her trailer. Sam was inside waiting when she opened the door.

Ignoring Tom, he looked directly at her and said, "We're going back to Carolina. Get packed."

CHAPTER THIRTEEN

Jerilyn always wondered what if.

In spite of Sam's violence that night, Jerilyn still could have made a different choice. She could have taken a different road with another man. She could only speculate how her life might have been different.

Once Sam did turn his attention to Tom, he didn't give him any opportunity. Sam was an ex-Marine who had survived combat. Tom, a young Airman, didn't stand a chance. Even when his friend Jack joined in, Sam left them both bloody and laying in the street.

The neighbors called the police and then the decision was Jerilyn's. All she had to do was say one word and Sam would have gone to jail and she could have had Tom. Her mouth was bleeding from Sam slapping her after he finished with the two men who were taken to the hospital. The policeman asked her and she just couldn't have her husband arrested.

At that point the men were technically intruders. She packed and they left for North Carolina at dawn the next day. Jerilyn would ask herself what if for the next twenty years. She never spoke to Tom again.

Sam had been in North Carolina the whole time working a construction job in Morehead City. He never explained why he didn't call or why he left in the first place. For some reason, he came back and collected his family.

Jerilyn, feeling defeated and beaten, never tried to understand. She turned cold toward Sam and merely tolerated his presence. She and the girls were going to survive no matter what. It was good to be home again. The fact she was with Sam really made little difference to her. A few weeks later she realized she was pregnant.

From the beginning Sam insisted it was not his baby.

"Get a goddamn abortion!" he screamed, slapping her across the room. "I won't support some fucker's kid!"

Sam was right. Jerilyn knew it was Tom's and wanted to call him.

She thought about it, but never got the nerve. It was easier to leave Sam and one weekend when he didn't come home, she packed the girls and herself and went home to her mother and father.

Sam was probably glad to see them gone. He never called to see where they were and Jerilyn considered it a blessing in disguise. She was pregnant with another man's baby and while she never admitted it to him, Sam knew. She thought she wanted to get an abortion. She even made an appointment at a clinic in Raleigh, but never kept it. She knew she could save her marriage by getting the abortion, but just never got around to it. Summer was ending and she was four months pregnant. Just after Labor Day she went to Richmond to live with her sister Ruth.

Tina began kindergarten and Anne Marie went to nursery school. Ruth was working in the shipping department of a furniture company and Jerilyn got a job in accounting. They split the rent on Ruth's two-bedroom apartment.

Jerilyn and the girls slept together in the same bed. She found herself feeling more secure even though she faced the uncertainty of being pregnant. She told her parents not to tell Sam where she was and she knew without their help he would never find her. It worked because by the end of October she was showing and in maternity clothes, but still no Sam. Her appetite had increased and she was feeling good.

Then she realized something she'd never realized before. It never dawned on her men were attracted to pregnant women.

Sam was all she had to compare against and he was never really romantic with her. When she was pregnant, he insisted she take care of him, but after the third or fourth month he had no use for her body.

She assumed she was ugly and all men felt that way. This was not the case with Brad Morrison, the head of the accounting department. He thought she was attractive and asked her to go with him to dinner and a movie. She accepted and they had a lovely time. He even kissed her goodnight when he brought her home.

Brad began asking her out several times a week. He was older than her, around thirty and divorced. She liked the way he treated her and especially the nice places he took her. All Jerilyn had ever been used to going to were bars. Brad never took her to a bar.

They would drink with dinner, but he never suggested they go to a club or roadhouse. They went bowling and saw a lot of movies. He even took her to Washington, D.C. to see Elvis the Saturday after Thanksgiving.

Work ended on Wednesday afternoon and Ruth and Jerilyn started that night preparing Thanksgiving dinner. Ruth was dating Stoney, one of the delivery drivers and had invited him. Jerilyn asked Brad. The little girls thought this was great fun and had new dresses and shoes for the occasion. They ate at four o'clock and it was a wonderful meal. Both of the men stuffed themselves, swearing they never had a finer meal.

The tickets to Elvis were Brad's surprise for Jerilyn. He announced it as she was pouring coffee after dinner.

"We'll have to stay over Saturday night. Can you watch the girls?" he asked Ruth.

Amidst shrieks of joy, Ruth agreed and it was a date.

Immediately, Jerilyn said she had nothing to wear even though Brad thought she was an absolute knockout at that moment.

For Jerilyn this was certainly one of the highlights of her life. She had grown up on Elvis and to actually see him in person was something she always imagined was out of her reach. They left Richmond at three in the afternoon and arrived at the Hilton Hotel, downtown Washington, D.C. just before four-thirty.

She had never been to Washington and Brad drove around pointing out the sights before checking in. The valet met them at the curb on K Street and the bellman took their bags up to the room. Even though she was tired, she was too excited to rest. In two hours she'd be seeing Elvis.

Brad ordered a light snack and a bottle of champagne from room service to hold them over until dinner. He made ten-thirty dinner reservations at La Promenade. Jerilyn bathed, did her hair and dressed. Brad finished one bottle of wine and ordered another, continually telling her how beautiful she was. He said it so convincingly she believed she truly was.

And then he was on the stage. She couldn't believe it. There he was and she imagined Elvis was singing just for her in the 'Warm Kentucky Rain' and how he did it his way. He was fat now, but she still loved him. She was fat, too. Then it was over and they announced Elvis had left the building. It was at that moment she first felt the baby kick.

Everything about the night was magical. They were seated as soon as they arrived at the restaurant and the waiter discreetly whispered Henry Kissinger was dining there at the moment. Brad ordered wine and ordered for both of them from the French menu. The wine made her tingle and the food was delicious. He insisted she have dessert and as it arrived, he opened a small box and placed it in front of her.

She opened it to see a beautiful white gold ring with a solitaire diamond.

"I love you, Jerilyn," he said to her.

"Please take this and marry me," he asked almost pleading with
her.

Jerilyn was totally shocked.

Before she left town with him, she made up her mind about several things. She would make love to him any way he wanted. She trusted Brad and wanted to please him as much as she could. She bought a
blue full-length flowing negligee to wear to bed, hoping it would hide
her fullness. But, this was something she never expected.

"I'm already married," she said.

"We'll get you a divorce. I'll pay for it. I love you and want to take
care of you."

She couldn't believe it. Here was a man she had never made love
with actually wanting to marry her. Her hand reached for the ring, but
drew back. Her eyes filled with tears.

"You don't know anything about me. If you did, you wouldn't
want me."

"You mean about this baby not being your husband's? Ruth told
me about it and how violent he was with you.

"Jerilyn, you're a good woman for not giving in to him and getting an abortion. This baby will be ours and he'll have my name. He'll
be my son, not Sam's."

Jerilyn began to cry as she took the ring from the box. "You're
crazy," she told him.

"Crazy about you," he said as he watched her place the ring on
her finger.

She never needed the blue negligee. He made love to her the
moment they returned to the room. He spoke to her the whole time
and swore he'd always love her. Jerilyn allowed herself to believe him.

The next week Brad hired an attorney and Jerilyn filed for a
divorce. Sam was served with the papers the week before her father suffered a stroke. Ruth and Jerilyn returned home with the girls. Their
father was not expected to live.

An old wives' tale passed on in the lore of the North Carolina
farmlands says if a pregnant woman is present at a death, she will have
a difficult and probably fatal delivery. The child, it is said, will be
marked and live a confused and troubled life. The child will never
know his true parents and in the end will take his own life.

Jerilyn didn't believe in old wives' tales and stayed to care for her father. A week after he came home from the hospital as Jerilyn was giving him a sponge bath, Ray Webb suffered a second massive and this time fatal stroke. He died in his daughter's arms.

Ruth and Brad came down for the funeral. Their sister Ellen came home from Indiana with her husband and children. Aunts and uncles assembled from across the state and began a wake lasting until the Sunday afternoon burial service.

It was a cold rainy January afternoon as the family gathered at the gravesite. The minister gently consoled Mrs. Webb and the children. In all, nearly thirty adults and children were present as the final words were spoken for their father. Finally it was over and the people all began to leave. Jerilyn was with Brad and Ruth when Sam appeared. He walked directly at her.

"Where do you get off having me served with divorce papers?" he hissed.

"You're nothing but a lousy whore!" he screamed at her.

People getting into cars stopped to stare. Sam was waving the divorce papers in Jerilyn's face and Ruth started screaming at him.

"You low-life piece of shit," Ruth said to him. "How dare you come here today when we're burying our father!"

"Shut up, you bitch. You're a whore just like your sister!"

Then Brad moved in front of Sam attempting to bring some peace to the situation. His movement between Jerilyn and him only served to feed the rage that was rapidly running out of control in Sam.

Sam never spoke to Brad. In a sudden and unconscious move, Sam crashed his fist into Brad's face. The blow was followed by four or five more.

Brad was knocked back into Jerilyn who fell to the ground. Brad fell on top of her with Sam pursuing him and trying to kick him in the head.

Instead of meeting his target, Sam was knocked off balance when Ruth attacked him. While his foot hit near his target, it missed just the same and managed to hit Jerilyn in her ribs. Sam recovered and punched Ruth in the face, knocking her off her feet. Then he proceeded to kick Brad in his back.

The rest of the family rushed in and grabbed Sam, trying to subdue him. Sam wouldn't stop fighting. In spite of four or five men grabbing at him, Sam continued kicking at Brad, half of the time hitting Jerilyn. Finally, the police arrived and Sam was taken into custody. An ambulance was called and then a second. Brad and Jerilyn were both taken to the hospital. Brad was unconscious and Jerilyn had begun to go into labor.

Sam was in trouble. When he was arrested, he was carrying a knife. With what he had done to Brad and Jerilyn, along with the knife, he was booked for felony assault.

Brad was still out cold when he arrived at the hospital. He had been kicked in the face and head many times. He had lost his front teeth and was suffering from a serious concussion.

Jerilyn went into labor at the cemetery and was bleeding. Several of her ribs were broken from the kicks she received while on the ground. Her head was cut open. Moments after arriving at the hospital she gave birth to an eight-pound boy.

Ruth, her own face swollen from a punch, stayed with her sister who suddenly was scared of the old wives' tale. Jerilyn verged on hysterics; sure she was going to die. When they finally placed her son in her arms, Jerilyn slept from exhaustion and fear.

Brad regained consciousness at six that evening. He had no idea where he was or any recollection of the past two days. His last memory was leaving work on Friday afternoon. His front teeth were gone and his face a swollen mess. He had not been in a physical fight since sixth grade.

Jerilyn woke just before nine o'clock. She woke to the sounds of firecrackers, sirens, and horns honking. It had been some day for her. They buried her father, her baby was born, her soon-to-be ex-husband attacked her, and now what? When the nurse came in, she told Jerilyn the Vietnam War was over. The government signed an armistice with the Vietnamese.

Sam Gardner was sitting in a jail cell when he heard the news. He greeted it with a flurry of obscenities.

Brad was transported to a hospital in Virginia on Wednesday. Jerilyn stayed in the hospital until the following Monday. Sam stayed in jail for over a week until his brother flew in from Illinois and posted his bail. Jerilyn named her son Michael.

She tried to call Brad, but couldn't reach him. She called Ruth and asked her to go by and see him. After all, they were engaged and she needed to be sure he wanted to be on the birth certificate as Michael's father.

Ruth had a difficult time getting to see Brad. When he finally did talk to her, she called Jerilyn immediately.

"He told me everything was off. He said to keep the ring, but he wasn't going to marry you and didn't want to talk to you."

And that was that, Jerilyn thought to herself.

Just like that, he was gone from her life. She decided to stay in Carolina. Ruth's boyfriend left her and a few weeks later she quit her job and came home.

Jerilyn's old friend Debbie was working in a knitting mill in Farmville and got Ruth a job. Jerilyn stayed home and took care of her mother and the children. At the end of April her divorce was final.

Summer came and Jerilyn signed up for Mother's Aid. There was always a man here and there. She didn't allow any of them too close, but she always had one around. Then summer ended and she got her own trailer. Ruth moved in to help out with the kids and the money and Jerilyn appreciated it. Then in November Jerilyn took a job at the Carolina Inn as night bartender. The money was good and there were a lot of men drinking there.

One was Charley Reed.

Jerilyn met Lee Stein first. Without Lee, she might never have met Charley because he was quiet and kept to himself. In a strange sort of way, Charley's reserve was appealing to her because it was different. She was used to men coming on to her. While she certainly did enjoy the attention, an attractive man who did not pursue her was quite a novelty. Lee Stein was just like the rest of them and she knew it even before she asked him for a ride home.

Jerilyn lived out the Stantonsburg Highway. The Carolina Inn was at the eastern end of the highway where it ran into the main route from Rocky Mount to Kinston. Jerilyn's trailer was five miles to the west. Beyond were Stantonsburg, Farmville, and Wilson.

Lee owned the Cadillac dealership in town and drove a white El Dorado convertible. Like the guys he drank with, he drank a lot of beer, talked too much and too loud. Like the other men at the bar, there was something missing that he was hoping to find somewhere other than in his own home. With Jerilyn, what was missing was simple. She was missing a man. On this particular night, Lee would be the man.

Excitement begins and ends. It is measured by time. Sometimes it lasts longer than others. It was all just a matter of seconds, minutes, and hours. In fairy tales, it never ends. That night was no fairy tale.

Lee was over in a matter of minutes and she was left to clean herself as best she could. He pulled up his pants and started the car. He tried to talk to her, but she knew he wished she would just disappear. He had to be home. His wife was probably waiting. Jerilyn looked at his face and decided he wasn't even that good looking. She didn't even bother to wonder why she did what she did. She all ready knew. He had been a man and that was enough.

The next night the bar was slow. Happy hour had the one or two customers. Only Bob Holtz and his two friends stayed on in the corner booth. All three of them were weekly regulars and guests at the Inn. Eddie Jacoby was a tax accountant from New York and Bruce Johannsen was Bob's boss from Raleigh. Bob lived in Goldsboro and was a farm supply salesman.

Jerilyn was sitting in the booth with the men when Lee walked in and sat down at the bar. Bob made a comment when he saw him. Jerilyn only caught part of it as she got up to serve him, but detected Bob didn't care for Lee very much.

Lee looked tired and wasn't talkative. He ordered a second beer for someone else who hadn't arrived yet. She served him and went back to the booth.

As she sat back at the booth, Charley Reed came in and Bob made another comment about Yankees and how they should all go home. The sound of his voice with the word Yankees immediately reminded her of her father. It made her smile.

"So you don't like Yankees?" Jerilyn teased Bob. She was looking directly at Eddie who was from New York.

Bob laughed realizing what he had done. "I don't have anything against Northerners," he said. "It's just the Yankees I can't stand and it starts with those two."

"Lee?" she asked. "What do you have against him?"

"Go try to buy a car from him and you'll find out. He comes down here and buys the Cadillac shop and thinks he's too good for us boys who lived here all our lives. It's a good thing for him and his right-hand man the Klan isn't as active as it used to be. We'd give them both a party."

"Oh, Bob," Bruce, his boss said. "You're just upset because your credit isn't good and you were turned down. It wasn't him. It was the bank."

"He's a goddamn Jew and his friend is an asshole."

"Well," Jerilyn sighed. "I guess that takes care of them."

"I don't like the guy with Lee either," Eddie said. "He's a mean son-of-a-bitch."

"How's that?" Jerilyn asked, looking him over as he sat at the bar.

"I tried talking to him once several months ago and to say the least, he was rather unsociable."

Again Bruce clarified what had actually happened. "You were drunk and running on at the mouth. The poor guy was tired and just didn't want to hear it. A lot of people would have decked you. He just moved."

"Who is he?" Jerilyn asked.

"Lee's sales manager, Charley Reed."

Lee and Charley began to laugh at something one of them said. Jerilyn got up and got each of them another beer. Lee paid her and when they finished the second round, they left.

The next night Lee came in alone. It was still slow and Lee sat with her in the booth she had shared the night before with Eddie, Bob, and Bruce.

"What are you doing sitting with those jerks?" Lee asked her.

"They say the same thing about you," she said.

"I guess they would," he said.

"Who was with you last night?" she asked.

"Charley, my sales manager. He used to work for me up in Washington."

"Oh," Jerilyn said, sounding interested.

"He's married," Lee added in a tone of voice calling her off. "He's had some tough times. He and his wife lost a baby."

"That's a shame," she said.

"Even in spite of that, he's happily married. He's not like me."

"Lee, I'm not sure anyone is happily married. You aren't. None of those men last night are. I wasn't. I'm not sure I've ever known anyone who was. Everyone wants something else."

"Well, he is," Lee said. "Leave him alone. I don't need him getting messed up. He makes me a lot of money every month. If he plays it straight, he has one hell of a future ahead of him."

As they sat there talking about Charley, Lee saw him drive up in his car.

"Here he is now," Lee said. "Get him a Bud. He's been at the auto auction all day and will be thirsty."

Jerilyn got up to get the beer. As she did, Charley came in and sat across from Lee.

"How did we do?" Lee asked as soon as Charley sat down.

About that time Jerilyn returned with a beer. When she put it down, she went back to the bar.

"Is this mine?" Charley asked pointing at the beer.

"Yes," Lee said. "How did we do at the auction?"

"We lost our ass," Charley answered with a straight face.

"I expected that," Lee said. "How bad?"

"Thirty-three hundred."

"Thirty-three hundred!" Lee said louder than he intended.

"Christ Almighty! We only had twenty-five in the whole lot of them!"

"That's right," Charley said beginning to lose the serious expression on his face. "I had to pay them eight hundred to haul the iron away. You told me not to bring any of it back."

The look on Lee's face was priceless. Charley winked and Jerilyn began to laugh.

"You're not funny," Lee said.

Charley began to laugh. "We made thirty-three hundred."

"You got thirty-three hundred?"

"No," Charley said. "I got fifty-eight. We made thirty-three hundred profit."

"How the hell did you do that?" Lee exclaimed.

"It's a junk market. Nice, big cars were bringing nothing. That's only temporary though. Everyone's running scared."

Jerilyn watched Charley finish his beer in three swallows and then looked to Lee who said to get him another.

Jerilyn realized from the conversation that Charley had done something extraordinary, but never heard Lee tell him so. Instead, Lee began talking about the troubles he had at the car dealership. It soon turned into an argument about the salesmen Charley had working for him. Jerilyn figured out the problem was the salesmen worked for Charley, not Lee, and finally Charley told him so.

"He's exactly the same as I was when you hired me," Charley said, talking about someone named George.

"Eddie Edwards wasn't my boss, you were. I was totally loyal to you. I'm sure that bastard felt the same way about me as you feel about George."

Lee was quiet and even though he didn't say it, he understood what Charley meant. Jerilyn brought them two more beers and then got herself a fresh cup of coffee. She sat down at the booth next to Lee.

"You've never introduced me to Charley," Jerilyn said to Lee.

She watched Charley's face. He paid no attention to her while he was pouring his beer into the glass. He continued to drink as if she had said nothing.

"Jerilyn Gardner, Charley Reed," Lee said ceremoniously.

"Nice to meet you," Jerilyn said.

"Of course, it would be," he said. He barely even looked at her as he spoke and his arrogance irritated her.

"Screw you," she blurted out.

"You wish," he said laughing.

She stood up and walked away, realizing almost instantly he was teasing her. She heard Charley laugh and was too embarrassed to go back. Charley finished his beer and got up to leave. She hadn't been paying attention to them, but was looking when he turned and winked at her. Then he turned back to Lee.

"You have more to lose than I do," he said to Lee. "Just decide whether it's worth it or not."

Jerilyn went back to the table and sat with Lee as they both watched Charley get into a white sedan Deville and drive away.

"What was he talking about when he left?" she asked.

"You," Lee answered.

Jerilyn didn't ask anything else. A moment later the bar was busy and when she looked up, Lee was gone, too.

At home that night Jerilyn thought about Charley Reed. He was young, successful and good looking. He had a certain confidence about him and a way that made her want to know him better. Even though he was sarcastic and teased, she liked the way he sounded, smiled, and even winked. Thinking about him made her feel good. She fell asleep wondering if she could have him.

CHAPTER FOURTEEN

CHICAGO, ILLINOIS
1992

Jerilyn Garner woke late. Her apartment was cold. It was snowing and she got out of bed to turn up the heat. It was December 11th and while Jerilyn hated the snow, she realized it was the time of the year to expect it.

A week passed since she spoke to or saw Chuck Ganley. She had not heard from Tina or Anne. Her sister Ruth was in the bar yesterday and sat through the football games with her. Ruth mentioned Tina was seeing someone, but didn't know anymore than that. Anne told her Tina had really fallen for him, but didn't know who he was.

Jerilyn made herself coffee and tried to remember if December 11th had any sort of significance. She thought about calling Chuck at his office, but changed her mind.

Instead, she sat back and sipped her coffee and thought about December 11th and remembered.

It was the time of the first energy crisis and Merle Haggard was singing 'If We Can Make It Through December.' By that time Nixon had stopped fighting the Vietnamese and was busy with Congress, fighting to survive his term. The fifty-five mile per hour speed limit was the law. It was December 11th and it had been raining for two days.

Jerilyn hadn't seen Lee or Charley Reed for a week. That night Charley came in with another young man whom he introduced as George. Jerilyn recognized the name as the young man they had spoken of the week before.

"Could we have two Buds, please," Charley asked her.

"Sure you can," she said. "What's the change? You're so polite tonight."

"I am?" Charley asked.

"That's right. Everyone comes in here wrapped up in presenting one image or another. They all forget about being polite. Your boss, Lee, he's the worst. He just walks in and demands his beer. Some people don't have any manners."

"I guess I'm just nice," he kidded.

"You are," she said not allowing him to make light of it. "You shouldn't joke about it or sell yourself short."

Her hair fell forward as she reached into the cooler. As she brought out the beers she brushed it quickly back into place with her hand. She filled their glasses and found herself looking into Charley's eyes. She realized she wanted something and hoped she might find it there. Jerilyn knew she was attracted to this man and suddenly found herself smiling at him as she poured him his second beer.

Outside the rains were still falling and began to beat against the front window with greater fury. The wind howled and the panes of glass vibrated at their force. Across the street the tall gas station sign rocked back and forth. George and Charley began joking about how nice the weather was.

As she poured them their third beer, Charley mentioned Lee had been gone, but was expected back the next day.

"So," she said attempting to show she wasn't interested.

Charley laughed out loud. "I feel the same way!"

George laughed and said they all would be better off if Lee stayed away for the rest of the month. Jerilyn nodded in agreement and left them to talk.

She was busy with other tables, but never took her eyes from him for long. He was wearing a suit and tie and had the look of success about him. Comparing him to Lee, she thought Lee should be working for him instead of the way it was.

When George left, Charley got up to play the jukebox. Jerilyn got him a fresh beer and moved him over to her table in the corner. She smiled at him as he stopped and realized the beer at the table was for him. She took care of the last remaining couple and then joined him.

She looked into his brown eyes. They seemed open like someone who had nothing to hide and gave her the feeling there was something there she could hold onto.

He spoke briefly of his wife. He didn't mention the baby they lost. She told him about her ex-husband and children. The children were great, but Sam was a jerk. She complained he never wrote, called, or sent support of any kind.

"He's never even sent his daughter a birthday card," she said.

Charley sat and listened.

She watched his face and eyes. At the same time Jerilyn felt him study her.

From the very first moment they sat together she knew his eyes seldom left her. She was aware of him watching her as she walked away from him to serve customers. She could feel him looking at her body and enjoyed it when she caught a glimpse of the expression on his face. She knew he was hooked, but she knew she was, too.

She tried to get him to talk more about his wife, but he wouldn't. As open and warm as he seemed, she felt something walled off in that area. She sensed an aloneness of which he would not speak. It was an area he kept closed and private. Without being told, Jerilyn knew he would force her to respect it.

The rain continued through the evening and before long it was closing time. He was the only person left.

"Will you give me a ride home?" she asked.

She knew he would. She had already called Ruth and told her not to come pick her up.

They didn't talk. He drove her across town in his Cadillac.

"Do you really want to go home?" he asked.

She didn't answer. They kept driving and before long they were in empty apartment.

"Who does this belong to?" she asked.

"One of my salesmen. He moved to Raleigh and left me the keys to turn in at the end of the month."

"This is large," she said trying to keep the conversation light. "Do you know what the rent it?"

"Two hundred including utilities."

"Electricity, too?"

"Yes," he said, taking her by the hand and leading her back to the bedroom.

She wondered what he was thinking. She could feel his hand gripping hers and she wondered if he would kiss her. He turned out the light and she turned toward him and wound up in his arms.

Jerilyn tried to recall that moment many times. She tried to remember how she wound up in his arms so easily and exactly what the first kiss was really like. She remembered a magical wave engulfing them both. It was special and the feeling could never be recaptured again or even remembered exactly.

His kiss was tender. She opened her mouth to his and the first caress lasted and lasted.

Jerilyn moved her hands up his back into his hair. She kissed him more passionately and he responded with increased intensity. His hands ran around and across her back and beneath her blouse to touch her bare skin. She shook as he brought them back to the front, lifted her bra and softly began to touch her breasts.

He led them back into the empty bedroom. Jerilyn stood there totally motionless as he slowly began to undress her. As he opened each button of her blouse, her breathing became more rapid.

Soon it was off her shoulders and he was on his knees kissing her breasts. He opened her jeans and she felt them as they were taken down the length of her legs. His mouth left her breasts and as he took away her panties, he kissed her stomach, legs, all of her. Her knees buckled, but he supported her with his hands as he held her body to his face. Jerilyn sighed and held his head with both her hands.

"Oh my God!" she cried out.

He brought her to the floor and continued to kiss and explore her body. His lips moved back across her and once more kissed her lips. She tried to open his pants, but his belt would not give.

"Open it for me," she said. It wasn't a passionate request. It was a demand. She wanted him.

He quickly undid the belt and her hands took him and gently moved his length and cradled him between her palms.

"You make me feel so good," she whispered to him.

"I'm glad," he answered. "I want to make you feel even better."

"Yes, do," she said. "Do."

Jerilyn helped him remove his clothes, taking time to look at each part of his body. She touched him everywhere and moved him onto his back. Silently, she took him into her mouth.

She looked up at his face to find his eyes closed. His face had the look of a small boy. It was the look of innocence and in spite of the acts they were sharing, Jerilyn had the feeling Charley was surrendering something to her he had never given before. He ran his hands through her long black hair as she continued loving him.

"Oh, I love that!" he sighed.

He brought her head to his face and kissed her again. She felt his naked body move on top of her.

Their lovemaking was slow and deliberate. He cared and she felt her passion for him rise, slowly at first, and then flood over her. He took time to please her. Of all the men she had known, this was the first who truly cared about her.

She opened herself completely and allowed him to touch her like no man ever had. Each time he thrust himself forward, she felt as if he was reaching her soul. It was as if she heard his body speaking to hers. She responded, answering she was ready whenever he chose.

With that signal he exploded, filling her wanting body with a warm love given freely. His body quaked and shook. She held him tightly and even as the flow ended, she felt it begin. It was a love like nothing Jerilyn ever would have again in her life. It was a love that would consume them both and not end, even with his death.

CHAPTER FIFTEEN

SUNSET, UTAH
1992

Cindy Ganely woke, alone.

She looked at the alarm clock. It was six a.m. She had a high school senior to wake up as well as her husband. It was December 11th and as she got out of bed, the significance of the date was more of a reality than ever before. Cindy met Charley Reed on this date years and years ago at a high school dance. She wondered what he might say if he were alive and knew what was happening to his son.

Cindy spoke with her son the previous night and there was no mistaking what was going on in his life. She tried to control herself, but she was a mother. He told her he was seeing Tina.

"What about her mother?" Cindy asked.

"What about her?" Charley asked her back.

"Are you seeing her, too?"

"No," he answered.

"You were though, weren't you?"

"Yes, I was, but what does that have to do with anything?"

"Does Tina know you were seeing her mother?"

"Yes."

"Does she know you slept with her?"

"Mother, I never said I slept with her."

"You did though," replied Cindy. "Does Tina know?"

"No."

"What do you think Tina would say if she knew?" asked Cindy.

"Why would you think she has to know?"

"Oh, honey, she doesn't have to know, but I believe her mother will tell her."

Cindy listened, as her son was silent. She knew him well enough to understand how he was trying to reason this out. He was an attorney and dealt with problems every day.

"Are you in love with Tina?" she asked.

"Yes," he answered quietly.

"What do you think her mother will do when she finds out?"

"I don't know," he admitted.

"Chuck," she asked. "How serious is this?"

"Serious enough," he answered, allowing his mother to realize some of her worst fears.

"Your father will never approve of her," she said. "Have you thought about that?"

"Mother, I don't care what he approves of or doesn't. I stopped caring about what he wanted when we had it out over law school."

Cindy remembered when Chuck announced he would be going to Duquesne University and his father forbid him to go. He insisted BYU was a fine school and wouldn't have his son attend a Catholic university.

When Chuck defied his father, a blow struck him down from his father's right hand. When Chuck rose from the floor, he was struck down again. He left home that night and never returned. It was the same night Cindy moved into her own bedroom.

"He is your father," she gently reminded her son.

"Sometimes I wonder," he said back to her.

"And what is that supposed to mean," she demanded.

"Oh, nothing like that," he apologized.

"He's not human, Mother. He treats us like we are property instead of his flesh and blood. I don't have any memories of him loving me. I only remember his hand and his voice and thou shall and thou shall not. What kind of a father is that? I'll never treat my children like that."

Cindy knew he wouldn't and she also knew his real father wouldn't have either.

As she spoke to her son, she realized she had a major dilemma. She didn't know Jerilyn at all and had no idea how much she knew.

Cindy was afraid of so many things.

Had Charley ever spoken to Jerilyn about her and the pregnancy? Did Jerilyn recognize Chuck as Charley's son, or was it just someone who resembled him? If she did suspect Chuck was the son of Charley Reed, what would she do when she learned she was not only thrown over, but for her own daughter, too?

While Cindy was dutiful and subdued, taking a back seat to her husband and his wishes, she recognized women like Jerilyn could be very deadly.

She was sorry she hadn't known Charley Reed better. Cindy remembered being in love with him and the days they spent together. It seemed like another lifetime now.

She remembered his tenderness and wondered what war was like for the sensitive young man who was the father of her only son. She wondered what he'd been like when he came back.

Cindy found herself becoming jealous of Jerilyn Gardner because she knew. Jerilyn had known him and had loved him and he had loved her, too. Now, she knew and loved his son, too. Cindy wondered what Jerilyn knew.

"So what do you intend to do about Tina's mother?" she asked.

"I don't know," he said. "I guess maybe I should tell Tina so it won't be a surprise if Jerilyn turns on us."

"How do you think she'll respond?"

"I don't know, Mother," he said. "It's not like I planned this or was seeing them both at the same time. I haven't even talked to Jerilyn since I started seeing Tina. Tina says she loves me. I guess I'll find out how much."

Cindy didn't like the way her son was talking. She knew when he decided he wanted something he could become quite single-minded.

"You are serious about her, then?"

"Yes, I guess I am."

"I'm not sure I approve either," she heard herself saying.

"Why?" he asked.

"You don't even know her. You're judging her by her mother. I certainly wouldn't want to be judged by Father."

"No, that's not it. You've only known her a few weeks. You know how I feel about quick decisions. I don't know where you get that," she said knowing full well he was just like Charley Reed. " I really believe you should go slowly."

Cindy knew he wouldn't. He was so much like Charley in that respect. He made up his mind and bam! He'd go right ahead and make the most of the situation. This single trait would probably make him a great attorney.

"I just want you to be happy, son," she said. "I'm your mother and I want what is best for you."

"I know," he said quietly.

"Promise you'll call me to let me know what happens," she asked him.

"I will," he said.

Julie was just finishing breakfast when Adam came to the table. Cindy had been talking to her daughter about college and what her friends were going to do after graduation. This was her baby and in many ways, her favorite of the four girls.

Julie was a pregnancy she dreaded, not to mention the unexpectedness of it. Now Cindy was reliving her senior year through her daughter and the excitement of where she was going to school after graduation.

Cindy ignored her husband as he sat at the table and began his morning ritual of thanking God for another day and the food his wife was about to place before him. Even has he voiced his prayers aloud, his hands clasped and his face raised looking to the ceiling, Cindy poured his black coffee and placed a glass of freshly squeezed orange juice before him. While he was busy thanking the Lord for his gracious bounty, Cindy wondered what was going through her daughter's mind.

Cindy watched and listened to the Mayor of Sunset, Utah ask for Divine Guidance for the day before him and wondered how many other men performed such a scene each morning before their families. He was still beseeching God for additional help as she began scrambling his eggs and frying the ham. She placed the frozen hash brown potatoes in the microwave and put four pieces of whole wheat bread in the toaster. As she poured him a large glass of milk, he thanked God for the last time.

Julie rose as her father ended his morning prayers. She kissed him dutifully on the cheek and spoke the well-rehearsed and memorized words. "I love you, Father. Have a nice day."

Adam Ganley, as he had spoken to each of his other four children, responded with as much sincerity as his daughter. "I love you, too, my daughter. Go with God."

It was a ritual.

Cindy listened as she had for over twenty-six years. So many times she questioned the necessity of the ritual.

It was almost as many times she retreated within herself, ignoring her own Catholic training, and submitted to the will and whims of her husband. This morning as she listened for perhaps the one-millionth time, Cindy truly detested the sight before her. Even as her baby kissed her on the cheek, Cindy found herself revolted at the sight of her three hundred pound husband clutching his half empty glass of orange juice.

Julie left for school and Cindy placed his breakfast in front of him. As was expected of her, she sat at the table and drank her last cup of coffee.

They seldom spoke anymore. Usually she would ask him if he had a preference for dinner. He seldom did as long as there was enough. She learned early on, Adam was a big eater. His eating habits bordered on sloth. Cindy considered him a slob and never regretted the day she left his bed. Having no one was better than what she had to endure.

While she sipped her coffee, Cindy watched him shoveling the food into his mouth as fast as he could. Some fell either back to his plate or landed on the front of his shirt where it began to roll from his chest to his stomach and then to the floor.

Once it hit the floor another ritual would begin.

Corky, an old male beagle that belonged to Chuck, would be laying in wait for his inevitable first treat of the day. Then, as always, Adam would try to kick the dog with his legs that were so fat it was surprising he could even move them. Out of frustration Adam would then curse the dog.

"Get away you damned beast of the earth! If I had my way, I'd shoot you this very day and be rid of you and what you stand for!"

With that Adam would glare at his wife, acknowledging one of the few times she openly defied him. What the dog stood for was mother and son going against his wishes and bringing the stray dog into their home.

The ritual brought a smile to Cindy's face. Her husband's aggravation was a small victory, but a victory just the same. Within minutes Cindy would get up and call the dog to the door, putting him out. As the dog went outside, her husband would curse the animal once more.

"When he left this house, I hoped his dog would go with him. Damn that dog!"

Cindy always ignored that statement. She remembered the girls all in open rebellion to their father when he wanted to rid his house of the beast.

"Damn you!" he cursed her. "You undermine me and turn my own children from my face. Damn you to hell!"

Cindy ignored his curses, enjoying her small victory.

As the dog went out and she closed the door, Adam chose to break their usual silence.

"What did your son want last night?" he asked.

The word 'your' stung her ears and brought both heat and color to her face. It had been a long time since Adam had chosen any sort of combat with her. It had been nearly five years since he challenged her openly. The word 'your' was still stinging her ears as she remembered him trying to force himself on her for sex. She remembered that night and wouldn't ever put it from her mind.

"Damn you, woman!" he screamed. "Your duty as my wife is to satisfy me!"

Cindy wanted none of it. As his enormous weight pinned her to the bed and as his fat fingers began to move on her, she remembered her father, a man who had no sons and taught her to throw a punch.

"Don't hit like a girl," her daddy used to tell her.

Even though she never made her dad pleased as she punched at his hands, the lesson came back to her and she broke her husband's nose. Adam never approached her again.

"What did he want," Adam repeated.

"He called to talk to me," she answered.

"If he wants money, he can go somewhere else. He'll have none of mine."

Cindy hated the way he spoke to her and hated the way he claimed everything for himself. She couldn't stand the way he made her feel insignificant and for one moment she was tempted to use what her mother had told her on her recent trip to Pittsburgh.

"If Chuck needs money, I'll give him my own," she answered defiantly.

"That's good," he said, food falling out of his mouth. "He'll have none of mine.

Again Cindy held herself in check.

When she returned from dinner that night in Pittsburgh, she confronted her mother with what she had learned from Charley's friends.

Her mother admitted what she had always known and what she had done. Cindy had not forgiven her mother and there was certainly no way she ever intended forgiving this pompous, self-righteous excuse for a man.

She thought of Charley Reed. She thought of him fondly and remembered another young man who liked her that Charley called Bozo. Charley was smaller than Bozo, but managed to blacken both of Bozo's eyes when he tried to make a grab at her at a dance. Cindy smiled.

"What's funny, whore?" her husband shouted.

"You, you fat slob," she answered him calmly. He had never called her a whore.

"I know!" he screamed at her. "I know I'm funny! All these years

I must be a real joke. You must really think I'm hilarious. I think I am! I have to be! Everyone would think I'm a joke! Me! Adam Ganley!

"I'm a joke! I've raised a bastard and given him my name. My own wife can only give me daughters. I have no son of my own! It's my curse for marrying a whore."

Cindy stood as the words still echoed through the kitchen. Tears filled her eyes. She was more angry than hurt. After the years of suppression and penance, Cindy finally felt ready to fight him on an equal standing.

"Don't you dare call me a whore," she said as she smashed her coffee cup to the table. The cup broke into pieces, coffee flying into the air and her left holding only its handle.

"There's a whore in the family," she said. "There certainly is a whore, but it isn't me. A whore is someone who sells himself. Someone who marries a pregnant woman on the provision her father sets him up in his own hardware business is a whore.

"It certainly isn't some dumb young girl who trusts and listens to her socially- conscientious mother and is married to an up-and-coming executive. I'm no whore! You're the whore, you self-righteous bastard!

"I've listened to you damn me, my son, and the dog for the last time. I'm sick of it. God damn you and I hope you rot in hell, you dirty son-of-a-bitch!"

Cindy stormed out of the kitchen and locked herself in the bathroom.

Finally, after hearing him start the car and leave, she came out. As she began to clean up the kitchen, she felt strangely different. At first it was hard for her to identify, but the longer she thought, she eventually remember.

"I'm from Pittsburgh," Charley told her as he left for the Army. "We're all fighters. We feel better when we've had a good fight. I'll be fine. No one can kill me, but me!"

Cindy remembered his words. As she showered and washed her hair, she couldn't get them out of her head.

Later, drying herself she stood before the mirror and looked at her body. Naked and clean, a mother of five, her body was still firm and beautiful.

She thought of Adam, fat and slovenly. There was no way she was a whore. She knew all in all she had probably done the right thing. She also knew the right thing didn't always make you happy.

It could only be what it was, the right thing even though in truth, it was wrong.

CHAPTER SIXTEEN

CHICAGO, ILLINOIS
1992

As Jerilyn began to run the dishwasher she thought about Chuck Ganley.

It had been nearly three weeks since she'd been with him. It wasn't a long time for her. In the past it might have been, but with all the concerns over disease and all the violence, Jerilyn found herself just a bit more selective and cautious. Her friend Bob crossed her mind and she wondered why she hadn't heard from him, too.

She went down the hall to the laundry room and placed a load of dirty clothes in the washing machine. As she came back into her apartment, the phone had just stopped ringing. She walked to the phone and waited. It didn't ring again.

Jerilyn went on with her housework and changed the sheets on her bed. Just as she began to run a bath, the phone rang again. It was Bob.

"I was just thinking about you," she said. "Did you just call?"

"No," he answered.

"Oh," she said wondering who it might have been.

"How are you?" she asked. "I haven't heard from you in three weeks."

"I'm fine, I guess," he replied. "I've been traveling, working hard. I never have time for anything."

"Where have you been traveling to?" she asked, making small talk.

She was hoping the conversation would come around to the reason she hoped he really called. Jerilyn did want him to come over as she listened to him rattle off the cities along the east coast.

"So, are you going to come over and see me?" she asked.

"If you want me to," he answered.

"Sure, I'd like it a lot."

"When?" he asked her.

"Give me an hour or so. I'm just getting into the tub and I've got some clothes in the wash."

"Wear something sexy," he teased her.

"Sure," she said. "How about something black and lacy?"

"Great!" he exclaimed. "See you about one."

As she bathed, she thought about Bob. She'd known him for probably four years or so. From the very beginning he told her he was married. It made little difference to her. The last thing she wanted was to be tied down to one man.

Bob had a family and a job and like most men his age, suffered from the frustrations of going nowhere in his life and a wife he felt was totally unresponsive to him.

"Why did you marry her?" she asked him one time.

"She wasn't always this way," he answered her.

"When we dated and then lived together, we couldn't get enough of each other. Every time we'd make love it was better than the time before. Even if it wasn't, she made me believe that it was.

"We got married and it was even better for a while. Then all of a sudden there were times she'd just tolerate me. Physically I had her body, but mentally she was somewhere else. I hated those times!"

"Did it happen often?"

"No," he remembered. "Not at first.

"I chalked them up to not being in the mood, but loving me enough any way. The years went by. There were the kids and I guess we just got used to each other. She always excited me, even when she was pregnant. She didn't want to kiss me a lot when we made love and I mean kiss me, you know, on the mouth. I wondered if I had bad breath.

"Making love without kissing kind of makes it like fucking a whore you've paid for. Whores don't kiss either. And why would you want to? You're thinking about all the cocks she's sucked that day and you can't kiss her. It kind of makes me feel she thinks that way about me. That's a hell of a thought," he said.

"It sure is," Jerilyn agreed.

"She wants to cuddle," he said after a moment.

"I call it snuggle," she said back identifying with him.

"Cuddling means I get to hold her and tell her how much I love her, but we don't make love."

"Don't you enjoy just feeling close to her?"

"Sure, I used to. But cuddling is for the middle of the night when it's cold or you've had a bad dream. Any other time is just a way to get things started and then not finish them. It's just another way for her to control things."

"Is that the way you see it?" Jerilyn asked him.

"Isn't that the way it is?" he asked back.

She didn't answer.

"Evidently it wears off faster for women than it does for men.

"In marriage sex becomes a function shared only when the wife wants to share it. She calls the shots. She's in control. Just like my marriage. If my wife found out I had you, she'd be crushed. She'd never understand and would divorce me for being unfaithful. She'd be right, but it would be her fault, too.

"I never would need you, if she needed me."

Jerilyn knew Bob was right about some of it. She remembered Charley telling her the same thing and she knew how she had been when she lived with her husband.

As she dressed she considered his complaint. She knew it was valid and knew most men could easily complain in much the same way. She also knew there were women just like her, happy to have those men on whatever terms they offered.

Jerilyn considered herself an intelligent woman and even saw the humor in the situation. It was natural birth control. Indifference began with the wife and eventually spread to the husband. As a result they had sex on fewer and fewer occasions and when they did, it was a purely physical release, not lovemaking. It all seemed rather stupid.

Jerilyn found something black and lacy. She also found stockings and a pair of high heels. She was feeling especially eager and made a point of putting on some special perfume. Just as she dabbed it in one of her secret places, her doorbell rang. She grew even happier and more excited as she walked to answer the door.

Tina Gardner considered herself as unlike her mother as any daughter had ever been.

It wasn't something she consciously became, nor was it even something she pointed out to people. Everyone, including her father, remarked at her uncanny resemblance to her mother. Tina never minded it. Her mother was very beautiful. But she knew that all similarities ended there.

Like the child of an alcoholic, Tina considered herself the child of a whore. For that reason she made herself extremely selective and was aloof.

In her early teens when she was faced with the idea of going along with the crowd and sleeping around, she chose to remain apart from the partying and sexual activity. Her sister, Anne Marie, was very much her mother's daughter, but Tina remained a virgin until her second year in college.

It was just before her twentieth birthday and although she dated, she had never been serious about anyone. In a way, Tina began to worry about herself. She knew she was normal enough, but she worried about her ability to love someone. Her choice to abstain made Tina wonder if some sort of damage hadn't been done to her psyche.

Her roommate, Mary Ellen, told Tina about her first lover. "I chose him," she said. "He was twenty-nine or thirty. I was fifteen."

Mary Ellen laughed.

"He thought I was my older sister and was in college. I babysat for him. He was divorced and had his son. I knew he was really lonely and I just made myself available to him. I'm glad I did it that way, too. He taught me a lot about making love."

Tina thought about what Mary Ellen said and after a time she chose a young psychology instructor she worked for part time. He was thirty, divorced, and quite handsome. He had come on to her several times, probably mostly in jest, but Tina felt she could turn it into something much more serious.

She asked for Mary Ellen's help.

"Why would you ask me?" she asked, teasing Tina. "From what you've told me, you have something of an expert in your family. If you need advice on swimming, you should talk to an Olympic Gold Medallist."

That crack really made Tina mad. Mary Ellen broke up laughing and Tina began to look at the whole thing as a humorous adventure. They joked and referred to it as The Deflowering of Tina.

"Will it hurt? What if I get pregnant? Oh, God, I don't want to get pregnant! Shouldn't I be in love with him?"

"Tina," Mary Ellen said. "You're weird.

"Don't worry about love so much. Let's just make sure he's no pig or into something kinky. We'll get you to my doctor and he'll fix you up with birth control pills."

That's what they did and several weeks later Tina went to bed with Jeremy.

Tina had no idea what her virginity meant to Jeremy. When she realized what it did to him and how he began to court her, she couldn't help thinking how foolish young girls were to throw it away over some pimply-faced teenager.

She liked the closeness and the secrets they shared. What started out to be a physical interlude rapidly developed into a full-blown love affair. Their days centered on where they would meet and how long it would be until they were together again.

It was the fall of the year and Chicago was a great place to be in love.

They walked along the north shore and went to see the Bears play. They spent an entire Saturday walking through the Museum of Science and Industry and even went to the circus when it came to town. At twenty, Tina was finally in love.

She moved in with Jeremy in December.

He was from California and had no immediate family in Chicago. Tina's family, though not really close, became his family and their group activities centered around happy hour at the bar where Jerilyn was working. As winter changed into spring, Ruth, her husband, Anne Marie and her boyfriend, Tina, Jeremy, and several of their friends made a weekly ritual of Fridays. Ruth began having a Sunday meal for the family and their activities extended through the weekend. Tina began to feel for the first time she truly had a family.

In early May Jeremy began acting strange. He was distant. It was as if he had something on his mind. Tina tried to talk to him, but it only made him withdraw even more. By the end of the month he wasn't even interested in making love to her and when she tried to talk about it, he'd get angry.

Mary Ellen was the only person she could confide in.

"He just comes home and goes to bed right after he eats. I've tried everything I know, including candlelight and champagne. I've tried to get him to go on picnics or even walk along the lake like we used to do. He's going to Washington, D.C. next week and doesn't want me to come along."

"He has someone else," Mary Ellen said.

Tina couldn't believe it.

"You don't know men very well," Mary Ellen told Tina. "Very few of them are faithful to anyone. They can't live without us until they get us. Once they get us, there's someone else they think they want more. They leave and go after her and it keeps on and on."

"That can't be true," Tina insisted. "I've seen men stay with the same women all their lives."

Mary Ellen laughed.

"Those women are far and few between. And it isn't the woman. It's the man.

"They find a woman who knows how to control them. She gives them some of what they want, but not all of it. Instead of giving him a life that's a banquet, she only feeds him small snacks. They stay hungry for her all the time. I guess the secret is to learn to control them with what they want most."

Tina was disillusioned. She didn't want to believe Jeremy had someone else.

"What can I do to get him back?" she asked.

"Nothing. Really," Mary Ellen said.

"Anything you try to do to bring him back will just push him away. If it were me, I'd leave him. That might shock him into reality and then you'd become what he wants most. If it did happen, and it's a long shot, then you're in control."

Tina couldn't do it. She said she didn't like games.

"People should stay together because they love one another, not because they deny something the other person wants or needs. What kind of love is that?" she asked.

"It's not love, Tina, it's just a hard cold fact of life," answered Mary Ellen.

"You're wrong. You have to be wrong," she said insisting on her point.

As usual on Friday they all met for happy hour. Jeremy had barely spoken to her all week and her hurt was turning into anger. When Jeremy kissed her mother hello and hadn't even kissed her goodbye that morning, she lost all control.

"You bastard," she said.

"You can hug and kiss my mother, but you can't even kiss me on the cheek. I've had enough of you," she cried. "I hope you and my mother will be real happy."

She left the bar and drove home. She packed all her things. By nine o'clock she had moved back in with Mary Ellen.

"Now we wait him out," Mary Ellen said.

Tina waited and he didn't call. The weekend passed and then the week.

She called her Aunt Ruth to see if they were meeting for happy hour and was told her mother was out of town so they decided to cancel. About noon on Sunday she went by Jeremy's to get some things she'd forgotten. She knocked and knocked but there was no answer.

Tina let herself in with her key. There were suitcases in the living room and when she walked into the bedroom she was hardly prepared for what she found.

"Mother!" she exclaimed.

In the evening when Tina met Chuck, her mind was far away from that Sunday morning. As she crossed Lakeshore Drive and entered the lounge in the Prudential Building, the wind howled in off the lake. She paused to look around the room and saw him waving at her. He was seated at a small table in the corner.

Tina felt her body fill with warmth. She smiled as she crossed the room to join him. As she sat down next to him, he placed his arm around her, drawing her close, and kissed her.

"I love you," he told her. "I couldn't get you out of my mind all day. I want you right now!"

Tina felt herself blushing as he spoke to her. She felt her heart pound at his words and found herself wanting him, too.

"God, you're beautiful," he told her. "If you love me, I'm the luckiest man alive."

"Maybe I'll just start calling you Lucky," she said teasing him.

He asked what she wanted to drink and ordered them each a white wine.

"How was your day?" she asked, knowing he had a big case that day.

"We won," he answered with that great smile of his. "The jury was out thirty minutes and came back in and ruled in our favor."

She reached out and placed her hand on his arm. "I love you so much," she said.

"I love you, too," he said as their drinks arrived.

Tina couldn't take her eyes away from him as they talked. She studied his face and found the longer she looked, the more she liked what she saw.

He smiled all the time. The smile made his whole face come alive and ran from the center of his face out to his ears. His hair seemed to shine along with his face. She thought she was a very lucky woman to have a man like this. Nothing else seemed to matter to her.

They finished their wine and had another. He grew quiet and she could sense he had something on his mind and was struggling with it.

"What's wrong, baby?" she asked.

Tina could tell by the look on his face Chuck found the word baby comforting.

"You can tell me. I love you. I really do. I want us to be able to share everything and we can't if you hold something back," she said.

"You're right," he answered seriously. "Only what I have to say might hurt you and I'd do anything never to hurt you."

"I believe you wouldn't purposely hurt me. I'm a big girl," she said.

"Well," he said. "It really and truly wasn't ever important, but you could make it important now. I worry about it because I want to marry you and I don't want anything to stand in the way of that."

Tina's heart began to flutter.

"Marry me?" she asked. "Are you proposing?"

"Yes," he said. "I want to get married if you'll have me. I want you to be with me. I want us to share our whole lives together. I want us to have children and worry over them together. You're the finest, most wonderful woman I've ever known and I feel like a piece of dirt because of what I've done."

Tina just looked at him waiting for him to tell her. She never asked.

"Before I met you, I was with your mother," he said.

Tina was still looking at him. Her expression never changed. Her eyes didn't blink. She sat perfectly still and looked into his eyes. She could almost feel what he was feeling and sensed a oneness between them.

"I know," she said carefully. "I knew it all the time. It doesn't matter.

"It was before me and it doesn't count. The only thing that matters is what happens from this point on. If I ever see or hear of you kissing or even hugging her, I'll never speak to you again. My mother is a tramp and I won't compete with her for my husband. She is totally off limits and if you agree, I'll marry you tomorrow if you want."

Chuck reached for her and pulled her close, kissing her right there. "I love you," he said. "I love you so much."

After paying for the drinks they left and took a cab to his apartment. He had his arm around her the entire trip and held her hand with his free hand as he gently kissed her on the ear. He whispered he loved her and then got silly about buying her an engagement ring.

When they finally got to his apartment, they both grew quiet and serious. They undressed each other in the living room and then sat on the couch and touched each other.

Tina listened as Chuck talked to her saying what he was going to do. At first he guided her hands, but soon she needed no help.

He got up and returned with a small bottle of lotion. Then he turned her on her stomach and began to rub the lotion across her shoulders and back. He placed more in the small center of her back and rubbed down across and between her buttocks. His hands were slow, firm, and warm. They were strong and massaged her. They rubbed in the lotion.

His fingers teased her, making her wet with wanting him. Tina's body shuttered at his touch. Then he turned her on her back and she was naked before him. He smothered her breasts in lotion and then rubbed her legs as he occasionally slid his finger deep into her. His mouth began to suckle her breasts and his fingers stayed at her center.

His mouth left her breasts and moved down her body and his hands opened her legs. Then his mouth was on her and she heard herself cry out.

Her hands reached out and grasped him, pulling him to her lips. As she climaxed, he rose and took her to the bedroom where he pulled back the blankets and sheet and laid her on the bed.

He entered her making love very slowly. When she cried out, repeating his name over and over, he finally released himself inside her. She felt him fill her with his love and held his body with her arms and legs until he stopped shaking and their breathing slowed.

"I love you," he said and then fell off to sleep.

He went soft inside her and she rolled from him, holding his head so he wouldn't wake. She thought of being married to him and having him love her like this again and again.

Her body was limp and satisfied. She had a smile on her face as she fell asleep. She slept until she felt him leave the bed.

Not quite awake, she heard someone knocking at the door. The clock next to the bed said five a.m. Then she heard a voice and she came fully awake. As she rose from the bed, her body was aware of the fact it was December. The bed was warm and the room cold.

Perhaps it was because Chuck had committed himself to her and she was now prepared to defend her den. She didn't bother to find a robe as she left the bedroom. Tina walked from the bedroom to the living room completely naked, expecting exactly what she found.

By the time she arrived in the living room, Jerilyn was already demanding to know who Chuck had here.

"Who is she?" she demanded. "Who is the whore?"

Jerilyn didn't see Tina at first. Tina stood in the doorway and a myriad of thoughts swept through her mind. She listened to her future husband attempt to explain and get rid of Jerilyn at the same time. Tina watched and realized her mother was drunk. The cold air surrounding her naked body gave her confidence as she spoke with a frigid arrogance.

"Mother!" she said sharply.

Jerilyn's attention turned to Tina's naked body in the hallway entrance.

"A woman your age should be home in bed, not waking young people out of sound sleep. He's mine. This time you've lost. Go home and get some sleep!"

Tina's face was like granite.

Jerilyn couldn't believe her eyes or ears. "You whore," was all Jerilyn could say.

Tina laughed.

"You're right. I learned at a young age from a real professional. Get out of here and don't come back, ever!"

Tina turned, showing her mother and Chuck her firm buttocks as she walked away and down the hall. When the door finally closed and Chuck returned to bed, Tina made him lay on his back as she straddled his body and made love to him. When it was over, they both slept.

Two hours later Tina woke, no longer a girl struggling to be a woman.

Chuck stood at the sink shaving. Tina was in the warm bathtub. She wanted to reach up and touch him, but only smiled instead.

"I love you," she said.

He smiled down at her. "I love you, too."

CHAPTER SEVENTEEN

"Listen," Ruth said to her sister. "I know what you're feeling, but he's not the man you knew."

"You've seen him," Jerilyn cried. "It's him. It's him and I'm losing him a second time and to my own daughter!"

"You're not losing anything," Ruth said. "You never really had him. He's just like all the others and you would have been tired of him in less than two months. There isn't any difference."

"Yes, there is," Jerilyn insisted. "You don't know! I don't know how, but it's him. He looks the same, smells the same, and kisses the same. Damn it, he even feels the same inside me. Don't tell me it's not him!"

Ruth had never seen her sister act like this. At six a.m. Jerilyn was at her front door, hysterical and completely drunk.

"She's trying to pay me back for Jeremy."

"I seriously doubt that," Ruth said trying to calm Jerilyn down. "I've known Tina all her life and she doesn't have a mean bone in her body. The girl only knows how to get hurt, not pay people back. That's not Tina's style at all."

Jerilyn continued to rave like a mad woman.

She refused to believe anything other than revenge motivated her daughter. She finally became so angry and frustrated she left because Ruth wouldn't agree with her.

Even though she was probably too drunk to drive, Ruth was glad to see her leave. In the sudden silence Ruth remembered the day that Jerilyn was told Charley Reed had been killed in an automobile accident. Her reaction had been much the same, even though it was more grief than anger. Just as she had that day, once more she suffered a loss.

In Ruth's memory Jerilyn didn't lose very often. Death had been an insurmountable obstacle. Another woman, even her own daughter, was something Ruth didn't expect Jerilyn would allow to defeat her.

Where men were concerned, Jerilyn usually had her way. But at the same time, Ruth was enough of a realist to bet Chuck Ganley would have an awful lot to say about the ultimate outcome. A man his age would in all probability choose the younger woman with whom he might have a future.

While Ruth felt sorry for her sister, she was glad for her niece. Tina deserved happiness and this young man.

Cindy Ganley was anxious when she woke that morning. Her son was on her mind. She had no way of knowing Chuck had experienced the scene in his apartment and was about to have a second and worse scene as he arrived at his office. Cindy decided to call him at work.

Jerilyn left her sister's home and drove to Chuck's office. The receptionist had no idea why she chose to wait for Chuck. She didn't have an appointment.

"I need to talk to you," Jerilyn said rising from the chair in the lobby as Chuck walked in.

He was startled by how suddenly she appeared before him and his body turned sideways as if preparing for a blow.

"Jerilyn," he said. "There really isn't anything to talk about. I'm sorry, but I don't have anything to say to you right now, and especially not here."

"You'll talk to me now or you'll pay for this later, you bastard!" she screamed at him in front of his associates and the receptionist.

Thelma Gates had been the receptionist at the law firm ever since her husband Jack had passed away and was a good-sized woman. As Jerilyn raised her voice, Thelma immediately stood and began to move between the young attorney and the enraged woman. In her ten years at the firm Thelma had never experienced such an enraged client. The north side law firm usually dealt with a better class of people, but as she had learned, legal matters had a way of bringing out the worst in everyone.

"You dirty bastard!" Jerilyn screamed.

Chuck was speechless.

Thelma moved between him and this crazy woman and her mere presence moved Jerilyn back to the door. "I'll have to ask you to leave," Thelma calmly said. "We cannot tolerate this type of behavior. This is a place of business, not a corner bar."

Jerilyn was being forced out of the office.

"Your father never would have treated me like this!" she screamed.

"Your father loved me! He never would have treated me his way!"

With Thelma in command of the situation, Chuck was leaving the lobby area. Jerilyn's last outburst stung his ears and he found himself wondering what she meant. There was absolutely no way Adam Ganley would ever have anything to do with her. What was she talking about?

The heavy wooden outer door slammed shut behind the two women as Thelma negotiated Jerilyn outside. There were a few more outbursts that the walls and the heavy door muffled. Several minutes of silence followed and Thelma finally returned back inside to the lobby.

"Thank you," Chuck said. "I don't know what I would have done without you. You're a real savior."

"It's all part of my job," she matter-of-factly answered.

"What case is she involved in?"

"No case," he answered. "She's about to become my mother-in-law."

Thelma's face never changed. She wanted to shake her head in dismay, but didn't. He was just another young attorney in her care. She would do her best to protect him at work, but she knew very well she wasn't able to protect him from himself.

"Young man," she said in a scolding tone. "Perhaps you should seek the advice of one of the partners before you rush headlong into that family.

"An ounce of prevention is worth a pound of cure," she told him.

Chuck put on his best smile. "I'm really sorry about the scene. I'll straighten everything out and it won't happen again. She is just upset."

"To say the least," Thelma said.

Tina was in her apartment taking a hot shower. She had taken a bath, but they made love again before he left for the office. She wanted to be clean for him. As the water pounded over her, she remembered the night before with her man.

Chuck was her man and he had awakened something in her, reached someplace, touched a part that no one ever had before. She remembered the whole night and especially their last lovemaking in the morning. Her mother probably had been still in the building, maybe just getting out of the elevator, as Chuck returned to bed and Tina reached out to make love to him. She could still smell herself in his hair.

She kissed his neck and then his chest. Her mouth ran across his navel and then beyond. She took him in her mouth and loved him. He cried out to her and she loved him like she had never loved a man before.

The phone was ringing as she stepped out of the shower. She was still tingling from the hot water and hot memories of last night.

"Hi, I love you," he said.

"Well, I love you, too," she answered.

"I certainly hope so."

"And I love the way you taste."

The last remark took him entirely by surprise.

"I never tasted a man before," she whispered. "You tasted great!" Chuck was speechless.

"I love you," she continued. "I really, really love you and anything you ever want, you can have with me. Just tell me and you'll have it. Just say the word."

"I want us to get married right away," he said. "Tomorrow, if it's all right. I want you and everything that goes with you. I want children and I want to make love to you all the time! I have to have you."

"I want you, too," she said detecting a rising fear in his voice.

"What's the matter?" she asked.

"Jerilyn was here when I got to work. She was crazy and called me all kinds of names and started saying things like she knew my father. She had to be crazy. How could she ever know Adam? Be careful, you might be her next target."

"Honey," Tina said. "I'll handle my mother. I'm not worried. She's been crazy before and if I have to, I'll call my father. He's always been able to handle her, but I doubt I'll have to. She doesn't want to mess with me over you."

"Why does this have to be so complicated? It's my fault because of her," he complained.

"All I want is to be with you," he said softly.

"I know," Tina said. "Me, too. But nobody ever promised it would be easy falling in love. We love each other and we can't lose sight of it, no matter what. If it weren't for my mother, we never would have met. You're the absolute best thing that's ever happened to me. I want to marry you, have kids, argue over what the kids are doing, and I want us to make up.

"I want to be there when you're sad, and I want to make you happy. We're going to have a great life. I promise. Please, don't worry about my mother."

"I love you."

"I love you, too," she said. "And I'll see you tonight at the Moosehead."

"Sure," he said.

"See you then."

Cindy was holding for her son. The phone system rang back to the receptionist every two minutes and Mrs. Gates politely came back on and asked if she'd like to continue holding. Just as Cindy was about to give up, Thelma came back on and said she could put her through.

"Mother!" Chuck was surprised to hear her voice. "How are you?"

"I'm fine," she said. "The question is, how are you?"

"I suppose I'm okay," he answered.

"I woke up worried about you," she said.

"Exactly what's going on?" she asked.

"Jerilyn's about half crazy. She found out about Tina and me and came into the office and made a huge scene. Mrs. Gates made her leave not too long ago. She was really a lunatic. She started saying my father never would have treated her like this. She was really way out there."

"That bitch," Cindy responded before she could catch herself.

Cindy felt rage engulf her and wished she were face to face with Jerilyn Gardner. How could Jerilyn have known, she asked herself.

Cindy fought to regain her composure and thought of Charley Reed. Here she was, speaking to his son who had just been confronted by their shared lover. What am I supposed to do, she said to herself.

"Mother!" Chuck said shocked by his mother's language.

"She is!" Cindy exclaimed. "I won't have her doing this!"

Chuck was at a loss for words. His mother had never reacted like this for any reason.

Cindy knew her son thought she was acting out of character, but at that moment Cindy realized something very terrible had happened to herself.

"Doing what?" he asked. "Does she really know Father?"

"Of course not!" she snapped. "How in the world would a woman like her know your father! Don't be ridiculous!"

"Then what," Chuck asked again.

Cindy didn't answer her son's question. Instead, she asked, "Son, how serious are you over Tina?"

Cindy listened to his voice. It was strong and confident and it told her he was very serious.

"And how serious is very serious? Does she feel the same way?"

"Yes, she does and we want to get married," answered Chuck.

It was exactly as Cindy feared. The last thing in the world she wanted to hear was that her son wanted to marry that woman's daughter.

"When?" she asked.

"Soon, Mother," he answered.

"Don't you think this is rather sudden?

"The two of you hardly know each other. Getting married is much more than just sleeping together. The normal problems you'll encounter test even the strongest marriages where two people have known each other and have done some planning.

"You're telling me the two of you are just going to rush out and get married and you haven't even given her crazy mother a second thought! Exactly what do you think she'll say? What do you think she might do?"

"Oh, Mother," he said sounding worn out. "In the first place Jerilyn is not really crazy. I know you look down on her because she works in a bar and she wouldn't fit in with your nice little circle of ladies. That doesn't make her bad or crazy. As for Tina and me, she'll just have to learn to accept it. Jerilyn's a smart woman, in time she will."

"Jerilyn will never accept you marrying her daughter," Cindy said emphatically. "She'll fight you and try to divide the two of you every chance she has."

"Mother, that's silly. She's an attractive woman and will forget about me in a month."

"Don't tell me it's silly. It isn't. She will never allow you to have a moment of happiness. She'll tell you and Tina things to confuse and destroy the two of you. She'll lie! She'll do anything she thinks she can get away with to break you up. You're asking for nothing but trouble."

Cindy wanted to tell him everything.

She wanted to tell her son that Jerilyn wanted his father, not him. She wanted to say his father, his real father, was dead. She wanted him to know that Jerilyn had been in love with his father and probably still was. She was in love with his memory and Chuck brought that memory to life for her.

Cindy knew Jerilyn would never allow her own daughter to steal Charley Reed away from her. Cindy was afraid of the woman for many reasons. She was afraid for her son's happiness and future and she was afraid of the anger stored inside her for years. Most of all, Cindy was afraid for herself. Jerilyn could expose her secret.

"Mother," Chuck said. "I have to be in court. I'll call you later in the week."

"Okay," Cindy answered, knowing there was no more she could say at this point. "I love you and only want what's best for you. Most of all, I want you to be happy."

Cindy poured herself a cup of coffee and sat down at the kitchen table. She had no one with whom she could discuss this problem. As she sat there, she realized something inside her was different.

She realized she didn't care about the outcome. She didn't want her son hurt, but she didn't really care about what happened to Adam or her. If Adam was told Chuck wasn't his son, so be it. In her mind it couldn't possibly make any difference.

He'd never treated Chuck like his son. It would only represent the loss of a possession and Cindy began to laugh to herself at the thought of leaving Adam and taking half of everything.

Adam and his possessions; it was laughable.

When Jerilyn left Chuck's office she managed to become involved in a traffic accident on Jackson Avenue. By the time the police arrived, she was totally hysterical. Even though the accident was clearly the fault of the cab driver running a red light, the officer placed her in the police car and even considered arresting her for disorderly conduct. As they towed her car away, she surrendered to what she considered a lousy morning and a much worse month.

Tina met her Aunt Ruth for lunch at Bennigan's. Ruth was worried about her sister and wanted to find out what was going on.

"This has nothing to do with Jeremy," she told her aunt. "I was in the bar at the Prudential Building with a girlfriend and there he was. He bought us both a drink and it all started there. Since then he's been with me and he hasn't phoned or seen Mother until this morning.

"He told me they went to bed together. Big deal! Who hasn't my mother slept with!

"He never told her he loved her or ever promised her one single thing. Not even a phone call or lunch! She has no business acting like this!"

"You're right, honey," Ruth said soothingly. "You'd be one hundred percent right if this was all it was to her. Do you know who Charley Reed was?"

"Yes. He was an old boyfriend of hers. I know Dad doesn't care to even hear his name."

"Your dad has good reason not to like hearing his name. He beat the hell out of your dad and threw him down four flights of stairs when you girls and your mother lived with him in Washington, D.C."

"What's that got to do with what's going on now?" asked Tina.

"Chuck Ganley looks, sounds and acts so much like Charley Reed they could either be twins or the same man. Your mother believes he's Charley Reed's son."

Tina could only stare at her aunt, not believing what she was hearing.

"That's foolish," she said. "He knows who his parents are. He even knows his mother was pregnant and had to leave college when she married his father.

"And besides, even if Mother were right, which is really far-fetched, what claim does she have over his son who is twenty some years younger than her?

"Do you and my mother expect me to step aside so she can pre-tend she's lying in the arms of her old lover, who's probably bald and fat by now, and pretend it's twenty years ago?"

"He's dead, Tina."

"So what! That's even worse. It's down right sick! I can't believe the two of you."

"Tina!" Ruth exclaimed. "It's not me. I think it's crazy, too. It's your mother."

Tina was irritated. "I'm sorry," she said. "I just don't understand it."

"Charley Reed is dead, isn't he?" she asked.

"Oh, yes," Ruth answered.

"No two people are the same. My Chuck is not her Charley. My Chuck and I are going to get married very soon. Mother better get it in her head and stop this silly behavior. I can't believe she could be this way.

"I won't have her trying to hurt innocent people with this busi-ness about Charley Reed's son."

Ruth nodded in agreement with Tina.

"Surprisingly enough that's the one place where she makes sense. I knew Charley Reed and he really loved your mother."

Tina didn't interrupt and sat quietly and listened.

"He loved you kids, too. Michael was still living with you girls then and he was Charley's little boy. He wasn't really Charley's son, but Michael acted so much like him. He picked up Charley's strut and walked exactly like him.

"Your dad was phoning your mother all the time, trying to find about you girls. Finally she gave in and phoned him back. I guess there was a week when she even thought she might leave Charley and go back with your dad."

"Why didn't she?" Tina asked.

"She really loved Charley, too. Your dad always messed over her. Charley was a nice guy, a salesman who made good money and your mom enjoyed being home, being a mother. They were going to be married and wanted more children."

"Why didn't they get married?"

"Charley wasn't divorced from his wife Joanna yet. You all were living in Washington, D.C. then and one day your father showed up when Charley was at work. As luck would have it, Charley came home early.

"Your father was a real bad ass back then. He used to beat up every man your mother went with within an inch of his life. Your dad was a Marine and tough as nails, but he met his match in Charley Reed.

"Charley had been in the Green Berets and all of them were really bad asses, too.

"Your father didn't like your mother and you kids living with Charley and I guess he told him so. That's when Charley physically threw him out and down the steps. It was one hell of a fight and your father came out on the short end.

"After that Charley kept thinking your mother was going to leave and I guess it made him next to impossible to live with. If they were out and your mother talked to someone, there would be an argument. He became insanely jealous to the point he couldn't even work. Finally, maybe to save himself, he took all of you back to North Carolina and left.

"That was when he started writing letters to your mother. She still has them all. She says it's all there; Chuck Ganley's mother's name and how she was a college student and he got her pregnant as he was going into the Army. She called and told him, but before he could get leave and come back to marry her, she married someone else.

"Several years later he ran into her mother in a department store in Pittsburgh and she told him her daughter had a three year-old red-headed son. Your mother says that girl is Chuck's mother and Charley Reed is his father."

"Aunt Ruth, that's really farfetched. No one in their right mind would believe that," Tina said.

"Your mother does," Ruth replied.

When Adam Ganley came home that evening, Cindy tried to speak to him about Chuck. She hoped he might get involved and talk to him about rushing into marriage.

"I've had nothing to do with him since the day he defied me and attended a Catholic law school. Nothing has changed and I don't want to know about him. As far as I'm concerned, he's not my son."

Cindy held back what she really wanted to say.

"You should talk to your mother. She's always had influence over young men."

"What are you talking about?" Cindy asked disgustedly.

"Just what I said," he insisted. "She was there with the money when her grandson needed money to go to law school."

He laughed and looked coldly at his wife.

"She was there with the money when her own daughter was pregnant and she didn't want her married to some soldier whose father was a policeman."

"What?" Cindy screamed.

"You heard me," he said. "Where do you think the money came from to start the hardware stores? You and Chuck were bought and paid for.

"The irony of it all is you gave another man a son and me only daughters. You never gave me my own son! That is God's punishment to me. I accept it."

"That's where you're wrong," she said. "You had a son and ran him off. He was yours and you blew it, you pompous ass."

Cindy couldn't believe her ears. All those years he knew Chuck wasn't really his son and he said nothing. He said nothing because her mother paid him off.

Cindy hated him for the first time in her life. She hadn't liked him. Now she hated him.

"I'm leaving you! I want a divorce!" she screamed.

CHAPTER EIGHTEEN

Marilyn George hung up the phone. She couldn't believe what her daughter had just told her. She was shocked. Her daughter had never spoken to her like this.

Cindy was always a devoted and loving daughter. In all her memory she could never recall a single instance of defiance which was why Marilyn was stunned at the language her daughter used. She poured herself another cup of coffee and phoned her daughter Andrea.

Cindy wasted no time and started to look for a lawyer immediately.

Adam wasn't even out of the driveway when her suitcase along with the yellow pages was thrown on her bed. Her bedroom door was still on the floor and there was still broken glass in the hallway. Passing before the dressing table mirror, her anger rose again as she noticed the bruise on her left cheek. No one had ever laid a hand on her and she was determined it would never happen again.

There had never been any kind of violence in her parents' home as she grew up and as a woman she restrained and controlled her husband's temper around the children. In Cindy's mind there was no excuse for his actions against her and then Julie today.

She knew she never should have screamed at him. She especially shouldn't have threatened him with divorce. From then on Adam was in a rage like she'd never witnessed.

He slapped her across the face with a blow so powerful it knocked her to the floor. She tried to roll away from him, but surprisingly in spite of his size, he was very agile.

He grabbed her hair, pulling her up to her feet, only to slap her again. He was screaming, calling her names she'd only heard in movies or when she was in college. Still holding her by the hair, his other hand grabbed the front of her sweater and actually tore the entire garment off her body.

"You've been no wife to me for years," he screamed. "You'll be one now! I'm your husband and it's my right! You'll be one now!"

For several seconds she broke loose and ran up the stairs to her bedroom. She could hear him thundering up the steps behind her. Cindy locked her bedroom door and ran to the phone to call for help. She could remember that she was afraid he'd kill her as she reached for the phone. As she dialed the emergency number, the door to her bedroom seemed to explode from its hinges.

"Put that damn phone down!" he screamed as he steadied his body and then rushed towards her. "Hang up right now!"

"Help me!" she cried out.

He hit her a third time. He pulled the phone from her hand and then the wall. He threw the entire phone away with his left hand and moved at her.

Cindy remembered the sound of the telephone crashing into the glass étagère next to the door. The sound of the breaking glass seemed to continue for a long time. It sounded like bits of hail striking one at a time as each piece of glass broke and fell.

She fell across the bed as he struck her and he smothered her body with his. Cindy was unable to move as the weight of his great mass immobilized her. His hands were all over her body as she tried to stop him. Cindy remembered the smell of his breath. It smelled of alcohol and Cindy hadn't known Adam to drink since college.

While his hands were trying to pull down her slacks, she heard her daughter begin to scream. She felt added weight on top of her already crushed body and saw Julie's face as she tried to pull her father away.

Cindy felt Adam rise up from her and watched as he turned and punched his daughter in her face.

"Get out of this room now!" he bellowed.

Julie fell backwards and landed in the middle of the floor strewn with broken glass.

While Adam's attention was turned to the seventeen-year-old, Cindy rolled off the bed. Julie stood up and came at her father once more. There was blood coming from her nose and her hands were cut and bleeding from the glass.

Adam rose against the girl's attack, but before he could strike her again, Cindy hit him across the back of his head with a five-pound dumbbell she used to exercise. The force of the first blow stunned him. He turned his head to see what happened and she struck a second time, causing him to fall to the floor nearly unconscious.

Julie ran to her mother and they heard the sound of people coming up the stairs. Realizing it was the police Cindy grabbed a robe.

Adam was lurching about on the floor trying to regain his senses as the two policemen entered the room. Recognizing him as the mayor, they helped him up and sat him on the bed.

Julie was screaming hysterically, demanding they arrest him.

"He's crazy! He tried to kill my mother! Arrest him! Look at me!" she screamed. "I'm bleeding!"

"Get him out of here," Cindy told both of the policemen. "Get him out now!"

Adam tried to stand, but was still disoriented. Cindy took her daughter into the bathroom and began to clean her up.

"I don't care if you have to drag him, I want him out of my room," she said from the bathroom.

Julie was crying. "He's crazy, Mom. Why did he hit me? Why was he hurting you? I don't want to stay with him. Mother, let's get out of here. I'm afraid of him."

Adam was still on her bed when Cindy came from the bathroom and she lunged at him. The younger of the two policemen stopped her.

"I said I want him out of here."

Adam rose while she was being restrained.

"You whore!" he said to her. "You whore. You were one when I married you and you've never changed. You're still nothing but a whore!"

As Adam walked from her room under his own power and went downstairs, the young officer was still holding Cindy.

"I want him arrested," she said.

"For what?" he asked.

"Look at this place," she demanded. "Look at me and look at my daughter!"

"Mrs. Ganley, we didn't really see anything. It's your word against the Mayor's."

"He tried to rape me!" she said.

"Calm down, please," he told her.

"Did he?"

"No," she answered. "He tried!"

"Mrs. Ganley, I'm not so sure the laws in this state recognize attempted rape of a wife by her husband. I want you to calm down and think about what you're saying."

"Look at this place!" she insisted. "Look at what he's done!"

"Mrs. Ganley, a man has the right to do what he wants with his own property in his own house."

"Look at me!" Julie cried coming out of the bathroom. Her face was already swelling from the punch she received. "I'm his daughter! Not some fucking piece of property! I want the bastard arrested."

The young officer's head snapped at the language Julie used. His cold stare would have been answer enough, but his words stung Cindy's ears when he spoke directly to her.

"No one is getting arrested here. We do not arrest the Mayor in his own home and I suggest you wash the little girl's mouth out with soap. I'm not going to be any plainer than that. Now relax and let this whole thing pass, both of you."

The police stayed for a while longer. The shift captain came by, but only spoke to Adam. Cindy and Julie went to Julie's bedroom, locking the door and moving a dresser in front of it. Adam didn't try to speak to either of them. He rose the next morning and left the house.

As she walked to the window to check he really had left, Cindy noticed it was starting to snow. She wasn't sure what she was going to do. She knew she wouldn't spend another night under the same roof with Adam. When Julie came into her room, she decided they'd fly to Phoenix and see her sister Lisa. But first she would see an attorney.

Cindy called the office of Marvin Galloway, the man Adam had defeated for mayor and a man who was not a Mormon.

Early that same morning it began to snow in Chicago, too.

By the time the alarm clock woke Chuck, there was already three inches on the ground. Since he had nothing important at the office, he quietly slid back in bed next to Tina. He always liked snowy days and was soon asleep again.

Jerilyn woke later that morning when Ruth called.

"Have you looked outside?" Ruth asked.

"No, why?" Jerilyn asked sleepily.

"Well, it's been snowing since early this morning and no one can get anywhere. I kept the kids home from school and I'm glad I did."

Jerilyn looked out the bedroom window and could hardly believe her eyes. "I can't remember when it has snowed like this," she said to Ruth.

"Are you okay?" Ruth asked.

"Yes, I'm fine," she assured her sister.

"Well, you had me worried," Ruth said.

"I know. I made a fool out of myself. I'm really embarrassed."

"That's okay," Ruth said. "We all still love you."

Jerilyn did feel embarrassed. In all her life, she'd never once acted like this over any man. She didn't understand her behavior, but she did know she had always ached over Charley Reed. Perhaps it was the chance to relive the past with a young man who surely was his son that made her crazy.

She went to her closet and on the floor in the back was a small trunk. Pulling it out, she opened it. It had been many years since she'd looked at the contents. On this snowy day Jerilyn thought she might find the reason she lost Charley Reed.

Jerilyn held his picture and studied his face.

His eyes had been so intense and his face could be hard one minute and soft the next. He'd been a little boy for her and at the same time a man for the world.

Charley seldom smiled, but the second picture was one of him and Michael and he was smiling. It had been taken on campus at East Carolina and the note on the back read 'Michael, 19 months and me.' It was in Charley's handwriting. It was summer in the picture and Charley was in a pair of shorts and a football jersey. The sleeves had been cut off. His arms were strong and Michael was laughing.

Jerilyn took out a third picture.

She remembered it well and could still feel some of the happiness they'd shared on a long weekend at Topsail Beach. It was one of Charley, the three kids, and herself standing on the beach. Michael was eighteen months, Anne Marie was four, and Tina six. Charley taught Tina and Anne to swim. Michael started to call him daddy and that was probably the weekend when she got pregnant.

Her IUD had been giving her problems and the doctor removed it. She was going to start the pill, but they had to use rubbers until she had her period again. Charley hated them, but agreed.

Saturday night they put the children to bed and sat on the balcony of their room, looking out at the ocean. They smoked some grass and drank some wine, then made love.

In her lifetime she remembered it as the single greatest time.

He lasted in her forever and she felt every single part of him. She opened herself completely to him and he totally filled her. Her body became his. He touched her everywhere and took her away. She remembered her mind swirling in a whirlpool of pleasure and her body receiving him time after time.

She continued to hold the picture and remembered him exploding in her. "I love you," she remembered crying out as he finally stopped.

"I love you," she whispered again as she dropped the picture

"Why aren't you with me now?"

There was no need for an answer. She knew so well. It came back almost as if she'd been watching a video of her life. She wondered what might of happened if she hadn't miscarried.

"Why did I do that?" she asked aloud as she picked up the fourth picture.

It was one of Charley and Bob Walker.

Walker had been his best friend, his partner, his teacher, and his student. The picture was taken just before Charley's birthday. He never knew she was pregnant. He turned twenty-eight and seventy people arrived at their townhouse on Indian Head Highway for a birthday party. The party started at seven on Friday night and didn't end until seven the next morning. Charley missed work. A lot of people never left. The party continued into the next day.

"How is it?" he asked her as he woke and made love to her in the afternoon. "How is it I become more excited each time I touch you?

"You know," he said. "More excited than the last and more in love with you than the first."

Charley was in the picture she held. He had a scotch in his hand, a smile on his face, and a beautiful woman kissing his cheek. Jerilyn tried to remember her name, but couldn't. Nevertheless, she looked at the smiling faces and still said, "You bitch!"

The fifth picture was Charley and Michael at a fort on the Potomac River. The sixth was at a welcome station on Interstate 95 in front of one of his cars.

The seventh was him asleep in bed looking like an angel.

Jerilyn held that picture and felt the tears begin to fall from her eyes. It had been her fault. The whole thing had been her fault from the day they first met until the day he died.

It had been years since she looked at the picture of him sleeping. It was taken at the Marriott just across the river from Washington, D.C. They had gone away together for a week and she snapped the picture the first morning. He never even moved when the flash went off.

She remembered placing the camera down and climbing back into bed where she moved next to him. Jerilyn remembered his tousled hair and the smile he gave her when she kissed his lips. She remembered him coming alive when she touched him. He was always a wonderful lover, but he was special in the morning.

The next picture was one of him at the Washington Monument.

The one after that was in a bar with him holding a Bloody Mary. There were enough pictures to remember what he looked like.

And then there were the letters to remind her of how he thought and spoke.

My Dearest Jerilyn,

Here I am in Denver. It took eight hours from Omaha. It was a long trip. I missed you. I remember our trip North in February. I hope the kids are fine. I wish I could talk to you.

Denver is at the foot of the Rocky Mountains. There's snow up there right now in July. I'm at the Holiday Inn and it has a revolving restaurant and bar. The bar is fine but the bartender isn't as pretty as you.

Was I wrong not wanting you to work? Why was I so jealous? I tried not to be, honestly, I truly did. I've never loved anyone like you. Christ! I doubt that I was ever even in love until I met you. God I miss you!

I talked to Walker last night. Both he and Mary yelled at me. Mary wants me to come back to Washington. She doesn't understand what I'm doing. Neither do I. I caused all this. I should have talked to you instead of doing what I did. It wasn't fair what I did to you and the kids. I don't blame you for not wanting to talk to me. I miss you and I love you. I'll never be able to forget you or the kids. I wish I could come back, but I understand. I'll try not to be a pest, but I hurt so much. It's all my fault. I'll always love you.

It's two a.m. my time, four a.m. yours. It's all over now and you're asleep. I'll always hate any man who touches you. I can't stand to think about it, but I can't stop either. What am I supposed to do? Where am I supposed to go? Maybe to hell, huh?

Jerilyn, I'm going to end now and try to sleep. I'll come back if you want. Call Bob or Mary. They'll tell me. I'll come right away. I'm sorry. I love you. I always will.

Charley

There were other letters. All of them said the same thing. They were on nearly consecutive days from Denver, Las Vegas, Los Angeles, San Jose, San Francisco, Lake Tahoe, Reno, Salt Lake City, Denver, Denver, Denver, and finally Pittsburgh.

"It makes no difference where I go. It makes no difference who I am with. All I do so think about you and when we were together."

Jerilyn placed the letter down and picked up another photo. Charley was in Walker's apartment at the bar drinking a beer. He was laughing and toasting whoever took the picture. He had an unforgettable face.

"God, I loved you," she said aloud. She picked up the letter again.

I'm enclosing something I've written. It's a short story and it's about you. I've called it 'The Woman Every Man Wanted.' Maybe I'll try and have it published. I'm sorry. I love you.

She held the story in her hand. It was still in the same sealed manila envelope that it arrived in years ago. Jerilyn had never read the story nor had she ever heard of it being published. For all she knew, she was holding the only surviving copy. She realized she possessed a part of Charley Reed that no one else may have ever known.

Sitting there she seriously considered opening the envelope and reading the story. It was an interesting title and she knew it was about her.

In a way it was quite flattering to know someone had written something about her. In another way she was afraid of some hidden secret it might hold. The idea of opening this forgotten story, as appealing as it might seem, was equally ominous. She gently placed it back in the box with the letters and pictures.

"It can stay where it belongs," she said aloud as she placed the trunk back in the closet.

Jerilyn rose and walked to the window. Outside it was still snowing. Staring out the window she finally spoke to Charley Reed.

"Wherever you are, baby, you should know it was all my fault. I made you jealous on purpose. I needed that attention from you. It was all my fault."

Hundreds of miles away in Pittsburgh, Marilyn George opened a letter that was twenty-six years old. It had a Ft. Benning, Georgia postmark. It wasn't addressed to her. It was to her daughter, Cindy. It was from Charley Reed.

As much as she tried, the old woman couldn't close her heart this time. For the very first time she questioned whether she had done the right thing. Angry over what her daughter said to her, she coldly tore each of the five separate pages into many small pieces. When she was through, she went into the bathroom and flushed them down the toilet.

While her mother was destroying Charley's last plea, Cindy Ganley calmly boarded a flight to Phoenix. She didn't look back and wondered why it had taken her so long.

CHAPTER NINETEEN

SEPTEMBER 11, 2001
NEW YORK CITY
4:45 P.M.

Tina Ganley was in a state of shock. She was trying to fight back her tears. She didn't want the children to see her cry. As much as she tried, she couldn't. And Kimberly, eight-year-old Kimberly, asked why she was crying.

"Is it because daddy is dead?" she asked.

She didn't know what to say. She just held onto her. Tina was alone with the children.

There was no news. Thousands in Chuck's building were missing and probably dead. Firemen and policemen who tried to rescue all of those people were dead. And when she came home there was a message on her answering machine. It was a message from Chuck.

"Honey," he began. "I love you."

Then there was a long silence. She could hear people in the background. They were crying and they were screaming.

"Something horrible has happened. I don't think I am going to get out of this.

"I thought I would grow old with you. I thought I'd see our children grow up and get married and have children of their own. It doesn't look like that's going to happen now.

"No matter what happens, know that I always loved you and always will. Tell our children how much I love them, too. I'm going to try and call my mother. When I'm done, I will call you back if I can."

He paused one more time.

"I love you, Tina," he said.

She wanted to call his mother and find out what he said to her. She tried to get a dial tone, but she kept getting a message all circuits were busy. It told her to please try again.

In that moment she wanted to despair, but something inside of her made her keep herself together as well as she could. She had to for Chuck and their children.

"Chuck, Chuck," she cried to herself. "What am I going to do without you? What did I do before I met you? It seems like you have always been with me."

But he wasn't and she thought back to when they were first together.

DECEMBER 22, 1992

Tina was excited when her father's wife, Jackie, called to ask if she would spend Christmas Eve with them at their home in Lombard. Tina asked if she could bring her fiancé and her dad's wife of six years thought it was a great idea.

"When are you getting married?" she asked.

"We haven't decided," she answered.

She didn't tell her, but she knew it would be soon.

"Is it going to be a big wedding?" Jackie asked.

"No. His family is from Utah and his parents are in the middle of a horrible divorce. His mother left and is in Phoenix with his sisters. His dad won't even speak to him."

"Oh," Jackie laughed. "Sounds just like our families!"

"You'll make your father very happy you're coming. I'll have to track down your sister and try to talk her into this."

Tina laughed. "I don't envy you. You know Anne Marie where Dad is concerned."

"I know," Jackie said. "It hurts your father, too.

"He really wants you girls to be part of our family and wants you to get to know the kids. They are your half-brother and half sisters. And, Tina, they're all so cute. You just have to love them. Little Sam is just like your dad. He even walks like him."

Tina's father and Jackie had three small children. Jackie had been good for him. He now controlled his drinking and began breaking out of his periods of depression and violence. He took a job, held it, and was promoted three times. Tina was old enough to appreciate how her father had really straightened out his life.

Anne Marie was another story.

Tina remembered her father's violence and drinking and so did her sister. Anne Marie hated him almost from the day they first went to live with him. She was stubborn and wouldn't even acknowledge him as her father. She insisted 'the man' was her daddy and called her father Sam.

She refused to change and finally left to live with her mother when she was thirteen. Since then they had been together only a handful of times. Even to this day, it was as if she never got over the loss of her 'man' and wouldn't allow anyone else to take his place.

To Tina he was a shadowy memory, some good and some bad. Tina associated the ocean with him and her mother crying when he died. Anne Marie's 'man' was the same person her mother believed Chuck Ganley was. She surprised even herself when she offered to call her sister and try to get her to come on Christmas Eve.

"I'd really appreciate it," Jackie said. "Your sister has never cared for me. I've tried, but she just won't let me get close."

"Don't take it personally. My sister is like that. She's fought Dad since she was born. You're his wife and in her mind you're automatically part of the war."

"Why is she fighting this war?" Jackie asked.

"I can't say for sure," Tina answered. "It's gone on as long as I can remember. I know Dad hates it and he just doesn't know how to stop the whole thing. Anne Marie has been fighting so long I'm sure she considers it the natural way of things. I'll talk to her and see what I can do."

Tina was very surprised when Anne Marie agreed to go to their father's for Christmas Eve dinner.

"I think it would be really nice," she said.

"Do you think they'd mind if I brought someone with me?"

"Of course not," Tina said. "Who?"

"Someone I work with. Ben is his name."

"I'm sure Dad would love it. I'm bringing Chuck. He's going to wind up feeling really old if we're not careful."

Anne laughed.

"Let's get presents for the kids and Dad. We'll really make us into a family for once. We're not going to have much with Mother this year. She's going to Florida tomorrow and staying until after New Year's."

This was welcome news to Tina. She told her sister they were all expected at seven for dinner and then they'd all go to church.

"Since when does Dad go to church?" Anne asked.

"Since Jackie said he would," Tina told her sister.

"My, my," Anne laughed. "So you can teach an old dog new tricks."

"It is humorous," Tina laughingly said. "Let's not look a gift horse in the mouth. He's happy now and we should be happy for him."

Anne asked if Tina was free for lunch tomorrow, but Tina said she was meeting Mary Ellen because she had something to discuss with her.

"Then I guess I won't see you until Dad's."

"I'll see you then," said Tina.

The next day Tina met her old roommate for lunch.

"What are you going to do?" Mary Ellen asked breathlessly.

"What do you mean?" Tina asked back.

"Are you going to have it?"

"Of course, I am. I could never kill our baby. We're going to get married anyway. We'll just do it sooner."

"Your mother will have a fit."

"There isn't anything I can do about that," Tina said.

"She's going to have to live with it just like his mother. Between you and me, I think she'll be the major problem. She's divorcing Chuck's dad and it's turned very ugly. I met her before Thanksgiving and she's so proper and straight-laced. No one is good enough for her son."

Mary Ellen shook her head. "You've got some problems ahead of you, girl. Getting married is going to be a big adjustment. Then having a baby on its way will be another one for you and him. Just add your mother and his mother to the kettle and you have one really interesting stew.

"When are you going to tell him?" Mary Ellen asked.

"Tonight," Tina answered.

"On the night before the night before Christmas," Mary Ellen observed. "Some Christmas present. What if he doesn't take it the way you expect?"

"Then I shouldn't be marrying him and I would have to say I've totally misunderstood our entire relationship."

As she said it, Tina knew she hadn't. Actually, she wasn't even apprehensive about telling him. She was excited, yes, but scared, no. For the first time in her life she really trusted someone.

"You're sure?" Chuck asked.

"Yes. I used two of those tests and then I went to the doctor."

Chuck's expression didn't change. He calmly stood and walked from the room without uttering a single word. Just as Tina was about to call out to him, he returned and handed her a small box.

"Then I guess you should have this now," he said to her with a smile on his face.

Tina carefully opened it to find a gorgeous ring with one prominent diamond in the center flanked by four smaller diamonds on either side.

"It's beautiful!" she exclaimed. "Absolutely beautiful!"

Chuck told her it had belonged to his grandmother. She gave it to him to give to his wife when he decided to marry.

"She made me promise that I would find someone just like you."

"You're not upset?" asked Tina looking up at him.

"About what?" he asked.

"About me being pregnant."

"Why in the world would I be upset? I think we should get married as soon as possible."

"I love you," she said pulling him towards her and kissing his mouth. "I'm the luckiest woman alive."

"I don't know about that," he said. "The day after Christmas we'll drive up to Lake Geneva and get married. It'll be beautiful up there and very romantic. How does that sound?"

Tina said yes and couldn't stop admiring the ring Chuck gave her. It fit perfectly.

"Did you have this sized for me?"

"No," he said. "Like I said, it belonged to my grandmother. She gave it to me when I was in law school and asked that I give it to my wife when I was ready to marry."

"I've never had anything as beautiful as this, Chuck. A ring like this is what every girl dreams about. It must be worth a small fortune."

"It probably is," Chuck agreed. "My mother's family always did have the bucks, but you're certainly worth it."

Tears sprang into Tina's eyes. She realized how lucky she was to have the love of this wonderful man. He was the best Christmas present ever.

That same night Jerilyn boarded a flight to Miami. She always hated the holidays and considering what had happened she decided to go somewhere it didn't look like Christmas. Florida would be her escape. This was her present to herself.

At the same time Cindy Ganley missed not having the feeling of Christmas around her. Her sister's condo was comfortable, but it wasn't her home and the artificial tree was far from the spruce Adam and the children used to bring down from the mountains.

Christmas music in the Phoenix sunshine just wasn't the same as listening to it while a fire roared in the fireplace. The barren mountains had no snow peaks and her baby sister was a woman in her thirties, not a little girl in her sleeper pajamas.

She thought of her son and remembered the Christmas he was given a Mattel M-16 toy rifle with a helmet and toy hand grenades. Something inside her turned that Christmas. She could still remember the feeling. It was the same feeling she had when she last spoke to her son's real father. It was a conversation she remembered vividly and relived many times as she watched her son grow to a man.

"What are you doing?" she asked Charley Reed.

"I'm in jump school," he answered. "Airborne! I'm a paratrooper."

"A paratrooper? Do you mean you jump out of airplanes?"

"That's right. Death from above!"

"My God, do you think you'll go to Vietnam?"

"I don't know. A lot of us will. But don't worry about me. I'll be okay."

When she saw their son with that toy she truly hated war for the very first time. Had it not been for the war, she probably could have married Charley Reed.

He was acceptable enough to her parents until he enlisted in the Army. So much emphasis was placed on staying in college then. She remembered how the professors were literally gods at the end of each term. They could send a young man off to war with a single failing grade.

She tried to remember all those young men, men very much like Charley Reed. They were lost and looking for direction. She thought about her part in Charley's life and wondered if she could have been the direction he might have needed.

Cindy couldn't help but compare him to Adam. They certainly were as different as night and day. Now over twenty years later, Cindy finally began to see what had been wrong all the time.

College had been Adam's escape. College and then her, his pregnant wife, kept him from going into the Army. He began his life on time without interruption and became the arrogant stuffed shirt he was.

Cindy envisioned Charley Reed as a fiery man who took nothing from any man. He was a man in the midst of life, dealing with it as it came, rather than looking for some angle in an attempt to control it from the outside.

Where Adam succeeded, Cindy knew Charley would usually fail. At the same time Cindy knew each of Charley Reed's failures only prepared him that much more for his eventual success.

Adam Ganley was a mass of flesh, sinking farther into his own loathsome pit of indifference with each day's passing. His life had never been interrupted. He had never experienced adversity. Adam had never learned the feeling of pain or the experience of losing. That's why he was so good at inflicting it.

Charley had to fight away from home and at home. She was sorry she hadn't known him and was sorry he hadn't known his son.

Cindy's Christmas present to herself was her freedom and a new beginning.

The next day was Christmas Eve. Chuck didn't go into to work so they stayed in bed together until late in the morning. Tina made breakfast and brought it to him in bed. They made love again and again. In the afternoon Chuck watched football and she went shopping for presents.

Tina could hardly take her eyes from the ring and nearly floated from store to store. She intended to surprise her sister, but when Anne Marie called at five o'clock, she couldn't hold it in. They talked about it for the next twenty minutes.

As they dressed for the evening, Tina watched Chuck's movements. His body was strong and she admired the shape and hardness of his arms and shoulders. She watched as he stepped into his pants and fastened them. She drew him close and inhaled his scent. It was clean and pleasant.

He brushed his hair straight back. It wasn't long, but at the same time was far from short. He had a proud and confident air about him. It gave her confidence just being with him. As she watched him pull the red sweater over his head, she knew deep inside her that this was the right man for her.

When they arrived at her father's house, Anne Marie was already there and was playing on the floor with little Sam. Little Mickey toddled right over to Tina with singular and deliberate steps, smiling the whole way. Baby Ashley was on the couch, making Anne Marie's boyfriend read her a book.

Jackie met them at the door and Tina noticed for the first time a strong resemblance to her own mother. Jackie was short with dark, long hair and had deep, beautiful eyes. Smiling warmly and hugging Tina, Jackie thanked her for helping to bring everyone together. Then she took Chuck's hand and thanked him for bringing Tina.

"Your father is in the kitchen making drinks. He must have spent a fortune on booze, so don't be shy. He has anything you could possibly want."

Anne Marie looked up and smiled at Charley. "Congratulations!" she said with a wink.

"Congratulations about what?" Jackie asked.

Just then Sam walked into the room with a tray full of drinks. "Yeah," he said. "Congratulations about what?"

Placing the tray down he extended his hand to Chuck. "Hello! I'm Sam Gardner."

Chuck took Tina's father's hand and looked him squarely in the eyes. "Chuck Ganley. I'm very pleased to meet you."

Tina watched the expression on her father's face change from a smile to one of shock.

Immediately, Tina knew what had to be going through her father's mind. Her future husband must certainly be a dead ringer for the man out of all their pasts. Tina moved between the two men and kissed her father.

"I'm so happy you invited us, Daddy," she said trying to sound like a little girl. "This is the very first time we've ever been together like this as a family. Isn't this just great!"

Sam let go of Chuck's hand and hugged his daughter warmly.

"Thank you for coming, Tina. Having you and Anne here is the best Christmas present I've ever had. What's all this about congratulations?"

Tina turned to Chuck and watched him start to blush. Then she held out her hand and showed Jackie and her father the ring.

"Why, Tina, it's lovely," Jackie said in awe.

Sam was silent.

He looked at the ring and then Chuck, then back at the ring again. As he was about to look at Chuck again, Anne Marie got up from the floor and joined in the group of people standing in the center of the room.

"Hey, let little Annie in here," her dad said.

"You know I hate to be called that, Sammy boy," she said half disrespectfully and half kidding, hitting him in his side.

"I'm sorry, Anne Marie," he said looking at Chuck a third time. "I just wanted to see if I could still get a rise out of you."

"Should I kick you like I used to?" she kidded. As Anne Marie reminded her father of their old battles, it seemed the situation passed.

"It's certainly one of the most beautiful rings I've ever seen! You have good taste, young man," Sam Gardner said, "Good taste in jewelry and in women. I'm happy for both of you."

Then he shook Chuck's hand again.

"Scratch these drinks," Sam said picking up the tray. "Baby, get the glasses. I'm breaking out the champagne."

CHAPTER TWENTY

SEPTEMBER 11, 2001
NEW YORK CITY
5:25 P.M.

Tina was shocked when the phone finally rang.

She was lost in the past as she started dinner. She started it like she had so many times before as she waited for Chuck to come home. She set the table, careful to have a place for him just in case.

How happy she would be if some miracle happened and he came walking through the door at six like he was supposed to. Tonight was special. She had news for him. Now she wished she would have told him before he left for work. She was pregnant again.

She hoped he would walk in, but inside she knew there was no hope. She saw the pictures of the building collapsing. She saw them and knew he couldn't have lived through it.

When she answered the phone it was Anne Marie.

"Everyone has been trying to reach you all day. Is there any news?"

She started to cry. She told her sister about the message on the answering machine.

"I haven't been able to call out," she said. "Your call scared me half to death. I didn't think the phones were working."

"Come here with the children," Anne said.

"I can't. You don't understand. It took me hours just to get home. This place is crazy. And I have to stay just in case. I have to be here and take care of things. Chuck would have wanted me to do that."

She caught herself talking about him in the past. She didn't want to, but she knew. She knew Chuck was dead. She began to cry some more.

"Then I'm coming there. I can take time off from work. I'll come there and help you. No planes are allowed to fly. I can drive."

"Would you?" Tina said to her baby sister. "That would be great. I don't know how I can deal with this alone."

"I am leaving tonight," she said. "Hang in there, sis."

Tina hung up the phone. She walked into the kitchen and looked out at the girls in the living room. She had the cartoon channel on the television. She didn't want them watching the coverage. They both knew their daddy worked in the 'big buildings.' She didn't want them seeing the pictures over and over and over.

At six-fifteen as was their custom, she and the girls sat at the dinner table and they said grace. Before they started, Kathy, the three-year old, asked if her daddy was coming home for dinner.

"Not tonight, honey," Tina answered.

She looked over at Kimberly who was staring down at her food.

After a quiet dinner the girls were having their ice cream and she started the dishes. Her mind was awash with memories. She thought about when they got married. Little did she know, at that very minute, so was her mother-in-law.

LAS VEGAS, NEVADA
DECEMBER 1992

Tina and Chuck didn't get married until the twenty-eighth. Cindy reserved a block of rooms at the Flamingo Hilton and Lisa took charge of buying the bride's dress and making arrangements for the ceremony itself. Julie called her sisters and one by one Cindy purchased additional plane tickets. Chuck's buddies, Brad and Mark both came. Brad brought his wife and Mark had his latest flame with him. By the time Lisa's boyfriend arrived, there were ten people, not including the bride and groom.

Tina was a beautiful bride.

Lisa helped her find a gorgeous wedding dress at a Second Time Around shop and Chuck rented a tuxedo. All the girls fussed over Tina. They fixed her long black hair on top of her head with loose curls hanging down the back. She wore a veil and Chuck gave her a bouquet of carnations and roses. As fast as it was put together, the wedding was lovely.

Everyone added something, even Brad who rented two limousines for the party. Lisa found a nice little wedding chapel and hired a photographer. She even arranged for Lou, her boyfriend, to walk the bride down the aisle. It was a happy time for everyone who was there.

Cindy watched the girls helping Tina get ready. There was love and happiness here. She couldn't help but compare it to when she married Adam. Cindy only remembered the cold dampness of the meeting hall in Pravo, Utah and how alone she felt.

Cindy remembered it was snowing. Her feet were wet and cold. The minister was very severe and interrogated her and Adam individually and then together. He told her she was a sinner and what she had done was wrong. He said she would pay for this sin for the rest of her life.

She remembered wishing her sisters could have been there. She thought about Charley Reed and how it could have been different. Adam's parents were there and they barely spoke to her. Cindy only wanted it all to be over.

It seemed very strange to remember that night from long ago. She was pregnant with the son who was now about to be married.

She walked down the hall to Chuck's room and knocked. Brad answered and let her in. Chuck was fussing with his bow tie. She crossed the room, kissed her son and whispered she loved him. At that moment all thoughts of the past left her and everything she had done suddenly made sense.

Cindy rode next to him in the limo and held his hand. Lovingly she looked at each one of his fingers and remembered examining them once before hours after he was born. She studied his face as only a mother can study the face of her son. Just as the car stopped, she brushed some hair from his forehead. Chuck took her hand and placed it on his arm as they walked inside.

"Mother," he said stopping just inside the door. "Thanks for everything."

Then he kissed her and went to stand at the altar with his best man and waited for Tina.

The music began and one at a time each of Chuck's four sisters came through the door and started down the aisle. Finally, Tina entered and Cindy felt tears well up in her eyes. She looked at her son, standing tall and proud and smiling at his bride. She thought of Charley Reed and how much his son looked like him.

The conversation she had with her son the previous day flashed into her mind. She told him about his real father and how she had come to marry Adam. Chuck had not asked many questions.

"Leave it to Grandmother," he said. "Always running everyone's life and manipulating events to suit her."

Chuck was quite matter of fact about the entire subject.

"Yes, I'm surprised," he told her. "But, you're still my mother and the girls are still my sisters. Father has spoken to me once in four years. You know I've never pleased him. So now he can kiss my ass and I don't have to feel guilty about it."

"You've always been a good son," she told him. "You've always made me proud of you. I'm proud of you now and I want you to be happy.

"I know I voiced objections about Tina for a number of reasons. That's in the past. I want you to know I trust your judgment and believe you are doing the right thing now."

"Thank you, Mother," he said.

His words echoed in her brain as Tina reached Chuck and they joined hands. Cindy watched his face as he told Tina he loved her. The tears were now tumbling down Cindy's cheeks as she watched them become one. She could see the love they had for each other and she was envious. She wished she could have had it.

Then they were married and Tina was hugging her, calling her mother and thanking her for everything. As everyone shook hands, kissed, and prepared to celebrate, it suddenly dawned on Cindy by this time next year she would be a grandmother. The thought made her laugh.

"I'm glad we did this," she told Lisa.

"So am I," she agreed. "This is great!"

And it was.

They all went to dinner and then to the bar in the casino to listen to the band play. The presence of the wedding party gave the lounge a different air and before long the entire place had become one big wedding reception.

Later in the evening, long after the party wound down, Chuck was alone in the cocktail lounge when his mother spotted him before turning in for the evening herself.

"Where's Tina," she asked him.

"Laying down," he told her. "The excitement has really worn her out. Her stomach is a little upset and she's got a headache."

Then he got serious.

"I guess I'm really married now," he laughed.

He laughed, but it wasn't a laugh of frivolity. It was a laugh of nervousness and apprehension.

Cindy laughed, too. She halfway sympathized with her son and certainly knew first hand how her daughter-in-law felt.

At least she had done a good job as a mother, she thought, bringing her son up to respect how a woman might feel from time to time. Of course, her son had always been sensitive, being the only son and eldest child with four younger sisters. She thought of Adam who was the youngest of eight.

Their wedding night was a disaster.

It never stopped snowing from the time they left the meeting hall until they reached their hotel in Salt Lake City. She was beginning her third month with Chuck and was starting to feel sick, then sleepy, and then sick again. She was alone and far from home and scared. In all her life she had never been this far from her family. She felt as if her own mother had sold her into bondage. Cindy was cold, afraid, and wondered who this stranger was she had married.

When they reached their room it was cold. The heat was on but the room was still cold.

"Can I get you anything?" Adam asked her.

"A small glass of white wine to warm me would be nice," she said.

She was shocked when he very blankly told her alcohol was forbidden by the Mormon faith. Cindy couldn't believe her ears. She admired his temperance, but this was total intolerance.

Then what happened next really turned her stomach. Adam insisted on his rights as a husband.

This was the same man who used to beg her for sex. He sent her flowers and had the pledges serenade her at the sorority house. He wrote her poetry that didn't rhyme and tried to sing to her when he couldn't carry a note.

She had listened to her mother because her mother convinced her she knew what was right. Now, as she sat with her son, she could still vividly remember it all.

Looking at her son, she loved the softness in his face. It was the same softness that had been in his father's. She remembered thinking to herself as she watched Charley sleep one morning, how in the world would he ever survive Vietnam?

He was an innocent striving to become evil. He was a mere boy hoping to be a man. He had great dreams, but she doubted he had the ability to achieve them. Charley Reed was a liar. What was more, he believed his own lies. As her mother warned, Charley Reed would fall dead in a war young American men had no business fighting.

"You're father was a hero," Marilyn George told her daughter. "He fought in the Battle of Midway. He flew from the carrier Enterprise and was shot down after he successfully attacked and helped sink a Japanese carrier. The carrier was one of the ones that attacked

Pearl Harbor.

"Your father spent thirty-seven hours in the Pacific Ocean until he was rescued. Most men would have died. Your father didn't. He lived and he came home to me.

"Now he's a captain of industry and I have you three girls.

"Is your Charley Reed cut from the same cloth as your father? Is he a hero or is he a coward? Will he survive Vietnam or die?

"Frankly, Cindy," she continued. "I believe he's a coward and he'll die. You'll be left alone with an infant and your life will be ruined. Adam Ganley will never see the Army let alone Vietnam. Why in the world would you ever want to make your life so difficult?"

What her mother said all made sense to her.

Even though Cindy was in love with Charley Reed, he was beneath her and he would die. The only logical way out of this was to marry Adam.

But the moment Adam physically grabbed her on their wedding night she questioned her decision. Did her father act this way toward her mother?

Cindy imagined her father gentle and warm and smelling clean like Charley. Adam was rough and cold as he undressed her on top of the bedspread with the lights and TV on.

Adam never kissed her.

His meaty hands grabbed first at her breasts and then roughly forced those fat little fingers inside of her. His breath still smelled of onions from the hamburger he'd eaten earlier. His body odor was strong and his perspiration dripped from his body to hers as he forced himself inside of her.

Never once did he say he loved her. Never once did he consider how she might feel.

And as he exploded inside her, groaning in his own pleasure, Cindy could still remember her only consolation was that she was already pregnant with Charley Reed's baby.

As he rolled off her and immediately fell asleep, Cindy knew she had made a mistake.

"I should have taken my chances with Charley," she said to herself as she lay awake in a strange place with an upset stomach.

Adam was next to her snoring. She knew he'd wake up and expect sex again. She wondered how this ever happened to her. She wondered how she'd ever survive. It was at that moment she closed herself off. Cindy felt truly trapped and it was the only way she would survive.

She felt that way until June 14th when Chuck was born. Ironically, it was his father's birthday, too.

Adam wanted to name the boy Abel. Cindy wouldn't hear of it and refused. She phoned her mother and she spoke to Adam. It was after that Cindy prevailed and he was named Charles Allen after Charles Allen Reed.

As she held their son for the first time, she quietly whispered a prayer hoping for the safety of her son's father.

She prayed to the God the nuns taught her about, rather than the God of Adam and the band of hypocrites to which he belonged. Her God was forgiving and loving. He wasn't the same God Adam used to condemn everything from movies to Pepsi. There were no Mormons fighting in Vietnam. Charley Reed was a Catholic and he proudly served.

There really was no way for either Cindy or Charley Reed to know that as the doctor first brought forth Charles Allen Ganley into the world, Charles Allen Reed replaced his Green Beret with a steel helmet, stood up, hooked up, stood in the door, and then jumped with the 601st Special Warfare Unit into the Republic of Bolivia.

It was June 14, 1967 and Operation Eagle Thrust was underway. By the end of October Che Guevara and nearly six thousand Cuban soldiers would die at the hands of 568 American troops and the Bolivian Army.

Funeral pyres would light the skies for the entire months of July, August, and September. And as they did the superstitious Bolivian Indians fled to the highest points of the mountains, believing the Inca god of revenge had returned after centuries of dormancy.

The President of the United States himself ordered no survivors, no remains, and no proof.

Sergeant Reed and many others became the vassal and the arm of Lyndon Baines Johnson. They followed orders. No mercy was given; no prisoners were taken. The young man with the soft face, the coward, the liar, had arrived. He was now a cold-blooded killer devoid of conscience.

As Cindy Ganley stood up from the wheelchair and carried her son to her husband's car, Charley Reed lifted his fallen comrade over his shoulder and carried the critically wounded man twenty-two miles to the medical evacuation station at Palomas.

As Cindy brought her baby home, she thought about his father. She examined their son. He had brown eyes and red hair just like his father. She undressed him and examined and even touched his tiny manhood. She couldn't help but think of the father as she touched their son. And then she took him to her breast to give him nourishment.

"How could this have happened to me?" she asked aloud, her son nursing at her breast.

And as she asked her questions, Charley Reed had a few also.

"How could this have happened at all?" Charley Reed cried out to anyone who might have been listening as he fell under the weight of his wounded friend.

"I love you," Cindy said to Charley Reed.

"Fuck this!" Charley screamed out.

"I love you, too," her son said as they sat together at the end of the wonderful wedding day.

"Thank you, Mother, for being here and telling me the truth and for all you've done," he said.

"I haven't done anything," she told him. "You deserved more than I've given you."

"What was he like?" Chuck asked his mother.

The question startled her even though she knew he would ask it sometime. It was late now and they were both tired. She wasn't sure exactly what to say to him.

"You look just like him," she said. "When you were growing up you would do things that reminded me of him.

"He was very bright. He could grasp things faster than anyone I've ever known. He wanted to be a lawyer and a pitcher for the New York Yankees. He never became either. He was a dreamer and when I became pregnant he wanted to marry me."

"Why didn't you marry him and just ignore Grandmother's wishes," Chuck asked.

"I was young and didn't know what I was doing.

"He was a very good young man, but he was in the Army. Vietnam was just really starting to get underway and I was sure he was going to die," Cindy said.

"Were you ever in love with him?" he asked her.

He asked it with a very different sound to his voice. As his mother, she knew the tone. He was sincere and knew he needed an answer.

"Honestly," she began. "From the first time I met him I was in love with your father. There was something very special between us. Maybe we were just kids, but I always knew he loved me.

"We didn't see much of one another. We lived in different states during most of our high school years. He wrote to me. He was quite the letter writer. He kept it up even when we both started college. I wasn't the writer he was, but he was never discouraged.

"He hung in there and then one day in my sophomore year in college, there he was. I was living in the sorority house and one of the girls said I had a guest downstairs. It was during the week in the evening.

"I hadn't seen him in nearly four years, but I knew him right away. I can't describe how I felt. It was almost the same as when I first met him, but it was different. It was more intense.

"I ran to him and kissed him and wouldn't stop. All of a sudden I was in love with him again."

"Did your parents like him?" Chuck asked.

"My dad did. My mother, you know how she is. If his father had been an important executive, he would have been fine. Even though both hers and dad's families didn't have a lot of money, she always acted like they did. She was always competing through us girls. That's why your Aunt Lisa and she don't get along so well.

"But they were always nice to him. Mother felt he was dangerous, but really in a way she was taken by him, too.

"He was very personable. People liked him very much. When I was in Pittsburgh in November, I visited with an old friend of his. Even today the people who knew him all still have kind words and funny stories to tell about him."

Chuck sat there and listened to his mother talk. He was intrigued listening to this for the very first time.

"Tina's mother can tell you more about him after you were born, but his friends said he was a Green Beret in the Army and won the Silver Star for bravery. He married a girl from the Washington, D.C. area. She could tell you a few things, too. I'm sure she could.

"He left her for Jerilyn. I guess he was in love with Jerilyn."

"How did he die?" Chuck asked.

"He was killed in an automobile accident outside of Emporia, Virginia. Your grandmother and I visited his grave in November and for me it was a very moving experience.

"All this time I thought he was alive. I imagined him out there and wondered what kind of life he was having. I wondered if he was happy or miserable like I was.

"I didn't know he was dead. I lived all these years expecting him to just show up like he did that evening at the sorority house.

"There were years I hoped he would. I hoped he'd come and take you and me and the girls away from Adam, away from Utah, and away from the Mormons. Your father was my imaginary knight in shining armor.

"Many times I wished and wished for him to come. He never did. There was no way for me to know he was dead. I always believed he was close by. He probably was the whole time, kind of like some angel watching over us. He was probably there helping me have patience and just survive.

"Charley Reed was a very special man to me. He truly was."

Chuck watched his mother's face as she withdrew into her memories. He could read the pain she was feeling at that moment and wished he could make it better for her.

He looked out into the casino at the people walking in opposite directions like two separate herds of animals each following the one in front of them, all with no general purpose or direction. He saw the blank look on each of their faces. Then he looked back at his mother.

Her expression was not blank. Her expression was alive and pained. Pain or not, Chuck knew his mother was finally alive once more.

"I was wrong," she said to her son. "I played it safe and I was wrong.

"How can you trade away six months of happiness for years of safe boredom?"

It wasn't a question that required an answer. Cindy had already answered the question.

"I was so wrong," she said. "I cheated you and I cheated your father. If it wasn't for me, he might be alive today."

"That's wrong, Mother," Chuck told her. "It was his time when he died. Whether he was with you, alone, or with someone else, he would have died just the same. You blame yourself because you weren't around. It's better you never knew. That way you had your knight in shining armor. If you ask me, it sounds like you still do."

Cindy remembered the tombstone setting atop his grave.

She tried to imagine his funeral. She couldn't. She couldn't remember the time of the year when he died. Was that important?

She doubted it. She had become preoccupied with the simple things, not really understanding the big ones. She wondered about items of detail and tried to place herself at the graveside.

"I'll always love him," she admitted to her son.

"My father will always love you," he said consoling his mother.

"Thank you," she said touching her son's face. "I appreciate that very much."

The wedding party went on even after the band stopped. Chuck went to bed with his new wife. Cindy sat alone for a long while.

Finally she went to bed at five a.m. As she slipped between the sheets and laid her head on the pillow, she thought of the skinny young man she met at a high school dance years ago. She remembered how good she felt with him. He used to share his dreams with her. His dreams all included her. They were serious dreams for their future.

Cindy lay there in bed drifting in and out of sleep. It was one of those times when dreams and reality blend with one another.

Charley Reed was with her. She could smell his aftershave. Her hand touched his soft cheek. His lips met hers and they kissed.

"I love you," he told her. "No matter what happened to us, I'll always love you.

"I'll love you till I die," he said. "I'll love you till then and even beyond. I will love you forever."

Cindy remembered teasing him. "Even when I'm old and fat?"

"You'll never be old and fat to me," he told her. "You'll always be the same to me as you are today."

"Really?" she asked.

"For sure," he told her.

Then she thought she was awake and he was a grown man standing next to her bed. Cindy couldn't believe her eyes. He was really there!

"The only thing I really regret is," he said to her, "I wish I could have seen you pregnant. My God! You certainly had to be an exceptionally beautiful woman when you were pregnant."

Cindy tried to speak to him, but couldn't. She was very sleepy and fought to keep her eyes open. She was afraid if she closed her eyes, he'd leave. She tried to speak, but was unable. She was afraid she'd lose him and held her arms out.

"Come lay down with me," she heard herself say.

"Take off your clothes and lay down. I want to make love to you. I haven't made love for years. It will be like it's our first time."

His face glowed.

She watched as he unbuttoned his shirt and took it off. She felt herself blush. He opened his belt and unzipped his pants. Cindy could feel her heart beating as he pushed them down his legs.

Immediately he grew hard and she watched as he stepped out of his pants. He pushed the sheet down below her feet exposing her entire body to him.

The bed moved as he joined her. His hand went to her face as he kissed her. His hands and mouth moved to her breasts. The feeling exhilarated her.

She felt herself becoming wet with wanting him. Her hands held his head as he continued to kiss her whole body.

Charley's face moved down to her center and his hands followed. Cindy was shocked. Adam never did this.

"I want you in me," she cried out. "I want you now."

She tried to pull his face to hers, but he resisted. She tried again and then he was gone.

Cindy lay in bed, her eyes open and staring at the darkness around her. She cried out for him and then realized she'd been dreaming.

Then, for no reason at all, Adam flashed into her mind and he was in a rage. She imagined the conversation that took place a couple of days ago between her mother and her soon-to-be ex-husband.

"I'm being thrown out of my own house!" he screamed at Marilyn George.

"Can't you control your own daughter? Why is this happening to me? I never should have listened to you!"

"Quit your complaining," Marilyn George told him. "You've had the world by the tail since you married Cindy. I set you up in business and I financed your campaign for mayor. You're the one who let it all go to his head.

"You were stupid and decided to fall in love with some slut you had on the side and then let yourself get caught. That took a lot of brains," she told him.

"You owe me!" he reminded her.

"Adam," Marilyn said in disgusted voice. "Those days ended a long, long time ago. I've financed you from the day you took Cindy.

"I don't hold with a man hitting a woman. My granddaughter told me you not only beat her mother, but hit her as well. As for being thrown out of your house, those are the breaks. You brought that on yourself. Don't look to me for help. I'm done. I won't get involved."

"But I'll lose everything. It's not right," he said.

"It wasn't right what we did either," she reminded him. "We did it just the same."

"But won't you do anything to help me?" he asked one more frantic time.

"No!" Marilyn George answered coldly.

Cindy lay awake remembering too much, sick with her own thoughts. She closed her eyes and moments later she finally drifted off to sleep. It was almost daylight.

CHAPTER TWENTY-ONE

WASHINGTON, D.C.
SEPTEMBER 11, 2001
6:09 P.M.

Since ten that morning the Central Intelligence Agency had snatched twenty-seven Arabs with ties to the hijackers. John Hughes was overseeing the activity. As new names came up, he dispatched operatives to pick them up and seize the assets at each of the locations.

The Federal Bureau of Investigation had a watch list and was in the process of taking measures to track down and detain those on the list. All twenty-seven were on the list and they were by now in custody. They were in custody, but no one knew it. And the interrogations continued.

Mohammed Abdullah was dead. He died around two that afternoon. The repeated injections of Sodium Pentothal finally stopped his heart. But it didn't happen until he had given them so much information they were able to immediately begin bringing in the rest of those they now had in custody.

He wasn't the only casualty that day either. Seven other Arabs died in various ways. One actually took his own life by swallowing a poison pill.

But the Arabs weren't as brave as the American public was being led to believe. They weren't all prepared to give their lives for their religion in some imagined Holy War. The majority of the ones the CIA had in custody talked without very much coercion.

And as they talked the full scope of it all was unfolding.

While the Arab men who were being tortured and beaten were painting the picture for the CIA, the American people were still in a state of shock. Everywhere those touched by what happened tried to escape their grief by falling back into the past and happier times.

Jerilyn was no different. When Anne Marie called her and told her about Chuck, she thought back to when Tina and Chuck were first married.

ST. PETE BEACH, FLORIDA
DECEMBER 25, 1992

Several thousand miles away daylight was almost upon the beach and Jerilyn Gardner was walking alone. She had been awake less than an hour and Bob never even moved when she left the bed. He continued snoring as she pulled on a pair of shorts and a football jersey, pausing at the side of the bed to watch him sleep.

It was the same Bob she'd known for years. His wife went to Hawaii for Christmas so Bob brought her to Florida. This was the first time in many years Jerilyn went away with someone.

Most of the men she'd known wanted to sit around some redneck bar and drink beer. Their idea of going away was to go fishing for a weekend.

Jerilyn never enjoyed those kinds of vacations. She liked nice hotels, fine restaurants, and a beach. Bob had given her that and she was his lover. It was a fair exchange.

She didn't feel bought and paid for. After all, they already were lovers so why shouldn't they be allowed to go off together? The only problem was even though she was with him, she was still lonely. And unfortunately, Jerilyn knew what loneliness was.

She enjoyed the early morning breeze and the sound of the waves rolling in on the shore. Jerilyn thought this was the nicest time of the day at the beach. She enjoyed the smells of the morning almost as much as she enjoyed the solitude. It was her time to be totally within herself. Jerilyn seldom examined her life, but this morning she was doing just that.

The sand felt good as she walked the beach barefoot. She remembered the Easter weekend she spent at Myrtle Beach with Charley Reed. They walked the beach on Easter Sunday morning and talked about getting married. She could still remember how much he wanted to marry her.

Charley Reed wanting to marry her scared Jerilyn half to death. Other men had wanted her and had been good to her. Charley Reed was the first one Jerilyn had ever been truly in love with and really wanted.

As she walked up the beach now, Jerilyn could physically remember the ache she had from wanting him. No other man had ever made her want him as much as she wanted Charley Reed. She was never able to have enough.

Each time he made love to her, she wanted him that much more. He became an obsession and she was terrified.

Wanting anyone that much gave them a power over her. And committing herself again was something Jerilyn preferred to avoid. When Charley handed her a ring and asked her to marry him, he blew her away.

The ring was beautiful and she said yes.

"I'll file for a divorce next week and we can get married this summer," he had said.

Fear of a commitment or not, Jerilyn had to say yes. She had to have him and it made no difference to her whether or not she was scared.

Jerilyn continued walking and remembered what happened to them.

They never stopped loving one another, but they became stubborn and stupid. She never realized Charley was so obsessed with her. Her fear of being left again scared her to death. It seemed they were doomed from the start. Had she known, had she been more perceptive, she might have been able to do something.

He always seemed so confident and powerful it had been hard to realize he was scared, too. To her he had always been what she expected in a man. When he finally collapsed, she misread the signs and believed he no longer loved her. Then, before she could realize how wrong she had been, he was dead.

He wasn't just gone. Charley Reed was dead.

He'd been a man of extremes and Jerilyn, even at that moment, was angry at the extreme to which he had gone.

She began to walk back down the beach.

The years since Charley's death piled one upon the other. They had been lived without much purpose. She'd given her children away. Michael was given to a childless couple in Dallas for money. Sam had finished raising the girls.

Jerilyn had lived for herself. Now she was middle-aged and sneaking off to Florida with someone else's husband. Nothing had changed! She was still living only for herself with no commitment to anyone. In her mind she thought it would always be this way.

How had it happened? How had she lost?

She was gone nearly an hour and a half by the time she returned to their room. Bob was awake and already showered. He was reading the morning paper out on the balcony and drinking a cup of coffee. Jerilyn walked through the room, kissed him on top of the head, and joined him, pouring herself coffee in the extra cup.

"I missed you," he said. "Couldn't you sleep?"

"I guess not," she said.

"Is it me?" he asked.

"Heavens no!" she laughed.

"It's this thing with Tina getting married and all that," she said. "She's already pregnant! I'll be a grandmother this time next year. What's more the father, my new son-in-law, is the exact double and most likely the son of a man I was very much in love with once."

"Really?" Bob asked. "What happened to him?"

"He's dead. Has been dead for nearly twenty years.

"But it's really a crazy life all the same. Now out of nowhere, his son shows up and marries my daughter. What a crazy life!"

Bob agreed. "It is a crazy life for sure.

"Look at me. I have a very successful law practice. I make in the six figures every year. I have a big house in the suburbs, a condo in Maui, a membership at the local country club and three grown married children. I have everything anyone could want, but I'm not happy. The only time I'm ever happy is when I'm with you."

Looking down at the pool below them, he continued.

"My wife dresses in another room and can't stand to have me touch her. We haven't made love in over two years and now she wants to spend her holidays away from me. I've really been thinking about this for a long time and I don't like it one bit.

"The greatest sex I've ever had has been with you. I can talk to you. I think you even find me interesting. I want to divorce her, Jerilyn, and marry you.

"I can't stand the thought of growing old alone. Married to her would be just that. Married to you could be new and exciting. We could travel and see things together. You'd be someone I'd enjoy taking places and coming home to. You'd make me the happiest man going if you'd say yes."

Then he handed her a beautiful diamond ring.

She was shocked. It was the very last thing she expected from him. For some reason, she never felt Bob might be really unhappy. She thought she was just something on the side where he found excitement. Now he wanted her to be his wife.

In an instant Jerilyn stepped back and looked at herself.

She had prepared herself to be alone, but now there was an alternative. It was a way out and she had absolutely nothing to lose.

Why not, she asked herself. Why shouldn't she have someone to take care of her?

"Bob, I'd love to marry you," she answered with a big smile on her face.

"When?" she asked.

"I can be divorced in a few weeks. We'll get married just as soon as I am."

"What is your wife going to say about this?" she asked him.

"I told her before she left for Hawaii that if she did leave, I wanted a divorce. She just laughed at me. She said we've been divorced for years. All we needed to do was divide the property. That I can do.

"This won't come as any surprise to her and will probably be the best thing I've done for her in years," he said.

Jerilyn watched his face as he talked. It was something she learned being married to Sam because his eyes usually gave him away. Bob's face was sincere.

His eyes were intense and beginning to fill with tears. She could tell he really did want to marry her. She liked him as a person and no matter what his wife took, he would still be able to provide for her. At last she could get out of the bar and begin to enjoy life.

Without saying another word, she took his hand and led him from the balcony into the bedroom. Jerilyn undressed him, enjoying the fresh soapy smell of his body and then undressed herself. The only way she knew to thank him was to make love to him. If she had given him the best sex of his life before, Jerilyn decided he hadn't seen anything yet.

Her mind began to remember years of being treated like a whore. If that was the way she'd been treated, then she must have been one.

As she began to gently caress him bringing him to a total state of erection, Jerilyn began to calculate a game plan.

The only difference between a dumb whore and a smart whore is the amount they demand and receive. Inside she laughed realizing she was able to give him more sex than he could physically or mentally stand. She knew giving him more and more would be okay for a while. Then she could begin to hold back. It would make him want her more. She could tease and tantalize him. If he liked stockings and high heels, he'd have them. She would give him anything he desired.

At the same time she'd be his wife and companion. She was still beautiful and could turn men's heads. He would be proud to be seen with her. She would be his trophy wife and at the same time she would control him with sex.

Jerilyn smiled as she straddled his body, looking at his face beneath her. How easy this would be, she thought. This man was hers. It would require no extra effort on her part and was actually quite pleasant. She guided him inside her and gasped.

"Oh, you feel good," he told her.

"And you do, too," she told him. "Honey, I'm going to enjoy having you all to myself whenever I want you."

"I just hope you want me a lot," he said.

She squealed in pleasure and swore she would.

"Oh, my God, you're good," she cried.

And then, even as she cried out, more for him than herself, her mind left the moment and watched from a corner of the room.

This is good, she told herself.

CHAPTER TWENTY-TWO

SEPTEMBER 11, 2001
7:32 P.M.

All of a sudden Tina's phone began ringing off the hook. Cindy called first and then Tina's mother, Jerilyn. The three of them cried and they all fell back into the solitude of their memories. Ironically, it was the same.

CHICAGO, ILLINOIS
JANUARY 1993

By the third of January the wedding guests and bride and groom returned to their homes. And by the end of the week life was going on as usual in Chicago and Cindy was making changes in Salt Lake City.

Cindy returned to Salt Lake City to attend a hearing regarding support and possession of the house. Julie was in her last year of high school and Cindy had no intention of moving her before graduation. Julie refused to go back to the house as long as her father was there. The hearing took less than an hour and her attorney got her everything he asked.

Both Adam and his attorney were taken back by the harshness of the judge when he heard Julie's testimony about how she was afraid of her father. Adam was told to be packed and out by six p.m. that night. He was further told he was not to attempt to contact either his wife or daughter without permission of the court.

"I recognize your position in the community," the judge said referring to Adam's position as mayor.

"I also recognize the police made no report and actually ignored Mrs. Ganley and your daughter and in my estimation placed them both in jeopardy. If there is even a hint of any such action or any violation of my order not to communicate, I will hold you and anyone else even remotely involved in contempt of this court. I hope for the sake of all involved that I make myself perfectly clear."

While they waited for Adam to move out, Cindy and Julie spent the day shopping in Salt Lake City. Both of them were happy to finally return home in the evening.

Meanwhile, in Chicago Bob filed for divorce and moved into Jerilyn's apartment. During the next few days Jerilyn and Bob found a lakefront condo and planned to move in February first.

Tina and Chuck stayed in his apartment just for the sake of convenience. Tina was graduating in May and the baby was due in August. They decided the best time to move would be June or July and maybe into a house.

In spite of the January snows that were unusually heavy, everyone seemed to settle into a routine that disturbed no one.

Cindy and Julie began their new life without Adam and the other girls began coming home on weekends, something they avoided when their father was there. Cindy even had an occasional glass of wine with her meals, usually toasting to a new beginning and a new life.

The Super Bowl was on the last Sunday of the month. Jerilyn no longer worked at the bar and Ruth invited her and Bob over for the day. She also invited Tina and Chuck.

"It's fine with me," Jerilyn said. "I guess it's time I begin acting my age and accept things the way they are. She's my daughter, he's my son-in-law, and I'm going to be a grandmother."

Ruth just laughed and kidded her calling her granny.

Tina on the other hand was skeptical. "I don't know. Dad wants us to come over," she lied.

"I'm not sure this is such a good idea. Mother has been against us since the beginning and why should I believe she's just out of the blue decided to change? I know Mother too well. She doesn't change and she doesn't forgive when it comes to men. Chuck has a big case he's working on and he really doesn't need this kind of aggravation.

"Aunt Ruth, maybe some other time without Mother. Chuck really does want to talk to you about Charley Reed. His mother admitted that he was his father and he wants to know about him," Tina said and left it at that.

Anne Marie called and tried to change her mind, but it was of no use. Tina didn't even bother Chuck with any of it. He worked at home every night and didn't need any turmoil at all. Tina suddenly became very protective of her husband.

She sensed this whole matter bothered him much more than he let on. In a matter of four months his whole life had turned upside down. He met her mother and then her. They fell in love. She'd become pregnant and they married.

During all of this her mother made a drunken scene at his apartment and then at his work. His own mother began divorcing his father and then he finds out the man wasn't really his father all along.

His grandmother who had always been on his side turned against him when he married too quickly and he found out she was behind the deception about his father from the very beginning. Tina decided to stand firm. All of this would take time to absorb and sort out. Her husband was going to have the time he needed. She would see to it.

They had just finished dinner. He helped her load the dishwasher and clean up the kitchen before sitting down with the case he'd been pleading that week. He told her they had two more days and it could go either way.

"You'll win," she assured him. "You're a winner."

"This is an important case," he said. "If I win this, I won't be in practice by myself. The law firm will stop making me pay rent to them and probably offer me a partnership. If it happens, we've got it made."

Tina was pleased with her husband and sat next to him and kissed his cheek.

"I love you," she said.

As she kissed him again the doorbell rang. "I'll get it," she told him.

When she opened the door, she was dumbfounded. It was her mother and a distinguished looking man. Before she could speak, Jerilyn handed her a very expensive bottle of champagne and walked into the apartment, pausing only to kiss her thoroughly surprised daughter.

Chuck was still sitting on the couch. He turned to see who was at the door. Jerilyn walked over and handed him a box filled with letters, pictures, and other papers.

"This will answer a lot of your questions about Charley Reed. He was a very special man. You'll see that as you read and maybe it will explain why I acted the way I did."

Jerilyn felt tears welling in her eyes and turned to her daughter.

"Tina, this is Bob. We're going to be married in March. I really wanted you to meet him."

Tina looked at the champagne and then at Bob and her mother.

"Come in," she said. "Take off your coats and we'll open this bottle."

"Your mother and I were hoping you'd say that. It's already chilled," Bob said, speaking for the first time.

Chuck stood and shook Bob's hand. He quickly recognized Bob as a very well known attorney and even acknowledged that he did recognize him.

"Thank you," Bob said with a genuine note of modesty. "I understand you're handling the DAT Systems case."

"Yes," Chuck answered.

"How is it going?" Bob asked with interest.

"Not bad," Chuck replied as Jerilyn and Tina hung coats in the closet.

The men went to the kitchen to get wine glasses. Tina listened as Chuck told Bob about the latest development that seemed to have stopped him at least temporarily.

"You don't have a problem at all, Chuck.

"The phone company lawyers played right into your hands and they don't even know it. There was a decision handed down in U.S. Court in Annapolis, Maryland in 1982 about the time of the breakup. It'll take them right out of the ballpark. It's listed as Kearney vs. Maryland Public Utilities Commission.

"My boy, you've got this one locked up," Bob said.

Tina watched Chuck's face light up as she served the wine. Bob's advice had been a godsend for him tonight and she happily drank with her mother as Jerilyn toasted her new son-in-law and her lovely daughter.

Tina watched her mother.

She could tell there was something different about her. Even the way she was dressed was different. She was wearing an expensive suit with matching heels. Her hair was done and she had a beautiful tan. More than that, there was a certain elegance about her mother she hadn't seen since she was a little girl.

The wine was excellent and Tina immediately liked Bob. She brought out their wedding pictures and proudly showed them to her mother and Bob.

Chuck relaxed for the first time in nearly two weeks. Tina saw him sink back into the couch, enjoy his wine, and laugh as she told a story about how nervous he had been.

For this she was grateful her mother and Bob had come by to visit. She was also thankful her mother suddenly became her mother and began to mend the fences.

Jerilyn and Bob didn't stay late. They left before ten and Chuck began to dig through the box Jerilyn gave him. Together Tina and Chuck looked at all the pictures and Tina was able to identify most and even remember some.

"My God, you do look just like him," Tina said to her husband. "No wonder Mom went nuts."

Chuck couldn't believe his eyes. "Look at his handwriting," he said. "It could be mine!"

"I remember him teaching me to swim," Tina said holding out a picture of her with Charley Reed in a swimming pool.

"Where was this taken?" he asked her.

"This had to be in Washington, D.C. when we all lived there," she said.

"Look at Anne Marie," she said handing a picture to him.

"Who is this?" he asked.

"Michael," she answered. Before he could ask more she told him who Michael was. "He was my brother."

"Was?" Chuck asked.

"Mother sold him for adoption to some doctor and his wife in Texas. I haven't seen him since he was four."

Then Chuck took out the large manila envelope and opened it. Inside he found another manila envelope that had been mailed to a post office box in Greenville, North Carolina and had never been opened. A note was stapled to it advising Jerilyn not to open this. It was a duplicate and could someday be proof as to who and when the story was written.

"Story?" Charley asked aloud. Then he pulled out six typewritten pages under the title 'The Woman Every Man Wanted.'

"Look," he showed Tina. "It's a story written by my father."

"Read it to me. Let's go to bed and you can read it to me there."

"Okay. That sounds like fun," he laughed.

Tina was in bed in no time at all with her pillows propped up and looking like a little girl waiting for her daddy to come tell her a bedtime story. As Chuck walked into the room, the feeling of dejavu came over her.

It was Charley Reed coming into hers and Anne's bedroom to tell them a story. She could remember wishing he was her father and that she was his little girl. She wanted him to hug her.

Tina could still remember the way he smiled. She wanted him to love her, but she was afraid he could go away. As her husband slid into the bed next to her, she remembered that he did.

"The Woman Every Man Wanted by Charles Allen Reed," Chuck began.

The apartment was growing dark as she sat alone and smoked cigarettes. There had been too many nights she sat alone. They had all been exactly the same. Then, she thought, many nights she hadn't. For Pat, all she saw before her was more liquor and the faces of the unnamed men in her future. At that point she wished the end were closer. At that point she even considered giving up.

As the little remaining light began to fade with increasing speed, she remembered Terry and imagined him sitting next to her. He was smiling the same wonderful smile of his that illuminated his whole face. He was holding a drink and gently sipping it. There had been so many evenings they sat together like this. Sometimes they would just hold hands in the dark. They always enjoyed one another. In her frantic search for someone to replace him, those were the times she missed most.

"I have something most men will never understand, let alone have," he said.

She agreed. Not really at first, but later for sure. It was after he left, then came back and hung on, then finally was gone for good. Once she realized, it was too late. He used to tell her beautiful things about life. In his own funny way he was quite an optimist.

"I laugh at the way we as people complicate such a simple thing as living. Just breathing air, in and out of our lungs with the heart pumping blood to all parts of our bodies." He'd laugh. "Then we invent love when we're really in heat." He'd continue to laugh and she'd realize he really wasn't laughing. Terry would begin to apologize for what he was saying. "It's not really heat, I guess. It's probably that we realize as a person we're so alone. That's when we reach out for someone and grasp, praying we can hold on. When we can't, we cry. Some people just give up and end it all. I believe it is ended when they do."

Tears always came to his eyes. Sometimes they'd be large, heavy tears filling his eyes and rolling across his cheeks and falling to the floor. Pat remembered how sensitive he was. She remembered how deeply he'd be hurt by her spoken words. She remembered the unspoken words hurting him more. He was so vulnerable to her.

"As long as I live," he once told her. "I'll love you. I know you. You're a hard crust of a young woman and might even be laughing at me right now. Laugh if you want, just don't forget. Someday you might reach the point where you won't want to continue. If it comes, just call me. Please call me. I love you now and I'll love you then."

She began to cry and buried her face in a pillow she pulled up from her lap. Whether they meant it or not, no one ever said that to her. No one had ever loved her enough to promise that. Pat knew Terry loved her that much. "I wish," she said to herself. "I wish."

"What's going to happen to the girls with you working nights? What about Michael? How will they grow up? Insisting you're a good mother isn't enough. What will they believe when they're eighteen, then twenty-two, and twenty-eight? Punishing yourself is one thing. What are you doing to them in the meantime?"

"My God!" Tina exclaimed. "This story is about them. He wrote this about them. It's unbelievable!"

Chuck looked at her and then continued.

Pat thought of the way it ended. Letters came from many different places and then occasionally he'd show up in town. It was about the time she began to expect him he stopped. He never forgot birthdays and Christmas was always special. There were always presents and cards, but the notes to her were distant without even a hint of himself. She began to wonder about him until it was nearly an obsession with her. Through it all Pat never broke. Not once did she try to call or find him. Instead, she let the days turn into other days and occasionally admitted to only herself she might have made a mistake.

"I love you," he told her one Christmas on the phone.

"I love you, too," she said to herself, never actually answering him.

She listened to the same silences he did. They seemed to last forever.

"Well, the hell with you then," he screamed into the phone before hanging up.

She wanted to cry but didn't. There were times she wished she had. At other times she wished she had called him back. She never did.

Pat was thinking about herself as she sat in the darkened living room. She realized she was the woman every man wanted to make love to, but not marry. Terry had, but for some reason she wouldn't let him. Maybe it was because he wanted her that caused her to force him to leave. In a way, she never really understood why.

"I'm sorry," she said to him after he hung up. "I'm so sorry," she said again. Then she finally cried. "I love you, too."

Tina stopped Chuck again. This time she was crying. Chuck looked at her and had tears in his eyes, too. His voice cracked as he tried to speak. Instead, he just squeezed her hand.

"I can remember Mother like that," she said. "She was always so lonely. She was the woman every man wanted."

Chuck continued to hold her hand as he read on.

The gentle moments picked at her and she wondered what she really wanted. Pat remembered the meanness that came after him and she remembered his own meanness. "I'll kill you," he screamed in his sleep. She wondered who he meant. She remembered holding him the last night they were together. He was deep inside her and when they were as close as they possibly could be she said, "I love you." She meant it. She really did love him. Then the next day he left.

Once she dreamed of a house with a husband, a little dog, and all of it becoming a home for the children. She even imagined another baby with Terry the beaming father and the man in that dream. She hadn't allowed him time to grow. She expected him to be strong all the time so he could hold them together. It hadn't been fair to him. He had weathered her marginal times but she was unable to do the same for him.

"I'm sorry," she said as she continued to clutch the pillow. "I wish I could have been something else." Pat realized if she had wanted, she could have been different. Other people and other things had seemed more important at the time. Her vanity never allowed her to yield to his kindness.

"I'm sorry," she said again. "I wish I would have been something else."

He loomed in her memory as a giant. Terry always believed he was average, but actually he was very exceptional. He was a contradiction and for that she loved him even now after all these years.

The lines on her face had changed to wrinkles and the wrinkled stomach turned to fat. Her gray hair was hidden with dye and she was missing two of her teeth. She was getting old.

"Hey, old woman!" he used to tease her. "I love you!"

"I know," she answered. "I know," she said again as she finished her drink and lit another cigarette. Pat remembered him in the days after they lived together. He ran back and forth across the country before he finally went home to Pittsburgh and started his own used car business. Friends of theirs said he was a success from the beginning. She knew it would be that way.

He was in town. She was in Louie's with Eddie Lee and he came in with an attractive blond who never took her eyes away from him. Pat never forgot the way he looked that night. Something was different about him, but she wasn't sure what it was. Terry seemed so alive, laughing and smiling, dancing and holding the blond girl to him. She woke early the next morning and looked at Eddie and felt so empty.

"Why?" she asked herself.

She still didn't understand. The blackness of the empty living room began to press against her. The open door leading into the August night seemed miles away even though it was only just across the room. Pat felt she was trapped. She remembered Terry telling her that one day she would feel the way she was feeling now. She laughed at herself and thought of how she doubted that the day would ever come. She was laughing, but then, not really.

The flowers he gave her one morning when he thought she was going to leave wilted and died before her eyes. Everything between them that had ever been sweet and tender soured and grew hard. Pat realized in another month she'd be forty-seven. She thought of the years when the kids were young and couldn't begin to even imagine forty-seven. She hated it and the being alone.

"Why?" she asked a final time.

Both Chuck and Tina were silent. She snuggled into his arms and he held her tight. There was no need to talk. Tina felt totally safe and peaceful in her husband's arms. She was the daughter of Pat and he was the son of Terry. The two of them had succeeded with their own love where their parents had failed.

His hands began to roam and caress her body. Tina sighed with pleasure and though she focused her attention on her husband, she couldn't help but think of Pat and Terry. She thought of their last night together and how Pat finally gave herself over completely to Terry.

Had Pat waited too long? Was that why Terry left the next day?

Tina cried out as the pleasures she was receiving from her husband began to build.

"I love you," Tina cried.

Pat had cried those very words.

As Chuck read her that short paragraph, it was as if Tina had been watching a movie. She could see Pat, a beautiful woman with her mother's face.

It was her face, too.

She had the kind of clean trim body men desired. She could see Terry, firm and muscular. He was a warrior and a survivor. If Pat was the woman every man wanted, Terry was the man every woman wanted.

Tina could imagine them making love. Pat's head turned from side to side. Her hands gripped his face and she kissed him. Through Chuck, Tina felt the pleasure Pat was receiving from Terry.

"I love you," Tina cried out.

"I love you," Pat echoed.

Then as both women climaxed at identical moments, all that remained was Tina and Chuck. They were breathing heavily; their lovemaking had never been so good.

"I love you, too," he said rolling to his side and pulling her body close to him. "I'll always love you."

She listened to her husband's pledge and remembered Terry had made the same pledge to Pat. Charley Reed undoubtedly made that pledge to her mother.

   As she relaxed in her husband's arms, Tina wondered if her mother had made a similar pledge in her life. Was that the reason her mother had been the way she was?

CHAPTER TWENTY-THREE

The next morning after Chuck went to court Tina called her mother. Her mind wouldn't rest. The story and the pictures woke memories of the man Charley Reed. They were little girl memories, but just the same they were unresolved memories. Tina found herself crossing over from a woman to a child and into the character of Pat. Tina realized Pat was her mother.

"Have you ever read this story?" she asked her mother.

"No," Jerilyn admitted.

"We did after you left. Wow, Mother, it is really some story."

"I'm sure it is," Jerilyn said.

"Charley Reed was a very smart guy. He had talent and probably could have been a great writer. He was a tremendous salesman and knew how to make money. He was a very special man, one I haven't forgotten, and definitely one I never will now that you've married his son."

"How did you know?" Tina asked.

"Look at the pictures and look at his handwriting. I heard his voice. It was like something on television. Twenty years later a man walks back into your life. He hasn't aged a day and he has no memory of you, good or bad. Everyone wants a second chance at something they feel they botched the first time around. Maybe it can be done right this time."

"Mother, I didn't know."

"I know you didn't, Tina," she said.

"But, I'm getting my wish. Seeing the two of you together last night was the fulfillment of that. I told Bob on the way home I'm finally at peace inside myself. You and he have given me that, each in equal amounts, both of you in different ways, too."

"That's nice to hear," Tina said genuinely.

"Thank you. I think I would like to read that story, finally."

"Whenever you want," she offered. "It's really something."

"I expect it to be," Jerilyn said.

As Jerilyn and Tina hung up the phone that morning, Marilyn George was changing planes in St. Louis, boarding a flight to Salt Lake City. It was not very often Marilyn left Pittsburgh, but his time she felt there was certainly a good enough reason. Two and a half hours later when the jet landed, her son-in-law, Adam Ganley, met her. Marilyn was not in a good mood.

"I should have flown first class. I forgot how uncomfortable it is back in coach. They don't even serve a meal anymore. Air travel has really gone downhill since my husband and I used to travel.

"Adam," she said turning her attention to him. "You've gotten as big as an ox, from the sounds of things, as dumb as one, too. No wonder Cindy is trying to divorce you," she said sharply.

Adam didn't know how to react. He nearly began to cry.

"Don't be such a wimp!" she scolded him. "You've gotten lazy. Join a health club and lose a hundred pounds or go to a fat farm. You have a few acres due for harvest."

"Oh, Mother," he whined. "You have no idea what this has been like."

"There's my bag," she pointed it out to him as they waited at the baggage claims area.

"I'm not interested," she told him. "You shit in your hat as far as I'm concerned.

"I'm here to save your ass and my investments. And, if your enormous ass was not so much involved in my investments, I'd cut you loose so fast your head wouldn't even have a chance to spin."

As they drove out of the parking lot Marilyn continued. "You damn Bible-thumpers are all alike," she told him. "You won't touch a drink, but you'll touch another woman and then blame God and the devil for it when you were nothing more than horny the whole time. You've gotten out of hand, Adam! When I fix this, if you so much as look the wrong way, you'll be out on the street with nothing."

"I have nothing now," he complained. "You should see where I'm staying. I slept in my office that first night!"

"You deserve it for being such an ass!" she reminded him.

"No one deserves what is happening to me!"

"You better decide how you're going to fix things with my grandson," she said. "As it sits right now, if anything happens to me, you're working for him."

"What!" Adam asked beginning to protest.

Marilyn stopped him cold.

"You wouldn't listen. When you started all that crap about him going to Brigham Young for law school and you disowning him if he didn't, you wouldn't listen to me. I tried talking to you, but you were too busy quoting the Bible and the teachings of John Smith. I was just some silly old woman who the Sacred Heart Sisters taught the Bible to better than anyone in the whole state of Utah.

"You seem to forget from time to time who you owe it all to and I had to see my investments were secure. My grandson is just like me. He has that killer instinct and he knows how to manage a dollar."

"I'm not too impressed with his decision-making process," Adam said. "He gets some nothing college girl whose mother works in a bar pregnant and then marries her."

"Careful, Adam," Marilyn warned.

"That nothing college girl is my grandson's wife and for your information she receives her Master's degree, something you always promised me you would get, this spring from Northwestern. Her mother may be a bartender, but certainly the girl never will. My grandson not only found a smart one, but a beautiful one, too."

Marilyn produced one of their wedding pictures and held it in front of Adam's face as he drove up the interstate into the mountains. It started to snow as they reached Sunset. Snowy weather always made Marilyn nervous and she insisted Adam slow down.

Cindy got home about three that afternoon. She had begun going to a health spa to exercise every day. She was through by one, but had gone grocery shopping. She had invited all the girls home for the weekend and she expected a houseful, especially if they brought their boyfriends. As she took the last bag of groceries from the trunk of her car, she saw Adam pull up in front of the house.

Cindy wasn't sure what to do. She had all the locks changed and even had an alarm system installed. She wasn't sure whether she should call the police, her lawyer or both. She left the garage and locked the kitchen entrance behind her.

Then the doorbell began to ring. Cindy froze in her steps. Julie was due home from school any minute. Adam might be drinking again and could be violent. Cindy wasn't sure what to do.

The doorbell rang again. She cautiously walked to the front of the house and saw that Adam's car was gone. Again the doorbell rang and someone began pounding on the door. Cindy walked to the door and looked out the peephole. At that moment her mother started screaming.

"Cynthia Lee George Ganley, open this door before I freeze to death out here!"

Realizing it was her mother, Cindy threw open the door.

"Mother!" she exclaimed. "What are you doing here?"

Marilyn walked into the house, leaving her bags on the front porch. Cindy stepped outside and looked around for Adam before bring the bags inside.

"I sent fatso away," Marilyn told her daughter. "He told me about the judge's orders. You have him scared to death. He's such a God damn wimp anyway and he's as fat as a whale."

Cindy was shocked to hear her mother utter an obscenity. At the same time she noticed something different about her face. Cindy wasn't sure what it was. She just knew something was different.

"I don't need a reason to visit my daughter," Marilyn said.

"Where are my granddaughters?" she asked.

"Julie should be home any time and the other girls will all be home tomorrow."

Marilyn was still holding the picture of Tina and Chuck that she had waved in Adam's face. She showed it to Cindy.

"My grandson found himself a beautiful and smart young woman to be his wife!" she said.

"I was always sorry you didn't name him after your father. He's smart like your father."

"He's smart like his father," Cindy said

"Bullshit!" Marilyn said.

"Mother!" Cindy exclaimed. "I've never heard you talk like this. What is the matter?"

"That lousy Charley Reed has pissed me off for years.

"I never had a son. I gave your father everything he ever wanted except a son," she said taking her coat off and throwing it over a chair.

"Daddy wanted a son?" Cindy asked.

"Don't be silly," Marilyn snapped back. "Every man wants a son. It's one of those proofs of manhood. Even that wimp Adam wanted his own son."

"He had his own son and he blew it," Cindy reminded her mother.

Just as they were about to argue, Julie came home from school. The inevitable was delayed until evening after the dinner dishes were completed and Julie was upstairs talking on the telephone.

"I want this divorce business ended," Marilyn told her daughter.

Cindy was shocked by her mother's bluntness.

"Would you like a glass of sherry to go with your coffee, Mother?" she asked.

"Since when is there alcohol in this house?" Marilyn asked.

"Since Adam is gone and it suits me very well."

"I want this mess over with," Marilyn demanded again.

"It will be very soon," Cindy assured her.

"Cynthia, that's why I'm here! I won't sit by and watch you destroy your family. You can't possibly know what you're doing. You're angry with Adam, but that will all pass. It's time to begin to mend and allow your marriage to heal. You've got to call off this divorce."

"Mother," Cindy said in a tone Marilyn had never heard from her daughter. "There is nothing left to mend. Our marriage is over and it will never heal."

"Never is a long time," Marilyn reminded her daughter.

"I know it is and I want nothing to do with him or my marriage to him."

"Why?" Marilyn asked.

"Why!" Cindy repeated. "You've been talking to him through all this and you're asking me why?"

Cindy was beginning to get angry.

"Mother! This is the end of the twentieth century. I won't have a man strike me or see a man strike my daughter. He had a lovely family, a good wife, and a nice home. That wasn't enough for him. He couldn't keep his hands off a little clerk in the hardware store. Then he got her pregnant and everyone in town knew because his little sweetheart kept the baby and gave it his name!"

"Cynthia! What is the matter with you?

"The business with the salesgirl was five years ago. You've been making him pay for that mistake ever since. You locked him out of your bedroom for those five years. What happened was only frustration, frustration that you very expertly created and nurtured each and every one of those years. You've hated him since the day he turned against Charles. You've made him pay for that along with his indiscretion. All these years you've been here in body but not in spirit. You've been anything but a wife to him. You're to blame for what happened that night. You've been laying the blueprint since the day you found out and your pride was hurt," Marilyn said.

"So what's wrong with that?" Cindy demanded. "You raised me to have pride! You raised me to be a lady. You taught me what to expect from a husband. You taught me what to demand. Are you trying to tell me now that I have five grown children that you were wrong or just lying to me?"

Cindy was angry and expected an answer from her mother. The eye contact between the two women was intense. Cindy expected her mother to fire back at her with everything she had.

Instead, Marilyn's voice grew softer, quieter, and even held what Cindy thought was a twinge of pain.

"You don't think I understand how you feel? I do. Things are the same no matter what part of whatever century you're living in. They always were and they always will be. Adam isn't any different than your father."

Cindy began to speak, but her mother stopped her.

"In many ways Adam has been a better husband to you than your father was to me," she said. Marilyn's voice started to quiver.

"Your generation is lucky. Your sister Lisa has a good job and is able to support herself and doesn't need a man for anything other than companionship. You, the money you've saved and your father's money will take care of you for years to come. You can sell this beautiful house and move to Arizona and take life easy. Women today don't know how easy they have it.

"Your father came home after World War II and we got married. We were high school sweethearts and we were going to have the best of everything. I was pregnant with you in a matter of months and your dad was just starting college under the GI bill. We had a one-room apartment and no money. He was always at the library. It turned out that he was seeing one of the coeds, too.

"I found out. I cried and cried and went home to my parents. I was living with them when you were born.

"When your father came to the hospital to see us, I forgave him. He graduated from college and went to work and I was pregnant with Andrea. That time it was a girl at the office.

"I was in the hospital in labor and no one could find your father. He was with her at her place. You just didn't get up and leave with an infant and a five-year-old. He was a good provider and I pretended it wasn't happening. I pretended, but I knew.

"Then Lisa came and your father changed. He was moving up in the company and his energy was going into his job. I became an asset to him and we were like a team. I was an extension of him and I helped further his career by becoming the perfect corporate wife. I did what he expected and he moved on up the ladder. Then he went out and fell in love."

"When?" Cindy asked in amazement at her mother's story.

"The year we left Pittsburgh. You were fourteen and you hated me. I'll never forget how you hated me. It was the only time I ever made your father do anything. I insisted he take a lateral move to get us away from that woman. He didn't want to do it, but I made him. He either moved us or I was going to divorce him. That move probably cost him the presidency of the company, but I'd do it all over again.

"What has Adam done to you that your father hasn't done to me? Hit you?

"Your father broke my nose when I was eight months pregnant with you. I didn't know anything, he told me, and didn't know how to treat a man. He punched me and my nose was broken and both of my eyes were blackened. My father was going to kill him.

"In Pittsburgh he pushed me and I sprained my ankle and broke my wrist. He said he hated me. I was his wife, but he said I was a bitch and he couldn't stand me."

"I can't ever remember you fighting," Cindy said truly astonished at her mother's revelations.

"Of course not," Marilyn said. "Your father never wanted you children upset. He didn't want to talk about it until he was drunk. Then it was different.

"He'd hold me down in bed if I wouldn't make love to him. If I wanted to breathe, I'd submit to him. You never realized how good you really had it. Your father was a great daddy, but he was a real bastard of a husband."

"I had no idea!" Cindy said.

"Why should you? I was never going to tell any of you. He provided for all of us before he died. When he was sick and knew he was dying, he was sorry for all the things he had done.

"He thanked me for staying with him and always finding room in my heart to forgive him. I knew he was dying and I didn't bother to tell him that I never had. To this very day, I've never forgiven him.

"So many times I wished I could leave. I was trapped like so many other women. In the end when you girls were grown and gone, all we really had was one another.

"Then it was different. He liked me and found me attractive and interesting. Can you imagine, after all the years!

"We traveled together and enjoyed our life as a married couple. Those years didn't make up for the first thirty, but they made them easier for me to accept. That's why I want you to fix things with Adam. In the end he's all you'll have and that is better than being alone."

Cindy didn't say anything. Her mother was very tired and went to bed. Cindy made sure the house was locked and went to bed also.

All she could think about was what her mother told her. She had always judged every man she'd ever known by her father.

Cindy remembered being fourteen and moving from Pittsburgh. She remembered her father telling her that he didn't want to leave either. Her thoughts of those times were blurry. That was the year she met Charley Reed.

She remembered turning fifteen in April and not wanting to leave her friends. Her mother was right. She did hate her. She hated her for the way she was treating her father and hated her for having to leave Charley. For some reason, Cindy knew her mother was behind the move from Pittsburgh.

Charley was her first real love. He fit her idea of what a man should be. Her dreams were his dreams.

Her own mother and father were high school sweethearts and her dad had gone off to war. Charley promised to graduate from high school and come for her. Everything happened too fast for her.

School ended and it was his sixteenth birthday. She made him a heart-shaped cake and promised to wait for him. Cindy remembered wanting to make love to him and how shy he was. Neither one of them knew anything, but somehow they blundered into their first sexual experiences. It was an innocent love and even then it was still very special to her.

Cindy wanted to bind him to her and that she did. Charley Reed wrote every day.

Cindy and her father both missed Pittsburgh that summer. In August she went back to visit her friends. She and Charley made love again. It was different that time. Where it was shy and tentative the first time, now there was more. Charley wasn't shy and he took control. She knew she was right. He was a man like her father.

Cindy lay in bed, giving in to sleep as she tried to remember what had happened. It was fuzzy. All she knew is they stopped writing and she didn't hear from him until he showed up at the sorority house. A lot of time was in between. It probably seemed endless then, but it had only been four years.

Four years in a life of forty-five was not much at all.

CHAPTER TWENTY-FOUR

The alarm clock went off and Chuck woke up feeling confident and ready for the day ahead. This was the last day of the trial and after following Bob's suggestion, Chuck was positive he would win. It was a good feeling.

He could hear Tina in the bathroom. She was sick. It was morning sickness and she was beginning to wake up each day with it. He was bothered by Tina having to begin her day being sick and silently wished there was something he could do. In a few minutes she emerged, forcing a smile and said she'd start the coffee.

After his shower Chuck came out into the kitchen. Tina was sitting at the table with a cup of black coffee in front of her.

"Are you sorry you ever met me?" he asked innocently.

Tina began to force another smile, but it struck her so funny she laughed genuinely instead.

"Why would you ask that?"

"If you hadn't met me, I never would have seduced you and you never would have gotten pregnant and you wouldn't be sick right now."

She laughed a second time.

"I don't mind being sick just as long as I have you around to say stupid things and make me laugh. I wouldn't change anything and besides, I seduced you. I just made it seem like you were seducing me."

Chuck was pouring himself a cup of coffee and noticed Tina had stopped laughing and seemed to be thinking about what she was about to say.

"What's the matter?" he asked.

"Oh, nothing. Really," she reassured him. "It's just that from the very first time I met you I wanted you. I knew you were with my mother, but I didn't care. It made no difference to me whatsoever. I wanted you. I never knew why.

"When you asked me to meet you for lunch and we started to talk, at that moment I knew you'd always be around.

"When we first made love I didn't worry about anything. I trusted you. I felt like I belonged in your arms and would always be there. From the beginning I've always loved you."

Chuck was overwhelmed by his wife's words. He left the coffee and walked over and kissed her.

"I love you," he said.

Just as he did Tina pushed herself from his arms and ran to the sink where she was sick again.

"I'm sorry," she apologized. "I didn't mean to do that in front of you. I'm really sorry."

Chuck held her again and wiped her forehead. "Don't worry about that," he said. "I love you and I want you feeling better."

Jerilyn and Bob were having coffee and they were talking about Chuck.

"He was magnificent yesterday," Bob said. "He held himself in until the very last. He finished cross-examining a witness and he knew the judge would ask for closing statements and then adjourn for a decision. I couldn't have done it better myself.

"Chuck had the decision prepared along with all the supporting material and made a motion for judgment based on the evidence given and prior precedents. When the judge asked which precedents he was talking about, he produced them. It was great!

"I'm going in today to see how the judge rules. Chuck hasn't left him much of a choice. He's a bright young man."

"Give credit where credit is due. You're the one who told him about the precedent," Jerilyn said.

"Sure I did," he said. "Anyone could have. It was the way he used it and his timing. That's what makes him good. He has it. He has that sixth sense. He knows how to go for the kill."

"So what is this all about?" Jerilyn asked.

"I'm going to court today and listen to the judge and help him celebrate afterwards."

"Okay, but what is this really about?" she asked again.

"I've been asked to leave the law firm," he said.

"Why on earth for?" Jerilyn demanded. "You're a full partner."

"I know," he said. "They're buying me out for more than a fair price. It's the divorce. They're afraid there will be a scandal and it will hurt them. I told them it was stupid, but they insisted so I agreed."

"So what happens now?" Jerilyn asked anxiously.

"Nothing, really," he told her. "I need to set up my own office. I'll keep all my clients so I'm not really losing anything, except for the support and monthly dividend.

"I'm working for a living again. It's kind of exciting and I'm thinking about asking Chuck to join me as my partner."

Jerilyn said nothing.

She wondered how he really felt. On the surface he seemed to be dealing with everything, but she wondered how it was deep inside him. The divorce definitely bothered Bob and now this. She reached across the table and held his hand.

"It's not much, but you'll always have me," she said.

"I'll do anything you need. I can answer phones and file. I can't type, but I can deliver papers for you. Anything you need, I'll do," she added.

"Thanks, honey," he said. "I appreciate it."

Just as Bob predicted, the judge ruled in favor of Chuck's client. Tina was in the courtroom and kissed her husband on the cheek.

"Congratulations," Bob said as he shook Chuck's hand.

"Congratulations to you," Chuck said back. "Without what you told me I would have been a dead duck."

Bob held his finger to his lips.

"Keep that to yourself," he said. "Everyone gets a boost now and then. If you get a chance later, I'd like to talk to you. I have a proposition that could make us both some money."

"Sure," Chuck agreed. "When?"

"Any time this morning," Bob said. "Come by my office."

"In an hour?"

"Sure. See you then."

Tina met her mother for lunch and asked what business Bob had with Chuck. Jerilyn tried to explain as best she could what had happened to Bob, but her anger over the matter was very plain.

"They're making him sell his interest in the law firm because of the divorce and maybe because of me. He's taking his clients and setting up a new practice and he's asking Chuck to come in as his partner."

"What do you think about that?" Tina asked her mother.

"Honey," she answered. "If our men can make it work, I'm all for it. Bob really likes Chuck. I can tell by the way he talks about him.

"Bob's never had a son and I believe he sees himself as a father who can teach the kid some tricks of the trade. Under the right circumstances it could be good for both of them and according to Bob, very financially rewarding. He is really excited over the whole thing."

"Well, Chuck certainly respects and likes Bob and said he couldn't have won this case without his help. Will it bother you at all if they become partners?"

"No," Jerilyn quickly answered. "Not one bit. That's all behind me now."

Bob offered Chuck an equal partnership and Chuck accepted on the spot. They went to lunch and over a few celebratory drinks they drew up the agreement. That night both of the men came home excited.

Chuck decided to take Tina out to dinner to celebrate. While she was getting dressed, he called his mother to give her the news.

"Why, Chuck," Cindy said. "That's wonderful news."

"What's wonderful news?" Marilyn asked immediately.

"Mother," Cindy said. "Just a minute."

Marilyn refused to be silenced.

"If it's Charles, I want to hear it from him. If it's wonderful news, I should be called first. I'm the head of this family now. Why am I always the last one to know everything? I should be the first."

"Mother!" Cindy exclaimed.

"What is the matter with Grandmother?" Chuck asked overhearing Marilyn's voice.

"I don't know," Cindy answered.

Marilyn rose from her chair and extended her hand to Cindy, demanding the phone.

"Let me talk to him. You never took good messages as a child. You'll just screw this up, too."

"Did you hear that?" Cindy asked her son incredulously.

"Yes," he answered.

"What's wrong with her?"

"I don't know. Just talk to her," said Cindy handing the phone to her mother.

"Charles! What is such good news?" Marilyn asked at once.

"Grandmother," he began. "I won a very important case today. I've been offered a partnership with one of the best attorneys in Chicago."

"What does this mean?" she asked.

Chuck was puzzled by the question. If anyone would understand what that meant, it would be his grandmother. Marilyn George had always been accused by her grandson as being a woman with a cash register for a heart.

"Why, Grandmother," he said. "It means I've made it. I'm writing my own ticket now."

"Well, I think that's fine," she said sounding mollified. "As long as you're happy, that's all that matters."

Cindy was listening all the while and wondering what was the matter with her mother. Was she drinking in her room? Cindy didn't know what she was doing, but she did know her mother was different.

"Is Gina there with you, Charles?" Marilyn asked.

"Yes, Grandmother, Tina is here."

"Let me say hello to her, son," she said.

"Mother," Cindy corrected her. "His wife's name is Tina."

"I know her name," Marilyn snapped back at her daughter. "I'm not a ninny. I won't be treated like an old fool!"

Cindy held her mouth. It didn't make any difference how old she grew. She would always respect her mother.

"Hello, dear," she heard her mother begin. Then without asking how Tina felt, Marilyn said what was on her mind.

"I wanted to know what your plans were for when the baby arrived?"

Cindy could only hear one side of the conversation and had no idea what Tina answered.

"No," Marilyn said. "I didn't mean that, dear. I meant as to how the baby would be raised. Didn't the priest make you sign an agreement saying you'd raise the baby Catholic?"

Cindy listened in shock to her mother.

"You weren't married by a priest?" Marilyn asked as if she didn't know.

"Dear," she said. "Charles was raised like his mother, a good Catholic. I can't imagine what you did to turn him away from his faith. All I can say to you is consider carefully the course you're plotting and change before it's too late for the three of you."

Evidently Tina had put Chuck on the telephone because almost immediately the entire tone of the conversation changed.

"Well, Charles," Marilyn said. "I can't say how pleased I am to hear about your good fortune. This is all so exciting. Imagine, you becoming a full partner and me becoming a great-grandmother. I always expected one of your sisters to make me a great-grandmother first. I never expected it to be you."

There was a brief pause.

"Yes, I love you, too," Marilyn said. Then without another word she hung up the phone.

Cindy couldn't believe what just happened. She wanted to shout at her mother but somehow held it in. Just when she thought she could control herself, her mother did it again.

"Cynthia Lee, I believe it's time to start dinner. I've had all the fast food I can stand. I'd like a home-cooked meal for a change. Your sister Andrea always makes sure I have my meals on time. I expect the same from you."

As Cindy was about to speak, the phone rang again. It was Chuck.

"What's wrong with Grandmother?"

"I'm not sure," Cindy answered.

"Is she sick or something?"

"I don't really know," she answered.

"Who is that?" Marilyn interjected.

"My attorney," Cindy lied.

"Well, I have something to say to him!" Marilyn shouted.

"Mother!" Cindy said raising her voice. "No!"

Cindy spoke to her son briefly and then went into the kitchen to start dinner.

Marilyn George was watching the news. She looked to her right and saw someone standing there. She looked again and blinked. She thought she saw her husband.

She called Cindy and looked back. It was her husband. How could that be?

She called for her daughter once more and reached for the cup of tea.

Cindy heard her mother call that time and walked into the family room. Just as she entered, she saw her mother fall forward onto the floor.

"Mother!" she cried, running to her. "Mother!"

Julie was in the kitchen helping with the dinner when she heard cries from the family room. She rushed in to find her mother turning her grandmother on her back.

"Call for help!" Cindy screamed. "Mother's had a heart attack!"

Cindy opened the collar of her mother's blouse and tried to remember how to administer CPR.

Within minutes the ambulance arrived and Marilyn George was receiving oxygen and on her way to the hospital. Cindy rode in the ambulance with her mother and held her hand. They were less than a mile from the hospital when her mother's eyes opened and looked straight at her. Marilyn tried to speak, but was unable. She moved her head and shook the mask from her face. Looking right at Cindy she spoke one word, a name.

"Charley," she said and then died as she clutched Cindy's hand.

It was just after two a.m. on Saturday morning when the phone rang in Chuck Ganley's apartment in Chicago.

"Hello?" he answered still half asleep.

"Charles, this is Mother."

"Mother," he said shocked to hear from her in the middle of the night. "Is anything wrong?"

"Your grandmother died tonight." Cindy's voice shook.

"How?" he only asked.

"It was either a heart attack or a stroke. It was probably a stroke. I should have known. I knew she was acting funny. I should have done something."

"Mother, it wasn't your fault. Don't do that to yourself."

"Oh, Chuck, I feel terrible."

"I know," he said. "I'll be on the next flight out to be with you and take care of things."

"Oh, thank you," she said.

"The last thing she said before she died was your name."

"I'll be there in a few hours. Rest now, Mother, I'll be there soon."

"I love you, son," Cindy said. "I don't know what I'd do without you."

"I love you, too, Mother," he answered.

After hanging up the phone Chuck left his wife still asleep in the bed and went out to the living room. He called American Airlines and made a reservation on a 6:34 a.m. flight to Salt Lake that would arrive there at 8:44 a.m. He returned to the bedroom and quietly packed. Then he went into the kitchen and started a pot of coffee and turned on the 24-hour news station from Atlanta.

CHAPTER TWENTY-FIVE

VIETNAM
MARCH 3, 1968

Saigon was the military headquarters for all of Vietnam. All of the American generals were headquartered in the city. In January as Tet began, the Viet Cong tried to kill as many of them as they could. They failed. Not one general was even wounded.

However, that was considered dirty pool in the way wars were to be fought. In retaliation, General Westmoreland ordered the North Vietnamese General Staff Headquarters bombed.

Sixty Navy bombers based on the nuclear-powered aircraft carrier Enterprise along with ten Air Force F-111B terrain-following bombers from Udorn, Thailand attacked the city of Hanoi.

The President himself had placed the entire city of Hanoi off limits. The plans for the attack had not been cleared. They were the brainchild of the staff officers in Saigon and when they were sent to the commander in the field, he immediately approved.

The commander's own home had been the target of a rocket attack, and while he survived, three of his servants were killed and six military police guards were wounded. Viet Cong sappers climbed the wall, came across the yard and even entered his bedroom. He had barely escaped and he gladly approved the orders.

"Now it's their turn!" he said to the other generals.

The plan called for a daylight attack. Sunday was just another day for the Vietnamese and intelligence reported they would all be in their headquarters by eight a.m. The bombing attack would begin at 8:30.

General Hap arrived only moments before General Vinh. Lieutenant Colonel Gnu met him at the curb.

"What is it, Gnu?" he asked. He recognized a distressed look on the subordinate's face.

"It's the 7th Division," he said.

Hap stopped him. "Inside," he ordered. "Inside now and nothing until we reach my office."

Their pace was quick. The office door burst open and then closed with a loud slam.

"What about the 7th Division?" he demanded.

"It was attacked by the American bombers six hours ago."

"How bad?" the general asked.

"There is hardly anything left. They hit our SAM emplacements and their explosions set Muang Ngoy on fire. An hour ago the civilian population was running through the streets trying to get to the safety of the jungle. Our men in the city say there are only a handful of our soldiers alive and they're wandering aimlessly as if they don't even know where they are."

General Hap sat down. He pressed the call button and his aide immediately appeared.

"Get us some tea," he told the soldier. As the man left the room, he looked back at Gnu.

"What of the 308th Division?" he asked.

"They're fine," he answered. "They checked in on time an hour ago."

"Where are they now?" the general asked him.

"They should be crossing the border in three hours. They will be outside of Khe Sanh by tonight."

"Good," he said. "I want the attack on Khe Sanh to begin tomorrow."

He looked to his watch.

"General Vinh and I have to meet with General Giap's aide at 8:30. I want you to come with us. You can answer questions that I might not have the answers for. First it was the 3rd and now the 7th Division. Nearly 16,000 men are gone in the wink of an eye. How can we explain that?"

"Is General Giap here?" Gnu asked.

"No," Hap answered. "He's with the chairman this morning briefing him on the offensive."

Hap looked at his watch again and then stood.

"Let's walk over to General Vinh's office. He needs to know about the 7th and then we'll meet with General Minh."

The two men left and began to walk out into the corridor.

Major Bernie Rosen was flying the lead F-111B. Captain Al Gushen was his weapons officer. They were traveling just under five hundred miles per hour ground speed and were at two hundred feet above the ground avoiding radar detection. They were seventy miles from Hanoi and closing from the southwest. Nine other bombers followed their lead.

At the same time Navy Commander George Meyers was leading the A6 Intruder Bombers in a western route south of Hanoi. They would follow the Air Force and concentrate on one target only. That target was the General Staff Headquarters located directly next to the People's Parliament in the heart of Hanoi. He knew this was a dangerous mission. By now the Air Defense Radar was tracking them. Hanoi was probably one of the best-defended cities in the world.

It was the F-111's mission to clear a path for the Intruders. They were to surprise the defenses, take out the radar and the SAM sites and give the Navy a pathway to their objective. The attack of the F-111's would begin on the outskirts of Hanoi on the radar that was at that very moment locked on the Intruders.

In Saigon General William Westmoreland crossed the hall to the men's room. He had been up most of the night with diarrhea. He'd been to dinner at General Thuc's house the evening before and was sure the chicken they served had been tainted. He was anxious to get the first results of Operation Eye for an Eye.

At 8:30 the three men entered General Minh's office. Air Force Chief of Staff General Vuong was there along with Russian Army Colonel Mikel.

"Be seated," General Minh said with a stern face.

As they sat, explosions could be heard to the west. They looked at one another as more explosions were heard. While no one spoke, each man wondered if they were under attack. They looked at one another. If they were being attacked, where were the warning sirens? Still, the explosions grew louder and closer.

The reality struck them that they were being bombed. It had to be what was happening.

"To the shelter!" Lieutenant Colonel Gnu yelled.

"Yes," General Vuong agreed.

As he did, the first F-111B roared over the General Staff Headquarters.

"Get down!" Gnu yelled again. "They're here! It's too late!"

The men all hit the floor. General Minh got under his desk.

Another F-111 flew over the building and then another, followed by yet another. As they did, the explosions began again. The last F-111 flew over them and then began bombing the targets to the east of the staff headquarters.

As the men got up from the floor, they had no idea at that very moment the city was blind. The primary radar defenses were gone and SAM emplacements were exploding. Then came the Intruders. The city's secondary defenses came to life. Anti-aircraft guns fired into the morning sky.

Commander Meyers followed a clear path of destruction created by the F-111's. He was over the Dong Da section of Hanoi and was following the tree-lined boulevard. He could see the National Assembly Building and the People's Park. Beyond the park was his target.

Anti-aircraft fire was intense. His wingman was hit. Black smoke was pouring from the aircraft. It was hit again and exploded.

"Oh, my God!" his weapons officer said.

"Shut up!" he yelled to the man sitting to his right. "Hit the fucking target! Concentrate on what we are doing! Do it now!"

They crossed the Nhue River and the weapons officer, finally calm, spoke. "They're away!" he said, referring to the twelve 500-pound bombs he had just released.

"Let's get out of here!"

Immediately Meyers took the jet aircraft into a climb and a sharp turn eastward toward the Red River. Anti-aircraft rounds exploded beneath him as he escaped the deadly skies over the city.

The bombs from Commander Meyers Intruder hit their mark. They hit the roof of the General Staff Headquarters and penetrated the ceiling of the eighth floor and continued on down through the building before exploding on the fourth floor.

The first explosions were two floors below and south of the office where the men were still recovering from the F-111's. That was the first and then payload after payload was delivered on the same target. The men in the office survived the first explosion, but the second came through their office. They were killed, as were ninety-six men, women, and three children who were at work with their mothers.

While that was going on, not all of the Navy pilots dropped their bombs on the headquarters. Before the ten-minute attack ended, they hit the General Confederation of Trade Unions and the Gia Lam International Airport, destroying a French 707 airliner, a Chinese cargo plane, and damaging the terminal building. Along with those targets, they also destroyed The People's Army Newspaper offices and print facility.

Those had not been designated targets, but as they saw their fellow airmen being hit, they purposely strayed and declared open season on the city. Hospitals and schools were hit. Every standing structure became fair game.

Later, when the losses of the day were tallied with twenty Intruders lost, twenty-two airmen killed, eleven captured and only seven rescued, they would all agree they did the right thing.

One would say, "It's war and we hit the enemy where he lived."

John Hughes was the first to find out what took place in Hanoi. He got on the phone and realized the generals had taken it upon themselves to set in motion a rogue operation they called 'Eye for an Eye.' He tracked down the units involved and then called Henry Townsend.

Henry Townsend immediately called the President as soon as he was told what the Saigon generals had done. It took nearly an hour to get through, but when he used the code name Archangel, things began to happen.

"They did what?" the sleepy President screamed in the phone.

"Are they out of their fucking minds?" he screamed.

"That son-of-a-bitch Westmoreland is done. I've never liked that motherfucker! McNamara stuck me with him. He's done!

"Get over here, Henry. I'll clear you through," the President said.

CHAPTER TWENTY-SIX

That night in Saigon the generals celebrated. Their strike on the Staff Headquarters in Hanoi was a success. While their only motive had been revenge, the immediate result wasn't the chaos they imagined.

In Hanoi subordinates gladly filled the vacancies above them. As they did, they all were promoted. And each of them, in their own way, set out to prove to the party leaders they were better strategists and leaders than their predecessors.

There was one other ramification the general staff had not anticipated. That perhaps was the most significant result of their unapproved action.

There had been a private deal about to unfold between the Johnson Administration and the North Vietnamese Government that would have ended the war and brought home the troops. General Giap, also headquartered in the destroyed General Staff Headquarters, was out of the building that morning, recommending they take the deal. He was meeting with Ho Chi Minh himself. The attack ended all hope it ever happening.

The North Vietnamese 308th Division crossed the border into South Vietnam around noon. They were thirty miles from Khe Sanh. The 545th SOG was following.

It was slow going for the North Vietnamese regulars. It was difficult traveling with the 572nd tank/artillery battalion as well as the 675th Artillery. They were sure they were still undetected and the night would be very welcome.

As darkness began to arrive, they had no way of knowing the B-52's were already on the way to destroy them. Refueled and reloaded, the B-52's were airborne and in contact with the trailing Special Forces unit.

Lance Corporal Mike Carson hated the night. It was at night the bombardment began and never let up. All he could do was stay as deep as possible and hope he didn't take a direct hit. At the same time, he had to be on the alert for the tunnel rats trying to get under the wire.

He couldn't help but wonder how he had gotten into this. He was sure he'd never survive. As he waited for the night, he wondered how could his life end in such a place.

As he went deep, the B-52's silently passed over the Marine stronghold. The 308th Division was within fifteen miles of the Marines when the bombs began to fall.

"Holy shit!" he exclaimed. "What the fuck is that?"

The southwest sky lit up. It was red at first, but as the intensity of the attack grew, it turned white. Even as far away as the Marines were, the sound of the continuing attack was deafening. One hundred six B-52 Stratofortresses dropped thirty tons of bombs each.

Metal tanks and artillery made of iron vaporized. Trucks loaded with men blew into a million pieces. The secondary ground explosions merged with those of the detonating one thousand-pounders. It was hard to imagine what it was like at ground zero.

Death and destruction was everywhere. The ground temperature exceeded two thousand degrees and even those who were not directly hit, literally boiled and were vaporized. Gasoline in vehicles exploded and the rubber tires melted. Fires erupted for what seemed to be no reason. With all of that, the bombs continued to fall as Stratofortress after Stratofortress took its turn in the pattern.

Mike Carson was aware the enemy shelling had stopped. He climbed to the top of the bunker and looked out. PFC Andre S. Bailey was next to him.

"They're B-52's," he said to Mike.

"Awesome," was all Mike was able to say.

Andre looked at him and agreed. He couldn't help but wonder what this was all about. As he watched the explosions continue, he knew men were dying, men who looked and talked differently from him, but men with desires and needs like him just the same.

"Awesome doesn't even begin to describe it," Andre said. "What we're looking at is hell from the other side of the mountain."

Upon his arrival at the White House Henry Townsend was taken directly to the Oval Office. As he entered the room, the President was seated on the couch facing him.

There was a large round coffee table between the couch and another matching couch. To the left of the sitting area was a fireplace with a fire burning. Above it was a painting of Franklin Delano Roosevelt. President Johnson had a bucket of ice and a bottle of Cutty Sark in front of him. A full glass was in his hand.

"Sit here in the rocking chair," he said to Townsend. He motioned to the wooden chair to his left. "It's convenient to the phone. We'll probably need to use it."

President Johnson poured scotch in a glass full of ice.

"Do you take water or do you drink it straight?" he asked Townsend.

As Townsend sat down he began to say no to the drink, but the old man erupted suddenly at the refusal.

"God damn it!" he said. "When I looked in the mirror this morning, I was still the President of the United States of America. If the President wants you to drink with him, you say whether you want your drink straight or with water!"

"With water," Townsend answered immediately.

"That's better," Johnson said to him.

He finished pouring the drink and handed it to Townsend. As he did, he offered a toast in the direction of the painting.

"To Franklin Delano Roosevelt," he said raising his glass to the painting over the fireplace.

Then he took a long drink. Townsend took a sip.

"He was the last great president this country had," Lyndon Johnson said.

"You're a great president, sir," Townsend said.

Johnson looked at him and smiled.

"Your civil rights legislation will insure your place in history," the man continued.

"Maybe," the President said. "This fucking war could do it, too."

Johnson continued looking at the painting of Roosevelt.

"He understood what it was to fight a war for the very existence of democracy. That's what we're doing. We have to stop the spread of Communism in our lifetime. If we don't, our very way of life will end and our children's children will live under Communist rule."

Johnson looked at Townsend. He was reflecting on what he was saying.

"Yes," he continued. "Franklin knew what it was like, just as I do. No other president in this century has had to feel the total impact.

"No other president," he repeated. "Not Harry Truman or Woodrow Wilson, not even Eisenhower had to feel this. It was just Franklin, and now it's me, too.

"It's fitting," he said. "I was elected to Congress because I backed his New Deal policies. He became my mentor in Washington and I delivered what he asked of me every single time. Now we're sitting where he sat and fighting a war like he fought."

Townsend looked at the painting. From where they sat it was looking down on them. He looked at the President and thought about the comparison he had just made. What would the Washington Post say if they heard the same thing?

Johnson took a long drink of his scotch.

"Now, tell me what these fucking generals have done."

While they were meeting in the Oval Office, Senator J. William Fulbright was preparing to appear on Meet the Press. As chairman of the Senate Foreign Relations Committee, he had become an outspoken critic of the Vietnam War.

In the past he had alluded to the President misleading the American people about the war. Today he was prepared to charge the President had lied about the Gulf of Tonkin incident.

"You can't use the word lie," his assistant cautioned him. "You're talking about the President of the United States of America."

"I don't care," Fulbright said. "It was a lie that to date has cost nearly thirty thousand American lives. There's no telling where this will end. We have these generals in Saigon talking about acceptable losses while boys are coming home in bags or maimed for life.

"Someone has to take responsibility for what has happened. If I sit back and say nothing, then I become the President's accomplice."

The senator from Arkansas stopped as if he was not only reflecting on the past, but the future as well. He was visibly silent for at least a minute.

The aide said nothing. He did not want to interrupt the generation of the thought.

"I'm an old man," Fulbright said to his aide. "So is the President.

"Soon we will both stand before our Maker. I'd like to be there to hear him try to explain to our Creator and Lord his reasoning on what a just war is versus an unjust war. I'd love to hear him make the analogy that North Vietnam is equated with Hitler's invasion of Poland.

"Daring to be presumptuous and not blasphemous, I can't imagine the Creator listening and pondering the President's words as he continues to explain that for us to parley with the Viet Cong would have been tantamount to another Munich."

Fulbright laughed to himself as he continued.

"I am sure that in all of His Wisdom, He will look down on the pitiful being before him. There will be no Oval Office or Great Seal. The Marine guards and the Secret Service won't be around. It will be just a naked Lyndon Baines Johnson standing in His Light and at that moment He will reveal to our President the treatment of slight and superficial resemblances as if they were full-blooded analogies, as instances as it were, of history repeating itself is a substitute for thinking and a misuse of history.

"John," he said addressing his aide by his name for the first time. "There is a kind of voodoo about American foreign policy. Certain drums have to be beaten regularly to ward off evil spirits. These are maledictions, which are regularly uttered against North Vietnamese aggression, the wild men in Peking, Communism in general, and President DeGaulle. Certain pledges must be repeated every day, lest the whole free world would go to rack and ruin."

The makeup people walked in at that moment and the Senator sat and reflected on what he truly wanted to say. In his mind he was sure what he wanted to say was right. At the same time he knew the limitations upon him. He silently admired Eugene McCarthy for his bravery and leadership. While McCarthy spoke out from his heart, he could only ask the American people speak out from theirs.

"John," he said. "I've been in politics too long."

As suddenly as the bombing began, it also ended. Charley raised his head. They were less than two miles away and a hot wind blew into their faces. The ground was hot and still glowing where only a short time before ten thousand living and breathing life forms known as human beings existed.

The rumbling was gone. It was replaced by silence. Even then in the silence it was as if he could hear dreams dying, the crying out of souls, and the end of so much.

Ten thousand of them were gone while the huge metal birds of prey returned to their roost far out to sea on the isle of death. He sat back and wondered what might be next.

He couldn't help wondering if his dreams might not be the next to be destroyed.

He looked at the other men. Could they hear the agony? Did they also wonder if they might not be next?

The President hung up the phone. He had been speaking to McGeorge Bundy.

"That's it. It's over and we have those four-star assholes to thank for it."

"What's over?" Townsend asked.

"Our deal with the North Vietnamese," he said.

"What deal?" Townsend asked.

Johnson spoke frankly. "We've been negotiating our withdrawal from the war. Averill Harriman has been maintaining a dialogue with the North Vietnamese in Paris. We finalized a rough draft last week. General Giap took it to Ho Chi Minh yesterday and they were discussing it when we hit the General Staff Headquarters. Giap feels we were trying to kill him.

"Now he and Ho Chi Minh are in hiding. They're talking about going to Peking and running the war from there so they'll be safe."

"What reason do our generals give for the attack?" Townsend asked.

Johnson shook his head.

"Because the Viet Cong attacked Westmoreland's residence and killed his favorite houseboy. That houseboy is the direct cause for the continuation of this war.

"The North Vietnamese now refuse to negotiate with my administration. They say we can't be trusted."

Johnson stood up and walked to a cabinet that held three televisions. He turned all three to the same station.

"I'll show you someone who can't be trusted," he said to Henry Townsend.

"Fulbright!" he said. "That backstabbing son-of-a-bitch is selling us out just like that queer bastard McCarthy."

As the President spoke, Fulbright was responding to a question from a panelist on Meet the Press.

"The United States cannot be expected to act as policeman for the world. Power tends to take itself for omnipotence. Once imbued with the idea of a mission, a great nation can easily assume that if it has the means, then it has the duty to do God's Work.

"He would never deny you the sword after He chose you to perform His Work.

"It is with this exaggerated sense of power and imaginary sense of mission that the Athenians attacked Syracuse, and Napoleon and then Hitler invaded Russia.

"In plain words they overextended their commitments and they came to grief," said Fulbright.

"Jesus Christ Almighty!" Lyndon Johnson exclaimed.

"My question is," Fulbright continued. "Can America overcome the fatal arrogance of power? Can our leaders accept that to criticize one's country is to do it a service and pay it a compliment?

"Criticism may embarrass the country's leaders in the short run, but ultimately strengthen their hand in the long run."

"Son-of-a-bitch!" Johnson roared. "Listen to him! He's a senator and he's talking like that. I can't believe my ears."

Johnson sat down and made himself another drink.

"What are you going to do?" Townsend asked.

"I'm going to replace that asshole Westmoreland. That means promoting him."

Johnson laughed out loud. He looked back at Franklin Roosevelt.

"The presidency isn't what it was when he was President," he said.

"You know, in 1944 he considered me for Vice President. It came down to Harry Truman and me. I was thirty-six years old and I was his choice. The party made him take Truman because of my age. Imagine, I could have been President then instead of now."

Richard Nixon was on Face the Nation that morning.

After losing in California when he ran for governor, he withdrew from politics. Now he was back and running for president. Even though he was on the ballot in the New Hampshire primary, he stated a primary win was not necessary. He felt that a minimum showing in the primary was all that was needed.

He said the party bosses would choose their candidate in 1968. Both he and Nelson Rockefeller believed that.

He further stated the American public was ready for a change. Change meant a Republican on a peace platform.

As the sun set on Washington, D.C., it rose on Saigon.

The President was drafting a reprimand to General Westmoreland while the General was eating breakfast. In the Soviet Union three men were launched into space. Their mission was to orbit the moon. An oil tanker ran aground off San Juan and split open. While this was happening in the world, the 25th Infantry left Saigon and began to travel north on Route 1.

The Communists wasted no time in giving the U.S. generals a response. Nine miles north of Saigon they struck in a well-planned ambush. Striking at the main body of the column, they destroyed twenty vehicles and two tanks. Forty-eight soldiers died and two hundred ten were wounded. Of those, one hundred sixty were removed from action and sent home. This was a defeat for the Americans and a victory for the Communists.

While that attack was going on, the 545th SOG, now in South Vietnam, was picked up by choppers and flown across the country to DaNang. There they were to have a few days off before being returned to the field. However, the ambush outside of Saigon, the attack on General Staff Headquarters, and the disobedience by the generals sent them back almost immediately.

Ambassador Ellsworth Bunker was ordered home to meet with the President.

CHAPTER TWENTY-SEVEN

MARCH 4, 1968

It was just before 1 a.m. when she walked down to the Oval Office. As she opened the door, she heard him talking to someone, but he was alone.

"Lyndon," she called to him. "Are you talking to Franklin again?"

There was no answer. It was as if he hadn't heard the question. He continued his conversation.

"You told me this would happen. There isn't anyone I can trust. My closest advisors and best generals have sold me out. I could have had this lousy war over in thirty days if they would have followed orders and left Hanoi alone.

"This is what Eisenhower and Churchill did to you before Yalta, isn't it? They sold you out. Like you, I can't trust any of them."

"Lyndon!" she called out to him again.

"Is that you, Claudia?" he asked into the darkness.

"Yes, Lyndon," she said. "It's me. Come to bed."

"Okay," he said. "That's a good idea. It's been a long day."

As he rose to his feet he took his glass of scotch with him.

"Good night," he said to the painting.

Lady Bird Johnson took her husband's arm and helped him to their bedroom.

Colonel Ladd arrived in Saigon from DaNang about the same time the 545th landed in DaNang. He was taken to Westmoreland's deputy commander, General Creighton Abrams. Abrams wasted no time once he and Colonel Ladd were alone.

"Are your people conducting secret incursions into Laos?"

"Sir," Ladd said. "I am not at liberty to divulge at this time whether any units under my command are or are not in Laos."

The answer took Abrams back.

"And by what authority do you refuse to answer my question?" he demanded.

"By authority of the President of the United States," he answered calmly.

"What?" he exploded.

He picked up the phone. "Is Bob Komer in his office?" he asked. He waited for an answer.

"Ask him to please step in on this meeting," he said.

Robert Komer was hand picked by Lyndon Johnson to be General Westmoreland's Deputy for Civilian Operations and Revolutionary Development Support. Robert Komer was CIA.

As Komer entered the office Abrams once more wasted no time.

"Do we have Special Ops in Laos?" he asked.

"Not by my authority," he answered.

"Colonel Ladd here has refused to answer me one way or the other under the authority of the President of the United States. If that's so, then your people are involved. Do you mean to tell me the CIA would have an agenda that left you out in the cold?"

"Hey," Komer said. "Anything is possible. I'm not lying to you."

"How can we find out?" Abrams asked.

"Call the President," Komer answered bluntly.

"No," Abrams said. "Call your people in Washington."

"What's this all about?" Komer asked.

"Frankly, our contacts in Hanoi report three divisions of North Vietnamese regulars have been bombed out of existence in the past sixty hours. Here at command headquarters we have no knowledge of this action. Hell, we had no knowledge of the three North Vietnamese divisions. Is there some other war going on that we don't know about?"

"Your guess is as good as mine," Komer answered. "I'll call Henry Townsend and ask him. He deals in a lot of Sneaky Pete business, but that doesn't mean he'll tell me. All I can do is ask. I'll get a coded message off right now. We'll have an answer by tonight."

Colonel Ladd was dismissed. He left the office.

Abrams looked at Komer.

"That bastard knows," he said. "He knows and he's not talking. We have a good thing going here. Operations like this can change everything."

Komer agreed.

"I'll find out if I can," he promised.

John Hughes received and decoded two messages for Henry Townsend that morning. The first was from Robert Komer inquiring about Special Operations in Laos and the destruction of three divisions. The second was from Colonel Ladd, Special Forces Headquarters.

It read: "Archangel in jeopardy. Headquarters Saigon inquiring as to mission of Uriel and whereabouts of Michael. Please issue instructions ASAP. Ladd"

Upon his return to DaNang Colonel Ladd sent the 545th to their next designated target. He decided they were better able to avoid detection in the field rather than if they were in DaNang or a Special Forces camp.

None of the members were happy about that. DaNang wasn't a bad town. It would have been nice to enjoy some local fun, but all they managed was a hot shower, a warm meal, and fresh uniforms. They were back in Laos by nightfall.

"Shit!" the captain said to Tankersley. "We all could have used the time down."

"You're right," he agreed.

Charley was there, but remained silent. He knew they were right. Since arriving in Vietnam they hadn't had a break. The entire country was under attack. It was the North Vietnamese version of blitzkrieg.

The generals in Saigon preferred to believe it was more like a small version of the Battle of the Bulge. Whatever they chose to call it, for the civilians and soldiers caught up in it, it only meant death.

He looked around at the eleven other faces. He was the youngest, but certainly not the most innocent. While they all were killers, he knew he had the blood of thousands on his hands.

Ho Chi Minh sat alone looking out the window into the darkness of the night. He sipped a glass of brandy and thought of his life. Privately he grieved the loss of his friends. Now only he and Vo remained from the group that took up arms against the Japanese.

He had been the political arm and Vo had been the military arm. Together, with the aid of many close friends, they overcame the Japanese, then the French, and now they faced the Americans.

Never before had he faced such overwhelming odds.

"More brandy, sir?" the servant asked.

"Please," the President requested.

He looked at the face of the servant. He had been with him a long time, but he couldn't remember how long.

"Where did we begin?" Ho asked. "When did you first come to work for me?"

"We were fighting the French," the servant answered. "It was when you were wounded. I was assigned to care for you."

"You've been with me ever since."

"Yes," he answered.

"Aside from Vo, you're my oldest friend."

"Friend, sir?" the man questioned. "I didn't know you thought of me like that."

"Yes," Ho said. "I have, but have not said it until now."

"Thank you, sir," the servant said. "I consider it a great honor."

"I've trusted you with my life," the President said. "I've trusted you and you've repaid me over and over with your loyalty. You have even saved my life when enemies tried to kill me. What more is friendship?"

"You humble me, sir. You humble me and you honor me at the same time."

The servant began to leave.

"Please stay," Ho asked. "I feel so alone tonight."

"I know," the man said consoling him. "These are dark days for our country."

"Yes," Ho said. "Our history is full of dark days. The Chinese are our natural enemies like the mongoose is to the snake. They help us now like the British and the French helped us against the Japanese. When the Japanese were gone, then we had to fight the French. When they were gone, it should have been the British, but instead it became the Americans. They are worse than any of the others."

"Even the Chinese?" the servant asked.

"Yes," he admitted. "The Chinese only want us as slaves. They need our crops and they need us as a protective buffer to the south.

"The Europeans and the Americans want our souls. They want to starve us physically and then emotionally.

"We are more than slaves in their scheme. They want us to be them. Like they've already done to so many of our people, we are to be their prostitutes, their allies who will fight their wars, be their pimps and their business partners. It never ends with them. They want to own us and in owning us, we will cease to exist and become them. We mean nothing to them."

The servant listened attentively as the President continued.

"The Americans are not to be trusted. They are liars. They

attacked our patrol boats and claimed we attacked them."

"But why?" the man asked.

"Because we were about to unite our country," he answered.

"The Americans and the Europeans set up Diem in the south. Diem was a Catholic like the American president. Vietnam is a Buddhist country, yet the Catholic minority leftover from the French was set up to govern our people.

"Our people did not want this European minority rule. As they were ready to throw it off, the Americans created a reason to intervene.

"First," he said continuing. "They sent the American advisors. Soldiers and special killers was all that they really were. We had no army before that. We had no need of one. The change was already taking place. The Americans stopped the change and then they attacked us.

"What's worse is they lied about the reason for the attack.

"They bombed our port at Vinh, destroying our patrol boats and our oil supply. We shot down two of their planes and that's how it began. We defended ourselves against aggression and terror.

"Now, in a matter of days, we have over a hundred thousand dead and our country in ruins. The American president wants to talk peace now after he has bombed and killed us. Why has he done that? Is it because he wants to prolong the division of our people?

"We will be reunited. We will be, even if it means my death and yours, too. In the end we will be one people again."

Ho Chi Minh didn't speak after that. He sipped his brandy and stared into the darkness. The servant stood by his side. His hand rested on the President's shoulder as he maintained the vigil.

Hundreds of miles to the south there was death. Where the two men stood at that moment there was only darkness.

General Vo Nguyen Giap on the other hand was not silent. He'd been drinking for hours and was outraged at the American attack.

"We were ready to withdraw our troops to above the 17th Parallel!" he repeated over and over.

"They were supposed to stop the bombing and killing. Instead they lied," he said as if he couldn't comprehend the overall result. "They lied!

"Why should I be surprised that they would lie to us? They've been lying to the world so why shouldn't they lie to us?

"We had an agreement. This could have been ended.

"Why? Why?" he asked.

The men with him only listened. They knew what it all meant. Then he finally said it.

"We'll fight on until the last American leaves. We'll wait and then Vietnam will be ours. We'll fight and then we will win."

CHAPTER TWENTY-EIGHT

MARCH 4, 1968

In Saigon Generals Westmoreland and Abrams sat down to dine with Ambassador Ellsworth Bunker and Robert Komer.

A lovely Vietnamese woman, who was no older than sixteen, poured the wine while a clean young man served them soup. As he did, he asked each man in turn how he liked his steak.

"Big T-bones," the Ambassador said. "They were cut this morning in Seattle and flown here on an SR-71.

"He does routine surveillance of the Soviet coast as he comes in. That's how we justify the flight and get our fresh meats and Alaskan king crab. Tonight's meal will cost the taxpayers about $40,000 a plate."

The men laughed and drank the wine.

"Did you get an answer yet?" Abrams asked Komer.

"No," Komer answered.

"Answer to what?" Bunker asked.

Westmoreland answered for him. "We have reason to believe the Special Forces are operating in Laos and directing secret Air Force bombing missions."

"How can that be?" Bunker asked.

"You tell me," Westmoreland said. "I'm the allied commander. I'm supposed to know all our actions in this theater of operations. It appears under special orders of the President we have several units running a cowboy operation.

"Hell! The other night they gave us support at Khe Sanh and damn near scared the shit out of the local commander. He thought World War III had started. He claims bombs fell for nearly fifteen minutes and took out what probably was a NVA Division, complete with artillery and armor.

"We had no knowledge of it or its movement, yet we destroyed it."

"Maybe it was a friendly UFO," Abrams joked.

"I'd buy that," Westmoreland said. "The only problem is Vietnamese Rangers reported seeing a Green Beret team rendezvous with two choppers and fly off toward the coast. If it wasn't for that sighting, I would buy the UFO theory."

"What's the purpose?" Bunker asked.

"You tell me," Westmoreland said. "You have the President's ear. He hasn't said howdy or fuck-you since I met with him in Washington last November. I had the impression then he was holding something back."

"Yes," Bunker agreed. "I know what you're talking about. I met with him. It's not just you. It's all of us. He's holding out on us all."

"Well, God damn it," Westmoreland said raising his voice. "Maybe he ought to cut us in instead of sitting there with his bottle of scotch and playing God."

On that day as the American leaders dined in Vietnam, the President's special message to Congress, 'Health in America,' was read into the Congressional record. He outlined a program that identified a high rate of infant mortality; the urgent need for more doctors and nurses; the soaring cost of medical care; the high number of accidental deaths; and finally, the need to launch a nationwide volunteer effort to improve the health of all Americans.

While his message was being read into the record PFC J. J. Cosgrove died of wounds before he could reach the MASH unit for treatment. He was twenty-years old and was from Alliance, Ohio.

President Johnson never knew about PFC Cosgrove. As the day closed and he sat alone in the Oval Office, he raised a glass of scotch in a silent salute to the men fighting in Vietnam.

MARCH 5, 1968

Hanoi wasted no time avenging their losses. Shortly after midnight five battalions of Viet Cong attacked the southern edge of Saigon.

General Westmoreland had just gone to bed. He was awakened and moved to a safe position. As he arrived, the other members of his staff were already there to meet him.

At the same time NVA regulars attacked Special Forces camps A-105 at Nong Son and A-103 at Gia Vuc. In each instance, over two thousand battle-hardened regulars attacked less than a hundred Green Berets. Without air support, both positions would have been lost. Nevertheless, casualties were high and a severe blow was dealt to I-Corps strike capabilities.

As news of the attacks arrived at Westmoreland's temporary head-quarters, he immediately ordered retaliation. Abrams agreed.

Both were still feeling the effects of the sumptuous meal and the large quantity of alcohol they had with dinner. In spite of that, they knew the target they wanted to hit. It would the eleven-acre dock area on the Red River only 1.8 miles south of Hanoi.

The 545th was overlooking a North Vietnamese supply dump. Incandescent lights illuminated the valley below. Trucks were lined up at the entrance to a tunnel, which entered the mountain where they were unloaded. People moved in and out of the mountain like ants. The Green Berets had been watching for hours.

Inside the mountain fourteen-year old Nyugen Gnu was unloading a truck loaded with mortar shells. He was conscripted for military service earlier in the week and this was the first time he had ever been away from home.

All of his life he lived with his family outside of Hanoi. They were river people. They lived on sampans and fished. Half the fish they caught they traded for rice. The other half they ate.

Since the Americans brought the war to his country, Nyugen watched as his brothers left home. There were three of them and they were never heard from again. Then the local leaders came for him. All he could do was hug his mother and father and say goodbye. He knew it was his duty to serve his country, but he would miss his home on the Red River.

Along with the sadness the war brought, it had also given him work. Until he was taken by the military, he and his friends worked unloading the ships loaded with war materials destined for the south. His father was a gang boss and his mother worked in the shipyard commissary. That entitled the family to rations they could obtain at the supply house. They received items like bread and dried meats. There was even an occasional bottle of plum wine, which his father enjoyed.

But it was all behind him now. He was far from home in a strange place. If there was any solace to be found, at least he was not fighting. Here he was safe.

The men on the mountain continued to watch. Another convoy of trucks arrived from the north. There were nearly fifty of them and they watched as yard managers moved them into positions to be parked and then unloaded.

"It's nearly three," Charley said to the captain.

"Make contact."

He turned on the radio and tuned to the frequency for the day. Then he began to attempt to contact the 185th.

"Michael, Michael," Charley began. "This is Uriel. Come in Michael."

He paused and waited for an answer. It came immediately.

"Uriel. This is Michael. Go ahead."

Once contact was made he gave them the daily recognition signal.

"Alpha, niner, bravo, three, delta, seven, omega, niner," he said to the wing commander.

"That's a roger," the wing commander replied. "Signal received and confirmed."

Immediately Charley began to give him the target information.

"Roger," he said once more as he received the information and read it back to confirm it.

"Correct," Charley acknowledged. "That's a roger."

"How close to the target are you?" the wing commander asked.

"Just above it," Charley answered.

"We're only minutes away and we're running low on fuel. We have to drop our loads and get out of here. How much time will you need to get away?"

Charley looked at the Captain. There was no need to speak. They both knew they wouldn't have enough time.

"Go for it now," Charley answered. "All we can do is hope you're dead on target. If you're off, we've bought it."

"We'll begin our run in three minutes. Good luck."

"Roger," he said. "Over and out."

As he turned off the radio, everyone knew the position they were in. All they could do was go over the opposite side of the hill they were on and go fast. The north side of their position was part of the target area.

They moved as fast as they could. It was downhill for nearly fifteen hundred yards. If they could make it to the valley floor, they would be less than a mile from the target. As bad as that was, there still was a small mountain between them and the place where the bombs were supposed to go. That was good. All that was left was the accuracy of the Air Force and the accuracy of the information he gave them. Any error could be deadly.

Breaking through the jungle going down the side of the mountain, they were desperately trying to escape their own bombs. They were trying to get away from the attack they had directed. Then it began.

Nyugen Gnu stopped for a moment to catch his breath. He stood up and looked around at the man-made cavern in which he worked. From the ground to the ceiling it was nearly fifty feet. Across it measured several hundred feet and the ceiling was braced with enormous supports that rose up from the floor and connected to cross braces. There were probably fifty or more of them and wooden shelving used for storage was built from one to the other giving added stability. Nyugen felt safe in the man-made cave.

Then the first bomb hit.

Thirty-seven B-52's attacked, dropping their bombs directly on the valley. By that time the 545th had several million cubic yards of rock and dirt between them and the target, but the earth shook so violently they were knocked to the ground and were unable to get up and continue. Trees crashed to the ground all around them as bomb after bomb hit its target. So many were hitting and exploding it seemed as if it was one continuous explosion. Once more the temperature in the jungle began to rise and fires broke out everywhere.

Then it ended. They had survived.

Nyugen Gnu was buried under the ceiling of the man-made cavern when it collapsed.

As the eastern horizon turned a dull orange in advance of sunrise, pilots aboard the carrier U.S.S. Forrestal received their briefing. All night the A-6 Intruders and A-4 Phantom II's were loaded with ordinance for the morning mission. Five hundred-pound incendiary bombs, along with air to ground rockets, were employed.

When the sun rose an hour later, the carrier turned into the wind. It was then the jets began to take off. Their destination was Hanoi.

Ho Gnu and his wife woke before sunrise. It had been a peaceful night. Their sampan rolled gently with the river.

The river was calm and the last of the large ships had tied up before midnight. Ho was to unload those ships that day. They were French cargo ships. There were three of them and they were loaded with Russian surface-to-air missiles taken on five days before at Vladivostok. They were the latest SAM III, capable of hitting the B-52's.

Because of recent bombings and the damage at Haiphong, the cargo ships had sailed up the river to Hanoi. The eleven-acre dock area was large enough to accommodate the largest ocean going cargo vessels.

North Vietnamese radar detected the American aircraft as they came in from the sea. It was a heavy concentration. There were sixty-eight of them and they were not disguising their destination. Sirens began to sound the warning in Hanoi. Anti-aircraft and SAM batteries went on alert.

Meanwhile, the Gnu's went about their business and started for work.

The President and General Giap were taken to bunkers for safety. Considering the events of the previous days, it was only natural to assume they were the targets.

As the City of Hanoi braced itself, the westerly flying aircraft suddenly turned south just before they reached the city. There they began their run on the port facility.

"Look at that!" Commander Mark Becker said to his weapons officer. "Three of them lined up for us."

Lieutenant Bob Wolfensperger was the weapons officer on board the A-4 Phantom II.

"Christ!" he exclaimed. "No one told us about them. Who do you think they are?"

"Makes no difference to me," Becker said. "They're in the target area and that makes them targets. Let's go get them."

The anti-aircraft batteries opened up, sending up a barrage of shrapnel against the American bombers. Four aircraft swept across the dock area at a time. Commander Becker's was the first of the groups of four and was followed by sixteen more.

"Hit the ships!" Becker told his flight as they began their run.

Wolfensperger was dead on target. The five hundred-pounders hit the first ship and then the second. The other jets hit the second and the third ships as well as the C and D storage areas. As they did, major secondary explosions erupted.

"Jesus Christ!" Becker said. "What the hell were they carrying?"

"Big stuff, obviously," Wolfensperger said.

"Obviously," Becker agreed.

Mr. Gnu and his wife were just getting to work. Mr. Gnu watched the jets come in. He was next to the first ship when it exploded. He was killed instantly.

His wife was killed when the second wave flew over dropping

their bombs. The commissary took a direct hit just as she entered the building.

That morning the last two surviving members of the Gnu family were killed.

Wave after wave of jets passed over the river port, dropping their bombs and firing rockets. The three French cargo ships exploded and were in flames. The first ship rolled over on its side. The second and the third exploded and broke into pieces, sinking in the shallow harbor leaving parts of them still exposed. All hands on all three ships were lost.

The devastation was total.

As the last four of the sixty-eight Navy bombers left the target area, the entire port was engulfed in flames. Secondary explosions from rockets, ammunition, and shells sitting on the docks were going off non-stop.

The strike was a total success. All aircraft returned safely.

CHAPTER TWENTY-NINE

Ambassador Ellsworth Bunker walked from his quarters in the embassy compound to his office shortly before nine a.m. His secretary phoned him earlier informing him an angry French Ambassador was on his way to see him.

"What's this all about?" Bunker asked.

"He claims we sank three French cargo vessels, killing all hands."

"Hogwash!" Bunker roared over the phone. "Call General Westmoreland's aide and find out what we have going on today. I'll be right over."

The French Ambassador was waiting as he entered. Before he could even speak to his secretary, the Ambassador got to private business. Bunker's secretary came to his defense.

"Sir," she interrupted. "I did as you asked and I believe Mr. Komer should sit in on your meeting."

"The CIA?" he asked.

Bunker looked at her with a questioning look on his face. Immediately he feared the worst. If the CIA was going to be included, he thought, we certainly must have sunk three French ships.

"Yes, sir," she insisted. "This is a matter in which he should definitely be involved."

As she finished speaking, Robert Komer entered the office carrying a manila folder.

"Gentlemen," he said. "Are we ready to meet?"

"I guess so," Bunker said, seeming as if he was at a loss for what was going on.

All three men entered Ambassador Bunker's office. As the men sat down, the French Ambassador began an angry tirade about American jets bombing and sinking three cargo vessels flying the French flag and killing all hands.

Before Bunker was able to answer, Robert Komer spoke.

"Andre, are these the same three cargo ships that took on the new Russian SAM III missiles in Vladovostok five days ago?"

He didn't wait for an answer.

"Andre, aren't those the same SAM missiles that are capable of hitting our B-52's? Furthermore, if a mistake was made and three French ships were attacked, what were they doing in the Red River port facility inside the Hanoi city limits?"

"The French Government and you are aware that any vessel in that area is not protected. They are at risk of attack at anytime."

"You have not bombed Hanoi in almost two years. Why now?" asked the French Ambassador.

"We bombed Hanoi two days ago. We hit the General Staff Headquarters in retaliation for the attacks on this Embassy and General Westmoreland's quarters. Yesterday one of our troop convoys was attacked, so we bombed the Red River port. Your ships were in the wrong place at the wrong time and they were legitimate targets."

Bunker sat back and said nothing. He realized the situation was already under control.

"What are we supposed to say about the ships? We can't just say they disappeared," said the French ambassador.

Komer smiled.

"It happens all the time. Say they ran into a storm at sea and are missing. We'll have our Navy assist in the search.

"This was a secret transfer of war materials. No one knew where they were in the first place. Otherwise, we will be forced to release these satellite photos of your ships being loaded with Russian missiles designed to kill American flyers. That will do the French tourist industry a lot of good this year when the American press begins calling for a boycott of everything that is French. Your wine might be outlawed just like Cuban cigars."

The French Ambassador swallowed hard. He didn't like what he heard, but he had been a diplomat long enough to know there was nothing he could do.

He stood and said, "I'll pass this on to Paris. I am sure they will not be happy about these events."

"All I can say, Andre, is to keep a lid on this. The American people are ready for a change. A major incident involving an allied nation trading war goods with the enemy will only polarize the people. We're trying to wind the war down. Something like this could lead to the total destruction of North Vietnam. I don't think any of us would want that."

The French Ambassador turned and left the room.

Within the hour he had transmitted all the pertinent information to Paris. He remained objective and didn't make any recommendations. He did understand what Komer meant. In his heart he truly did understand.

Once he was gone Bunker said it was time they spring into action.

"All we've done is delay this thing. Once Paris gets hold of this, it could easily turn into a full-blown crisis. We should inform Washington the position we took and our success with it."

Komer agreed.

"By the way," Bunker said. "You were magnificent when you produced those satellite photos. No one else, not even the Russians, have that capability."

Komer laughed and said, "We'd better meet with Westmoreland and Abrams. Our stories should be the same."

While the four men sat to have lunch, Pairs woke to the news of the American bombing. DeGaulle, the seventy-seven year old French President, was outraged. He called for an immediate meeting with Prime Minister Georges Pompidou.

"This is an outrage!" he screamed. "The Americans have purposefully attacked French ships. This is an outright act of war and we have established ourselves as a neutral nation in this conflict. They are forcing us into this war!"

Pompidou watched the old man's face. He'd known him for many years and believed eventually reason would overtake his anger.

"Charles," he asked. "How can we claim to the world our neutrality when we have openly opposed the presence of American forces in Vietnam? How can we make that claim while ships under our flag deliver weapons of war to the American's enemy?

"A case could be made against us that we are indirectly killing American soldiers by our actions. If anyone has committed an act of war against the other, it is us against the Americans. We have been profiteers in our self-proclaimed neutrality."

DeGaulle considered Pompidou's words. They did not quell his fury. He was still outraged at the loss of French lives and the destruction of the ships.

"Then what am I to do?" he asked.

"What do you believe you can do?" Pompidou asked back. "Do you want to break diplomatic ties with the Americans? Should we expel the Ambassador?

"We could attack their bases in Germany and England and declare war on them. Should we plunge headlong on a path from which there is no return, a path that can only undo all the good you have done?

"Tell me, Charles. Is that what you want?" asked Pompidou.

"No! No! No!" the President said. "It's not what I want. The Americans must pay for what they've done. I must do something."

Pompidou smiled.

"There is something," he said.

"What?" DeGaulle asked.

"The American dollar," he answered. "We can attack them through their own dollar. It is better than a military adventure. It is hurting them where we can hurt them most."

"How can we do that?" DeGaulle asked.

He did not understand the financial intricacies of the world economy. He was a warrior. He was a war hero and a leader. He was not an economist like Pompidou.

"Charles," the Prime Minister began. "All these years you have guided our republic so skillfully and you have never understood the true secret to our success."

DeGaulle was puzzled.

"You expelled American and NATO forces from our soil. You kept England out of the Common Market and opposed the direct threat to our productivity. Actually, the true secret to our productivity has been the American dollar."

"How is that?" DeGaulle asked.

"Every American dollar is backed by twenty-five cents in gold. The French franc is backed by the American dollar. The price of gold is determined in American dollars. Today an ounce of gold is six dollars and seventy-five cents in American dollars. Now follow this.

"We can begin to convert our American dollars to gold. We will devalue our currency exactly seventy-five percent. In doing that we will drive up the price of gold and increase the value of our gold reserves.

"If we can start a world-wide run on gold, we will be attacking the American dollar and reap enormous profits at the same time.

"We can do this! We will be warring on America without ever firing a shot."

DeGaulle was old, but he caught on immediately.

"How high do you think gold will go before the Americans can get off the gold standard?" Pompidou asked the President.

He did not wait for him to answer. "Forty-five dollars an ounce? Fifty? Who can say? The gold market will go crazy."

DeGaulle did some longhand calculations and began to laugh. As he began, he laughed harder and harder.

"We devalue our currency and for every franc we have today it will take four to buy the same amount tomorrow. How long will it take for gold to get to $50?" DeGaulle asked.

"Two weeks," the Prime Minister answered.

"So in two weeks our treasury will be worth thirty-four times more than it is worth today. Then we can hold half of our gold in reserve and convert the other half back into American dollars at $45 an ounce and make one franc worth exactly one American dollar. We win our war in two weeks without ever firing a shot."

"Yes, Mr. President."

DeGaulle began to laugh again.

"Send a secret letter of protest to Washington through their Department of State. Make the wording angry and fill it with the usual threats. At the same time, start turning all our dollars into gold."

CHAPTER THIRTY

MARCH 5, 1968

The French wasted no time. Their American dollars were held in three New York banks. As Pompidou's assistants prepared a strong letter of protest, he personally woke their New York financial representatives.

There was a six-hour time difference between Paris and New York. He made no apology for the time of the call. He was direct and instructed each representative to convert all French-held American dollars to gold the moment the doors opened for business.

"Every single dollar," Pompidou repeated. "Do I make myself clear?"

In all three instances each man said he understood. They didn't ask why. Each man rose immediately and prepared, just as a soldier prepared to go into a dawn attack. And in reality, that is exactly what it was.

France was declaring war.

Within hours the French were poised to spring into action. The French Ambassador in Washington was awakened by a phone call from the Prime Minister. The letter of protest was already in the Embassy decoding room and Georges Pompidou instructed the Ambassador how he wanted the matter handled.

"Phone Secretary Rusk. Wake him if you must. Stress the importance of the situation. Let him believe we are preparing to take strong measures."

"What sort of measures?" the Ambassador asked.

"It makes no difference," Pompidou said. "Use your imagination. All you are is a diversion. Keep him occupied with this matter until ten a.m. your time."

"Yes, sir," the Ambassador said.

"What's going on with the French?" Tom Swanson asked his CIA contact, Miles Wilson.

"We've had five encrypted calls originating from the Prime Minister himself. Four of them woke people. Three were in New York and one in Washington. Then there was a coded message to their cryptography section in the Embassy."

Tom Swanson was a U.S. Information Agency monitor at Fort Meade, Maryland. He was the liaison to the CIA and supervised twenty others who worked the graveyard shift monitoring overseas phone calls coming into the country. He gave them a heads up when unusual traffic occurred and when necessary, he would alert other parts of the government.

"I don't know for sure. The scuttlebutt is we bombed three of their ships outside of Hanoi yesterday," Wilson replied.

"How bad?"

"Bad. All hands were lost and the ships sank."

"So this is going to be a day of protests and letters. They'll do the U.N. and the President will have to apologize for this unfortunate situation," said Swanson

"You got it," Miles Wilson said.

Tom Swanson decided the situation was nothing to bother anyone else with. He considered the French activity routine in view of what happened.

London picked up on the French activity, too. They were able to intercept the calls to the French financial brokers. They understood the true scope of what was unfolding.

Prime Minister Harold Wilson woke up the British Ambassador in Washington. Immediately, Sir Patrick Dean realized the seriousness of the situation.

In November the pound was devalued from $2.80 to $2.40. It was a move they were forced to make when the French blocked their entry into the Common Market. Had they not acted decisively, millions of British jobs would have been lost and their economy thrown into a state of chaos.

"What do you think they are doing?" Wilson asked his old friend.

"It seems obvious," Sir Patrick said. "They're attacking the American dollar and the American gold reserves."

"But why?" Wilson asked. "Why would they purposely set out to disrupt the economy of the free world?

"They could throw the world economy into chaos and give the

Russians the opening they have been waiting for. This could start World War III."

Sir Patrick was a realist. He may not have liked what the results were and he probably wanted to believe that they couldn't even happen. Still, he faced the situation square in the face and told his friend what he believed.

"The French are a nation of whores," he said matter-of-factly. "And Charles DeGaulle is the largest.

"The French are out for themselves and the rest of us be damned! They don't care who they trade with. If it is not us or the Americans, then it will be the Russians or the Chinese. They see this as an opportunity to control the gold reserves of the world."

"What can we do to protect ourselves?" Wilson asked.

"Do the same as the French and beat them at their own God damned game."

"But the pound is backed by the American dollar," Wilson said.

"It could easily become every man for himself before this is over," Sir Patrick told his friend. "We'll have to back our own currency with our own gold reserves instead of American dollars."

"If it comes to that, we are facing an international disaster," the Prime Minister said. "We cannot be a party to that."

Wilson became silent.

"I'll have to think this through," he said. "I'll call you back."

"If the French move, we'll have to go, too. You'd better get everyone on your end ready."

As their conversation ended Tom Swanson once again communicated with Miles Wilson.

"Something is up. Now we have Harold Wilson calling Sir Patrick Dean. We have another Prime Minister of one of our allies waking up the Ambassador to the United States. Right now Sir Patrick is waking his staff for a meeting in forty-five minutes. The French staff is meeting at this moment."

"What were they talking about?" Miles asked.

"They were using scramblers. It will take an hour to break it and convert it to something understandable."

"How about the French?"

"Same thing," Swanson answered.

"Our French translator is out sick. I was going to wait for the day shift, but now I think this is getting serious. Who do you have that can do French?" Swanson asked.

"At this hour? No one.

"This is more than what we originally thought. And I can't notify anyone until we know what they are doing," Miles said. "Get back to me as soon as you know something. Then I'll pass it on."

In the meantime, the American Ambassador to France was summoned to the Prime Minister's office. He was told about the sinking of French ships while they were docked at the Red River port. A formal letter of protest was conveyed to him.

While that was happening, Ambassador Bunker notified the Department of State in Washington. Secretary Rusk was awakened and informed of the situation. In turn, he made an unsuccessful attempt to wake President Johnson.

"I'm sorry, Mr. Secretary," Walter told him. "Mrs. Johnson told me in no uncertain terms that the President was not to be disturbed unless the Russians were attacking with nuclear missiles and it was an all out war. Unless that is the case, I'll tell him you called."

"What time are you to wake him?" the Secretary of State asked.

"Six-thirty," the old man answered.

"Clear me at the gate. I'll be in the Oval Office at six-thirty five."

"Yes, sir," the old man said.

No sooner did Rusk hang up and his phone rang again. It was the French Ambassador requesting they meet.

"I can't see you until ten," he said, giving no indication he already knew what he had on his mind.

"We must meet earlier," the Ambassador said.

"Impossible," Secretary Rusk said. "Ten is the earliest I can see you."

"This is important," the Ambassador pressed. "We must meet. We must meet now!"

"I'm sorry," Rusk said holding the phone away from his ear. "I'm on my way out right now. Even if our two countries were on the verge of war, which I am sure we are not, I could not meet with you. I can have Undersecretary Katzenback meet with you if it is so important that you speak with someone. "

"No," the French Ambassador said. "I will meet with you at ten."

At six a.m. Henry Fowler, Secretary of the Treasury, was awakened. James Duesenberry was on the phone.

"Henry," he began. "At nine a.m. this morning the French are going to convert all their American dollars to gold."

"What?" Fowler asked. "Why?"

"I don't know why, but I know they are going to do it."

"How?" he asked.

"Morris Wiesenberg phoned me minutes ago. He's one of the three registered agents for the French government. He's been instructed to convert the dollars he controls to gold. Fortunately, he is more loyal to us than the French."

"Thank God!" Fowler said. "This could be a real disaster for the monetary system. I'll phone Rusk. He should inform the President."

"Yes," Duesenberry agreed. "I'll stand by in case you need anything else."

"Good idea," Fowler said. "Have Wiesenberg stand by, too. See if you can get the names of the other two agents."

Secretary Fowler hung up and immediately phoned Dean Rusk. Rusk was already in route to the White House so Fowler had White House communications reach him in his limousine and patch him through.

"What's so important?" Rusk asked.

"The French are going to make a run on the gold supply using their American dollars at nine a.m. today."

Rusk was silent as he digested the information that was just supplied to him.

"Did you hear me?" Fowler asked.

"Yes," Rusk answered.

"Come to the Oval Office right away. I'm meeting with the President at 6:35 and you should sit in with your information. We have some major events unfolding."

"Okay," Fowler said. "I'll get moving right now. I'll get there as soon as I can."

When the Secretary of State arrived at the White House, he was expected but was asked to wait for the President. He wasn't taken to the Oval Office. Instead, he was left waiting in the hallway. He waited until seven when Secretary Fowler arrived. At exactly seven a Marine guard came for both mean. Instead of taking them to the Oval Office, they were escorted to the Cabinet Room.

As they entered, they immediately saw the President. Then they both recognized Ramsey Clark, Cyrus Vance, and Gardner Ackley.

"Good morning," the President said. "Please take a seat."

Dean Rusk was taken totally by surprise. He believed he was the messenger. Now it appeared he was only a participant.

"Thank you for being so prompt," the President said as if he had summoned them.

"Our command in Vietnam bombed the Red River dock facility in Hanoi this morning. In doing so, they destroyed three French cargo vessels loaded with Russian SAM III missiles. All hands were aboard at the time and all were lost."

The President ignored the loss of life. He went on to the heart of the matter.

"The Russian SAM III is a new generation of missile able to hit our B-52's at a previously unreachable altitude. Those missiles had to be destroyed.

"Now the French are going to make an attack on our gold reserves by converting all their American dollars to gold. They currently have twenty-nine billion dollars. Converted to gold, that is 828 million ounces of gold. That would deplete our gold reserves by eighty-two percent.

"Simply speaking, the American dollar would be worth eighteen cents and the western monetary systems would collapse," the President told them.

"Now, gentlemen. What do we do?" he asked.

Cyrus Vance spoke first and asked, "How and when will the French convert their dollars?"

"Their monetary agents in New York have been instructed to do so beginning at nine this morning," the President answered.

"Who are these agents?" Vance asked.

"We don't know," the President replied. "I have the FBI working on that right now."

"Mr. President," Dean Rusk said. "Henry spoke with one of the three agents at six this morning."

"Yes," Fowler said. "I didn't speak with him directly. Jim Duesenberry spoke to Morris Wiesenberg, one of the three agents. He is getting us the names of the other two."

"These are American citizens?" the President asked.

"It seems they are, sir," he said. "By now Jim probably has their names."

"Get them, Henry," the President said. "Use the phone over there."

Johnson looked at Ramsey Clark and spoke.

"I want all three men picked up and detained before they can begin their transactions."

Clark was taken back.

"Mr. President," he protested. " Call it what you want, but we are in fact arresting these men without warrants. What are the charges and for what reason? Are we suspending due process?"

"God damn it!" Johnson screamed, banging his fist on the table. "This is an attack on the United States by a foreign power. To hell with due process! If I say pick the bastards up and detain them, then do it! You figure out the justification. Just get them and get them fast."

Ramsey Clark was an attorney, but he was an American, too. If the President of the United States of America wanted three citizens arrested or detained, he would find the grounds to arrest them.

"We'd better get the FBI to handle this," Ramsey said.

"Yes," Johnson agreed. "Call Hoover at home. Tell him this is a matter of national security."

He paused and then he continued, "And immediately freeze all French accounts in this country. I don't want them to be able to touch a penny."

"Yes, sir," Clark said.

He went to the phone and contacted J. Edgar Hoover, Director of the FBI.

Fowler produced the other two names. "Bernard Schwartz and Allen Stern," he said.

"Wiesenberg has cooperated fully with us and is prepared to be taken into protective custody," he added.

He handed the names of all three men, their firms and the banks that controlled the accounts to Ramsey Clark. Ramsey Clark relayed the information to the Director of the FBI.

"These men must be taken into custody no later than 8:30 a.m. before the banks open," Clark said.

Clark listened and said, "Charges?

"Espionage," he said without hesitation. "Arrest them for suspicion of espionage. Hold them and they are to speak to no one. They are to have no lawyers, no calls, nothing. I want them cut off from the world."

The phone next to the President rang. Gardner Ackley answered it.

"Just a second," he said.

"Sir Patrick is outside."

"Have him come in," the President said.

As Sir Patrick Dean entered the room, Ramsey Clark ended his call and returned to the table. No one rose and no one exchanged pleasantries. Lyndon Johnson looked up at the British Ambassador and told him to take a seat. It was an order and not a request. Then as the Ambassador sat down, he began.

"This morning the USIA and the CIA intercepted and decoded a conversation between you and Harold Wilson. The conversation was about Great Britain converting American dollars to gold. I believe the phrase used was something to the effect you said it was every man for himself.

"You said that, didn't you?"

Sir Patrick didn't answer. He looked the President in the eye and said nothing.

"Let me tell you," the President continued. "If Harold Wilson, Queen Elizabeth, the Beetles, or even the Rolling Stones convert one American dollar to twenty-five cents in gold, the United States of America will look upon that action as an act of war.

"You tell that sniveling bastard Wilson he'd better watch himself. The CIA has a file on him and half of his closest people and if we put it in the wrong hands, it will be the end of his government. What we have on him would make Christine Keelor look like a Girl Scout and Profumo like a monk."

"Do I make myself clear?" the President asked coldly.

"Yes, Mr. President," Sir Patrick Dean said.

"Good. Now convey the message to your Prime Minister."

Sir Patrick Dean stood and left the room.

Secretary Rusk looked at the President in disbelief. Cyrus Vance broke out into laughter.

"Now that's what I call diplomacy," Vance said.

"The hell with those limey sons-of-bitches," the President growled.

"We've bailed their asses out in two wars, supported the pound, and sucked a hind tit in trade so they could stabilize unemployment. Now the fact they even consider being opportunistic at our expense is beyond belief."

"Sir," Henry Fowler interrupted.

"Yes?" the President answered.

"Freezing French assets in the U.S. will account for 85% of the dollars they control. We have no way of stopping them with the dollars in banks abroad."

"How much is that?" he asked.

"Just over four billion," Fowler answered.

"If they convert to gold, what will happen?" the President asked.

"Conservatively, by mid-March gold will be trading at forty-five dollars an ounce," Fowler answered.

The President looked at Ackley. "Do you concur?"

"Yes, sir, I do."

"What do you suggest?"

Fowler was definite in his answer.

"Revoke the gold cover as soon as possible."

Johnson thought. He closed his eyes and leaned back in his chair.

"Unless I invoke the War Powers Act, something like that has to go through Congress. We're going to have a lot of opposition on both sides of the aisle to that. And if I use War Powers, we must have a valid explanation, something they will buy."

Lyndon Johnson looked down at the table. He thought for a moment. Then he picked up the phone.

"Schedule a luncheon here at the White House today at noon. Call Speaker of the House McCormack, Wilbur Mills, and Gerald Ford. You had also better call Senators Fulbright, yes, you heard me, and Dirksen, Mansfield, and Morse. Also, ask the Vice-President to attend. Yes, noon."

He looked up at the men in the room. "Thank you for coming.

"I'm sorry I stole your thunder, Dean," he said to the Secretary of State. "We didn't have any time."

"How did you find out?" he asked the President.

Johnson smiled.

"Thank you for coming," he answered.

He picked up the phone once more. "Send in Secretary Clifford."

Within moments the President and the Secretary of Defense were alone in the room. The President began.

"Our generals in Saigon have placed us in a bad situation."

"I heard about the French ships," Clark Clifford said.

"Good," Johnson said. "Then we can cut through the bullshit.

"Where do they get off bombing targets I personally placed off limits?"

"I don't know," Clifford answered.

"Well," the President said. "We're going to damn well find out! Call Westmoreland and Abrams at home. I want both of them here in the White House on Friday. I want them here and I want answers."

"I'm sorry about this, Mr. President," Clark Clifford said.

Johnson looked up at him and told him he was excused. When he was gone, he picked up the phone one more time.

"Come in now," he said.

Almost instantly Henry Townsend appeared.

"Did you hear it all?" he asked.

"Yes, sir," he said.

"Good. Thank you very much. The extra time probably saved us. Now we will deal with General DeGaulle."

Then the President thought of something.

"Henry?" he asked. "How difficult would it be for your spooks to interrupt trading on the Gold Market today?"

Henry smiled.

"When do you want it to happen and for how long?" he asked.

"Until further notice. Crash the system before it opens."

"Consider it done," he said and smiled as he left the room.

It was three-thirty in the afternoon when Prime Minister Pompidou phoned President DeGaulle and reported the bad news.

"Our agents have been taken into custody and our American assets are frozen."

"What?" DeGaulle demanded. "This is an outrage."

The British Prime Minister had been likewise informed an hour before and his reaction was the same.

"A total outrage!" Harold Wilson voiced to his Ambassador.

"Who does Johnson think he is? Maybe we'll tell the Americans to take their bases out like the French did. What will he say then?"

"I believe, Harold," Sir Patrick said. "He will remove them and in a very crude way tell us to kiss his ass. We would be the losers. We would lose the annual income that we depend upon."

Wilson thought for a moment and then resigned himself to quiet acceptance of the situation.

DeGaulle, however, did not.

"We'll convert all the dollars we hold outside the United States. We'll buy dollars on margin, convert them and drive up gold on the London market anyway. We'll begin immediately."

While DeGaulle imagined saying 'immediately' would get things rolling, for him immediately meant two days.

That day, March 5, 1968, for unexplained reasons the Gold Exchange closed at 3:35 p.m. London time. The following day, March 6th, an IRA bomb threat kept the exchange closed the entire day.

The French were precluded from beginning their campaign until March 8th.

In the meantime, President Johnson gained two days.

His luncheon on March 5th was received well. House Ways and

Means Chairman Wilbur Mills would begin the legislative process.

The price of gold held at $35 and ounce until March 12th when it began to rise. On March 12th when it hit $44.36 an ounce, the United States of America revoked its pledge to cover dollars to gold. They did it retroactively back to March 5th.

Faced with a worldwide monetary crisis, British banks closed in order to stem the rush on gold.

DeGaulle had overextended the French economy and was forced to devalue the franc and lost face in the eyes of the world.

During that period of time, March 6 to March 14, 1968, the Wednesday morning newspapers reported advertised specials on pork loins at forty-five cents a pound. They would also report that Richard Nixon pledged a Republican president would end the war.

Eugene McCarthy, a Democratic candidate for President, placed his peace candidacy on the line before the Minnesota Democrats in three thousand precinct caucuses.

The Allegheny River was clogged with ice and 55,000 members of the Glass Blowers Union, on strike for eight months, asked for more meetings with management.

Not a single newspaper in the United States or any news service in the world reported the freezing of French assets, the sinking of French ships, or that three American citizens who were agents for the French were arrested.

Thursday's papers reported forty-nine American lives lost, forty-four Marines and five Air Force crewmen, killed when the VC downed a C-123 at Khe Sanh with .50 caliber machine gun fire.

President Johnson announced he would not enter state primaries and forty-two teachers were arrested while walking picket lines in Pittsburgh.

President Johnson asked Congress for aid for the American Indians and the first reporters entered Hue. They reported it looked like a city that bled to death.

The newspapers and the wire services failed to report the 545th was ordered farther north into Laos to the Plaine Des Jarres. There was no account given of how they covered nearly two hundred miles on foot in enemy territory and were in position on the March 16th to transmit data for a series of new strikes.

While they were moving into position, the B-52s were grounded for repairs and the installation of new electronic countermeasures designed to evade and defeat the Russian SAM III missiles.

The papers from Friday, Saturday, and Sunday were filled with news from Vietnam that was several days to a week old. They reported U.S. losses mounting and told of twenty-one miners who were trapped in a Calumet, Louisiana salt mine being found dead.

On Monday the GOP leaders sent Governor Nelson Rockefeller a letter urging him to announce his candidacy for President. An Oregon prison riot was quelled and Robert Kennedy said he would not run for President.

St. Bonaventure, 23-0 in basketball, was slated to meet North Carolina on Friday. The men of the 545th had already covered half the distance to their objective and the airmen from the 185th Bomb Wing were on R&R in Honolulu.

On Tuesday Senator Fulbright and Dean Rusk clashed openly during a Senate hearing on Vietnam. Eugene McCarthy charged Lyndon Johnson has cast a pall of fear over the American people by his Vietnamese policies.

In Poland students battled police. Teachers in Pittsburgh returned to class after an eleven-day strike. It was not reported that General William Westmoreland finally arrived in Washington five days late. However, when he did arrive and announced his arrival to the White House Staff, the President ignored him and made him wait for a meeting.

Wednesday's papers reported the results of the New Hampshire primary. Eugene McCarthy ran strong, receiving 39% of the votes on the Democratic ballot. Richard Nixon overwhelmingly won the Republican side. A massive storm swept across the north.

That day General Westmoreland met with the President of the United States at 10 a.m. in the Cabinet Room. Clark Clifford, Dean Rusk, General Wheeler, Chairman of the Joint Chiefs of Staff, and Dick Helms, Director of the CIA were also in attendance. At the meeting Lyndon Johnson fired Westmoreland and promoted him to a position in the Pentagon.

General Abrams was to take over the command in Vietnam.

CHAPTER THIRTY-ONE

MARCH 19, 1968

Following the meeting, General Westmoreland was excused and the National Security Council met. The subject was the Plaines des Jarres. They immediately referred to a meeting of the NSC nearly five years before. General Wheeler read the following into the record.

"Mr. President," he began.

"Summary Record of the 511th National Security Council Meeting

"Washington, April 10, 1963, noon.

"Mr. McCone read a summary of current intelligence on Laos, noting that we were dependent almost entirely for information from Kong Le sources. Therefore, we should take the information he had summarized with some caution. Under Secretary Harriman was asked by Acting Secretary Ball to present the State Department's recommendations.

"Mr. Harriman said he agreed with the analysis which Mr. McCone had presented. He noted that the Pathet Lao forces had been unsuccessful so far in undermining the Kong Le neutralist forces.

"In an effort to bring to an end the hostilities in the Plaines des Jarres and to maintain Kong Le's position, Mr. Harriman recommended that we:

a. Continue to supply Kong Le forces in the Plaines and Meo tribesmen in the area surrounding the Plaines.

b. Encourage the British to put pressure on the Soviet Union in the hope that the Russian Ambassador in Vientiane will tell the North Vietnamese and the Pathet Lao to stop the attacks on neutralist forces.

c. Put pressure on the French to take a firmer stand, including instructing their military mission in the area to support Kong Le and Phoumi forces.

d. Continue detailed planning for the reintroduction of U.S. military forces into Thailand if it is decided to so act in the future.

e. Consider whether at a later time we should openly use Phoumi forces. Mr. Harriman reported that the ICC would be visiting the Plaines today and apparently will take further action to halt the fighting. Secretary Rusk, from Paris, recommended that we ask the King of Laos to commit his prestige in an effort to halt the Pathet Lao attacks on neutralists. Mr. Harriman said the King was a very weak reed and probably would not be useful in this situation.

"A proposed draft letter to Khrushchev on Laos was not presented to the President for consideration because of developments which indicated that fighting might be now under control.

"The President indicated his support of the actions recommended by Mr. Harriman. He commented on the fact that the ICC would be visiting the Plaines des Jarres and that supplies were getting through to Kong Le forces. He asked Admiral Anderson for the details of these U.S. shipments. Admiral Anderson listed the ammunition, supplies, and food that had been flown in to Kong Le forces in the past few days.

"Mr. Harriman recommended that the discussion of Vietnam be omitted in view of recent developments which indicated that the problem discussed in the State paper was not as urgent as had appeared earlier."

"Mr. President," General Wheeler said. "Those efforts all met with failure. It is time to bomb the Paines des Jarres and put an end to all of this. Five years have passed and the North Vietnamese are using this as a staging area for forays and assaults on our forces using the Ho Chi Minh trail."

Lyndon Johnson sat silent. He knew what was in the works and said nothing.

In the meantime, the 545th moved into position. They moved past the ancient and giant earthenware jars. Charley marveled at them. They gave the area their name, The Plains of the Jars. The 545th crossed the plains. They continued to the border with North Vietnam.

General Wheeler continued his synopsis of the area.

"In violation of, yet somewhat protected by the neutrality of Laos accorded at Geneva in a 14-nation protocol conference July 23, 1962, the North Vietnamese and supporting Communist insurgent group, the Pathet Lao, lost no time in building strategic strongholds of defense in Northern Laos and establishing a steady flow of manpower and material to their revolutionary forces in South Vietnam via the Ho Chi Minh Trail on the eastern border of the Laotian panhandle.

"As a result, the Royal Lao sought help from the U.S. in stopping both initiatives. It was strategically important to do so, although every initiative had to be cleared through the U.S. Ambassador at Vientiane, so that the delicate balance of 'look-the-other-way-neutrality' engaged in by the nations involved, including China, could be preserved.

"Defense of non-communist activity in Laos generally falls into three categories:

1) U.S. Army and CIA's bolstering of the Meo (Hmong) army led by General Vang Pao;

2) Strategic U.S. Air Force bombing initiatives on the Ho Chi Minh Trail (Operations Commando Hunt, Steel Tiger, etc.);

3) U.S. Air Force bombing initiatives in northern Laos (Operation Barrel Roll, etc.) both against Communist strongholds there, and in support of the Royal Lao and Gen. Vang Pao's army."

Again, Lyndon Johnson said nothing.

As he sat silently, the 545th established contact with the enemy. Their target was COSVN, the Central Office for South Vietnam head-quarters. It was the central supply depot and staging area for men and materials destined for South Vietnam. This was the beginning of the Ho Chi Minh Trail. This was the head of the snake.

The supply depot sprawled across the Plaines for miles. They had two days to plot the extent and prepare detailed information on anti-aircraft defenses. Once Archangel did its job, then the F-105 Thunderchiefs based at Ubon Air Base in Thailand would be ordered in to finish off what was left. The Air Force knew it had a mission. The destination was secret. They wasted no time.

Sergeants Dewberry and Hayes took the southern perimeter, while Sergeants Campbell and Tankersley took the northern most points. They maintained radio contact and sent back information to Sergeant Reed who was plotting everything on a map. Captain Van Name oversaw the operation and kept a careful record of the various units and materials being observed. While that was happening, the rest of the unit was doing reconnaissance for SAM missile sites.

While the men on the ground were accomplishing all of this, the meeting in the Cabinet Room ended without any resolution. Lyndon Johnson remained silent. He and Henry Townsend had already identified this one attack as Operation Rolling Thunder.

"Mr. President," Townsend said. "This attack will be unlike the previous ones. Instead of coming in as a concentrated wave as we have in the past, the B-52 F's will come in single file, each dropping its load on its own designated target. In that way we will have maximum effect and deal the enemy the greatest possible amount of devastation short of using nuclear weapons."

The President listened attentively as Townsend began to detail the targets for him.

The first day produced a wealth of information. The area was well protected. The North Vietnamese had hardened defenses and it was obvious they were there to stay. Carefully each site was mapped, identified as to type, and then given a coded tag number so it could be referred to with ease when the damage assessment was done.

At the end of the first day Charley raised his radio antenna and began transmitting to a CIA listening post in Thailand. From there it was relayed to Washington and Anderson Air Base in Guam where the B-52s were based.

The second day gave up even more information. In fact, it produced so much new information regarding enemy troop strength and the different types of weapons available to them, the decision was made to keep the 545th on post for an additional three days.

Their attention was directed to the east and the roads that were used to transport materials from North Vietnam. Once more they began a new mapping process. As they did, they identified key targets such as bridges and tunnels. They were going after the supply line and they were going to knock it out.

For five days the 545th remained undetected. Finally, just before midnight on March 24th they were told to begin back to a location near Paksane on the border with Thailand. There choppers would meet them and take them out.

The B-52s were on their way and they had just crossed a tributary of the Mekong River when the attack began. As the 545th made its way south, they were especially careful. They were in enemy territory and they had to arrive at their destination undetected.

And as the attacks began the North Vietnamese had an idea there was a possibility American troops were operating around them. They began to search for them.

In an effort to evade the enemy the 545th divided itself into smaller parts all heading for the same destination.

Mater Sergeant Dewberry led the group of four Charley was in
along with Billy Campbell. It was slow going, but as they were about
to cross a ridge several miles from the extraction point, they encoun-
tered a unit of North Vietnamese Regulars.

There were perhaps a dozen of them and instantly they were
involved in a firefight. They attacked with small weapons fire and
Charley Hayes responded with the Browning automatic rifle. The
results were devastating. Five of the enemy fell allowing the team to
move away.

They were fighting on the ridge of some smaller hills, foothills
to the larger mountains that were to their west. It was early morning,
perhaps four a.m., and the full moon was sitting atop the mountains in
the distance. Below the ridge were the plains leading to their destination

As quickly as they had attacked, the North Vietnamese broke off,
allowing the four men to descend the hills to the farmlands below.
They had no way of knowing they were walking into more battle-
hardened North Vietnamese soldiers. Dewberry was the N.C.O.I.C.
and led them into the elephant grass toward the landing zone where
the choppers were to pick them up.

It rained hours before and the grass was wet. The smell of dampness hung over the lowlands and as they started across, their uniforms
picked up the moisture from the tall grasses. As they reached the center of the grassy area, the trailing North Vietnamese once more opened
fire.

The four men returned fire and called to the rest of their A-team
for help. As the answer came in promising help within ten minutes, the
larger force struck them head on. Somehow the four men fought and
evaded the superior forces.

Dewberry had them divide into two groups of two and work to
each flank as the two North Vietnamese forces met with one another.
This was an ambush tactic the men had used before with great success.
The superior forces would join together and then become pinned down
by a deadly crossfire and barrage of hand grenades.

Each group was to station itself at a precise location to avoid placing itself in the line of the other's fire. The key group, led by Dewberry,
would open fire first, firing for ten seconds.

Five seconds later, the second group, Charley Reed and Billy
Campbell, would then open fire.

264

THE FIRST TERRORIST ACT

Fifteen seconds later Dewberry and Hayes would throw hand grenades into the enemy's midst to be followed by the second group doing the same thing.

Fifteen seconds after that both groups, aware of the other's exact location, would move in and finish off any survivors.

While their combined timed attacks were deadly, the battle-hardened North Vietnamese Regulars fought back and attacked in the directions of the flanking ambushes.

Charley and Billy dove to the ground, crawling into the cover of thicker grasses. The dampness nearly choked them as they both lay clutching the earth.

Charley could hear the sound of bayonets sweeping back and forth as the enemy moved through the grass searching for them. And then as he nearly choked on his fear, he rose and fired point blank into the faces of four men who searched for him.

To his left he caught the shadow of two men with the full moon at their backs. Charley wheeled and fired again. In a fraction of an instant as they both fell to the ground dead, Charley realized he had killed Hayes and Dewberry.

The North Vietnamese Regulars opened fire. At the same time and to his right the rest of the arriving A-team rose and shot the enemy riflemen. Billy Campbell and Charley both dropped to the ground, afraid the arriving American soldiers might fire upon them.

The silence of the night returned and was unbroken. Charley wanted to cry out, hoping he hadn't fired on his friends. But he knew he had, and he had done so with his usual deadly accuracy.

No one asked any questions. They assumed the enemy had taken out Hayes and Dewberry. They carried their bodies with them and met the arriving choppers. Charley Reed kept the secret of what happened to himself.

The following day the F-105 Thunderchiefs began pounding what remained of the headquarters area. They attacked what the B-52's missed and they began taking out the bridges and roads leading to the staging area. The 545th stood down and was replaced in the field by A-437.

In Washington the President was treated to photos of the successful bombing missions. And while he smiled to himself, Henry Townsend and John Hughes had to deal with a problem. The problem was the surviving members of the 545th.

CHAPTER THIRTY-TWO

WASHINGTON, DC
MARCH 30, 1968

Henry Townsend left the problem of the 545th to John Hughes. He was conferring with Colonel Ladd's attaché as to upcoming missions. They were scheduled to do reconnaissance into North Vietnam the night of April 2nd. They would be scouting out an enemy ammunition dump near Xom Bong, twenty miles north of the DMZ.

"Perfect," Hughes said to himself.

He picked up the phone and called a friend of his in the French embassy.

As he made his phone call, Henry Townsend was meeting with the President. The President was troubled.

"Vietnam is killing us," he said to Townsend. "No other question so preoccupies our people. No other dream so absorbs the 250 million human beings who live in that part of the world. No other goal motivates American policy in Southeast Asia.

"For years, representatives of our Government and others have traveled the world seeking to find a basis for peace talks. I've tried to bomb them to the peace table."

"And you've done a damn good job of it, too," Townsend said to the President.

"Yes," he said. "We've dealt him blow after blow and I have offered to end it all. I've continually made the offer that the United States would stop its bombardment of North Vietnam when that would lead promptly to productive discussions, and that we would assume that North Vietnam would not take military advantage of our restraint. It hasn't worked.

"Their attack during the Tet holidays failed to achieve its principal objectives. It did not collapse the elected government of South Vietnam or shatter its army as the Communists had hoped.

"It did not produce a general uprising among the people of the cities as they had predicted. Hell, the Communists were unable to maintain control of any of the more than thirty cities that they attacked. And they took very heavy casualties. Look at the loss of men they had.

"But they did compel us to move certain forces from the countryside into the cities. They caused widespread disruption and suffering. Their attacks, and the battles that followed, made refugees of half a million human beings. They are, it appears, trying to make 1968 the year of decision in South Vietnam, the year that brings, if not final victory or defeat, at least a turning point in the struggle."

Henry Townsend sat back. He could see the man's mind working. He could see how troubled he was over the war and the fact that he was unable to end it. He listened as the President continued to speak.

"This much is clear," the President said. "If they do mount another round of heavy attacks, they will not succeed in destroying the fighting power of South Vietnam and its allies. But tragically, this is also clear. Many men on both sides of the struggle will be lost. A nation that has already suffered twenty years of warfare will suffer once again. Armies on both sides will take new casualties. And the war will go on.

"There is no need for this to be so," he said. "There is no need to delay the talks that could bring an end to this long and this bloody war."

"What do you propose doing?" Henry Townsend asked.

"I'm going to renew the offer I made last August to stop the bombardment of North Vietnam. Those damn Generals blew it for us.

"I am going to ask that talks begin promptly, that they be serious talks on the substance of peace. I am going to ask that during those talks Hanoi will not take advantage of our restraint. I am prepared to move immediately toward peace through negotiations. I am going to offer that this action will lead to early talks and I am taking the first step to deescalate the conflict. We will reduce substantially the present level of hostilities.

"I'm going to do it and begin doing so unilaterally, and at once.

"Tomorrow I am going to order our aircraft and our naval vessels to make no attacks on North Vietnam, except in the area north of the demilitarized zone where the continuing enemy buildup directly threatens allied forward positions and where the movements of their troops and supplies are clearly related to that threat.

"The area in which we are stopping our attacks includes almost ninety percent of North Vietnam's population, and most of its territory. There will be no attacks around the principal populated areas, or in the food-producing areas of North Vietnam."

Townsend couldn't believe what he was hearing. This President had just completed nearly a month of the most deadly secret bombing in the history of warfare and now he wanted to talk peace. What a strategy!

"Even this very limited bombing of the North could come to an early end," Johnson said. "It could if our restraint is matched by restraint in Hanoi. But I cannot in good conscience stop all bombing so long as to do so would immediately and directly endanger the lives of our men and our allies. Whether a complete bombing halt becomes possible in the future will be determined by events. My main purpose in this action is to bring about a reduction in the level of violence that now exists."

Johnson looked at the man.

"What do you think?" he asked.

"How are you going to go about this?" Townsend asked.

"I am designating one of our most distinguished Americans, Ambassador Averill Harriman, as my personal representative for such talks. In addition, I have asked Ambassador Llewellyn Thompson, who returned from Moscow for consultation, to be available to join Ambassador Harriman at Geneva or any other suitable place just as soon as Hanoi agrees to a conference.

"I am going to call upon President Ho Chi Minh to respond positively and favorably to this new step toward peace."

"Considering the losses Archangel has been handing them, I would think Ho Chi Minh would jump at this offer," Townsend said.

"You would think so," the President said.

"What is the South going to say about all of this?" Henry asked.

"Fuck them!" Johnson said coldly.

"There has been substantial progress, I think, in building a durable government during these last three years. The South Vietnam of 1965 couldn't have survived the enemy's offensive of 1968. The elected government of South Vietnam survived that attack because of us and is rapidly repairing the devastation that it wrought.

"The South Vietnamese had better know that further efforts are going to be required. They are going to have to expand their own armed forces, move back into the countryside as quickly as possible, increase their taxes, select the very best men that they have for civil and military responsibility, achieve a new unity within their constitutional

THE FIRST TERRORIST ACT

government, and include in the national effort all those groups who wish to preserve South Vietnam's control over its own destiny.

"I am tired of the same old excuses. It is time to put up or shut up."

Townsend offered some information.

"Last week President Thieu ordered the mobilization of 135,000 additional South Vietnamese. He plans to reach a total military strength of more than 800,000 men. He said to achieve this the government of South Vietnam started the drafting of nineteen-year olds on March 1st. On May 1st the government will begin the drafting of eighteen-year olds.

"Last month, ten thousand men volunteered for military service. That was two and a half times the number of volunteers during the same month last year. Since the middle of January, more than 48,000 South Vietnamese have joined the armed forces and nearly half of them volunteered to do so. All men in the South Vietnamese armed forces have had their tours of duty extended for the duration of the war and reserves are now being called up for immediate active duty."

"Interesting," Johnson said. "Give me that again."

As Townsend repeated the information, Johnson carefully wrote it down. The two men spoke candidly.

"We need to accelerate the re-equipment of South Vietnam's armed forces in order to meet the enemy's increased firepower," Townsend said. "This will enable them progressively to undertake a larger share of combat operations against the Communist."

Johnson agreed. Then he talked about our commitment.

"On many occasions I have told the American people that we would send to Vietnam those forces that are required to accomplish our mission there. So, with that as our guide, we have previously authorized a force level of approximately 525,000.

"As you know, some weeks ago, to help meet the enemy's new offensive, we sent to Vietnam about 11,000 additional Marine and airborne troops. They were deployed by air in forty-eight hours, on an emergency basis. But the artillery, tank, aircraft, medical, and other units that were needed to work with and to support these infantry troops in combat could not then accompany them by air on that short notice.

"In order that these forces may reach maximum combat effectiveness, the Joint Chiefs of Staff have recommended to me that we should prepare to send during the next five months support troops totaling approximately 13,500 men. They recommend a portion of these men will be made available from our active forces. The balance will come from reserve component units which will be called up for service."

"Sound thinking," Townsend said.

Johnson looked at the other man.

"I have no intention of widening this war," he said.

"The United States will never accept a fake solution to this long and arduous struggle and call it peace. They won't after the men we lost. We can't have another Korea.

"No one can foretell the precise terms of an eventual settlement. My objective in South Vietnam has never been the annihilation of the enemy. It has been to bring about recognition in Hanoi that its objective of taking over the South by force could not be achieved.

"I think that peace can be based on the Geneva Accords of 1954 under political conditions that permit the South Vietnamese, all the South Vietnamese, to chart their course free of any outside domination or interference from us or from anyone else."

Johnson and Townsend continued to speak until finally the President excused himself.

"I have a speech to write. I am making some decisions today that could bring about an end to the war. I have some tough decisions to make," he said.

Henry Townsend stood and excused himself.

QUANG TRI CITIES
CAMP A-155
MARCH 31, 1968

Charley Reed was listening to the transistor radio that his father sent to him. The President of the United States was speaking.

"Finally, my fellow Americans, let me say this:

"Of those to whom much is given, much is asked. I cannot say and no man could say that no more will be asked of us.

"Yet, I believe that now, no less than when the decade began, this generation of Americans is willing to 'pay any price, bear any burden, meet any hardship, support any friend, oppose any foe to assure the survival and the success of liberty.'

"Since those words were spoken by John F. Kennedy, the people of America have kept that compact with mankind's noblest cause.

"And we shall continue to keep it.

"Yet, I believe that we must always be mindful of this one thing, whatever the trials and the tests ahead. The ultimate strength of our country and our cause will lie not in powerful weapons or infinite resources or boundless wealth, but will lie in the unity of our people.

"This I believe very deeply.

"Throughout my entire public career I have followed the personal philosophy that I am a free man, an American, a public servant, and a member of my party, in that order always and only.

"For 37 years in the service of our Nation, first as a Congressman, as a Senator, and as Vice President, and now as your President, I have put the unity of the people first. I have put it ahead of any divisive partisanship.

"And in these times as in times before, it is true that a house divided against itself by the spirit of faction, of party, of region, of religion, of race, is a house that cannot stand.

"There is division in the American house now. There is divisiveness among us all tonight. And holding the trust that is mine, as President of all the people, I cannot disregard the peril to the progress of the American people and the hope and the prospect of peace for all peoples.

"So, I would ask all Americans, whatever their personal interests or concern, to guard against divisiveness and all its ugly consequences.

"Fifty-two months and 10 days ago, in a moment of tragedy and trauma, the duties of this office fell upon me. I asked then for your help and God's, that we might continue America on its course, binding up our wounds, healing our history, moving forward in new unity, to clear the American agenda and to keep the American commitment for all of our people.

"United we have kept that commitment. United we have enlarged that commitment.

"Through all time to come, I think America will be a stronger nation, a more just society, and a land of greater opportunity and fulfillment because of what we have all done together in these years of unparalleled achievement.

"Our reward will come in the life of freedom, peace, and hope that our children will enjoy through ages ahead.

"What we won when all of our people united just must not now be lost in suspicion, distrust, selfishness, and politics among any of our people.

"Believing this as I do, I have concluded that I should not permit the Presidency to become involved in the partisan divisions that are developing in this political year.

"With America's sons in the fields far away, with America's future under challenge right here at home, with our hopes and the world's hopes for peace in the balance every day, I do not believe that I should devote an hour or a day of my time to any personal partisan causes or to any duties other than the awesome duties of this office, the Presidency of your country.

"Accordingly, I shall not seek, and I will not accept, the nomination of my party for another term as your President.

"But let men everywhere know, however, that a strong, a confident, and a vigilant America stands ready tonight to seek an honorable peace, and stands ready tonight to defend an honored cause, whatever the price, whatever the burden, whatever the sacrifice that duty may require.

"Thank you for listening.

"Good night and God bless all of you."

CHAPTER THIRTY-THREE

WASHINGTON, D.C.
MARCH 31, 1968

The President finished his speech. He walked into the Oval Office and closed the door behind him. A new bottle of scotch was in the corner with a full bucket of ice. He filled the glass with ice and then with scotch. He looked up at the portrait of Franklin Delano Roosevelt and raised his glass.

"Here we are, old friend," he said. "Here we are."

He took a drink from the glass.

"I'm giving up the job I always wanted. I'm giving it up because I don't deserve it. All the good I've done; the Poverty Program, Civil Rights, even keeping the economy going in spite of a war, none of it matters because it is all based on a lie."

Lyndon Johnson took another long drink of his scotch.

"It started out wrong and all I can hope for is I can save it. How did it all come to this? Tell me, Franklin. You were my mentor. How did it all come to this?"

He looked at the portrait as if he expected an answer. He looked at it and waited. No answer came. He looked down at the glass. All that was left was the ice. He poured himself another glass of scotch and drank that one, too.

"I did this," he said to the portrait. "I really did. I caused it all."

As he drank his scotch, it all ran through his head. Averill Harriman secretly dealing with Raul Castro in 1962. Then there was the plotting in 1963. The military industrial complex was so powerful. They wanted the war and Kennedy was against it. He remembered it all. He remembered how he was their boy.

They courted him and they told him he would be President for ten years. He could finish out Kennedy's term and then have two of his own. It seemed so simple. He had to do nothing. All he had to do was remain silent and then aim the investigation in the wrong direction. Considering Bobby was in line after Jack, and then Ted after him, he knew he had no other choice if he was ever to be President. And he knew he had to be. He had to because Franklin had told him he would be. It was as simple as that.

Being President was everything. Now he was and as he looked back into the darkness behind him, it was nothing. It was nothing at all. He realized it for the first time when he received the letter from a maid who quit her job in the White House. He looked at it lying on his desk and he read it once more. It was dated March 29, 1968 and he received it the following day.

Dear Mr. President,

I quit my job because I can no longer work for you. I know I am giving up a lot. It makes no difference. My son, Woodrow Smith III, Corporal Woodrow Smith III, was killed in Vietnam.

He was a fine young man. He was his mother's only child. He was my only child, Mr. President. And now he is dead. He is dead and you sent him to die. You sent him to die in your war and I know your war is built on a lie.

I can no longer change your dirty sheets on your bed. I can no longer pick up your dirty underwear and vacuum your floor. I can't because I no longer respect you. I no longer respect you not only because of what you have taken away from me, but for what you have taken away from so many others.

All the fancy speeches in the world, all the nice programs you establish, all of the other high minded and good things you do cannot make up for the evil you have wrought on this nation. Every single tear shed by a mother and a wife is your damnation and you will deserve it all.

I was proud to work in the White House but you made me ashamed. You made me ashamed that I was a part of all of this pain and horror. I will not judge you. One greater than you will judge you. May He have mercy on your soul.

Ruby Smith

He knew Mrs. Smith. He knew her well. He greeted her and he trusted her. And then he thought back. He thought back to 1964 when she overheard his conversation with General Wheeler. He was in his bathrobe and she was making the bed.

"God damn it, General," he roared into the telephone. "I don't give a flying fuck that you can't provoke them. Get it started and get it started now. If they won't come out and fight, attack the little slant-eyed bastards and claim they attacked us. We need this war and we need it now."

He thought back. He thought back to a classified report done by Dale Andradé and Kenneth Conboy. They told the whole truth. That's why it was classified and hidden.

He remembered it well.

In July 1964, Operational Plan 34A was taking off, but during the first six months of this highly classified program of covert attacks against North Vietnam, one after the other the missions failed, often spelling doom for the commando teams inserted into the North by boat and parachute.

These secret intelligence-gathering missions and sabotage operations had begun under the Central Intelligence Agency in 1961, but in January 1964, the program was transferred to the Defense Department under the control of a cover organization called the Studies and Observations Group (SOG). For the maritime part of the covert operation, Nasty-class fast patrol boats were purchased quietly from Norway to lend the illusion the United States was not involved in the operations.

To increase the chances of success, SOG proposed increased raids along the coast, emphasizing offshore bombardment by the boats rather than inserting commandos.

In Saigon General William C. Westmoreland, the new commander of Military Assistance Command, Vietnam (MACV), approved of the plan and SOG began testing 81-mm mortars, 4.5-inch rockets, and recoilless rifles aboard the boats. On July 30th Westmoreland revised the 34A maritime operations schedule for August, increasing the number of raids by "283% over the July program and 566% over June." Most of these would be shore bombardment.

That very night the idea was put to the test.

Under cover of darkness, four boats (PTF-2, PTF-3, PTF-5, and PTF-6) left DaNang, racing north up the coast toward the demilitarized zone (DMZ) and then angling farther out to sea as they left the safety of South Vietnamese waters. About five hours later they neared their objective: the offshore islands of Hon Me and Hon Nieu.

Just before midnight, the four boats cut their engines. To the northwest, though they could not see it in the blackness, was Hon Me; to the southwest lay Hon Nieu. The crews quietly made last-minute plans and then split up.

It was twenty minutes into the new day July 31st when PTF-3 and

PTF-6, both under the command of Lieutenant Son, considered one of the best boat skippers in the covert fleet, reached Hon Me and began their run at the shore. Even in the darkness, the commandos could see their target. It was a water tower surrounded by a few military buildings.

Suddenly, North Vietnamese guns opened fire from the shore.

Heavy machine-gun bullets riddled PTF-6, tearing away part of the port bow and wounding four South Vietnamese crewmen, including Lieutenant Son. Moments later one of the crewmen spotted a North Vietnamese Swatow patrol boat bearing down on them. There was no way to get a commando team ashore to plant demolition charges; they would have to do what damage they could with the boats' guns.

Illumination rounds shot skyward, catching the patrol boats in their harsh glare. But the light helped the commandos as well, revealing their targets.

Holding their vector despite the gunfire, the boats rushed in, pouring 20-mm and 40-mm fire and 57-mm recoilless rifle rounds into their target. In less than twenty-five minutes the attack was over. PTF-3 and PTF-6 broke off and streaked south for safety; they were back in port before 1200.

At Hon Nieu, the attack was a complete surprise.

Just after midnight on July 31st, PTF-2 and PTF-5, commanded by Lieutenant Huyet, arrived undetected at a position 800 yards northeast of the island. Moving in closer, the crew could see their target, a communications tower, silhouetted in the moonlight. Both boats opened fire, scoring hits on the tower and then moving on to other buildings nearby.

The only opposition came from a few scattered machine guns on shore, but they did no damage. Forty-five minutes after beginning their attack, the commandos withdrew. The two boats headed northeast along the same route they had come, then turned south for the run back to South Vietnam.

Within days Hanoi lodged a complaint with the International Control Commission (ICC), which had been established in 1954 to oversee the provisions of the Geneva Accords. The United States denied involvement.

In response the North Vietnamese built up their naval presence around the offshore islands. On August 3rd the CIA confirmed, "Hanoi's naval units have displayed increasing sensitivity to U.S. and South Vietnamese naval activity in the Gulf of Tonkin during the past several months."

At about the same time, there were other secret missions going on.

Code-named Desoto, they were special U.S. Navy patrols designed to eavesdrop on enemy shore-based communications, specifically China, North Korea, and now North Vietnam.

Typically a destroyer specially outfitted with sensitive eavesdropping equipment carried out these missions.

Until 1964, Desoto patrols stayed at least twenty miles away from the coast. But on January 7th, the Seventh Fleet eased the restriction, allowing the destroyers to approach to within four miles, still one mile beyond North Vietnamese territorial waters as recognized by the United States.

The first such Desoto mission was conducted off the North Vietnamese coast in February 1964, followed by more through the spring. In July, General Westmoreland asked that Desoto patrols be expanded to cover 34A missions from Vinh Son north to the islands of Hon Me, Hon Nieu, and Hon Mat, all of which housed North Vietnamese radar installations or other coast watching equipment.

The stakes were high because Hanoi had beefed up its southern coastal defenses by adding four new Swatow gunboats at Quang Khe, a naval base seventy-five miles north of the DMZ, and ten more just to the south at Dong Hoi.

Because the North Vietnamese had fewer than fifty Swatows, most of them up north near the important industrial port of Haiphong, the movement south of one-third of its fleet was strong evidence that 34A and the Desoto patrols were concerning Hanoi. Westmoreland reported that although he was not absolutely certain why the Swatows were shifted south, the move "could be attributable to recent successful 34A operations."

In reality there was little actual coordination between 34A and Desoto.

During May, Admiral U.S. G. Sharp, the Pacific Fleet Commander-in-Chief, had suggested that 34A raids could be coordinated "with the operation of a shipboard radar to reduce the possibility of North Vietnamese radar detection of the delivery vehicle." The Commander-in-Chief, Pacific, Admiral Harry D. Felt, agreed and suggested that a U.S. Navy ship could be used to vector 34A boats to their targets.

The lack of success in SOG's missions during the first few months of 1964 made this proposal quite attractive. But by the end of June, the situation had changed. Covert maritime operations were in full swing, and some of the missions succeeded in blowing up small installations along the coast, leading General Westmoreland to conclude that any close connection between 34A and Desoto would destroy the thin veneer of deniability surrounding the operations.

In the end the Navy agreed and, in concert with MACV, took steps to ensure that "34A operations will be adjusted to prevent interference" with Desoto patrols.

This didn't mean that MACV did not welcome the information brought back by the Desoto patrols, only that the two missions would not actively support one another.

On July 28th, the latest specially fitted destroyer, the Maddox (DD-731), set out from Taiwan for the South China Sea. Three days later, she rendezvoused with a tanker just east of the DMZ before beginning her intelligence-gathering mission up the North Vietnamese coast.

The Maddox planned to sail to sixteen points along the North Vietnam coast, ranging from the DMZ north to the Chinese border. At each point, the ship would stop and circle, picking up electronic signals before moving on. Everything went smoothly until the early hours of August 2nd. It was then intelligence picked up indications that the North Vietnamese Navy had moved additional Swatows into the vicinity of Hon Me and Hon Nieu Islands and ordered them to prepare for battle. This was almost certainly a reaction to the recent 34A raids.

At 0354 on August 2nd, the destroyer was just south of Hon Me Island. Captain John J. Herrick, Commander Destroyer Division 192, embarked in the Maddox and concluded that there would be "possible hostile action."

He headed seaward hoping to avoid a confrontation until daybreak. Then he returned to the coast at 1045, this time north of Hon Me. It is difficult to imagine that the North Vietnamese could come to any other conclusion than the 34A and Desoto missions were all part of the same operation.

The Maddox was attacked at 1600.

Ship's radar detected five patrol boats, which turned out to be P-4 torpedo boats and Swatows. When the enemy boats closed to less than 10,000 yards, the destroyer fired three shots across the bow of the lead vessel. In response, the North Vietnamese boat launched a torpedo.

The Maddox fired again. This time to it fired to kill.

It was accurate, hitting the second North Vietnamese boat just as it launched two torpedoes. Badly damaged, the boat limped home.

Changing course in time to evade the torpedoes, the Maddox again was attacked, this time by a boat that fired another torpedo and 14.5-mm machine guns. The bullets struck the destroyer; the torpedo missed. As the enemy boat passed astern, it was raked by gunfire from the Maddox, killing the boat's commander.

The battle was over in twenty-two minutes. The North Vietnamese turned for shore with the Maddox in pursuit. Aircraft from the Ticonderoga (CVA-14) appeared on the scene, strafing three torpedo boats and sinking the one that had been damaged in the battle with the Maddox.

The Desoto patrol continued with another destroyer, the Turner Joy (DD-951), coming along to ward off further trouble.

On the night of August 4th, both ships reported renewed attacks by North Vietnamese patrol boats.

The President knew this second attack didn't occur and was merely reports from jittery radar and sonar operators, but at the time he took it and used it as evidence that Hanoi was raising the stakes against the United States.

As far as the headlines were concerned, that was it, but the covert campaign continued unabated.

During the afternoon of August 3rd, another maritime team headed north from DaNang. Four boats, PTF-1, PTF-2 (the American-made patrol boats), PTF-5 and PTF-6 (Nasty boats), were on their way to bombard a North Vietnamese radar installation at Vinh Son and a security post on the banks of the nearby Ron River, both about ninety miles north of the DMZ. Each boat carried a 16-man crew and a 57-mm recoilless rifle, plus machine guns. PTF-2 had mechanical troubles and had to turn back, but the other boats made it to their rendezvous point off the coast from Vinh Son. PTF-1 and PTF-5 raced toward shore. For twenty-five minutes the boats fired on the radar station, then headed back to DaNang.

PTF-6 took up station at the mouth of the Ron River, lit up the sky with illumination rounds and fired at the security post. The rounds set some of the buildings ablaze, keeping the defenders off balance. Scattered small arms sent tracers toward the commandos, but no one was hurt. Just after midnight on August 4th, PTF-6 turned for home, pursued by an enemy Swatow. Easily outdistancing the North Vietnamese boat, the commandos arrived back at DaNang shortly after daybreak.

North Vietnam immediately and publicly linked the 34A raids and the Desoto patrol, a move that threatened tentative peace feelers from Washington that were only just reaching Hanoi.

The President had made the first of several secret diplomatic attempts during the summer of 1964 to convince the North Vietnamese to stop its war on South Vietnam, using the chief Canadian delegate to the ICC, J. Blair Seaborn, to pass the message along to Hanoi.

After the Tonkin Gulf incident, the State Department cabled Seaborn, instructing him to tell the North Vietnamese "neither the Maddox or any other destroyer was in any way associated with any attack on the DRV (Democratic Republic of Vietnam, or North Vietnam) islands."

This was the first of several carefully worded official statements aimed at separating 34A and Desoto and leaving the impression the United States was not involved in the covert operations.

The U.S. Navy stressed that the two technically were not in communication with one another, but the distinction was irrelevant to the North Vietnamese. Both were perceived as threats and both were in the same general area at about the same time.

CIA Director John McCone was convinced Hanoi was reacting to the raids when it attacked the Maddox.

During a meeting at the White House on the evening of August 4th, President Johnson asked McCone, "Do they want a war by attacking our ships in the middle of the Gulf of Tonkin?"

"No," replied McCone. "The North Vietnamese are reacting defensively to our attacks on their offshore islands. The attack is a signal to us that the North Vietnamese have the will and determination to continue the war."

It took only a little imagination to see why the North Vietnamese might connect the two. In this case, perception was much more important than reality.

The North Vietnamese Ministry of Foreign Affairs made all this clear in September when it published a "Memorandum Regarding the U.S. War Acts Against the Democratic Republic of Vietnam in the First Days of August 1964." Hanoi pointed out what Washington denied:

"On July 30, 1964, U.S. and South Vietnamese warships intruded into the territorial waters of the Democratic Republic of Vietnam and simultaneously shelled: Hon Nieu Island, 4 kilometers off the coast of Thanh Hoa Province and Hon Me Island, 12 kilometers off the coast of Thanh Hoa Province."

It also outlined the Maddox's path along the coast on August 2nd and the 34A attacks on Vinh Son the following day. Hanoi denied the charge that it had fired on the U.S. destroyers on August 4th, calling the charge "an impudent fabrication."

SOG took the mounting war of words very seriously and assumed the worst.

They assumed an investigation would expose its operations against the North. Both South Vietnamese and U.S. maritime operators in DaNang assumed their raids were the cause of the mounting international crisis, and they never for a moment doubted that the North Vietnamese believed the raids and the Desoto patrols were one and the same. And it didn't take much detective work to figure out where the commandos were stationed. The only solution was to get rid of the evidence.

A U.S. Navy SEAL (Sea Air Land) team officer assigned to the SOG maritime operations training staff, Lieutenant James Hawes, led the covert boat fleet out of DaNang and down the coast three hundred miles to Cam Ranh Bay, where they waited out the crisis in isolation.

Cam Ranh was a sprawling logistic center for material bolstering the war effort, but in the summer of 1964 it was only a junk force-training base near a village of farmers and fishermen. Until the ICC investigation blew over a week later, the commandos camped on a small pier. Then they boarded their boats and headed back to Da Nang.

At the White House, administration officials panicked as the public spotlight illuminated their policy in Vietnam and threatened to reveal its covert roots. President Johnson ordered a halt to all 34A operations "to avoid sending confusing signals associated with recent events in the Gulf of Tonkin."

If there had been any doubt before about whose hand was behind the raids, surely there was none now.

In Saigon, Ambassador Maxwell Taylor objected to the halt saying, "it is my conviction that we must resume these operations and continue their pressure on North Vietnam as soon as possible, leaving no impression that we or the South Vietnamese have been deterred from our operations because of the Tonkin Gulf incidents."

But the administration dithered, informing the embassy only that "further OPLAN 34A operations should be held off pending review of the situation in Washington."

As far as the State Department was concerned, there was no need to review the operations.

"We believe that present OPLAN 34A activities are beginning to rattle Hanoi" wrote Secretary of State Dean Rusk, "and the Maddox incident is directly related to their effort to resist these activities. We have no intention of yielding to pressure."

Of course, none of this was known to Congress, which demanded an explanation for the goings-on in the Tonkin Gulf. On August 6th, Secretary of Defense Robert S. McNamara met with a joint session of the Senate Foreign Relations and Armed Services Committees. He explained that the North Vietnamese had initiated combat with the U.S. Navy and described the attack on the Maddox.

"This is no isolated event," he said.

"They are part and parcel of a continuing Communist drive to conquer South Vietnam."

McNamara did not mention the 34A raids.

Senator Wayne Morse, a Democrat from Oregon, challenged the account and argued that despite evidence that 34A missions and Desoto patrols were not operating in tandem, Hanoi could only have concluded that they were. But Morse did not know enough about the program to ask pointed questions.

"I think we are kidding the world if you try to give the impression that when the South Vietnamese naval boats bombarded two islands a short distance off the coast of North Vietnam we were not implicated," he scornfully told McNamara during the hearings.

McNamara took advantage of Morse's imprecision and concentrated on the Senator's connection between 34A and Desoto, squirming away from the issue of U.S. involvement in covert missions by claiming the Maddox was in international waters and not involved in belligerent activities.

"I was not informed of, was not aware of, had no evidence of, and so far as I know today had no knowledge of any possible South Vietnamese actions in connection with the two islands Senator Morse referred to," he said.

Although McNamara didn't know it at the time, part of his statement was not true.

Captain Herrick, the Desoto patrol commander, did know about the 34A raids, something that his ship's logs later made clear. And, of course, McNamara himself knew about the "South Vietnamese actions in connection with the two islands," but his cautiously worded answer got him out of admitting it.

The fig leaf of plausible denial served McNamara in this case, but it was scant cover. Hanoi was more than willing to tell the world about the attacks, and it took either a fool or an innocent to believe the

United States knew nothing about the raids. Despite McNamara's nimble answers, North Vietnam's insistence that there was a connection between 34A and the Desoto patrols was only natural.

Despite Morse's doubts, Senate reaction fell in behind the Johnson team and the question of secret operations was overtaken by the issue of punishing Hanoi for its blatant attack on a U.S. warship in international waters.

On August 7th the Senate passed the Tonkin Gulf Resolution, allowing the administration greater latitude in expanding the war by a vote of 88 to 2. Senator Morse was one of the dissenters. The House passed the resolution unanimously.

Lyndon Johnson looked back. He thought about Ruby Smith's letter. Why shouldn't she feel that way? America's Vietnam War had begun in earnest.

Within the year, U.S. bombers would strike North Vietnam and U.S. ground units would land on South Vietnamese soil. But for a band of South Vietnamese commandos and a handful of U.S. advisers not much had changed.

The publicity caused by the Tonkin Gulf incident and the subsequent resolution shifted attention away from covert activities and ended high-level debate over the wisdom of secret operations against North Vietnam.

In the future, conventional operations would receive all the attention. This was the only time covert operations against the North came close to being discussed in public. For the rest of the war they would be truly secret. He saw to that.

Lyndon Johnson looked up at the portrait. He knew he had committed the second terrorist act when he allowed it all to be set in motion. He provoked the war with North Vietnam even more than when he allowed John Kennedy to be assassinated.

He poured himself another glass of scotch and sat back in his chair. The room was dark and he was drinking with his friend, Franklin Delano Roosevelt.

He had just given up the Presidency.

QUANG TRI CITIES
CAMP A-155
MARCH 31, 1968

Charley Reed looked into the darkness. He couldn't get his friends out of his mind. He couldn't shake the fact that he had killed two of his buddies.

He left the bunker and was out on the fence line. He was armed with a .45 caliber automatic side arm. Even though the fence line was a dangerous place to walk, he didn't care. Dying was the least of his worries. In a way, it would almost be a release.

He had just listened to the President of the United States of America say he wouldn't run for re-election so he could bring peace to Vietnam. He thought it was an admirable thing to do, but at the same time he wondered at his motives. He wondered if the President wasn't looking for some sort of release, too.

"Is the old bastard feeling guilty over all the lives we are taking?" he asked out loud.

As he did a single round fired from beyond the fence line went passed his head. He hit the ground.

"That will teach me to talk out loud to myself," he said to himself.

A second round was fired and he saw the muzzle flash. He fired five rounds in return and then rolled across the ground to cover.

Someone cried out in pain. One of his rounds had hit its target. As he cried out, the perimeter lights went on and sirens began to sound. He saw the man lying on the ground. An AK-47 was at his side. He moved for the rifle and as he did, Charley fired again. That time he hit him squarely in the head. He was killed instantly.

About then the MP's arrived. Charley pointed to the dead sapper on the other side of the fence line. He went back to his bunker and tried to sleep.

First his friends and now the enemy, he thought to himself.

"When will it be me?" he asked. "When?"

CHAPTER THIRTY-FOUR

QUANG TRI CITIES
CAMP A-155
APRIL 2, 1968

It had been a mistake, a terrible mistake.

He knew it was. They could have just as easily killed him. When he saw them standing there in the grass, they were drawing down on him. It was a reflex action to shoot. He had been trained to react as he had. Fate had given him the advantage of a heartbeat instant and the use of that advantage allowed him to stay alive.

As he lay there on his cot, tears came to his eyes. He had stolen his friend's life. He hadn't meant to steal it, but he had just the same. Moments later he drifted off to sleep again. And as he slept, he dreamed once more.

He was home in Pittsburgh, walking up his parents' street to their house. It was the house in which he grew up. The street was dark and it seemed to be summer time. He could smell Fred Roberts' honey-suckle as he walked past his house. His own yard smelled like freshly cut grass and he paused to inhale and savor the smell.

He always liked that smell along with the dampness. It must have been August. The dampness in the western Pennsylvania hills always smelled like this in August.

He entered his parents' home without using a key. The door was just open.

The house was empty. He called out to his parents, and then to his brother and sister. No one answered so he went upstairs to his bed-room.

He heard noises downstairs. There weren't any lights on in the house. As he went down the stairs to the living room, the street lamp shown through the window across the floor and into the dining room. He turned from the dining room to enter the kitchen and it was then he could hear a noise from the cellar steps.

It was the sound of feet running up the wooden stairs and then they suddenly stopped.

For several seconds there was nothing, but then he heard the click of the light switch on the steps being turned off. He remembered that light switch. The house was old and the switch had its own distinctive sound.

And then he was there in the kitchen. It was Dewberry!

He was long and thin and his head was turned and twisted around to the back. Charley could still somehow see his face. It was horrible. His eyeballs were out of his head, almost hanging there. He was wearing a tan coat with patches on the sleeves. He grabbed at Charley.

Charley tried to run, but was frozen with fear.

When he finally moved, he stumbled over the chairs behind him. Dewberry kept coming toward him. Charley crawled over the chairs and out of the dining room, but Dewberry was gaining on him.

He could smell the man's rotting flesh as a foot kicked him in the side. Charley cried out and crawled for the front door.

Again a foot crashed into his side. Charley doubled up in pain. A third time the foot connected with his side, knocking what was left of his wind from him. Charley rolled to his back and looked up at the hideous face of Dewberry.

"Die, you bastard!" Dewberry screeched.

Dewberry was holding a rifle with a bayonet on the end. He slowly raised it and prepared to lunge downward.

"No!" a voice screamed.

Charley recognized the voice and turned to look at the doorway. It was Chuck Hayes. Unlike Dewberry, Hayes was not deformed and rotting. He was as Charley remembered him.

Chuck was in uniform, his green beret cocked perfectly on his head. He was holding his combat .45 and had it aimed at Dewberry.

"If you move, I'll kill you," he said.

"Charley, come to me."

Dewberry just laughed. "I'm already dead, you asshole!"

Without saying another word, Dewberry changed the direction of his intended attack. Instead of Charley, he thrust the bayonet into Chuck Hayes' stomach.

Charley Reed rose to his feet. "No!" he screamed out. "No!"

He jumped on Dewberry who flung him aside.

Dewberry repeated a second thrust into an astonished Chuck Hayes. Again, Charley Reed attacked Dewberry, only to be cast aside once more.

Dewberry turned to Charley and aimed the rifle at his face.

"Die, you mother-fucker!"

"No!" Charley screamed out and woke himself.

He was shaking all over. Looking at the clock, he realized it was time to get ready for the night's mission. Slowly he got out of bed and began to dress. He put his feet on the floor and stepped into water.

Charley was in an underground bunker and the rains ran down into it and collected on the floor until the water was several inches deep in places. It rained off and on all day and he slept as one storm followed another. When the light outside faded, he woke and with the rest of the men went up for chow. It was Marine Corps chow. Their cover and guards were a company in the Third Regiment of the Third Marine Division.

As usual, Charley sat with Billy Campbell after the Marine private filled his plate with food. Their rations weren't bad. Even though the camp was designed to give the appearance of a temporary operation, the Sea Bees constructed it and the underground bunkers were reinforced concrete. There were generators for electricity, which gave them a lot of comforts including cold beer and fresh food.

Supplies came in from Phu Bai by chopper every morning. At the same time the camp perimeter was a veritable no-mans land with a cleared one hundred yard kill zone in all directions. There were claymores and booby traps in the jungle beyond that. The NVA had attempted penetrations in the past, but were repelled by the heavy fire brought to bear by the camp and Army artillery located in the hills to the west. After those probes the enemy bypassed the compound, assigning it little importance because of the lack of observable activity in and around the camp.

That night the darkness ran down out of the hills between the valleys and covered the plains and coastal jungle to the east. When the rains ended, the clouds disappeared into the hills and stars began to fill the moonless night. Billy Campbell sat across from Charley and as usual, complained about the food.

"Just like Mom used to make," he'd joke. Then after hardly any pause at all he'd add, "Except she didn't shit in it!"

Laughing, he would keep right on eating. Charley always smiled and Billy would grin, his mouth still full of food.

Billy Campbell was an unlikely looking killer. His soft sandy hair, brown eyes, tender complexion, and small delicate hands gave him the appearance of a high school boy just outgrowing acne rather than a blooded veteran of a secret strike force.

"What day of the week is it?" Charley asked him.

"Does it bother you?" Billy asked him back.

"Of course, it bothers me," Charley answered. "They're all the same. They're all damp and dark and you never see a newspaper. I never thought I would miss reading a newspaper."

"Not that," Billy said. "Not that part at all. The killing," he asked. "Does that bother you?"

Charley looked out the open tent into the darkness. "Of course, it does," he answered. "Anyone it doesn't bother is sick or dead."

"Are you afraid?"

"I'm afraid all the time," Charley admitted. "I'm afraid right now. Hell, I'm afraid to use the damn crapper!"

"What?" Billy asked looking puzzled.

"Yes," Charley reinforced. "I'm afraid of this shitty food and then I'm afraid to shit.

"Haven't you ever noticed the first places they go whenever they hit us? In order, they take out the latrines, the mess, and the command post.

"Somewhere in the Pentagon there's a major, his name is probably Major Nick Nichols. He's some lazy, overweight yes man who'll never made lieutenant colonel and his job is keeping track of how many buy it while taking a shit!"

Billy looked at Charley in disbelief.

"I can see it now," Charley continued. "Every morning he walks into some general officer and gives the statistics on deaths while shitting. Think about it! Every one of us has dysentery half the time and we're either in or waiting by the latrine. Hit it any time of the day or night and the slopes have five to ten kills. Multiply that by a couple hundred camps, times seven days a week, and Major Nick becomes a pretty important non-entity."

"You're crazy!" Billy said with a grin.

"Sure, I'm crazy," Charley agreed. "We're all crazy, but I'm not dying on any shitter. I hold it all day and shit when we're out. I shit just before we get back, too, just in case."

"You could get it while you're out there squatting," Billy suggested.

"No," Charley said. "I keep my Colt .45 in my right hand and I dig my knife into the ground and balance off that with my left hand. I switch my pistol to my left hand while I wipe and button up. I've got it down to a science."

"Get serious," Billy said, irritated with Charley.

"I am serious," Charley said changing the tone of his voice. "We're all scared. We should be. We could die any minute."

"Well, what are we supposed to do?" Billy asked.

"Stay afraid, I guess. Maybe that keeps us alive."

Billy thought about it for a minute. He wanted to talk. Something was bothering him. After they finished eating, they walked the camp perimeter.

"I remember the Captain getting it," Billy said. "He was hit in the back and had a surprised look on his face. He tried to cry out, but for some reason he couldn't. He didn't fall and they hit him again. Then he went down.

"The Sarge tried to get to him, but they fired on him, too. They hit him in the head and it exploded. His head just exploded and they both were down.

"I wanted to help, but I was frozen. Then I realized they were dead. I looked around for you and then we fought our way out."

"That bothers you?" Charley asked.

"Yes," Billy answered.

"Well, it bothers me, too. I guess that's the difference."

"What do you mean?" Billy asked.

"We knew them. They were our buddies and we loved them. The slopes don't mean anything to us. Killing them doesn't bother me. I hate them. I hate all of them."

Billy disagreed. "It bothers you. It bothers you in a different way than you even realize, old buddy."

"How's that?" Charley asked.

"The fact that the killing doesn't bother you is bothering you. That's why you joke about it and say you hate them. They're the enemy. You don't know them so how can you hate them?"

Charley had no answer. They walked back to the bunker and prepared for their mission.

Just before midnight, they boarded the UC-1A helicopter, which took them north into enemy territory and across the DMZ. From the landing zone the unit of men proceeded north toward the suspect ammunition dump. Billy Campbell was on the point. Charley Reed was drag man.

Billy's job was to detect the enemy as soon as possible and prepare the main body. Charley was the unit's eyes in the back of its head. He was responsible for any attack from the rear as well as providing cover fire in the event the unit was forced to retreat.

Keeping to his routine, Charley notified the lieutenant he was dropping back for several minutes. Billy Campbell, hearing the lieutenant give Charley permission, gave a chuckle over the radio with a smart little comment. Charley smiled to himself, but didn't answer. In a matter of minutes he was through and double-timing to get back to the men ahead of him.

He was within twenty-five meters when he slowed down and began to move into position again. There still was some ground to cover before he was back in his position. It was at that moment when the jungle in front of him erupted with the sounds of exploding mines and automatic weapons fire.

The explosions came from three directions, all in front of him. They began to the left and then moved across the front and ending to his right. Then a second series of explosions began.

In the light he saw the men in front of him fall.

He leveled his M16 and started moving to his right, but was knocked to the ground and felt a stabbing pain in his left collarbone. His right hand never released its grip on his rifle. A burst of gunfire seared the air above his head as he crawled from the trail into the jungle brush.

There was a second burst of gunfire and the jungle fell all around him.

As if by instinct, his training kicked in and he crawled away at irregular angles. That saved his life when the enemy soldiers threw grenades where he was supposed to be rather than where he was.

Charley Reed rolled onto his back and raised his weapon and fired a full burst at the approaching enemy soldiers, killing two of them. The pain in his collarbone was so sharp and so excruciating he almost passed out.

He rolled back on his stomach and as he did, he felt something sticking in his shoulder. Charley grabbed at the object sticking to him and pulled it away. In an instant of revulsion he realized he was holding a bloody human hand that was still wearing a gold wedding band. He vomited as he flung it away and crawled in the opposite direction.

The events on the morning of April third were no accident. It was a planned ambush. Everyone was supposed to die.

Everyone was supposed to, except Charley Reed survived.

For three days, including the third of April, he evaded the enemy. The enemy reported all killed inside of North Vietnam. Command had no reason to believe otherwise. He was given up for dead along with the rest of the men.

Then, on the morning of the third day, he walked back to his base camp. He walked out of the jungle into the free fire zone a hundred yards from the camp wire where he finally collapsed.

When he finally did regain consciousness, his face was bandaged and he could see nothing. His left arm was bound to his body and he had very little mobility. He didn't know he was in a MASH unit and being readied for transportation to DaNang. Charley had no way of knowing that he'd been missing in action for nearly three days and at one time had been reported captured by the North Vietnamese.

He had no memory of the ambush.

All that, plus the days alone in the jungle, was gone from him. He remembered talking to Billy Campbell and then waking up. There was an aching pain in his left side near his neck and his left wrist seemed to throb as his heart pounded. Finally, someone spoke to him. It was a corpsman.

"You're okay, man," he said. "You're in Con Thien and we're sending you down to DaNang. You've got some broken bones, but that's all. Everything is still there and it all works."

Charley didn't speak. He didn't even try. He listened to the specialist tell him that he had three fractures and he'd been brought in by a Marine search and kill unit that found him near the camp.

The corpsman's words made him try to think. All he remembered was being the last man to board the chopper. Billy Campbell had been laughing and a few of the others joked, too.

Then reality hit him as hard as the pieces of the bodies had when he was knocked to the ground during the ambush. Charley remembered the explosions and the gunfire. He remembered crawling off into the jungle and finding the hand stuck to him.

From that point on, his memory was blank.

At DaNang he was placed on a huge Air Force C-141 Starlifter and flown to Clark Air Force Base in the Philippines. There in the hospital they set his jaw, which evidently was also broken. The bandages were taken off his face and he was even allowed to sit up in bed.

Through it all Charley Reed never spoke, not one word, nor did he try.

Within days he was out of bed walking around. There were a lot of facilities for him to use, but he just sat at the window looking out toward the flight line on the base.

WASHINGTON, D.C.

On April 20th the C-141 Starlifter landed at Andrews Air Force Base and he was taken by ambulance to Walter Reed Army Hospital in Washington, D.C. From the moment Charley was assigned a bed in the ward, he caused a stir.

He was assigned to a ward for wounded who were recovering and eventually would be discharged from the hospital and the Army. He was not in that category. He didn't belong in that ward and no one understood why he was there.

The military runs on schedules and expectations. Hospitals in the Army, especially Walter Reed, were not any different. Each man in C Ward was given an expected date of discharge as well as an expected date of separation from the service. Charley Reed, aside from needing some bridgework on his upper left jaw, had no physical injuries requiring hospitalization. The head nurse immediately decided Charley belonged in an enlisted man's barracks at Fort Meade, not in C-Ward.

"He's not scheduled for separation for two and a half years," she complained to Lt. Col. Grigsby. "His date of discharge from here is unknown. We have no patients in his category on this floor. He should be reassigned."

Lt. Col. Bertrum Grigsby was a career medical officer. He was far from the best doctor in the world, but he was a military man and he went by the book. He didn't actually practice medicine anymore. He was an administrator and in his own eyes considered himself to be a fine one. What the head nurse said made sense to him and he intended to find out why Staff Sergeant Reed was in his hospital.

"I'll examine him myself," he told her. "Get his file and bring it to me. Then give me ten minutes and bring him to my exam room."

"Yes, sir," she replied, obviously pleased with his decision.

The fracture to Charley's jaw was minor and before he left Clark Air Force Base, they had removed the restraints to the jaw. When the nurse came for him, he was sitting on the edge of his bed staring out the window.

"Sergeant," she said. "Colonel Grigsby wants to see you."

He didn't respond to her. He just remained sitting there looking out the window.

"Sergeant," she repeated.

Again he appeared not to hear her. She took his arm and pulled him to his feet, leading him to the exam room where he was equally unresponsive.

The head nurse expected some sort of recognition from him, but he avoided looking at her and not only wouldn't speak, but he wouldn't even utter a sound. When Lt. Col. Grigsby came in, Charley was oblivious to his presence.

"Sergeant Reed," he said in a forceful voice. "Unless you're unable to, it is required military custom to rise when an officer enters the room."

Charley Reed just continued to stare at the floor.

"Sergeant!" Grigsby said again louder. "Did you hear me?"

Charley still continued looking down at the floor and didn't acknowledge the officer. Grigsby walked behind him and loudly clapped his hands behind the sergeant's right ear, causing Charley to jump with surprise.

"You can hear me!" Grigsby said in a commanding voice. "I expect you to pay attention and conduct yourself properly."

Charley Reed never moved. His eyes were fixed on a single tile on the floor.

"Nurse!" Grigsby screamed.

As the nurse entered the room, Grigsby exploded, "Get him out of my sight!"

"There's nothing wrong with you!" he yelled at Charley Reed. "I'll have you out of my hospital tomorrow! Do you hear me? I said tomorrow!"

Charley never moved. He never responded to the officer either.

The nurse took him by the arm and led him back to his bed. As she began to speak to him, his head raised and he looked directly into her eyes

The force of his stare left her speechless. It was an icy stare, cold and penetrating, and there was no need for any words. He continued staring for nearly fifteen seconds, then sat down on the edge of the bed and looked out the window.

The head nurse warned the other nurses to watch him and even spoke to Captain Kirsch who was the doctor on duty.

"Just what I need," Paul Kirsch thought to himself.

As he stood outside the ward looking in through the glass, he saw Charley Reed get up from his bed and cross the ward to pick up a magazine which had fallen on the floor for a fellow soldier. Charley handed it to the man, smiled, and patted him on the arm. He returned to his bed without ever saying a word. When he saw that, Paul knew then Charley Reed would cause no problems. He began his rounds.

He saved Charley for last.

As Dr. Kirsch approached, Charley was still sitting on the edge of the bed. The nurse followed and began to tell the doctor the injuries Charley had sustained. Then she informed him that Charley had not spoken since being wounded.

"Where was he?" the doctor asked.

"All the information about that is missing," the nurse told him.

"Missing?"

"It's just not here," she said.

"Is he in the Army or Marines?"

"I don't know. I assume it's the Army. He's a staff sergeant and his name is Charles A. Reed. He's twenty-two years old, five feet eleven inches tall, one hundred sixty-five pounds."

Captain Kirsch walked up to Charley Reed and placed his hand under his chin, raising his head. Charley's eyes met the doctor's and seemed to relax just a bit, letting his guard down for the first time.

"Is there anything I can get you?" the doctor asked.

Charley didn't speak, but he did shake his head no.

"Why don't you stretch out and get some rest. It'll take you a few days to get used to the time change. Everything is going to be turned around for you until then."

He showed Charley the call button and told him he'd be back in the morning.

"If you need anything, just press this and the nurse will come. You're home now, son, so just relax."

Charley stretched out on the bed and the nurse covered him. He watched the doctor leave the room and then closed his eyes. In a matter of moments, he was asleep.

The usual staff meeting the next morning discussed patients and their conditions. It was the head nurse who brought up Charley Reed. When she said there was nothing wrong with him and he needed to be moved out, Captain Kirsch immediately raised an objection.

"I disagree," he said.

"You're looking at him from the wrong perspective. His body might not be so damaged it requires our attention, but the person inside is. Haven't you noticed that he doesn't talk? My God! That young man is bleeding right before your eyes and you can't see it!"

Grigsby sat silently as the younger doctor disagreed with the nurse. She looked to him for support, but none came. What she heard was certainly different than what he said the day before.

"Sergeant Reed does not belong in C-Ward if we compare him to the other patients. I'm the first one to admit that. I don't want him here, but I have no choice. I've been told he stays and we deal with him. Since you seem to be his champion, Captain Kirsch, he's your responsibility."

It took Charley nearly a week to adjust to the time difference. The cast came off his wrist and forearm and the collarbone was healing to the point there was very little pain. He'd been to the dentist and they gave him a temporary bridge and took impressions for a permanent one. He was able to walk the floor and watch television in the day room. In that week Charley began to realize the war was over and he was home. While he began to relax, he still didn't talk.

One day turned into the other, but during that time as the days passed, he never thought about his family. While he sat in the day room watching television, it was as if his emotions had been erased and now he had to start all over. His parents and younger brother drove down from Pittsburgh the next weekend. The appearance of his family on Saturday morning caused no change in him at all. They brought him clothes and shoes and some food.

His mother tried to act as if nothing was wrong.

Charley sat and didn't say a word. He watched her as she spoke, but acted as if his father and brother weren't even around. At one point he closed his eyes and yawned and his parents decided he was probably tired.

They returned the next day and his father told him how they spent Saturday afternoon sightseeing. They had already checked out of their motel and were on their way home as soon as they left him.

Charley was allowed on the grounds and they walked outside. It was spring and the smell of the air made him feel good. His mother held his hand and asked if he could talk to her. Charley didn't respond to her question. He just held her hand and kept walking. At noon his family left, saying they'd see him soon. Charley went back to his room and sat on his bed the rest of the day.

The next week Charley became even more responsive to the world around him.

He put on the clothes his mother brought and wore them around the hospital. He spent hours pushing other patients around the hospital in their wheelchairs and just helping them. Charley had his own money and walked down to the gift shop and snack bar. He brought Lee Renzuli, a soldier who lost both hands, an ice cream cone and held it while the man ate. The nurses liked him. He was no trouble at all and was really quite helpful.

His parents returned two weeks later. It was Mother's Day weekend. He was allowed to leave the hospital with his family.

While Charley still wasn't talking, he smiled at his mother and even had a present for her. The improvement was obvious and he responded well to the restaurants and being around people away from the hospital. That night he returned to the hospital and slept well. He was awake the next morning and ready when his parents came for him.

They found a Catholic church and went to Mass. Afterwards they all went to breakfast and then back to the hospital. It was a beautiful Sunday and Charley walked the grounds with his father.

"This is good for me," he said to his son. "I should walk like this every day. Do you walk every day?"

Charley didn't speak. He only nodded his head.

"You should," his dad continued. "Do you know when they plan to release you?"

Again Charley didn't speak. He only nodded negatively.

His father bit his lower lip. He always did that when he was angry or irritated.

"They can't very well release you, Charley, if you don't talk. And they certainly can't use you in combat if you don't talk."

He watched his son for any sign, but there was no change. They walked a bit farther and he looked at his son again.

"I want to know," he asked. "Is it because you ran away that you aren't talking? Is it because you were a coward? Is that the reason?"

Charley stopped and turned to his father. He had tears in his eyes and his fist was clenched at his side. He started to grit his teeth, but a pain stabbed through the left side of his jaw.

He didn't answer.

Instead, he turned and walked away from his father. He didn't stay on the walk but went directly across the grass to where the car was parked and his mother and brother waited. Charley shook his brother's hand, kissed his mother, and then went into the hospital. He went to his bed by the window and sat on the edge. He could see his parents' car leaving the parking lot.

Tears began to run down his face as he thought about the questions his father asked. Charley wanted to scream out, but couldn't. The directness of his father's questions hurt him deeply. They hurt because his father had asked them and they hurt because he didn't know the answer.

Charley Reed watched the car drive away, realizing he honestly didn't remember.

CHAPTER THIRTY-FIVE

Charley continued sitting on the bed after his parent's car drove away and was out of sight. He watched a suburban transit bus drive up to the main entrance of the hospital. People got off and people got on and the bus drove away. Charley opened his footlocker and took out several changes of clothes. He placed them in a brown paper bag along with his toothbrush and razor.

Sitting on the edge of the bed he watched another bus come and go a half an hour later. A half an hour after that there was still another bus. When the next bus arrived, Charley Reed got on and paid the forty cents fare. The bus took him to downtown Washington at Pennsylvania Avenue and 14th Street. There he took another to Landmark Shopping Center in nearby Virginia.

Charley only knew two people in the Washington, D.C. area. They shared an apartment off the Shirley Highway and worked at the Navy Annex. They were two girls from Pittsburgh, Cookie and Judy, whom he knew from high school. When the bus stopped at Landmark, he got off and walked down Duke Street to the Princess Gardens Apartments. It was Sunday afternoon and he doubted if they would even be home. But he was in luck.

When he knocked on the door, Cookie answered. Charley Reed was the last person she expected to find at her front door. The last she heard he had gone to Vietnam. She didn't know he was back.

"Charley!" she said with a big smile.

Charley just stood there holding his paper bag. With his left hand he indicated to her that he couldn't talk. Instead, when she invited him in, he wrote on the brown paper bag what had happened. He asked if he could stay awhile and she agreed.

"You can sleep on the couch," she said. "Are you hungry?"

Judy came in later. She'd been out with a guy who was stationed at Ft. Meade. That evening they stayed in and drank rum and coke.

The next day the hospital realized he was gone and called his parents in Pittsburgh. Lt. Col. Grigsby said Charley would try to go home and wanted his parents to know that he was AWOL. Captain Kirsch objected to Grigsby reporting Charley as AWOL, arguing Charley should be considered a mental patient.

"The nature of his disorder is mental. He's not mentally ill, but he is emotionally ill. There's a fine line; I know that. But, he is sick and really isn't responsible. Leaving him listed as AWOL could put him in jeopardy or someone else if they try to bring him in."

Grigsby reconsidered and reported him as a missing mental patient who was not dangerous. Charley's parents agreed with Grigsby. They were sure he would return home. Two weeks later no one had heard from him.

Charley was still with the girls, cooking and cleaning for them, spending his days next to the swimming pool. He finally relaxed.

The girls didn't mind having him around. He slept on the floor inside the living room walk-in closet. He joked and referred to himself as their houseboy. He had so much to say he used up a small tablet in no time.

His birthday was in the second week of June and they celebrated by going down to Georgetown. They spent the evening bar hopping and drinking.

When they were out on the street, he walked into the night nurse from C-Ward. She recognized him immediately and looked around for the military police that regularly patrolled K Street.

Charley let Judy and Cookie know what happened and they left immediately. It was then Charley realized he was far from free. As they drove back to the apartment, he knew he had to go back.

The following Monday, Charley got off a bus and went back to C-Ward at Walter Reed Army Hospital. The staff immediately considered placing him in a more secure section of the hospital, which would inhibit his free movement, but Captain Kirsch argued against it.

"He's come back. That tells us he trusts us or he's at least ready to trust us. If we lock him up, we could lose him for good."

Grigsby thought for a moment.

"I've had the Department of Defense calling me about him. They want to do a full-blown ceremony at Arlington Cemetery and decorate everyone in his unit. Now that we have him back, we can't afford to lose him. I want him out of the ward and into a private room. Take his civilian clothes away from him. I want him in uniform. You're responsible for him!"

Captain Kirsch understood what Grigsby was saying and took it seriously.

"You've got to promise me, Charley, you won't take off again," the doctor said. "Grigsby wants me to put you in the detention section. If you'll give me your word that you won't take off, I'll move you into a private room instead.

"He wants me to take away your civilian clothes and put you in uniform. I won't do that either, but you'll have to sign out of your room to specific places and state your expected time of return. Will you agree to this?" he asked.

Charley wrote: "Grigsby's a lazy asshole who's afraid to get out of the Army and set up a private practice."

"I know," Kirsch laughed. "I'm not. I'm just trying to do my time. Now, I need your word."

Charley agreed and he moved into a private room. From then on Charley spent three hours a day in sessions with Kirsch and other doctors.

It was just after the fourth of July when Charley first spoke. It happened suddenly one afternoon as they were walking across the grounds.

"Why?" he asked.

Even though he was surprised, the doctor was expecting Charley to speak at almost any time and in much the same manner as it happened.

Quietly, he answered, "Because that's the way it is."

Charley looked at the doctor and smiled as if he had been able to speak all along. The doctor smiled back at Charley with the same tenderness a father might give his young son who spoke a new word. He ran his hand over Charley's head, messing his hair.

"Now that you can talk, Grigsby's going to want you to get a haircut and trim your sideburns."

Charley laughed aloud.

"We don't have to tell him," he said.

"Yes, we do."

"I can forget how to talk again," Charley teased.

"Don't try to blackmail me," Kirsch said. "I have to tell my commanding officer."

"He's a lazy ass!" Charley said, getting hoarse from not using his voice in so long.

Kirsch didn't tell Grigsby right away. He was afraid Charley might do exactly as he threatened. When he finally told Grigsby, he had to explain himself.

"He could have stopped talking. We both know that and I seem to be the only person he trusts. At this point he doesn't even trust his parents. I'm trying to bring him back to reality as fast as possible."

"Then do it," Grigsby said irritably. "Just get the job done! I'm tired of Charley Reed. I want him out of here."

Charley Reed went along with whatever Captain Kirsch asked. He got a haircut and started wearing his uniforms. By the middle of August, Charley was allowed to go down to Cookie and Judy's for the weekend. The Captain tried to get him to go home for the weekend, but Charley didn't want to see his parents.

One day in September they were walking. It was a breezy afternoon and Charley was as relaxed as he had ever been at the hospital.

"Will you tell me how you really feel?" Kirsch asked.

"About what," Charley asked back.

"Just whatever you feel. I'm curious about your feelings in general and really, even though you've done everything we've asked, you are still withdrawn from it all. I would like to know what you think of everything."

Charley was not quick to answer. He looked back at the hospital, noticing the trees surrounding it. The building nestled into the scenery perfectly. As he looked, a squirrel ran across the lawn and up a tree.

"I like squirrels," he said.

"Why?" Kirsch asked.

"Oh, because they're cute little animals running around on their tiny legs. They don't seem to do anything besides eat and play. I wonder if they're happy?"

Answering his own question, Charley decided they were.

"They don't know anything else. I don't see how they could be unhappy. They're doing what nature planned for them. Of course, they're happy."

Captain Kirsch agreed.

"What about you?" he asked. "Are you happy?"

"Sure I am," Charley joked. "I'm just pleased as punch to be here in this hospital. What young man wouldn't be?"

"What do you think about them wanting to give you the Silver Star?"

"Big deal," Charley answered. "What's the Silver Star? It's a hunk of metal they made into a medal. I come home and I get it. My friends don't come home and they get it, too. Where's the consistency? Either they should get it for being dead or I should get it for being alive. I think the whole thing stinks."

Kirsch listened as Charley let loose.

"I'm sure a piece of metal and some ribbon will keep Billy Campbell's wife warm at night. But excuse me," he said.

"Oh yes! I almost forget about the ten thousand dollar government life insurance policy. And, yes, the government will send the Sarge's kids to college. Benefits are better than getting your man back. Big Brother goes out and finds a war to fight and if you die, it will take care of everything."

"You sound very bitter," the doctor said.

"No, I'm not bitter! Why should I be? After all, I'm the one who's alive. I came home so, of course, I'm happy. I'm a hero! They're going to select me for reenlistment. Why should I be bitter? I'm alive and don't forget that!"

The doctor said nothing.

A squirrel darted down the trunk of a tree. It was just in front of them and as it reached the ground, it suddenly stopped and moved its head from side to side. The small squirrel scanned the area searching for danger. Its attention became fixed on the two men. As they approached it seemed frozen, but scarcely a heartbeat later it turned and ran back up the tree.

"I don't think you have any reason to feel like this," the doctor said. "You volunteered for what you did. No one forced you to become a Green Beret. You could just have easily been a clerk-typist and never left the United States."

Charley Reed laughed.

"In a way you're right. We all volunteered."

"So what's your complaint?"

Charley became serious as he answered. "We were lied to about why we were fighting. I'm not stupid. I've been watching television since I came back. We were told we were fighting Communism, when all along we were in a war that someone here started when we decided to keep a corrupt government in the South. We were put in the position we had to kill people who weren't on any side. That wasn't right and we were part of it."

"Charley," the doctor said. "You make it sound like none of you enjoyed killing those people. That isn't the way you told me it was. You made it sound like you enjoyed the killing. Now you're complaining. Which way is it?"

"What are you trying to do?" Charley asked.

"If you're trying to make me contradict myself, I think you can.

Haven't you ever believed in something and then changed your mind?"

"I guess so," the doctor answered.

"What do you mean, you guess so? Did you or didn't you?"

"Well, yes," Kirsch said.

"I have. So what? So that's where I'm at," Charley said.

"Where?"

"I've changed my mind about how I feel toward all of this. All you have to do is watch television or read a newspaper and you see what's happening. We have people killing people in Asia. That's a war. But, what about here in our own country?

"Martin Luther King and Bobby Kennedy have both been killed for their beliefs. Is this a war, too? What about Chicago? Was that a war?

"What's it going to be like at the Pentagon this weekend? We're bringing the 82nd Airborne in for that one. Think about it! We're using the Regular Army to control American citizens. Are we at war in this country or what?"

"So, Charley, I guess if I let you out this weekend, you'll go join the protestors at the Pentagon?" Kirsch asked.

"Now you sound like Grigsby," Charley said.

That made the doctor laugh.

"Really? Do I?"

"In a way you do," Charley said, laughing at himself.

They walked around the tree. Above on the safety of a limb, the squirrel watched them walk back to the hospital. Charley took the doctor's arm as they walked.

"You don't have to be a protestor to be against the war."

Charley stopped and the doctor stopped, too.

"That's the problem with this," Charley said. "The wrong people are protesting the war. My parents and the parents of those boys up in C-Ward should be marching on the Pentagon instead of a bunch of college kids who just don't want to serve in the Army. Those are the protestors this country needs, not some selfish kids who don't want their lives interrupted.

"What do they care about Chuck Hayes who only wanted to finish college and take care of his parents? Now all he is to them is just another number to talk about in their political science classes.

"The government says he's a hero. Well, I'll protest that the rest of my life. He deserves to be a live man, not a dead hero.

"I'll protest that and every parent in this country should protest right along with me."

The doctor looked at Charley, amazed at his long speech. They started walking again.

"The whole war is a lot of bullshit!" Charley screamed. "It's bullshit!"

Tears were running down his face. He was full of anger and frustration while at the same time, he continued speaking.

"This government of ours is a scary thing. It brainwashes you into thinking we're right and everyone else is wrong. It has young men begging to die for some myth and condemns anyone who won't. And everyone in the country buys into what they say one way or the other. Eventually, we all do what they say."

"They?" Kirsch asked.

"Yes," Charley answered. "They! That's the most terrifying part. No one knows who they are, but everyone does what they say."

"You're not serious," the doctor said. "This is America!"

"So what?" Charley asked him. "So fucking what!

"We're nothing special. Doctor, get out from under the mushroom and open up your eyes. It's easy to sit here in Washington and say we're right. Give up your cushy job and volunteer for Vietnam and then tell me we're right."

Paul Kirsch stopped walking. Charley Reed stopped with him. The doctor turned to the soldier and looked into his face. It was a young face with eyes that knew more than their age.

"If you really feel this way, then why did you join and why did you fight?" the doctor asked.

Charley was quiet as he answered.

"Because I didn't know any better and then when I did, I wanted to live."

That weekend nearly two hundred thousand students and war protestors surrounded the Pentagon. War-hardened veterans of the United States Army defended it. Every soldier carried live ammunition and every student believed the guns were empty. Paul Kirsch was at the University of Maryland football game and Charley Reed was confined to the hospital.

When the crowds and the soldiers went home that night, it rained. By ten the next morning, it was forty-five degrees and fall arrived. In the days that followed, the leaves began to change and fall from the trees.

A tailor visited Charley Reed and several days later two custom-made uniforms were delivered to his room. The next day he received notification of the upcoming awards ceremony at Arlington Cemetery.

Charley was upset and the doctor came to his room.

"I saw a movie the other night," Charley said to the doctor.

"It was one of those late night movies you never knew they even made. The king's wife picks out this soldier in her husband's army. They have all these captives lined up and the idea is this soldier is supposed to show them how to die. She walks past the men in the army and stops to ask this one if he believes in Allah. He says he does. She smiles and tells him to go and die with glory. The dumb ass climbs these steps and slides down a steel blade and is cut in half. All the people cheer."

"So what's the point," the doctor asked.

"That's what tomorrow is all about," Charley said. "All these people are going to cheer because nine men slid down the steel blade and were cut in half."

"What do you intend to do about it?"

"Nothing," Charley said.

"I just had to get it out. It's the way I feel, but I won't embarrass you and act like a jerk. I'll make you real proud of me. Wait until you see what a good little soldier I can be."

"That's good," Kirsch said. He thought for a moment.

"Will you answer a question for me?"

"Sure," Charley said.

"Why haven't you told your parents about tomorrow?"

"Because I don't want them here," he said.

"But why?" the doctor asked.

Charley just shook his head and would not answer. The doctor knew better than try to force an answer so he changed the subject.

"What if they send you back to Vietnam?" he asked. "They could, you know."

Charley looked him right in the face.

"I wouldn't go."

There was a pause and the doctor hesitated. "Seriously?" he asked.

"Serious as a heart attack!" Charley said.

"They can stick Vietnam up their asses. I'm not going back to give those bastards another chance to get me killed."

"That's no way for a hero to talk," Kirsch chided. "You're getting the Silver Star tomorrow."

"They may give it to me," Charley said. "They can't make me proud of it or even keep it.

"I won't cause any trouble, but I don't want it and I don't want to fight their war. Let the generals go fight! If those bastards started dying, the war would be over in a week. As for me, I'm through!"

"You know they can make you go back if they decide to do so," the doctor said.

Charley just shook his head.

"I'll go to jail first if it ever comes to that. I'll use their Silver Star against them. They won't do a damn thing to me."

"I can't understand why you feel this way," the doctor said.

Charley looked at the doctor almost in disbelief.

"I don't want to die. Can't you understand that?"

"You're a soldier. Don't you understand that?" Kirsch asked.

Charley shook his head again.

"You make it sound like just because I'm a soldier I'm expected to die. What's with you? What is your job anyway? Is it to find out if I'm crazy or just crazy enough to go back and die? Why don't you go in my place?"

The doctor laughed. "I'm trained to do something else, Charley. I'm no killer."

"You're wrong!" Charley said.

"It doesn't take any special training to kill. All you have to do is kill once. From then on it's really easy. You're not any different from me. You're in the same Army that I am and you should have to kill the enemy and take your chances, too. I really resent what you're implying, Doctor"

"I'm not implying anything," the doctor said, realizing he had become too involved in the conversation. "I appreciate what you're saying. Everyone wants to live. I was just trying to point out what is expected of me and what is expected of you is different."

"Now you really sound like Grigsby!" Charley said.

"You have to understand," Kirsch said. "I have to sound like Grigsby. It's my job to make you face what's more than likely to be ahead of you. In that respect, I am Grigsby."

"So that's your job," Charley mocked him. "Get me healthy and ready to go back."

"That's what any doctor's job is. In my case, it's more getting you mentally to the point of where you were than anything else."

Charley laughed.

"Then I'm already dead and you're a failure. I'll never be there again."

"Charley, that's not facing the reality of the situation. You can't run away from reality."

Charley looked at the doctor. The expression on his face remained unchanged. It was the same expression he would wear the next day.

"You say I can't run from reality. When that reality is lining up bodies of the dead for television for the folks at home and for some fat-assed flat-topped general who just flew up from his villa in Saigon, I'd rather dream. When reality is putting my friends in body bags, I'm not interested in that either.

"Keep your reality. I don't want any part of it."

"But you can't run away from what's there," the doctor said.

"I can if I want to.

"I will," he added defiantly. "And as I do I'll be facing reality better than any general. I'll face it better than Grigsby could ever do. They live in the dream world. They live there and their dreams are nightmares. Their dreams created Vietnam.

"What's really scary is Vietnam is only the beginning unless we stop them. I want no part of their dreams. If it takes running away to be safe, I'm a coward."

"Charley," the doctor said to him. "You're no coward. You're probably one of the bravest young men I've known. Knowing you has been one of the highlights of my life. I'll never forget you."

The next day began as a sunny October morning. A barber was in Charley's room just after breakfast. When Charley told him how he wanted his hair cut, the barber politely stopped him.

"I'm sorry, Sergeant Reed. I've been instructed how your hair is to be cut. If there's a problem, I can call my commanding officer."

As Charley was about to throw him out of the room, Captain Kirsch looked in. Charley bit his lip and allowed the man to cut his hair. The haircut ended and the barber left.

Within a few minutes, a major appeared to help him dress as well as brief him for the ceremony. At noon the major had him in a reception room in the Ft. Meyers Officer's Club.

He wasn't alone. The families of his dead comrades were there also.

A buffet lunch was put out for anyone who was hungry and in the corner there was a bar. Two hours remained before the ceremony and Charley wasn't especially comfortable being there with the people in the room.

"Get yourself a drink or two," the major said. "Just don't over do it."

Charley walked to the bar. He was aware of the eyes following him as he crossed the room. He took care to look straight ahead and avoid any eye contact. He had no idea what he would do or say if any of them came up to him. He went to the bar and ordered a bourbon and ginger ale.

"Do you have Wild Turkey?" a voice asked from behind him.

"Yes, we do, sir," the bartender answered.

"Good," the voice said. "I'll have a glass of Wild Turkey with no ice and a bottle of cold beer. Budweiser, if you have it."

"Yes, sir," the bartender said.

Charley took his drink from the bar and was about to walk to an empty corner when a hand rested on his shoulder.

"You're Charley Reed," the voice said.

Charley turned and met Alexander Hayes. The man's voice carried across the room. Other people recognized the name Charley Reed and walked to where they were standing.

Charley's fears were never realized.

Everyone was happy to meet him. They knew him from letters sent by their sons and husbands. They all had questions. Charley tried to answer them with kindness and affection.

There was a young woman with light brown hair, holding a baby. She said nothing, but she listened to every word. Then when everyone else finished, she asked about her husband, Billy Campbell.

"He was a fine man," Charley told her. "He was my friend and the night he died he talked to me about you. He told me how beautiful you are and how much he loved you. He hated being away from you and the baby and wanted to come home."

He looked at the rest of the people and with tears in his eyes spoke to them.

"They all were very brave men. They were my friends and I loved them. I'm sorry we are all together like this. If I could, I'd trade places with any one of them so you wouldn't have to be alone. I would."

Charley wiped his face. Tears were running down his cheeks and he couldn't breathe. He went back to the bar and found a napkin and blew his nose. Everyone else was crying including the major.

Then it was time to go to the cemetery.

Clark Clifford, the Secretary of Defense, was presenting the medals. There was a color guard, flags were flying, and an armed contingent guarded the nine graves. Charley Reed took his place and came to attention upon command.

A general stepped forward and read the specifics and circumstances of heroism for the men of the 545th Special Operations Group. Then, one at a time, their names were called and a mother, a father, or a wife would step forward to accept an American flag and the Silver Star.

Finally, they called Charles Allen Reed.

After taking two steps he came to attention again and received his medal. He saluted sharply and returned to his place. The bugler played taps and then the honor guard fired a gun salute into the air. The general stepped forward and dismissed the formation.

Charley Reed watched as everyone began to leave. A photographer came up and congratulated him. Charley was polite and thanked him.

Without anyone noticing, he removed the medal from around his neck and held it in his hand. He started to walk back to the car that brought him. About half way there, a girl who was about twelve came up and asked if she could take his picture. He asked where she was from and she said Ohio. She took the picture and thanked him. She turned to go back to her parents. They were only sightseers and hadn't come for the presentation.

"What's your name?" Charley asked her.

"Sharon Haller," she answered.

"What part of Ohio are you from?" he asked.

"Cleveland," she answered.

"Well, Sharon Haller," he said. "Here's something to take back to Cleveland with you and keep. Don't tell anyone I gave it to you until you get home."

He handed her the Silver Star and walked to his waiting car.

CHAPTER THIRTY-SIX

WASHINGTON, D.C.
OCTOBER 1, 1968

Henry Townsend was in the Oval Office on Tuesday morning at seven sharp. He opened his briefcase and took out a folder. It was marked 'Operation Eagle Thrust.'

"Sir," he began. "Of the 568 ground forces employed in this operation, only ten survive today."

He went on to elaborate. "Two are officers and the other eight are enlisted men. The officers include a major and a captain. The enlisted men are made up of four master sergeants, three sergeants first class, and one staff sergeant.

"Of the enlisted men, three are in country at this time, four in the Philippines, and one here in Washington, D.C. He has been in the mental ward at Walter Reed and was awarded the Silver Star last Thursday. The three in country are easily dealt with, as are the four in the Philippines. Even the one here in Washington can be dealt with and no one would suspect a thing. The Airmen who participated, eighty-six of them, they are another story."

"Stop!" the President said. "Stop it right now."

Henry stopped.

"Is there something wrong, sir?" he asked.

"You know there is," Johnson said back to him. "I'm trying to stop the killing and look at what we are doing."

"But, sir," Townsend said. "This is in the national interest. These men know too much. If any one of them ever talks, the result could be devastating. If Jack Anderson got his hands on any piece of what happened, the reverberations would go back as far as Truman."

Johnson shook his head.

"I don't care," he said. "It stops and it stops now.

"Starting a war is one thing. I can go along with the secret commando raids on the enemy and I can go along with the secret bombing missions in neutral countries. But we consorted with our enemy and that's too much."

Townsend stopped the President.

"Excuse me, sir," he said. "It happens all the time. The North Vietnamese have been of great assistance to us in eliminating the men who participated in this action. It was necessary. It had to be done."

"I don't care," the President insisted. "It's over. The ten who are left and the Airmen are to be left alone. Do I make myself clear?"

"Yes, sir," Townsend said.

Henry Townsend closed the folder marked 'Operation Eagle Thrust,' put it back in his briefcase and closed it.

"Is there anything else, sir?" he asked.

"No," the President said.

Townsend left the Oval Office and returned to Langley. On the way he made a phone call. John Hughes was waiting for him in his office.

As soon as Henry entered the office, Hughes could tell something was wrong. He could tell by the look on Townsend's face. It was always transparent when there was a problem. He knew better than to ask. He waited. It didn't take long.

"The old man has lost his nerve. He's gone soft on it all. He's taking this peace initiative to an extreme. I should have seen it coming. I should have. He's gone soft."

"What do you mean?" Hughes asked.

"The sanctions stop immediately. His order."

Hughes got a funny look on his face.

"What's the matter?" Townsend asked.

"Major Reilly was killed this morning. A bomb exploded in his office in Saigon. It killed him and an aide."

"Tough shit!" Townsend said. "Good. That leaves nine of them. Maybe the Philippine guerillas can get the three over there and that will leave us with six. As for them, maybe a building will fall on them or they will die in a plane crash. It happens all the time."

Hughes listened attentively.

"We can't do it. The old man won't let us, so we better not get caught. Maybe the odds will work in our favor for once. That's the way it has to be."

John Hughes understood. He left his superior's office. As he walked back to his desk, he remembered how it all began. This was the

310   THE FIRST TERRORIST ACT

first real activity he had been involved in and he worked hard to see everything went off the way it was supposed to.

DECEMBER 2, 1966

He was a green recruit when he accompanied Henry Townsend as he traveled to Toronto. They stayed in Toronto for two days where they secretly met with two Cubans.

During those meetings that took place in a room at the Royal Prince Hotel, they got right to the point. The Cubans wanted concessions from the Johnson Administration. In return, they would turn over certain information the United States government wanted.

"This could be beneficial to us all," a man named Raul told them at the first of three meetings.

He made no bones about what they were after.

"You must turn down the military pressure on us in Cuba. We must have assurances that you will not invade or sponsor an invasion."

"That's all been taken care of," Townsend told Raul. "Kennedy took care of that when Khrushchev took the missiles out of Cuba. He promised we would not invade at that time."

"That was a man who we both know is dead," Raul answered back. "We both know how he was killed and who killed him. We depended on the new administration easing the tensions with our government. They have not. They have, on the other hand, reinforced your garrison at Guantanamo. That forces us to reinforce also and have more men in our army, something we can ill afford."

"What about your Russian allies?" Townsend asked. "Can't you get assistance from them?"

Raul continued to be frank.

"We both know that without a major military presence our Russian allies pay us lip service. They support us militarily, but we realize if an invasion ever came, they would not risk a nuclear war with you. We know their promise is a paper promise. That is why we need assurances from you. If anyone owes my country a debt, it is certainly your President. He has not lived up to what he promised."

Townsend corrected Raul.

"He promised nothing. He said he would see what he could do. Being president in the United States is not like being president in Cuba. We have the Congress to deal with and we have our military. We cannot overnight change something that has gone on now for over half a decade."

"We understood that. We knew nothing would happen overnight. But you have made things tougher on us when we depended on the gradual reestablishment of trade between Cuba and the United States. That has not happened and it does not seem that it will happen. We need that trade so we can pay for the improvements we are making for the people of Cuba. We are on the verge of bankruptcy and the Russians have no available cash to help us."

Townsend continued to listen with a blank face.

"When you needed our assistance, we were there for you. We gave you what you needed. We gave you our fall guy and we sat back and said nothing. We said nothing when it would have been very easy for our President to come forward and expose what you did.

"We did not and we have no intention of doing so. The man was an enemy to us all. He was a fanatic and we are better off without him.

"But," he said. "There must be some price for that silence. There must be some payment for our help and our silence."

Townsend said nothing. John Hughes was astonished at the frankness of the Cuban.

"What can I relay to my principals?" he asked Townsend.

"Raul," he said. "I'm not in a position to say anything at this time. I will have to be in touch with my superiors and see what arrangement we can make with you. May I have a day?"

"Of course," Raul agreed.

He and the man with him left the room. As soon as they were gone, Townsend turned to Hughes.

"You are now part of something a very select few know anything about," he said coldly.

"I had reservations about bringing you. I had reservations about allowing you to sit in. However, just as I was trained and allowed to rise in the agency by my angel, I will be yours.

"I asked for permission to bring you inside of this small circle of control. Permission has been given. Now you are my responsibility and I have chosen you to eventually succeed me in my position. The actions we take today will have ramifications years from now. That is why it is important you understand everything that took place and is about to take place.

"Do you have any questions?"

Hughes remembered how he was afraid to ask any questions.

"No," Hughes answered. "It is obvious what he was talking about. At this point it is probably better not to know any details. If it becomes necessary for me to know, I am sure you will fill me in."

Townsend smiled at him.

"Very smart of you, my boy," he said.

Townsend brought Hughes with him when he took a cab to a house in a residential section of Mississauga. It was a safe house, a house occupied by an agency agent who dealt with various Middle Eastern factions. He had secure communications in the house and Townsend called in and relayed exactly what the Cubans were looking for. They didn't wait for an answer. They went back to their hotel, ate and went to bed.

The following morning a courier knocked on Hughes' door. He identified himself with a code word and Hughes gave the reciprocal. When he did, the man handed him an envelope. He closed and locked the door behind him and immediately knocked on the connecting door between his and Townsend's rooms. When Townsend opened the door, John handed him the envelope.

"Come in," he told Hughes.

Hughes did as he was told and followed his superior.

"Have some coffee," he told Hughes. "I'll decode this."

Hughes watched as his boss took out a single piece of paper. It was not a complicated process and the simplicity was what made it so fool-proof. There were key phrases indicating certain actions. Most of the actions were anticipated and as he read the seemingly innocuous message, he was, in fact, receiving instructions from the President of the United States himself.

The men met at noon in Raul's room.

"My government is prepared to, under the proper circumstances, ease the pressure on your government," Townsend said.

"We are also prepared to transfer an amount of money into an account that will cover your balance of payments for this year. We will do it on a timely basis in order that you do not default on your loans. We will use funds that were we froze when Batista left the country.

"You understand this has to be done surreptitiously. We cannot afford to have anyone know we are giving your government aid of any kind. The losses our businesses took when you nationalized American holdings are enormous. If they found out what we were doing, it would be the end of this administration."

Raul nodded his head in agreement.

"Aside from your silence on our operation, what else are you prepared to give us?" Townsend asked.

Raul smiled.

"El Gato," he said.

Townsend was very matter of fact.

"Now we are solving a problem of yours. That in itself should be payment enough."

Raul smiled again.

"There's more."

"And what might that be?" he asked.

"The SAM III guidance system. We have SAM IIIs and we can give you what you need to defeat it. It is now able to hit your B-52s.

"You will have to go to Havana to get them. I have already made arrangements for you to travel tonight. Here are your papers and passports. I have taken the liberty of preparing them for you."

"I will have to get permission and I will have to get the information about the transfer of funds. I will turn the information over when the transaction is complete."

Raul agreed. They met one more time and had dinner together. Townsend said everything was a go.

At midnight on the second day, they boarded an Air Canada flight using the false credentials Raul gave them and flew to Havana.

WASHINGTON, D.C.,
THE OVAL OFFICE
DECEMBER 4, 1966
1:00 A.M.

Lyndon Johnson was alone drinking a glass of scotch. The only light in the room was the small one illuminating the portrait of Franklin Delano Roosevelt. The President was intoxicated.

"I'm dealing with the devil again," he said.

He took a heavy swallow from the glass.

"Who did you have to deal with? The Russians? The Brits? Or was it those fucking French sons-of-bitches?"

He looked at the portrait hard. It was as if he was hearing something or was at least expecting to hear something.

"The fucking Japs," he said. "You provoked those bastards, didn't you?"

He looked down into his glass and took another drink.

"I know you did, Mr. President. You all but admitted it to me. You provoked them just like I provoked the North Vietnamese. You needed a reason to get us into the war and you provoked them. You just never expected them to hit us where they did. You thought they would go after MacArthur in the Philippines. You never expected them to hit Pearl Harbor. That's why you had the aircraft carriers out to sea. You were going to send them against the Japs in the Philippines. When they hit Pearl and we lost the fleet, then they had you. You couldn't relieve the Army."

He laughed.

"Dealing with the devil is always a fuck job. You can never win. I dealt with that son-of-a-bitch once and now I'm doing it again. This time is an extension of the last time. I should have expected it. I really should have."

Johnson finished his drink and fell asleep in his chair.

Henry Townsend and John Hughes were only a few miles east on the Air Canada flight heading to Havana.

Chapter Thirty-seven

Havana, Cuba
December 4, 1966
5:32 A.M.

The Air Canada jet landed with twenty passengers. When the jet came to a stop and the doors were opened, six armed soldiers boarded the aircraft. John Hughes was not as experienced as Henry Townsend, but it didn't take much to see the presence of the armed men visibly bothered his boss.

"What the Christ is this?" Townsend said under his breath.

The men came directly for them. And as they approached, John Hughes suddenly realized they might have been setup. Pictures of an international incident, being arrested as a spy in a Communist nation, went through his mind. He held his breath as the first man came up to their seats.

"Senor," the officer said. "We have a car waiting for you."

Townsend nodded his head and stood. John Hughes did the same. The soldiers with the officer stood aside while Townsend and Hughes followed the man from the jet. It was raining and it was still dark. Carefully they went down the steps to the tarmac and crossed to the black Russian limousine waiting for them. As soon as they were inside, the doors closed behind them and they were whisked away from the airport.

The lights of the city were in the distance and the ocean was to their left as they were driven to what seemed to be some type of country estate. They passed the gates and the guards and in a matter of moments, they stopped in front of a grand entrance. The doors opened for them and a man in a uniform asked them to please follow him.

He led them up the steps through an imposing entrance into a magnificent foyer and great room. Hughes could only imagine the dignitary who lived in such a place. He wouldn't have to wait long. They were led up an impressive staircase to the second floor and into a large room with an enormous mahogany table surrounded by large stuffed chairs.

"Gentlemen," the man who was leading them said. "Please be seated."

Two chairs were pulled back on the far side of the table next to the seat at the head. He directed them to those particular seats. They did as he told them.

"Coffee?" he asked in a polite but businesslike manner.

Both men accepted.

He immediately produced two cups and saucers and a Sterling Silver pot from which he served them coffee. Immediately, another man put fresh milk and sugar in front of them.

"Would either of you care for cream or sugar?" he asked.

Townsend declined, saying he took his black. Hughes asked for cream. As the man poured the milk in Hughes cup, he also stirred it for him. Then when he was done, the milk, sugar, and coffee were removed. All that remained on the table were their cups and saucers.

As they sipped the coffee, they were alone in the room except for a man stationed at a doorway directly behind the seat at the head of the table. Neither man spoke to the other. They both remained totally silent. Then the door opened and as it did, the mystery about where they were and whom they were meeting with ended. In walked Fidel Castro. He was carrying papers with him.

As he entered the room in a brisk walk, Townsend and Hughes rose to their feet.

"No need to rise, gentlemen," he said in perfect English. "Please, stay seated."

Both men did as he asked.

He walked to his chair and the man who was standing by at the door pulled it back for him as he sat down. Then, as soon as he pushed it in for his President, he left the room. The only people remaining were the two Americans and Fidel Castro. He wasted no time getting to the point.

"Thank you for traveling so far to visit with me," he said.

Hughes looked into the eyes of the man he had known as an international villain and murderer of thousands. He found a very charming and charismatic man.

"My brother, Raul, is satisfied we have come to an acceptable arrangement. It was important that you come here and meet with me personally because we cannot afford to have middle men involved in such a sensitive matter."

Townsend nodded his agreement. The men continued to listen.

"Will our funds be made available immediately?" he asked.

"Yes, sir," Townsend answered. "At the open of business today, Zurich time, this account was made accessible using the following number and password. One hundred million American dollars are now available for your use. That should more than cover your debt service and give you a cushion for comfort. Mr. Johnson wanted it that way. He appreciates your assistance in the past."

Townsend passed Castro an envelope. As he did, Castro passed Townsend the papers he brought with him when he entered the room.

"The SAM III operational specifics," he said. "My experts tell me this is everything you will need to deal with your new problem."

Townsend took the papers and thanked the President. Castro nodded and then got right to the point.

"I have a serious problem," he began. "His name is Ernesto Che Guevara."

Immediately, Hughes recognized the name. He remembered the Agency paper on him. It was taken from a description by one of his contemporaries.

It read: "Guevara grew up in a regimented society. He saw the unfairness of the American's evaluation of the oppression inflicted by the military tyrants in Latin America and declared a personal war against it. Born Ernesto Guevara de la Serna on June 14, 1928, in Rosario Argentina to Ernesto Guevara Lynch, a Civil Engineer of Irish descent, and Celia de la Serna of Spanish descent. Ernesto was the eldest of five children of the middle-class family with strong liberal tendencies. During his childhood, Ernesto developed bronchial asthma, a choking sensation that would always accompany him. As one stood next to him, one could hear a wheezing sound coming from his lungs whenever he got too uptight about anything that didn't go his way.

"Although he was called cold and inhuman by his enemies, Ernesto was warm and compassionate toward those people deprived of fundamental social and economic privileges. The latter was a dominant part of his life; the part that made him the world's most known insurrectionist. He was a man that trembled with indignation at the sight of any injustice committed against the poor.

"In 1952, El Che disengaged himself from his school work to tour South America with Alberto Granados, a pharmacist and a biochemist. The journey started on a motorcycle and ended-up in hitch-

hiking. They visited Chile, Peru, Colombia and Venezuela. It was in
Peru where for the first time Ernesto 'Che' Guevara came in close
contact with South America's Indian masses. He saw how the Indians
of the Peruvian high plateau, whose ancestors were the great Incas,
were being exploited and brutalized by foreign investors. Later on he
cried when he saw the brutal inhumanity of the lepers in San Pablo
Leprosarium, located along the Amazon River. After spending a few
weeks around the Leprosarium, Ernesto returned to Argentina where
he resumed his studies at the Medical School in Buenos Aires.
Granados stayed behind as an employee of the Leprosarium.

"However, after his graduation from Medical School, El Che
once again set out to visit Granados and tour other countries of Latin
America. In Guayaquil, Ecuador, he met Ricardo Rojo, Argentinean
attorney who had been expelled from his Country by dictator Juan
Domingo Peron. Rojo convinced Ernesto to go to Guatemala where
a real social revolution was taking place. That's where I met Ernesto
'Che' Guevara. I was in Guatemala City with a group of students trying to convince the people of Guatemala to fight for their democratic
elected government, under the presidency of Jacobo Arbenz.

"Arbenz was elected by promising land to the landless Indians
who were dying of starvation. As a result, he expropriated 225,000 of
uncultivated acres of arable land from the American Fruit Company
who was monopolizing Guatemala's agriculture. The move became
too much to bear by the American Secretary of State, John Foster
Dulles, also a stockholder and an attorney for the American Fruit
Company. Therefore, in March 1954, Dulles accused the Arbenz government of being a Communist regime and succeeded in forcing the
AOS members to prepare a mercenary invasion force in neighboring
Honduras. Che recognized the necessity of the land reform, and supported Jacobo Arbenz' actions against the American Fruit Company
and tried to organize a fighting force to resist the CIA-sponsored invasion of Guatemala. However, his efforts availed him nothing. The people and the Guatemalan Army, whose high echelons sold out to the
CIA, refused to fight. The Arbenz government collapsed ahead of the
invasion. For El Che, it was a personal failure that nearly cost him his
life. Luckily, he was given asylum in the Argentine Embassy in
Guatemala City. Later arrangement was made to secure him a guarantee of safe conduct so he could travel to Mexico City. While in
Mexico City, El Che married Hilda Gadea Acosta, a girl he first met
in Guatemala while she was working for the Arbenz government. A
female child was born out of the marriage and all went smoothly until

Ernesto met Raul Castro, Fidel's brother.

"However, immediately after Che met Fidel Castro, who at the time was preparing the plans for the Cuban invasion out of the Hotel Imperial in Mexico City, Guevara managed to talk himself into the plan as the troop physician. The sixty-two men invasion force left Mexico in a 43-foot yacht named Gramma on November 25, 1956, from the port of Tuxpan. After landing in Cuba, Ernesto 'Che' Guevara rose to the rank of major.

"Less publicized than his legendary epoch as a guerrilla, Che Guevara's work as one of the builders of the new society represented a very fruitful period in his life. Che's talents in that context were already apparent during the battles of the Sierra Maestra, where he organized workshops of weaponry, tailoring and shoemaking and the production of bread, beef jerky, cigarettes and cigars as logistical support for the guerrilla campaign. Then in late 1958, he led one of the forces that invaded central Cuba, capturing Santa Clara. That was the decisive victory of the war against the forces of Fulgencio Batista. After the revolution, El Che held various positions in government from where he oriented Cuba industry towards socialism, establishing concepts that ranged from the infrastructure to the smallest production unit. He was the driving force behind socialist planning, creatively applying to this system the principles, criteria and objectives identified with Fidel Castro, although he was not interested in power. Then, in April 1965, Che wrote the following letter to Fidel Castro:

"I formally renounce my position in the national leadership of the party, my post as minister, my rank as major, and my Cuban Citizenship... other nations of the world call for my modest efforts.

"In mid-1965, Che wrote his parents: Once again I feel between my heels the ribs of Rosinante; once more I must hit the road with my shield upon my arm. I believe in armed struggle as the only solution for those peoples who fight to free themselves, and I am consistent with my belief. Many will call me an adventurer, and I am, only one of a different sort; one of those who risks his skin to prove his platitudes. It is possible this may be the finish. I don't seek it, but it's within the realm of probabilities."

Hughes was pleased that he remembered the paper on Che Guevara.

"Ernesto," Castro said, "is a true revolutionary. Unless he has a war to fight or a society to remake, he is not happy. He is now in Bolivia attempting to overthrow the government. I do not want him to return from Bolivia. It is in both of our interests he does not return.

You have the ability to see that he doesn't."

Townsend and Hughes immediately understood what Castro was saying. Guevara, in his time in Cuba with the Cuban people had become as popular as the President. In recent days with the shortages and the embargo taking its toll, many people began to quietly grumble that the Revolution was failing. Castro feared Guevara might lead a movement to overthrow him. He feared that he would be successful, too.

"The men with him," Castro said. "They are loyal to him. None of them need come back to Cuba either."

"I understand," Townsend said.

"This must be kept at the highest levels only," Castro said.

"Yes, sir," Townsend agreed.

"All communication will be directly between you and my brother, Raul."

"Fine," Townsend said. "Mr. Hughes here with me today may fill in for me from time to time, sir."

Castro looked Hughes up and down. He smiled. Hughes remembered thinking how out of character he thought it was for a dictator to smile.

"That will be fine," he agreed. "I have had your Mr. Hughes checked out already. He is very acceptable."

Hughes was taken back by the idea that Castro already knew about him. He wondered how secure our security really was.

With that, Castro rose. Townsend and Hughes rose, too.

"Thank you for making such a long trip, gentlemen. I trust our arrangement will be fruitful for both of our governments.

"Your return flight is waiting for you. We have delayed their departure so you can return as soon as possible. My car will see that you arrive safely."

Fidel Castro turned and left the room.

A man appeared and led them down the stairs outside to the car. It was daylight now and John Hughes marveled at the beauty of the tropical island. They entered the car and they were whisked back to the airport where the jet was waiting. The car drove up to the jet and the men got out and went up the stair.

The documents for the SAM III missile were safely in Henry Townsend's brief case.

LANGLEY, VIRGINIA
OCTOBER 1, 1968

John Hughes remembered those first days. When they returned to Washington from that trip to Havana, the wheels of the system went into action.

The activity was designated Operation Eagle Thrust and units of the Special Forces were chosen to participate along with select detachments of the Air Force. Then, after choosing the units that were to participate, orders were cut for training at camps and bases in the Canal Zone. That would serve as their cover.

In the days and months that followed, John Hughes traveled regularly to Toronto. He met weekly with Raul Castro and important details about troop strengths and locations of the Cubans in Bolivia were being passed onto the United States. By spring they were ready to move.

ALEXANDRIA, VIRGINIA
OCTOBER 10, 1968
5:30 A.M.

The young woman opened her eyes and looked at the clock on the nightstand. It was five-thirty. At first she didn't know exactly where she was, but in only a few seconds she remembered making love with Charley. She was in a motel with him.

They'd met in a Georgetown bar several days before. She was a secretary for the FBI and remembered seeing him on the news being decorated by the Secretary of Defense. They had gone out to dinner the night before and wound up here.

Quietly she left the bed and went to the bathroom. When she returned, she found her slip and after putting it on, she got back into bed and listened to Charley's regular breathing. She closed her eyes and allowed her mind to drift.

Charley Reed was in a deep sleep and now he was beginning to dream. Ten of them were moving in from the west, coming down out of some rolling hills. They were cautiously moving through the tropical growth until finally they reached the valley floor covered with elephant grass. Three hundred yards away was a small village and the unit of men silently moved towards it.

As they crept across the distance in the darkness, Charley remembered playing army as a boy and sneaking up on his playmates in much the same way. Only he knew what he was doing wasn't play.

They expected to encounter the enemy. Just after one a.m. they surrounded and entered the sleeping hamlet, waking the residents and forcing them to the center of the village. The young men of the village were all gone. Only old people, women and children remained. This told the unit they were in an enemy village.

It always amazed him how a whole village would fight and support the enemy. He never understood how they could turn their backs on the Saigon government and go against their own people.

The village leader was an old man with a white beard, very few teeth, and no hair on the top of his head. The captain and sergeant took him behind a hut and questioned him. Meanwhile, everyone was held under guard in the center of the town. Six soldiers searched through the meager possessions in each household.

As the questioning continued, the old man cried out in pain. An old woman sat on the ground and began crying with fear. A baby suckled at its mother's breast as a little girl began to cry along with the old woman.

Charley could feel the tension building as they completed the search of the village.

Someone found a Viet Cong flag and took it to where the captain was questioning the old man. There were more cries of agony and then the sound of three shots. Immediately, silence engulfed the village.

Then the old woman screamed. Three of the older children broke from the group of people and started to run. The sarge came out from behind the hut.

"Kill them!" he ordered. "Kill them all!"

He pulled his side arm and shot the children as they ran past him.

"Kill them!" he screamed again.

Charley felt the hate rise within him. He turned and aimed his M-16 at an old man and fired. The old man was thrown back and fell motionless to the ground.

Gunfire erupted and filled the night. Women fell to the ground and screaming children began running into the elephant grass beyond the village. The sounds of automatic weapons continued to fill the air until there were only torn bloody bodies lying dead on the ground.

The baby was still at its mother's breast. A round had blown the left side of the mother's face and head away. On all sides of the dead mother were the rest of the villagers. Their bodies were twisted and bloody, some on their backs, others in contorted positions.

Charley stepped over the bodies and along with the others, began to set fire to the bamboo and grass huts. It didn't take long before the entire village was in flames.

The soldiers were moving back toward the hills when enemy fire came at them from the elephant grass. It was coming at them from three sides and they had no choice but to fall back into the burning village.

The heat and smoke in the village was so intense the men could barely breathe. Charley was coughing, trying to make his way through the village when he tripped over a body and fell onto another. Charley was looking directly into the eyes of a dead woman.

"No!" he screamed. "No! No! No!"

His screams woke the young woman and scared her. She jumped out of bed and turned on the light, calling his name. He continued to scream and then abruptly sat up in the bed.

"Oh, Christ!" he said, trying to bring himself back to reality.

"Are you all right?" she asked, afraid for him.

"Are you all right?" she repeated. "You were screaming."

Charley looked at her standing in her slip by the bed. Her blond hair was in her face and she was so beautiful. Suddenly he remembered making love to her and found himself wanting her again.

"I'm okay, honestly," he said. "I was dreaming. I'm sorry I frightened you. Please, come back to bed with me."

She turned off the lamp and got back into bed. "What were you dreaming?"

"The war," he answered.

"Tell me about the war," she said holding him.

"Nothing special," he said. "Just something that happened to me when I was there."

"Do you want to talk about it?" she asked as her body moved against his.

He turned on his side to face her. His hand ran through her hair and held the back of her head. His other hand ran the length of her body as he kissed her.

"Not really," he said. "It's something I haven't dreamed about before. It's better left forgotten."

She felt him grow hard against her and she knew he wanted to make love again. She responded to him and they made love. It was slow, soft, and it was gentle. When they were through, they fell asleep in each other's arms.

Charley didn't dream anymore.

CHAPTER THIRTY-EIGHT

ALEXANDRIA, VIRGINIA
OCTOBER 10, 1968
11:30 A.M.

Charley and Beth woke up around ten. They showered and went to breakfast. She was curious about his dream and asked him about his military service.

"What happened to you after you finished all of your basic training?" she asked.

"I went home to Pittsburgh and stayed there for a week. I was in jump school and a few other things. I was going into intelligence because I could learn languages, but they had other plans.

"They sent me to language school first. Then I went to the John F. Kennedy Special Warfare Center at Ft. Bragg, North Carolina and became a Green Beret."

"Was it tough?" she asked.

He smiled.

"One hundred men will test today, but only three win the Green Beret."

"Then what did you do?" she asked with a smile.

"I was sent to the Canal Zone with the First Special Forces in April of 1967."

"What did you do there?"

"Trained in the jungles, drank bourbon, and fought with the Marines."

Beth sat and listened to his story.

"After that," he said. "We went to Bolivia."

"Bolivia? Why there?"

"There was a revolution going on and we were supporting a dictator named Barrientos. Five hundred of us airlifted from the Canal

Zone to the grasslands in southeastern Bolivia."

"We sent American soldiers to Bolivia last year? Boy, I never knew that."

"Well, yes and no," Charley answered. "We weren't American soldiers while we were there."

"Well, who were you?" she asked.

"We were private citizens."

"How could that be? You were all in the Army!" Beth exclaimed.

"No one had any identification. We had no insignia of rank or indication of who or what we were on our uniforms. We carried foreign-made weapons and were under the command of the CIA on special orders."

"I've never heard anything about it," Beth said, shaking her head.

"Of course, you haven't," Charley told her. "You weren't supposed to hear anything."

"How long were you there?"

"We went in at the beginning of June and stayed until the middle of October."

"What did you do?"

"Killed Cubans and the guerillas," Charley answered her.

"You just went in there and killed people?"

"Sure," he answered. "Our job was to find the guerillas and kill them all. We had to maintain a very low profile. The Bolivians were to be the ones to take credit for the military victories."

"Are you serious?" she asked again.

"Of course, I am," he said. "I was there when Che Guevara was captured. I watched them beat and torture him and then put him against a wall and shoot him. They took pictures of his dead body and then burned it, along with about one hundred fifty others."

"My God, Charley, you're serious."

"I am," he said.

"Who beat and tortured him?" she asked.

"We did."

"American soldiers?"

"That's right. Soldiers and CIA agents."

"Why?"

"There were still more guerillas out there and we wanted their positions and strengths so we beat him."

"Did he tell you?" she asked.

"Yes," Charley answered. "He talked and the information he gave us was good, too."

Beth watched Charley as he talked about being part of the group that tortured and killed Che Guevara. He told the story without emotion of any kind. It was difficult for her to imagine the same young man she made love to was able to kill without emotion or thought.

"I find it hard to believe American soldiers could torture someone to make them talk."

Charley just laughed.

"The torture didn't make him talk. It was the fear of dying that did it. We told him we'd let him live if he talked."

"You guys lied to him."

"Sure we did. Why wouldn't we?

"We had already lost three hundred men and we didn't want to lose any more. It could have been any one of us, so no one cared what we did to end the whole thing. We weren't going home until they were all dead."

"So you lied to him to get him to talk?"

"Sure. You know what you have to do and you do it."

"Didn't you feel bad?" Beth asked.

"When he cried and begged for his life, I guess I did.

"He wanted a priest, but there weren't any around. It was just as well because we would have had to kill the priest, too. I felt a little funny, but once we shot him that passed. A gunshot is final and when the sound of it gradually fades, after enough of them, your personal feelings fade, too."

Charley thought for a moment. Beth watched and knew there was more he wanted to say. She waited quietly.

"We made him a figure in history by killing him. We made him larger than life when in fact he died a coward.

"If we hadn't killed him, he would have been just another good solider. This way he became a hero to the revolutionaries of the world.

"Haven't you ever seen an urban picture with the word 'Che' scrawled across a wall in paint? He already has his name and his picture in the Encyclopedia Britannica and a page and a half about his life. I saw it. It's there.

"We were born the same month and day. He was born June 14, 1928 and died October 8, 1967. He was thirty-nine years old when he died."

"You mean killed," she corrected him.

"Killed," he conceded.

"And that doesn't bother you?"

"No," he said. "Not at all. What does bother me is that we shot anyone who was wounded and couldn't get out on their own."

Beth was speechless. She just stared at him, unwilling to comprehend what he said.

"You mean our own men?"

"Yes," he admitted.

"My God, Charley, why?"

"Orders. We were all expendable. If we couldn't walk out, we were left behind."

"Americans don't do that!" she insisted.

"Americans do that," he assured her.

"Maybe when your father was in World War II, we didn't do that. This was 1967 and a different time. We'd been fighting Asian wars long enough to learn from them. A wounded or dead soldier is a dead soldier. We were there to search and kill. We took no prisoners and gave no quarter.

"We annihilated a force ten times our size in less than three months in a tropical rain forest at altitudes equivalent to the mountains in Colorado. The insects and snakes were as bad as the enemy. We were sick the whole time we were there."

"What on earth did they tell the families of the men who were killed there?" she asked.

"We were all in the Special Forces. Our families knew we were all mobile and they were told they were killed in Vietnam."

"I can't believe it!" Beth said in astonishment. "How could our government do something like that?"

"Easy," he said.

"I'm sure no one in Washington or any place else ever lost a minute sleep over any part of the operation. It began, took place, and ended. We came home and they reported a special unit of the Bolivian Army surrounded and killed Guevara. I read about it all in Time magazine."

Charley remained incredibly calm as he told Beth the story. She looked into his eyes and found an unusual emptiness as the story ended. It was as if he truly didn't care about what he had done.

She remembered his words about how they had made Che Guevara an historic figure. She thought about what Charley was saying.

There was nothing personal involved. It was a job and the soldiers did it, and somehow the story had never been told. Evidently, they were all remarkable men.

Later that day they were at Beth's apartment. Charley laid his head on the pillow and cuddled against her naked body. She felt the warmth of him and listened to his breathing as it slowed. He was asleep and without guilt.

Beth wondered about what her country was doing to innocent young men. She wondered about what it had done in a country where it had no business ever being in the first place.

"A lie is still a lie," she said to him. He was asleep and did not hear her as she spoke.

"You lived your lie and I'm living mine."

She thought about her boyfriend who was in Vietnam. She looked at the man next to her and suddenly he was the only one who mattered to her. She drifted off to sleep and began to dream.

Charley was already dreaming.

Buddy was his friend since Fort Benning. It was Buddy who asked him about the phone call.

"Is everything all right?" he asked.

Charley remembered telling him about Cindy and that she was pregnant.

"What are you going to do?" Buddy asked.

"Why, marry her," Charley answered immediately. "I've been in love with her since I was fifteen. I want her and I want our baby."

Charley remembered telling Buddy and meaning every word. Then Charley had to face him when he returned from Indiana. Somehow Buddy understood and didn't ask beyond the second short answer.

"She married someone else," Charley finally admitted.

"It's probably just as well. I'll die soon anyway. I'll never survive the war."

Charley Reed wasn't alone in that thought. Every young man felt the same way.

The young men in America were divided into three separate groups. There were those who were physically unable to serve. There were those who were mentally unwilling to serve. Finally, there were those who did serve. The last group accounted for only one out of every five men.

Buddy and Charley were still together when the Special Forces began Operation Eagle Thrust. It was a secret operation starting with the gradual deployment of men and equipment into the Canal Zone. Charley and his friend were among the first sent. They were part of the 601st Special Warfare Group.

Through the summer equipment was sent to the friendly Bolivian government and by the end of July the second phase of the operation was ready.

Major Beckwith boarded the jet assisted C-130 with the men of the 601st, 603rd, and the 614th. It was a steamy June evening and as the engines warmed, the men who waited to board could hear the millions of frogs croaking love songs to one another.

Charley, Buddy, and one hundred twenty more men boarded the transport that would take off into the west and make a gradual left hand turn and begin the fourteen hundred mile trip southward to Bolivia. Six and a half hours later they were over the drop zone.

"Stand up!" the major shouted as the men loaded with ninety-six extra pounds of combat gear stood up at the same time.

"Hook up!" he commanded as the men almost all at the exact moment attached the metal clip of their rip cord to the cables running the length of the aircraft on either side.

Then, as they all were facing the rear of the aircraft anticipating the unknown, the back door slowly opened. It was hydraulically operated and moved with a precision Charley Reed found himself admiring. It came down, opening an avenue into the blackness of the South American night. The chill of the late winter night moved forward through the transport until Charley and Buddy both felt the bite of the air.

"Stand in the door!" the major shouted and the entire group took five steps forward toward the door.

A buzzer sounded and a red light began to flash.

"Go!" the major shouted. "Go! Go!" he repeated over and over again.

Charley Reed came to the door and then left the aircraft. Buddy Hoogan followed him and both men assumed a tight body position as they waited for the jolt of the parachute when it opened and filled with air. Moments later they hit the ground with incredible force.

By that point their eyes had adjusted to the blackness and they could both see more men still falling to the ground. They had landed on an almost endless grassy plain in the southeastern part of the country. It was a star-filled moonless night and each soldier silently went about taking down and concealing his parachute. Within minutes they were formed into three separate units and began the four-kilometer march to a village north of them. The 601st assumed the position on the west side of the village and at 0400 hours the attack began.

The 614th invaded the center of the small town while the 603rd swept in from the east and circled to take the northern sections.

Charley and his unit set up along a line to the west and waited. They watched as small explosions illuminated the night and the sound of automatic weapons fire broke the silence surrounding them.

It wasn't a large town. There were no more than thirty buildings made of wood or adobe. The information supplied to the invading force said there was a group of over two hundred guerillas using the town as a base of operations and re-supply for the rest of the Cuban-backed forces.

Their mission was to eliminate this position.

The battle continued within the town and seemed to be moving closer to the 601st. Then, as the town was in flames and the explosions continued, silhouettes of armed men appeared running at the position the soldiers had taken.

No one fired or moved. Each man held himself in check until the escaping force was close enough that the faces of the terrified enemy could be seen by each and every one of the attacking men.

"Fire!" the captain screamed and Charley Reed took down four men in the first instant. He took aim and fired at men who turned and began running parallel to the line the 601st had taken. More men fell and the firing continued.

"Cease fire!" the captain commanded and the men immediately stopped and reloaded. The next command was to move forward and check the dead and wounded.

"No prisoners!" Charley heard the captain order and he understood what was expected. They moved through the bodies and insured each of the fallen enemy was dead. The ones that weren't dead were shot in the head.

"Sir!" someone called out to the captain. "Women and children, too?"

"I said no prisoners!" the captain repeated.

The answer was followed by the sound of four shots from a .45 automatic. It suddenly dawned on Charley they were to kill everyone. It was later on when he truly understood the scope of that command.

The 601st had no killed or wounded, but the 603rd and the 614th did. There were no provisions for removal of the dead or treatment for the seriously wounded. As they found out later, even a minor wound would become serious when they moved into the jungle and forest areas. The wounded were shot, too.

Charley didn't know what to think as he helped pile the bodies, enemy and American alike, in a pile and burn them.

In the following weeks, the three groups moved together as a single search and destroy force. They moved out of the grasslands into the forest.

They had several encounters with fringe elements of a much superior force by virtue of numbers alone. The Americans followed them through the villages and towns of eastern Bolivia and everywhere they were told the same story about the so-called Army of Liberation.

The people of the towns were always looted of whatever meager possessions they had including blankets, food and livestock. The women and young girls were raped and the men forced to join the revolutionary cause. If they resisted, they were shot. Che Guevara's army was nothing more than a massive group of bandits and scum, preying on the innocent peasants.

As the South American winter changed into September and spring began, the strike force was finally in position to cut off the enemy forces' escape into Guevara's Argentinean homeland. With Air Calvary support, the September 19th ambush wiped out an enemy force which had grown to nearly two thousand. Fighting unarmed and poorly trained bandits, the American casualties were very light.

Again, all the dead were burned in a common pyre.

There were other groups of Americans in other parts of the country. The engineers had built an airfield in the southeastern grasslands and supplies were stockpiled in the area. More forces swept down from the mountains in the west driving the revolutionary forces toward the point where the American strength was the greatest.

On October 6th, the forces met just outside the town of Cotoca, a hamlet of less than a thousand. It was only nine kilometers east-southeast of Santa Cruz, the provincial capital.

Charley's strike force drove into the heart of Cotoca on October 7th and captured a slightly wounded Ernesto 'Che' Guevara who was more than willing to surrender to the Americans rather than the Bolivian Army.

Later, Guevara would realize it really made no difference. Guevara was forced to talk, revealing the location of his second-in-command, Raymondo Rodriquez.

On the morning of the next day, the hero and partial architect of the Cuban Revolution was placed against a wall and shot. His bullet-riddled body was photographed and then burned with the last of his men.

A week later, the last of the enemy was cornered near Cochabamba and eliminated. In the last action of Operation Eagle Thrust, Buddy Hoogan was shot in the back by enemy fire.

It was then that Charley Reed disobeyed orders and began the one hundred kilometer hike with his wounded friend on his back. He managed to stop the bleeding and somehow Buddy managed to stay alive in spite of being dropped and falling to the ground every time Charley stumbled.

Two days later when Charley struggled up the ramp of the C-130 transport, placing his friend in the arms of the black man who was the air force loadmaster, Buddy had lapsed into a coma.

"Don't let them kill him," Charley begged Sergeant Poole. "Promise me you won't let them shoot him!"

"Hey, man," the loadmaster said. "The war's over. Get in and we'll get both of you out."

He called for a medic who boarded the plane. The plane took off a half an hour later.

Daylight was beginning when Charley woke next to Beth. They were wrapped in several blankets, their naked bodies still touching. He looked up to find her awake, watching him.

"Good morning," he said.

As he said it, he believed he was finally safe. He had no idea that John Hughes was having him watched.

Chapter Thirty-nine

Washington, D.C.
The Oval Office
October 11, 1968,
9:08 P.M.

The President was seated in a large stuffed chair when Henry Townsend entered the room. He had a glass of scotch in his hand. The television sets were off and the lights were low giving the room a sense of peace, even though a world of turmoil was swirling outside. The Presidential election was underway and Humphrey and Nixon were slugging it out. The main issue was the war and it seemed that Nixon was winning.

"Come in and sit down, Henry," the President said.

He poured him a glass of scotch identical to his own. Townsend wondered how many others ever had any President of the United States make them a drink. He was sure it wasn't many. Henry took the drink and sat across from Lyndon Johnson.

"There have been some accidents," the President said.

"I understand Philippine guerillas killed three of our people. I also understand two more were killed in Vietnam. So am I correct that now there are four non-exempt survivors of Eagle Thrust?" the President asked.

"Yes, sir," Townsend confirmed.

"Good," he said. "Leave it that way."

"Sir?" Townsend asked.

"Leave them alone. They are brave men and I don't want them touched. If your men are involved, order your men to stand down on them."

"Yes, sir," Townsend said.

Then he stopped. "But, sir, may I point something out?"

"Henry," he said taking a drink from his glass. "There's nothing to point out. Those men are not to be harmed. The sanctions you have ordered are now rescinded. Are we clear on that?"

"Yes, sir," Townsend said.

Then Johnson changed the subject.

"What do you think about the election?" he asked.

"It's a tough one to call," Townsend replied. "Wallace can be a spoiler."

"Bullshit!" the President said. "Nixon has it hands down. The North Vietnamese know it and that's why they are refusing to negotiate in good faith. They think they can cut a better deal with Tricky Dickey. They are in for a big surprise.

"If there ever was a war hawk, it's Nixon. The little bastards haven't done their homework on him. If they were ever going to get a deal, it would have been with me. This war will go on and on and on," he said.

"More boys will die and my legacy of public work will be overshadowed by this lousy war. Instead of being remembered for three Civil Rights Bills and my war on poverty, I will be remembered for this."

He took a long drink from his glass. Then he added more ice and more scotch.

"And why?" he asked.

He didn't wait for an answer. He answered the question himself.

"Just because I had to pay off the people who put me here. All those boys died because the War Industry and my friends wanted to be paid back."

His gaze drifted off to the portrait of Franklin Roosevelt.

"Money and power. Kennedy had it all and they hated him for it. They would have put up with him if he had played ball. He wouldn't and he paid the price. You and I sat back and let it happen."

"What were we going to do?" he asked. "Sir, we had no control."

"Didn't we, Henry?" the President asked.

"No, sir, we didn't," he said. "Everything was already in motion when we were brought in. He was going to die no matter what. If it wasn't one way, it was going to be the other. They would have taken Air Force One down if they had to. They wanted the war and he didn't. There was going to be a war one way or the other. If you would have stood in the way, they would have killed you, too, and the Speaker would be the President today."

Johnson laughed and took another drink.

"Old Sam as President. I could see that.

"And everyone thinks the President has so much power. Bullshit," he said. "Bullshit!

"I have power as long as they allow me to have power. And it will be that way for every President who follows me into this office, too. The same people bent on creating a new world order and a new world government will see to that. One day they will put their own men in this office and that's when the American people will really get fucked.

"When they did what they did, they set something into motion that will grow on them and ultimately consume even them in their ivory towers of power and safety. Before this is over no one will be safe anywhere. Someone will decide who lives and who dies, Henry, and that's why we have to stop what we are doing. We are no better than they are. We are an extension of them and I don't want to be any-more."

Henry Townsend had another drink with the President and left shortly after eleven. As the limousine drove him to his home in Chevy Chase, Beth Rathsman walked into the ladies room in a downtown nightclub.

Charley had to pull duty as Commander of Quarters at Fort Meade that night so she went out with two of her girlfriends. As she left the stall and walked to the mirror to check herself out, a woman came up from behind her. In a single movement she cut across her throat with a small knife. Beth fell to the floor, gasping for her life. In a moment, she was dead. The woman turned and walked out of the ladies room and disappeared into the crowd.

Henry picked up the phone and called John Hughes.

"The President has ordered a stand down on the eagles," he said.

"What?" Hughes asked.

"He has ordered an immediate stand down. Do I make myself clear?"

"Yes, sir," Hughes said. "I'm going to have to recall our people. We have action going on as we speak."

"Stop it. I don't care how. Just stop it now!" Townsend ordered. "Call me back and let me know the status."

"Yes, sir," Hughes said.

He walked out of his office and went to the small situation room where he ran the operation.

"What's the status?" he asked.

"One down," the man at the console reported.

"Stand down on the rest," he said. "Call our people back."

"Yes, sir," the man answered.

"I want to know when you have made contact and the orders are understood. I want to know immediately."

He went back to his office. He sat down in his chair and picked up the folder.

"Four of them left with Roger Knigge and Charley Reed here where we can get them," he said. "Four left and now we stand down. This is bullshit."

Within moments, the orders were given and confirmed as being received. It was relayed to John Hughes and he relayed it to Henry Townsend.

"The four eagles are safe, but the one bird was taken out," he said.

Townsend did not comment.

"Thank you," he said. Then he hung up the phone.

WASHINGTON, D.C.
SEPTEMBER 11, 2001
6:37 P.M.

John Hughes could still remember that night as if it happened the day before. He remembered tracking the men through the years. Two were discharged, one stayed in the military, and Reed was sent to a training base as a drill instructor.

Once he tried to have Reed sent back to Vietnam figuring his luck would have to give out sooner or later. Reed refused to go.

The Army was faced with a dilemma and the fact that before he left office, Lyndon Johnson awarded Reed the Distinguished Service Cross, the second highest award the military can give, only served to exacerbate the situation. Reed was adamant and the Army backed down. They let him finish out his time in the service as a drill instructor.

Reed got over the loss of his girlfriend Beth. Two years later, he married Joanna. They seemed happy enough. A year and a half after they were married, they had a baby boy who died two days after he was born. From that point on it was it was down hill.

He finished college and moved to North Carolina where he sold cars with a friend who owned an automobile dealership.

Hughes never lost track of him or his activities. He followed his extramarital affair with Jerilyn Gardner. He waited and bided his time until the day came when he could finish what he started.

The moratorium on the sanction held the rest of Johnson's life. When he died suddenly of a heart attack at his Texas ranch on January 22, 1973 and with Henry Townsend retired, John Hughes took it upon himself to complete the old business.

McLean, Virginia
January 23, 1973

John Hughes was cleared through the front gate at the CIA in McLean, Virginia just before ten in the morning. He parked in the north lot and walked to the main entrance where he was once again cleared through security. Ten minutes later he was in his supervisor's office, explaining what happened.

"Reed was one of the active participants in Operation Eagle Thrust. This was an operation conceived by the Pentagon to be carried out under our supervision by certain units of the Army. Counting support and engineering, over a thousand men took part in the operation. It was classified top secret.

"As of October 31, 1967, seventy-two had survived. The rest had become bona fide casualties in Vietnam, victims of accidents, and various other acts. The survivors were given exempt status."

"Exempt status?" the supervisor asked.

"Yes. At first any officer who was a West Point graduate and above the rank of captain still on active military duty or participating in one of our operations was exempt. President Johnson changed that. As of October 1968, all survivors became exempt. That left us with multiple security risks.

"Of the seventy-two survivors, twenty-seven were still on active duty and were eliminated through military accidents and unfriendly action in Southeast Asia during the next two years.

"During that same period we arranged accidents, drug overdoses, and suicides, thus having seventeen of the exempts eliminated without suspicion. Since then, all but two of the exempts have died of various natural causes. We verified the remaining twenty-six through various means.

"This man, Charley Reed, is unfinished business. Now that Lyndon Johnson is dead, I want to complete what we started. There is no reason to leave loose ends untied."

His supervisor agreed with him.

"What are you going to do about this one?"

Hughes looked out the window.

"He has a lot of problems ahead of him. We're seeing to that right now. Within a week, he'll commit suicide."

The supervisor nodded his head in agreement and Hughes returned to his own office. Already he knew the wheels were in motion.

WASHINGTON, D.C.
SEPTEMBER 11, 2001
6:55 P.M

John Hughes finished his phone call. Two more of the Arabs were dead. Before they died, they gave up a wealth of information and names. CIA operatives were already in the process of finding those people and bringing them in for interrogation.

Then he turned his attention to something else. He brought up the file on Charley Reed and had agents busy getting more information on him as Charley Hayes. He ordered phone surveillance on his home and on his businesses.

The file was an old one. It ended the year Charley Reed died with a copy of the death certificate and clippings from the local newspapers that told about how he was killed in a fiery automobile crash. Hughes backed up in the file and read through the known associates section.

He began reading aloud.

"Bob Walker - Oxen Hill, Maryland. Jerilyn Gardner - Greenville, North Carolina. Lee Stein - Greenville, North Carolina. Joseph Kelly - Erie, Pennsylvania. Walter Davenport - Raleigh, North Carolina."

Hughes held the file in his hand and stood up. He was safe, deep underground in the command center. He was calling the shots as to who was and who was not being picked up.

"Where are you going to run?" he asked aloud. "Where will I find you and how am I going to let you kill yourself?"

John smiled, knowing he would enjoy this job. This was why he joined the Company. Tying up loose ends from the sixties was going to be an interesting diversion.

Ken O'Brien knocked at his door and John told him to come in.

"Sit down," Hughes said, taking a seat himself.

"Where are we?" he asked.

"He has problems," O'Brien said, smiling at his boss.

"We found years ago he took out a Small Business Administration loan using the name Charles Wilson Hayes and Hayes' social security number. The loan has been paid off, but he violated federal laws in falsifying documents to obtain funds from a federal lending institution. He has been filing false income tax returns for years, even though they are financially accurate. There are numerous state charges that can be brought against him for falsifying his applications for driver's license, business license, not to mention various fraud statutes."

"That's good," Hughes said. "That gives us justification for picking him up. Even though he doesn't look like a fucking Arab, this is exactly how they would have played it and he fits right into our deep-cover mole routine. He can be a sympathizer. He can be a paid mercenary. We can kill him with justification.

"Who are you working with on this?" Hughes asked.

"Brown. The U.S. District Attorney in San Francisco."

"Is he a good man? Can we trust him?"

"He owes me," O'Brien said. "I helped him with some less than legal deposits of money and drugs so he could get a conviction in the Fontana case last year."

"Yes," Hughes said, remembering the nationally publicized case. "That was good work. That's how I want you to get this guy. Use the RICO statutes and get him on federal racketeering charges. Put some pressure on your man. I want us to get this thing rolling. Our boy is a loose canon and if he knows or even suspects we're onto him, he could hurt us."

"I understand," O'Brien said. "When do you want him terminated?"

"The sooner, the better," Hughes said.

"He can resist and shoot it out with us. We can make links to militia groups. Is there any one we want to take out? Link him to them and we can get them all at once."

He picked up an 8 x 10 photograph of Charley Reed and Bob Walker sitting together in a bar in Alexandria, Virginia. The date on the back of it was 1971.

Hughes smiled.

"You're mine," he said. "You ass belongs to me."

He felt good. This was a job he wanted.

It wasn't because he hated Charley Reed. No, it was because he understood the American people could never know what happened in 1967.

Charley Reed not only knew, but he was a witness to it.

He took part in Operation Eagle Thrust. It had been American planning and execution at its very best. American soldiers defeated a force many times their size commanded by the most famous revolutionary leader of the time, a leader who had written books on guerilla warfare.

Che Guevara was larger than life. He had been a medical doctor and had traveled to North Vietnam and advised General Giap on how to fight the American Army. He'd been to the Congo and created the Patrice Lamumba Division. Guevara had done all that, yet when we wanted to, we took him.

Charley Reed was in the very group that did it.

Charley Reed was there when Guevara was questioned. Charley Reed understood Spanish and he certainly heard the questions that were asked about the Kennedy assassination. And if he heard the questions, he certainly heard the answers, too. In itself, that was a threat to national security.

And he saw him shot, too.

What a story it would make if it ever came out! Charley Reed could embarrass the government and get the entire country angry.

The obvious question would be how we were able to carry out such an efficient and covert operation in such a short period of time when the Vietnam War, which was going on at the same time, was run with such inefficiency. How were we able to defeat a superior force and yet not win against the North Vietnamese when we had all the power and might of our military arsenal at our disposal?

John Hughes thought of the city somewhere above the command center. What was happening up there? How were the people dealing with the disaster? What was Charley Reed thinking?

It was at that very moment he realized this was a secret not even the President of the United States knew. It was his job to keep this secret.

Charley Reed knew the whole story. Charley Reed had to die.

CHAPTER FORTY

Pittsburgh, Pennsylvania
September 11, 2001
7:07 P.M.

Cindy sat and thought of the attack that took her son.

For some reason she kept thinking of her mother and her mother's funeral. Her mind wandered back to the past.

The priest was reading the Litany of the Saints and everyone was answering with the proper responses. Cindy held her son's arm and mindlessly gave the answers to the litany she had been taught by the nuns when she was in the third grade. Her mind became numb. Those few months were some of the worst in her entire life.

When her father died, she wasn't sure she could ever get over it. Her father always represented security to her. When he died, all she had left was her mother and now she was gone, too. She was divorcing her husband. When Julie left for college, she'd be alone.

Cindy's hand clutched the firm arm of her son. She smiled up at him as he looked at her lovingly. On his other arm was Tina, his wife. One generation ended as another prepared to begin with the birth of their first child.

Cindy remembered feeling very old and tired as she repeated after the priest. She remembered being here with her mother this last November to visit Charley's grave. It seemed strange to have her mother buried so close to Charley Reed.

Cindy remembered at her mother's funeral she looked across to the edge of the hill where he was buried. She saw a man standing there watching them. It had started to snow lightly and his frame was erect against the gray sky behind him. He was standing very close to where Charley was buried. For a moment she found herself wishing it was Charley.

Shaking her head, she tried to concentrate on the service for her mother. Andrea was weeping out loud and Lisa was biting her lower lip. Some things never changed.

Lisa tried so hard not to show any emotion. Whenever she felt she might, she bit her lower lip. Andrea, on the other hand, was very emotional. When the family moved from Pittsburgh, Andrea cried for a week until she was so sick she had to be put in the hospital. But, these sisters were all she had left and she told herself even though they were both grown women, they were still her baby sisters and she was still their big sister.

Cindy remembered looking back to where the man was standing. He was still there and it was still snowing. She wondered why he came on a day like this and what he was doing over there by himself. Cindy watched as he turned his head. First she saw a profile and then a view of his face straight on. Even though he was fifty yards away, she gasped and squeezed her son's arm. The man stood there looking directly at her for what seemed to be minutes, but was actually only seconds.

Then he walked from the graves to his car parked on the side of the road. As she watched him come closer, her heart began to pound. He turned his back to her and got into the car. She was astonished at the resemblance. Then the car with the California plates drove away. And then the Monsignor concluded the graveside service.

She never forgot him. It was as if a ghost came to visit her on the day of her mother's burial. She wondered why.

The next day was the reading of her mother's will.

She remembered Chuck when he arrived at the lawyer's office. He was taken into a large conference room. She was there along her sisters, Andrea and Lisa. Andrea's husband, John, was with her. Julie sat on one side of her and Chuck on the other. Chuck took her hand as they all sat silently.

The attorney walked into the room and introduced himself. Without any ceremony, he opened the will and began immediately. The reading of the will was very matter of fact. Marilyn had very specific instructions.

She had cash left from her husband's estate. The cash was divided between all of the grandchildren and was to be held in trust until they began college. The money was for college and if they didn't attend, they had to wait until they were twenty-five to get it.

Marilyn's house was to be sold and divided between Cindy's two sisters and herself. Her car was to be given to her cleaning lady. Then there was a long list of jewelry specifically described and listed as to which daughter was to receive it.

Marilyn George owned an extensive portfolio of stock and life insurance. It was to be divided equally between Cindy, Andrea, and Lisa. There was one exception and that was the exception that shocked everyone.

Marilyn George owned one hundred percent of the stock in Rocky Mountain Hardware. She acknowledged her son-in-law, Adam Ganley, who with her money had built a prosperous business. She willed him ownership of a key-man life insurance policy having a cash value in excess of one hundred sixty thousand dollars. Ownership of the stock and the business was given to her grandson, Chuck Ganley.

It was her mother's irony that always astonished Cindy. She gave Adam's business to her grandson. When news of what she had done reached Adam, he had a massive heart attack and died instantly. Cindy no sooner buried her mother and she had to return to Utah to bury her husband.

In the following months, Cindy sold the home in Utah and bought her mother's home from the estate and paid off her sisters. She moved back to Pittsburgh after Julie finished high school. She moved into her mother's house and changed nothing. And then the years passed.

They passed until today, September 11th.

She was finally alone. She was alone still living in her mother's house after all of those years. In her mind it seemed very fitting. What better place than this to live out her punishment?

So many people came around, all of them concerned about her. She didn't mind them. There were all those years she had been alone. While people were around, her mind couldn't drift.

But now, as evening came and they went home, she was finally alone and she couldn't help herself. She thought of Adam and she thought of Charley. It had been so long ago.

Adam never made her feel like a woman. He made her feel awkward and uncomfortable. She couldn't naturally respond to him like she had with Charley. She knew now there had been something about Adam she resented. Making love to him was a duty. It was not fun and she resented him for it.

The resentment buried itself within her and even though they had four daughters, she never once allowed herself to let go and fully enjoy the act of making love. It was never the way it should have been and it was her fault. She knew it.

The natural and warm lovemaking with Charley was so completely different from anything she ever experienced with Adam. With Charley she closed her eyes, held him tight, and let herself give and receive in full pleasure. He touched her and she responded to him. He touched places inside of her no one ever did or could again.

With Adam, her eyes never closed and the more he wanted her, the more she secretly hated him. In punishing him, she also punished herself. She didn't mind one bit.

Right now, after all the years, she made the comparison. Cindy remembered promising herself as she packed to leave and marry Adam that she wouldn't compare. She wondered why she made such a stupid promise to herself. Cindy knew the answer as she grieved for her son and thought of his father.

As she sat in her mother's rocking chair with a cup of tea, she spoke out loud to her dead mother.

"Why, Mother? Why couldn't I have the man I loved? Why was it so important I marry Adam?

Cindy waited, almost expecting her dead mother to answer. She waited, but heard nothing. Except for the sounds of the fire crackling, the house was silent.

"Why?" she screamed, spilling the hot tea on her bare knee.

"Damn!" she screamed.

It was quite out of character for Cindy to do something like that. It was even more so when she flung the cup at the fireplace, smashing it to pieces.

Cindy wiped the tea from her leg using her bare hand. She looked at the pieces of the cup. It was one of her mother's favorites. It was part of a coffee serving set she saved for special occasions.

Cindy looked at the saucer she was still holding and threw it against the brick fireplace, too. As it shattered and the pieces fell to the floor with those of the broken cup, Cindy smiled. Now the set was incomplete. It was no longer perfect.

"Look, Mother, I've ruined your coffee set," she said aloud. "It's not perfect anymore. It's incomplete! I suppose I should to go to town and order a replacement. That's what you would do. Should I do the same Mother?"

Cindy waited for an answer. She laughed hysterically.

"I think I won't. I think not only won't I fix it, but also I won't tell anyone the set is broken. Only you and I will know the set is incomplete.

"Lisa won't care. She never did have any time for your sets of fine china and porcelain dolls. Lisa cared about life and that bothered you, didn't it?"

Again Cindy listened for an answer, and again there was only silence.

"I tried, Mother. I tried, but I failed miserably. I listened to you, but you were wrong. How does it feel, Mother?"

She demanded in an even louder voice, "Tell me, Mother! How does it feel?

"You were always right. Everything you did was always right, wasn't it? You had the perfect marriage, didn't you? I know you didn't think so, but you made sure everyone else believed it.

"Then you had three perfect daughters.

"What happened to Lisa, Mother? How could your baby run off with a drummer in a band and become an airline stewardess? That wasn't very perfect, was it?"

Tears began to run down Cindy's face.

"Maybe I should have listened to my little sister."

Cindy remembered packing to leave with Adam. Even though Lisa was a lot younger, there had been so much discussion and tears in those days, she knew what was happening.

"If it was me," Lisa told her, "I wouldn't listen to Mother. I'd marry Charley. I like him. He likes bunny rabbits."

Cindy remembered the bunny rabbits and she remembered her little sister being so sincere.

"I should have listened to Lisa," she said to her mother.

"I should have, but it wouldn't have been perfect! I was your perfect daughter. I did what my mother told me. I didn't like it, but I did it.

"You paid off Adam to take me and keep me perfect. I wasn't ever supposed to know, but I always did. I knew and I hated you both for it. Did you know that, Mother? I hated you both!"

Cindy stood and went over to the broken pieces of china. Bending down, she carefully picked up each separate piece. It took several minutes, but when she stood, Cindy had even the smallest fragment of the broken china.

She walked to the kitchen and dropped the pieces in the trash. She brushed her hands against one another and then opened the cupboard and took down the remaining pieces of the set. Looking around she found a box large enough for the saucers, cups, and coffee server. Then she took each piece and carefully wrapped them in paper and cushioned them in the box. When the last piece was packed, Cindy went back to the cupboard. She had a smile on her face.

"Let's see," she said. "We can't send an incomplete set."

Looking through the cupboard she found one she was sure would do. It was a large black and gold coffee mug with 'Superbowl IX Pittsburgh Steelers' written on it.

"This will do," she said aloud.

Then she packed it with the others, taking the same care as before.

She found a piece of paper and a pen. She wrote in her usual neat penmanship:

Andrea,
This was Mother's favorite coffee set.
She would want you to have it.
Love, your sisters,
Lisa and Cindy

Cindy sealed the box, addressed it, and laid it by the door so she could take it to the post office.

"There, Mother," she said. "We've sent your serving set to the only perfect daughter you ever had. We should have called her Marilyn Jr. instead of Andrea.

"Yes, Mother," Cindy continued as she walked into her mother's bedroom. "Andrea was your perfect daughter. You had the beautiful Catholic wedding for her. All of your friends and all of father's business associates came. You had the wedding announced in the Pittsburgh Press. Why, she even married a banker's son! You didn't have to buy him off like you did with me."

Cindy sat on her father's side of the bed. She tucked her left foot beneath her as she sat looking at the pillow on her mother's side.

"I hated Adam, Mother. I always hated him. I loved Charley, but you wouldn't let me have him. Were you jealous of me? Is that why I couldn't have him? Did you wonder what it was like to be with a man you really loved and wanted? Is that why you wouldn't let me have him?"

She stared at the pillow, her teeth clenched.

"I liked it, Mother," she said. "I liked it with him when I was young, too. I've always liked it with him, but you wouldn't let me have him.

"I was a good daughter," she said as her voice trailed off into almost a whisper.

"I didn't want to embarrass you or father so I did as I was told."

Cindy stood up from the bed.

"Now that his son is dead, he is finally gone, too. He's finally gone, Mother, and he won't be back. Not ever, Mother," she said as she turned and left the bedroom.

Cindy went back to the rocking chair in front of the fire.

"He told me that I'd never let him be part of my life, Mother. I told him he was wrong, but maybe he wasn't. He was right, Mother. He was right."

She looked into the fire and started to cry.

"His son is dead and I'm a selfish bitch just like you, Mother. There wasn't anything for him with me. You always said he wasn't good enough for me. You were wrong! I wasn't good enough for him.

"He was a kind, gentle man. He hurt, Mother, and didn't have anyone to help him. He hurt and yet he helped other people and didn't complain. He didn't have anyone to complain to, did he? He didn't have anyone, Mother. He didn't even have his own son. You were terribly wrong about him."

The tears were still running down Cindy's face. She sat alone in her mother's house.

CHICAGO, ILLINOIS
7:25 P.M.

Chuck's obvious death in the horrendous attack on the World Trade Center was a blow to everyone. It was more of one to Jerilyn than she imagined. What was Tina going to do?

With the jets grounded, she couldn't even go to her daughter and be with her. She ached for Tina, but there was something more. There was something beyond Chuck's death. His dying brought back the memories of his father.

Jerilyn was sitting on the edge of the bed in her panties and bra. She was getting ready to go out with Bob. Even in spite of the events of the day, Bob had a business dinner they could not escape. She was holding her pantyhose, getting ready to put them on, when her thoughts drifted to Charley Reed.

She remembered living with him in Washington, D.C. and how hard he tried to make a life for them. She remembered him borrowing money just to pay the rent and buy groceries. He was using his credit cards for gasoline and to buy drinks when they would go out at night. All the while she stayed home and took care of the children.

Maybe she had too much time on her hands. Maybe she was never meant to be a housewife. The more he did, the more she was restless.

She called a guy back in North Carolina and called Sam in Illinois. She called them every day for a week before she realized how much she really had with Charley. She watched the children begin to depend on him more and more. Finally, Jerilyn realized she needed him, too.

Charley used to come home from work and talk to her. She would make them vodka martinis and they would sit together on the couch. Sometimes he would rest his head in her lap. During those times his mind would drift and she would ask him where he was.

"No where in particular," he answered one time. "I was just thinking about us."

"What about us," she asked him.

"What's going to happen to us and where will we be in a year?"

"You think about things too much," she said.

"I'm sorry," he answered her. "I worry. I have this fear I'm going to lose you."

Jerilyn remembered him saying that. She didn't tell him not to worry or tell him he was imagining things. Instead, she said nothing. She turned off the television and put on the stereo.

"Come here with me," she said, bringing him down on the floor with her.

It was one of those rare times when she broke down and cried in his arms. She knew he was confused and as she cried, she admitted she wasn't sure what she really wanted.

"Maybe it would be better if the kids and me just went back home. We're all such a burden on you and you're working so hard."

Charley wouldn't hear of it. He was the one who started out asking for reassurance and ended up giving it to her. He reassured her and she said nothing back. He lived in constant fear that she would leave him. She knew that and in a way, enjoyed it.

"What's your problem?" she would ask him.

"I love you," he said. "I don't want you to leave. Doesn't that mean anything to you?"

Again, she said nothing. Instead, she looked out the balcony window at the trees. "I'm here," she said.

She was irritated with him.

"What else do you want? I don't understand."

"I want you to love me," he pleaded. "I want you to stay with me and love me. I want us to be happy. Doesn't that make sense to you?"

Jerilyn stood up and walked away from him.

"Where are you going?"

"To wash dishes!" she said.

"Why won't you answer me?" he pleaded with her.

"When you act like a man instead a little boy, then I'll answer you."

Jerilyn was in the kitchen and had begun to run the water, rinsing off the dishes before putting them into the dishwasher. Jerilyn remembered Charley got up and followed, shouting at her.

"What in the name of hell is that supposed to mean?" he asked in a much louder voice.

She turned and met him face to face before he could come through the doorway of the kitchen.

"Exactly what I said!" she screamed in his face. "Since we moved here you've been nothing but some whining little kid. You come home, eat, and go to sleep on the couch. Then you wake up and expect me to fall all over you. Every time I turn around or bend over you're ready to climb on me."

"Listen to you!" Charley shot back. "Just listen to you! The Queen of the Carolina Inn! Miss Hot Pants complaining about getting laid too much! This is unbelievable! What would every man in Greenville, North Carolina say if they could hear you now? If I walked into the Carolina Inn and said Jerilyn Gardner is complaining about getting too much sex, I'd be called a liar!"

She remembered how angry she felt.

Charley walked past her and make himself a drink.

"You must really hate me," he said to her.

"I don't hate you," she said. "I just don't understand you."

Charley looked into the glass he held in his hand, swirling the vodka and the ice cubes.

"What's there not to understand?" he asked.

"You make a big deal out of other men. I'm here with you. You have me! I'm with you and I love you. You have this idea you have to be some tremendous stud, performing morning, noon and night.

"Love isn't sex and sex isn't love. You don't know the difference and even right now, you don't believe it. You're insecure and you expect me to fix it for you. I can't! Only you can fix it for yourself."

She turned her back to him and looked out the window. Charley looked out the window, too, and escaped into his past. He watched a squirrel run across the lawn and up the trunk of a tree.

"You're right," he said softly. "I don't understand love. I understand sex and to me that's love because I don't cheat when I'm in love."

"What about five years from now?" she remembered asking him. "What about twenty years and I'm not so pretty anymore?"

Yeah, what about it, she asked herself, looking at the pantyhose in her hands.

She looked up at Bob who was in a pair of boxer shorts and a white tee shirt. His belly hung over the shorts and his arms were soft. But it didn't matter any more. Bob loved her.

It was then that she realized so had Charley.

CHAPTER FORTY-ONE

GREENVILLE, NORTH CAROLINA
FEBRUARY 11, 1973
7:07 P.M.

John Hughes arrived at the Holiday Inn just after six. He followed Charley Reed from Washington, D.C. He missed him the day before. Reed left for North Carolina unexpectedly. An agent running his credit card activity traced him to this hotel.

At that moment Charley Reed was meeting with Jerilyn Gardner. They had broken up at the end of the summer and it had been months since they had seen one another. They met at Darryl's.

Charley walked into the bar just after seven. She was there waiting for him. She didn't see him come in. He stood in the doorway and just watched her until she finally looked up to see him.

"Hello, tough guy," he said in a gentle way. His face broke into a full smile as he took her hand.

"Tough guy?" she asked. "What does that mean?"

He just smiled and never did answer the question.

"You really look great, Jerilyn," he told her.

She smiled back at him. "You look good yourself."

"Thank you," he said. "And thank you for meeting me."

"You didn't think I would?"

"I wasn't sure."

"Well, how long are you going to be in town?" she asked him.

"Just a day or two," he said. "I came down to see Lee. He called me."

Jerilyn relaxed in her seat, realizing it was nice to be with him again.

"Where are you staying?" she asked.

"With Joanna," he answered without hesitating.

"Are the two of you going back together?"

"No," he said.

"Don't you want to?"

"I don't really feel like talking about it," he said.

"Why?"

"Oh, a lot of reasons. Besides, she says she doesn't love me, so why would I want to be with her?"

"Do you believe her when she says that?"

"Why not? When I was with her she didn't treat me like she loved me. If she had, I might never have needed you."

Jerilyn listened to what he said.

"You're right," she said. "You told me, but I never believed you about Joanna."

Charley changed the subject. "How are the kids?"

"Just fine," she said. "Tina is in first grade. She's really cute, too. She's a real little lady."

"I'll bet," Charley said.

"She talks about you all the time. When I look back at it, you were really good for her. You taught her to print her name and you made her feel safe. Thank you for that."

Charley was a little embarrassed when she thanked him.

"I didn't do anything special," he said.

"You loved her. That was more than any man ever did for her. And you gave her confidence in herself. That was the biggest thing.

"After her father left us she didn't have any. Even before she started kindergarten, she felt inferior to the other kids. You taught her how to print and in school she became somebody special because she already knew. She was the teacher's helper, helping the children who were having trouble printing."

Charley smiled.

"And what about Anne Marie?" he asked.

"Bigger and meaner," Jerilyn replied.

"She's not mean," Charley objected. "She's a good kid. She's stuck there in the middle between Tina and Michael and doesn't know where she belongs. She's bad just to get attention."

Then they talked about Michael and she told him he was potty-trained. Her sister Ruth had trained him.

"I was wrong about Ruth," Charley admitted. "She comes on strong, but she's got a heart of gold. She deserves more than what life has given her."

"She likes you," Jerilyn said. "If I get depressed, she talks about you and tries to cheer me up."

"Does it?"

"I make her stop," Jerilyn said. As she spoke she saw something in his face. She noticed what she said seemed to hurt him.

"Michael is awfully cute. He laughs real loud and smiles all the time. Michael misses you more than the girls. You were his first daddy and he really loved you."

Charley looked down at the floor. She noticed he still had a full beer in front of him.

"Why aren't you drinking," she asked.

"I don't know," he said. "Do you think I'm sick?"

"No," she said reaching for his hand.

"Are you working anywhere?"

"No," he answered.

When she asked what he was doing, he shrugged his shoulders and said, "Sitting here talking to you and just taking everything as it comes."

"Are you going to do anything?"

"Lee wants me to come back to work for him. But I don't know," he answered. "I don't have a job and I guess I'm going to need one pretty soon."

"He has another sales manager, doesn't he?" she asked.

"Yes, Jake Adler," he answered.

"Is he going to fire him?"

"No," Charley answered. "He wants me to handle used cars and work the auctions. Right now Lee and Jake do that for the most part."

"Won't Jake think of you as a threat to him?"

"Probably," Charley said seeming unconcerned.

"Why don't you work for someone else?

"You're so much better than Lee. You shouldn't be working for him. You'll do what you want, I know, but you don't have any business putting up with the way he is. You're better than that."

She watched his face and how he began to warm towards her. The subject changed and they began to talk about how it had been for them. She talked about his jealousy and he talked about how she flirted. She remembered how she thought he had other women and how emphatically he denied it.

"I didn't believe you then and I still don't," she said with a pout.

"I know," he said. "But you're wrong. I had opportunities, but I never once did."

She remembered how she didn't believe him and how it really

made him angry.

"Oh, there must have been others," she told him. She was testing him. She wanted to know for sure.

"No, there weren't," he insisted. "You were all I ever wanted or could handle for that matter."

He laughed as he spoke about it. She remembered him laughing.

"You used to complain about me having a martini and falling asleep. What do you think it would have been like if I'd been out doing some other woman in the daytime? I would have been dead!"

Jerilyn still argued with him.

"Look," he said. "I was busy trying to sell cars to keep us going. You used to sit by the pool all day and then complain to me when I came home. Imagine how I felt when I was out there working, trying to make money."

"You told me you had money," she said.

"I lied," he admitted. "I was trying to impress you. I worked for every penny. I was up to my ass in debt and I was supporting you like a queen and at the same time you were calling other men, telling them how miserable you were. You never told me you were pregnant. I never knew until you miscarried."

"I didn't know if I wanted another baby," she said. "I had three."

"But it was mine," he said.

"Yes. But I didn't know if I could depend on you and in the end, I couldn't. You brought me back here and dumped me in my brother's front yard."

"At least I didn't leave you stranded like Sam did in Illinois."

"But the kids," she said. "They loved you and you never thought about it. You just walked away!"

"They loved me, but their mother didn't."

"I did," she said. "I loved you. I just couldn't love you the way you wanted me to."

"All I wanted was for you to only want me so I wouldn't worry every other minute."

"You acted like a little boy," she said. "I was with you and no one else. For some reason you never understood that. You wanted more than what I could give you. You wanted to own me. All I ever wanted you to do was love me."

"That's all I wanted," Charley said quietly.

A tear came out of his eye and ran over his cheek. He looked away and wiped the tear off.

"It looks like we messed up," he said.

Jerilyn drank her beer and stared across the bar. Her jaw tightened as she thought about what he said. She reached over and placed her hand on his wrist. She knew what he was saying was true and she knew if she wanted, she could have him again. All she would have to do was say the words.

"We used to talk," he said. "We just never really communicated. You told me you loved me, but you just never made me believe it."

"You wanted too much, Charley. You wanted it all at once. You were too impatient," she said.

Charley just stared at her.

"It was my fault. I'm sorry," he said. "I blame myself because it didn't work."

Tears filled his eyes as he apologized.

"You're the only woman who can do this to me. I still love you."

She said nothing. She looked at his face and ran her fingers along his forearm and felt the ripples of his muscles as they tightened.

"Are you still my baby?" she asked.

"Always," he answered. "You know that.

"Do you miss me?" he asked.

"Yeah," she said smiling. "I miss you a little."

"Really?"

"No, I miss you a lot," she admitted.

He picked up her hand and kissed and kissed it.

"I love you," he told her.

"I love you, too," she said.

Charley smiled. "Then let's stop all this and go back together."

"I can't," she said. "I just can't.

"But why?"

Jerilyn looked at him and forced a smile. "We're no good for you. You'd be unhappy again."

Charley understood what she said, but didn't want to believe it.

"If we tried, we could," he said.

"That's it, baby," she said. "We would try for awhile, but we wouldn't make it last. It wouldn't work."

They talked longer and then he left. It was the last time Jerilyn saw him.

Charley left the bar and went outside. As soon as he walked out, he ran into Joanna in the parking lot. She was outside waiting for him.

"I should have known you went to see her," she said. "Nothing ever changes. You are in town one day and you have to go sniff her out."

Charley didn't try to defend himself. What good would it do?

356 THE FIRST TERRORIST ACT

Joanna already had her mind made up.

She opened her car door and pulled his suitcase out. She threw it on the ground.

"Go stay with her," she said. "Don't ever call me again. I don't ever want to see you again."

Joanna got in her car and drove away.

Charley picked up the suitcase and put it in his car. He looked back at the bar. Jerilyn was still inside. He turned and walked back inside.

She was sitting at the bar with a man. She was holding his hand and they were talking. Looking at her face he knew. It was over for them. He turned and walked away. Jerilyn never knew that he came back. She never knew.

As he walked to the car and drove away, suddenly going back to work for Lee Stein didn't matter. He had all of his clothes in the car and he had a full tank of gas. Charley turned and drove past the Holiday Inn and out into the country. He started north for Washington.

Charley didn't mind driving. It gave him a chance to get lost in his thoughts. He thought about Jerilyn and he thought about Cindy.

"Where is Cindy George?" he asked out loud. "Where is my baby?"

Charley remembered a blustery November Saturday. The snow was squalling as he walked from the bus station, across the bridge over the river, across campus and another mile to her home. He could still remember ringing the bell and Marilyn George answering and then yelling at Lisa to get away from the door.

Even after all these years, the icy tone of her voice never seemed to fade. He'd been calling all week and she had stopped every call. Now she was in the doorway, blocking him.

"I told you yesterday morning not to bother. All you've done is waste your time and money by coming here. She's gone and she's married someone else and there's nothing you can do about it. The best thing you can do is turn around and go back where you were."

"But she's having my baby!" he protested.

"Nothing she has belongs to you and the sooner you understand that, the better for all of us. Now, leave before I call my husband."

"Go ahead!" he said.

"Good!" she said back to him. "If you're not gone in thirty seconds, I'm calling the police."

He remembered the door slamming in his face and the wind penetrating his cotton uniform. The walk back to the bus station was longer than the one to the house. As he crossed the campus he could hear the roar of the crowd in the football stadium. There were thousands of people celebrating in unison and he was alone, denied access to a woman he loved and the baby that was theirs.

He was alone then just as he was alone at that moment. Slowly he guided his car on to Interstate 95. He was getting tired.

He was on the interstate highway for about a half an hour. He saw a sign for Emporia, Virginia and he took the first exit. Immediately, he saw a Holiday Inn and he stopped there for the night. After checking in and taking his bag to the room, he went to the bar. He sat down and ordered himself a beer.

"It's good to get off the road," he said to the bartender.

They exchanged polite words. The bartender asked where he was coming from and Charley answered him.

Next to him were a man and a woman. The man was big and rough looking. The woman looked cheap. She was wearing a short skirt and a tight sweater.

The man got up and went to the rest room. As soon as he left, the woman smiled at Charley and said hello.

"You're going to Washington, D.C.?" she asked.

"Yes," he said, "Oxen Hill, actually."

"What do you do up there?" she asked.

"I sell cars," he told her.

"My boyfriend drives truck," she said. "He's in town over night. We haven't seen each other for two weeks."

"Good for you," Charley said to her.

About that time the man came back to the bar. He introduced himself as Dan. He also introduced Carla.

Charley settled in and tried to relax. He continued talking to the man and the woman. The bar filled up and before long they had gone through quite a few beers.

Charley got up and went to the rest room. When he returned there was a fresh beer waiting for him.

"You're a nice guy," Dan said. "We bought you a beer."

Charley took a drink of his beer. He remembered how good it tasted and how it seemed to finally relax him. He took another long swallow and sat back in the barstool. Charley felt himself become lightheaded and sleepy.

"Wow," he said to Dan. "This one is really hitting me. I'm going to have to call it a night."

The bartender was standing there when Charley got up to go

back to his room. As he did, his legs began to give out on him and he nearly fell to the floor. Dan caught him.

The bartender was immediately annoyed.

"I'll take care of him," Dan offered. "I'll get him back to his room."

"Thank you," the bartender said. "We don't need this shit in here."

Dan and Carla supported Charley as they walked him out of the bar and down the hallway of the hotel. Charley's room was 154 but they took him to 133 instead. As they opened the door, they took him to the bed and allowed him to fall across it. Charley was unconscious.

Carla laughed. She went through his pants pocket and emptied them.

"Two hundred in cash and credit cards. We hit a good one, honey," she said.

Dan laughed, too.

"Get his room key. We'll see what he has there."

"What about him?" she asked.

"He's out for at least twelve hours. I slipped him enough to take down two men."

The two of them left room 133 and placed a Do Not Disturb sign on the door. They went to room 154 and opened it. Immediately, Carla saw the car keys on the dresser. When she picked them up, she cried out.

"A Cadillac!" she said in amazement. "He said he sold cars. I didn't realize what kind he sold."

She looked out the window and sure enough, there was a red Cadillac El Dorado with Maryland plates in the parking lot. Meanwhile, Dan was going through his suitcase.

"Nice clothes," he said.

He took off his shirt and tried on one of Charley's.

"Look, babe," he said. "Just my size, too."

Carla looked at Dan with the shirt hanging open. She walked over to him and unbuttoned his jeans. She dropped to her knees and pulled his pants down around his knees and began to suck him. Dan held her by her head and pumped himself into her mouth. Then suddenly he pulled her up and threw her on the bed.

He struggled to get out of his jeans. His boots had to come off first. Carla pulled down the covers and the sheet and began to get undressed. Dan, finally naked, joined her on the bed where he pounded himself inside of her body. It was a definite high for both of them having sex in someone else's room.

While Carla went into the bathroom to clean herself, Dan dressed and lit up a joint. He looked at Charley's wallet and stuck it in his pocket.

Carla came out of the bathroom in her panties and bra and took a long hit off the joint. She continued to dress and Dan packed up the suitcase. They walked out of the room, leaving the room key on the dresser. They went out, opened the door to the Cadillac and drove away.

They went down the road to another bar. It was packed. They continued drinking and made the acquaintance of a truck driver. After an hour or so Carla lured him out into the parking lot. She took him to the back seat of the Cadillac and as he was getting his pants off, the door opened. When he turned to see what was happening, Dan hit him across the face with a blackjack, knocking him unconscious. Quickly he took his cash and pulled him out of the car. He dropped the man's wallet on the ground next to him.

"Let's go south," Dan said to Carla.

"Are you okay to drive?" she asked.

"I'm fine," he told her.

She slid over in the seat next to him and undid his pants.

"He got me horny again," she said. "I want to suck your cock."

Dan continued driving the car as Carla pulled him out of his pants and began sucking on him. As he made the left hand turn on to Interstate 95 to go south, he didn't notice he was going up the off ramp for the northbound lane. As Carla picked up speed at what she was doing to Dan, the Cadillac accelerated. It was going sixty-five miles an hour as Dan looked back for traffic. All he could see were the taillights of the northbound traffic. He didn't see the eighteen-wheel tanker coming straight at him.

The Cadillac was going just under seventy miles and hour when it hit the tanker loaded with gasoline head on. The force of the two vehicles colliding at the speed they were traveling caused the tank to rupture and the gasoline to explode. Everyone in the two vehicles was killed instantly. The flames engulfed three other vehicles following the tanker and the people in those cars were killed, too.

Sirens filled the night air. Rescue vehicles came to the scene. No one involved survived. It took four hours to put out the fire and the northbound lanes of Interstate 95 remained closed for the next two days.

Around noon the next day Charley Reed woke up in Room 133.

There was noise in the hallway. He tried to ignore it. Then the maid knocked on his door and opened it.

"Check out time is noon," she said to him when she saw him lying on the bed. "Are you going to be staying on?"

"No," he said.

Then the maid volunteered what all the noise in the hallway was about.

"One of the guests was in a horrible accident last night," she said. "Mr. Reed in 155 got on the interstate going the wrong way and hit a gasoline tanker head on. Fifteen people, including him, were killed. They are in his room right now."

Charley couldn't believe what he was hearing. His room was 155. What room was he in?

He looked over at where his suitcase should have been; instead there was a small gym bag. When the maid left the room, he went over and opened the bag. In it was a wallet belonging to Daniel Mathew Colella. There were car keys and some clothes.

He turned on the television and the news. Pictures of the crash scene were on the noon news. He went into the bathroom and washed his face and did what he could. Gathering his wits about himself, he left the room, taking the bag with him.

The car keys were to a General Motors automobile. He walked past room 155. There were police officers in the room looking around. He went out into the parking lot where he saw an older Chevrolet Chevelle four-door sedan. He walked up to the car and inserted the key. The door opened. When he put the key in the ignition, the car started up immediately. As he looked down at the passenger seat, he saw a woman's small pocketbook stuck down in the seat. He pulled it out. It belonged to Carla Marie Williams. As he looked at the picture on the driver's license, the night before began to come back to him.

"They drugged me and then robbed me. They stole my car and were involved in an accident. They think it was me. They think I am dead."

And they did.

John Hughes was at the scene visiting with a Captain in the Virginia State Police.

"There is no way anyone in that automobile survived," the Captain told Hughes.

Charley went through Carla's wallet and found two one hundred dollar bills folded up neatly behind pictures of two little boys.

"She kept some getaway money," he said to himself. "Good for me, bad for her."

He checked the gasoline in the car. The tank was full. Slowly he drove the car out of the parking lot and followed the detour signs that led him to Interstate 95 north. Cautiously he went up the on ramp and started north in the car. Charley had a lot to think about.

Meanwhile, John Hughes closed the file on Charley Reed.

"It's a shame," he said to himself. "It would have been a pleasure to take out such a talented man."

CHAPTER FORTY-TWO

RICHMOND, VIRGINIA
FEBRUARY 12, 1973
5:36 P.M.

How does someone make a decision like this?

Charley Reed was asking himself that question over and over. He could have ended it all easily. All he had to do was walk into room 155 and introduce himself. He could have, but he didn't.

He checked into a Holiday Inn along Interstate 95 and tried to sort things out. He checked in as Dan Colella and paid cash for the room.

Joanna didn't want him. She filed for divorce and he signed the papers. He signed them when he was there with her two nights ago.

He got in late and she let him sleep on the couch. He didn't want anything from her. He'd hurt her enough. So when she crawled under the blanket to be with him, he was surprised.

He tried to talk to her, but she wouldn't let him. She wanted to make love to him and she took control. All he had to do was lay back and let her. He did exactly that.

It was different. It was sexual. In fact, it was more sexual than it had ever been between them. Joanna, it seemed, always held back. It seemed like she was tolerating him because she felt it was her job. At least that was the impression Charley had and he hated it. Each time he made love to her was less satisfying than the last. That was the reason a woman like Jerilyn appealed to him.

But this time was different. She was aggressive and she wanted him. It was the first time she not only wanted him, but needed him, too. The couch was too cramped, so they moved to the floor.

She pushed him on his back and turned her body around and straddled him. She took him in her mouth as she forced herself down on his face. Charley responded and they took their time pleasing one another. Then she turned around and sat down on him. She cried out as she climaxed immediately and ground herself into him. And then it started all over again.

He rolled her on her back and began to pound himself into her. She held on to him, wrapping her legs around his hips and cried out in pleasure. She climaxed two more times and he kept pounding himself inside of her. And as he finally exploded inside of her, she cried out telling him for the first time ever how good it was.

"I can feel you coming in me!" she cried out. "I can feel it way back inside of me and it feels so good."

It was different from any time they had ever been together. It was a truly pleasurable experience and Charley didn't know what to say. Joanna cuddled up to him. They were both still naked and she didn't run off to the bathroom to clean him out of her as was normal. No, instead she just stayed there with him, running her hand through the hair on his chest. Then she talked to him.

"If we wouldn't have lost the baby," she said. "If he hadn't died, do you think we could have made it?"

"I don't know," Charley said truthfully. "I'm kind of screwed up."

"That's partly my fault," she said. "If I was the wife you expected, you wouldn't need anyone else."

Charley didn't answer. He didn't have to. She was right.

"I never loved you enough," she said. "You needed more than I could give you."

"What happened tonight?" he asked.

"I don't know," she admitted. "I just wanted you. I wanted you for me and I had to have you. I didn't care what you thought of me. I wanted you and I wanted all of you."

Charley listened as his wife made her admissions to him.

"I don't know why it was like it was and why it was different tonight. I really don't know."

They lay there in each other's arms and she began to touch him and arouse him again.

"Come to bed with me," she said.

They went into the bedroom and made love. That time it was slow and tender. They cared about one another and she cried out in pleasure as he gave her his unconditional love. And then they slept.

When he woke, she was already up and out. She was off to work. She hadn't left a note and he didn't know how to take what had happened between them. He looked in the dining room. He had signed the divorce papers the night before and she left them on the table. Now they were gone.

She must have taken them with her. She was serious about the divorce, he believed. Last night was an aberration. It was one last time for old time's sake. He had no idea what it did to her. He had no idea of the thoughts that were going through her head that day. He showered and dressed. Then he went in to see Lee Stein.

Jerilyn was working days. He went in at lunch and saw her. She agreed to meet him later that day. That was when Joanna saw him and they had the scene in Darryl's parking lot.

Now here he was, driving someone else's car, running away.

He went down to the bar. His head was still cloudy from the effects of whatever they gave him the night before. He only had one beer and then he went back to his room and went to bed. When he woke the next morning, he made up his mind. Charley Reed was dead. He was going to leave him that way.

That day he drove straight through to Boston. The next day he found himself a job as a bartender.

The following day Charley Hayes came back to life.

WASHINGTON, D.C.
SEPTEMBER 11, 2001
11:55 P.M.

The command post beneath the Potomac River was deactivated. The threat had passed and the directors returned to their offices in the McLean Headquarters. John Hughes was glad to be back with his view of the river and the city to the south. It was a much more comfortable place to administer and run what they were currently involved in.

Ed Manion, Deputy Director of the Central Intelligence Agency and his direct supervisor, sent out a summary of the day's events following the collapse of the World Trade Towers.

10:45 a.m. All federal buildings in Washington, D.C. are evacuated.

10:46 a.m. Secretary of State Colin Powell cancels his visit to South America, heads back to the United States.

10:48 a.m. Police confirm the plane crash in Somerset County, near Pittsburgh, Pennsylvania.

10:53 a.m. New York postpones that day's primary elections.

10:54 a.m. Israel closes diplomatic missions worldwide.

10:57 a.m. New York Governor George Pataki announces the closure of all state government offices.

11:02 a.m. New York City Mayor Rudolph Guiliani calls on citizens to remain at home and announces the evacuation of lower Manhattan.

11:18 a.m. American Airlines confirms the loss of both Flights 11 and 77. The number of people on both flights totaled 156.

11:26 a.m. United Airlines confirms Flight 93 crashed in Pennsylvania.

11:59 a.m. United Airlines confirms the crash of Flight 175.

12:00 p.m. The United States closes the border with Mexico.

12:04 p.m. Los Angeles International Airport evacuates because it was destination for two of the hijacked aircraft.

12:13 p.m. The New York Stock Exchange announces U.S. markets will remain closed Sept. 12.

12:15 p.m. San Francisco International Airport, destination of one of the hijacked aircraft, is evacuated and closed.

12:15 p.m. The FAA reports 50 remaining aircraft in U.S. airspace.

1:04 p.m. President Bush, from Barksdale Air Force Base in Shreveport, Louisiana, promises United States will punish those responsible and that the U.S. military is on high alert around the world.

1:27 p.m. Washington, D.C. declares city in state of emergency.

1:44 p.m. The Pentagon announces two aircraft carriers will leave the U.S. Naval Station in Norfolk, Virginia and head to the New York area.

1:48 p.m. President Bush leaves Barksdale Air Force Base for Offutt Air Force Base in Nebraska.

1:50 p.m. Washington Dulles Airport is closed until Sept. 12.

2:00 p.m. Canada suspends all major airline flights.

2:21 p.m. Fifty-three people are reported injured in the Pentagon crash.

4:30 p.m. President Bush departs Offutt Air Force Base for Washington, D.C.

5:20 p.m. Building 7 of the World Trade Center, a 47-story structure, collapses.

6:54 p.m. Marine Force One lands at the White House carrying President Bush, who immediately heads for the Oval Office.

7:30 p.m. Agency Emergency Command Post is deactivated. Return

8:30 p.m.   to normal procedures at a Category Four Alert Status.
8:30 p.m.   President Bush addresses the nation from the White House, declaring he will make no distinction between the terrorists who committed the acts and those who harbor them.
8:35 p.m.   President Bush holds a National Security meeting.
9:12 p.m.   Central Intelligence Agency stands down to Category Three Alert Status.

This is the end of the day's activities.

WASHINGTON, D.C.
SEPTEMBER 12, 2001
6:15 A.M.

John Hughes spent the night in his office. In times of crisis it was normal for the directors to do just that. The washroom was equipped with showers and lockers where extra clothes were kept. He rose, showered, and dressed. The second day began.

He prepared the report for the Director that was to be taken to the President of the United States. It would, without a doubt, implicate Osama bin Laden and his terrorist network as the authors of the previous day's attack.

He looked at the file on Charley Reed. He knew, for the moment at least, it would have to wait.

He worked through the early hours of the morning and at nine sharp he was in the Director's office, accompanied by Ed Manion, delivering the report.

"Thank you," the Director said. "This is what the President needs. It is exactly what he needs. Good job."

As they left the Director's office and walked down the hallway together, Manion questioned him about the men they were detaining and questioning.

"What are you doing with them?" Manion asked.

"Getting information," he answered.

"How are you getting that information?" he asked. "That report contained details I had never seen before and was totally unaware of."

"It's called deniability," Hughes told his boss. "If anything blows up, you are off the hook and it is all me."

"That still doesn't answer my question," Manion pressed.

"The old fashioned way," Hughes answered. "One knuckle, one

joint at a time."

"I don't like this," Manion said.

"I knew you wouldn't. That's why I left you out of the loop. But it has accomplished its purpose. We know beyond a shadow of a doubt who is responsible and who their accomplices are. We have their cells and we have their funding sources. If we want to, we can shut it all down in a half an hour."

The words John Hughes spoke scared Ed Manion. He knew Hughes and the men who were working for him were out on their own. They were out on their own in much the same way as the agency used to operate until the Congress reined them in. Now it seemed many of the agency section chiefs, one of his in particular, without higher approval had taken it upon themselves to proceed in a way expressly forbidden by Congress and the President of the United States.

While Ed Manion wanted to forbid any further activity, he knew better. While he was Hughes supervisor on paper, Hughes was too powerful for him to oppose. All he could do is look the other way and accept the deniability Hughes offered him.

As the day progressed, Manion issued another summary of the day.

12:43 a.m.   Reports circulate of investigators searching Logan Airport in Boston. The Boston Herald reports the existence of five possible suspects.

8:11 a.m.   New York City Mayor Rudolph Guiliani announces the rescue of firefighters and police officers from the rubble of the World Trade Center. The number would total six firefighters and three police officers by the afternoon.

8:15 a.m.   The United Nations announces it is removing workers from Afghanistan. Workers fear local revenge attacks should the United States attack Afghan targets.

8:40 a.m.   The Pentagon is still burning and reports are confirmed that the World Financial Center is on fire.

8:45 a.m.   European markets halt trading for one minute in silence in memory of the events of the previous day.

9:05 a.m.   Announcement made that Washington Dulles will reopen at 3 p.m., Sept. 12 in order for people to collect luggage and vehicles.

9:30 a.m.   Agency Director meets with President Bush.

9:53 a.m.   After 80 bodies are retrieved, the Pentagon says it is unlikely any more survivors will be found.

10:06 a.m. Congress reconvenes. Both Republicans and Democrats denounce the September 11 attacks.

10:50 a.m. President Bush labels attacks an "act of war."

11:20 a.m. The FAA decides to extend the ban on all U.S. air travel indefinitely.

11:58 a.m. The Pentagon evacuates because of fire, but declares building safe soon afterwards.

1:07 p.m.   The FBI searches a downtown hotel room in Boston for suspects. Investigators also question several people in Florida.

1:10 p.m.   American Airlines distributes passenger lists.

1:48 p.m.   United Airlines distributes passenger lists.

2:20 p.m.   Flights rerouted during and after September 11 attacks given the go-ahead to travel to their original destinations. All other flights are still grounded.

2:40 p.m.   Authorities stop Amtrak train from Boston heading to Providence, R.I., and take three into custody, Reuters reports.

2:57 p.m.   The White House announces it has credible information indicating the White House and Air Force One were possible targets of the September 11 attacks.

5:57 p.m.   The FBI arrests five people in Providence, Rhode Island.

6:16 p.m.   The FBI arrests seven people in Seattle, Washington.

6:34 p.m.   The FBI arrests two people in Dallas, Texas.

8:23 p.m.   Information is received that the tunnels and bridges in New York City are targets September 13th.

9:13 p.m.   Additional information is received regarding the Sears Tower as a possible target.

This is the end of the day's events.

CHAPTER FORTY-THREE

NEW YORK, NEW YORK
SEPTEMBER 13, 2001
4:05 A.M

Tina Ganley couldn't sleep. She was sick to her stomach.

She walked around in the dark, checked on the children, and poured herself a glass of apple juice. It seemed to be the only thing she was able to keep down. She was pregnant again. She was at her doctor's when the jet crashed into the first tower.

"What am I going to do now?" she asked herself. "I don't even have a dead husband to bury. He's just gone."

She had gone through the motions. She went down and posted his picture on the walls in different places in the city. With the picture, she left her phone number. She was one of thousands who clung to that single shred of hope. Like the rest of them, she knew the truth. It was an exercise. That's all it was.

She sat down at the kitchen table and started to cry again. It seemed all she did was throw up and cry. She was glad the children were asleep. It upset them when they saw her cry.

"Can't you sleep?" Cindy asked her daughter-in-law.

She didn't turn the light on. She knew Tina was crying and wanted to allow her some privacy. She wanted to cry herself.

"No," Tina said.

She appreciated her mother-in-law coming to be with her. Even though there was nothing anyone could do, just having her there meant everything to her.

"I heard you get up. Are you sick?"

"Yes," she said. "And pregnant, too."

Cindy said nothing. She wondered how this could have happened. The horror of it all was beyond belief. But she faced it.

Chuck was gone.

He was her first born and probably the child she loved the most. Chuck had been a good and loyal son and she knew she would always miss him.

At that moment across the country, Chuck Hayes was closing the bar. Alicia phoned him around midnight. She was in a motel near St. Louis. She was anxious to get to Washington. It was all she talked about. Charley understood. He knew her very well.

She was attempting to cover her pain with work. The only problem was she had to get to work before she could do it. That was why she was so anxious.

"How are you?" he asked.

"I'm fine," she answered him.

"Really? I'm sorry I let you go alone. We could have driven straight through and you could be there by now."

"It's better this way," she said. "I have a lot to think about."

"I know. How are you holding up?"

"I'm okay. Really, I am," she said, sounding like she was trying to convince herself.

"I worry about you," he said.

"Don't, honey. I'm a big girl and I can take care of myself. I'm tough, too."

"I know," he said. "That you are."

She began talking about some information she was getting from sources within the government.

"The FBI can't locate a lot of these suspected terrorists. They've just dropped off the face of the earth. And the body of a Mohammed Abdullah was just taken out of the East River in New York. He was on the top of the FBI's list of people to detain. Something is going on," she said.

Charley was quiet as he listened to her. She kept talking and he listened.

She was going to get up early and keep on going. The most important thing to her was reaching Washington. She said this was the biggest break in her career. This was her chance to get back what she had lost.

"Well?" she asked. "Aren't you happy for me?"

"Sure," he answered. "I'm happy things are turning out for you."

"You don't sound like it," she said.

"I'm tired," he said. "And maybe I'm getting old. This was okay before, but now I just need you and want you here with me."

"What brought this about all of a sudden? What made the ice man thaw?"

Charley didn't answer.

"Really," she said. "All of a sudden you finally decide you need me? Isn't it a little late?"

"I don't know," he answered. "Is it?"

He was silent a moment and waited for her to say something, but she didn't.

"If you're asking me," he said. "I guess it is."

"Seriously, Charley," she said. "You know how I've felt. You've just wanted me here for you whenever you felt like it.

"You've done your thing and I've done mine. We've tried but it really hasn't worked. We share a house and we share a bed, but we don't share a life. You go off for weeks at a time and I'm here. I've never tried to force you into anything. I thought sooner or later you would see what you had, but I guess I was wrong."

"I suppose I could say the same thing," he said. "We haven't been all that good for or to one another, I guess. I did want to go with you. I said I needed you. What more do you want?"

"Charley, I have a job. I can't do that and worry about what you might need or want to do. I have to put that first right now."

"Yes," he said. "I understand."

" I'll stay in touch," she said and then hung up.

As he locked up and turned off the lights, Charley sat and thought about her. Alicia always wanted big things for herself. Now she had her break and she was on her way.

"If you love something, let it go," he said out loud. "If it doesn't come back, hunt it down and kill it."

He laughed at himself and felt lonely. And as he did, he more or less welcomed the old feeling back. It was with him for years. It was with him because he chose it to be.

Charley turned on the burglar alarm and left the building. He locked the door behind him and walked to truck. As he got in and turned on the ignition, he was unaware of the two men who were watching him.

Cindy didn't go back to bed. She made coffee and turned on the television to watch the continuing coverage of the disaster. Tina sat with her and dozed on the couch.

When Kathy began to fuss around six-thirty Cindy went in and took care of her.

"Can I watch cartoons, Grandma?" Kathy asked.

"Sure, honey," Cindy said. "You have to be very quiet. Mommy is sick."

"Okay," the three-year old said. "I'll be very quiet."

"First I am going to make your breakfast. What do you usually have?"

"Cereal," she said. "I have cereal with bananas."

Cindy smiled and began to cut up a banana. Cindy looked down at the little girl. She was dark and the picture of her mother. Kimberly, on the other hand, looked exactly like Chuck. She even had his red-dish-blonde hair.

She no sooner had Kathy sitting down and eating when Kimberly came in.

"Good morning, Grandmother," she said.

"Hello, honey. How did you sleep?"

"I was dreaming about Daddy."

Cindy didn't say anything. She looked away as tears came into her eyes.

"He was telling me he loved me."

"Did he say he loved me, too?" Kathy asked.

"It was my dream, silly. He'll come and tell you in your own dream," she told her sister.

"I hope he comes soon," the three-year old said. "I miss him. I want him to come home."

Cindy touched Kathy's head.

"We all do, honey, but he is with God now. He can't come home. God needs him to work for Him in heaven."

She tried to get Kimberly some breakfast, but she insisted on tak-ing care of herself. She made her breakfast and sat at the table with her sister.

Cindy poured herself another cup of coffee and sat with them. She remembered her girls at the breakfast table and she remembered their older brother. Years of breakfasts in their home passed through her mind.

What a loss. What a senseless loss, she thought to herself. She wanted to cry, but she held it back for the sake of her granddaughters. It was about that time the telephone rang.

Cindy answered it. It was Jerilyn checking on Tina.

"She's asleep," Cindy said. "She's been up most of the night. She is having trouble sleeping."

"I'm glad you're there," she said. "Have her call me if she feels up to it."

"I will," Cindy said.

When she hung up the phone, Tina walked into the kitchen.

"Who was that?" she asked.

"Your mother. She is worried about you."

"Thank you for talking to her. I'm not up to it. She is more than I want to deal with right now."

Tina walked over to where Cindy was sitting and patted her on the shoulder.

"Thank you for coming. I'm glad you're here."

Cindy reached up and took Tina's hand and squeezed it.

"You're very welcome, dear."

Moments later the phone rang again. This time it was Anne Marie, Tina's sister. Once more Cindy said Tina was sleeping and she would have her phone when she woke. Tina tried to sip some tea, but wound up going into the bathroom where she threw up again.

Cindy found some cartoons for Kathy. Kimberly went back to her room and made her bed and dressed herself. There was no school that day so she put on her play clothes and entertained herself. It was a little after nine when the phone rang again. Again, Cindy answered it.

"Mrs. Ganley?" a man's voice asked.

"Yes," she answered out of habit, not realizing the call was for Tina.

"This is Jack Michaels from the Today Show. I am sorry to bother you in your time of loss."

Cindy didn't respond immediately.

"Are you there, Mrs. Ganley?" he asked.

"Yes," she said.

"We are aware that your husband was attempting to help several of the people who were trapped on the higher floors of the World Trade Center. We were wondering if you would be willing to be interviewed?"

Cindy was taken back by the call.

"Who is this?" she asked.

"I am Jack Michaels from the NBC Today Show. I'm an associate producer. This is very real."

"Okay," she said. "How did you know about Chuck?"

"Several of the people on his floor made calls. His name was mentioned time and time again. He was organizing everyone, trying to get them down. It seemed futile, but everyone we've talked to seemed to believe he was giving those with no hope some anyway.

"Even as the building collapsed, one person was talking to a family member who said he was trying to lead them out. We have interviewed at least twenty people who have mentioned his name."

Cindy was silent at first. She tried to think about what the man on the other end was saying. Of course, Chuck would have done something like that. Even when it was hopeless, he would never have given up. She remembered him telling the people not to jump.

"Mrs. Ganley?" the man asked.

"Yes," Cindy answered.

"You will do the interview?" he asked.

"No," she said. "You don't understand. Chuck was my son, not my husband. You want to talk to his wife. You need to talk to Tina. I'll get her."

Cindy went in and got Tina.

"You need to take this call," Cindy said. "It's someone from the Today Show about Chuck."

Tina took the phone and listened as the man on the other end explained to her what he wanted. Tina was silent as he told her what he had already told Cindy.

"I don't know," she said. "May I have your phone number and can I call you back? I want to speak with my mother-in-law about this."

Tina turned to Cindy when she hung up the phone.

"They're saying Chuck was some kind of a hero," she said.

"You're surprised?" she asked.

"No," Tina answered. "Not really."

She thought for a moment and looked at her mother-in-law.

"What should I do?" she asked. "They want me on their show tomorrow."

"It's up to you," Cindy said. "Are you up to it?"

"I don't know," Tina answered.

"Call the man back and see what he has in mind," Cindy suggested.

OAKLAND, CALIFORNIA
SEPTEMBER 14, 2001
8:15 A.M.

Charley had been up for an hour. He was finishing his second cup of coffee and was intermittently watching Katie Couric and Matt Lauer on the Today Show. It was the only morning show he really cared for. While he liked the young woman on CBS, Jane Clayson, he absolutely hated Bryant Gumbel. He thought Gumbel was the biggest jerk in the world. ABC was his second choice. He didn't think there was anything wrong with them. He just liked Katie and Matt better.

As the commercial ended, Katie came on and began playing a recording of a phone call. It was a call from one of the people trapped in the South Tower of the World Trade Center. It was a woman telling her husband how a man named Chuck Ganley was trying to get them out. She was in the midst of explaining how he had already taken them down fifteen floors, past areas that were burning, trying to get them out. Then there was a tremendous roar and the phone went dead. The building had collapsed.

"This was a man who refused to give up hope," Katie said. "He was a man who gave people who had no hope their last chance at trying to survive. He did this while people on his floor were jumping out of windows to their deaths."

Charley was paying attention. All the stories of heroism touched him. He knew if it was him and he was trapped on one of those upper floors, he wouldn't have given up either. He admired the man they were speaking of instantly. It took great courage not to give up.

A picture of Chuck Ganley came up on the screen.

Charley looked and then he looked again. Chuck Ganley was a younger version of himself. The resemblance was so remarkable Chuck Ganley could have easily been his son.

"Today we are joined by Chuck Ganley's wife, Tina; his two children, Kimberly and Kathy; and his mother Cindy George Ganley."

Charley sat watching the television stunned.

After all these years his life, the life he ran away from was there in his face. Even after thirty-five years he recognized her. He would have recognized her anywhere. It was Cindy. It was his Cindy and Chuck Ganley was the baby that was his.

Katie was interviewing Cindy and she was recounting their last telephone conversation. The television camera went to the two girls.

Kimberly was eight and Kathy was three. His son had daughters. He had granddaughters.

Tina was talking. She was explaining that she was at the doctor's office as the jets crashed into the towers. She said she was pregnant and her husband never knew. She was going to tell him when he got home from work that night. He never came home.

Then the interview was over.

"God damn it!" he said. "Why the hell didn't I tape it?"

The rest of the day he thought about the interview and the son he never knew. He called information and got phone numbers. He got the phone number of his law firm and he found his home phone number. The home phone had a Park Avenue address.

"He was a successful lawyer," Charley said to himself. "Of course, he would have been. Cindy and that old witch of a mother of hers would have seen to it."

He called the local television station and asked if he could get a copy of the interview. The woman he talked to said she would see if it was available and told him to call back the next day.

In the meantime, he couldn't get it out of his head. Seeing Cindy after all of those years was more than he was ready for. He checked information for her address and phone number, but there wasn't one in the New York City area. Then he remembered Katie said Chuck called her at her home in Pittsburgh. Sure enough, there was a North Hills address and phone number. And, he noted that it was in her name.

"No husband," he said to himself. "She's a bitch just like her mother no doubt."

As he said it, it also dawned on him that his son was named Chuck. Cindy named their son after him. He wondered what that was supposed to mean. He wondered, but deep inside of him he knew. Deep inside of him, he knew she loved him. At least she loved him when their baby was born and she loved him enough to name a son after his father.

Charley wondered if she had ever told their son about him. He wondered if Cindy ever tried to find out about him. He had so many questions he wanted to have answered. Around five he began to drink and feel sorry for himself.

When Alicia called around eight he was pretty drunk.

"What's the matter?" she asked.

"Nothing much," he said.

"Well, what have you been doing?"

"Sitting around watching television and drinking," he said.

"I'm here in Washington," she said. "I start work tomorrow."

"Great," he said, really not meaning it.

There wasn't much else to their conversation. She wanted to talk, but Charley didn't. She knew him well enough that when he was moody not to press the issue. She said goodbye and hung up the phone.

As the phone disconnected the two men outside were listening. They had monitored all of Charley's phone activity that day.

"This fucker doesn't sound like much of a terrorist," Terry Schmid said to Mike Hampsey.

"No, he doesn't," Hampsey said. "That's what makes them good. Moles are supposed to come off like anyone else. This guy, if he is a mole, is one of the best. Nothing has phased him and he just sits in there and watches television and drinks."

"Who said this guy is a mole anyway?" Terry asked.

"Comes right from the top," Mike answered. "John Hughes himself. He has us on his ass. He wants to know everything about this guy."

"If Mr. Hughes wants to know everything about this guy, then Mr. Hughes will know everything there is to know. His slightest wish is our command."

The two men laughed and continued the surveillance.

WASHINGTON, D.C.
SEPTEMBER 15, 2001
7:25 A.M.

Alicia Masters walked into the national news center. She had driven across the country and was ready to pick up and relieve the overworked staff that had handled the grueling days and nights since the eleventh.

She went directly to makeup and was briefed on what was expected of her. At eight o'clock she went on the air and Charley was awake in California watching her.

CHAPTER FORTY-FOUR

OAKLAND, CALIFORNIA
SEPTEMBER 15, 2001
5:35 P.M.

Charley couldn't get the interview off his mind. Earlier that day he called the television station and they made a copy of the Today Show for him. They charged him fifteen dollars, which he gladly paid.

He drove into his parking place at the piano bar and went in the front door. As soon as he walked in, his manager approached him.

"Hey, boss," Al Poole said to Charley.

"Hi, Al," he said. "What's up?"

"Two men were in here when I opened up, asking about you."

"Me?" he asked. "What did they want to know about me and who the hell were they?"

"They were asking questions like how long you've owned the place and who your friends were."

"What did you tell them?" he asked.

"Nothing," he said. "You know me better than that. That's why you have me here. I cover your backside, boss."

"Who were they?" he asked.

"Some kind of government types. I asked them for identification, but they wouldn't show me any. At first they made out like they were cops, but I can spot a cop a mile away. They weren't cops. They were Feds. Are you up to date on your income taxes? They might have been IRS. I don't need them coming in one me with a full cash register seizing it."

"My taxes are all paid," he said.

He went up to his office, but the fact people were asking questions bothered him. He always maintained a low profile. He didn't need questions.

He took the video of the Today Show out of his briefcase and placed it into the VCR in his office. He turned on the television and pressed the play button on the remote control. As it came on, he ran it fast forward to the interview. When it came on, he slowed it down.

Charley froze the picture of Chuck. He studied his face. It was his face. It was his face when he was younger. There was no mistaking him for his son.

Then he played it on. He looked at Tina and her children. The oldest girl, Kimberly looked like her dad. The youngest looked like Tina. Charley found himself smiling. They were his granddaughters.

Then he came to Cindy.

"Cindy," he said out loud. "Why did you do this to me?"

He froze the picture of her on the screen. Carefully he studied her face.

"What has your life been like?" he asked.

"Have you been happy? Were you satisfied? Did you have everything you wanted?"

He kept looking at her.

"You're fifty-four now. Your birthday is in April. Then you'll be my age. Then you'll be fifty-five. How do you like being old? Do you still have sex?"

He laughed.

"Do you even like it?" he asked. "Maybe you're all dried up and don't do it anymore. Are you one of those women, Cindy?"

He continued to run the interview and listened to her voice. He closed his eyes and he remembered. Her voice was still soft and kind. It hadn't changed. And as he listened to her voice, it did something to him. There was something about her voice that excited him. It always had. It always had and he had forgotten. Now, sitting there listening it all came back to him.

He remembered the way she spoke to him and the way she held him. He remembered the way she used to tickle his cheeks with her eyelashes. He closed his eyes and he could almost remember the way she smelled.

And then Katie was talking and Cindy stopped. He opened his eyes and looked at the television. He had to go see her.

The planes began flying the day before. His car was in Washington, D.C. and she was in New York. He thought it out and while he was, the phone rang. It was Alicia.

"Are you in a better mood tonight?" she asked.

"Yeah," he said. "I'm better."

"They are sending me on assignment to New York and then I'm going to Hamburg, Germany," she told him. "They want me to cover the arrests over there."

"Sounds important."

"It is."

"Where are you going to leave the car?" he asked.

"I'll leave it here in the parking garage," she said. "Why?"

"I'm going to come east for a few days on business. I'll pick it up and drive it home if you don't need it."

"Sure," she said. "When I leave for New York, I can leave the keys at the front desk. Or, if you are going to be here before Tuesday, you can stay with me for a night."

"Let me see what I can get out of here. All the flights are pretty well backed up from what I'm hearing. I'll let you know."

When they hung up, Charley began checking reservations on the Internet. There was nothing out of San Francisco until Wednesday, but he did find a flight out of LAX on Sunday afternoon, direct to Dulles International. The only problem he had was there were no available flights to Los Angeles.

"Take the train," he said to himself. "Take the night train and then take a cab to the airport. You'll be there in plenty of time."

He went home and packed a bag. When he went home, he was followed. The two men following him assumed he was in for the night and broke off surveillance until the next morning. They were gone when he returned to the bar and had one of the waitresses drive him to the train station in Oakland.

At midnight the train left for Los Angeles. Charley fell asleep as the train made its way south.

NEW YORK CITY
SEPTEMBER 16, 2001
11:35 A.M.

Cindy had just returned from church when the phone rang. She answered it, but no one said anything.

"Hello?" she said a second time.

There was still no answer, but the line was open. She was sure someone was still on the line.

"Hello?" she said a third time. Then the phone connection was broken.

John Hughes sat in his office in Virginia.

"What the hell did he want with that phone number?" he asked.

CALIFORNIA

In the meantime, Schmid and Hampsey took up surveillance once more outside Charley's house. They aimed the antenna at the windows of his home. There was nothing stirring inside. There was no television or radio playing. Schmid went up to the garage and looked in. The truck was gone. Hayes wasn't there.

"We're fucked," Hampsey said. "We had better report in."

As they reported in, Charley was getting out of a cab at Los Angeles International Airport.

He took his single bag and walked up to the ticket counter. There he purchased the round trip ticket, even though he was only going to use one way. He went through a personal search and had his bag searched. Then he was cleared through security and allowed to proceed to the boarding area. He got into line to clear the last security point beyond which only ticketed passengers were allowed.

Flight 1243 from St. Louis had just arrived at Gate 21A at Los Angeles International Airport. In the first class section of the Lockeed L1011 were Senator John Young and his companion, Teri Sunderland.

Senator Young was one of the major proponents for a new and very severe bill limiting the rights of immigrants and temporary visitors to the United States. He was in California for a speaking engagement. Then they were off to Hong Kong for a two week fact-finding trip which was nothing more than a glossed over vacation.

Teri had never been to the west coast and was excited. John, who was separated from his wife, would enjoy being in Hong Kong out of the public eye and away where he could just simply enjoy himself and Teri.

It was a very pleasant flight. The stewardess in first class was especially friendly and very attentive. The champagne was fair and it made Teri giggly and rather playful. She was like a little girl who was being taken to the zoo for the first time. Just being with her made John feel like he was a young man again.

John put on his suit coat and picked up his briefcase. Teri placed her arm in his as they started down the aisle to the exit from the aircraft.

It was a full flight and the jet way was congested with the exiting passengers. As they emerged from the jet way into the gate area, the congestion seemed to double. They continued to walk arm in arm through the secure area into the terminal itself.

"There's our driver," Teri said to him, pointing to a man in a black suit. He was holding a sign with the name Michaels.

They started toward the man when John heard a pop and felt a burning sensation on his right ear. There were two more pops and Teri fell backwards into him, making him stagger and lose his balance.

Someone screamed and then John fell to the floor with his ear ringing and burning at the same time. Teri fell with him and he felt the pressure of someone stepping on his chest. Then he lost consciousness.

A local television station had sent a reporter with a cameraman to cover Senator Young's arrival. As the Senator emerged from the security area, the camera was running.

The reporter started in his direction as the first gunshot blew off the Senator's right ear. Teri was hit by the next two shots and was thrown back into the Senator.

As they both fell to the floor, a man sprang from the paralyzed crowd and leaped over the fallen bodies and attacked a dark-skinned man with a moustache. The dark-skinned man still had a gun in his hand when the man hit his body.

The gun discharged two more times and then, as if in slow motion, the attacking newcomer brought a fist up from his side and hit the man with the gun in the neck directly on the Adam's apple. The force of the blow was tremendous.

The dark-skinned man, obviously Middle Eastern, was immediately immobilized. The gun fell from his hand as his eyes rolled back in his head. His mouth opened slightly, all color left his face and he fell to the floor. Then the attacking newcomer delivered a second blow of equal force, but it was unnecessary. The Middle Eastern man was already dead.

The crowd was in a panic. Police with guns drawn took over the area. The man who delivered the lethal blows to the would-be assassin was handcuffed and led away into a secure area.

Medics appeared and began working on the gunman, the Senator, Teri, and two others who had been wounded by the stray bullets. Within moments Teri and the gunman were pronounced dead and the Senator rushed to a hospital in a state of shock from loss of blood.

The reporter, Marie Van Arsdale, continued her commentary throughout the entire time. She was already behind police lines and had footage of the entire attack from beginning to end.

Immediately, national news picked up the story. Marie Van

Arsdale's footage was an exclusive for her network. The coverage of the World Trade Center and the New War was interrupted by what had just happened in California.

"The attacker," the commentator began, "was identified as Ali Mufstafa Iber, an Iranian who came to this country in 1978. Iber owned a gas station and convenience store in Santa Ana and lived in Orange County.

"The hero of the day was mistakenly handcuffed and taken into custody by police, but was later released. He is shown here leaving the police headquarters and he declined to speak with the press. He has been identified as Charles Wilson Hayes, a businessman who lives in Oakland, California.

"The hero of the airport attack," the commentator reported, "is fifty-five year old Charles Wilson Hayes of Oakland, California. Mr. Hayes is the owner of a piano bar in California and a Vietnam veteran, which was made obvious by the way he stopped the terrorist.

"Mr. Hayes, pictured here, was at the airport, ticketed on a flight to Dulles International. Mr. Hayes has declined to be interviewed since being released by the police."

Cindy Ganley hadn't heard about the assassination attempt on Senator Young and stopped to watch the report.

She frowned and squinted her eyes. She couldn't believe what she was seeing. The man on the television was like looking at a picture of her son. The picture wasn't the greatest in quality, but the resemblance was remarkable. As the story line changed, she shook her head and went on with what she was doing.

In Chicago Jerilyn and Bob had just returned home. They were laughing over an incident at the cocktail lounge where they'd been all evening.

"How about a drink before bed?" Bob asked.

"Sure, why not," Jerilyn answered.

"I'll slip into something more comfortable," she said seductively.

"Good," Bob teased. "Put on those black high heels. You don't need anything else except the high heels."

"Not even my garter belt?" she teased back.

"If you feel like it," he said.

Jerilyn laughed and went into the bedroom and undressed. Feeling playful, she took his advice and only put on her black high heels.

Bob didn't see her as she walked into the room. He was looking at the television and the story being covered was the assassination attempt of Senator Young.

"Oh, my God!" Jerilyn exclaimed. "It's Charley Reed!"

CHAPTER FORTY-FIVE

LOS ANGELES, CALIFORNIA
SEPTEMBER 16, 2001
5:02 P.M.

The last thing Charley ever wanted to do was get involved in a public spectacle. He was minding his own business standing in line to clear security when he saw the Iranian man pull out his gun and begin to fire.

Charley didn't see the television crew. He didn't see the reporter and he was unaware that a United States Senator was arriving. Charley didn't even know who Senator Young was. All he saw was a man firing a gun into a crowd of people and he reacted as if by instinct.

The police took him into custody. He was a hero. He saved the Senator's life, but they handcuffed him behind his back and knocked him around as they shoved him into the backseat of a police car. One cop hit him in the back of the head with his fist.

He was fingerprinted and photographed. It was the first time he'd been fingerprinted since the service. When they ran his prints, they would find out who he really was.

He was thankful the news crew was there. The footage it shot cleared him. In less than two hours, he was freed. He was freed and everyone wanted to talk to him. All he wanted to do was disappear.

Somehow he got to the train station and fortunately for him a train was leaving for San Francisco. As he sat back and finally relaxed, he knew his life had been altered. He realized what he had run away from was finally catching up.

He caught a cab at the train station to his club. He slipped in the back way and went to his office. The keys for his truck were in his desk. He was getting them when Al walked in.

"Jesus, boss. You're all over the news."

"I know," he said. "It sucks."

"What are you going to do?" he asked.

"I'm going to get the hell out of here for awhile. You're going to have to take care of things."

"I have you covered," he said.

"Thanks," he answered.

He looked at him for a minute and nearly let him in on his secret. Then he caught himself. He had always kept it to himself. He never told anyone, not even Alicia, and she was closer to him than anyone.

"What?" Al asked.

"Nothing," he said. "This will get worse before it gets better. Just play dumb and everything will be okay. If you have any problems, call my lawyer. He'll handle everything and see you have what you need."

"Where are you going?" he asked.

"It's better you don't know. I won't call you here. I'll call you at home."

Al didn't understand.

"You're a big time hero. Why are you running away?"

Charley just looked at him. He wanted to tell him, but it was too involved and it was too complicated. He just wanted to get out of there and be on his way.

He kept cash in his safe. He opened the safe and took the cash, about six thousand dollars, and put it in his briefcase. Charley closed it and went out the back way and got in his truck.

When he drove to his home, he found a crowd of people at his front door. He drove around the block and parked. He went through the backyards and made his way to the kitchen door. He unlocked it and went inside. He left the lights off. He didn't want anyone to know he was home.

Meanwhile, other things were happening.

There is no way to deny the American news media once it decides a story is news worthy. The story of Charles Hayes, hero of the Senator Young assassination attempt was one of those stories.

Marie Van Arsdale was a southern California girl who majored in communications at UCLA and took her first job at the TV station where she still worked. The idea of the reluctant hero was very intriguing to her.

She saw this man react when hundreds of people either were paralyzed or ran and hid for their lives. She was only feet away from the gunman as he fired. She caught his eye. He had spotted her and was actually turning to shoot when Charles Hayes attacked him.

What an amazing man he was to be able to kill another man with a single blow from his hand! Marie's eyewitness report was on every news broadcast in the country. Everyone was asking for information about the Hero of LAX as he was being called. Marie decided she would get the first interview with this man who kills with his bare hands and shuns the spotlight afterwards.

Marie's producer was intrigued, too.

"Do what you have to. Get the story," he told her.

She started that evening at the police department as she gave her account of what happened at the airport. She found out from a friendly police officer that Hayes was a Vietnam veteran. He had been in the 545th Special Warfare Group, the Green Berets! Slowly his biography emerged.

He was born in Boston and attended Brown University, but never graduated. He owned businesses in northern California and owned a home in Oakland. He was divorced and lived with a nationally known newsperson.

Marie had his home phone number, but every time she called it was busy. She guessed he probably took the phone off the hook.

A busy phone didn't discourage Marie. She caught a flight to San Francisco and rented a car. She bought a good bottle of wine and went right to his front door. Almost immediately she realized that wouldn't work, as there were over two hundred people along with the police on his driveway and lawn. If she couldn't interview him, she would interview his father. He was still alive and was living in Boston.

Charley needed to rest before he left. He checked all the doors to make sure they were locked and then he went to sleep.

He slept until six on Monday morning. There were still people outside. He showered and packed a few more things. Then he quietly left the way he came. He started his truck and drove away.

Later that day Marie Van Arsdale landed at Logan International Airport and took a cab across the bridge to the north side of town. She was going to the home of G. Alexander Hayes, Charles Hayes' father. She was in for the shock of her life when the old man answered the door. He was black!

Stammering she spit out her opening question. "Are you Mr. Hayes?"

"I sure am," he answered. "What can I do for you, pretty lady?"

"Mr. Hayes, I'm sorry to intrude on you at home. I'm Marie Van Arsdale from station KLAC-TV in Los Angeles and I'd like to speak to you about your son, Charles Wilson Hayes."

"Please, come in," the old man said. "What would you like to know?"

Inside she found a small, but neat home. As he showed her into the living room, the pictures on the mantle over the fireplace answered half of her questions. But, she had to hear it for herself.

"Mr. Hayes, where is your son?" she asked.

"Why, dead," he answered, shocked she didn't already know.

"He died March 22, 1968 in Vietnam in the service of his country. He saved his best friend's life and was awarded the Silver Star for heroism by Lyndon Johnson himself."

The old man handed her the medal and the Presidential Citation from the mantle.

She looked back at the mantle and saw an 8 x 10 photograph of a strikingly handsome young black man in the Beret of the Fifth Special Forces. Her entire body tingled as she looked into his eyes. It was as if he had reached out and touched her hand.

Goosebumps covered her body and she tried to look away. She tried, but was unable to stop staring. Then her attention was drawn to another photograph in a frame next to the one of Charles Hayes.

Marie stood and walked to the mantle and took down a group photograph including Charles Hayes. There, next to him in the picture, was unmistakably the same man who saved her life at the airport.

"Who is this?" she asked excitedly. "Who is this man next to your son?"

"That was his best friend. That's Charley Reed."

"Where is he now?"

"Dead," Mr. Hayes answered.

"They're all dead. Every single one of those fine boys is dead. They all died in the war, except Charley Reed."

"What happened to him?" she asked.

"He never got over the war and drank himself up. He was killed in a car accident. He should have been buried in Arlington cemetery with his friends, but his mama would have none of that. She had him brought home and buried in Pittsburgh. I know because I went to the funeral. He was the last link I had to my boy."

Tears began to fill the old man's eyes.

"Could I come back again tomorrow?" she asked.

"Sure," he answered. "Just call first because I might be around the corner at the gin mill."

"Thank you very much," she said. Then she asked to use the phone to call a cab.

September 17, 2001
12:10 P.M.

Jerilyn Gardner began drinking vodka at noon and angrily insisted Chuck Hayes was Charley Reed. When they first showed his press conference on the front lawn, she was positive.

"Why that dirty son-of-a-bitch," she said to the television. "That dirty son-of-a-bitch."

Jerilyn Gardner wasn't the only woman to recognize Charley Reed on television either.

Joanna Reed, Charley's ex-wife, was living in Potomac, Maryland. She dropped a pitcher of ice tea when she saw him on television. He was telling the news people he had nothing to say. There was no mistaking his voice. His was one of a kind.

Her younger brother Rollie ran from the living room to see if his sister was okay.

"What's wrong?" he asked.

Joanna didn't answer, but pushed her way past him and walked directly to the television. Her eyes confirmed what her ears heard.

"Why you dirty son-of-a-bitch," she yelled.

"Who?" Rollie asked his sister.

"Him!" she screamed, pointing at the television.

"Who?" he asked again.

"Him!" she said. "That dirty son-of-a-bitch, that's who!"

"Who the hell is he?" Rollie asked puzzled.

"Your ex-brother-in-law!" she said. "That's who!"

"My ex-brother-in-law is dead!" Rollie said.

Joanna Reed looked back at the television one more time and then at her brother.

"Not hardly!" she answered. "If anyone could come back from the dead, it's him!"

Rollie looked at the man on the television. He was a young boy when he came to live with his sister and her husband Charley. Their parents died and Joanna became his guardian.

Even after all these years, he still lived with her because she didn't think he could take care of himself. What did she know! He could do it, but it was nicer to live with Joanna and let her do all the worrying.

Rollie liked to take life easy.

"I'll kill him," Joanna Reed vowed. "He'll wish he died in that car accident!"

Rollie looked at the man on the screen and smiled. It sure looked like Charley.

Even as his sister vowed to kill the man with her bare hands, Rollie looked forward to meeting him again. Charley was quite a legend to him. Charley Reed was hero to Rollie. He was a man who won the Silver Star and had fought his way back alone against insurmountable odds. His legend had always been something Rollie liked to remember. Charley had been good to him and Rollie liked him when they lived together.

As Rollie was thinking all this, the President of the United States announced that Charles Wilson Hayes was an outstanding citizen who placed his own life in jeopardy to save the Senator. For that, Charles Wilson Hayes was to be awarded the Medal of Freedom.

Charley had just left the state of California and was listening to the news on his radio.

"Jesus Christ!" he exclaimed in annoyance. "All this bullshit over one lousy raghead! I'm sorry I ever stopped him!"

As he continued driving, the full impact of what had happened and what he was returning to hit him. Many, many, many years had come between him and his old life. He thought about it.

First there was Cindy, then Joanna, and then Jerilyn. He wondered what had happened to them. They all were women he once loved. All of them had been women every man wanted, yet he was never able to possess.

As he drove into the night he imagined he heard a voice. He ignored it at first, believing it was his mind playing tricks on him. He decided he was just tired. Then it spoke again.

It sounded like the voice of an old woman. He rubbed his eyes, shook his head, and continued to drive. He looked down at the speedometer. The cruise control was set at seventy-five. He ignored the old woman's voice and increased the speed to eighty-five. He refused to allow his eyes to leave the road.

"You nothing!" he heard out loud.

He knew he was alone, but he heard it again.

"You nothing!"

Charley continued to drive and decided he should find a rest area and pull off to sleep.

"You heard me, you worthless piece of nothing," the voice said again.

Almost at once, Charley Reed recognized the voice. He remembered arriving in West Lafayette, Indiana to take his girl away only to be confronted by a sniveling father and a cruel mother who spoke in the same vicious tone of voice, calling him a worthless piece of nothing.

Charley Reed looked to his right and there seated next to him in the passenger seat was Marilyn George.

"You worthless piece of nothing," she said to him.

"I was right. I was always right about you. You killed your best friend. You don't deserve to live. You're nothing. You're a worthless piece of nothing and I always knew it!"

Charley believed this must be a dream. He was scared because he was driving eighty-five miles an hour and having a dream at the same time.

"This is no dream!" Marilyn George said to him. "You always were an asshole and you always will be."

"Fuck you, bitch," Charley heard himself say.

Marilyn began to laugh and laugh. The sound made chills crawl up Charley's spine. It was the laugh of a witch directly from the bowels of hell.

"I'm dead, you worthless asshole, and your name was the last word I ever said!"

Charley Reed listened and then looked at the woman seated next to him. He knew this must all be a dream.

"Fuck you," he said again. "This is my car and get the fuck out, you dirty bitch. I hated you when I was fifteen and I hate you now. Get out of my life!

Shaking all over and angry as hell, Charley Reed pulled into the next rest area. He calmed himself down and went to sleep for the rest of the night.

CHAPTER FORTY-SIX

By two that same afternoon Charley Reed was crossing Colorado. He'd been driving since the rest area and decided to stop and get a room somewhere in Missouri. It had been a long time since he'd been on the road.

For years he put those times behind him. He even managed for a time to convince himself it was all a dream. The California sunshine and lifestyle helped make it easy to do what he had done. The distractions helped ease whatever feelings of guilt he felt at first. Then as he bought the bar and began learning the business, a new direction was the answer. The rest took care of itself.

He prospered and grew until Sunday when he made the mistake of being in the wrong place at the right time and doing the right thing. Now, he would have to do what he never wanted to do before, face himself.

How had it come to this? Where did it begin and how had it ended?

Charley continued driving. He had plenty of time to think. He knew where it began. Now that these years stood up to face him, he knew exactly where it began.

Jerilyn and Joanna came to mind and he wondered what became of them. He wondered about his parents. The world he walked away from was in front of him several thousand miles away. Each minute he was a mile closer to what he left.

As he changed the CD in the player, he thought about Cindy George and why he had the dream last night about her mother. There was a lot to consider behind him and more ahead. Charley began singing with the music.

It was about that time Anne Marie called Tina.

"How are you holding up, sis?" she asked.

"Decent, I guess," she said.

"Here's something for you that will take you mind off of things for a few minutes."

"What's that?" she asked.

"Mother," she answered.

"Have you seen the story about the man in California who stopped an assassination attempt on the life of a U.S. Senator?"

"Yes," Tina said. "What about him?"

"Mother saw him and swears up and down it's Charley Reed," said Anne Marie.

"Is she drinking?"

"Is she ever!" Anne Marie laughed. "Bob can't believe it. He's never seen her like this. He doesn't know what to do with her."

Tina laughed thinking about it.

"Have you seen the man she's talking about?"

"No. They stopped running the story by the time I heard about it. Considering the fact that Charley Reed was positively identified years ago, it's impossible the man she saw was him."

"Yes, I agree," Tina sighed.

"But if it was," Anne Marie said almost dreaming out loud.

"But if it was," Tina finished. "We could get to meet him. He could meet his granddaughters and they would have something of their father."

"Imagine what our mother would do!" Anne Marie exclaimed.

"I wouldn't want to think about it," said Tina laughing at the thought.

"What would Cindy do?" Anne Marie asked.

"Oh, God!" Tina said. "What a thought! They'd both drive us crazy!"

When Tina got off the phone, Cindy was standing there.

"That was my sister. Mother believes the man who saved the Senator's life in California is Charley Reed. Have you seen the story?"

"Yes," Cindy said.

"What do you think?" she asked.

"I think it's him, too," she said. "I saw him and I think it is Charley Reed without a doubt. If you saw him, you would think so, too. I don't see the humor in it at all."

Charley Reed stopped at the Holiday Inn in Springfield, Missouri in the evening. He was anxious over the publicity he received before he left California and wondered if it was still going on.

Once in his room he turned on the twenty-four hour news station from Atlanta. Then he called room service and watched television for an hour and a half until he was satisfied there was no mention of the incident at the airport Sunday afternoon. He ate and finally relaxed, believing he was rapidly becoming yesterday's news as each hour passed.

Charley changed the station to one with continuous movies and then turned out the lights. Even at his age, Charley Reed was still afraid of the dark and when he was alone preferred to leave on the television for company as well as light.

He sat up in bed sipping a glass of wine and felt drowsy. His mind wandered as he placed the glass on the bedside stand and laid his head on the pillows. He thought of his past as Charley Reed. In particular, he thought of the women in his past.

There had been Cindy, Joanna, and Jerilyn before he died.

He laughed to himself. His death was quite fortuitous as far as he was concerned. It eliminated a world of problems while at the same time allowed him to repay a debt.

He thought of Jerilyn and how the sound of her voice alone would excite him. For the first time in many years, he thought about making love to her and how easy it was for her to become his obsession.

As he fell off to sleep, he was remembering the first time they made love. In sleep his dreams took over and he was still with her. He remembered her still young and beautiful. Her body was firm with soft and sensuous skin. He was touching her and then he woke.

Charley woke and found himself staring at the ceiling in his room at the Holiday Inn. On television a man and a woman were arguing over something. She was crying and he was angry. It was morning and it was becoming light.

In Boston Marie Van Arsdale was preparing for the day. She had stumbled on a story the likes of which she had never heard before. There were hundreds of Vietnam stories over the years, but none like this. She was going to get old Mr. Hayes on video and then she'd track down Charley Reed's past, ending with Charley himself. This was her big chance and she knew it. At seven-thirty she phoned Mr. Hayes and asked if she could come over.

"Sure," the old man answered. "I always have time for a pretty girl."

At nine-thirty she arrived with a cameraman. Before the old man could object, she explained.

"I want a film of this so we can get some recognition for your son and his unit. It's been over thirty years and people forget. This way there will be a record so everyone can remember."

When he agreed, Marie sighed with relief, realizing she was over the first obstacle. She immediately had the camera running so Mr. Hayes wouldn't have the opportunity to change his mind.

"This is Marie Van Arsdale," she began. "I am visiting with Mr. G. Alexander Hayes of Boston, Massachusetts.

"On March 22, 1968, Mr. Hayes' only son was killed in action in Vietnam. He was later decorated for bravery and posthumously awarded the Silver Star for Gallantry in Action."

Marie moved from Mr. Hayes' side to the mantle where the pictures sat. The camera was still rolling as she picked up Chuck Hayes' picture.

"Charles Wilson Hayes was just twenty-two. He was a high school basketball star and attended Brown University. Like so many other young men of the time, Chuck Hayes searched for direction and purpose. Disillusioned with college, he left school and enlisted in the Army in early 1966. He was twenty-two years old."

The camera focused closely on the 8 x 10 of Chuck Hayes in uniform.

"Mr. Hayes," she said walking over and sitting next to the old man. "Did your son speak to you about his decision to leave school and join the Army?"

"Not before he done it. Just after he done it. His mother, rest her soul, and I were pretty disappointed. No one in our family had ever even graduated high school, let alone gone off to college. We were all really proud of the boy. Then the way he just up and quit, it pissed me off."

Mr. Hayes caught himself and put his hand up to his mouth. "I shouldn't be talkin' like that in the movies. Did I screw the damn thing up?"

"No, Mr. Hayes," Marie said. "You just tell me the way you remember things. Don't worry about that. It's okay."

He continued, reassured by the pretty young woman.

"It was tough for him. He was a bright boy, but college was different for him from high school. He told me that he was studyin' his ass off and his best grade was only a C. That was discouragin' for him and he couldn't keep his scholarship with those grades and we didn't have the money to keep him there. He just went off and joined the Army."

"How did you feel about that?" she asked.

"I thought it was good for him. I was a sergeant in the Marines in World War II. I fought on Saipan, Iwo Jima, and Okinawa against the Japs. One Chinaman was as good as another as far as I was concerned and I was proud of my boy servin' his country."

"You were proud, Mr. Hayes?" she asked in a surprised tone.

"Sure I was. Why wouldn't I be?"

"It was 1966, Mr. Hayes," Marie reminded him. "It was the heart of the Civil Rights Movement. Even in the early years of the war, it was obvious the poor blacks were fighting the war in greater numbers than the middle-class whites. Didn't you resent that even a little?"

"Resent, shit!" he said, raising his voice.

The old man stood up and walked to the mantle. He stooped as he walked. He picked up the group picture of Chuck's Green Beret Unit and brought it back to Marie.

"Look at this picture of Chuck's unit," he said handing it to her. "Count them. Just count them. There's eight white boys in there, my son, and the captain who was a Chinaman. If that ain't equal opportunity, I don't know what is!"

Marie started to speak, but Mr. Hayes interrupted her.

"Listen here, pretty lady," he said. "You was probably still in diapers when these boys went off to war. Don't you tell me what it was like then! I ain't so old and feeble I don't still remember.

"It wasn't perfect, far from it. But I always had a job and I always fed my wife and the boy. I was a janitor in the Boston schools for thirty years. I got my job when an old Irishman retired. When I retired, a Puerto Rican got my job. It wasn't the best job in the world, but it was a job and I was damn good at that job, too.

"I was proud of what I did, takin' care of those children and those teachers. My son would have been a teacher if he'd lived. That ain't no discrimination in my book.

"I don't want to hear that shit. Me and a lot more like me is tired of little girls like you and sissy draft dodgers taking pictures of these lazy asses standin' on street corners doin' nothing. Let them get a job!

"If there ain't no jobs in Boston, let them up and go to where there is jobs. I came here from North Carolina with my daddy when I was ten. They can go pick tobacco if there ain't nothin' here. They can join the Army. I'm tired of hearin' all this crap about gettin' somethin' for nothin'."

Marie realized she needed to change the subject and she took the second picture from Mr. Hayes' hand.

"What unit was this, Mr. Hayes?" she asked.

"That's the 545th Special Warfare Group. Green Berets, every one of them."

"Here is your son," she said, pointing with her finger as she held it for the camera to see. "Do you know the names of any of the other men here?"

"Let me see," he said. "I used to know them all. Next to my boy was his best friend, Charley Reed. I told you about him the other day. This one is Billy Campbell. The Lieutenant is O. K. Kim and this one is the old sarge, John P. Tankersley. Here is Dewberry. This is Harold Maille and the other two are Lloyd Booth and Ben Webbinger."

Marie shook her head in wonder. "That's amazing after all these years you can still remember all their names."

"Why?" Mr. Hayes asked.

"Everyone remembers George Washington, Paul Revere, Ulysses S. Grant, Black Jack Pershing, George Patton, or Douglas MacArthur. They were all heroes and leaders. These boys were, too, and they deserve to have someone remember them. That's my job since I retired, remembering these boys."

"Are they all dead?" Marie asked.

"Yes, Miss," he answered sadly. "Every one of them is dead. Nine of them were killed in combat and one of them died in an automobile accident after the war."

"Who was that?" she asked, motioning the camera in closer.

"Charley Reed," he answered. "My son's best friend."

"This is him here," he said pointing with his finger.

The camera got a perfect close-up of Charley Reed smiling with his arm around Chuck Hayes.

"Him and my son really loved each other. He used to come and see me after he was back and out of the hospital."

"Charley Reed was in the hospital?"

"Yes. He was in Walter Reed in Washington, D.C."

"Do you know how he was hurt?"

"Sure," Mr. Hayes said. "About a month after my son was killed the enemy ambushed the rest of them. Everyone was killed except Charley and he fought his way back."

"Fought his way back?"

"Yes," Mr. Hayes answered. "It took him two days and he killed fifty of them. He was all busted up inside, but he crawled back fightin' the enemy the whole way. They gave him the Silver Star, too, just like my boy. They gave all of them the Silver Star. They were all heroes, every single one of them."

Marie was ready to ask another question when Mr. Hayes stopped her.

"Look," he said. "I'll be happy to answer all your questions, but I go around the corner every day at this time to D.J.'s, my gin mill. You're welcome to come with me and bring your man with the camera, too. I'm gettin' awful dry and need my mornin' refreshment."

Marie agreed and they walked with Mr. Hayes through the alley to D.J.'s Lounge a block away. When they entered the door, Marie realized she and Fred, the cameraman, were the only white people in the place. She stopped in her footsteps at the surprise. Mr. Hayes took her arm and brought her into the building.

D.J. was tending bar and extended a greeting.

"Alexander, you're late. What have you been doing and why are you bringing 60 Minutes with you?"

"This ain't no 60 Minutes," he said back. "This lady is doin' a story about my boy and his buddies."

"Chuck and Charley?" D.J. asked, pointing to the picture of the two of them above the bar.

"Sure, Hayes answered. "The rest of them, too."

"That's great. That's just great!" D.J. repeated.

"Here," Mr. Hayes said to D.J. "Cash this for me while I take a walk and shake hands with an old friend."

Marie watched as Mr. Hayes handed D.J. a check from First Interstate Bank in California for five hundred dollars and then walk away. D.J. took the check and counted out the cash on the bar for his friend.

"Alexander is one lucky man," D.J. said to Marie.

"Before he was killed Chuck set up a retirement fund for his dad. He gets a check like this every week. Between this and his pension and social security, Alexander is doing real well."

Marie didn't say anything, but knew it seemed very odd that a twenty-two year old college dropout had the funds and the smarts to set up any kind of deferred compensation plan for his father. The number of the check, 3434340, and name of the bank was large enough to read and for some reason stuck in her memory. As Mr. Hayes returned to the bar and pocketed his cash, Marie opened her purse and wrote the number and name down on the first scrap of paper she found.

"Give me the usual, D.J. and give the pretty lady and her man with the camera whatever they want," Mr. Hayes said.

"Nothing for me," Fred said with a grin. "I can only do one thing at a time."

"Same here," Marie added.

Alexander would have none of it.

"If you want to interview me, have a drink," he said to Marie.

"You," he said to Fred, "you're right. The picture would probably come out shaky."

"What'll it be?" D.J. asked her.

"A Bloody Mary, I guess."

"Fine," D.J. said and made the drink.

"What do you want to know about next?" Mr. Hayes asked.

He swallowed a shot of Wild Turkey and then took a healthy gulp of beer. D.J. poured another shot of bourbon to replace the one he'd finished.

"Tell me about Charley Reed," she asked him, watching his face for any expression out of the ordinary.

The old man swallowed hard. He picked up the glass of beer and finished it. Then he looked directly into her eyes as if he was trying to read her motives.

Glancing back at the bar, he said, "D.J., when you get a chance I need another glass of beer."

Then he looked back at her and asked, "Why do you want to know about Charley Reed?"

"He was your son's best friend," she said as she took a small sip of the Bloody Mary. "You said he came to visit you after he was out of the Army. I want to know if he gave you any special insight into what happened."

The old man downed the second shot of Wild Turkey and again took an enormous gulp of beer.

"You know," he said, looking directly into her eyes.

Marie was at a loss for words. She wasn't sure what to say. She was very much aware he was watching her closely for a reaction. She gave none and only looked directly back into his eyes. Marie didn't nod or shake her head. Her silence was all the indication she gave him, one way or the other.

"I know you know," he said. "How?"

"I just do," she answered. "That's all that really matters."

"You're right," he said.

Thinking for a moment, he reflected on what she said and then gave her a big smile. "You're going to tell the story whether I tell you or not."

Marie said nothing.

"I'll tell you just so you get it right."

Then he began. "Charley Reed first came to see me about six months after he got out of the Army. My wife was dyin' of cancer and things weren't so good for me. They weren't so good for him neither.

"At first he just talked about Chuck and what good friends they was. I already knew that. Chuck wrote about him all the time.

"Chuck owed his life to Charley. Charley went back to pull Chuck out of a burning C-124 at Lon Binn when they first got there in January. He pulled him out and then dragged him across the damn airfield to cover while they was under attack. He saved my boy's life.

"Chuck was unconscious the whole time and came to in a bunker not knowin' how he got out of the plane. Charley Reed loved my son. I want you to tell that for me," he said as tears came into his eyes.

D.J. poured him another shot and he drank it down.

"That's the trouble with you people," he said. "You only dwell on the bad. The good ain't news. The bad you can make a lot out of while the good ain't nothin'.

"We were drinkn', Charley and me. We were drinkin' a lot. I was pouring him the Wild Turkey and he was matchin' me drink for drink and then he takes out this gun. It was a .45 and he cocks it, throwin' a round in the chamber.

"It was a big-assed old pistol and the hammer was back and ready to pop.

"Then he slides the gun to me. We was in my kitchen at the table and he slides it across and tells me to kill him! I couldn't believe my ears, this boy tellin' me to kill him.

"I asked him why and that's when he tells me he killed my son. There I was, my wife dyin' of cancer, and this young man confessin' he killed my son and handin' me a loaded gun so I can kill him."

"How did he say he killed your son?" Marie asked.

She glanced back to be sure the camera was rolling the entire time.

"It was an accident in one of those early mornin' fire fights while they was comin' back from an attack across the border in North Vietnam. Everyone was shootin' at everyone else and I guess Chuck had aimed at Charley by mistake and Charley fired first before he realized who he was shootin'. When he got to me, he was one screwed up young man."

"How did you feel when he told you?" she asked quietly.

"I didn't want to kill him," Mr. Hayes said. "I felt sorry for him havin' to live with that inside him. I felt sorry for him 'cause I knew how he felt. I had the same thing happen to me on Saipan. I knew exactly how he felt. I got the boy to the VA for help so he could live with himself and I kept that pistol. I still have it."

"What happened to Charley?" Marie asked.

"He was okay for awhile. He came and stayed with me when my wife passed away and helped me an awful lot. He called me when he got married. His wife was a strange one.

"Charley married bad. That woman didn't want him or no kids. Then he fell in love with some pretty black-haired girl from North Carolina. He was off and on with her when he was killed."

"What happened to his wife?"

"Like I said, she didn't want him. When Charley died she just went on with her life, I suppose. Charley became my son for two years and took the place of Chuck and I loved him like I loved my own boy."

Tears filled the old man's eyes and began to roll down his cheeks.

"I went to Charley's funeral in Pittsburgh. I had to tell his parents what happened to their son so they wouldn't be havin' bad thoughts about him. Charley Reed was a good boy. He never intentionally hurt no one, except in war and that was war. He was just doin' his duty."

Alexander Hayes stared at the door as he stopped talking. It was as if he expected someone to walk in at any minute.

"I've been back to his grave a couple of times," he said.

"Where is he buried?" she asked. "I can end this piece at the grave."

"Queen of Heaven Cemetery," he answered. "It's a half an hour ride from the Pittsburgh airport. The cab drivers all know where it is. It ain't hard to get to at all."

Marie had what she wanted.

The story Alexander Hayes had told her was just the beginning. The story was even better than she imagined and she knew there was still much more to uncover.

Alexander Hayes was getting pretty drunk and it was just noon. Marie felt sorry for the old man and kissed him on the cheek when she left. Outside in the car Fred asked where they were off to next.

Pittsburgh was her answer.

CHAPTER FORTY-SEVEN

Charley Reed arrived outside Pittsburgh at seven in the evening and took a room at the Greentree Radisson for two nights. This was the first time he'd been back to Pittsburgh since going to California years ago. He had no idea what had happened since then. Were his parents still alive? He had a brother and a sister. What of them?

He checked the phone book in his room for his parents. There was no listing. Charley knew they would never move away, so he had to assume they were dead. His brother Jerry wasn't listed either, but he was able to find his sister at the same old address.

It was Pittsburgh. Few things ever changed.

As Charley showered, Marie Van Arsdale and her cameraman, Fred, checked into their rooms at the Greentree Holiday Inn. Both hotels were located in the south hills of Pittsburgh just off the Parkway West, next to one another on the other side of Greentree hill.

Marie called Los Angeles and excitedly told her producer about the interview and footage they had and the direction in which the story was developing.

Meanwhile, Charley enjoyed the feeling of being refreshed and in clean clothes. He was happy to be out of the car and he found the bar rather enjoyable. He wasn't especially hungry, so he decided to sit at the bar and drink his meal.

It had been a long time since he'd done that, but he decided it wasn't all that bad of an idea. Pleased with his decision, he happily ordered another drink.

Charley finally managed to relax after his third drink. He felt his mood lift. He wasn't sure if it was the alcohol or just being back in his hometown. There was always something different about Pittsburgh and its people. It was something he liked.

As he sat at the bar, he realized he was more than relaxed. He felt at peace.

Charley knew he wasn't drunk and also knew the few drinks he had could never have given him this feeling of well being. It was a feeling totally new to him and from wherever it came, he was grateful. With no idea of what was ahead of him, he sat and sipped his drink, just watching the people around him.

Andrea and John Watson were among the people in the lounge. It was Andrea who first noticed Charley seated at the bar.

"John," she said. "Look at the man sitting at the bar."

John put down his drink and looked in the direction his wife spoke.

"Where?" he asked.

"Over on the left on the other side," she answered.

"My goodness," he said. "He looks just like Chuck."

"Yes, he does," she said.

John wanted a closer look. He stood up and walked directly to where Charley Reed was seated. He couldn't believe his eyes. He wanted to speak, but he didn't know what to say.

The man at the bar was nearly an exact double, but older. The difference in their ages wasn't noticeable from a distance, but up close you could tell. John guessed the man's age to be a few years older than himself.

Charley watched John walk up to him. He could tell the man wanted to say something, but at the last second changed his mind.

"Hi," Charley said to him. "Do you need something?"

"No!" John said embarrassed. "My wife and I are sitting over there and we commented on how much you look like our nephew."

Charley laughed.

"I'm a little too old to be your nephew. He must be a good looking man though," he said with a grin.

"Yes, I guess you are," John agreed. "Unfortunately he was killed in the World Trade Center last week.

"I'm John Watson," he said extending his hand. As he did, he noted even their voices sounded the same. It was uncanny.

"Chuck Hayes," Charley answered, shaking John's hand.

"I'm sorry to bother you," John told him.

"It was no bother," Charley said. "I'm sorry about your nephew. Have a nice evening."

John returned to his wife and told her what happened.

"Did he tell you his name?" Andrea asked with suspicion.

"Yes, he did," John said.

"Was it Charley Reed?" she asked.

"No," he answered. "It was Chuck Hayes."

"Are you sure?" she asked her husband.

"Of course, I'm sure," he said. "If you don't believe me, go ask him yourself."

Andrea looked up and he was gone.

Charley had gone back to his room. The drinks made him tired. He turned out the lights in the room, leaving the television set on, and got into bed. Then the reality of where he was hit him.

He had come home.

He wasn't sure who he had come home as. When he left California the thought wasn't even in his mind. All he intended to do was put a lot of miles between himself and the news people.

Looking back, he realized he could have just gone to Las Vegas. There was something else, a reason he had yet to understand that brought him here.

Now that he was here, who was he? He told the man in the bar he was Chuck Hayes. Why not Charley Reed? Was Charley Reed really dead or had he just taken time off from life?

Charley moved his head around on the pillows and smiled to himself. He liked that, taking time off from life. It was a quick explanation and probably could be accepted by anybody if it was only six months or a year. The fact he had taken nearly thirty years off from life was a totally different story.

Had he just taken the time off or was Charley Reed really dead?

Only he could answer the question and he could only do that when he was ready. He closed his eyes and drifted off to sleep. Regardless of who he said he was, his dreams were still the dreams of Charley Reed, not Chuck Hayes.

Marie Van Arsdale checked out of the Holiday Inn the next day just after eight a.m. The directions they were given to the cemetery weren't complicated and they arrived there just after nine o'clock.

Marie wasn't used to the February chill covering the hills of western Pennsylvania. She was shivering as the wind blew up the hill to Charley's grave from the highway below. Fred, who was on loan from the Boston affiliate station, laughed at her as her teeth began to chatter.

"Why don't you sit in the car and stay warm while I set up?" he suggested to her.

"Good idea," she answered.

As Fred got everything ready to shoot, he noticed the graves were all from the same family. Charley Reed's was the oldest, and then there were the parents. They died within two years of one another. Then there was Jerry J. Reed, evidently another son, younger than Charley. Fred wondered if there were any other children or if this was the whole family.

Marie got out of the car and walked to where Fred was preparing to shoot the piece. Marie noticed a freshly dug grave not more than fifty yards away. While this part wasn't a major segment of her report, it was important in the respect it would show the extent Charley Reed had gone to appear dead. As she stared at the grave, she realized this small segment would only expand the story more. The grave raised many more questions.

Was there a body buried there? If it wasn't Charley Reed, who was it and how did they really die? Was it someone Charley Reed had killed? Had he killed the person buried in his place? Was this an unsolved murder of someone who was missing for nearly twenty years?

There was no limit to where this story might lead. Marie understood what this could mean to her. Then, as she imagined herself as an anchorwoman on the evening news, she faced reality.

If Charley Reed was a killer, and she had seen him kill with his bare hands in the airport, why wouldn't he kill her to keep from being exposed?

The very man who had saved her life now seemed to pose a very definite threat. Yet, if this story was ever to be told in its entirety, it could only be done so with an interview with Charley Reed.

Fred interrupted her train of thought to tell her he was ready to shoot. A half an hour later they were through and getting ready to go to Emporia, Virginia where Charley Reed supposedly died. As they packed up, a procession of cars started up the hill and out of the parking lot where they fell in line behind the hearse. They drove off and ignored the car passing them coming in the opposite direction. They didn't see it stop and they didn't see the man get out.

Wearing a bright red sweater, Charley Reed walked up to his own grave. His questions about his family were answered by the presence of the three other gravestones.

He felt a pain in his stomach and a lump in his throat as he looked at the graves of his parents and his brother. He felt overwhelming guilt for what he had done. He felt selfish and inconsiderate. It had never occurred to him what his actions might have done to anyone else. He had only thought of himself and how he felt. It was all so easy; he'd never even thought to look back.

Now everything was finalized for him and there was no looking back.

As Fred and Marie drove to the airport to catch a flight to Washington, D.C., she had a brainstorm.

"Let's go to the Vietnam Memorial, The Wall, and film there at Chuck Hayes' name. It'll make a great cut in after what we've just shot," she said.

Fred agreed saying it was a great idea.

Charley was looking over the edge of the hill down at the road. He wondered who had chosen the location for the graves.

It had probably been his mother and he imagined her saying that he would like the hillside and the road below. She was right, he did. As he looked down at his own gravestone, he wondered where he might be buried next and what might be said as an epitaph the next time.

And what of the son-of-a-bitch buried in his place? What of his family? Were they dead? Was this guy ever missed?

Charley watched the funeral procession wind up the hill. As it drove past his parked car, he coldly put the man buried in his place out of his mind by concluding he'd gotten what he deserved. It was that stranger who had directly intervened to affect the direction Charley's life had taken.

Charley turned and watched an entire family get out of the cars and follow the priest and the casket to the freshly prepared grave. The women were crying and the men were silent and solemn looking. There were children and probably brothers and sisters of the deceased.

Burial of the dead was a family matter, just as births and weddings. Charley Reed had no family and didn't participate in the burial of his own parents. While he had been able to deal with his own problems by becoming his dead friend, how would he now deal with what he had failed to bring to his own family as a son?

As he thought of his own responsibilities as a son, he watched a young man in the family of people at the gravesite who reminded him very much of himself. The young man looked to be with his mother, wife, and sisters. The mannerisms of the young man could easily have been his own at that age had there never been a Vietnam. Charley stood alone at the graves of his mother, father, and brother, silently participating in the burial going on fifty yards away.

Marie Van Arsdale and Fred arrived at The Wall at one p.m. They filmed the segment on Charles Wilson Hayes.

Charley Reed was back in the hotel at the bar having his second beer. He had no thought of food. He wasn't hungry. He was having his own wake for his family. The keys to car were in his room and he could get as drunk as he wanted.

He hadn't been able to erase the thoughts he had that morning. He wondered who had come to his parents' and his brother's funerals. Who had come to his and what it was like?

He sipped the beer and tried to think of something else, but his mind wouldn't move. He'd never been to his own grave before this. In all the years he'd been gone, he never thought about having a place where his body was buried. It never occurred to him that somewhere there was a gravestone with his name on it and people who loved him might visit it.

Charley felt very selfish as he though about his parents. He wanted to imagine they visited his grave. He tried to imagine if they felt sadness. Did they cry over him or were they relieved he was gone?

Charley wanted to believe his death was simple for everyone. He was sure in a very short time everyone had forgotten. After his visit to the cemetery, he wasn't so sure. A chill swept over his body and the cold grave stones in the cemetery flashed before eyes.

CHAPTER FORTY-EIGHT

WASHINGTON, D.C.
SEPTEMBER 21, 2001
8:43 A.M.

John Hughes exploded, "What do you mean you don't know where he is?"

He listened to the voice on the other end of the phone. He wasn't happy.

"If he's gone, track his fucking credit cards. He has to be using credit cards if he is moving around. We are the goddamn CIA! We ought to be able to do that."

He slammed the phone down.

At ten o'clock Marie Van Arsdale was in Greenville, North Carolina with Lee Stein. She found his name in the police records as the person who brought Joanna Reed to identify the personal effects and the car when Charley Reed was supposedly killed in the automobile accident. He was the Cadillac dealer at the time of the accident and Charley Reed worked for him at one time.

"Charley was my sales manager," Lee said. "He worked for me when Rollie, that's Joanna's little brother, came to live with them because the parents died. I helped them get Rollie into a special school. You see Rollie was a little slow and needed more attention."

Marie watched the man's face as he sat in the high-backed leather chair. It was an old face with lines of experience. Obviously he was very successful judging by the magnificent southern-style home in which he lived. A new Cadillac was in the driveway and there was an old black maid who answered his front door.

"Mr. Stein," Marie said. "I'm doing a story on Charley Reed's Vietnam unit. I wanted to interview his wife. Would you know how I could get in touch with her?"

"Please, call me Lee," he said. "She's in the phone book in

Bethesda, Maryland."

He caught himself.

"It might be Potomac, Maryland. My wife and I don't speak to her that often. She calls once in a while. We don't call her," he said with a strange tone to his voice.

"After Charley died she wasn't much of a mother to her little brother. Actually she wasn't much of one before he died either."

"How is that?" Marie asked.

"Charley wasn't living with her at the end. He was gone just less than a year when he was killed. He was on his way back here to check on Rollie. She had her hands full with him.

"She'd leave him alone too much. He got hurt once, I can't remember exactly what it was, but anyway the hospital called me when she took him in because she didn't have any money. I guess they thought Charley still worked for me or something.

"When I saw her at the hospital that day she said she was tired of acting like a mother and just wanted to be responsible for herself. She wanted Rollie placed in a home. Anyway I went up to the hospital, the old one. She was there and the boy's face was all cut up. I signed for her so he could be treated and then I went back and called Charley."

"Where was Charley living then?"

"He was up north with some girl. He always had someone."

"I'm getting the impression you don't like Joanna Reed very much," Marie said. "Why is that?"

"Because she was selfish," Lee Stein said.

"She was a quiet, pretty little girl who only cared about herself. She never asked for anything. She didn't care about things. She liked plants and books and treated Charley like he was something to be watered and put on a shelf. She never wanted to have a baby of their own. She was something. She took care of Rollie about the same. She'd sleep all the time and began ignoring both of them. Then, Charley began looking around."

"He started seeing other women?" she asked.

"That's right," Lee said. "That's when he met Jerilyn Gardner. It was a few months after Rollie came to live with them."

"Where is Jerilyn Gardner now?" Marie asked.

"I don't know," Lee answered. "After Charley died, she was pretty upset. She was in the bars every night. Then she went away. When her mother died a few years ago, she came back for the funeral and I heard she was living in Chicago. She was always on the move. She was all wrong for Charley."

"What was Charley Reed like?" Marie asked. "You evidently knew him better than most people."

"Yes, I knew him," Lee said. "You're right, probably better than most, too. I gave him his first job right out of the Army. We were in Washington, D.C. then, working at Capitol Ford."

"Was he married to Joanna then?"

"Yes, he was and even then he wandered from time to time. I'm not sure if it was ever right between them."

"Did he move to North Carolina with you?"

"No," Lee said. "Not at first. He came down about two years later."

"How was he? Did he like it here?"

"Whether he liked it or not would be hard to say. Charley was always troubled. He was a hard worker and honest, but there was a problem somewhere. It was the kind of problem you couldn't pin down or touch. It was at the root of everything that bothered him and it was always there."

"Did he ever talk to you about it?" Marie asked.

"No," Lee told her, shaking his head. "But Joanna did once. She was afraid. He was having horrible dreams and she wanted him to get help. Charley wouldn't go."

"What kind of dreams did he have?"

"Like I said, he never talked to me about them. Bob Walker probably knew. Charley liked him and stayed friends with him right to the end."

"Where is Bob Walker?"

"He's probably still in Washington, selling cars somewhere."

Marie thanked Lee Stein and left. Her next stop was obvious. She knew she was on a real hot story and the next few days would wrap it up for her. This was her big break.

Marie Van Arsdale reached her hotel in Arlington, Virginia at four in the afternoon. Just as Lee Stein said, Joanna Reed's number was listed in the phone book. Marie freshened up and then began to phone her every half hour until finally reaching her just before seven.

Marie was very practiced at introducing herself and getting to the point of her business. It took very little convincing for her to get Joanna Reed to agree to see her.

"I'll come by at eight-thirty," Marie said after getting directions. "Thank you very much."

Marie was there on time and anxious about this particular interview. As she paid the cab driver, Marie wondered what kind of woman she would find. Lee Stein didn't think much of her, but she was about to find out for herself.

When the door opened, a woman who could have stepped out of a '60s news clip greeted her. Joanna Reed was a woman who evidently still thought she was twenty.

Marie entered the townhouse. It was decorated in bright colors with posters on the walls. A fat black cat slept on a rocking chair in the corner and as she scanned the room, she noted there was no television.

She had some classical music playing and the room was full of books. There were built-in shelves on two walls and they were packed from end to end. Huge cushions were thrown around the wooden coffee table in the center of the room near the fireplace. There were two other rocking chairs besides the one the cat occupied. A high-backed couch was on the wall opposite the fireplace. A knitted afghan was folded across the back of the couch and more cushions in bright colors were on each end. An open book laying face down was on the table by one of the rocking chairs.

"Can I take your coat?" Joanna asked Marie.

"Yes, thank you," Marie answered.

As she slipped it from her shoulders and Joanna took it to the closet, Marie noticed framed pictures on the mantle. One was of Charley with a young boy at the ocean, probably Rollie.

Joanna Reed was wearing a long simple cotton dress with ruffled shoulders and long sleeves. It was burgundy with little yellow flowers and green leaves on it. Her feet were bare and Marie was surprised at the woman's slim and youthful body. Her hair was long and straight.

"How ever did you find me?" Joanna asked.

"Lee Stein in Greenville told me you were listed in the phone book. I was there this morning and took a chance by calling when I got here."

Joanna laughed a throaty sarcastic laugh when she heard his name.

"Good old Lee Stein," she said. "He's always been one of my greatest fans."

She handed Marie a glass of wine and offered her one of the rocking chairs by the fireplace.

"How can I help you?" Joanna asked.

"I'm here about your husband, Charley Reed."

"Was that him I saw on the news last week?" she asked.

"I believe so," Marie said. "He saved my life. I was the reporter that character was about to shoot when he stepped in and attacked him."

"I saw the pictures and couldn't believe it! Rollie was here for dinner and I told him that man was either Charley or Charley's double. Even the way he threw the punch, I was sure. I've seen him fight before and I remember."

"It seems we're in agreement then," Marie said.

"I'm doing a story on the man who saved the Senator's life as well as my own and who knows how many other people at that gate. The man who did that has a valid California driver's license and has had one since the year Charley Reed was killed in an automobile accident.

"He has no arrests outside of a speeding ticket two years ago. He owns a piano bar in the San Francisco area along with other businesses. He lives in Oakland and has never been married since coming to California from Boston about the time Charley Reed died. He lives with a television reporter named Alicia Masters and has for the past two or three years. He is using the name Charley Hayes."

Joanna listened as Marie continued.

"Charley Hayes is originally from Boston. I went to Boston and met his father, Alexander Hayes. Alexander Hayes is a black man whose son was in the 545th Special Operations Group, the same unit as Charley Reed."

"I couldn't verify that for you," Joanna said. "He never talked very much about the war to me.

"I met him after the war and he was a training instructor. We were married during his last year and a half in the service, but I never knew anything about what happened before I met him. He had horrible nightmares, but would never talk about them. He closed that part of his life out completely."

"I went to his grave in Pittsburgh," Marie continued. "I found out his parents and his brother are dead.

"I went to Emporia, Virginia and I discovered the man who was in the automobile accident was over six feet tall. Charley Reed was only five feet eleven inches tall. Lee Stein said the body was burned beyond recognition and he was identified by his wallet and the car he was driving."

"Yes, that's right," Joanna said. "They wouldn't even let me see him he was burnt so bad. I couldn't say whether it was him or not. We weren't living together at the time. He came by to see Rollie, but that was the extent of it."

"Lee Stein said he was on his way back to help you with Rollie. Is that right?"

"So Lee told you that! It is and it isn't."

Joanna leaned forward in the rocking chair.

"He was coming back to tell me how to take care of Rollie, but he was coming back for me, too. He was going to take us back up north with him because I was having so much trouble here and I couldn't afford to move. His death took care of that. He always was a good provider."

"I don't believe he is dead," Marie said.

"From what I saw on television, I would have to agree with you," she said coolly.

"But you have to understand, Miss Van Arsdale, that part of my life is gone. That was a long time ago. I cried when they said he was dead. I wore black to the funeral and I cried because we never had a chance to make it up."

Joanna stopped to finish her wine. She looked directly at Marie and carefully selected her words.

"Charley Reed loved Rollie and me. I can understand him going away and not calling. That would make a lot of sense, especially if you knew the way he thought. I find it hard to believe he just turned his back on his whole life. If he's been alive all these years and he's never tried to find out about me or anyone else, I'd be careful. There might be something very wrong with him."

"What do you mean by that?" Marie asked.

"Look," Joanna said. "If that was Charley, he did kill someone with his bare hands, right?"

"Yes," Marie answered. "That was justifiable. He's a hero. He saved many lives by acting the way he did."

Joanna shook her head.

"You don't understand at all. Charley Reed was a trained killer. He never told me exactly what he did because it was too horrible for him to face. To him there wasn't any justifiable or unjustifiable killing. To him killing was killing and it was something he was very proficient at doing. How do you ever make someone stop once they've started? Charley may have gone away for a reason and we might not want to know any part of it."

Marie didn't understand.

"When we were married," Joanna said, "he was still in the service and he started to sleep walk. I was such a sound sleeper that I never realized he was gone.

"It was the dead of winter and he'd get out of bed and wander around the neighborhood. We'd go to parties or visit the neighbors and they'd talk about a Peeping Tom and how the police were trying to catch him. I had no idea until I woke up one night to see Charley walk into the other bedroom and get dressed.

"I said something to him and it was as if I wasn't even there. He never heard a word I said. His eyes were open and he left and locked the door behind him. An hour later he came back. It was scary, very scary. The next night it was the same thing again and I followed him in the car. He walked for miles and then came home."

"What happened? Did he get help?"

"No," Joanna said. "He hated the doctors and he warned me to keep my mouth shut. He was always afraid they'd find out there was something wrong and put him in the hospital."

"How did you live with that?" Marie asked.

"I didn't have to," Joanna answered. "The sleepwalking stopped and then he got asthma. Now we know what it was. Then they didn't have a name for it. It was a classic case of delayed stress with the sleep-walking followed by asthma.

"He was so troubled, but he absolutely refused to get help. Charley was sure he could work it out on his own."

"If the man in the airport was Charley Reed, then you believe he may be still troubled?" asked Marie.

"I'm not saying yes, but I sure wouldn't rule it out. I lived with him for five years off and on and I know what he had inside of him. It was thirty years ago, but I can't see how it would have gone away. You don't solve emotional problems just by changing your identity."

Joanna got them another glass of wine. They sat and talked about Rollie and they talked about their jobs and what it was like trying to manage a career. Marie found herself really enjoying the other woman.

She glanced at the mantle over the fire. There was a picture of a young man. He had blonde hair and features that strongly resembled Charley.

"Who is the man in the photograph?" she asked.

"Tommy, my son," Joanna said.

"You remarried?" she asked awkwardly.

"No," Joanna said blankly. "He is Charley's son. When he was killed, I didn't know I was pregnant. It happened the night before he died. His last gift to me."

Lee Stein hadn't mentioned they had a son. Joanna picked up on it.

"Lee Stein never believed Tommy was Charley's son. There is no mistaking it. Tommy is just like his father. He has his same mean temper," Joanna said.

Just after eleven o'clock the door opened and another woman walked in, closing the door behind her. Joanna stood up from her chair and walked to the woman in the foyer who was unbuttoning her coat. When Joanna kissed the other woman on her mouth, Marie nearly dropped her glass of wine.

"This is my roommate, Ellen," Joanna said, introducing her to Marie.

After the casual introduction and a little conversation, Marie called for a cab and left the women.

Hours later Joanna Reed slid from between the sheets and picked up her housecoat from the chair in the corner of the bedroom. She looked back at Ellen sprawled across their bed and listened to the steadiness of her breathing. Joanna walked back to the bed and pulled the blanket up over the woman. She bent down and kissed her forehead and then walked out to the living room.

There was still a small amount of wine left in the bottle that she shared with Marie Van Arsdale. She poured it into her glass and went over to the couch and tucked her feet beneath her. The black male cat walked across the back of the couch and rubbed the top of his head against hers. He purred and Joanna reached back and stroked his body, feeling it vibrate beneath her touch. She thought of Marie Van Arsdale and what she was doing.

She remembered seeing Charley on the television. Joanna knew him at once just by the movements of his body. There had been many times she wished she could have erased him from her memory, but so much of him still lingered. Every time Charley Reed thundered back into her conscious mind, she wished she could forget.

Joanna had learned to live with his thundering times, it was the tender side of him that cut her deeper than Charley ever imagined. Then on the eleven o'clock news he was there.

After thirty years he was back from the grave.

She looked at the phone across the room and wondered what she would do if it rang and it was Charley. She sank into the corner of the couch and pulled the afghan over her legs.

She remembered living in North Carolina and being asleep on the couch. They were not living together. The living room lights were on and the book she was reading had fallen from her hand and was open on the floor. The phone began to ring and she woke. It was Charley and she asked what time it was.

"Around one," he answered. "I'm here. I just got into town. Can I come over?"

She remembered hesitating, knowing he would stay and they would make love. She remembered wanting to make love to him.

"Okay," she answered.

Joanna remembered waiting for him and how she was nervous. She walked around the living room trying to decide what she would do. She wished she had eaten something and went to the kitchen to see what was already made, but there was nothing. She walked back into the living room and waited.

She looked at the clock and wondered where he was when he called. Joanna remembered being jealous when she thought he was in one of the bars where he used to drink and meet his women. If that was so, he was only minutes away.

The doorbell rang and he was there. She remembered him standing in the doorway and how he seemed taller to her. She wondered if she should kiss him or just step aside and let him enter. She remembered the sheepish look on his face as he spoke first.

"Hi! I'm here."

"So you are," she said, not really knowing what to say.

He kissed her on the cheek and then walked into the house.

"You have a nice tan," she told him.

"Thanks."

"You've been lifting weights, too," she said looking at the muscles in his arms and across his chest. "You always liked to lift weights."

"Thanks," was all he said.

"Do you want to see Rollie? He's probably asleep."

"Please, I'd like to."

They walked back to Rollie's room.

"I brought him a present," said Charley. "Well, I'll just put the present here and he can have it tomorrow when he wakes up. Boy, he sure is getting big, twelve now, isn't he?"

"Yes," answered Joanna.

They returned to the living room and sat together on the couch and talked about so many things. When she looked at Charley, he was smiling. She watched him look around the room and wondered what he was thinking. She wondered if he missed her and wanted to come back. She remembered wanting to ask, but wouldn't. Instead, she asked how he had been.

"All right," he answered.

"Just all right?" she asked, sensing something in his voice.

"I still have the dreams," he admitted.

She could still remember how surprised she had been when he

mentioned the dreams. She could remember waking up and not knowing what to do. She would ask what he was dreaming about, but he
never exactly told her. He would talk about dead bodies and killing, but
everything was always vague. There was never anything really definite.

"Do you remember them better now?" she asked.

"Yes," he answered.

"Tell me about them," she said. "I'd like to know."

Normally he would have refused or changed the subject. He
might even have lied to her, but that night it was different. Joanna
remembered him wanting to confess in a way. He looked so vulnerable and she knew it was why he had come to her.

"They're ugly," he began. "They're about me and I'm not sure
what I am and what I've done."

"What do you mean?" she asked.

"When I was in the hospital, my parents came to visit me."

"I didn't know you were in the hospital," she said.

"I know. I never told you. It was after Vietnam and I didn't talk.
I mean I didn't say a word for months. My father asked me if I had quit
talking because I'd been a coward and run away from the battle."

"What happened?" she remembered asking him.

"I was the only one who came back," he told her.

"We were killers. We were killing and they got us. They got
everyone, except me. I was missing for three days and when they found
me, I wouldn't talk. They had me in the hospital and my dad thought
I was a coward because I was alive."

She watched him as he closed his eyes and sort of held his breath.

"What he said to me could be true," he said to her honestly.
"There's no way for me to know. I've blocked those days completely
from my memory. I just don't know. All I have are these dreams and
I'm killing a lot of soldiers and I'm running away."

"It doesn't sound like you were a coward to me," she said. "It
sounds like you were fighting for your life."

"I know," he said. "The last dream I had I ran away, but everyone
was already dead. There really isn't anything I can do. I'm running, but
I'm running to live. I've never remembered that before, but I do now.

"I'm running and I'm fighting. I'm killing a lot of them. I gouge
one's eyes out and he's screaming. I can remember jamming my fingers
into his eye socket and digging into his head. Blood is gushing out and
soaking my hand. My fingers are holding his head and I'm beating
him with my other hand.

"Then he dies and for some reason, I stay and sleep. The next morning I wake and he's still there, dead and stiff. His hands are extended out in agony and I just crawl away from him."

"And that's what your nightmares are about?" she asked incredulously.

"Just this latest one," he said.

"Sometimes I'm shooting at women and children who are trying to run away."

"Did you ever do that?" she asked.

"I think," he said, "I think I did during those three days, but I'm not sure."

"Charley, how could you do that?" she asked looking at him.

"I don't know. In the dream I'm there and I'm doing it."

Joanna remembered looking at Charley and realizing she had never really known him. She had known a quiet person who used to erupt into loud anger. As he spoke to her that night, she realized there was more to him than she ever knew.

They sat in the living room in silence for a long time.

"Time for bed," she said to him.

She fixed the couch for him and went down the hall to her bedroom. She pulled the blankets back across the bed and then slipped out of her housecoat and began to get into bed. For some reason, she didn't. She went back down the hall to check on him. He was getting undressed.

She watched as he pulled his sweater over his head and then unzipped his pants. He slid them down his body and then turned totally naked and got under the blankets on the couch.

She remembered going back to her bedroom and how much she wanted him. She remembered how she couldn't get him out of her mind. She could still remember how much she wanted him.

He was still wounded and it was the first time she ever really knew that. Joanna wanted to make it right for him and she knew she had to show him how much she loved him. She got out of bed and went to him.

Within minutes she was breathing hard. He was holding her and moving inside her body. As he did, she was more than just a recipient of the act of making love. She was giving back at the same time and receiving that much more as she did. In a very strange way it had scared her and when they were through and he had fallen off to sleep, she remembered how defenseless she felt.

As she sat there on the couch reliving these memories and thinking about her conversation with Marie Van Arsdale, she wondered if he would call her. She sat there thinking about what she would say to him.

But the phone didn't ring and finally she went back to bed and cuddled up next to Ellen's soft body. She closed her eyes and thought again about making love to Charley that night in North Carolina.

CHAPTER FORTY-NINE

WASHINGTON, D.C.
SEPTEMBER 22, 2001
7:22 A.M.

John Hughes thumbed through the reports on his desk. He smiled to himself when he came across a reference about the FBI's inability to find certain suspects.

"We are going to keep it that way, too," he said.

He looked at the files sitting in the right corner of his desk. There were seventy-two of them. The information each person provided was invaluable. The FBI wouldn't have been able to extract what his men had accumulated.

No, his men used different techniques.

While FBI suspects were sitting in jail cells refusing to talk, the terrorist suspects his teams took into custody all talked. Some took longer to talk, but in the end they talked. They all talked.

Then he thought about Charley Reed. He picked up the folder with a recent photograph of him paper clipped to the front.

"Where are you?" he mused. "Why aren't you using your plastic? You should be living it up. You don't have that much time left."

Later that morning Marie Van Arsdale found Bob Walker. He was at work. He didn't want to talk there so they went across the street to a bar.

"I believe Charley Reed is still alive," she told him.

"How's that possible," Bob Walker asked.

She reached into her purse and produced ten photographs.

"These were taken at the airport in Los Angeles last Sunday," she said to Walker.

He took each of the photographs and spent perhaps thirty seconds with them, one at a time. When he finished, he looked up at her and didn't say anything.

"Is it him?" she asked.

"Yes, it's him," Walker answered.

"Where is he?"

"I don't know."

"Well, if he doesn't want to be found," Walker said, "he won't. He's an amazing man. He was my best friend."

"Yes," Marie agreed. "Everyone I've spoken to has said that."

"What's he doing?" Walker asked.

Marie filled him in on what she knew and then proceeded to question Walker on what he could tell her about his friend. Bob told her about Charley arriving in Washington, D.C. years ago.

"It was the first of May," he said. "He had Jerilyn and her three kids with him. They took a room at the Holiday Inn on Glebe Road. Charley was a real operator. He got right on the phone and had a job selling cars in less than an hour.

"He went out after that and rented a three-bedroom condo. By the end of the week he had it furnished with new furniture, a bar, a color television, and a stereo. He just walked in and set up this little family. It was incredible. I couldn't figure out how he did it so fast or even why."

"He must have been in love," Marie said.

"Oh, he was in love all right. He was sick in love. He had it bad.

"We had a birthday party for him. His birthday and my wife at the time had birthdays on the same day. It was a combination house warming- birthday party and they invited about forty people, three different groups actually.

"They started showing up around seven on Friday night. The first ones to arrive were the straight people who were mostly neighbors and a few old friends Charley knew from high school and college.

"Then the alcoholics came. They showed up around nine-thirty and were people we worked with and knew from the car business, along with their women.

"Then finally around ten-thirty, the freaks arrived. They were longhaired and pretty unconventional. Some of them were bikers we knew through a couple of topless dancers we used to see every now and then. Others did any number of jobs from landscaping to washing cars at the dealerships we worked.

"It worked out for the best," Bob continued. "About the time the freaks arrived, the straight people were leaving. The ones who stayed didn't last long once we set up a projector and began showing porn flicks. The joints started getting passed around and the music was turned up louder. There were three kids there and they slept through it all.

"Jerilyn enjoyed herself! She was smoking and partying with everyone. That woman really knew how to party and Charley watched her like a hawk. He didn't trust her very much."

Bob stopped to take a long drink of his beer.

"Why was that?" Marie asked.

"Jerilyn was one of those women who had to flirt with every man she met. She had to have the attention and it used to send Charley over the edge. He was sure she was sleeping with other men, but I never knew she actually did it. It was all mostly in his imagination, but she didn't help things at all."

"What do you mean?"

"Jerilyn could have laid it out the way it was. He probably would have believed her. She never did that. She thrived on the attention of other men. What happened between them was her fault."

Marie watched as Walker lapsed into silence.

"What are you thinking about?" she asked him.

"I'm trying to figure out how he managed to make everyone think he was dead," he said. "Charley was good, but that's a trick even for him."

"I'm sure it's quite a story," she said. "The more I find out about him, the more I'm fascinated. What did he ever tell you about Vietnam?"

"That's funny," Walker said.

"Funny in what way?" Marie asked.

"If you consider how close we were, he really didn't tell me very much at all. I knew he was there and I knew he fought. He was a killer and he had horrible dreams. He seldom spoke about it, but Vietnam was always there. It was in everything he did."

"Was he violent?" she asked.

"Yes, he was," Walker answered. "Not with me or with people he knew. But there were times when he'd go out and look for fights."

"He would?" Marie asked.

"Sure," Walker told her. "He used to go to this redneck bar called the Vienna Inn. It was just over the hill from where he lived and whenever he couldn't stand it anymore, he'd go there."

"How did he pick fights?"

"He didn't have to. The fights came to him," Walker remembered.

"All he did was show up. He had a handlebar moustache and long hair down to his shoulders. Some rednecks always made fun of the way he looked and he'd knock the hell out of them.

"He was quite a fighter and after a while they barred him from the place. He started hurting too many customers and one night he fought inside the bar instead of out in the parking lot."

Walker stopped and looked at the woman.

"Listen," he said. "If Charley is still alive, I would take it slow if I were you. Charley always had his reasons for everything he did. If he decides he doesn't want you in his business, you might have a big problem."

"You're the second person who's told me that," Marie confided.

"Pay attention then. We know Charley Reed and he isn't anyone to mess with. If he's chosen to drop out and change his name, whatever was bothering him probably is still there. If that's true, he can be dangerous to you and to himself," Walker warned.

"Personally, I think you seem like a nice lady. If you do it right, maybe he'll talk to you. If you don't, you'll have problems. Use my name. It might work for you. If you do get to talk to him, tell him where I am and that I want to see him."

"Sure," Marie agreed. "I can do that."

News organizations across the country began to catch on. The local station in Los Angeles began running Marie's pieces on the Hero of LAX. By Friday they were buzzing at the scoop.

The Washington Post found a photograph in their archives of Clark Clifford awarding Charley Reed the Silver Star. They planned to run it on the front page.

The CNN news organization was the most active. Within a half an hour of the story first airing, they began running their own piece on the Hero of the LAX assassination attempt.

Using footage of the airport scene, plus quotes from Marie Van Arsdale's report, they managed a minute and a half at the top of the next hour. Meanwhile, their extensive network of reporters and freelancers began to glean the country for more information and tried to get the first interview.

In New York the network realized they really had something in this story. Public response was incredible.

"Get that broad here in New York this afternoon," the vice president of news demanded. "I want her and all the footage she didn't use. We've scooped the country and I want it to stay that way for as long as we can ride this piece. Find this guy and let's get the first interview!

"In the meantime, I want a new piece for the evening news and expand the original fifteen-minute report to thirty minutes or even forty-five. I don't care. Do enough for an hour and I'll get P&G to sponsor it. I don't care what it takes! Just do it!" he exclaimed.

Marie never did see her footage on the air. She was asleep when it ran in the Eastern and Central Time zones. She was on her way to the airport when it was carried in the Pacific Time zone.

"You've hit it big, young lady," her boss in Los Angeles said to her as she drove to the airport. "This is everyone's dream. The Network asked for you.

"You walked into the story of a lifetime and the network likes you. When you get there, you're going to have your own ideas. All I can say is keep them to yourself. If you don't play ball, they'll take the story away from you and give it to one of their own people."

Marie listened with a certain amount of disbelief. This was her story all the way and now she was being told it no longer belonged to her.

"This story is bigger than you," he continued.

She listened on her cell phone.

"You brought it to life, but now it's just like anything else. You're not going to have any control over where it goes from here. All you can do is sit back and watch. You're lucky they're letting you be part of it. Do you understand?"

"Yes," she said, but she didn't appreciate it.

She understood how big it was. In spite of her relative youth in the industry, she realized how insignificant any reporter really was. She could be replaced. She thanked her boss for the advice.

While all this was happening, Charley Reed drove across the Cabin John Bridge, leaving Maryland and entering Virginia. In the old days the highway he was on was Interstate 495, the Capital Beltway. Now, the numbers had changed and the old four-lane loop around the city had nearly tripled in size.

"The capital of the world," he exclaimed to himself as the high-rise hotels and condos of Vienna came into view.

As he continued along the expressway, he recognized the exits to Fairfax. He remembered selling cars in Fairfax when he first got out of the service. That was when he met Walker.

There were many uncertainties in Charley's mind at that moment. It all started over his son. He wanted to find out about his son, Chuck Ganley, and he was going to go to where he thought he could. Then the airport thing happened. As a result of one act, it seemed he was being forced to return to the world he left years ago.

He didn't exactly know how to start. Being in Pittsburgh was sort of a start. But he needed something else.

For some reason he felt like Walker would still be around. He exited on Gallows Road and crossed over the highway. Then after a series of turns, he drove up to the front of the house Walker's father built and left to him when he passed away.

Charley stopped and got out of the car. He looked at the trees towering over the houses along the street. They were probably over a hundred years old. It was exactly as Charley remembered. He walked up to the door and rang the bell.

There was no car in the driveway, but Charley took a chance that Mary would be inside taking care of the house or making dinner. For some reason Charley assumed they would still be married. He rang the bell again, but there was no answer. Then a voice called to him from the next yard.

"He's not home," an older woman called to Charley. "He's at work."

Charley turned to recognize the schoolteacher who had lived next to Bob Walker years ago.

"Hi!" Charley said to the woman. "Do Bob and Mary still live here?"

"Bob does," the woman answered. "Mary left him a long time ago and remarried. Bob will be at work now. He doesn't get home until ten or eleven usually."

"Do you know where he works," Charley asked. "I'm an old friend of his and haven't seen him in a long while."

"I thought I recognized your face," the woman said. "He sells Fords for the dealer in Springfield. It's at the first exit on 95 below the beltway. Do you know where that is?"

"Yes," Charley answered. "I know exactly where it is. Thank you very much."

It took about fifteen minutes to drive to Springfield and the Ford dealer was just off the exit. Charley drove in, parked and went into the showroom. It didn't surprise him when he was told Walker was at lunch.

"I'm an old friend of his," Charley said. "Where does he eat lunch these days?"

"He's probably at the Daulphine Steakhouse," the car salesman told him. "I can give you directions."

Charley smiled and thanked the man.

"I know where it is. Thanks."

As Charley drove to the restaurant, he realized that as much as some things changed, they stayed the same.

The steakhouse was actually a topless bar. Bob and Charley used to drink there. In 1971 they were thrown out because Walker was giving drugs to the dancers. Walker had gotten his drugs mixed up and gave a dancer a downer instead of an upper and she wound up sleeping instead of dancing. That mistake forced them to move downtown to the Board Room and Archibald's. After all these years, the Daulphine was still there and Walker was back.

Charley opened the door and entered the bar. His eyes took a few moments to adjust from coming in out of the sunlight. There was a dancer on a stage to his left and sitting on a stool at one end of the stage was Walker.

Charley recognized him immediately. Walker hadn't changed at all.

His old friend was watching the dancer and didn't see Charley as he walked across the room and along the back of the platform to where he was seated. Charley wondered what to say or do. He couldn't think of anything special, so he did nothing.

He took the empty stool next to his friend and sat down. Walker's attention was fixed on the dark-haired young girl who was dancing directly in front of him.

A cocktail waitress came up to Charley and asked him if he would like a drink.

"Yes, please," he answered. "A Lite for me and bring my friend here another Bud."

Still Walker paid no attention to Charley. The beers were delivered as the song ended. Walker was whispering something in the dancer's ear when the waitress placed the Budweiser in front of him.

"This is from the gentleman next to you," she said.

Walker turned to find Charley Reed sitting next to him. As he did, his face remained expressionless. Even though he had spoken to the reporter and was told his friend was alive, Bob Walker long ago had buried his friend. In his mind, at least until that moment, Bob Walker still considered Charley Reed dead. Walker remained totally motionless and silent.

It was Charley who spoke first.

"At least say hello or hit me," he said to his friend.

"Oh, my God!" Walker exclaimed. "She was right!"

He came off the stool and hugged Charley.

"You're alive!"

The dancer and the cocktail waitress looked on, both shocked by Walker's display of emotion.

"I can't believe it!" he said, letting go of Charley and shaking his hand. "Look at you! You look great! You really do. I can't believe it! You're really here, just like the old days!"

Walker turned his attention to the dancer.

"Baby!" he said to her. "This is my friend Charley. He's the one I was telling you about. Look at him! He's back from the dead."

While this was going on, Charley paid for the beers, giving the waitress an extra dollar for herself.

"Charley, my man!" Walker exclaimed. "I just can't believe it! Are we ever going to party today!

"This is my peachy pie, Connie," he said, introducing him to the dancer.

Charley Reed just laughed. He had come home.

Walker would always be just Walker. Anyone else might have been angry, but Walker was just happy to have his friend back. That's the way Walker was and to Charley Reed it felt good.

At four p.m. Eastern time, Charley went to a pay phone outside and called the bar. Al Poole answered, picking it up on the first ring.

"Al, what's happening?" Charley asked, beginning to feel the beer.

"A lot, boss," Al answered. "The feds came in about two o'clock looking for you. They came with a subpoena wanting the numbers of all our bank accounts and any account you can sign on."

"What kind of feds?" Charley asked.

"I don't know, but they had federal marshals with them. They want you for questioning."

Charley's head cleared immediately.

"What happened?" he asked.

"Nothing. I called your lawyer, Mr. Abraham, and he talked to them and they left. He told me it was urgent that he talks directly to you. The sooner, the better," he said.

"Okay, Al," Charley said. "I'll call him."

Marie Van Arsdale got out of a cab on West 57th Street. She

looked up and down the street at the skyscrapers. She was here, New York City! She had finally arrived.

At the information desk in the lobby she introduced herself. The young receptionist was very businesslike, but did manage a smile.

"You're expected," she was told. "Take the second elevator on the left to the thirty-fifth floor. Someone will meet you when you get off."

"Thank you," Marie said as she turned to find the elevator lobby.

On the appropriate floor the doors opened and a young woman who identified herself as Molly was waiting for her.

"Everyone has been waiting for you. This is quite a story," the young woman said as Marie followed her down the hall.

"It's the first time in years we've had a true scoop on everyone in the entire industry. As of right now, only CNN and the Washington Post have anything. Your station at home is giving the story to the LA Times, but outside of that everyone else is in the dark. We've given the other networks limited approval to use your footage. So as it stands right now, we're it!"

Marie followed her through a doorway into a secretary's office.

"Why don't you put your bag there with the coats," Molly told her.

Marie did as she was directed and continued to follow Molly as they entered the office of the Senior Vice President of News. Jason Snyder stood as the women entered the oversized room. At his back was a bank of windows with a magnificent view of the Manhattan skyline.

"Marie," he said assuming first name informality. "This is a great pleasure to finally meet you."

Marie stepped forward and extended her hand to her new boss.

"While you're with us Molly will be your assistant."

He walked over to the couch and chairs positioned around a polished wooden coffee table and asked them to be seated with him. On the table was a phone and he picked it up and pressed the intercom button.

"Mary, would you please ask Dan to come to my office."

He didn't wait for an answer. The commanding tone in his voice, while still pleasant, was such that he certainly expected compliance. Then he turned his attention to Marie.

"What is your impression of this Reed fellow?" he asked directly. "Is he some wild man who is out there waiting to explode or is he some bona fide hero?"

"He saved my life, Mr. Snyder. I'd like to think he's a hero."

Jason's face grew pensive. He considered Marie's words for a moment and then nodded his approval.

"A hero he is then," he said, slapping his knee with his hand.

The door opened and Marie saw a very familiar face enter the room. Out of sheer respect she rose to her feet.

"Dan," Jason said. "This is Marie Van Arsdale."

The anchorman's face broke into a smile as he extended his hand to her.

"Sir," Marie stumbled. "This is really my great pleasure to meet you."

"Thank you, Marie," he said. "Please call me Dan. We're going to be working together very closely for the next week. Just call me Dan."

"Thanks," Marie said. "Yes, sir, Dan."

Jason chuckled at the schoolgirl awe Marie had for the top-rated anchorman on network news.

"Molly," Jason said. "We have two hours until we're on the air. Get with wardrobe. I want the professional young businesswoman image for Marie. Gray business suit, dark blue sweater or blouse will do fine with her coloring. Get her set up with makeup. I want her hair up. We want to see her neck and ears. She's a fresh face. I want everyone to trust her."

He smiled and then turned his attention to Dan.

"We've decided to do this Reed guy as a hero, Dan. He did save Marie's life. That qualifies him, I suppose," he said seriously.

"We want to key in on the footage of the old black man and what we pulled out today from our people in L.A."

He turned to Marie.

"You edited out the checks he got from California. They were from First Interstate Bank and we found they've been coming since 1975. The old man had a small pension and his social security, but these checks let him live very comfortably. The trust officer at the main bank in Los Angeles automatically drafts on an account in the name of Charley Wilson Hayes each month and sends a check to the old man. It's almost as if he was paying to use the name of his dead friend."

Jason changed his line of thinking as he turned back to Dan.

"I want five minutes at the end of tonight's news. I want you to introduce Marie and then run the footage of the airport. I want the country to see our boy take out that low-life terrorist scum. I want Marie live saying how he saved her life as well as the lives of countless others that afternoon.

"Do a picture of Hayes, the dead soldier, and then his father. Then do a still of Reed. Use the Washington Post photo of him getting the Silver Star. I think then we can use the idea of him stealing his friend's name. Close with a statement to the effect that there is more coming tomorrow. I want an exchange between the two of you on camera and I want Marie to ask our hero on the air for an interview."

Jason didn't wait for any exchange of ideas. He said what he wanted, then stood and walked back to his desk where he sat and began dialing the phone. The anchorman and the two women left the office.

As the meeting concluded, one of the tapes of the morning's first story about Charley Reed was taken from the studio on the tenth floor. The tape was placed in a white plastic garbage bag and then in a paper shopping bag from a local department store. Fifteen minutes later it was passed to a government agent who was waiting on the street corner outside the building.

While the two friends sat at the topless bar and drank beer, the nightly news featuring Marie Van Arsdale began. Bob and Charley were drinking as the footage of Alexander Hayes was being shown to the country. Marie and Dan were telling the country about this Vietnam veteran who was the LAX airport hero and had been supporting an old black man all these years.

Alexander Hayes was sitting in his gin mill as the news came on.

"God damn," the old man said. "That's him. That's Charley Reed for damn sure. I'd know him anywhere. He's back from the dead. Good for him. Good for him," the old man repeated.

John Hughes was still in his office at seven that evening. The stolen videotape had just been delivered to him and he was reviewing it with Scott Jenkinson, an agency expert on voiceprints and identification.

"Is this good enough quality?" he asked Scott.

"No problem," he answered. "This is better than what I usually have to work with. I can match this to anything. What do you have in mind?"

"I want that part, right there, duplicated."

Hughes was referring to a shot at the police station when Charley Reed was telling Marie Van Arsdale to leave him alone.

"All I want is his voice. Then I want you to get it over to U.S.I.A. tonight. I want this loaded into 'Rosie' and I want him located. I am to be notified night or day. This has the highest priority."

As Scott Jenkinson left the office, Hughes shook his head in irritation.

Jenkinson didn't fit the image of a career man in the security services of his country. He was a short man with a beer belly. He wore glasses and was balding. Worse than that, he wore a beard sticking directly out of his chin, perhaps a full inch long.

Hughes didn't understand why Jenkinson was not compelled to conform. Still, even Hughes made allowance for Jenkinson. He was a true genius.

He had come to the Company from the U.S. Information Agency. It was Scott who conceived and implemented 'Rosie,' a top-secret eavesdropping system. Rosie scanned the nation's phone system, ferreting out keywords in conversations. Once a keyword was identified, automatic recording and automatic tracing devices were activated.

Then one of several hundred inside investigators would review the conversation and recommend appropriate action. Since coming to the Company, Scott had improved 'Rosie' to identify a voiceprint, which was like a fingerprint being unique to a particular individual.

At eight-thirty that night 'Rosie' had a print of Charley Reed's voice and along with scanning for thousands of keywords, she listened to long distance phone conversations, waiting for a match of the print.

As John Hughes went to bed, he knew shortly he would have Charley Reed.

CHAPTER FIFTY

When Connie got through with work she went with Walker and Charley back to Walker's house. They stopped at the store and bought beer, wine and T-bone steaks.

"Just like the old days!" Walker said to Charley as he reached for the shoebox he always had sitting under the coffee table. Walker took out the papers and the grass and began rolling a joint.

Connie got the two men each a beer and poured herself a glass of wine before sitting on the couch next to Bob.

"Connie's a Pennsylvania girl," Bob said to his friend.

"Really?" Charley said. "What part of Pennsylvania?"

"Warren. Do you know where that is?"

"It's right up there close to the New York border, about twenty miles from Jamestown."

"That's right," she said.

"What's your last name?" Charley asked.

"Now it's Wright, but before I got married it was Knapp."

Charley nodded as Walker lit the joint and passed it to him. Charley took a hit from the cigarette and immediately sneezed. Then Charley sneezed again.

"Some things never change," Walker laughed.

"If it's good shit, he sneezes. We used to test the shit that way," Walker told Connie as he took the joint from Charley and passed it to her.

"What happened between you and Mary?" Charley asked Walker.

"You know me," Bob answered. "I'm a miserable son-of-a-bitch and I'm always in trouble, so she left. She took the kid and split."

"You had a kid?"

"A girl and she's beautiful."

"What's Mary doing?"

"She's married and has a few more kids."

Charley looked at his friend. He had always taken him exactly the way he was. That's why they were friends. They never harmed one another and they never asked anything of one another. They enjoyed each other, smoked a little grass together, and talked about their women. Because they had a friendship like that, Walker and Charley were able to take up exactly where they ended. In fact, nothing had ended and when they sat down for their meal, Charley toasted their friendship.

"To us then, to us now, we're still the same," he said as he touched his wine glass to Walker's.

"And to Connie," he continued. "The most beautiful woman I've ever seen you with."

The men drank their beer and talked. Charley was back and he was comfortable.

"What about that boy of yours!" Walker said to Charley.

Charley didn't know what Walker was talking about.

"What do you mean?" he asked.

"Tommy," Walker said. "Tom Reed, your son."

"I have a son?" Charley asked in disbelief.

"Yes," Walker reaffirmed. "You sure as hell do and you should see him. I think he looks just like you, not Joanna."

"I have a son! You know my son!" Charley exclaimed. "This is unbelievable! This is great!

"Where is he? How is he?"

"The kid is great," Bob said. "He's bigger than you. He's probably six three and weighs about two twenty-five. But he's yours. There's no doubt about that."

"What about Joanna? Have you seen her?"

"I see her in Georgetown every now and then. She never remarried. She lives up in Maryland with some woman."

"She must have been halfway decent if Tommy turned out this good."

"Shit!" Walker said. "She did all right after you died, I mean went away. You have to hand it to her. The kid is a D.C. cop."

"What?" Charley asked.

"That's right," Walker said.

"Actually, he sought me out. Tom wanted to know all about you. Joanna must have saved your things for him. He said he had your Green Beret and your jump boots and all kinds of stuff like that."

"I've got to go see him."

"Now?" Walker asked.

"No, tomorrow. Do you have his phone number?"

"Sure. I'll call him after we eat. I'll go with you if you want."

"I'd like that," Charley answered.

Charley couldn't believe it. A son, he had a son!

After dinner they smoked another joint and Walker called Tom Reed. Tom answered the phone. When Walker said who was with him, he could hear the excitement in the young man's voice. Then Charley got on the phone.

"Hello, son," Charley said.

"Dad? Can I come see you?"

"Yes. We can see each other tomorrow. I'll spend as much time with you as you can stand."

"When and where?" Tom asked.

"Just a second," Charley said to his son.

"Where should I meet him?" he asked Walker.

"Meet him at the Daulphine."

"What time is good for you?" he asked Tom.

"Noon," Tom answered.

"Well, meet me for lunch in Springfield."

"Sure," Tom agreed. "Where?"

Charley told him and gave him directions and then hung up.

"This will work out fine," Walker said. "Tomorrow is my day off and I have to go in to finish up some paperwork. You can ride down with me when I take Connie in and spend the day with Tom. We can come back here tomorrow night and have dinner."

Charley liked the idea. They drank and smoked some more before going off to bed.

As he closed the door and got out of his clothes, he remembered all the times he had stayed with Walker. He remembered sleeping on a mat by the door in an apartment Walker had in Suitland. He remembered the nights when he would wake out of a nightmare and his friend would be sitting there rolling a joint so Charley would calm down. He remembered Walker just listening and trying to understand.

Charley appreciated Bob Walker for those times. Walker had never tried to judge him and he certainly was not judging him now. Charley got between the sheets of the bed and enjoyed the safety of his friend's home. In the darkness he could hear Connie crying out in the throes of passion.

Charley smiled and fell off to sleep.

Marie Van Arsdale had just finished dinner. Jason had insisted she have dinner with him and she was very much aware of the absence of an invitation to Dan or Molly. She went by the hotel to shower and change. At nine a limousine called for her at the entrance of the hotel. They went to a quiet bar near the office and had several drinks. Jason drank martinis and she sipped a scotch and soda.

Marie was flattered by the attention of such a powerful man. From the bar they went to one of the many restaurants in Manhattan that cater to the famous and powerful. At the restaurant Jason was very attentive and interested in her.

"So tell me," he said. "Who is Marie Van Arsdale?"

"I'm just someone who right now thinks I'm in over my head and is scared to death."

Jason smiled.

"That's a very honest answer," he told her. "If you want to make it in this business, you have to wear a mask to hide how you really feel."

Marie sat quietly and silently worried she had said the wrong thing.

Jason chuckled, imaging what was going through her mind.

"You're refreshing," he said. "As bad as it could be for you, you're safe with me. It's refreshing to be with you. Tell me about you. Where did you go to school? What do you like? I want to know you."

"I'm not anything special," she answered. "I went to UCLA and received my degree in journalism. I went to work for KTLA-TV the month I graduated. I did the mail, wrote copy, worked in wardrobe and makeup. I did whatever they needed until one of the other girls got sick. Actually, she overdosed on cocaine and I had to fill in for her. From then on I was doing stories. I always tried hard and I think I did a good job."

"You did," he assured her. "Your station manager sent me a portfolio of you. I was very impressed."

"Thanks," Marie said, feeling very much out of her league in Jason's presence.

"You don't have to thank me," he told her. "If the story wasn't any good, you wouldn't have been called here. If you didn't do a good job with Dan tonight, you wouldn't be here now. I decided to give you a shot."

"And?" she asked.

"I told you," he said. "You made it. If you hadn't, you would be on a jet back to KTLA-TV right now."

Marie was surprised at the man's frankness. She understood she was on a fast track but she didn't realize exactly how fast it really was. Jason's comment brought the situation into clear reality. Marie understood she had one shot and one shot alone. She had passed that test.

Marie wondered what the next test would be and when it would come. She was experienced enough to understand one test was not going to end it. This was her chance and she made up her mind no matter what it took, she would pass.

"Tell me more about yourself," Jason said. "I want to know about you."

"I'm not married," she said. "I never have been. I lived with an older man when I graduated, but it ended because I worked all the time and wasn't interested enough in him. He was divorced and wanted someone who was there for him all the time. As much as I liked him, I wasn't ready to do that for anyone. I have my career and right now it comes first."

"You're smart, Marie," he said as he inspected a bottle of champagne the waiter delivered to the table.

"Right now your career is all that matters. You have plenty of time for a commitment later. While young women your age are busy making families, you're carving out a place for yourself in a very harsh and selective industry. Right now, as we sit here and talk, you are being evaluated and scrutinized. Every single mark on your face, the tone of your voice, and the ease you have in front of the camera is being assessed. I've seen women sent down only because they were too perfect. They were so perfect they had no personality. This is a very funny business."

Marie listened and said nothing. While she considered herself experienced with men, she had never been so subtly propositioned before.

She knew what sexual harassment was, but Jason was an expert and she couldn't exactly pinpoint his intentions. While she believed she knew, she still was not sure. She wasn't sure until the limousine took them back to her hotel and he stepped out on the curb with her.

"Thank you very much," she said.

"Think nothing of it," he said as he took her hand and walked her past the doorman into the lobby.

"I want to see that you have the room I ordered for you."

Now Marie was sure what was expected of her and she made no move to resist.

They took the elevator to her floor and Jason took the room key from her and opened the door. She walked into the dark room and Jason closed the door behind them. The curtains were open and the lights from the buildings around them illuminated the room.

Marie walked to the foot of the king-sized bed and removed her coat. Without hesitating, she took off her sweater. Jason had already removed his suit coat, tie and shirt. Marie waited for him to touch her, but he didn't.

He slipped out of his shoes and then removed his pants. She watched as he took off his shorts and was naked except for his calf-length socks that he left on. He went to the side of the bed and pulled back the covers.

Marie waited and when he was in the bed, she continued undressing. She unzipped her skirt and stepped out of the half-slip. Then she removed her bra, still standing at the foot of the bed in her high heels, panties, and pantyhose.

Marie could see his eyes in the darkened room. She could feel him staring at her body as she finished undressing and joined him in the bed. She realized neither one of them had spoken since they entered the elevator. She felt nervous as she cuddled next to him. He was half-sitting up in the bed.

"That's fine," he said to her in a low gravelly voice.

The voice startled her. She had never heard that voice before.

"Touch me," the voice said.

Marie looked at his face to be sure it was really Jason talking.

"Touch me gently and make me hard."

Every man Marie had been with had already been hard. She had never known a man who had watched her undress and still was not excited. Still, she did as she was told and touched him. As her hand moved to him, she had a second shock.

He was enormous. Her hand ran across his length and attempted to close around him, but was unable.

"Use your other hand, too," the voice said.

Placing her second hand on him she wondered how she could ever accommodate this. She touched him and he became semi-erect, but he never truly reached a state of complete erection.

"That's nice," the voice said. "Now kiss it."

Marie did as she was told. She moved her body around so her head was in the proper position. Then as she started, he turned on the bedside light so he could watch her.

"That's really nice," the voice said.

She didn't look at his face. She was afraid she might find someone else, perhaps some evil being into which Jason had been transformed.

"Keep doing that, but turn your body around so I can see you," he said.

She did as he asked.

"Open your legs," he told her.

Again, she did as he asked.

"Now touch yourself."

Marie touched herself. She felt like she was an exhibit on display for his pleasure.

"Do it faster," he said to her as he pulled his huge member away from her face. "Use both of your hands! Open yourself so I can see you!"

"Faster!" he demanded. "Faster!"

She felt herself responding to her hands and watched as he continued stroking himself.

"That's great!" he said. "I'm going to be there soon. Don't stop!"

He brought his body close to hers and rose to his knees. The entire time he was still stroking himself.

"Now!" he screamed and began to climax and directed himself so it flowed onto her body.

"Oh!" he sighed with pleasure as Marie took her hands away to wipe her thighs.

"Don't!" he commanded her as his hand held hers fast.

"I want it! Don't waste it!"

Then his mouth finally touched her only to lick his juices from her body.

Marie watched in disbelief. He finished and immediately began to get out of bed. He said nothing the entire time he dressed and never even looked at her.

She had the feeling she might not have even been in the room. Then when he finished dressing, he left. Marie lay on the bed, completely stunned at what had happened. Then she slept.

At seven a.m. the hotel woke Marie Van Arsdale. She felt disoriented and didn't know where she was. She rewound her memory to recall what had happened only hours before the wake-up call. As she showered and dressed, she wondered how she would ever be able to face Jason. She reminded herself she was a professional. Whatever happened she could handle it.

Molly called her at seven thirty.

"I'll pick you up at eight-thirty in front of the hotel. I'll be in the limousine Jason took you to dinner in last night."

At precisely eight-thirty the limo arrived and Marie walked out of the hotel. She wondered if Jason would be in the car, but Molly was alone.

"How do you like your coffee?" Molly asked as the driver closed the door behind Marie.

"With cream," Marie answered.

Molly took the coffee pot from the holder and poured her a cup.

"Did you enjoy dinner?" she asked Marie.

"Yes," Marie answered.

"I've spoken with Dan this morning," Molly said. "He reviewed the tape of last night's broadcast. We're to go shopping today. He wants you in a navy blue suit and a white blouse tonight. He wants you to have five minutes ready that will key in on Charley Reed just before the automobile accident and how Emporia, Virginia blew it.

"He wants another personal appeal to Charley Reed to come in and meet with you. He said to tell you to be prepared to run with this yourself. We had tremendous response last night and he's really excited about where we can go with this story.

"Also, Jason wondered how many other Charley Reeds are out there and said that perhaps you might slant your appeal to them, too."

Marie was stung by Jason's suggestion. She was sure he would never speak to her again after what had happened between them.

"Jason is very impressed by you," Molly told her.

"That really excites me. You're my big break. This story is yours and you're mine. I want you to know that I'm here to see that you're a success. If you're a success, I'm a success. If there is ever anything I do that you don't like, please tell me. I'll change. I need this job and I'll do whatever it takes to support you. You're on the inside track with Jason and that hasn't happened in a long, long time. I'm with you all the way!"

They toasted their alliance with their coffee cups. Moments later they were delivered to the front entrance of the network headquarters.

"Jason's given you an office next to Dan's," Molly said as they walked through the lobby. "I'm your assistant and I have the office leading into yours. I know the office he's given you. You'll love it!"

Molly opened the door into Marie's office.

"This is your office," she said taking Marie into a large room with windows looking out onto the city. There was a huge desk, sitting area, and computer workstation.

Marie was speechless. The office was much, much more than she expected. She walked to the desk where a dozen white roses were sitting in a vase. Marie took the card from the flowers and read it.

"Thank you," it began. "Prosper and grow with us. You're important to me. I'm here. Jason."

CHAPTER FIFTY-ONE

'Rosie' was designed by a genius. The design was perfect, but no matter how perfect or well conceived, it depended on the main power supply and the auxiliary when the primary power was out. Therefore, USIA tested the auxiliary power system every Tuesday at eleven a.m. On this particular Tuesday the transfer switch malfunctioned and 'Rosie' went down.

Charley Reed was still at Bob Walker's house. At exactly eleven o'clock he called his lawyer in Los Angeles. They didn't talk long. Charley told him to execute the resignation letter he had left on file and leave Al in charge of the businesses.

"Keep them out of the books and the checking accounts, Abe," Charley instructed his lawyer.

They had planned for this day. Abe was the only person who knew Charley's secret. He was the one who arranged to send old Mr. Hayes the monthly checks.

They developed an escape where Charley resigned as president and a series of holding companies took over running the businesses. Abe and Al knew Charley owned the last holding company in line and was still calling all the shots.

Each holding company had a supply of cash available for Charley to use as he needed. It was something he hoped he would never have to use, but it was there just the same. Now he was glad they had planned ahead.

As he finished his last sentence, 'Rosie' came back up and immediately identified his voice. The program designed by Scott Jenkinson locked onto the phone number at Bob Walker's house. It isolated the other party in Los Angeles, but did not get an exact location.

Charley hung up and went out to his car and drove away. He went to Springfield and parked across the street from the Daulphine Steakhouse. It was just a few minutes past noon when he walked in and took a table just to the right of the stage. A redheaded girl named Lisa was dancing. Charley was nervous and excited at the same time. Charley ordered a beer and asked for two menus in anticipation of his son's arrival.

Charley finished his second beer when his son Tom walked into the bar. They recognized one another immediately and Tom walked to the table as his father rose to his feet.

"Tom," he said as he extended his hand to his son.

Tom took his father's hand and shook it. "Dad," he said.

Charley held his son's hand and looked into his eyes. Tears filled Charley Reed's eyes and he pulled his son to him, hugging the larger young man.

"Son," he said. "I hardly know what to say. You look like your mother."

"Yes, some people say so," he answered. " But she says I have your temperament."

"Good," Charley said. "That's why you're not a wimp like your uncles."

Tom laughed as he returned his father's embrace. They sat down together and Charley ordered them beers. At that moment Walker came in and joined them. The three of them ate, drank and talked all afternoon.

Charley asked his son if he had any questions.

"I know what you've been doing," Tom said. "That reporter has let the whole country know what you've been doing."

"What did your mother have to say when I came back from the dead?"

"She doesn't say much. She told me you were my father when all the business at the LA airport started. The reporter came to see her and then me. She told me about the reporter, but never said much about you. She never has. Grandfather told me about you before he died. Mother gave me a picture of you and some of your stories and letters. She told me you were in Vietnam, but not a lot more than that."

"What's she doing now?" Charley asked.

"Working for some doctors. She runs their office."

"She's never remarried?" Charley asked his son.

"No, of course not," Tom answered. "You know about Mother."

Charley looked at his son and shook his head.

"Mother lives with another woman," Tom said. "She always has. That's why my grandparents raised me. She's a lesbian."

Charley looked at his son in disbelief.

"Really?" he asked.

"Yes."

"My parents raised you?"

"Yes," Tom said.

"That explains why you're a cop," Charley laughed.

"Of course," he said.

"And your mother is a lesbian?"

"Yes," he said repeating himself.

"I never knew that," he said and shook his head in puzzlement.

Walker stood up from the table.

"I told you she was strange," he said to Charley. "I could never put my finger on it, but I knew she was strange."

Walker went to sit at one of the stools around the stage, leaving Charley and Tom alone at the table.

"I never knew it," Charley repeated to his son.

"Well, she is," Tom assured him.

Tom had a thousand questions. He wanted them all answered at once. They had another beer and then another. They kept talking and ignored the girls on the stage taking off their clothes. The afternoon slipped away.

Tom told Charley about going to college and playing football at the University of Maryland.

"You went to college and you're a cop?"

"Sure," Tom said. "Why not?"

"I don't know," he answered. "Why not?"

They both laughed. It was at that point Tom Reed knocked his beer over on the table and managed to spill his father's over as he grabbed for his.

"Oh, shit," he said, beginning to feel the effects of the alcohol. "I'm a real jerk today!"

"You're fine, Tom," Charley said. "It isn't every day a father and son find one another."

"You're right," Tom agreed. "You are one hundred percent right."

"Your father is always right," Charley joked with his son.

"Of course!" Tom agreed, sticking his hand in the air to be slapped.

"You're the best dad I ever had," he added.

"The best dad, but not the best grandfather. Grandfather Donald was a good man!"

Charley looked over at Walker who was still sitting at the stage.

They smiled at each other.

There was a bond between the two of them. It extended beyond normal life experiences. That was why they were still friends after all this time. It was a bond of love only one man can feel for another.

Tom wasn't just Charley's son at that moment. He was Bob's, too. Charley wanted to cry out with sheer happiness. He wanted to tell his friend he loved him. But Charley was a man and knew he couldn't. He looked his friend in the eye from across the room and what remained unspoken was understood. Charley wiped the tears from his eyes.

By this time John Hughes had isolated the addresses of the phones Charley Reed had used. Ken O'Brien was in his office and they were planning their action.

"The first address is in Falls Church. It's Bob Walker's home. He'll be staying with Mr. Walker."

"And the second one?" O'Brien asked.

"It's a pay phone in a shopping center in Springfield. He called San Francisco and talked to his lawyer. Walker is the key. Take him at Walker's."

"Tonight?" O'Brien asked.

"Can we afford to wait?" Hughes asked back. "That broad is running stories about him every day. We need to end this now. He needs to go away. And if he moves, who knows when we'll get a chance like this again.

"Walker has always been a small-time drug user and dealer. Make it look like a drug deal gone bad. Kill everyone who's there. Take Sallak with you. A job like this is right up his alley. Use Weird Harold as a backup, just in case."

The network news came on at six-thirty Eastern Time. During the day the decision was made to lead with the Charley Reed story. Newspapers across the country picked up the story and Jason realized what a hot item they alone were holding.

Marie ran the story on her own. She used the segments with Tom Reed, Joanna Reed and Bob Walker.

John Hughes did not bother to watch the news. He went home secure that the Charley Reed problem was solved.

Tom Reed was too drunk to drive so Charley loaded his son in the car and drove him to Walker's. Connie rode with Bob and they picked up lobster tails and filets for dinner.

Charley had the salad made and the table set by the time Connie
and Bob got there. Tom was watching television. While the four of
them got dinner ready, Ken O'Brien was preparing his men.

From the agency armory they checked out three of the new MAP-
21s. This was the military assault pistol, a handheld machine pistol
that fired nine-millimeter ammunition and was considered by the
Pentagon to be the most deadly close-in weapon in existence. It was
authorized only to specialized units of the military and government
agencies such as the Secret Service, FBI and the CIA.

Ken O'Brien worked with Reid Sallak and Weird Harold before.
Harold Johnson looked like the all-American guy, but was a world-class
sneak. He was an expert in assassinations and generally liked shooting
people in the back.

Sallak was called Reid the Rat in agency circles. He was a short,
grotesque man who always aspired for much greater things within the
agency. But there was always something slimy about him and his superiors really had no use for someone like Reid. He was a necessary tool
and they tolerated him. Reid Sallak was type they used on missions
where the agent was expendable.

"We'll wait until they go to bed," O'Brien said to Sallak and
Johnson.

"Reid, you and I will go in through the kitchen door. There's no
deadbolt on it and it's a straight shot into the living room, and then into
the bedrooms."

Ken O'Brien had gone to Walker's house earlier, posing as a meter
reader. He gained entrance through the kitchen door and found the
room where Charley Reed was staying. He pointed to a drawing of the
house.

"Reed is in this bedroom and Walker will be here. Walker will
probably have a woman with him. Reed could possibly have one, too.
There are to be no survivors."

After dinner Tom Reed was ready to pass out. Charley helped his
son into his bedroom and put him to bed. Charley came back out into
the living room where Connie and Bob were smoking a joint. Charley
poured himself another glass of wine and sat on the loveseat across
from them.

Outside Harold Johnson drove the government Ford Crown
Victoria past the house and parked two doors down the street. From
their position they could watch the living room of Walker's house as
they waited for them to go to bed.

"Does he have a dog?" Sallak asked.

"No," O'Brien answered.

"Damn," Sallak said. "I hate dogs. I don't mind killing them!"

O'Brien ignored Sallak.

"I want you to cover the outside," he said to Johnson. "Take care of any neighbors or the police if they stumble into the action. I want no witnesses, no survivors."

"You've got it," Harold Johnson assured him.

O'Brien looked at Sallak.

"There will be three people in there, two men and a woman. Before we leave I want a body count."

"You've got it," Sallak said.

They sat in the car and watched the lights in the house.

It was eleven-thirty when Connie and Walker decided to go to bed. Charley had fallen asleep on the loveseat and was turned on his side. Connie covered him with a blanket before she turned off the lights.

"There they go," Sallak said.

"Give them a few minutes to get settled in," O'Brien said.

Connie and Bob went to bed and began making love. Connie was exceptionally loud. Charley woke up and realized where he was. As he did, the three men were outside the house.

Charley allowed his eyes to adjust to the dark before getting up and moving to the couch where he could stretch out. He was thinking about taking off his clothes when he thought he heard a noise out back. He lay perfectly still as he listened. Then he heard the kitchen door open.

Bob and Connie were in the throes of making love and never heard the two men open the door and move through the kitchen.

Charley Reed was perfectly still. His head was turned and he could make out the forms of the two men as they crept toward the living room. He heard them whisper to one another, but couldn't distinguish what they said. He was able to determine they were both armed. Charley did not move.

Outside Harold Johnson hid between a pine tree and the house. No one could see him from the street, but he was able to watch the front of the house, the driveway, and the street from both directions. He was in the perfect position to cover anyone who might decide to take a look and see what was going on.

The two agents entered the living room and turned left toward the bedrooms. They didn't see Charley Reed stretched out on the couch. They didn't see him as he rose up behind them. They were leaving the living room and entering the hallway when like a cat, he sprang through the air and landed on their backs.

Immediately, he shouted for his friend.

"Walker! Walker!" he screamed. "There are men in here. Get your gun!"

The impact of his attack knocked Ken O'Brien down the hall, past the bedrooms occupied by Walker and Connie and his son. Reid Sallak fell to the ground beneath Charley's weight and turned to defend himself.

Charley screamed out as he attacked the man underneath him. They wrestled with the weapon and rounds discharged into the ceiling before Charley tore it from Sallak's hands.

Ken O'Brien had dropped his weapon and felt around in the darkness for it. He had a .45 automatic as a backup, but he continued to search for the MAP-21.

Charley Reed jammed his right index finger into Reid Sallak's eye. Sallak shrieked out in agony as Charley Reed pushed through the eye socket. He grabbed Sallak's head with his left hand and in a smooth and practiced motion snapped his neck. At the same time, Ken O'Brien grabbed his weapon and leveled it on the forms wrestling in the hallway.

Bob Walker heard Charley Reed scream out. Then he heard the explosion of automatic weapon fire, followed by the sound of a man crying out in pain.

Ever since he first turned state's evidence against Hudson and his buddies who were dealing cocaine in a deal to keep himself from going to prison, Bob slept with a loaded shotgun under his bed. He rolled off the bed and pulled the shotgun to him.

Ken O'Brien fired at the men on the floor, but Charley Reed rolled out of the line of fire. O'Brien's burst hit the motionless form of Sallak.

Walker knew Charley was unarmed and came out of the bedroom and fired in one motion. The impact of the twelve-gauge hit O'Brien's left side and tore off his arm. He fired the second barrel and hit O'Brien in the gut, throwing him across the room and into the hall.

Connie ran naked from the bedroom, past Bob and into the living room. Hearing the shotgun blasts, Harold Johnson kicked in the front door and shot Connie as she ran directly at him. Her body was thrown into the television set as if she were a rag doll.

Walker was reloading as Johnson killed Connie. He stepped into the living room and fired blindly. Johnson fired back.

Charley rose to his feet and stepped over Sallak's dead body. He could see O'Brien motionless against the opposite wall. He turned the corner into the living room.

Walker's second volley was deadly. Harold Johnson had been blown through the front picture window and was dead on the front lawn. But Johnson had been equally efficient. Bob Walker was on the floor, his eyes staring blankly at the ceiling. He was dead.

Charley turned and ran to check on his son. Tom was still passed out and had not stirred. He had not heard a single shot. Knowing that his son was safe, Charley returned to his fallen friend.

"Bob!" he said. "Bob!"

There was no answer. Charley knelt and cradled his friend's head in his arms.

"Bob!" he cried.

"Don't die," he said, beginning to cry. "Don't die."

It was too late. Bob Walker was dead.

"Don't die," Charley repeated. "I love you. You can't die! Not you! Please, don't die. You can't!"

Walker's body remained motionless. His eyes were staring into infinity and Charley realized there was no use. He pulled his friend to him and kissed him goodbye. Then he laid him gently back on the floor and went for his son.

"Tom!" he said excitedly as he shook the large young man. "Tom! Wake up! We've got to get out of here right now!"

Tom Reed didn't move and already Charley could hear sirens in the distance.

"God damn it!" Charley screamed, but his son only snored.

The sirens were getting closer and Charley stood and left the room. He walked through the living room and outside to the driveway. Walker's car blocked in his car.

He looked down the street and saw the lights of the police cars coming up the street. Charley got in and started his car. Unable to back out of the driveway, he drove forward under the carport into the back yard. He maneuvered through the trees into the yard of the house behind Walker's and then down the side to the next street where he finally turned on the lights and sped away.

Charley Reed turned north on the beltway and finally began to breathe normally. He checked the rear view mirror constantly. It was clear. He turned on the radio and drove north toward Maryland

His friend was dead and he was forced to leave his son behind. Once more Charley Reed had successfully evaded and survived.

The adrenalin pumped through his veins, keeping him tense and alert. It did not occur to him until he was near Damascus, Maryland what had just happened.

"Who were they?" he asked himself.

He had no answer.

At the next exit, he pulled off and sat alone in the car. He was exhausted, but felt too worn out to sleep. He had too many unanswered questions.

Sleep was a long time coming.

CHAPTER FIFTY-TWO

WASHINGTON, D.C.
SEPTEMBER 24, 2001
4:22 A.M.

CNN was the first news network to realize that the Bob Walker who had been killed in the suburban Virginia gunfight was the same Bob Walker who Marie Van Arsdale highlighted the evening before on her newscast. They also realized that the Tom Reed the police had in custody was the same Tom Reed who was Charley Reed's son.

The other networks slept quietly as CNN comprehended what was being written off as a drug deal gone bad was all tied to the LAX assassination and its hero, Charley Reed. As the sun rose in Charley Reed's eyes, they were already running a story. It was a story that asked questions the authorities were declining to answer.

As CNN broke the story Marie Van Arsdale's phone began to ring.

"Hello?" she said coming out of a sound sleep.

"You need to get to Washington. All hell has broken loose down there and your boy, Charley Reed, is in it up to his eyeballs."

Marty Sporror had just fallen asleep for the third time since midnight. The baby began to cry. He was cutting teeth and it was his night to get up with him. Karen moved only when the phone rang for the fifth time.

"Hello," Marty answered.

"Inspector Sporror," the voice on the other end of the phone said. "This is Agent Paul. We have a situation developing that is either a government hit or a drug deal in which stolen government automatic weapons were used."

Marty Sporror made two phone calls and realized the MAP-21s were issued by the CIA armory within the past twenty-four hours. It didn't take him long to realize there were three dead government agents and no one had any idea what they were doing when they were killed.

He also took into consideration the two dead civilians in their own home, both naked as if they had been invaded and aroused from their bed. A third civilian was taken out of a sound sleep and claimed he knew nothing. A fourth civilian had escaped and was at large. The situation was out of control and unmanageable.

Joanna Reed was asleep when the phone woke her.

"Mom," her son said.

"Yes?" she answered.

"It's Tom. I'm in jail and I need help."

"What happened?" she demanded.

"I don't know," he said. "I was with Charley Reed and when I went to sleep everything was fine. When I woke up, everyone was dead. Dad was gone and the police had me handcuffed."

"You were with your father, Charley Reed?"

"Yes," he answered.

"Where are you?" she asked impatiently.

"Falls Church Police Station," he answered.

"I'll be right there," she said and hung up the phone.

The police were unable to identify the three dead men. They had no way of knowing they were government agents. They found the car they had driven and identified it as a vehicle registered to the government motor pool.

The big find was the weapons. If they were stolen, finding them was a feather in their cap. If they weren't, then it meant something else. The police were not sure how to deal with that possibility.

John Hughes woke when the phone began to ring.

"Yes," he answered and immediately recognized his supervisor's voice.

"What happened?" he asked.

"What went wrong?" Ed Manion asked him.

John did not know what he was talking about.

"Your men are all dead," Manion said. "The police have traced their car to the government motor pool and are asking questions about the weapons."

Charley Reed woke as the sun rose. At first he didn't know where he was, but soon the reality of the night before hit him. His friend was dead and he was not sure why.

He wondered what Walker might have been doing to have killers come in the middle of the night. Charley thought of the killers he had known and their methods.

If it were drug related, they just would have kicked in the doors and started shooting. If Walker owed them money, they never would have tried to take him at home. They could have had him any time he walked in or out of the Daulphine Steakhouse.

No, Charley thought. This had to be something else. It was too professional to be anything involving the old days. Then Charley remembered the automatic weapons.

They were not the run of the mill automatic weapons. They were special and even though he had only glimpsed them, he knew the average drug punk didn't have access to that kind of firepower. Charley wondered if it was the government. He also wondered what Walker could have done to warrant a government sanction.

Charley Reed took a chance and drove to a pay phone in a shopping area. It was seven-thirty where he was, four-thirty at Al Poole's house. Charley had to talk to someone and Al was the man. He dialed through using his credit card. After the sixth ring, Al answered.

"It's me," Charley said avoiding the use of names.

"Where are you?" Al asked.

"Just some place," Charley answered.

"Are you okay, man?"

"No," he answered. "It's gotten pretty hot. Someone hit my buddy and his girl last night. They nearly got me in the process."

"No shit?"

"No," Charley said. "For real."

"Christ," Al said. "It's dangerous out there. Get your lily white ass back here."

"You know I can't," Charley said.

"What are you going to do?" Al asked.

"I'm going to lay low," he said. "I'm going to get away from here."

"Where will you go?" he asked.

"I'm not sure, Al. I wanted to call and let you know what was happening just in case anyone else comes looking. I'll call you this afternoon as planned."

Rosie immediately identified Charley Reed's voice and keyed in on his location as well as Al Poole's. John Hughes was already in his office and USIA opened a secure link to the Mayfair Corporation so it could transmit the conversation and pull all material in its memory on Al Poole.

As Hughes listened to the conversation, he glanced over the information on Poole and could hardly believe what he saw.

"Holy shit!" he exclaimed out loud. "What next!"

There he was, larger than life, one of the airmen in Operation Eagle Thrust. He was a loadmaster for the Air Force and somehow they missed him.

He picked up the phone and called his operative in Los Angeles.

"I have a job for you," he said to the sleepy voice on the other end of the phone. "This is highest priority."

He gave the operative Al Poole's name and address.

"Elimination with extreme prejudice," he said. "This is to be completed no later than ten a.m. today and he is at this address now."

Hughes hung up the phone and opened his desk drawer. He took out a nine millimeter automatic and inserted the silencer and a full clip. He listened to the tape again.

"You're out there," he said. "I'm going to get you even if I have to do this myself."

He picked up his phone and called Lou Locante.

"Come to my office," he said. "I need you."

Ed Manion sat in his office at the McLean headquarters. He was on the phone with the Assistant Director. It was a one-way conversation with the other man doing all the talking and Ed Manion listening and agreeing.

"You're right," Manion said. "I realize that, but I think if we stop it here, it can't go any farther."

Manion listened again.

"No. Once he's out of the picture it has to stop. He's been operating on his own," he said.

He paused to listen, tapping his pipe in an ashtray.

"I realize that, but no government agency can get any higher than Hughes once he's out of the picture."

Manion listened again and then ended the conversation.

"Fine," he said. "It will be done this morning."

He hung up the phone and took time to fill his pipe. He carefully packed the tobacco before striking a match and lighting it. He looked out the window at the wooded grounds. At times like this, it was the only thing he enjoyed about his job.

Ed hated the Assistant Director of the agency. In his estimation Tom McMann was a tin god with a complex over being short. Ed often doubted the man's competence and felt many of the agency's problems were the fault of McMann and seven or eight others.

In the past the agency seldom sanctioned its own people. Now with leaks and blunders, it was happening with dangerous regularity and Manion didn't like it.

Manion unlocked his bottom desk drawer. He withdrew a metal box and unlocked it. Inside was another case holding a small metal aerosol can. He placed it in his inside jacket pocket and rose from his desk.

Standing, he picked up the phone and ordered an agent with a car to meet him at the side entrance immediately. Then he called Hughes and asked that he meet him at Property Ten in thirty minutes.

"Fine," John said. "Will this take long? I have some business to attend to."

"No," Manion said. "I just need a few minutes for a face to face."

Hughes agreed to meet and turned to Locante.

"Find Property Ten," he said.

Immediately Locante found the location was the parking lot of an Arlington restaurant.

As he closed his book of properties and put it away, Ed Manion went upstairs to Tom McMann's office. It was just after nine a.m. and the secretary was down the hall. No one saw him enter and no one saw him leave. Then he took the side stairs down to where a new agent was waiting with a car.

Moments later McMann's secretary found him slumped over his desk, dead from an apparent heart attack.

The young agent drove Manion to the location. He got out of the car as they arrived. Manion walked over to Hughes and Locante and got into the back seat of Lou's car.

"What's up," Locante asked his boss.

He turned to face him and Hughes turned around also. Immediately, Hughes saw what was happening.

Ed Manion withdrew the aerosol can from his pocket and sprayed it in Locante's face. Lou's head fell against the window of his car. Then he turned it on Hughes.

Hughes reacted too fast for Manion. He opened the door and rolled out onto the pavement. He continued to roll until he could get to his feet behind the safety of another car. He drew his pistol.

Ed Manion, knowing he missed Hughes, closed the car door behind him and quickly returned to the car where the young agent was waiting. He got in from the passenger side with his pistol drawn and shot the man behind the wheel. Calmly, he pushed his body out into the parking lot and drove himself back to the office.

John Hughes watched as the car drove away. He didn't bother to look back. He walked down the street and found a cab.

Al Poole stepped from the shower and took a heavy blue towel from the wall rack and began to dry himself. When he was finished, he wrapped the towel around his mid-section and walked into the bedroom. He glanced at his clock. It was six thirty-two. He slipped his pants on and walked to the kitchen.

"Who the hell are you?" Poole asked the strange man sitting in his kitchen.

The stranger pulled a nine-millimeter pistol and fired at Al Poole, hitting him five times before standing and leaving the house.

Al Poole's wife, Stephanie, heard the crash as his body fell backwards into the dining room. He grabbed for the table, pulling the tablecloth and centerpiece to the floor. She called his name and heard the back door close. She ran to the dining room to find her husband unconscious and bleeding on the floor.

At six forty-nine the ambulance arrived at the Poole residence. Al, who had been shot five times at close range by a high velocity pistol, was still partially conscious. He had gone in and out several times. He knew he was losing a lot of blood and when he was conscious, told Stephanie what to do. She helped save her husband's life in those first moments.

"Baby," he said to his wife. "Tell Charley that it was him they were after last night, no one else, just him. Tell him I know why."

"What?" Stephanie asked her husband, believing he must be delirious.

He didn't answer her. He lost consciousness and then came back.

"Eagle Thrust," he said to Stephanie. "I should have known all the time. Tell him Eagle Thrust. He'll understand. Make sure he knows."

"Don't die!" Stephanie cried. "Hold on!"

"I won't," he said, falling in and out of consciousness. "Make sure Charley knows. He'll call. Stay here and tell him."

Al grabbed her arm with incredible force.

"Promise me!" he demanded of his wife. "You have to promise me!"

"I promise," she said and then he passed out and lapsed into a coma.

The medics loaded Al Poole into the ambulance and transported him to the hospital.

Stephanie did as she promised her husband. She didn't stay home, but she did leave Charley a message. On the telephone answering machine, she changed the message.

"I'm sorry we're not here to answer your call," it said. "There is an emergency. If it's you, Charley, Al said to tell you Eagle Thrust. Otherwise, I will be at the hospital. Leave a message if you need us."

As she finished her message she broke down and began to cry.

Charley Reed drove back into the city. He parked his truck near the Lincoln Memorial. The end of September in Washington, D.C. was a nice time of year. He appreciated the warmth of the morning sun as it flooded in through the window. He looked around. The street was empty as he got out of the car. That was all right with him. He didn't want anyone around when he did what he felt he had to do. As he started to walk across the street toward The Wall, the time was nine forty a.m.

As Stephanie was finishing her message on the answering machine, Charley Reed was at the Vietnam Wall and had placed his hand on the name of the old sarge, John P. Tankersly, Jr.

"I miss you," he cried, tears running down his face.

He walked a few more steps and found Charles Wilson Hayes.

"I tried," he said to the marble wall. "I tried to give you your life.

"God damn it! I would have married a black woman if I could have found one that would have had me," he laughed.

He knew Charley Hayes would have laughed, too. Charley Hayes was like that. He was a stand up guy and would have known Charley was sincere.

"I love you," he said to the name on the wall.

"I'm sorry I killed you," he cried.

"I'm so, so sorry. I wish it had been me instead of you. If I could do it over, I would have let you fire first. I wish I would have died instead of you."

Charley stood there touching The Wall and crying when a hand gently rested on his shoulder.

"Are you okay, brother?" a man's voice asked.

Charley turned to find a bearded man with glasses, wearing an Army fatigue jacket, looking into his face. Charley was still crying and as he looked back into the man's face, he broke down and deeply wept. For the first time since he was a little boy, he accepted the arms of another man.

"No," Charley choked.

"Help me. Please help me!" he cried, collapsing into the arms of the man who appeared out of nowhere.

"I'm here," the man said. "It's okay. I'm right here."

Charley realized he was embracing a man he didn't know and pulled back.

"Who are you?" he asked.

"I'm Gary Martyn," the man answered. "I'm a volunteer who works here. I'm here for people like you who just need someone."

Charley wanted to pull back. He wanted to run and hide once more. He looked up the Mall to the Washington Monument and then into the gray-blue eyes of the thin bald man.

He didn't run. Instead, he stood firm for the first time since he had been a soldier.

"Thank you," he said. "I'm glad you're here."

"Come on over," Gary said. "I have some coffee. Have a cup with me."

Charley went with the man and shared his coffee.

"I was a Marine," Gary said. "I was over in the beginning and served down in the Mekong Delta region. My friends' names are over there on The Wall. I was just like you when I first came here. Another fellow helped me. His name was Roger Knigge. He helped me a lot."

"We never had a chance to say goodbye to them," Charley said.

"You're right," Gary agreed.

"They were there and then they were dead. I owed one guy money. I never got a chance to pay him back. I gave it to a bum on the street," Gary said with a laugh. "He probably drank himself to death!"

Charley laughed, too.

"Hey, you're Charley Reed," Gary said.

Charley nodded.

"I've been following the story about you. I heard what happened last night. Are you okay?"

"Yes," Charley answered. "They killed my friend."

"I heard," Gary said. "Your son's okay."

"He slept through the whole thing. He was so drunk he never even moved. I tried to get him up and take him with me, but there was no way," said Charley.

"His mother was on television this morning and she was hell with the police. She wanted him out and right then and there," Gary said.

Charley stayed with Gary for a few more minutes. They talked and they talked. Charley told him how he dropped out and what he had been doing since 1973.

"Go get your life back," Gary said. "You tried giving your friend his life. Nice thought, but that isn't what he would have wanted. Get your own life back, man."

Charley thanked him and left.

Charley wondered if the police were looking for him. If they were holding Tom, he was sure they wanted to talk to him also. But then, they didn't know who he was. He could still travel with some immunity. He drove out to Dulles so he could catch a flight to New York.

He put on a pair of dark glasses and calmly walked across the concourse to the ticket counter. It was ten thirty-five and the shuttle from New York had just unloaded its passengers and they were coming out of the secure area. As Charley stood reading the monitor for departure information, Marie Van Arsdale walked up to him.

She was alone. She didn't have a cameraman with her and wasn't as intimidating as she had seemed in the past. Charley recognized her and bit his bottom lip as she confronted him.

"Are you leaving?" she asked.

"Yes," he answered, no longer afraid of her or what she could do to him.

He felt an inner strength he had not felt in years. He was always smart and he had always been quick. Since he became Charley Hayes, the fire that used to rage within him had gone out. It had to, because he knew he couldn't draw attention to himself.

Now that he was back, so was the fire and with it came his strength.

It was the strength that allowed him to carry his wounded comrade to the airfield for evacuation. It was that same strength which allowed him to evade the enemy and avoid being captured. It was in him again and he felt powerful.

"The police are looking for you," she said so quietly her voice was barely audible.

"There's one just down the ramp. Why don't you go on down and point me out? You've exposed me to the whole blasted country. What's one cop?"

"I don't want to do that," she answered. "I just want to talk to you."

"So talk," Charley said. "I'm trying to get to New York. I don't know what I'm doing beyond that. If you don't turn me in to the cops, I'll be glad to drop you off where you're going. Flying isn't the best idea judging from what I see at this place. You can ask me whatever you want. If I feel like answering, I will. If I don't, I won't."

"That's fair," Marie said.

As she extended her hand to him, she was paged.

"Are you going to run away if I answer the call?"

"No," he answered. "I'll wait."

Marie smiled at Charley Reed and left to find the nearest red courtesy phone. When she returned Marie seemed excited.

"I need to speak with you," Marie said to Charley with a sense of urgency in her voice.

"What about," Charley asked.

"Al Poole's been shot. He's still alive, but it is very serious."

"My God, how?" Charley asked.

"No one knows," she answered. "It was early this morning, California time. He'd just gotten out of the shower and gone into the kitchen. His wife didn't hear any gunshots."

"Oh, God!" he exclaimed. "Stay here, Marie. I have to call Stephanie."

Charley didn't wait for an answer. He left her standing there and crossed the lobby to the phones.

He called Al Poole's house for the second time that morning. The phone rang three times and as it started the fourth ring, Stephanie's message began.

He very nearly hung up when the recorded message came on, but he caught himself. Then he heard the message Stephanie left just for him.

Without saying a word, he hung up. He looked across the lobby at the woman and thought about leaving her there. He thought about the message and suddenly understood everything.

No one had been after Walker. It was him they were after and it didn't take him long to realize somehow they were able to use the telephone to find him. What he didn't understand was why they would hit Al. He also didn't understand how Al knew about Eagle Thrust. He didn't understand, but somehow Al knew and now he might die as a result of it.

Charley still had not moved. He looked at Marie. Marie was still holding her overnight bag. Without asking if she needed help, he took it from her and started out of the airport.

"My truck is just across the way. It's not far at all," he said.

"Did you get through?" Marie asked him.

"No," he said. "I didn't, but Al did."

"What?" she asked.

"Never mind," he said. "I'm not ready for you to put it on the news yet."

Marie made one more shot at what he meant.

"Just tell me where you want to go and be glad I'm even talking to you. When I'm sure what's going on, you'll be the first to know," he said. "I need you to help get my son released. When you do that, then we'll talk."

Charley drove her to the K Street offices of the network. Marie busily wrote down phone numbers where she could be reached and she gave him a cell phone, too. Charley took them, but doubted he would be calling her for a while.

CHAPTER FIFTY-THREE

Charley pulled the truck to the curb so Marie could get out.

"I'd appreciate it if you would take it easy on me," he said to her. "People are starting to get killed now that you've got your big break. Maybe you should back off and see where this thing is going. I think if you did, you would find out the story you could end up with is a lot larger than some kid who ran away to California."

"What do you mean?" Marie asked.

"If I live through the next week, you'll get your interview and I'll tell you a story you will find hard to believe and impossible to substantiate.

"Stay close to Al Poole, get my son out of the hands of the police, and find out about Operation Eagle Thrust. And when you start finding out, be real careful or else you might have some visitors with automatic weapons come by one evening."

Marie got out of the truck a little different woman. She had spent an hour with the man who saved her life. While driving in from the airport, he alluded to a much larger story.

Charley Reed promised to tell her the story, too.

Lou Locante's body was found just before noon. The Arlington Police had just discovered the bodies of two men in a parking lot. One was dead from an apparent heart attack while the other was dead from a gunshot wound. It was at that moment people began asking questions.

When Marty Sporror started for lunch, he was alerted to the deaths of three more government agents. It didn't fit that two CIA agents would die of heart attacks within hours of one another and a third of gunshot wounds.

What was happening?

It was noon when Charley started north on Interstate 95. New

York City was several hours away. Fortunately for him, he had put his suitcase behind the seat of his truck when he went to meet Tom the day before. He smiled at small things that made his complicated life a little easier.

He looked down at the cell phone on the seat.

"It's the damn phone," he thought. "They must be able to key in on my voice."

"But why? Why after all of these years?" he asked out loud.

"Eagle Thrust," he said. "I was there and they are afraid of what I know."

Then he knew why they hit Al.

"My God, he was the loadmaster," Charley said out loud. "He was there, too. When I called him I gave him away. They must have missed him."

Now he wished he could talk to Marie Van Arsdale. He looked at the cell phone once more and knew he couldn't risk it.

John Hughes stayed out of the office. He phoned several of the men under him and was given the news that Tom McMann was dead.

"He had a heart attack," he was told.

"That was no heart attack," he said back. "Ed Manion killed Lou Locante and one of his own people. He tried to kill me, but he missed. We've got to stop him."

"How?" Bill Thurby asked.

"I don't know," he said.

Then he asked if there was anything else on Reed.

"No," Bill answered.

"Shit," Hughes said. "Keep me posted if anything happens."

Marty Sporror went to the Director's office just before lunch. Their meeting lasted for just under an hour. They discussed the events of the night before as well as that morning in California. Both agreed everything seemed to center around Charley Reed.

During their talk, they became aware of the fact the FBI had no record of Charley Reed. Then when they ran Al Poole they found the same thing.

"How is this?" the Director asked Sporror. "We're the FBI. Anyone who has ever been arrested or served in the military is in our fingerprint files."

"Evidently everyone except those two," Marty said.

"If we don't have records on Reed and Poole, how many more

don't we have in our files? And who the hell took them out of our files? You can't sit there and tell me those two men served in the military and their records never made it here."

Marty didn't answer.

"Of course, they were in our records!" the Director insisted. "Someone removed them! Someone in the Bureau removed them for the CIA!"

"Can we be sure it was the CIA?" Marty asked.

"Who the hell else would it be? This has all the markings of their work. They eliminate the records and then they eliminate the men.

"Everyone is disposable to them. They're just not as efficient as they used to be. They've missed twice in the past twelve hours and managed to get six of their own killed in the process. This whole thing really pisses me off!"

Marty sat and listened.

"I want to know who inside this Bureau was working for them or is still working for them. I want to know!" he roared. "I want to know that and I want these killings nailed down. By the end of the day I'm going to be on the carpet in front of the Attorney General and I want some answers, Martin."

"Yes, sir," Marty said as he stood to leave.

At Poole was still in surgery while Marty Sporror considered the reports of the latest deaths. He had lost a great deal of blood and the doctors fought to stabilize this condition. They were afraid of shock as well as the bleeding that they were having trouble stopping. Stephanie was in the waiting room, still wearing her nightgown with a raincoat over it.

Marty Sporror had an agent at the hospital where Al Poole was taken. He was there to speak with Mrs. Poole and gather any information he could.

He wanted to match the ballistics on any of the slugs they might take out of Poole. Marty was told they didn't expect Al to live. At one o'clock California time, Al Poole's condition was stabilized. Agent Frelke phoned Washington and gave his report over the phone.

"What about the bullet samples?" Marty asked.

"SFPD is doing the work on them now. We got three of them and they will fax you the results as soon as they are done. That should be within an hour."

"Have you talked to the wife?"

"Yes. All she heard was her husband falling.

"The trigger used a silencer. There wasn't any reason for this as far as I can see. Aside from working for Reed, there's nothing. He is a middle-aged, middle-class, working man. He's very loyal to his boss and insisted his wife stay and give Reed a message when he called."

"What message was that?" Sporror asked.

"The wife couldn't remember. She's quite upset. She left it on the phone recorder. If you call, it should still be on it. She hasn't left the hospital all day."

"Fine," Marty said. "I'll call their house and see what it is. Have the police put a guard on him in the hospital. I don't want them coming back to finish the job."

Sporror hung up the phone and dialed the Poole residence in California. After the third ring the message began and Marty listened. When it ended, he hung up the phone and wrote down two words. Moments later he was with the Director, telling him what he had learned.

"More than just two people have been eliminated from our records," Marty reported.

"We're working on it right now, but in 1970 it appears over a thousand people were taken out of our files. Even using our computers this is a very tedious task and a lot of guessing is involved.

"It does seem most of the individuals who have been removed were Special Forces types in all four branches of the military. The CIA used Special Forces in their operations before the shake-up in the mid seventies.

"Reed was a Green Beret and Poole was an Air Force loadmaster. It is very possible they crossed paths and if that is true, then it's probable it was in an operation known as Eagle Thrust."

The Director picked up the phone and called the Pentagon.

"This is the Director of the FBI. I want to speak with General Decker."

He placed his hand over the phone and spoke to Sporror.

"Good work. I mean it. Do we stand any chance of finding out who removed the names?"

"I'm not sure," Marty answered. "It was a long time ago."

"Bill!" the Director said to the General in the Pentagon. "I'm on a secure line to you. I need information on an operation called Eagle Thrust."

He listened and then spoke again.

"No. I don't know when it took place or where. This is a hunch, but I'd guess it was a CIA operation using Special Forces personnel that needed Air Force support. Probably in Vietnam."

He listened again.

"I know, but you've got to help me out and get around that. If I go to the Attorney General, the Company will find out and destroy what little evidence may be left.

"Right now we have six dead company agents, two civilians dead, one wounded and probably dying, and one civilian marked to die who is on the run. We're sitting on a situation ready to explode in our faces if we don't manage it."

He listened once more and thanked the General on the other end before hanging up the phone.

"Marty," he said. "If Eagle Thrust ever existed, Decker will come through for us. Now, how are you doing trying to find Charley Reed?"

"Not well," he answered. "We have no where to start. He disappeared into the night. The local police departments are looking for him, but only as a material witness. If he leaves the immediate area, he's clean.

"It'll be touchy if any of our people try to take him. He won't have any way to distinguish our men from the ones that tried to hit him. He's dangerous enough unarmed. By now, he's probably armed."

The Director shook his head in understanding.

"How do we go about letting him know we only want to protect him?"

Marty shrugged his shoulders.

"That in itself is about as difficult as finding who removed his name from our files."

CHICAGO, ILLINOIS
11:55 A.M.

At his suggestion, Jerilyn agreed to meet Bob for lunch.

"Where should I met you?" she asked when he called.

"Somewhere so we can drink," he told her. "I'm ready today."

They agreed on a downtown restaurant and met just before noon. Bob kissed her as she sat down at the table. He had a vodka martini in front of him and had been playing with the olives on the plastic toothpick. When the waitress came over, Jerilyn ordered a Bloody Mary.

"Is anything wrong?" she asked Bob.

"Of course, there is," he said. "Don't you know there's something wrong? You should! This has been going on for a week now."

"What?" she asked.

"You know damn well what," Bob insisted.

"What?" she asked again.

"This Charley Reed thing," Bob said. "I've lived with this thing since the airport deal in Los Angeles and I'm tired of it!"

"Calm down, honey," Jerilyn said. "This has all been my fault and I'm sorry. I should have been able to keep myself under control, but I guess with all that's happened I just sort of lost it."

"Yes," Bob said. "You did and you got me caught up in it with you."

"I know," she admitted. "I'm sorry.

"You have to imagine what all this has done to me. I was just getting satisfied with my life when Chuck Ganley appeared. He brought back all those memories of Charley Reed. Then Tina got pregnant and married him and she started blaming me for things I did and didn't do when she was growing up."

"Every child blames their parents for one thing or another," Bob said.

"I know," Jerilyn said. "In this case she was right. Everything Tina said was true and I never faced it until she made me.

"I started to face what a lousy person I had been. I tried to make it up to her all these years and I was doing a good job of it until Chuck was killed. I blew it with her. I should have gone to her and been there for her, but all I cared about was our life. She is really angry with me and now Charley Reed comes back from the dead."

"That's what I don't understand," Bob said as he finished his martini and ate the olives.

"What's not to understand? You knew about him."

"I knew about him, but it was so long ago. I don't understand why you've reacted the way you have now."

The waitress arrived with another martini for Bob and Jerilyn waited for her to leave. It gave her a moment to consider her answer. Should she be honest with Bob or should she just tell him what he wanted to hear?

In the past Jerilyn had always told men what they wanted to hear. The only one she had not done it with was Charley and she lost him. Jerilyn was unsure. She wondered if she would lose Bob. When the waitress left, she answered.

"Because it was never really over between the two of us," she said truthfully. "The only other man to ever just walk away from me was Sam. Charley was coming back to me when he was killed."

Jerilyn caught herself.

"I mean supposedly was killed and now all of a sudden he's back."

"Is there something I don't know?" Bob asked. "Have you been seeing him? Have you talked to him?"

"No," she said.

"Then I don't understand. Do you love me or do you love him?"

"I love you," she said.

"What about him?" Bob asked her.

"I hate him!" she blurted out.

Bob studied her face and tried to understand what she said.

Jerilyn finished her drink.

"That's right," she said to Bob. "I hate him and wish he was dead again!

"It just isn't fair. He should have stayed dead. I put my life in order and was making peace with my children when he came back."

"So?" Bob asked.

"I don't understand why this has anything to do with you. He evidently doesn't want you. You don't want him. Why is our life so upset?"

"Because I think he is going to go to Tina," she said. "She has his grandchildren."

"Still, Jerilyn, I don't understand. None of this makes any sense to me. If we're in love with one another, the past should be the past. Tina is a grown woman and can and will do as she pleases. Why are you so upset over Charley Reed? What is he to you?"

"He's nothing to me. Not any more, he isn't," she said. "I just want to know why he never came back. He said he was coming back and he never did."

"Then ask him!" Bob said. "Ask him, find out, and get on with your life. When you get on with your life then I'll be able to get on with mine. Just do it soon! Do it real soon!"

Charley was quiet as he drove north. He wasn't listening to the radio. He was lost in his thoughts.

"The story of Operation Eagle Thrust," he said to himself. "The story of Buddy Hoogan and the men who are still missing in action."

He remembered Buddy.

When they landed in Panama from Bolivia, Buddy was taken to the hospital. Charley was brought up on charges for disobeying a direct order. There were no particulars accompanying the charge. Charley offered no defense. He pleaded guilty and signed the Article 15 and lost a stripe.

Buddy was sent to Walter Reed and Charley didn't see him again until the next spring when he came back from Vietnam.

He used to visit Buddy and sit with him in the hospital. Charley couldn't speak and Buddy was in a coma. Charley always felt Buddy knew he was there. By this time Charley had his stripe back.

It was when Charley was living in Washington, D.C. with Jerilyn and the kids that they moved Buddy from Walter Reed Hospital to the Veterans Hospital in San Francisco.

Charley visited him whenever he could at Walter Reed. Now they had moved him across country to where his family lived. Little did Charley realize at the time, in another year he would run to the west coast to start a new life for himself.

When he did, Buddy was his only friend. Charley sat with him several times a month, talking to him, telling him what had happened to him. Sometimes he would read the newspaper to Buddy and on those days a nurse would bring in some of the blind patients so they could listen.

Charley Hayes was a regular at the Veterans Hospital and the staff grew to expect his visits. It was in early 1979 that Buddy Hoogan caught pneumonia and passed away. Buddy's family had moved and Charley was all the man had left. He saw to the burial and the monument.

As he drove north toward New York City, he missed Buddy Hoogan.

When the news came on that night, Marie did a report live from the Washington studios. Her report centered on the killings at Bob Walker's house and the shooting of Al Poole.

She interviewed Joanna Reed who was irate over the police holding her son. Marie was able to report that Tom Reed was released just before the broadcast began. What she didn't report was what Joanna Reed told her about Operation Eagle Thrust.

"That name doesn't mean anything to me," she said.

"He said you would know," Marie said to her.

Joanna shook her head.

"The name doesn't ring a bell with me. He didn't take part in any special operations in Vietnam that I know of, but he did before he went there. It was when he was in Panama."

"What year was he in Panama?"

"1967," Joanna answered. "He went in the spring and didn't come home until November."

"Did he ever say what happened?"

"No, not directly, he didn't."

"What do you mean by that?"

"Nightmares. He had nightmares and sometimes when I'd wake him he would talk to me. Some of them weren't from Vietnam. I got the impression it was somewhere in South America."

"Anywhere in particular?" Marie asked.

"No," Joanna said. "I never knew specifically. Whenever I asked him any questions, he wouldn't answer them. He wouldn't talk to me about the war."

Marie thanked Joanna Reed and left to prepare for the evening broadcast. When she finished, she consulted with one of the research people in the Washington bureau.

"I want information on all military actions that took place in South America in 1967. I'm interested in border wars, revolutions, anything like that."

As she made her request the phone in the office of the Director of the FBI rang. It was General Decker.

Hughes sat and listened as the General gave him the information he had requested. When he was finished, the Director thanked him and rang Marty Sporror's office.

"Come here, please," the Director requested.

Sporror came immediately.

"Sit down," the Director told Marty.

"General Decker has just called me. Operation Eagle Thrust was a top secret CIA operation that took place in 1967. Units from the First Special Forces, the Seventh Special Forces, and the Military Air Command took part. It originated in Panama, but from there not even the Pentagon has any records.

"Evidently this was one of the most secret operations of the entire period. Decker said this came directly from President Johnson and only a handful of people were involved. Not even the Joint Chiefs of Staff knew about Eagle Thrust."

"That was secret!" Marty commented.

"Yes," the Director agreed. "Decker said outside of the CIA, it's unlikely anyone would know."

"Except for Charley Reed and Al Poole," said Marty Sporror. "I'll make sure we put our own people on Poole as guards."

"Do more than that," Hughes said. "I want our people to take over the case now. I don't want any blunders. I want our best and most trusted people.

"If the CIA has been in our files, this is a matter of national importance and secrecy. If it's true, they have the ability to be in the files of every part of our government and know things they have no right to know.

"Even if it happened twenty years ago, it still happened. We have to expose that fact and see it never happens again."

Marty understood what the Director was saying. No one had the right to destroy public or government records, not the CIA or the President himself.

He wondered what Eagle Thrust could have been. Was it some secret action the military carried out for the CIA? It had to be, but where and why? The use of the military in a foreign country without proper authorization was and always has been against the law. What gave the CIA the right to operate outside the law?

He walked back to his office to find the reports on the deaths of Tom McMann and Lou Locante. Both died of apparent heart attacks. McMann had been sixty, Locante forty-one. Both had physicals within the past year and neither one had any record of heart disease or even high blood pressure. McMann played tennis regularly and Locante played rugby. None of it fit.

Neither of the two men was a heart attack candidate. If that was so, then why?

Marty had been a policeman all his life. He was more than just a policeman. He was a trained investigator and a good one, too. He held both reports in his hand and sensed there was something very wrong. All of his training and experience told him he was right. Placing the reports back on his desk, he picked up the phone and ordered an autopsy on both men.

"What are we looking for?" the voice on the other end of the phone asked.

"I'm not sure," Marty said. "Maybe a chemical or foreign substance that could induce a heart attack. Look for needle marks, anything that might be out of the ordinary."

He hung up the phone and made preparations to assume control of the Al Poole shooting in California. Picking up the phone again, he gave orders to the Los Angeles based agents.

"I know," he said agreeing with the agent in California. "Use national security as a reason. They don't need to know anything else."

When he finished, he sat back and thought about Charley Reed. He wondered what might be in his mind. Marty wondered about the man who had inadvertently become the center of national attention.

Was he alone? What did he think and where had he gone?

Marty Sporror picked up a black and white photograph of Reed and studied the face. Charley Reed was the key to the secret of Eagle Thrust and the killings and deaths that had occurred.

Yes, Marty thought, all this began when you were exposed. You are the key and I need you to unlock the door. I need you, but where do I find you?

Several hundred miles away Charley Reed took a room at a Holiday Inn just off the interstate. Charley was tired. He needed to sleep.

CHAPTER FIFTY-FOUR

"I'm miserable!" Joanna Reed screamed. "You've been making my life miserable ever since that son-of-a-bitch came back from the dead. It's not my fault! I have nothing to do with it and you have no right taking it out on me!"

Ellen just looked at her. They had been arguing since last night. It was all over Charley Reed.

"Technically you're still married to him," Ellen said. "How do you think that makes me feel?"

"I am not married to him. We are divorced. I have the papers to prove it," she shot back.

"How am I supposed to feel knowing I love you and he's around?"

"Tell me," Ellen said. "I'd like to know what I'm supposed to do when he shows up to take you back."

"If he does, which I really doubt it, you can help me cut the son-of-a-bitch's balls off!" Joanna screamed out in frustration.

"Since when can he show up and claim me? Get some sense, woman! He's been gone for years. He's let me believe he was dead when all the while he's out in California doing his thing, not giving me a second thought. He didn't even know he had a son. I want to see him only one more time and that will be to spit in his face.

"I can't understand what's gotten into you. Why are you suddenly so insecure? I'm here. I'm not going anywhere. I like what we have.

"All the time I was with him I couldn't stand it. The greatest day in my life was when they told me he was dead."

Joanna Reed had just finished a grueling day. She was at the police station all day dealing with them and the press. They didn't release Tom until eight when Marie Van Arsdale made them look like a pile of boobs on the national news. Then she came home to a jealous lover. She didn't need this. It was like when she was married to Charley.

Ellen finally calmed down. She apologized. They went to bed

and cuddled with one another. One thing led to another and then they made love.

Joanna liked the soft and tender love, but Ellen wanted reassurance. She was like a man and she was demanding. As she had with Charley, she tolerated Ellen until she was satisfied and fell asleep. Joanna didn't sleep. She wasn't tired.

She remembered meeting Charley Reed, just back from Vietnam. He was out of the hospital six months and it seemed like he was in control of everything around him.

He was the opposite of her father and that impressed her. No one in her family ever talked. Charley talked about everything and he had so many ideas. When she met him, he became her hero. Joanna was still a virgin.

They didn't talk about sex in her home. Her mother told her it was something she probably would not like, but to have a man, she had to do it.

With Charley sex was fun. They ran off to motels or made love in his car. They went places together and then they got married. That was when he changed.

He had the dreams. He drank and he began fighting in the bars. Some nights he didn't come home and other nights when he did, she wished he hadn't.

They moved back to the Washington, D.C. area. He was supposed to go to school and she took a job with the Department of Navy. He never even enrolled that year.

Instead, he took a job selling cars. That was when he met Lee Stein and Bob Walker. She couldn't help making the comparison even after all those years. As good as Stein was for him, Walker was that bad.

She knew she shouldn't blame Walker. Charley was always a big boy and wasn't led around by others. Walker became his running partner and from then on it was downhill.

They drank in the topless bars in Virginia and the District. They were both driving brand new cars given to them by Lee Stein. Walker kept Charley supplied with marijuana. Poor Lee was their sales manager and he had a hard time keeping track of them.

So did Joanna. Walker and Charley were inseparable and it seemed he only came home to sleep and at times he didn't even do that.

It went on through the fall, into the winter, and finally through the spring. Charley was getting worse. Lee Stein left and bought his own dealership in North Carolina and Charley followed Walker from one job to another.

There were car dealerships all around the beltway and they moved every month or so because they were either fired or were offered a better deal. By the end of spring, she had enough and took control.

It was simple enough. He either quit selling cars and went back to school or she was leaving.

Charley didn't have any trouble understanding her so he quit and went back to Pennsylvania and enrolled in the same school he had flunked out of six years before. He lived there alone that summer and she joined him in the fall and started school herself.

Joanna remembered them as good days. Charley settled into being a college student and actually began to calm down. Their lives became simple and within a year and a half they both graduated.

By then Charley was selling cars again. Walker was driving up on the weekends and Lee was calling and asking Charley to come to North Carolina. Joanna wanted Charley to teach or go on to law school.

His friends wanted him to sell cars. Just after Christmas they moved to North Carolina and Charley became Lee's sales manager.

It didn't seem to matter any more. She took a job at the local university. Charley was home from ten-thirty at night until seven the next morning, six days a week. On Sundays they would go to Lee's house where the men drank beer and talked about the car business. Joanna did not mind much. Charley came home every night and he was three hundred miles from Bob Walker.

During that time she lost interest in sex. She consciously began to dislike sex. She wasn't sure whether it was sex with Charley or just sex in general. Anyway, it really didn't matter to her and it became the point of most of their fights. No matter what the reason seemed to be, sex became the main issue. She tolerated it, but she did not like it.

Then she got pregnant. Joanna hated herself for it.

Charley took her out on a Saturday night and they were both drinking. She was drunk and they danced and drank more. Then they went out to the parking lot and Charley took out a joint for them to smoke. They sat in the Lincoln, listening to the music and smoking a joint, and the combination of it and the alcohol swept both of them away.

Charley kissed her and touched her breasts through her blouse. Then his hand was under her skirt and in moments her pantyhose were off and she was lying on the seat with her husband inside her.

She remembered how her brain was crashing around as he pounded himself in her body. She remembered trying to keep her self-imposed resistance and how she couldn't. She gave herself over to the pleasure of having him. She let herself go and gave herself to him.

Then there was the explosion of their climaxes. She held onto her husband. She licked the sweat from behind his ear as his breathing slowed. Joanna remembered being flooded by him.

That night was different from any other. Her body controlled her mind rather than the other way around.

She cleaned herself with a tissue in the car and then dressed. They went back into the bar as if nothing had happened. She didn't douche like she did at home and as a result, the one thing she feared most happened. She became pregnant.

Joanna clearly remembered being pregnant and how she just hated Charley. There were times she wished she would have a miscarriage and then there were times she found herself becoming excited. She knew it was her body trying to control her mind. She hated it. She could be happy and then she would be angry. No matter how she felt, one thing was certain. She hated Charley Reed.

The baby was born in August. It was a boy. He lived two days. What was right between them before was wrong from that point on.

Charley met Jerilyn Gardner four months later. Three months after that Charley left her and moved to Washington, D.C. He took Jerilyn and her three children with him and he was back selling cars with Bob Walker.

Joanna had mixed emotions about those times. She could not remember why she hated him so much while she was pregnant and then missed him when he left. She remembered she didn't want him back, but she didn't want Jerilyn to have him either.

He came back from time to time. The Jerilyn thing was over by the next winter and Charley was confused about his life.

The United States pulled out of Vietnam and all the college students celebrated. Charley was with her that night and she remembered holding him in bed as he cried.

She asked what he was crying about, but he couldn't tell her. She didn't ask again. She just held him until he slept. They woke the next morning, had sex, fought, and then he left. Then she found him at Darryl's with Jerilyn.

Joanna never saw him again.

Charley was killed in the automobile accident and she found out she was pregnant again. She became a widow, and then a lesbian. She didn't miss men and she certainly did not miss Charley Reed.

Joanna thought of all those years he lived while allowing everyone to believe he was dead. She thought about what it must have been like for him. She couldn't help but envy him.

Charley Reed walked away from everything and now they were trying to bring him back. Joanna remembered her husband. She knew how stubborn he was. She clearly remembered how fierce he could be and she wondered if Charley Reed would let them bring him back.

She knew him well enough to know it was his decision. No one could force him to do anything he chose not to do. She smiled.

Good, she thought. Let someone else deal with him. She felt that with all her heart and remembered feeling like that thirty years ago.

Ed Manion had been up most of the night. He always enjoyed the early morning, but this particular one was not greeted as cheerfully as others. Ed sat with the files of all the men who had taken part in Eagle Thrust.

He was reasonably sure the records he had were the only ones in existence. If he destroyed these, there would be no way of ever proving the operation took place. All the Charley Reeds in the world could only talk about an action that could never be verified.

Ed sat in his overstuffed chair looking out the bay window in his den. The eastern sky was beginning to change color as dawn approached. He took up his pipe and filled it with tobacco and then packed it before striking a match. He drew in the first mouthful of smoke and slowly exhaled.

His pipe was one of the few pleasures left in his life. Since Betty died three years ago his life was empty. His daughters were married and living in cities far away in distance and in thought. They both made their dutiful phone calls on Father's Day and at Christmas. Otherwise, unless one of them got pregnant, he didn't hear from them.

Looking out at the yard and trees he wondered why his daughters should give him any more than they did.

There really was no reason. When they were children, he was always off on some station in the Middle East. He missed their First Communions and their first piano recitals. Betty always went to those functions and she was always around to fill in for him. It was sad, he thought, the Agency and its business had been more important to him than his children.

All he had now was the Agency and as he looked at the box of records, Ed wondered what kind of choice he had made.

It was a choice made in the name of national security and at the time he felt the welfare of the country was more important than the needs of one individual. Now Ed found he was second-guessing his decision. He was alone; his wife dead, his children gone and all that was left was the Agency.

Did the Agency care?

He doubted it. He was as expendable as Lou Locante. No one cared that Lou was dead. No one would have cared if he had killed John Hughes either. But, he didn't. He missed.

There never had been room for individuals in the Agency. Ed always accepted it and realized in the event of a problem he could easily be out on his own. Now, after all these years, he questioned what he had accomplished.

Ed Manion scanned his career in the fight against Communism and terrorism. Had he been able to defeat it? Had he been able to contain its spread?

No, he answered himself. Not really, and he even doubted if he had been able to make even the slightest dent as the world leaders spoke their lies and hypocrisy.

Ed remembered Vietnam and how the President lied about the Gulf of Tonkin incident.

He remembered the Bay of Pigs and the Cuban Missile Crisis. There was the Kennedy assassination, the Diem assassination, the Martin Luther King assassination, and finally the Bobby Kennedy assassination.

There was the fall of Chile and the fall of Nicaragua. There was Iran and El Salvador, Lebanon and the killing of Anwar Sadat.

All world events rumbled through the floors of the McLean headquarters while bureaucrats maneuvered and positioned themselves for the next promotion. They all wanted that special station or that next review.

Ed Manion sat alone and wondered what it was all for.

He looked at the box of records and then back out the window. It was nearly dawn. The sun was about to rise and Ed drew more smoke from his pipe.

Ed Manion watched as the sun rose over the horizon. He reached for the phone and dialed the number he had held in his hand since just before three a.m. He listened as the switching station made the connection and the phone began to ring. Before the third ring a man answered. It was Marty Sporror.

"This is Ed Manion," he said to Marty. "I have something you can use in your investigation."

There was silence for a few seconds and Ed waited for the FBI agent to speak.

"Okay," Marty said. "When can we meet?"

"Now," Manion answered.

"Where?"

"Come to my home now and you'll get what I have."

"Are you going to need protection?" Marty asked.

"Not unless you tell someone or my phone is tapped," Ed answered.

"Is your phone tapped?"

"I don't know," Manion answered. "Come now in case it is."

"Fine," Marty said hanging up the phone.

Twenty minutes later Marty got off Interstate 66 at the Vienna exit and drove the residential streets to Ed Manion's home. He pulled down into the horseshoe-shaped driveway and stopped in front of the garage. As he got out of the car, he could see Ed Manion standing in the door.

Marty followed Ed through the house to the den and accepted a cup of coffee.

"Have a seat," he said to Marty.

"Well, either my phone isn't tapped or they were asleep on the job."

Marty nodded.

"You did an autopsy on Tom McMann," Manion said.

"And Lou Locante, too," Marty said.

"What were the findings?"

"Heart attacks," Marty answered.

"Both of them?"

"Yes," Marty affirmed. "Cocaine induced heart attacks; both of them exactly the same. We think a concentrated aerosol caused it. Have you ever heard of anything like that?"

Ed looked at the aerosol can lying on its side next to his pouch of tobacco.

"You know I have."

"They were Agency hits, weren't they?" Marty asked.

Ed nodded his head.

"I made them," he said.

"My God, why?" Marty asked.

"The answer to that question is in the box on the floor under the table."

Marty looked down beneath the coffee table. A brown cardboard box was filled to the top with files and computer papers.

"It's all there," Ed said. "Everything you always wanted to know about Eagle Thrust and couldn't find out."

"Is there a file on Charley Reed in there?" Marty asked.

"No," Ed answered. "I have it here."

He reached down to the floor next to his chair and picked up two manila folders.

"His is here along with Alexander Poole's."

"Do I get them, too?" Marty wanted to know.

"Sure," Manion answered. "They're yours along with the other thousand or so."

"What makes those two so special?" Marty asked.

"They're the only ones still alive." Ed Manion said.

"Al Poole died last night," Marty told him.

"That's too bad," Manion said. "I would have prevented it if I had acted sooner."

Marty watched the man's face. He appeared strangely calm and it made Marty uncomfortable.

"Why did you call me?" Marty asked.

"With McMann gone, you're in line to be one of the top three men in the Agency. This is your big break, even if you did make it happen yourself."

"Yes," Manion agreed smiling.

The sun rose and shone over his shoulder as he laughed to himself.

"I guess this is my big break."

He paused, thinking for a moment and then spoke to the FBI agent. "I guess it just came a little too late.

"It isn't important to me anymore. I can't remember what it was all about. I don't know who the good guys and the bad guys are any more. They are all the same.

"When McMann told me to eliminate Hughes and Locante, none of it made sense to me. The good guys aren't supposed to kill one another. Only the bad guys kill one another and no one ever told me I was one of the bad guys."

Manion turned in his chair toward the window and looked into the sunlight.

"The French sold arms to the Vietnamese when we fought and the French were our allies. The Israelis spy on us and we're supporting them. At the same time the Brits and the West Germans build a plant for the Arabs that can produce poison gas. The Arab princes support Osama bin Laden and then one of them comes to this country and tries to give us ten million dollars.

"Now we finally realize the Russians are our best allies. I've spent my whole life fighting the Russians and I guess I've spent my whole life in vain."

Marty nodded at the man.

"The world has changed," he said.

"No," Ed said. "The world is still the same. The rules changed, that's all. They changed and no one told me."

"What do you mean?" Marty asked.

Manion still had his back to the FBI agent.

"I wasn't in the country when Eagle Thrust took place. I was in Lebanon. I helped pass information along so the Jews could win the Seven Day War.

"Eagle Thrust was an excellent operation. It was conceived by brilliant military men and carried out by the bravest of the brave of our young men. They did their duty. They did it efficiently and succeeded against superior manpower in totally foreign surroundings.

"To reward them for their success, we sent them to Vietnam and placed them all in harms way. In some cases, we even leaked information to the enemy so they would be killed. Charley Reed's unit, the 545th Special Operations Group, was ambushed on information given to the enemy leaked by our operatives.

"No one was supposed to survive, but somehow Charley Reed came out of it in one piece. The ones that weren't killed there, we hit here in the USA."

Manion stopped and cleared his throat.

"That's a goddamn shame," he continued. "A brave young man fights in secret, then fights in Vietnam, and then comes home in one piece to be killed by agents of his own country."

Marty didn't say anything. He sat and listened.

Manion wiped his face.

"Some reward, wasn't it?"

Marty didn't know how to respond and before he could comment, Manion continued.

"When Hughes first called me, I didn't know what Eagle Thrust was. He told me there was some unfinished business, some loose ends and I approved the action.

"By the time I realized what it was all about, we had dead people in Falls Church. Then there was Poole and when I asked McMann, he told me all this was necessary.

"Imagine," Manion said. "It was necessary to kill American heroes.

"He ordered me to kill Hughes. I missed Hughes and Locante got in the way. But I killed McMann first and then I stole the files.

"I killed them in the Agency's computer, too. What you have is it. Use it any way you feel you need."

"What about you?" Marty asked.

"Don't worry about me," Manion said. "I'm an old soldier. We don't die. We just fade away."

Marty thanked Manion and stood, picking up the box of files.

"Here," Ed said. "You'll need these."

He handed Marty the files of Charley Reed and Al Poole.

"Thanks again," Marty said.

He started to leave and then stopped, turned to the man and asked, "Are you sure you're all right?"

"I'm fine," Manion said.

Marty left the room and walked to the front door.

Ed Manion sat looking out into the morning. He heard a car start and drive away. He reached toward the table his pipe and tobacco were on, but did not pick them up.

He reached beyond them and took the metal aerosol in his hand. He stood and walked into the bedroom where he picked up a picture of Betty and the girls. It was taken the year he was in Lebanon, the same year Eagle Thrust took place.

He sat in the loveseat across from the bed and looked at the portrait. He thought of Betty and the last time he made love to her.

They made love and then they fought. He went to work and then got the call she had been killed in an automobile accident. Ed always was sorry about that fight. He was sorry he never had a chance to tell Betty he had been silly and it was all his fault. He was sorry he never had a chance to say how much he loved and cherished her.

"I'm sorry," he said to Betty. "I love you. I wish I knew you could hear me. I wish I knew if you forgave me."

He thought of his girls and wondered if he should call them. He thought about it and realized it was not Father's Day or Christmas.

He pulled the portrait to his chest and raised the aerosol. As he did, the phone began to ring, but he didn't hear it. His finger pressed down and the concentrate sprayed in his face. He couldn't help but inhale and experience the flash shooting into his brain.

The phone rang seven more times. When it stopped, Ed Manion died.

CHAPTER FIFTY-FIVE

With Ed Manion dead, John Hughes now had a clear field. He took over the entire section and stepped up efforts to find Charley Reed.

"I don't want any loose ends. That girlfriend of his is one. He's lived with her long enough that he had to have told her," he said to Larry Coleman.

"Take care of her."

They sent a message to CIA operatives in Germany. They were ordered to arrange an accident for Alicia Masters.

Marie Vans Arsdale picked up the phone after the seventh ring. She had been working on Eagle Thrust for three days without a break. Everything she found led to the CIA and finally someone who Dan knew suggested she call at the Department of Justice. He told her about the results of the autopsies on the two agents.

"Are you saying the two deaths are connected with Eagle Thrust?" she asked.

"No," the informant answered. "I'm saying the Agency hits are connected with Eagle Thrust."

"Really?" she asked.

"Look," the man continued. "No one knows anything about Eagle Thrust. We know it took place in 1967. It started in that year and it ended in that year. We can trace expenditures assigned to Eagle Thrust, but we don't know what it was.

"It was approved by Lyndon Johnson, but no where is it ever mentioned in any of his papers. None of the Joint Chiefs of Staff know anything about it other than it was a Company operation in conjunction with the military.

"We can't find anyone in the military who took part in or even supported Eagle Thrust. Even the base commander in Panama where

Eagle Thrust originated is dead.

"We hit one stonewall after another and when we try to access CIA computer records, all references to Eagle Thrust have been deleted. We have reason to believe the one dead Company man, McMann, was the mastermind of the operation."

"Who was the other one?" Marie asked.

"Locante," he answered. "He was the caretaker of the files. His job was to see this operation, and probably a lot of others, stayed dead. When Charley Reed came back to life, it was Locante's job to see Eagle Thrust didn't."

"Is Charley Reed safe now that Locante and McMann are dead?"

"I can't answer that," he said. "Remember Locante and McMann are both victims of hits themselves. I would say now that they are gone, Poole and Reed may be the only two people alive who know anything about Eagle Thrust."

"Poole is dead," she told him.

"I didn't know," he answered.

"Who at the CIA can I speak to?" she asked.

"I'd be careful contacting the CIA," he told her. "You could place yourself in danger if you get a hold of the wrong person and you lead them to believe you know too much."

"I'm a television journalist. They wouldn't dare touch me."

"Have you ever heard of Dorothy Kilgallen?" he asked her.

"No," Marie answered honestly.

"Well, little girl," the informant said. "Call Dan and find out before you start shaking the wrong trees. She thought she was safe, too. In all likelihood, she was dealing with many of the same people we are talking about."

The informant broke off the conversation. He didn't say goodbye or wish her good luck. He just hung up.

Marie spoke to Dan who told her the hard cruel facts of life regarding the world of intelligence, spies, and national security. Then he told her how to go about speaking to an information officer and even suggested that she call early the next morning.

"Morning is best. You catch them off guard. They patch you through to the Duty Officer who is usually at home. He sits on any breaking news. Your conversation is recorded so watch what you say. Generally, they are pretty helpful. It's worth a shot until we can find more information which I believe is unlikely."

Marie called the CIA the next morning just after six a.m. Her call was patched through to Ed Manion who never answered the phone.

She called back and complained so they tried again.

When Ed Manion didn't answer the second time, a ground security officer was sent from the McLean headquarters to check on the Duty Officer. Forty-five minutes later the security officer reported back that Manion was dead.

With his death, only two men in the Company with knowledge of Eagle Thrust remained.

Marty Sporror did not return home.

He took Interstate 66 into the city, crossed the Potomac and drove up Constitution Avenue to the FBI headquarters. He called his assistant from his car and told him to come to the office immediately. Marty was there only about ten minutes when Jimmy Johnson walked into the room.

"What's up?" he asked.

Marty turned to find his young assistant wearing a sweat suit, tennis shoes, and a Redskins ball cap. He placed his hand on the box containing the files and smiled within himself, feeling a sense of accomplishment.

"Eagle Thrust," he said. "Probably the only information on it anywhere."

Jimmy felt a surge of excitement rush through him.

"Sit down," Marty said. "We have some reading to do."

Meanwhile, Charley didn't know what to do.

He was afraid to use credit cards and he was afraid to use the telephone. He wanted to meet his son's widow. He wanted to see his grandchildren. He also wanted to see Cindy.

What was he to do? Should he just show up and knock on the door? He didn't know what was the right thing to do.

To complicate matters Marie Van Arsdale was still running her stories. His face was very recognizable and several people had already asked him if he wasn't the person they had been seeing on the news.

Finally, he decided going to her front door was the only way.

He had a Park Avenue address. He parked and walked to the building. It was a little after ten in the morning. A uniformed doorman met him.

"May I help you, sir?" he asked.

"Yes," Charley said. "My name is Charley Reed. I'm here to see Mrs. Ganley."

"Is she expecting you?" he asked.

"No," he answered. "I'm a family member."

The doorman took a second look. He immediately saw the resemblance to Chuck Ganley.

"Just a second," he said as he phoned upstairs.

"Mrs. Ganley," he began. "A man is here to see you. His name is Charley Reed. He says he is a family member."

There were moments of total silence. Tina was taken by complete surprise. Then she responded to the doorman.

"Send him up," she said.

Charley took the elevator to the fourteenth floor. It seemed to take forever and he was anxious over what he was going to say.

When the elevator door opened, Tina was waiting for him in the hallway. He didn't have a chance to say anything. She threw her arms around him and hugged him instantly.

She took Charley by total surprise. It had been years since anyone greeted him like that and the surprises were just beginning.

While he knew she was his son's widow, he had no idea that she was Jerilyn Gardner's daughter and the little girl he took care of when he lived with her.

They visited for several hours.

"Cindy went back to Pittsburgh several days ago," she said.

Charley nodded his head.

"How are you doing?" he asked.

Tina forced a smile. Charley could tell she was holding back the tears.

"I'm coping the best I can," she said. "It's just so hard with the girls and their questions. I was okay when Cindy was here. She took care of the girls and did so much for me."

"I know," Charley said.

He recognized the sadness that filled her. She did the best she could to conceal it, but it was still there and as hard as she tried, it came through.

"I'm sorry," he said.

She started to cry and fought it. Then she apologized.

"You don't have to apologize to me," he said.

She did anyway.

"Where are you staying?" she asked.

"I was in a hotel, but I checked out this morning."

"Then you can stay here. You'll be safe here because no one has any idea of a link to us."

"I don't want to put you in any danger or bring the press in here," he said.

"You won't if you just stay here and don't use the phone," she said. "Besides the girls will want to get to know you. You're their grandfather. I know you'll be one who cares about them, too. My dad is always too busy to have anything to do with them. He has his own new family to worry about. We don't seem to count. He finally called yesterday. How long has it been? A month already?"

"I guess it has been that long," Charley agreed.

She told him to park his truck in Chuck's parking place and bring in his bags.

"Are you sure?" he asked.

"Yes," she said. "I insist."

He did and settled in. They visited the rest of the morning and on into the afternoon. Around two-thirty she realized the time.

"I have to get the girls. Do you want to come along?"

"Sure," he said.

He walked with her to pickup Kathy at nursery school. Kathy was a doll. She looked just like Tina. She had her dark almond shaped eyes and her complexion. Kathy's hair was long, the way he remembered Tina wearing hers as a girl.

"This is your grandpa," she said to Kathy.

Kathy didn't hesitate or draw back. Immediately, she went to Charley and held out her arms for him to pick her up.

"You look like my daddy," she said.

Tina took a second look and realized he did.

Charley didn't put Kathy down. He carried her in his arms as they walked over to meet Kimberly. When she saw him holding her sister, she froze in her steps.

"It's okay," Tina said to her daughter. "This is your daddy's daddy. He's come to visit us."

Charley smiled at the girl.

"Hello," he said. "You must be Kimberly. Your mother has told me all about you. Is it all right if I stay with you and your mother for a few days?"

"You look like my dad," she said to him.

"So do you," he said. "That must mean we look alike, too. What do you think?"

Kimberly wasn't as openly affectionate as Kathy, but she did hold Charley's hand as they walked back to their home.

Charley never put Kathy down. He carried her for nearly ten blocks. He enjoyed the feeling of holding her in his arms.

As the afternoon changed to evening and Tina started dinner, the girls had hundreds of questions. They came from every direction about every imaginable subject. Patiently he listened and patiently he answered them with kindness and love. It was a new experience for him.

He settled in and played with the girls while Tina made dinner. Finally, she called them to the table.

"Sit here," she told Charley.

"That's Daddy's chair, Mommy," Kathy said.

Charley stopped where he was and didn't make a move to sit down.

"Don't you think Daddy would want his daddy to sit in his chair if he wasn't here, honey?" she asked.

Kathy thought about it and decided it would be okay.

"Yes," she said. "Daddy would like that."

"Is Grandpa going to say grace the way Daddy did?" Kimberly asked.

"Will you?" Tina asked.

Charley nodded and he began with the sign of the cross. He watched as the three girls made the sign of the cross, too. Then he began.

"Bless us our Lord for these Thy Gifts, which we are about to receive. Through Thy Bounty, through Christ Our Lord, Amen."

They all blessed themselves again with the sign of the cross. Kimberly looked up at Charley from across the table.

"Did you teach that to my daddy?" she asked.

"No, honey," he said. "I would guess his mommy did."

Tina smiled at Charley.

"Chuck was raised a Mormon," she said. "After we were married we both joined the Catholic Church and were married in the church. Our first wedding was in Las Vegas at Christmas time. We wanted the girls to grow up with a religion and it was Cindy's and we chose it. Cindy did teach him the blessing, but after he was a grown man."

Charley smiled back at her.

"Thank you," he said. "Thank you for sharing that with me."

After dinner, he tried to help her with the dishes.

"No," she said. "The girls and I do the dishes. You go to the living room, read the paper and watch the news. It's time for it to come on."

Again Charley did as he was told. He realized there was some a sort of solace being taken from his presence both at dinner and now in keeping with a routine they had as a family until September 11th.

He sat in the chair his son used to sit in and watched the news.

The news anchor began:

"Tonight's news begins with a note of tragedy for the news industry. Our lead story is the death of reporter Alicia Masters. She was killed in an automobile accident in Hamburg, Germany."

"Oh, no," he groaned. "Oh, no."

Tina walked into the room as the story was being reported. She didn't understand the link between the woman and Charley until his picture came up on the television screen and the relationship between the two of them was explained.

"I'm so sorry," she said to him.

Charley's face was buried in his hands. He looked up at Tina.

"Thank you," he said watching the explanation of what happened.

"Oh, God," he groaned. "When is this going to end?"

Kathy heard him say that and came out and climbed up on his lap.

"Are you sad Grandpa?" she asked.

"Yes," he said. "Grandpa is sad, but it has nothing to do with you, sweetie."

"Did someone you know die? Is that why you are sad?"

"Yes," he said. "That's why."

"My daddy died and I'm sad. So is Mommy," she said.

Charley held her and forced back his tears.

"Then we all can help each other," he said.

"I'll like that," Kathy told him. "You smell like my daddy, too."

For the next several days, Charley got into a routine. He was coping the best he could with the loss of so many people close to him. At the same time, he had to be strong and be there for Tina. She was a widow with two children and was pregnant with a third. She was his daughter-in-law and she needed his help.

The days turned into a week. They were good for one another and Charley was filling a void for her and the girls. One evening he helped her put the girls to bed. He sat down on Kathy's bed and read her a story.

Tina watched and listened to him, remembering him doing the same thing for her so many years before. The sound of his voice and his presence were reassuring to her. Once the girls were finally asleep, she decided she needed to rest, too.

"Good night," she said. "Thank you for everything."

"No," Charley said. "Thank you."

Charley Reed couldn't sleep. He sat at the window looking out at the city. He thought about everything that happened to him.

His mind crossed the years separating him from the moment.

Tina had been wonderful. She accepted him immediately.

Charley couldn't believe how much she resembled Jerilyn. She was the picture of her mother. She was a picture of Jerilyn Gardner.

Tina wasn't sleeping either.

She was tossing and turning. She thought about how she knew his face as soon as she saw it. It was a face she loved both in the present and in the past. It would have been her husband's face twenty years from now and it was a face she loved as a little girl thirty years ago.

His was a kind face. It had loved her when she was bad as well as when she was good. She remembered touching it when it was rough and stubbly. She remembered it soft and smooth as he carried her from the car and into her bed. Now, it was there with her.

How could it be so, she wondered to herself.

She remembered them going back to live in North Carolina without him. Then she remembered her mother crying and saying he was dead. Tina understood what dead meant and cried, too.

Her sister Anne Marie asked why she was crying and when Tina told her, she cried. She was only seven, but she could still remember her mother blaming herself for the fact he was dead. Now, he was there with her. He was there and obviously very much alive.

She got out of bed and walked out into the living room.

"Can't you sleep?" he asked her.

She didn't answer. She hugged him. She hugged him for what he was to her and what he was doing at that time.

In that moment she remembered the years after him. She remembered Eddie Lee, her mother's boyfriend, who had touched her and made her touch him. She remembered going to live with her father and the women he had and how they treated her and Anne.

Charley Reed was the father she dreamed of having and now he was back. She didn't really know how and she really didn't care. Throwing her arms around him she hugged him around the neck.

"I always wanted you to be my father and now you are," she cried out.

Charley Reed put his arms around her and tried to hide the tears in his eyes. What a week this was for him! In spite of all that had happened, all of a sudden he had a family again and there were people who cared about him.

"Oh, Tina," he said to her. "You can't imagine how much that means to me."

They sat down on the couch. They had been careful with one another, but suddenly Tina wanted to know everything about him.

Tina asked him if he had gotten married again.

"No," he answered.

"Why not?" she asked.

"No real special reason," he said. "I guess I never was really lonely enough. There were women who wanted to marry me, but I just never did. You might find this hard to believe, but the years have really gone fast. I've been busy running my business and haven't thought much about marriage."

They talked about her brother and Tina said she'd like to find him. Charley nodded his head as he listened. He remembered Michael and wondered where he was even as they spoke.

Sitting with Tina, he couldn't help but remember being with Jerilyn and the kids.

"What do you remember about me?" he asked her.

"I remember taking car trips with you. We went to the beach in a white car with a huge back seat. We ate at a restaurant over the water with picnic tables and then we went to a fort.

"I can remember stopping at a Dairy Queen and sitting between you and Mother on the way home. I must have fallen asleep because you carried me upstairs and put me in bed. I can remember you kissing me goodnight.

"We were all happy when you were there. We felt safe and you were good to us.

"When you were gone, Anne Marie really missed you. She cried at night because she was afraid of the dark. She used to say monsters were in our room and only you could kill them.

"Mother wasn't happy after you were gone and I suppose things were pretty hard for her.

"Then there was a boyfriend of hers, Eddie Lee. I remember he smelled bad and we didn't like him. He drank all the time and would scream at mother to keep us away from him.

"He really didn't like Michael and I can still remember them fighting about money and how much we were costing him. He wasn't a very nice man," Tina said with a strange sound in her voice.

"After that we went to live with my father and then my grandmother, and then my father again. Anne never forgot you and I think that's just amazing. She was only four. You really made an impact on her."

"Does she still remember me?" he asked.

"She thinks she does. Chuck stirred her memories of you. She talks about going to a car wash with you and being scared and how good you make her feel. There was a clown, too.

"I can remember the clown frightened Anne. You yelled at the clown and Anne just sobbed in your arms and then I remember the police coming."

Charley smiled at Tina.

"I was a little over protective that day," he said. "The jerk in the clown suit just walked up behind her and picked her up. It scared her half to death and I'll never forget the shriek she let out. My God, it went right in my bones!

"I grabbed her right out of his arms and shoved him into one of those brick planters full of flowers. He banged his head and cut himself and security called the police. They were going to arrest me until your mother arrived with her arms full of packages and your brother."

Charley laughed remembering.

"She set them straight. You told her what happened and she wanted the guy in the clown suit arrested for attempted kidnapping and anything else she could think of! It was quite a scene!"

"I remember that!" Tina exclaimed.

"Anne does, too, and you've always been her protector. She used to tell Dad you were going to come back from heaven and beat him good."

"Why would she say that?" Charley asked.

"They never got along. She ignored everything he said and defied him every time she could. Anne took an immediate dislike to him and it's never changed.

"To this day, they don't get along very well. If he walked by her and she thought she could get away with it, she'd trip him and I think he'd do the same thing. It's that kind of dislike."

"That's incredible," he said. "I can understand her, but your father, too?"

"Oh, he's just as childish at times as she is when it comes to their feud. He's fine with everyone else, except her. This has been going on so long it's actually become humorous."

"What's Anne Marie like?" he asked.

"Don't get me wrong," Tina said. There's nothing wrong with her. She's beautiful and really good-hearted. She's just kind of wild. She's a real party girl and can go forever."

Charley laughed again.

"Anne Marie sounds like your father. He was the party guy. He used to forget to come home. That's why your mother divorced him. He never knew when to quit or how."

"He's different now," Tina said. "He's married to a really nice lady and they have three children. Dad's very devoted to them."

Charley looked out the window.

Sam Gardner had settled down. He held a job and he had a wife and three children.

Charley remembered Jerilyn blaming the war for the way Sam was. She tried to get him to tell her what it was like for him, but he was silent.

Then she turned her attention to Charley whenever he had his dreams, but Charley also stayed silent. He remembered her frustration when he'd say he didn't want to talk about it. He remembered her anger, saying he was just like Sam.

Charley patiently understood Jerilyn even though all the while he never understood himself.

"Your father sounds like he's done a pretty fair job of putting his life in order. Did he get outside help?" he asked.

"He used to go to a Vietnam Veterans group every Thursday and he met a man there from Rockford who really helped him. It was years ago. He went for over a year and even became pretty good friends with him.

"We went out to his house one Saturday for dinner. Even Anne Marie liked him and I did because Dad was always better when he was seeing him. His nightmares stopped and he only drank at home and not that much. It was such a major change that all of us really got involved."

"Did he stay that way?" Charley asked.

"Yes, he did. He changed. He got a job and kept it. He got married and now he's finally happy."

Charley looked away again. He was happy for Sam Gardner. His war was finally over.

He sat up in the overstuffed couch and took Tina's hand in his.

"You can't begin to imagine what being here with you has meant to me," he said. "Just seeing you again has been great. I can't believe it."

There were tears in his eyes as he spoke. Tina looked at him and then away with tears in her own eyes. When he loosened his grip on her hand, she wasn't ready to let go. As he wiped his eyes, she smiled. It was a smile of appreciation and tenderness. Tina placed her other hand on top of his and held it between both of hers.

"You're very sweet," she said. "I'm glad you are here. With all that has happened, I am really glad you are here."

Charley was glad, too.

But he knew it was dangerous for Tina and the girls if he stayed.

He had to leave soon. As much as didn't want to, he knew he must. At the same time, as much as he tried, he couldn't help living in the past.

Tina cuddled up against him and dozed. As she did, he stroked her hair. He stroked her hair and thought back to another time.

He remembered Jerilyn standing at the window of the Key Bridge Marriott in Washington. He drove up from North Carolina to meet her and the girls when they returned from Chicago.

The grown woman sleeping on his shoulder was six and asleep next to her sister.

Charley was sitting in the bed drinking a glass of wine. Jerilyn was naked, looking across the Potomac River at Georgetown. She lit a cigarette and the glow of the match illuminated the beauty of her body.

Even though they had just finished making love, he wanted her again. Charley always wanted Jerilyn. It seemed he could never have enough of her.

She was different from Joanna. Joanna was a clean young girl who shared recipes with his mother.

Jerilyn was a woman who captivated him.

From the first time he saw her, he wanted her. Once he had her, he had to have her again and again. Beyond that, Charley had to not only have her, he had to possess her. She became his obsession.

She was such an overwhelming obsession that even when he had her, he was never really convinced he did. She became his personal illness. It was an illness that consumed all his waking hours to the point where he thought of nothing other than her. He was unable to work and became insanely jealous.

He imagined her with other men and died a little inside every time he did. Charley wanted her, but never really understood how he could.

He shook his head.

"Wake up," he said to himself. "Wake up and go to sleep."

"I need to go to bed," he said out loud.

"Me, too," Tina said.

She kissed him and went to her bedroom. Charley got up and went to bed also.

As he sat on the bed in New York City, he remembered how years ago the young man on the bed in Washington, D.C. had been unable to separate sex and love. To him it was all the same.

How could he have been so wrong?

For Charley Reed at that moment, he was glad he was able to separate the two and appreciate each one for exactly what it was and what it meant. He laid his head on the pillow and tried to sleep.

CHAPTER FIFTY-SIX

While Charley Reed dropped out of sight, Marie Van Arsdale was in a state of shock. She had to report the story of Alicia Master's death and as she did, she remembered the warning the man gave her and the reference to Dorothy Killgallen.

Could it be true?

It was more than a coincidence that the one woman who lived with Charley Reed would suddenly be killed in an automobile accident days after his best friend was gunned down in his home by people who appeared to be federal agents.

She phoned the authorities in Hamburg. The first two men she spoke with put her off. Finally, she reached someone who spoke with her, but was very guarded.

"The Federal Government is involved in this investigation," he said.

"Something is very bad about this one. It doesn't seem like your run of the mill accident. It looks like a planned accident," he told her under a promise of confidentiality.

At the same time Marty Sporror and Jimmy Johnson dug into Operation Eagle Thrust. They were in total astonishment at the numbers they had developed through the week. The files they scanned were like some underworld hit list.

"The only thing they didn't do was line them up against a wall and gun them down," Jimmy said.

Marty shook his head. "It's just unbelievable."

Jimmy Johnson was astounded.

"Why did they do this?" he asked.

"They didn't want anyone to know what we had done. If you kill everyone who took part in the operation, there's no one who can say it ever happened and tell about it." Marty answered him.

"So many of these men are still listed as MIA," Jimmy said. "Where are they? What happened to their bodies?"

Marty shook his head.

"What was this operation anyway? What were they doing that was so important they felt compelled to do this?" Jimmy asked.

Marty began to tell him the story.

When he woke up the next morning Tina could tell something was bothering Charley.

"I need to get in touch with Marie Van Arsdale," he said to Tina.

"How are you going to get in touch with her?" she asked.

"She wrote down about ten phone numbers when I saw her in Washington. I want you to call and set up a meeting for me."

"Okay," Tina said. "I can do that.

"What are you going to tell her?"

"I'm going to give her the story of her life. If she thought I was a story, this will make me look like a Saturday morning cartoon."

"Why?" she asked.

"For Al Poole and for Alicia," he said.

He paused for a few seconds.

"They had it on the news. He died the other night. And they killed her, too."

Charley gave her the number and told her what to say. The phone rang only twice when Marie answered.

"Marie?" Tina asked.

"Yes," she said.

"This is Charley's daughter-in-law. Don't say his last name, please. We both know who he is."

"Okay," Marie said.

"He wants to talk to you."

"When?" Marie asked excitedly.

"He's ready now."

"Where are you?"

"We're are in the city. He wants it to be in a safe place."

"He can come here," Marie said.

Tina checked with him and Charley didn't want to go there.

"Ask her to meet me at Mickey Mantle's. Tell her I'll be at the bar," he said.

Tina did exactly that.

"When?" Marie asked.

"Eleven forty-five at the bar," she said.

"No camera crew!" she told the reporter.

"Fine. I'll be there," Marie said.

"All right. See you then," replied Tina.

Tina wanted to go along, but Charley wouldn't hear of it.

"It's too dangerous," he said.

Marie Van Arsdale hung up the phone.

"This is it!" she said to herself.

At exactly eleven forty-five that morning Marie walked into Mickey Mantle's Bar and Grille to find Charley Reed sitting at the bar. He was drinking a beer.

"Hello," she said to him.

"Hello yourself," he said.

"I'm sorry about Alicia," she said.

"You should be scared, too," he said to her. "It should show you what they are able to do."

"Do you believe she was killed?"

"Don't you?" he asked.

She didn't answer.

"You should," he said. "They killed her because they were afraid of what they thought I might have told her."

"And what is that?" she asked.

Charley didn't answer her right away. He changed the subject.

"Thank you for helping my son," Charley said to Marie. "I saw the news and I was impressed with the way you took on the police department."

"I felt I owed you," Marie said. "I spoke with Tom after we got him released. He's a fine young man."

Charley shook his head.

"Some reunion with his father. I get him drunk and very nearly killed."

"Those were government agents. Why were they trying to kill you?" Marie asked.

"Why did they kill Al Poole?" Charley asked instead of answering her question.

"Is it Eagle Thrust?" Marie asked.

"What have you been able to find out about Eagle Thrust?" Charley asked her.

"Not much," she said.

"I didn't think so," Charley said.

He looked at the tape recorder Marie had placed on the bar. Then he looked at her, his face very sober.

"Let's move to a table."

They did and she placed the tape recorder on the table.

"Turn that on," he said. "I'll tell you the story. How you'll ever verify it is your problem."

Then he began.

"In June 1967 the American Army invaded Bolivia with the approval of the Bolivian government. Che Guevara was leading an army of revolutionaries. During the next five months, we killed every single one of them."

"How many was that?" Marie asked.

"Six thousand," Charley answered.

"What happened to the bodies?"

"We burned them," Charley said.

"Che Guevara, too?"

"Yes. We captured him in early October. We interrogated him, tortured him and interrogated him again. We got what we wanted and then we killed him."

"You interrogated him?" she asked. "What did you want to know?"

"I didn't personally. Some guys from the CIA did. One was named Hughes, the other was Manion."

"Ed Manion?" Marie asked.

"I don't know. It was always last names with them. Any way, there were a number of things they wanted.

"From a military standpoint, we wanted to know where the rest of his men were located. We wanted to know the locations of their supplies and we wanted information regarding the supply lines and drops.

"The CIA had questions about Cuba, Russian military in Cuba, Russian missiles in Cuba, and," he said stopping short.

"And what," she asked.

"The Kennedy assassination," Charley finished.

While Marie and Charley were meeting in New York, Marty Sporror took out three six-inch tapes, each capable of recording for four hours on either side. The first tape was in a box and labeled 'Guevara Interrogation – Kennedy Assassination.'

The second tape was 'Guevara Interrogation – Missiles and Locations.'

The third was 'Guevara Interrogation – Cuban Military and Island Defenses.'

He held them and then showed them to Jimmy. Jimmy's eyes

opened wide as he read the labels. Then Marty handed him 8 by 10 black and white photographs of Guevara's bloody face.

There was one of him tied to a chair, his nose broken and shirt covered with blood. Another showed two soldiers walking him to a wall.

Then, in what was a sequence of photos, he was tied to a post and the next showed him screaming out and being blindfolded. There was a photo of the firing squad getting ready and then another of the squad shooting Guevara.

Then there was the famous photo of his bullet-riddled body. This photo was the one reproduced in enormous quantities and circulated throughout the world, giving proof Guevara was actually dead.

Marty passed the last photograph to Jimmy and then sat down in his chair. Jimmy took it and sat also.

"He had become a living legend," Marty explained to Jimmy.

"In 1966 we weren't sure where he was at any given time. He was reported to be in the Congo. He founded the Patrice Lamumba Regiment and trained them to overthrow the government. Then he was in Hanoi and Moscow. He was a phantom. They reported him everywhere there was unrest and the time right for rebellion. When he went to Bolivia and we had the chance to get him, we took it."

Jimmy listened. He was a small boy in 1967. He had never heard of Che Guevara. Neither had Marie Van Arsdale.

"He was the mastermind behind Castro's victory over Batista in Cuba," Charley said to Marie when she asked who he was.

"He even wrote a book on guerilla warfare. He was a medical doctor, too. He was quite a learned man. And he was a pig," Charley said.

"When we captured him, he was in a one room adobe hut with two little girls. They were all naked. The girls weren't any older than eight. He had raped both of them and was sleeping. He'd told them if they ran away he would find them and cut off their legs. They were terrorized and afraid to leave.

"Imagine that! Two eight-year-old girls! Some learned man! He was a pervert and a coward!"

Charley looked down at the tape recorder.

"Che Guevara cried and begged for his life. He didn't stand up to the torture any better than any other man could. He was supposed to be this fearless military leader. It was easy to be fearless against unarmed peasants and Indians who only had sticks to defend their daughters and wives.

"The great military man, the man of the century as he was called, was a lousy bandit who stole the meager belongings of starving people. After he took everything they had, then he liberated them!"

Jimmy Johnson asked Marty Sporror a question, still not able to put it all in order in his head.

"Why all the secrecy? We were already fighting a war in Vietnam. Evidently this came off without a hitch."

"Think about it," Marty reminded him.

"Think of all the laws that were violated. These weren't Marines. These were U.S. Army Special Forces. There was a press blackout and from what I can gather, we didn't take any prisoners."

"What happened to the prisoners?" Marie asked Charley

"There weren't any," he answered.

"How could it be there weren't prisoners?"

"We shot them and then burned their bodies."

"What about our own wounded?"

"We shot them and then burned their bodies."

"Our own men?" she asked in disbelief.

"Yes," Charley said. "Our own men."

"My God, what did we tell their families?"

"That they were killed or missing in action in Vietnam," Charley said.

He looked away out the window toward Central Park.

"Think about it," he continued. "The CIA fighting secret wars all over the world and when we lost a man, he was either dead or missing in action in Vietnam. Use the same group of men over a period of time and attrition brings the number of those men down. As the number decreases, there are that many less to worry about talking."

"Are you saying our MIAs aren't in Vietnam?"

"I'm not saying anything of the kind. I'm saying I know some of them died and were left behind in South America."

"My God!" Jimmy Johnson said.

"No wonder they want Charley Reed so bad. Charley Reed is it and they have no way to control him."

"That's right," Marty said. "Then Poole turned up and they hit him after they missed Reed."

"How did they know where Reed and Poole were?" Johnson

asked.

"They were using 'Rosie' at USIA. They got a voiceprint of Reed and when he came on, they traced him. That's how they found out about Poole. They realized Poole got by them years ago and they killed him."

Marty looked at Jimmy.

"The Director has his work cut out for him. This will be interesting to see what the big boys decide to do with it. How can they tell the American people we fought a secret war and then killed everyone who fought in it?"

Marie rose and put on her coat.

"When are you leaving New York?" she asked.

"Soon," Charley answered.

"Where are you going?"

"It's probably better that you don't know. I'll be in touch from wherever I am. I won't be able to talk. I can answer questions with sounds indicting yes and no, but once my voice is on then we all are in trouble."

She returned to the studio and asked to see Dan. She played the tape for him.

"It's a story we can't verify. If we can't verify it, we can't run it. From what I heard in there, if the wrong people know that we know, our lives are in jeopardy."

"What about Charley?" Marie asked.

Dan looked out the window.

"What about him?"

"He'll be killed."

"You can do the story then covering his death."

Marie made no comment. She always believed it was her job to report the news and inform the public. It was not a matter of picking and choosing to her. It was a matter of reporting the best possible story at the time.

It was a duty to tell the truth, a responsibility to protect the little person from the rich, the powerful, and even their own government.

Dan told her something she didn't like and Marie wasn't happy. She knew the news was a business. It was ratings, sponsors, market shares, and who looked the best every night. It was not the content. It was who could capture as many homes every evening as possible.

Marie looked at Dan whose head was turned away.

"Where shall we eat tonight?" he asked her.

Marie didn't answer. She was certainly not thinking about food.

Marty Sporror sent Jimmy Johnson home. He catalogued everything and then locked it up in the vault. He left a memorandum for the Director before finally going home. He checked his watch. It was just before ten.

Tina and Charley turned off the lights and went to bed. Before they went into their bedrooms, they checked on the girls.

"What's going to happen?" she asked.

"I can't say," Charley answered her.

"I'm afraid for you," she said.

"Don't be afraid," he said. "It's just all the talk about when I went to South America. It always has been unnerving to me whenever I think about it. It can be very upsetting.

"Sleep tight, Tina," he said.

Marty Sporror undressed quietly, trying not to wake Karen. He felt guilty he wasn't around to help her with the baby. She always seemed to understand when he had to work. She understood the importance of his work.

As he got into bed next to her, he thought how she couldn't possibly understand how important his work that day really was. Marty closed his eyes and realized a part of the United States government, probably with the approval of a former President, broke the law, violated the Constitution, and murdered brave American soldiers.

Marty wondered how this could have happened.

As he lay there in bed, he realized what he learned might never be told. He knew it probably could not be told. No President would ever allow the story to be told. No President could ever admit one of his predecessors had taken part in such an action.

Marie Van Arsdale was having trouble sleeping because all she could think about was Charley Reed and the incredible story he told her.

She knew the survival of a man who placed his trust in her depended on the story being told. Dan had no intention of ever telling it.

That meant the worst for Charley Reed. Marie was upset and when she finally did sleep, it was not a sound or peaceful rest.

She woke at three, again at four, and finally at five she got up and took a shower. She dressed and took a cab to the office. Even though she knew Dan did not want to run the story unless it was verified, she decided to have something ready just in case.

For the next three hours, Marie edited Charley's tape to include the key parts in his own voice and then wrote her own commentary. She prepared the script for the teleprompter and then numbered and catalogued the four and a half minute spot.

Also, while she was there, she made several copies of the hour-long interview with Charley Reed. She knew Dan would want the tape so the story would never get out.

Charley thanked Tina and told her he had to leave. She didn't want him to go, but he insisted. He knew his presence posed a danger to her and the girls.

A half an hour later he was crossing the bridge into New Jersey. He started west toward Pennsylvania. As he drove on, the reality of the situation confronted him.

What he could not understand was his own feeling of well being. He was running from government killers who in the past month and a half had already tried to kill him and had managed to kill Bob Walker, his girl, Alicia and Al Poole. They nearly killed his son, Tom.

Charley realized he wasn't worried so much about himself. He had been a warrior once and even after his time of fighting ended, he still lived the life. In living that life, he accepted death as an inevitable fate. He didn't welcome death, but he didn't fear it either.

In many ways, death might even be a welcome thing.

Maybe it was because of the warrior mentality and the fact he had lived on the run all these years that he now had a well feeling about himself. Maybe it was returning to familiar surroundings. In any event, Charley Reed was relaxed even though he knew his life was in danger.

At ten in the morning Marty and the Director met with the Deputy Attorney General of the United States. Marty had been with the Director since breakfast and he gave the head of the FBI a thorough briefing.

"What about the three tapes?" the Director asked him. "Did you listen to them?"

"No, Sir," Marty answered. "Time was short. I probably could have squeezed them in, but the labels identifying them indicated they could very well be national security items.

"I have always believed it is our job to protect national security. I didn't have the need to know what Eagle Thrust uncovered. I did have the need to know what Eagle Thrust was."

"Very good," Director Hastings told him. "You used excellent judgment. The existence of those tapes definitely casts a different light on the whole matter."

"In what way?" Marty asked.

"Why, it justifies the actions of President Johnson and the CIA," he said. "Che Guevara was the third most powerful man in Cuba, behind Fidel Castro and Raul Castro. If we had the opportunity to capture him outside of Cuba with the invitation of a friendly government, I believe the President acted properly.

"It was a secret operation and the CIA had an obligation to protect the integrity of that operation. If those tapes contained information vital to the defense of our country, enormous latitude could be taken in the name of national security."

Marty Sporror made no comment. He had known Director Hastings for nearly fifteen years and always respected him as a law-abiding enforcement officer. Never in all those years had Marty heard the Director intimate anything even having a hint of an illegality.

He wondered to himself why the mere mention of national security made career-government officials believe the Constitution of the United States, as well as basic human rights, no longer applied. The principle of the greatest good for the greatest amount was the principle they all seemed to use in the name of national security.

Nathan Seeburg rose as Marty and Director Hastings entered his office. He walked from behind the enormous wooden desk and enthusiastically shook both men's hands.

"Come over here and sit down, please," he said leading them to the couches over by the fireplace.

For the next half hour, Marty summarized Operation Eagle Thrust and the subsequent elimination of the men who took part in the operation.

Deputy Attorney General Seeburg listened. He didn't ask any questions. He didn't take any notes. It seemed once the enthusiastic handshake ended and the man settled on the couch across from them, he was unmoved by the story, even the fact nearly three thousand Americans were killed in the name of national security.

Finally, Marty told him that even as they spoke, Charley Reed was probably still fleeing from the CIA. He waited for the Deputy Attorney General to rise up and demand Reed be given federal protection. Seeburg said nothing.

Instead, he sat and remained completely expressionless. When Marty finished, the Deputy Attorney General stood and thanked him and Director Hastings for coming by and then they left.

"What happens now?" Marty asked the Director once they were outside.

"We wait," Hastings answered. "Until we're told, we do not move. As far as we're concerned, the investigation is over."

"What about Reed?" Marty asked still confused.

"What about him?" Hastings said.

Marty did not ask again.

When they were back at headquarters, the Director went to his office and Marty returned to his. Sitting at his desk, he read the report of Ed Manion's suicide.

Immediately, he questioned whether it really was a suicide. Then he thought about meeting with the man a little more than twenty-four hours ago and the tone of his voice.

Marty had the feeling then that something was ending for Manion. Evidently, it was more than just Manion's job.

Jimmy Johnson came into the office while Marty was thinking of Manion.

"How did it go?" he asked.

"It didn't," Marty answered.

"What do you mean?"

"The Deputy Attorney General sat and listened to everything I had to say and then thanked me."

"So?"

"So, that's it."

"What do you mean?" Jimmy asked.

"Exactly what I said," Marty told him.

"You mean we're not taking any action? We're not going to do anything to protect Charley Reed?"

"No."

"What did Director Hastings say?"

"Wait until we get orders."

"So we stop here?" Jimmy asked incredulously.

"That's right," Marty sighed. "Our job was to find out what was going on and what Eagle Thrust was. We did that. Thank you very much."

"But laws are being broken by a government agency!" Jimmy said.

"That's right," Marty answered. "Director Hastings seems to feel it's okay as long as national security is involved."

"What?" Jimmy asked.

"National security is the key. As long as national security is involved, you can get away with murder," Marty said.

Jimmy stood there hardly believing what he was told. His time in the Bureau had been spent upholding the law. He found it difficult to understand when the FBI stood back and allowed the law to be broken.

Marie Van Arsdale met with Dan at eleven and he asked her for the Charley Reed tape.

"Why?" she asked.

"I spoke with the Deputy Attorney General this morning and he asked I forward the tape to him. He feels the national security of the United States is involved."

"You spoke with the Deputy Attorney General?" she said sounding impressed.

"Yes," he said. "Nathan D. Seeburg and I go way back together. Old Nate and I used to chase around the bars together when he was just a young ambulance chaser. I think it would be best if we end this Charley Reed story tonight.

" I think we should focus on the investigation of him in Los Angeles. We should talk about how they are considering bringing racketeering charges against him and link Al Poole's death to drugs. That will explain Walker's death and why Reed is on the run."

Listening to Dan, Marie realized she had to do as he said. She had no choice.

Dan spoke to the Deputy Attorney General of the United States. He could pick up the phone and speak to a Cabinet level official. Obviously, he was a very powerful man. Dan not only reported the news, he had the ability to manufacture the news, too.

Yes, she thought to herself, it certainly was manufacturing with the direction and collusion of the highest-ranking law enforcement officer in the entire country. Marie handed Dan the tape and then excused herself by saying she had a lot of work to do to get ready for the new broadcast.

Marie went back to her office and prepared for the new slant on the story. She began and then began again and again.

She had her assistant get her background information on the U.S. District Attorney's investigation. They pulled out Bob Walker's criminal record and began to weave the story into the news.

CHAPTER FIFTY-SEVEN

It was just before three when Marie Van Arsdale's phone rang. When she recognized the voice on the other end, she was shocked.

"What do you want?" she asked.

"What have you done with Eagle Thrust?" the voice asked.

"Nothing," she said. "I can't verify the story."

"They're throwing Charley Reed to the wolves," the voice said.

"What do you mean?" she asked, realizing she was part of what he was talking about.

"The FBI has recovered the files of over a thousand men who took part in Eagle Thrust. As of right now, all but three are dead. Charley Reed is one of them. The other two are in the CIA and they are the ones trying to kill him.

"The FBI took the recovered information to Deputy Attorney General Seeburg this morning. He is taking no action and is leaving Charley Reed with no protection. They're going to allow the CIA to kill him."

Marie knew the man on the other end of the phone was verification. It was not textbook verification, but it was a second source. Dan and then Jason originally canned the story because it couldn't be verified. If she could keep him on the phone, she would have a thin sort of verification.

"Don't hang up," she said.

There was a desperate tone to her voice. Without telling him, she turned on the tape recorder installed on her phone so she could have a record of important phone conversations.

"I talked to Charley Reed yesterday," she said. "I need to verify some of the things he told me. Can you do that for me?"

"Yes," the man said.

"Was Operation Eagle Thrust a military invasion of Bolivia?"

"Yes," he answered. "I told you that yesterday."

"I know," she said.

"Was it sponsored by the CIA and was it against a revolution backed by Cuba, led by Che Guevara?"

"Yes," he said.

"Did the American soldiers capture Che Guevara?"

"Yes."

"Did they interrogate him and ask him about the Kennedy assassination?"

"Yes," he said.

As she asked her questions, he realized she had indeed spoken to Charley Reed.

"Did they interrogate him regarding Cuban military and island defenses?"

"Yes," he said.

"Since Operation Eagle Thrust was concluded in October 1967, is it true the CIA has been eliminating the men who took part in the action?"

"Yes," he said.

"Did Charley Reed take part in Operation Eagle Thrust?" Marie asked.

"Yes."

"Is his life presently in danger?"

"Yes."

"Did Alexander Poole take part in Eagle Thrust?"

"Yes."

"Is that why he was killed?"

"We believe so," he answered.

Marie was silent, not quite believing she had the verification she needed. She couldn't believe this man had called her unsolicited. She wondered why.

"Thank you," she said.

"Why have you done this?"

"Because," he began, "there's something evil in our government."

"What's that?" she asked him.

"It's called national security," he said.

"Over a thousand men were killed directly or indirectly as a result of Operation Eagle Thrust. The excuse we're given and the way it is justified, all the way to the President of the United States, is national security.

"They're telling us basic human rights and the Constitution don't apply when national security is involved. Well, I have a question I want you to ask them for me."

"Sure," she said. "Anything you'd like."

"I want to know who determines what is in the best interest of national security and what isn't? Is it the Director of the CIA? Is it the Director of the FBI?" he asked

She didn't answer him.

"Who do you think it should be?" he asked her.

"I don't know," Marie answered honestly.

"I don't either," he said. "I wouldn't even begin to make that kind of decision."

"Neither would I," Marie said.

"That's right," he said. "And you know why? We're rational human beings just trying to do our jobs.

"My God!" he exclaimed. "We aren't any better than the Nazis! The Deputy Attorney General just shrugged his shoulders this morning. He and the Director of the FBI feel what happened has been done in the name of national security!"

"Are they taking any action?" she asked.

"No," he said. "When Charley Reed dies, Operation Eagle Thrust dies, too."

Operation Eagle Thrust and the sake of national security would bring death across three generations. The very people within our government entrusted with the safety of the citizens of the country were all sitting by doing nothing.

"So it doesn't matter," she said to the voice on the other end of the phone.

"No," he admitted to her.

"What are we doing? What is our purpose in all of this?" she asked.

"I don't know," he said. "It's depressing to me."

"It must be," she agreed.

"How long have you been in the Bureau?"

"That's none of your business," he said. "You understand that."

"Yes," she laughed. "I do. I just want you to know I consider you a great patriot."

"Thank you," he said. "But that's not why I'm doing this."

"Why, then?" she asked.

"It's time for the killing to stop. This operation should have ended years ago.

"We have some misguided people in high positions in our government. Those people need to be identified and run out. If I can help expose them and save some innocent lives, especially a man who only did his duty, that's all I want."

"Thanks," Marie said.

"Your welcome, lady," the man said and then he hung up the phone.

Marie Van Arsdale sat for a few minutes before she even moved. Then she reran the tape and listened to the phone conversation. She listened and then listened again.

What a brave man, she thought. What a good and honest man.

Marie Van Arsdale prepared for the evening news broadcast. Jason left the office early and Dan was in Washington, D.C. for a Presidential dinner and reception at the Kennedy Center. Marie was anchoring the news by herself. When she called for a change on the Charley Reed story, no one thought anything of it

Jimmy Johnson returned to his office on Constitution Avenue just before four-thirty. He didn't check his messages. Instead, he walked into Marty Sporror's office.

"What's up?" Marty asked.

Jimmy reached into his pocket and withdrew a typed letter. He placed it on Marty's desk. Then he placed his identification, his weapon, and his building entry card on top of it.

"I'm resigning," Jimmy said.

Marty Sporror was shocked. Jimmy's resignation took him totally by surprise. The fact Jimmy resigned was the shocking part; the reason was not.

As he sat there holding the resignation, Marty considered doing the same thing. He considered it, then wondered what good it would do. He decided he probably could accomplish more by staying and fighting from within and he pointed it out to Johnson.

"I've had enough," Johnson said.

"This isn't the Bureau I thought I joined. We have experts falsifying evidence and we have people selling information to the Mafia. Now we are sitting back and allowing the CIA to kill people and I don't just mean Charley Reed."

"What are you talking about?" Marty asked.

Johnson produced a list of names. They were men who were being sought by the FBI for questioning in regard to the World Trade Center attacks.

"The ones marked with a red checkmark are dead."

"What?" Marty asked.

"They're dead. The CIA killed them while they were interrogating them, or they committed suicide to keep from being forced to talk. But they're dead just the same, and dead is dead."

Marty didn't answer him.

"I'm done. The list is a gift to you."

Johnson turned and walked out of the office.

Marty realized he had to stay and make a difference. As he decided he would stay, he wondered where to start. He looked at the list and then he looked down at the report on Ed Manion's suicide.

What was next?

Maybe there would be an automobile accident and Charley Reed would be killed. Yes, he said to himself. That would be it. It would happen and then there would be no one else except for the two CIA agents. Charley Reed would slip away just like Al Poole.

Marty picked up the phone and called the Bureau's operations officer.

"Jack," he said. "This is Marty. I need someone located."

Marty listened and then spoke again.

"Yes. I need him fast. The CIA is probably already after him. If we don't get to him and put him under our protective custody, he'll be dead."

There was a pause while Marty listened and then he continued.

"I know," he said.

"I know," he said again. "Thanks."

"Yes, I want it in all states. He's driving his car the last we knew and we haven't had any trace of him since the shooting at the Walker house."

Marty listened once more and then spoke.

"Fine. I'll send down the particulars."

He hung up the phone and took out his file on Charley Reed and walked the file down himself.

By the time the evening news came on, the national information system that shared police and FBI information had Charley Reed's picture and the description and license number of his car. The instructions were to take him into protective custody and hold for the FBI.

The only problem was Charley Reed was driving his truck. His car was in a parking garage in Washington, D.C. While they were looking for Charley Reed's car, he parked his truck in front of Cindy Ganley's home.

He got out of the truck and walked up to the door. He rang the bell and waited. Moments later, Cindy answered the door.

"Remember me?" he asked.

Cindy bit her bottom lip.

"Yes," she said. "I remember you. Come in."

Chapter Fifty-eight

In her opening segment Marie said nothing about the Charley Reed story, but when she returned after the commercial break, she led off with the most powerful story she had ever been associated with.

"Good evening," she began. "A shocking story has been confirmed today.

"In August 1967 the CIA, using nearly three thousand men on active duty in the U.S. Army and the U.S. Air Force, responded to the request of the Bolivian government to invade Bolivia and defeat the revolutionary forces in their country being led by Ernesto Che Guevara. Guevara was a former Cuban military leader and number three man to Fidel Castro during the Cuban Revolution.

"In an interview with Charley Reed yesterday, confirmed by FBI sources today, Reed took part in Operation Eagle Thrust, which defeated and annihilated the revolutionary forces as well as the capture, interrogation, torture, and execution of Che Guevara."

The commentary ended there and excerpts of the recording were run. As Charley heard his voice, he watched a file film of Che Guevara. The recording ended and then Marie Van Arsdale came back on.

"Of the thousand men taking part in Operation Eagle Thrust, nearly six hundred men were casualties in Bolivia, but were listed as killed or missing in action in the Vietnam conflict. The CIA, under the authority of then President Lyndon Johnson, carried out this deception.

"Since Operation Eagle Thrust ended October 29, 1967 all but three of the men taking part in the operation have died from causes ranging from war, to murder, to drug overdose, to accident.

"As late as last Wednesday, Alexander Poole, a staff sergeant in the Air Force in 1967, was brutally murdered in the kitchen of his home by a person or persons unknown. Charley Reed was nearly a victim of an attack that cost the lives of two friends and very nearly the life of his son. Our sources in the FBI have stated the dead attackers were using registered government weapons and were in the employ of the CIA."

Marie paused and made strong eye contact into the television camera for the viewing audience.

"Deputy Attorney General Nathan Seeburg has had this information since this morning at ten o'clock Eastern time. As of this broadcast, neither Deputy Attorney General Seeburg nor any government agency has acted to protect Charles Reed, a brave soldier, and an American citizen."

Marie stopped and looked directly into the camera. The network broke away for a commercial.

Marie walked off the set. The crew surrounded her. She just broke one of the most exciting stories of the decade and everyone was surprised. Only two or three people were aware of the substitution she made. She couldn't believe the impact the story made right there in the studio.

"The switchboard is going crazy," one of the assistant producers told her.

"As soon as the story ended, we were hit with a flood of telephone calls. Everyone wants to know more. They want to know what's being done.

"They want to know about brothers, husbands, and sons reported killed or missing in 1967. That story has opened up the floodgates. You hit a nerve and the American people are screaming out."

Marie went to the dressing room and took off her makeup and began to change her clothes. She was about finished when the producer knocked on the door.

"Yes," she said.

"Marie, when you're finished dressing, could I meet with you please?"

"Sure," she said.

"Where?"

"Your office is fine," he said.

Marie finished dressing and went up to her office. The producer was waiting for her and two of the assistants were with him. The producer was sitting in the chair behind her desk and rose when she entered.

"I spoke with Jason," he said. "He told me he didn't approve the story on Operation Eagle Thrust. He said he specifically told you not to run the story."

Marie nodded, indicating what he was saying was true.

"Jason told me to fire you.

"He said you were to get only your personal items and be out of the building in half an hour. Then he told me to tell you to get the next jet home. He said to say you were done for all time. He said he'd see to that.

"I'm to remind you of our copyright contract with you and I'm to escort you to the door and advise security you are not to return.

"Do you understand?"

"Yes," she said, her voice cracking with emotion.

Marie quickly packed what few personal items she had in her desk. As she walked out of the office and down the hall to the elevator, she felt like crying. Marie knew she couldn't show any tears; she was a professional.

She had verified the story and once she did, she ran it. Because she told the truth instead of the lie Jason wanted, she was fired and her career ruined. It was not fair, she thought.

She wanted to cry, but refused to give them the satisfaction. Marie got off the elevator and walked directly to the front door without stopping or looking back. When she was out on the street, she turned and walked away from the building. Instead of hailing a cab as she had in the past, she wanted to walk.

She never did stop for a cab. She walked back to the hotel and went up to her room to pack.

Marty Sporror was on his way home when Marie Van Arsdale went on the air. He had no way of knowing she was going to break the story. He didn't know she even had the information.

Director Hastings called for Marty at home. Karen answered and told him Marty wasn't home.

Tom Reed was with his mother in her townhouse when Marie Van Arsdale's broadcast came on the air. Joanna Reed could hardly believe what she was hearing.

She remembered Charley's nightmares and the violence. She remembered him walking in his sleep and how she would wake in the middle of the night and find him gone. In many ways, it had been as hard on her as it had been on him. She had no idea what she was letting herself in for when she married him.

Tom listened to the entire report without saying so much as a word. He listened to the part about the killing of Bob Walker and

Connie Knapp. He heard his name and realized how close he had been to being killed, too.

"He saved my life," he said to his mother.

Joanna thought about it and was angry.

"He almost got you killed," she said.

"I don't think that's fair," he told her.

"I know you don't like him. He didn't know they would send someone after him. How can you blame him for that?"

"I don't know," she said. "I blame him for leaving me and then thinking he can just walk into your life after all these years."

Tom was quiet. He listened to his mother and inside he thought what a short memory she must have.

Tom did not blame his father. He blamed her.

When his father was gone, she gave him to his father's parents. He always wondered what was wrong with him. Other boys his age lived with their mothers. Their parents were either divorced or their fathers were dead like his. In either case, they still lived with their mothers. He never knew anyone who lived with their grandparents. Tom remembered how he hated being different.

"Did he ever talk to you about being there?" he asked.

"Once he did," she said.

"What did he say?" Tom asked.

Joanna didn't want to remember that night, but for her son she did. As she remembered, she could not help but lose some of the hate and anger she felt for Charley.

"You must remember," Tom said. "Tell me about it."

"Tom," she said. "Your father didn't talk about the war to me very often. When he did, he talked about a lot of things at once and tried to be vague. A lot of the things he told me were incomplete or changed around. He admitted that to me many times."

"Tell me about the one time you remember," Tom asked again.

"He didn't talk about specifics," she said.

"We were in college together and someone had written 'Che' on a wall and it really made him mad."

Tom listened as his mother told him the story.

"I mean really mad," Joanna said. "He was swearing and using language I'd never heard put together in the combinations he used."

Tom laughed, listening to his mother talk about his father.

"I didn't understand what one name written on a wall could do to someone to make him so angry.

"He started telling me who Che was and what he stood for and why stupid college students had no right to put his name anywhere."

"What was Dad like?" Tom asked.

"He was a wild man. It upset him for nearly a week. He got into a fight in a bar that day and nearly sent the guy he fought with to the hospital. Your father was just crazy.

"That night," she continued, "he had horrible nightmares.

"He was speaking Spanish and I never knew he could speak Spanish. I'd heard him speak Vietnamese in his sleep, but never Spanish. He was screaming and really carrying on. It was so bad I woke him and I didn't like to wake him up ever."

"Why?" Tom asked.

"Because, she answered. "Waking your father could get you punched in the mouth. He woke up violently. He was always scared and he might believe he was in danger and try to defend himself. You shook him and ducked out of the way."

"What happened when you woke him?"

"He swung at me, but I wasn't in the way."

"Did you talk to him?"

"Yes," she said. "I talked to him. I asked him what he was dreaming about and he told me. I wished he hadn't."

"What did he tell you?" Tom asked.

"Really, Tom," she asked. "Why is this so important to you? What do you want to know for?"

"Because I almost was killed over it," he said to her. "If you know, tell me."

Joanna collected her thoughts before she began.

"It was like the girl said on the news. He went to South America and fought the Cubans. I guess he fought them for a few months and then one night, quite by accident, captured Che Guevara.

"Your father told me he was with two really young girls. I mean young, Tom. Like less than ten years old. It really disgusted him.

"It bothered him years after it was over. I guess they weren't going to leave any witnesses and the soldiers were ordered to shoot the little girls. Your father was one of those soldiers."

"Why would he have to shoot the little girls?" Tom asked in disbelief.

"Probably for the same reason they tried to kill you and your father," Joanna said. "Someone decided they never wanted the story to get out."

"Well, it's out now," Tom said.

"Yes, I guess it is," Joanna agreed.

"What else did he say?"

"He was there when the boys from the CIA came to interrogate Che. He told me they really worked him over. He didn't say much about it, but he said it went on for nearly two days straight.

"At one point they thought Che might die, so they let him rest. I guess what they did to him was so brutal your dad actually threw up while it was going on.

"The other night at Walker's house, the one agent had his neck snapped. No one even has to tell me," she said. "That was your father's work. He was violent like that when we were married. The wars he fought did that. Once he was a peaceful young man."

"If he was so violent, why did you marry him?"

"He wasn't like that when I married him," she said. "He was hurting and I didn't know it."

"What do you mean?" he asked his mother.

"When I married your father, he seemed so clean and strong. He was my hero and I depended on him for everything. There wasn't anything he couldn't do. He was a great athlete."

"He was?" Tom asked surprised. He was genuinely curious and this was one of the few times she had ever told him about his father.

"Yes, he was. You got that from him, not me. He loved sports. He was a quarterback for the flag football team his last year in the service and he played on the softball team, too."

Tom enjoyed listening to his mother talk about his dad. He sat and watched her face, realizing for the first time in years she was remembering happy times they shared when they were married.

"What happened?" Tom asked.

"He was hurt," she said.

"I never knew he was hurt inside. He looked okay. All the wounds outside healed. He didn't even have any visible scars on his body. I never even thought he might have trouble living with some of the things he had done.

"I was young and didn't know any better. I lost respect for him and hated it when he touched me. I eventually hated him."

Tom looked at his mother's face. He appreciated her honesty and thought he was beginning to understand something about her.

"Do I remind you of him?" he asked. "Is that why you didn't want me around all the time? Was I that much like him?"

Joanna looked at her son and was saddened and surprised by the directness of his questions. She didn't know how to answer him. She never wanted to even consider the questions he had just asked.

When Marty Sporror got home, he was surprised when Karen told him Director Hastings had called. He immediately thought someone called and told Hastings about the Bureau bulletin he had put out on Charley Reed.

"What does he want calling you at home?" Karen asked.

"I don't know," Marty said. "Director Hastings doesn't make a habit of calling people at home."

"Are you in trouble?" Karen asked.

He forced a smile.

"Maybe," he said. "Why don't I call and find out for sure."

Without hesitating or even taking off his topcoat, he called the Director at his home.

"Martin," the Director said. "I'm glad you called back so promptly. Thank you."

"What's up?" Marty asked.

"Have you seen Marie Van Arsdale tonight?"

"No, sir," he answered.

"Someone in the Bureau gave her information on Eagle Thrust and Charley Reed."

"Jimmy Johnson," Marty said.

"What?" the Director asked.

"Johnson resigned this afternoon," Marty told his boss.

"You're probably right," Hastings agreed.

"That's history now. We have bigger problems."

"How?" Marty asked.

"The bitch accused us of doing nothing to help Reed. We need to cover our asses and cover them fast!"

"They're already covered," Marty replied.

"How so?" the Director asked.

"At five this afternoon I put out a nationwide bulletin to pick him up and place him in protective custody. I did it under my authority and at risk of losing my job. I realize it was against your orders, but I did what I thought was right."

"Great!" Hastings said. "You just saved our collective assess.

"We can issue a statement we purposely leaked the information about Reed and put out a bulletin just before she went on the air. We'll say we want Reed to come in from the cold, so to speak, so we can protect him. We're going to come out of this smelling like roses. Thank you, Martin. Good work!"

Once Marie Van Arsdale got to her hotel room she broke down in tears. She knew what she was risking when she did the opposite of what Jason told her to do. She knew the risk when she took it. It was just that she couldn't get the face of the beautiful young pregnant woman out of her head.

When she listened to Charley Reed in his hotel room, she realized as good as the United States was for the majority of the people, it was cruel and heartless to the people it didn't care about or those who had outlived their usefulness. Charley Reed was one of those who were no longer useful.

Tina would be a witness and she didn't serve their purposes either. Marie wouldn't be able to live with herself if she sat back and did nothing.

She would eventually have hated herself had she lied like Jason told her to do. Instead, with the verification of Charley Reed's story, she ran it and told the truth. She did what was right and she lost her job.

Marie opened her suitcase on the bed and began packing. She was folding her blouses when the phone rang.

"Hello?" she said hesitantly.

"Marie Van Arsdale?" the man on the phone asked.

"Yes?"

"This is Martin Vanderburn with CNN. I saw your program tonight. I'd like to talk to you about coming to work for us."

CHAPTER FIFTY-NINE

For Cindy, when she opened the door and saw Charley, it was a little like a dream come true and a lot like a slap in the face. She didn't know what to say. She didn't know how to explain what she had done to him years ago. Calmly, she invited him into her home.

Charley entered and she closed the door behind him. She reached out with her hand and touched him on his arm.

"I'm sorry," she said.

Charley looked and her and said nothing. What could he say? He understood the pain she was feeling. She had just lost her son. There was no body to bury and no real way for her to make a final closure within herself.

Now, he was back.

He understood it even better now that he had been with Tina. His presence was as reassuring as it was hurtful for Tina. Evidently, his son had many of his own mannerisms. Being around him in many ways was like being around Chuck. But as nice as that might have been for a time, it was equally unpleasant and painful. His presence reminded them of what they had lost.

Similarities aside, nothing could ever bring back the man who was taken away from them.

"I'm sorry," she said again.

"I know," he finally answered. "I know."

She wiped some tears from her face.

"You look great," she said. "You are fit and you have all of your hair."

"Of course. What did you expect?"

"I don't know," she answered honestly. "I really don't."

She reached out and took his hand.

"Come in and sit down with me."

Charley followed her into the living room.

It was a large room with a bay window that looked out into the front lawn. A field stone fireplace was at the opposite end on the wall with a heavy wooden mantle above the opening. A comfortable looking sofa was in front of the window with a polished coffee table in front of it. Opposite the table was a matching love seat. Near the fireplace were a wooden rocking chair and a recliner. Large original paintings of seascapes hung on the walls and pictures of her children in gold frames were scattered about the room on the end tables and the mantle. A large scented candle was in the center of the coffee table.

"This is lovely," he commented.

"Thank you," she answered.

"Have a seat," she offered.

Charley sat down in the love seat. Cindy sat opposite him on the couch.

"I saw you on television. I saw Chuck's picture and I knew," he said quietly.

Cindy nodded. It was a nod of agreement.

"I knew right away."

"I was flying here when I got in that mess at the airport," he told her. "If I hadn't seen you and pictures of Chuck, I would still be in my safe little existence back in California."

"So I did it to you again," she said in a broken voice.

She tried to clear her throat and hold back the tears at the same time.

Charley laughed a small laugh. It made him smile and close his eyes at the same time.

"I guess you did," he said. "You always did have my number."

Cindy nodded again. Once more it was one of agreement. Cindy looked at his face and realized the tremendous strain he was under.

They visited for hours. She told him about Chuck and she told him about her life. He shared his with her, too. Then he realized the time and said he should be going.

"No," she said. "You're staying here."

"Won't the neighbors talk?" he joked with her.

"The hell with the neighbors," she said back to him.

Then he asked if he could watch the news.

"I want to see what that news broad is going to say about me tonight."

They went into the family room and she turned on the television. When Marie Van Arsdale broke the story Charley exploded.

"Holy shit!" Charley exclaimed, rising to his feet. "She did it!

She really did it! I can't believe it! The chick stuck her neck out and did the story."

"What does this mean?" Cindy asked.

"It means I'm close to being safe," he said.

"Once the story is out and people believe it, no one needs to kill me anymore."

"When will that be?" she asked.

"Soon," Charley said. "Real soon."

Cindy watched his face.

"Are you all right?" she asked.

Charley sat back down and took his time answering. He swallowed and took a deep breath.

"Yes. I'm fine now. I can't believe what she did."

"I know," she said.

"How are you?" he asked, looking over at Cindy.

"I'm okay, I guess," she answered him.

Charley was quiet for a while. He turned off the television and changed the subject.

"What was he like growing up?" he asked.

"He was a nice boy. He was never a problem and everyone liked him."

"Did he play any sports?"

"Yes," Cindy said remembering. "He was just like you. He wanted to play everything, but really didn't fill out until he was seventeen."

"What did he play?"

"Baseball," she said. "What else?

"He was a pitcher, too. I never missed a single game. I couldn't help but think of you when I watched him. He was so serious out there."

Charley remembered back while Cindy told him of their son. He remembered being in love with her when they were just teenagers. He remembered wanting to pitch for the New York Yankees and wanting to marry her.

"He was a skier, too," she said. "Living where we did, you had to ski or it was a long winter.

"He was built like you, lean and strong. He had a good mind. He was so smart it scared me sometimes.

"He'd look at me and then he'd look at Adam and try to see who he took after. You never met him. But, he was you from the day he was born. Each year he looked more and more like the Charley Reed I was in love with, and each year I wondered what became of you.

"I always wondered about you, but I never did anything about it. I had him and it was better that I didn't know."

"Why was it better?" he asked.

"Because I wasn't happy," Cindy said.

"Why didn't you do something about it?"

Cindy didn't answer the question. Instead, she continued talking about their son.

"He asked me the same thing. He was in college then. He was just a freshman and home at Thanksgiving. He didn't like the way Adam treated me and even told him about it. The two of them had words and I finally had to get between them."

"So?" he asked expecting an answer to his question.

"We were a Mormon family," she answered.

"You were a Catholic," he said back to her.

"I was a Catholic, but the children were all raised in his faith."

Charley understood what she was saying and even understood why things were the way she described. What he couldn't understand was why her husband didn't care about her happiness.

"Adam only cared about himself," Cindy said. "I knew that almost from the very beginning. I wanted to leave just before Chuck was born."

"Why didn't you?"

"My mother stopped me. I told her what I was going to do and she tried to talk me out of it. I had my mind made up and the day I was going to leave, she flew out to Salt Lake to stop me. The next day I went into labor and then I couldn't go anywhere."

"Where would you have gone?" Charley asked.

Cindy looked out the window.

"What difference does it make now? I didn't leave. I had four children by him."

"You're right," Charley answered. "It doesn't make any difference now."

Cindy knew he was hurt and felt cheated.

"I'm sorry," she said. "I made a mistake. I really did love you."

"Don't worry about it," Charley told her. "That Charley Reed you were in love with died.

"He died when he woke up in a hospital bed in the Philippines and couldn't remember what happened to him. The Charley Reed who came home wasn't any good for anyone. That's why it wasn't any great loss when he finally died."

"What do you mean?" she asked. "People loved you. You had

friends and a nice family. What happened to you?"

"I don't know," he said. "Maybe I quit like you did."

"Quit!" Cindy said, wanting to be angry with him.

But she knew in a way he was right. She had quit. She took the easy way out and married Adam instead of Charley. She stayed with Adam even though she didn't love him. Even when she caught Adam cheating on her, she didn't divorce him. Cindy only threw him out of her bedroom.

"You're right," she admitted. "I did quit.

"I quit early and raised my children. What I should have done and what I did, are two different things."

"That's the story of all our lives," Charley said sadly. "There's so much I should have done. The time just kept passing by and I kept making excuses for myself and each day seemed to turn into a year. I was successful in business, but I've been a failure in life."

Cindy listened and agreed with him about how fast time passed.

"All of the children grew up too fast. They were babies yesterday and now they're as old as I feel. I know I'm older. I just don't feel like I am."

"Who does?" he asked.

"I just feel stupid that I've wasted half my life."

Cindy looked at the time. She smiled at Charley.

"You're going to take me out to dinner," she said.

"I am?"

"Yes. I'm meeting Julie at eight. You are going to be my escort."

"Julie?" he asked.

"My baby and Chuck's sister. She was his favorite and he was hers. She has really taken this hard. Seeing you might cheer her up."

Chuck parked his truck in the driveway and brought in his suitcase. Cindy put him in a guest room and he washed up and changed his clothes. When he came downstairs, Cindy had backed her car out of the garage and was waiting for him. She handed him the keys.

"You drive," she told him. "We're going to the Greentree Inn."

Charley knew the area. They passed South Hills Village and Mount Lebanon High School. The area was familiar to them both. South Hills Village was a huge mall built where there had once been a golf driving range. Mount Lebanon High School was where Cindy and Charley would have gone to school had they not both gone to Catholic high schools. He turned left on Cochoran Road and then right onto Greentree Road.

"Are you sure you want to do this?" he asked her.

"Yes," she said. "I want you with me.

"I know how uncomfortable you feel. When I saw you on television, I was uncomfortable, too. I even resented you a bit. It was Julie who reminded me how you must be feeling.

"She reminded me of how I felt about you once and how you hadn't done a thing to hurt any of us all these years. She said if anyone had been truly hurt, it was you. When I thought about it, she was right. I need you to be here with us. This is probably the most terrible month of my life and I want you with me."

Charley had tears in his eyes. He looked straight ahead, hoping Cindy couldn't see him cry. Soon the tears ran down his face and Cindy reached out with her hand and wiped them away. He turned his face to her and forced a smile.

Cindy began to cry, too.

Charley reached out and touched Cindy's face. Even though they didn't say it, they knew what it was all about. Together they cried for the loss of their son and for the loss of their chance together many years ago.

"Okay," he said to her.

It was just before eight when he pulled her car into the parking lot. Julie was inside waiting for her mother. She was surprised when she walked in with a man.

"Julie," she said. "This is Charley Reed, your brother's father."

Julie stood there with her mouth open. She was taken by surprise.

"I could tell," Julie said, extending her hand to him.

As he took it, she suddenly hugged him. "I'm glad you're here. I really am."

Charley held the young woman and closed his eyes to keep from crying again. Cindy joined the two of them, putting her arms around them both.

"They can't seat us for an hour," Julie said to her mother.

"Oh, my," Cindy said.

"They have a bar," Charley said.

"They sure do," Julie said.

"What's wrong with the bar?" he asked.

"Nothing," she said. "The bar is fine."

Cindy was surprised, but she said nothing. She went along with Julie and Charlie. Julie took his arm and stayed with him as they walked into the bar.

Charley went to sit on the end, allowing the women to sit together, but Julie wanted him in between herself and her mother.

Julie ordered a vodka and tonic, Cindy ordered a glass of white wine, and Charley ordered Johnnie Walker Black on the rocks.

As she sat on the barstool, Cindy thought about another time she had been in a bar. She had a glass of wine then, just as she was having now. She had been with Adam and she was still in college.

It was the night she told him she was pregnant with his child. She realized the irony of it all. The first time she lied about a baby who was yet to be born. Now she was with the real father following his son's death after he had grown to be a man.

The lie and its impact on their lives made her cry.

Charley was sitting at her side and put his arm around her shoulder. He said nothing. She put her face his shoulder and sobbed. Charley's other arm surrounded and held her until she eventually quieted.

Julie didn't say a word. What could she say?

Charley reached for a clean bar napkin and wiped Cindy's eyes and face for her. When he finished, he tenderly kissed her on the forehead.

"Thank you," she said to him.

She looked up at his face. It was strong and handsome. It was a face that felt pain, yet was able to smile even as it was hurting.

Cindy could not help but remember that same face many years before, young and innocent. Now, it was marked with lines of time, pain, sorrow and strength.

"You've kissed me four times today."

"Except for our son, you're the only man to kiss me in years. I like it," she said as she took his face and kissed his cheek.

Charley was embarrassed and surprised

In a move that surprised both Julie and Charley, Cindy took a huge drink of her wine. In a moment her glass was empty.

"I'd like another glass of wine," Cindy said.

"Sure," Charley agreed and he ordered himself another drink, too.

"What happened to us?" she asked. "What was wrong with our generation? What didn't our parents know we needed? Why are we like this today?"

"Wow!" Charley exclaimed. "That was a mouthful to ask all at once. Where should I start?"

"Start with you and me," she said, looking into his eyes.

"Why did I do what I did? Why didn't I marry you?"

Julie was surprised at her mother's bluntness. She wondered if it was the wine.

Charley's voice was gentle, filled with compassion and tenderness.

"I told you the past is the past. The decisions we made then are already done. There isn't any way to go back and live them over. Even if we could, we'd probably do the exact same thing again.

"Somewhere, everything that happens in our lives is written down. We have a free choice to do what we want. It's just that the writer already knows what we're going to choose. All we can do is learn by the good and the bad choices and make the most of it."

"So what are we supposed to do?" she asked.

"Just like I said," Charley told her. "There's not a blessed thing we can do to change anything up to this very instant. Take right now and decide what you want for your life and get it. Nothing else matters."

Cindy sipped her wine and watched his face.

He was right; the past was gone.

Cindy wasn't sure what she wanted or even needed, but she did know this man made her feel better. She had just endured the most awful thing a mother can endure, hearing her son was dead.

Chuck had been his son, too.

Cindy realized he probably was feeling the same way and also feeling cheated by life. Or was it cheated by death?

She continued to watch his face and remembered the tenderness and passion they had for one another long ago. Then there was Adam, her husband. There had never been passion. There had never been tenderness. But, what could she expect from an arranged marriage?

Julie excused herself and went to the rest room.

"Why are you here?" she asked him. Her head was light from the wine.

"Because you needed me.

"And because I needed you, too," he said, his eyes filling with tears.

"What am I supposed to do?" she asked him.

"What do you want to do?

"I'm not young like I was," she said.

"Neither one of us are, Cindy."

"I mean I'm older. I've had five children. My body isn't like it was." Cindy dropped her gaze from his face and looked out into the distance.

"I'd probably disappoint you. I haven't been with a man in a long time."

"Do you want to me with me?" he asked quietly.

"Yes," she said.

Charley did not say another word.

Julie returned. Then they were seated and had dinner. Julie was full of questions. Charley answered them as best as he could.

Cindy was glad. She had been right. Charley was the medicine Julie needed. It took her mind off of her brother at least for the time they were at dinner.

He paid the bill and they went outside. They said goodbye to Julie and started home.

Cindy sat next to him as he drove and her heart was pounding. When the car finally stopped in the driveway, he took her into his arms and kissed her.

The kiss was different from any he had given her that day. He held her with an intensity that made them both tremble. His mouth covered hers and his tongue slid between her lips and into her mouth.

Her hands held his face and ran across his ears and through his hair.

"Come on," he said breathing heavily as he broke the embrace.

When they entered the house, they didn't bother turning on any lights. He took her hand and led her upstairs into her bedroom to the foot of the bed.

"Should we be doing this?" she asked.

He didn't answer her. Instead, he slid her coat from her shoulders and let it fall to the floor. Once more he took her into his arms and kissed her.

Cindy's mind flooded with emotion and passion. She was in a man's arms and her body was catching fire from the strength of their desire for each other.

His hand ran up her back and gently unzipped her dress. He slid the dress from her shoulders and pushed it to the floor. She stood there in her slip and high heels as he kissed her again and again.

Then he pulled the slip over her head. He was still fully dressed as he laid her down on the bed and unfastened her bra. She closed her eyes while he kissed her again and his mouth left hers and went first to one breast and then the other.

Her nipples grew hard and she felt herself quicken with desire for him. Then his mouth left her body and he was pulling her hose and her panties down her legs. Cindy felt the cool air of the room and tried to turn on her side and cover her small belly. His mouth was on her skin, gently kissing all of her.

"Oh, God!" she cried out.

"Oh, God!" she cried again and her body shuddered as his lips brushed her skin.

Then he was gone from her.

Cindy opened her eyes to watch him undo his shirt and take it off, allowing it to fall to the floor. His chest was broad and the muscles in his arms stood out as he opened his pants and pushed them down his legs.

The years of indifference with Adam evaporated as every inch of her being came alive. She reached out and touched him. She heard him gasp as he fell to the bed across her body.

He kissed her again and again and she cried out as her whole body shook from the center of her soul.

She could feel his hardness rest on her stomach and wanted him more than she had wanted anything in so long. When Charley entered her, she could feel him fill her body and Cindy felt a man for the first time in many years.

"I love you," she cried out.

"I love you," she said as she had years before.

His body thrust forward and when he was as far inside her as he could reach, she felt him stop and raise his face from her shoulder. She opened her eyes to find his face directly above hers. His eyes were open and watching her face.

"I love you," she said again.

"I love you, too," he said staring into her eyes. "I always have loved you."

She reached up and pulled his mouth to hers. As she kissed him, she felt him explode and their love mingle.

Her body had never been so open or vulnerable. It had never felt so good. Her hands ran through his hair and across the bare skin on his back. His body collapsed within her and she accepted him. Cindy felt his heart pounding against her breast and then he rolled off to one side.

"I love you, Cindy," he said once more before his eyes closed and his arms pulled her close. Then he fell asleep.

"I love you, too," she whispered as she lay cradled in his arms. Tears filled her eyes and rolled down her face. "I love you and I always have."

They slept peacefully.

Cindy Ganley woke first and looked at the man next to her.

She was overtaken by the sadness of losing her son and began to cry. The tears were silent. Her brain screamed out in agony, yet the room was still silent. Tears ran across her face and soaked the pillow.

An inch away from her was her lover and the father of her dead son. Her body shook with her grief. Her hair grew wet from the tears she was unable to stop. She wanted to scream out and tell the world how much she hurt. It was all so unfair! She didn't understand how it could come to this.

Charley Reed did not hear her cry.

He was not there when his son was born and he never saw him learn to walk. She watched his face as he slept.

Why didn't he hate her?

He never knew his son. All he knew of him was that he was taken from this earth in a horrible tragedy.

Cindy watched his sleeping face as she continued to cry. It was the face of the man her mother said would not do for her. Now everyone was gone, except this man and his face.

Cindy touched him as he slept. His body was warm and his skin soft to her hand. She touched his arm and traced the outline of his muscles down to the elbow. Then she touched his check, his ear, and then his hair.

Everything about him seemed gentle, even the roughness of his unshaven face.

Her finger ran down the side of his neck and then across his chest. She felt her body cry out for him as her fingers took him and stroked him to life. Cindy held him in both her hands and as his eyes opened, she kissed him.

"I want you," she whispered. "I want to feel you inside me again."

Charley rolled over onto her boy and entered her once more. He filled her and she cried out into the silence of the room.

"I love you," she cried. "I love you. Promise you'll never leave me!"

"I promise," Charley answered.

Cindy pulled his face to hers and kissed him.

"Thank you," she said and kissed him a second time.

Charley's hands took her face and kissed her on the mouth, holding her to him. She was surprised as he kissed her like this and felt something inside her respond to him.

"Everything will be okay," he promised her.

CHAPTER SIXTY

Cindy didn't want him to leave. She knew people were looking for him, but she didn't care.

"You're safe with me. No one knows how we are connected. As long as you don't use a telephone or a credit card, no one has any idea where to look for you."

Charley listened to her and settled in. Actually, staying with her was very pleasant. They made love like they were kids. They sat by the fireplace in the dark with only the light of the fire and a lone candle. They drank wine and snacked, not worrying about anything. Inside her house, they were safe from the rest of the world.

Julie visited regularly. Occasionally they went out for dinner, but for the most part they kept a very low profile. The stories continued and Charley's face was all over the news.

Meanwhile, Marie Van Arsdale, now with CNN, kept pounding the story. She was relentless. The national soul had been touched and there was outrage over the thought that American boys, American soldiers, were abandoned by their own and left in a foreign land while their families were lied to as to their disposition.

The government had no choice. It was denying an Operation Eagle Thrust ever took place and the denials were coming from the highest sources. Even with their denials, polls conducted by the media showed the people didn't believe the official stance on the matter.

But with all stories, the life of any story depends on what new fuel can be fed to feed the fire. Without Charley Reed to verify it personally, the story began to die. While the bombing increased in Afghanistan and the War on Terrorism continued, Marie's attempts were soon overshadowed and forgotten. In a matter of two weeks, she went from prime time to doing the news in the middle of the night.

One week turned into two weeks and then three. No one knew or even suspected they had spent one night together. Everything seemed natural with Charley helping out in a bad situation.

Charley sank into a stuffed chair next to the fireplace.

"That was my father's favorite chair," Cindy said. "You look a little like him sitting there."

Charley tried to remember her father. He couldn't put a face with the tall, serious man he remembered. All he was able to bring back was a man driving a black Ford sedan, talking to him about why he believed Charley did not like geometry. Charley remembered the man as being very intelligent. He wished he could have known him better.

"Do I really?" he said.

"A little," she said walking across the room to him.

She sat on the arm of the chair and kissed his cheek.

"I used to sit on his lap and kiss him just like this," she said continuing to kiss him on both sides of his face.

"I really miss him sometimes," she said.

"Do you miss him now?" Charley asked.

"A little," she admitted. "You're here and it has really been a blessing to me. I'd like to think my father had something to do with you coming when I really needed you."

Charley's teeth clenched as he listened.

"What's wrong?" she asked.

Charley's head drew back. His eyes looked directly into hers as he remembered sitting on the telephone talking to her when they were fifteen. She was a daddy's girl then and was always self-centered. Why was he surprised to find nothing had really changed?

Now she was looking to him to take her father's place.

Charley felt he should consider that a compliment. But, in spite of the compliment, he couldn't help resenting how she seemed to assume everything good that happened was exclusively for her in this time of need only she seemed to be experiencing.

"Did I say something wrong?" she asked. "I felt your whole body clench when I said my father sent you to me. Does that bother you?"

"No," he answered trying to smile at her.

"For all we know your father did. Maybe it was your mother. I don't know. I just know I'm here and as happy as we should feel, we can't because of what has happened."

"I know," she said. "But you are here and that helps me so much."

"I'm glad," Charley told her. "It's important to me to be here and help you. I've always enjoyed helping people. It's nice to be able to help someone I love. I just wonder what you think about me."

"I don't understand," she said as she rose from the chair and sat on the hearth of the fireplace. "I told you how I feel about you. I've shown you how I feel about you. I don't understand what you mean."

Charley's eyes closed as he collected his feelings and put them into words.

"When we were fifteen," he began. "You were my first love."

"We were lovers. It was only one time, but we were the first for each other. Weren't we?"

"Yes," she answered. "We were."

"That was special," he said. "As I grew up and you moved away, I never forgot you."

"And I never forgot you either," she said.

"I know. I realized that when I came to see you before I went into the Army. As soon as I saw you, I knew nothing had changed. Those days we spent together proved it to me. I never doubted it."

"So?" she asked.

"Then you called me and said you were pregnant. Did I hesitate or ask if you were sure it was mine?"

"No," she answered.

"I know," he said to her. "That never even crossed my mind. I knew if you called me, the baby was mine. I knew you'd never do anything like that to me."

Cindy looked away from him. She knew what was next.

"I called," he said. "I wasn't allowed to talk to you. I came to your house and your mother told me you had married someone else."

Cindy looked back at him, expecting his rage. It never came.

"I wanted to marry you. Did you know that?" he asked.

"Yes," she admitted.

"You didn't want to marry me."

Cindy shook her head in agreement.

"I wasn't good enough or you didn't love me?"

Cindy shook her head again and said, "It wasn't either of those reasons. I did what my mother told me. Today I don't understand why. But I did it and I can't make excuses."

"Believe it or not, Cindy," he said. "I can accept that. I don't have any problems with what you did."

"You don't?" she asked. "Why?"

"Because I know how the story goes after the broken-hearted soldier walks off into the blinding snowstorm."

Cindy leaned forward on the edge of the hearth.

HAROLD THOMAS BECK 533

"How does it go?" she asked. "I've always wanted to know what happened to you."

"You did?" he said apparently surprised.

"Yes," she said as she saw tears began to run down his face.

"I thought you didn't care."

"Is that what this is all about?" she asked.

"Yes," he said.

"Why?"

"Because I can handle everything if I knew you wondered about me."

Cindy wanted to laugh with relief, but didn't because he was crying.

"You dope!" she said.

"What do you think went through my mind every time I held our son?

"What do you think I thought watching him grow up, looking more and more like you every day? How do you think I felt when he was the star Little League pitcher and when he became a lawyer?

"How could I help but think about you? I thought about you all the time, but who could I ask? It wasn't until my last trip here that I found out about you."

Charley looked down at the floor when she looked at him.

"I made my mother go with me to your grave. I wanted her to share it with me."

"Did she?" Charley asked.

"No, she didn't care. It only made her feel much more right. The story I heard even made me believe she was right."

Charley raised his head and looked at her.

"She was," he admitted, surprising even himself.

"I would have been wrong for you. You did the right think, Cindy."

"How am I supposed to believe that?" she asked.

"Because," he began, "I changed. I was hurt and I was different.

"I was angry and I wouldn't have been any good for you or our son. It's better our son never felt the hurt or the anger that was inside me. I would have wound up hurting both of you instead of the people I did hurt."

"Does that include Jerilyn?" she asked.

"I suppose it does," he said. "It includes Joanna, too. It could have just as easily been you and Chuck."

"Oh, baby," Cindy said as she stood and knelt in front of him.

She took his face in her hands.

"How could this have happened?"

Charley looked at her and placed his hands over hers.

"It's easy. It's called war and what it does to people. It's called the hypocrisy of our government and how they lied to all of us.

"It's the democracy hypocrisy," he joked. "There's so much you don't know."

"Tell me," she said. "I want to know."

"I was raising babies when you were fighting. Tell me so I can know, too. Tell me about you. Let me heal you, Charley," she said as she kissed him.

An hour and a half later a fire was roaring in the fireplace and they were wrapped in a blanket on the floor. Both of their bodies were warm from lovemaking and Cindy's hands were gently tracing the lines of his body.

"After you walked away in the snowstorm, what happened next?" she asked.

"I went home and stayed for a week. Then I went to the John F. Kennedy Special Warfare Center at Ft. Bragg, North Carolina and became a Green Beret."

"Was it tough?" she asked.

He smiled.

"One hundred men will test today, but only three win the Green Beret."

As he said it to her, he remembered saying it once before. He said it to Beth. And as he remembered saying it to Beth, he then remembered how she had been murdered and how it had never been solved and seemed so senseless. He couldn't help wondering now if her death hadn't been part of the same filthy business he was involved in presently.

"Then what did you do?" Cindy asked.

"I was sent to the Canal Zone with the First Special Forces in April of 1967."

"What did you do there?"

"Trained in the jungles, drank bourbon, and fought with the Marines."

Cindy sat and listened to his story.

"After that," he said. "We went to Bolivia."

"Bolivia? That's the story Marie Van Arsdale told? The one they are denying now?"

"Yes," he said.

As he admitted it was and as he talked to Cindy, he knew he'd had the same conversation many years ago. Still, he continued.

"There was a revolution going on and we were supporting a dictator named Barrientos. We were airlifted from the Canal Zone to the grasslands in southeastern Bolivia."

"We sent American soldiers to Bolivia in 1967?

"Boy, I never knew that," Cindy said.

"We did," he said. "We were there, but we were in the employ of the CIA."

"How could that be? You were all in the Army!"

Charley smiled.

"No one had any identification. We had no insignia of rank or indication of who or what we were on our uniforms. We carried foreign-made weapons and were under the command of the CIA on special orders."

"I've never heard anything about it," Cindy said, shaking her head.

"Of course, you haven't," Charley told her. "No one did. It was above Top Secret."

"How long were you there?"

"We went in at the beginning of June and stayed until October. We were there to kill Cubans," Charley said.

"You just went in there and killed people?"

"Sure," he answered. "That's what we did."

"Are you serious?" she asked again.

"Of course, I am," he said.

"We captured Che Guevara and I was there when they beat and torture him and then put him against a wall and shot him. They took pictures of his dead body and then burned it, along with about one hundred fifty others."

"My God, Charley, you're serious."

"I am," he said.

"Who beat and tortured him?"

"We did."

"American soldiers?"

"The CIA did it."

"Why?"

"There were still more guerillas out there and we wanted their positions and strengths so we beat him. And there were other things they wanted to know."

"Did he tell you?" she asked.

"Yes," Charley answered. "He talked and the information he gave us was good, too."

"I find it hard to believe American soldiers could torture someone to make them talk."

Charley just laughed.

"The torture didn't make him talk. It was the fear of dying that did it. We told him we'd let him live if he talked."

"You guys lied to him."

"Sure we did. We had already lost three hundred men and we didn't want to lose any more. It could have been any one of us, so no one cared what we did to end the whole thing. We weren't going home until they were all dead."

"So you lied to him to get him to talk?"

"Sure. You know what you have to do and you do it."

"Didn't you feel bad?"

"When he cried and begged for his life, I guess I did."

Charley thought for a moment. Cindy watched and knew there was more he wanted to say. She waited quietly.

It was then he told her about the prisoners and the wounded. When he told her that it held for the American wounded, too, Cindy was speechless. She just stared at him, unwilling to comprehend what he said.

"You mean our own men?"

"Yes," he admitted.

"My God, Charley, why?"

"We were there to search and kill. We took no prisoners and gave no quarter. We annihilated a larger force in less than three months"

"What did they tell the families of the men who were killed there?" she asked.

"We were all in the Special Forces. They were told they were killed in Vietnam."

"I can't believe it!" Cindy said in astonishment. "How could our government do something like that?"

"Easy," he said. "How can they do what they are doing right now?"

Charley remained incredibly calm as he told Cindy the story. She looked into his eyes and found an unusual emptiness as the story ended. It was as if he truly didn't care about what he had done.

Charley laid his head on the pillow and cuddled against her naked body. She felt the warmth of him and listened to his breathing as it slowed. He was asleep and without guilt.

Cindy wondered about what her country had done to innocent young men. She wondered about what it had done in a country where it had no business ever being in the first place.

It all seemed so large to her and then she remembered her own life in 1967. There was a baby and a man she didn't love. She lived the same kind of lie Charley Reed had.

"A lie is still a lie," she said to him.

He was asleep and did not hear her as she spoke.

"You lived your lie and I lived mine."

Charley fell into a deep sleep. Cindy did, too. They had been asleep for several hours when he began to dream.

"No!' he screamed. "No!"

Cindy reached for him.

"It's okay," she said. "It's okay."

"No," he said in a quieter tone.

"It's okay," she said again as Charley lay back down.

He was shaking and she held him to her.

"It's okay. You're safe."

"I know," Charley said.

"What was it?" she asked.

"The fifth dream," he answered. "My fifth dream."

"What's it about?"

"The war," he answered. "It's the only one that won't go away."

"Do you want to talk about it?" she asked.

"I wasn't a coward," he said. "I never was a coward, not in war any way."

"What?" she asked.

"The fifth dream, the final dream, the last dream," he said.

"Me with my hands covered with blood, blood up to my elbows, blood warm and flowing, covering my sweat-stained, urine-smelling clothes and none of the blood is mine.

"There I am, drunk on blood and killing just to kill. I loved how it felt and I laughed each time there was another slaughter.

"I didn't fight to survive. I fought to kill and I loved it.

"It probably would have been better if I'd been killed. I'm not sure I belong anymore. I haven't since I came back and I'm not sure I am brave enough to be me any more."

Cindy listened to Charley as he rambled.

"You're the bravest man I've ever known."

Cindy held Charley in her arms. He was shaking with fright and she pulled him tight against her body.

"I know you're scared," she said. "I'm scared, too. You came back for a reason and now I'm here for you. We'll take care of each other. We have to."

Charley relaxed in Cindy's arms. He began to breathe normally and smelled the clean fragrance of the lovely woman. He tried to speak, but Cindy stopped him.

"We'll be fine," she told him. "Now that you're here, we're not going any where."

Charley listened to her voice. Charley closed his eyes and sighed. Cindy's hand ran through his hair. Charley's heart cried out, realizing the bond that was being fused between them.

Cindy held him until he fell back to sleep.

CHAPTER SIXTY-ONE

In the weeks following Marie Van Arsdale's story and her move to CNN, many in the government thought Operation Eagle Thrust would take care of itself. While it was no longer a hot media item, it was still a sore spot in many places in the government, all the way to the highest levels of the administration. In mid-November it was an open and festering wound.

Charley Reed had evaded the best efforts of the CIA to kill him and those of the FBI to find him.

Mary Sporror was in limbo until his phone rang at three a.m.

"Martin," the Director said when he answered.

"Yes, sir. What can I do for you?"

"I'm sorry to disturb you at this hour. There is a meeting at the Department of Justice at six a.m. I want you to attend with me. My car will call for you at four a.m. We need to talk before we meet with the Deputy Attorney General and the Director of the CIA."

"Yes, sir," Marty answered. "I'll be ready."

He showered and dressed. At exactly four a.m. the Director's limousine stopped in front of his home. Marty walked out to the car as the driver opened the door for him. Director Hastings was inside waiting for him. Seated next to him was the Director of the CIA, Stewart Lerner.

Marty remembered Lerner. He had only met him once, but he knew him by reputation. He was known as a cold-blooded politician and ruthless individual.

He was short, overweight, bald, and a compulsive cigar smoker. To Marty he was a repulsive egomaniac, which was reconfirmed for him in the first moments.

Marty was in the car and seated. When he was introduced and extended his hand to Lerner, Lerner took out a cigar and ignored the younger man.

"I'm sorry," Lerner said to Hastings, speaking as if Marty was not even in the car with them. "I have a hard time buying that he's saved us. It was his man who leaked to the news broad and then he went against your orders and what you and I agreed on."

The car was dark and Marty was glad because no one could see his face. Had it been daylight, they would have been able to see the anger and disgust. Instead, it was only minutes after four in the morning and they were being whisked away to a meeting.

"I have the utmost faith in Martin," Hastings said to Lerner.

"You fail to take into consideration Johnson resigned and the circumstances of his resignation led Marty to believe the entire case might have been compromised. I was unavailable for consultation and in the Bureau we allow our people to act when they consider their actions are in the best interest of the Bureau.

"Under those circumstances, Martin's action took the wind out of the news woman's sail. His actions allowed us to save face."

Lerner spoke immediately.

"In the Company our people don't act unless they are authorized by a superior. I'm not impressed by your man's action."

"Were you impressed by Ed Manion's action?" Marty asked.

"It was Manion who broke the case for us in the first place," he added.

Lerner ignored Marty and said nothing. He lit his cigar and filled the car with smoke.

Marty crossed his arms across his chest and tapped the fingers of his right hand on the .44 magnum he was carrying beneath his jacket under his left arm.

The car crossed the Potomac River and started passing government buildings. The driver took them directly to the Department of Justice and drove to the receiving entrance. The car came to a stop and the driver got the door for them.

Lerner got out first, then Hastings, and finally Marty. Lerner knew where he was going and the other two men followed. He had obviously been here before, perhaps yesterday afternoon when he made his agreement with Hastings.

Marty checked his watch. It was four forty-five. He thought the meeting was at six.

They took the elevator to the top floor and went down the same hallway Marty was in several weeks before. They walked to the Deputy Attorney General's office and entered. Nathan Seeburg was already there seated behind his desk. Seated on the couch was an Army general whom Marty recognized as a member of the Joint Chiefs of Staff.

"Fine," Seeburg said. "The meeting is still set for six. He's going to want answers and we better have them. Please sit down and, Lerner, put out that disgusting cigar."

For the next forty-five minutes, Marty sat and listened to the four other men discuss the events that brought them all together. He didn't speak because he wasn't spoken to by any of the men. He realized his only purpose in being there was whomever they were about to meet expected him also.

They all discussed what Marty was going to say when he was asked questions. They discussed their own answers and when they finished, the Deputy Attorney General looked directly at Marty.

"Mr. Sporror," he said. "Do you have any questions?"

"No, sir," he answered.

"Then we're all in agreement on the story," Seeburg said.

Looking directly at Lerner, he asked, "What do you have out there moving on Reed?"

"Nothing," Lerner replied. "The woman he lived with was killed in an automobile accident in Hamburg, Germany. It's a shame. She didn't know anything. She had quite a future."

"What about Reed?"

"We don't have any leads on him. He has fallen off the face of the earth. He hasn't used a telephone or a credit card in over a month. We have to go with the FBI bulletin and hope some local police department grabs him and we can pick him up.

"When he left New York, we lost him. Right now he could be anywhere. With this amount of time elapsing, it is highly unusual for anyone to avoid us. We usually have something on them by now.

"He paid for his hotel bill on his credit card," Lerner continued. "That's the first time he did that. We assumed he must be short of cash, but he hasn't used it since. We put an alert in on the card if he tries to use it again. As of midnight, we had nothing."

Marty listened and knew exactly what he was hearing.

"What about the newsgirl?" the general asked.

"She's done," Seeburg said. "Snyder fired her and CNN picked her up. But the War on Terrorism has overshadowed all of this.

"Jason worked with us on follow-up. He's covering us and she comes off as a rookie who got too anxious. She's losing credibility with CNN. Before long, she'll be gone."

As the Deputy Attorney General talked to the Chief of Staff and General of the Army, Martin Sporror realized the men in the room with him were flaunting the Constitution they swore to uphold and defend.

He looked at Director Hastings. There was no question in his mind. The Director was as much a part of it as Lerner and the others. They expected him to be part of it, too.

He was expected to tell their story and not the truth.

He thought about Karen and the children. All his life he had done the right thing and stood for something. He thought about the woman Lerner's boys killed and what they planned for Reed. How could he go along with these men? If he did, he was no better than the Agency killers who first went after Charley Reed.

"Okay, gentlemen," Seeburg said. "It's time to go."

Marty stood when the other men stood and left the room when they did. They took the same elevator down and they walked to the receiving entrance where their cars were waiting.

"Martin," Seeburg said as they walked outside. "Ride with me."

Marty got into the limousine after the Deputy Attorney General and sat next to him facing front. The driver closed the door behind him and he looked out at the other two cars. The general's car pulled out first, then Director Hastings, and last the one he was in.

"When this is over, Martin," Seeburg said, "I'd like you to come over to Justice.

"The position of Chief Investigator has been open for several months. I believe you're the man we need for the job. It will be a substantial increase for you. You'll be on an equal level with Lerner and Hastings and have your own men working for you."

Marty made no reply and knew a response wasn't required. No one would expect him not to want the job. It was a bribe and he recognized it for exactly what it was. He wondered what sort of bribery had turned the four men with him in this lie.

The three cars turned left and started up Pennsylvania Avenue. Marty wondered where they were going, but before long he realized he was expected to lie to the President himself. The cars turned left once more and drove through the gate to the White House. Marty checked his watch. It was five-fifty a.m.

The cars came to rest in front of the President's residence. Marines in dress uniform opened the doors and the five men stepped out and were led into the White House to the room where they were to meet the President. Marty watched the other four men who seemed perfectly at ease. They had all met the President before and probably all had experience in lying and deception. For Marty, this was something new. This would be a first for him and he was nervous.

The door opened at exactly six a.m. and the President of the

United States entered.

Marty had seen many pictures of the President. He voted for him and believed he was an honest man. He believed in his policies and he was solidly behind him with what he was doing in his War on Terrorism.

Standing there in his presence, Marty wondered what the man would say if he knew of the treachery discussed less than an hour ago. Then the Deputy Attorney General introduced him and he shook the President's hand.

"Please be seated," the President said and the men all sat.

A steward entered the room and served the men coffee. The man was old and he was black. Marty wondered how long the black man had worked here. This was something America didn't see on the news, just like the meeting he just left.

"I appreciate all of you coming here at this hour," the President said. "I have a full schedule today. And, our War is going into the next phase today.

"I know this is unusual. I chose this early hour because the news people are all still in bed. I was advised that they all stayed up late last night trying to get information. It's a safe bet they're asleep."

Everyone laughed at the President's comment about the news media. Then the President changed his tone.

"This is serious, Mr. Lerner," he said while holding a file in his hand. "I read this before I fell off to sleep last night. Are there any other situations like this in our system?"

"No, sir," Lerner answered. "This was unique in itself and because what the operation set out to do was accomplished, the administration at the time felt it was necessary to protect the integrity of the situation at all costs. It was set in motion at the time and was to remain for perpetuity. At the present time, we have dismantled that order and I can assure you, Sir, nothing else like this exists."

"Fine," the President said.

"What are we doing about the man who has survived our best efforts to do away with him?" he asked Hastings.

"At the present time, Sir, we have bulletins out in every one of our field offices. The bulletin has been circulated to all police departments instructing them only to take Mr. Reed into protective custody."

The President nodded in approval.

"We have your quick thinking to thank for that, Mr. Sporror," the President said. "Your gut feeling was correct and you saved the Administration a real black eye. I can't thank you enough for your fast thinking."

Marty nodded at the President.

"Thank you, sir," he said.

"General, are there any records anywhere on this operation?"

"No, sir," he answered.

"I would like those three tapes," the President said.

"Sir," the general said. "We've searched for those tapes and we doubt their existence."

Lerner joined in and agreed with the general. "I'm not saying they didn't exist, Sir. At this time we've been unable to turn them up in any of our searches."

"And you, Mr. Hastings. What about the FBI?" asked the President.

"No, sir," Hastings answered. "Nothing."

Marty listened to the three men lie directly to the President while the Attorney General stood by and said nothing. He realized by his own silence, he was no better than any of them.

"Then we have to assume the part of the newswoman's story concerning the tapes was incorrect?"

"That's right, Sir" Lerner said.

The President looked down at his desk and shook his head.

"I don't understand it," he commented. "These news people are so ambitious. They open up quite a story, actually reveal things to me that would have remained hidden. Then they enhance the story to the point of actually lying."

Marty looked at Hastings whose face was expressionless. He looked at Lerner who was smiling. The general was acting solemn and Seeburg appeared to listen intently to every word the President spoke.

In an instant Marty remembered everything he had been taught about good and evil, truth and deceit. He was ashamed to be associated with the men who were purposely lying to the President.

"Sir," he said, speaking to Director Hastings.

"Are we speaking about those six-inch reels?"

Hastings' face changed color. He never expected Marty to speak, let alone contradict him in the presence of the President.

"What six-inch reels?" he asked.

"Perhaps you never saw them," Marty said. "They are in a large brown envelope and because of the amount of material I passed on to you, they would have been easy to overlook. I'm sure they are catalogued in the inventory of information we received."

"Where did you receive this information?" the President asked.

Marty looked at Lerner and felt nothing but contempt and answered the President.

"Ed Manion, one of the Assistant Directors at the CIA. He called me to his home last month on a Sunday. He had this material and asked me to safeguard it. He was concerned about the safety of Mr. Reed, Sir. He believed Mr. Reed and the material were in danger.

"Sir, I concur with Mr. Manion," he told the President.

"Where is Mr. Manion?" the President asked Lerner.

"Sir," Lerner said. "Manion was depressed for several years since the death of his wife and shortly after meeting with Sporror, he committed suicide."

The President looked at Lerner. He seemed animated as he leaned forward in his chair.

"We seem to have an unusual number of deaths in our top intelligence gathering agency these days," he said sarcastically.

Then he turned to Marty.

"Martin," he began, reaching for a pad and pen at the same time. "Did Manion appear depressed to you?"

"Depressed isn't a word I would use, Sir. I would rather use the word disappointed."

"How so?" the President asked.

"We spoke for nearly an hour," Marty admitted. "Disappointed is the word I would use. He was troubled over our attempts to kill Mr. Reed. It bothered him, what we did to the men who took part in Operation Eagle Thrust. I got the impression that he was a major player and was feeling guilty over what he did in the name of national security."

"It bothers me, too, Martin," the President said.

"Yes, sir," Marty responded.

The President turned his head to look directly at Lerner. As he continued speaking to Martin, he carefully watched the Director's face.

"What do you suggest we do, Martin?" the President asked.

"Sir," Marty began. "There's nothing we can do about the past. We need to protect Mr. Reed and end the killing."

"I'm under the impression it has ended."

"A woman who lived with Mr. Reed, a nationally known news woman, was killed in an automobile accident in Hamburg, Germany. The German police say the accident was suspicious."

"Really," the President said, still watching Lerner who was visibly uncomfortable.

"Sir," Marty said. "If you would call a news conference and ask

Reed to come in, I believe he would.

"We could properly, once and for all, debrief him and let him go on with his life. Otherwise, Sir, I'm afraid he won't allow himself to be taken easily. I fear he has armed himself. He was a well trained soldier and even unarmed, he has proven to be quite formidable."

"The tapes, Martin," the President asked. "Are they labeled as Miss Van Arsdale reported?"

"Yes, sir," he answered.

"Have you listened to them?"

"No, sir."

"Why not?"

"I considered them a matter of national security and felt I did not have the need to know."

"Very good," the President said.

Then he looked to Director Hastings.

"Mr. Hastings," he began. "I would like you and Mr. Sporror to return to your offices and gather all the material turned over by Mr. Manion. Take special care to see that everything is collected and make special note of anything that might have been misplaced with an expla-nation signed by you. Have Martin deliver the information back to me no later than eight this morning."

Then he looked at Marty.

"Martin, come alone and be sure you have everything."

"Do you understand?" he asked the two men.

"Yes, Mr. President," they both answered.

"Very good. You're both excused. I will see you at eight, Martin," he added.

Hastings and Marty rose and left the room. They walked through the halls of the White House behind the Marine escort and out to their car.

During the ride across the city to their office, neither man spoke. Marty waited for Hastings to say something, but he made no comment. Even as they went directly to Hastings' office, the Director said noth-ing.

Once in the office, the Director opened his desk and removed three labeled tapes. Then he searched for a large brown envelope.

"Here," he said finally speaking. "Write whatever you feel is nec-essary on this."

"I believe it should remain blank," Marty said.

"Okay," Hastings said.

He looked at Marty.

"Would you care to tell me why?" he asked.

"Lerner is a pig," he answered without hesitation. "So is Seeburg.
"You've always been so much better than them. I couldn't sit by and allow you to sink down to their level. The Bureau stands for something. As long as you're the Director, you are the Bureau. Jimmy Johnson quit because of this. I can't let it go any further. It has to stop here."

Hastings looked down at his desk.

"I suppose you think I should feel ashamed," he said quietly. "I don't. We were doing the right thing. You have no idea the damage you've done.

"You seem to think everything is black and white. It isn't. And you think you can make a difference. You can't. What is going to happen is carved in stone. There will just be different people doing it now."

"What do you mean?" Marty asked.

"Lerner and Seeburg aren't calling the shots. Neither is Ashcroft. If you think they are, you are kidding yourself. The directors beneath them are the real power.

"You think you can save this Reed guy. You're wrong. Reed is going to go one way or the other. He knows too much. Even if he hadn't been there for the Guevara thing, they still would have gone after him. We would have gone after him."

"Why?" Marty asked.

"TWA Flight 800," he answered. "He's an eyewitness. He was on US Air 217 and saw the missile come up from the ocean. He is the only surviving eyewitness. He knows the center fuel tank story is false. As long as he was Charley Hayes, he was never going to say a thing. Now that he is Charley Reed and if he gets a forum, he is going to tell the world."

"Flight 800 was brought down by a missile?" Marty asked incredulously.

"Of course, it was," he said. "Everyone in the Clinton Administration knew it. And the Egyptian airliner that went down in the Atlantic was a suicide attack. Both of them were Al Queda attacks. We knew it and we kept it from the public. There are certain things the unwashed masses don't need to know."

Marty couldn't believe what he heard.

"You've withheld information from the public? You knew it wasn't safe to fly all these years and you've sat back and done nothing?"

"There are larger things to worry about," Hastings said. "There is an agenda that was being allowed to play out. An embassy bombing here, a destroyer bombing there, an airline crash, even a Federal Office Building, what difference does it make? Think about it.

"Alone they meant nothing. There wasn't enough collateral damage. Two or three hundred people at a time didn't mean much. It took something the magnitude of the two World Trade Towers crashing down to the ground. It took them using our own airliners against us. It took it being played out on national television and the whole world watching.

"It took the threat of an atomic bomb being smuggled into this nation and being detonated to wake up the American people. It took the unleashing of anthrax against the population at large to make them angry. Without any of it, they never would have gone along with the war."

"I can't believe what you are saying," Marty said in disbelief.

"Why? What surprises you about any of it? You've played a key role in deceiving the American people."

"How is that?" he asked.

"You were in on the investigation. You are the one who came up with the center fuel tank theory. We led you to it.

"If the American public knew it was a missile, they would have wanted better protection. If they suspected the Egyptian airliner was a suicide attack, they would have wanted closer scrutiny. They can accept mechanical failure. They can't accept terrorism. Things had to unfold the way they did. We had to sit back and allow it to happen."

Hastings laughed.

"Go tell the world. Go ahead! Who's going to believe you? We have the bad guys tied up in a nice neat package. They did exactly what we wanted. We're at war with the world and it isn't going to end soon. Everything we've waited for has come to pass."

Handing the large box to Marty, he said, "This is everything."

"Thank you," Marty said as he took the box.

"Let me tell you something. Let me let you in on a big secret. The President is going to make a good show of this. He is going to act like he is concerned and he wants to do the right thing.

"But he's going to do as he's told, just like the rest of us. He isn't in control. There are much larger people who are calling the shots and he knows it just like Bill Clinton did. They do as they are told."

Marty took the box and left the office. Marty looked at his watch. It was seven twenty-five a.m.

As he drove to the White House, he couldn't get Hastings' words out of his head. Was what he said true? Had they allowed the terrorists to act? Did they know? Could they have stopped them?

When Marty walked into the President's office, it was exactly eight a.m. He was carrying the box containing the only surviving information about Operation Eagle Thrust.

"Place that here, next to my desk," the President said.

Marty did as he was told.

"This might interest you," the President said, handing him three signed letters.

Marty took them from the President. They were letters of resignation from Stewart Lerner, Nathan Seeburg, and General William Decker. Marty looked up at the President and smiled.

The President extended his hand to him and then spoke.

"Thank you, Martin. Thank you for being an honest man."

Marty shook the President's hand.

"Sir," he said. "May I ask you something?"

CHAPTER SIXTY-TWO

The President of the United States held a surprise news conference at nine-thirty a.m. Eastern Standard Time. He announced the resignations of the Deputy Attorney General, the Director of the CIA and the retirement of the Vice-Chairman of the Joint Chiefs of Staff.

"These resignations and the retirement are effective immediately. As of now, their successors have not been determined and you will be advised as soon as they are chosen."

The President paused for a moment and looked across the room at the reporters. Then he turned his face directly at the television cameras and removed his reading glasses.

"In recent weeks," he began, "a television reporter broke a story about a military operation that took place in the 1960s. She suggested because of his involvement and knowledge of the action, a man was in danger of being murdered by his own government.

"I will neither deny nor affirm the report. I will say right now that this government will not participate in or condone the murder of its citizens. As President, I am sworn to uphold the Constitution and guarantee every citizen has the right to life, liberty, and the pursuit of happiness. I am here right now to guarantee the right to life of this man.

"I am asking Charles Reed to contact the nearest office of the Federal Bureau of Investigation. I will personally guarantee his safety. Wherever you are, please call us immediately, Mr. Reed."

The President turned to Marty Sporror who was standing off to the side with a Secret Service agent. He motioned to Marty to join him.

"Effective immediately, Inspector Martin Sporror is joining my staff as National Security Advisor. In accepting this post, Mr. Sporror is taking leave from the FBI and will undertake the job of examining, scrutinizing, and overseeing our intelligence community, both on a domestic and an international level. He will meet with me on a weekly basis and advise me of any and all developments in this area. His job will be to insure various intelligence-gathering agencies operate within the confines of the law. At the same time, Mr. Sporror will be responsible for Mr. Reed's safety as well as the prompt restoration of the man's civil liberties."

While the President spoke, Cindy was sitting on the edge of the bed watching and listening to every word. When the President finished, she turned to Charley who had finished his shower and was standing in the hallway with a towel wrapped around him.

"How much did you hear?" she asked him.

"Everything from the resignations on," he answered.

"What do you think?"

"I don't know," Charley said. "I didn't vote for him. I thought he was a clown. I hated his father. But on the other hand, I voted for Lyndon Johnson and Richard Nixon, too. It's entirely possible that when it comes to presidents, I might not be the greatest judge of character."

Cindy smiled at Charley.

"So what are you going to do?"

"Maybe nothing," he answered.

"What?"

"Maybe nothing," he repeated. "I want to wait this out. It could be a trap. How can I be sure?"

"Honey," she said. "The President of the United States guaranteed your safety."

"Yeah," he said. "And Richard Nixon was going to end the war in Vietnam, too."

Marty Sporror shook hands with the President and left for his office at the FBI. He knew all of this was very sudden and if he was to locate Charley Reed, he couldn't afford the luxury of time to set up a new base of operations.

At the FBI he had ready access to the information he needed to complete his mission. His security rating had been increased and under orders from the President, he had access to virtually everything.

Once in his office he picked up the phone and called the US Information Agency. He asked for the director. When he had him on the phone, he asked for information regarding 'Rosie.'

"Rosie is a classified government project," the director answered him.

Marty smiled as he held the phone in his hand. In the past, one agency was able to block another whenever there was an investigation. Now he was above all that and was working directly for the President.

"My authority comes directly from the President. Check it out. I'm coming to you right now so don't leave for lunch. I expect you to have what I need when I arrive."

When he arrived and was cleared through gate, he was immediately taken to the director's office. It was well into the lunch hour, but the man Marty wanted to see was there. So was Scott Jenkinson.

"Thank you for seeing me," Marty said.

The director didn't bother to acknowledge Marty's pleasantry. Instead, he went directly to the matter before them.

"Scott Jenkinson here can tell you everything you need to know about 'Rosie.' She's his baby. I also assume this is about the Charley Reed business. Here is our file on him. We've had him under surveillance for well over a month, closer to two."

Marty picked up the file and looked through it as he listened to Scott brief him. The briefing lasted almost ten minutes. He listened and didn't ask any questions. When Scott stopped talking, he was still holding the file in his hand.

"Continue the surveillance," Marty said. "I'm to be called on a twenty-four hour a day basis if he is detected. No one else, as of this moment, is to be notified. Only me.

"Do I make myself clear?" he asked.

Meanwhile, Cindy and Charley ate lunch. They sat in the family room and watched television. There was a newsbreak at three between soap operas and the story of the day was the President's news conference. Once more, Charley heard the President ask him to call the FBI. Charley listened but made no attempt to look for the number of the nearest FBI office. Instead, he told Cindy he was going to go for a ride. He needed some time to himself.

Cindy understood when Charley left. She was tired anyway and wanted a nap. As soon as the door closed, she laid down on the couch.

As she closed her eyes, she thought of the week he'd been with her. She liked it. It was comfortable.

She thought about what a kind man he was and how when she was with him, she was at peace. She wondered about that feeling and tried to compare it to love. There really wasn't any difference, she thought. Loving the right person and having them love you back produced a feeling of peace.

Charley went to a neighborhood bar. He sat down and ordered a beer. There were four men sitting at the other end talking about football. The Steelers were doing okay. The television was on and one of the news channels was reporting to the otherwise empty lounge. Sipping his beer, he watched the report on the weather and then sports.

For the first time since he allowed the world to believe he was dead, Charley wondered what would happen to him. That question brought back a thought that hadn't occurred to him in as many years. He looked at the bottle of beer and felt uncomfortable as he questioned why he was even alive.

Why was he alive? Why didn't he die in the ambush like the others?

He always felt he was supposed to die then. He was positive he should have died, but because of some fluke, he was in limbo just wandering through life.

He tried to have a marriage, except the woman didn't love him. Then he met Jerilyn and maybe she loved him too much for her to accept the fact she did. All of it was painful and all of it only convinced him he did not belong.

Charley drank his beer and asked the bartender for another. Why hadn't he thought about this until now? Why now?

Was it because Charley Reed was alive again?

Was it because Charley Reed had died in the first place?

As he asked himself those questions, he understood. As he understood, he knew the truth. Finally, he really did know the truth and he wondered why it had been so difficult.

The truth, he said to himself. Just the plain old truth and it had been so difficult for so very long. Now, all of a sudden it was simple.

He was a liar.

Yes, Charley admitted to himself, he was a liar.

He lied to Cindy George when he spent those days and nights with her. He lied to her as Cindy Ganley when he showed up at her front door. He lied to Joanna when he met and courted her. He lied when he was married to her. Then there was Jerilyn. Charley thought about Jerilyn and how he lied to her. He wondered why.

"People love you," she shouted at him once. "Why do you have to worry everyone? Can't you just accept their love? Isn't that enough for you? What's wrong with you anyway?"

Charley remembered he didn't have an answer for her. He remembered knowing she was right and hating her for it. Remembering, he hated that, too!

It was easy dying.

He remembered how it was the easiest thing he ever did. He woke up in the motel room and saw on television that he had been killed in an automobile accident. He saw pictures of his car, a pile of burned and twisted steel, and even saw his charred remains being removed in a body bag. It didn't dawn on him what had happened at first. Then the maid told him.

"At last," he said. "I'm free."

And as he spoke those words, the weight seemed to be lifted from his shoulders. As it lifted, he realized there was another chance for him. For once in his life, he was not lying anymore.

He did not have to lie.

All he had to do was allow everyone to believe what they wanted. It was different for Charley, allowing people to believe what they wanted. He was used to telling them what they needed to believe.

This time was different. It served him best to say nothing. In doing so, Charley Reed finally died and as he died, Charley Hayes was reborn.

A debt was being repaid.

It was simple enough. It was a life for a life. The lying was over and Charley Reed could finally rest in peace.

All the years passed and he appreciated the lies that he never had to tell. Charley saw the humor in what happened. Charley Hayes had been a black man and everyone knew how they lied! He laughed. It was Charley Reed who was the liar and he was a white man. By lying and becoming Charley Hayes, a black man in reality, Charley Reed never had to lie again.

It was then Charley Reed realized the ultimate lie.

All along, he had been lying to himself. He lied to himself and believed what he said. Instead of hating women because they were all stupid bitches, Charley Reed wound up hating himself.

In doing so, he knew he deserved to die.

He knew he should have died with his friends. Life beyond their deaths was his own personal hell and as he lived it, he grew to hate each single breath, each minute, each hour, and each day. The passing of Charley Reed managed to free him to finally live.

Every time there is a birth, there is a death. Charley Hayes died a second time when Charley Reed was reborn. He fought it, but it was inevitable.

It was like a gigantic flood just washed over and swept everything away. When the waters receded, Charley Reed was there, naked and exposed.

Charley Hayes's second death was quiet and without violence. He went to bed one night and just never woke up the next morning.

That was the morning Charley Reed came back to life.

Charley asked for another beer. The news was still background for the empty bar. As his beer was served, he heard a familiar voice ring in his ear.

"This is Marie Van Arsdale," the voice said.

"The President today acknowledged the United States government participated in a program to silence veterans who took part in Operation Eagle Thrust. While the particulars of Operation Eagle Thrust remain classified, we have been able to identify the following casualties as a result of an effort to eliminate Charley Reed."

The television screen changed to a picture of Bob Walker.

"Scott Robert Walker, Bob Walker, a Washington area car salesman. Long-time friend of Charley Reed."

The picture changed again.

"Connie Knapp, a dancer and girlfriend of Bob Walker's. Both were killed during an attack by three CIA operatives, who were also killed and still remain unnamed as of this news broadcast."

Pictures of Lou Locante, Tom McMann, and Ed Manion appeared on the screen.

"These three CIA administration personnel all died under mysterious circumstances within days of the shootings at the Walker residence."

The television picture changed back to Marie Van Arsdale. Charley was watching the report as he sipped his beer.

"Alexander Poole," she reported as his picture came on the screen, "took part in Operation Eagle Thrust and was employed by Mr. Reed in his California-based businesses. Alexander Poole was shot to death in the kitchen of his home the morning after the shootings at Walker's."

Then Charley felt a cold emptiness come over his body as Alicia's picture followed Al's.

"Alicia Masters, news reporter and girlfriend of Mr. Reed's, was killed in an automobile accident in Hamburg, Germany. German authorities have indicated the accident is suspicious."

Charley held his face in his hands. A feeling of guilt swept over him when he realized the friends he had just lost.

"This is all my fault," he said out loud.

"I beg your pardon?" the bartender asked him.

Charley looked at the young woman.

"Did you say something?" she asked again.

"No," he said. "I did, but I was talking to myself. That's a bad habit, I guess."

"Just so you don't answer yourself," she said with a laugh. Then the television caught her attention.

"That's you," she said to Charley.

The four men at the bar heard her and looked at the television. Instantly, they agreed with her.

Charley looked at the television and saw a photograph of himself on the screen as Marie continued the report.

"Today the President assured Mr. Reed's safety and asked him to contact the nearest FBI office. As of this broadcast, Mr. Reed has not contacted anyone. His whereabouts remain unknown."

The report ended and Charley drank more of his beer.

"Was that you?" one of the men asked.

"No," Charley answered with what he hoped was a grin. "I'm much better looking than that guy."

The other men laughed, but the bartender disagreed.

"He sure looked like you," she said.

"I know," Charley answered. "My wife says so, too. If it's me, she's in for a real surprise."

Charley quickly finished his beer and left a tip on the bar. He went out to his truck.

Charley Reed had never been so alone in his life.

Since the first night in Bolivia, his life had begun to decline. It went down and down, always seeming to place him farther from the people he wanted to be close to. At times it would level off; sometimes it seemed to improve. The improvements could go on for years and he might even believe it had finally ended and he was cured.

In every case, it was only a mirage. It was only a hoax. No matter what he did and no matter what he accomplished, he would always be in second place, on his way down. There was no way for him to ever win. The system would see to that.

Charley remembered Arlington Cemetery. He remembered the Secretary of Defense filling in for the President that day. He remembered Lyndon Baines Johnson begged off because he had a cold.

At the same time, Charley remembered John P. Tankersley, the old Sarge, who had a cold the night he was killed. Clark Clifford didn't stand in for him. If he wouldn't stand in for the old Sarge, then why did he do it for the President? Tankersley showed up, so should have Johnson.

Charley knew the answer. None of it was ever important. It was only a way to get votes or stay in power. To those people nothing ever mattered very much.

As Charley looked back on it, nothing really mattered at all.

He sat there in the parking lot with the engine running. He made no attempt to leave. All of a sudden, nothing mattered to him either. This was not a new feeling. He was alone. No one else cared.

Sitting in the driver's seat, Charley felt defeated. He reached under the seat for the 9mm Beretta he took from the man he killed in Walker's house. Calmly, he placed a bullet in the chamber. The gun was now armed for the first shot as well as however many others remained in the clip.

"Why?" he asked aloud.

No one answered.

"Why?" he asked again.

Still there was no answer and in the silence, he turned the pistol on himself. He opened his mouth and put the barrel firmly on his bottom lip. He brought his mouth down and closed around the cold steel. His thumb flirted with the trigger as his brain wondered if he had enough guts to explode the shell through the back of his head.

The trigger was cold as his thumb ran across it. He could feel it move slightly as he increased the pressure. He wondered how long the pull on the trigger was.

It moved a little more and Charley felt a surprising calm sweep over him. He knew he was only millimeters away from ending his life and was prepared to welcome the sound of one final gunshot.

Then, as he was ready to finally pull the trigger the rest of the way, he stopped. He withdrew the barrel of the pistol from his mouth.

"What use are you to me?" he asked aloud.

No answer came back.

Charley looked up at the roof of the truck and tears began to fill his eyes. Why had he always cared more than everyone else? Why did it have to be like this?

Charley could not answer his own questions. He sat and stared at the roof and then looked at the pistol he still held in his hand. He smiled. It was not a Colt .45 like the one he carried for a sidearm, but it was a military issue just the same.

He decided he would not end his life.

The sun was setting in the west and shining directly in his face.

"I love you," he said as he looked into the swirling ball of fire.

He waited for an answer, but it never came. He waited awhile longer and then knew what he waited for would never come.

He knew life would go on with or without him. He unloaded the pistol and looked out at the late afternoon sky.

"If no one cares," he said, "I do!"

He looked into the burning star once more. He turned off the truck and went back to the bar.

Marty Sporror walked back to his office when the phone rang. It was the President.

"Yes, sir," Marty said.

"Martin," the man began. "This whole filthy business really upsets me and I'm sure it does you, too."

"Yes, sir," Marty said, agreeing with the President.

"What bothers me," the President said, "Is the ease with which people allow themselves to be seduced in the name of national security.

"Seeburg got involved with Jason Snyder. He's the vice president in charge of news who fired Marie Van Arsdale. The young woman did this nation a service by breaking the story. Jason Snyder and Nathan Seeburg tried to bury it. They would have allowed our own brand of Murder Incorporated to continue unchecked. I want Jason Snyder's head," the President said angrily.

"Yes, sir," Marty answered.

"I want you to get in touch with Wally Joselyn. You can reach him at the DAK Corporation in New York City. He's Chairman and he is also a board member of the network. Tell Wally I want Snyder out."

"Yes, sir," Marty said. "It will be my pleasure."

"CNN is quite an organization," the President mused.

"In what way?" Marty asked.

"Giving that Van Arsdale woman another chance in spite of Snyder trying to blackball her."

"They're their own people," Marty said. "They can afford to be. They're big enough."

The President laughed.

"Yes," he said. "Wealth and power does open a lot of doors that are otherwise closed. Even the ones that stay closed, you just buy the whole damn building."

Marty laughed.

"Martin, get in touch with the Van Arsdale woman."

"Yes, sir," he said.

"I want the American people to know the whole story. She did us a great service and I want her rewarded."

"Yes, sir," Marty replied again.

"Tell her everything."

"Even about the killings in the seventies?"

"Yes," the President said. "Everything."

"Yes, sir," he said.

"Let her have a day on everyone else. Give her the exclusive. She deserves it. She placed her career on the line when she broke the story. It took a lot of guts on her part to jeopardize everything when she had finally made it to the top. Too many people just go along. She didn't and neither did you. You and Marie Van Arsdale are the heroes in our country today."

"What about Charley Reed?" Marty asked.

"He's a victim. He's been one for a long time. Imagine, allowing everyone to believe you were dead just so you could go off and find peace."

"I can't imagine, Sir," Marty said.

"He's quite man. I'm looking forward to meeting him," the President said.

"Really?" Marty asked.

"Yes," he said. "I've been reading a lot about him. He was a true soldier."

"He still is," Marty said. "He survived the CIA's best at the Walker house. He survived and they didn't. It was sudden and unexpected and he still survived."

"Yes," the President said. "With young men like that you wonder why we didn't allow them to win the war in Vietnam."

"I know. It seems like we cheated them, doesn't it?" Marty asked.

"Yes, Martin," the President said. "I know exactly what you mean. I wonder how many other Charley Reed's are out there hiding from themselves and hiding from the world."

"I don't know," Marty said.

"I don't either," the President answered him. "We owe it to them to try to help them through. We owe them an awful lot."

"How do we repay them?"

"I don't know," the President said. "I don't think they expect to be repaid. I think all they want is a fair shake. I think they expect someone to protect them from this enormous government we've created. They need someone to stand between them and the professional bureaucrats who regulate and control their lives.

"You and I forget that. We're both in our own niches and it's difficult for us to relate to the man who served us and now is a logger in

Pennsylvania for six or seven dollars an hour, simply trying to support a wife and two children.

"Who know what that man lives with? What are his fears? What does he enjoy?

"He's like you and me, but he's different. He has that incredible pride in what he's done. He has pride, but he has shame, too.

"When I read this Eagle Thrust material I was ashamed. I was shocked and I was ashamed."

"Sir?" Marty asked.

"Imagine," the President said. "How could any leader sanction Americans killing their own wounded?

"That's what always separated us from the rest of the world. That's what made us great. We were better and in being better, I honestly believe God was on our side. This period of time we've just come through is in doubt. I'm not sure God is with us anymore. He might be sitting back and deciding if we're at the end of the line like the Roman Empire. Perhaps I'm one of the last of the Caesars."

"No, Sir," Marty said. "I wouldn't look at it like that."

"This Eagle Thrust thing has really upset me," the President admitted. "I didn't need it on top of September 11th. We are trying so hard to do this War on Terrorism properly. We are trying to show the world who we really are and then I get hit square in the face with this.

"We've lied in the name of national security. There are several thousand men still unaccounted for from the Vietnam War. I seriously wonder how many of them are laying buried in places like Bolivia and the Congo along with who knows where else, while their families still believe they could be held hostage and suffering in Southeast Asia?"

"I don't know," Marty answered.

"I don't either and I'm the President. I should know and I don't. What does that tell you?"

Charley Reed was sitting at the bar when Marie Van Arsdale's report came on again. Once more the bartender insisted he was indeed Charley Reed. Again he denied it. Moments later Julie joined him.

"I recognized your truck. I thought Mom would be with you. You two are inseparable lately. Where is she?" she asked.

"She's home taking a nap."

"I saw you on the news. I didn't realize how famous you were."

"Don't say it too loud," he told her. "I've been trying to convince these people it isn't me."

"Why?" she asked.

"I don't want anyone to know where I am. It could be dangerous for your mom and anyone else around me."

He changed the subject.

"Can I get you anything?" he asked.

"I'll have a beer like you," she said.

Charley had another beer and ordered one for Julie.

"I'm not afraid," she said. "I'm proud of you. The Silver Star, the Purple Heart, and the Distinguished Service Cross, I can hardly believe I am sitting here with a decorated war hero."

"I'm not hero," he said. "I was a kid and I was scared."

"Well, I'm proud of you," she told him, moving closer and resting her head on his shoulder in an affectionate manner.

"You're my brother's father. That kind of makes us special and you are the closest thing I have to a father now. I'm glad you're here."

Charley looked away. She didn't see him wipe the tears out of his eyes.

They sat and talked. An hour later the story ran again and once more the bartender made her comments about how he had to be Charley Reed.

As he began to deny who he was, Julie objected.

"Of course, he's Charley Reed," she said to the bartender. "He's only trying to protect me. The dirty bastards have been trying to kill him. He doesn't care about himself, but he does care about me."

The men at the bar heard her as she spoke to the bartender. They rose from their bar stools and walked around to where he was sitting.

"I want to shake your hand," the man in the flannel shirt said.

"I do, too," the one in the hunting coat said, as did the other two men also.

Charley rose and shook their hands. Tears filled his eyes and began to run across his cheeks.

"Thank you," he said. "Thank you very much."

He was crying and his nose was running as he tried to control himself.

"Thank you," he said again as the largest of the four men hugged him and began to cry, too.

At the beginning of the next hour Marie Van Arsdale led with a new story.

"Network Vice President and Chief of News, Jason Snyder, was fired today in an unprecedented directive of the Board of Directors. This move by the Board, directly bypassing President Marc Katz, forced his own resignation."

As the report came over the air, Charley and Julie were sitting with a group of new friends. Charley was laughing, listening to the men tell their stories. Julie sat watching Charley's face as it finally came alive.

"I like having you here. You remind me so much of my brother," she said. "You would have liked him."

"I'm sure I would have," he answered her.

CHAPTER SIXTY-THREE

Julie and Charley went back to the house. Cindy was just getting up from her nap. She kissed her daughter when she saw her and squeezed Charley's hand.

"Did you have a good nap?" he asked.

"Yes," she said. "I did. It was nice."

"Good," he said.

"What were the two of you doing?" she asked.

"Julie saw my truck and stopped in. I was down at Larry's."

"I've never been there," she said.

She looked at her daughter and then she smiled.

"Have you eaten?" she asked.

"No," Julie said.

"You can eat with us. Dinner is in the oven."

As they sat down to eat, John Hughes was on a US Air flight to Pittsburgh. An agent was notified by someone at a local radio station that had been contacted by a bar patron who claimed Charley Reed was there drinking with a young woman. It was the only sighting of Reed and Hughes, realizing Reed was originally from Pittsburgh, took the report seriously. A team was hastily assembled and they were meeting him when he landed.

But the radio station wasn't the only part of the media contacted. The same bar patron called a television station and as the local news broke, the story about him being seen at a local bar ran along with his picture. He was in the middle of his meal as the story ran.

"Damn it," he said when he heard the story. "I have to go."

Cindy looked up at him as he rose from the table.

"Why?" she asked. "You're safe now."

"No, I'm not," he said.

"The President guaranteed your safety."

Charley tried to laugh, but was unable. There was nothing to laugh at. All he could generate was cynicism.

"The President can't guarantee anything with these people. I worked for them. I know them. They've missed me too many times to let me go. As long as I am here with you, both of you are in danger.

"Julie, you can't tell anyone you saw me. They will come for you and your mother. Too many people close to me are dying and I couldn't live with myself if anything happened to either of you."

Charley packed and began to leave.

"Where will you go?" Cindy asked.

"Don't worry. I have a place in mind that should be safe enough. I can't tell you. It would put you in danger."

John Hughes flight landed at seven thirty. At that moment Charley Reed backed his truck out of Cindy Ganley's driveway. As Hughes and the three men with him made their way to the parking lot and out of Greater Pittsburgh International Airport, Charley Reed negotiated the streets, making his way to McKnight Road and then north to Interstate 79.

It took them the better part of the next hour to drive across town into the North Hills to Larry's Sports Lounge. As they went in, Charley was turning east on Interstate 80.

The same bartender who served Charley Reed was still on duty. When Hughes showed her his government identification, she became defensive.

"We're here to help him," Hughes said. "He's in danger and we want to take him into custody and keep him safe."

"He looked safe enough to me," she said.

Hughes ignored her answer.

"Was he alone?" Hughes asked.

"No," she answered. "He had a woman with him."

"Can you describe her? Was she young, middle aged, old?"

"She was in her late thirties," she lied.

Something about Hughes didn't sit well with her. She had been a bartender most of her adult life and she was always able to size up a phony immediately. While this man was indeed a government agent, she didn't believe him when he said he wanted to insure the man's safety.

"What was the color of her hair?" he asked.

"It was bleached blonde," she said.

Once more she lied. While the woman with him was blonde, it was not bleached blonde. For whatever reason, she decided she wanted to mislead the man who was asking the questions.

"She had a rough look about her."

"Have you ever seen her before?"

"No," she said. "She's never been in here before. She didn't even sound like she was from around here. She was tough."

"What about him?' he asked. "Did he say where he was staying?"

"No," she said. "It was the first time I ever saw him, too. I thought the picture on the television was him, but he denied it. He denied it several times until she finally admitted it was. As soon as people recognized him, they left."

Hughes and his men spoke with the other patrons who were in the bar when he was there. None of them told them much. The most information was received from the bartender. Hughes thanked her, saying she was a big help.

She nodded as the men left the bar.

"Do you believe her?" one of the men asked Hughes.

"Sure," he said. "She has no reason to lie."

The man agreed.

"Reed and the woman were passing through. If we check hotels in the South Hills, I think we will find him. He wasn't from this part of Pittsburgh and people in this town stay in their own area. He would have gone home or close to it. He was probably just over here for something and stopped in for a few drinks before going back across town. He was probably just waiting for the traffic to die down."

While Hughes and his men started back to the South Hills of Pittsburgh, they had agents checking hotel registrations across the city. It didn't take them long to discover that he had stayed at the Radisson off the Parkway in Greentree days after the incident at LAX. He paid his hotel bill with cash.

"Keep checking," Hughes told his people. "He's here somewhere and he's probably either paying in cash or using the blonde woman's credit card."

Hughes had no more left Larry's Sports Lounge, than agents from the local FBI office walked in.

"How many of you guys are looking for him?" the bartender asked. "Four men with government identification just left."

She was careful to tell the FBI the same thing she told the other men. She suspected they might be double-checking her story.

Charley got off Interstate 80 and started north on Route 8. He made his way into the mountains and continued to drive north out of Franklin along the Allegheny River. He remembered driving the river road with his father as a boy and then a young man. He remembered the Boy Scout Camp in Tionesta as well as the places they used to go to hunt and fish.

As he passed through the towns, Oil City, then Tionesta, and finally Tidioute, his father was in his mind. He thought of the hours and the days they spent in the forest together and how his dad taught him to fish and fire a gun. He didn't know it at the time, but as he looked back, he realized all of those times taught him how to survive.

It was around ten when he turned off Route 62 and crossed the bridge into Tidioute, Pennsylvania. He made the turn at the flashing light and pulled his truck into a parking place in front of the Hotel Tidioute.

He went into the building. It was old like the rest of Pennsylvania. He remembered one time they had rooms and as he sat at the bar and ordered a beer, he asked the woman behind the bar if they still rented rooms.

"Yes," she said. "We rent rooms. They're thirty dollars a night."

"Can I get one?" he asked.

"Sonny," she called to the man seated at the end of the bar. "This fellow wants a room."

A large bearded man got up from the barstool and came around behind the bar and walked down to the place where he was seated.

"Hi, there," the man said to Charley. "How many nights?"

"Just tonight, I think," he said. "I just need to get off the road."

Sonny nodded his head.

"Where are you going?" he asked.

"Really," Charley said. "I'm not sure. This is the first time I've been up this way in years. My father and I used to hunt and fish up this way."

"Where at?" Sonny asked.

"Marshburg," Charley said.

Sonny smiled.

"I know where Marshburg is. My friend owns a place up there. His name is Buddy. It's called the Rainbow Inn."

Charley shook his head in surprise.

"I know the place! My dad used to take me there."

"So the old joint is still there," he mused. "That was the first place I ever was served a beer in my life."

"The old place burned down. Buddy rebuilt it back where the motel was," Sonny said.

Charley felt comfortable. He had come home. He was greeted with the old Pennsylvania hospitality. As he filled out the guest card and put his cash out on the bar for his room, Sonny had a request.

He handed him a magazine.

"If you get up that way, tell Buddy I am going to come up there and kick his ass. He dropped my ad this month."

Charley took the magazine and promised he would deliver the message.

Sonny told him to pull his truck around back and told him how to get to his room. Charley finished his beer, parked his truck around back, and found his room. He locked the door behind him and in less than a half an hour he was asleep.

Meanwhile, John Hughes checked into the Wyndham Hotel near the Greater Pittsburgh International Airport. Once in his room, he relaxed. It was eleven and he needed a drink. He went down to the lounge off the lobby and sat at the bar. Right away the woman tending bar asked him what he would have.

"Do you have Johnnie Walker Black?" he asked.

"Yes," she answered.

"I'd like it neat," he told her.

He sipped his scotch and wondered where Charley Reed could be. Was he in Pittsburgh or did he leave when he realized the media was aware he was there?

"He's gone," Hughes said to himself.

Just then the news came on and the lead story was the President and then Reed being sighted in Pittsburgh. They were in Larry's Sports Lounge interviewing the bartender. The woman told KDKA television the same story she told him.

"It must be true," he said. He studied the bartender's face in the television story.

"This is her moment of fame. She doesn't want to blow it."

He had his initial doubts. He detected something in her voice that made him believe she was lying. He intended to go back and question her alone. But then he changed his mind. He decided she was truthful with him. He laughed. It saved her life.

He wondered about the woman with Reed. Who was she? Was she an old girl friend? Was she a new one?

He finished his drink and had another. His cell phone rang and he answered it.

"Mr. Hughes," the voice said. "We have had negative results on our search."

"Scramble," he said to the man on the other end as he walked away from the bar. As he said it, he pressed a key on his phone that immediately scrambled the telephone conversation.

"Go ahead," he told the man after they had scrambled.

"We have two nights stay at the Radisson before he left for Washington, D.C. We have two other nights. One in New Jersey following his time in Washington, D.C. and one night in New York City. The only time he used a credit card was the night in New York City. He paid cash for his rooms every other time."

"Have you checked smaller hotels?" Hughes asked.

"No, sir," the man said. "Reed has a definite pattern. The cheapest hotel he stays at is a Holiday Inn. He avoids the others."

"I want them checked, too. I want them all checked. Do I make myself clear?"

"Yes, sir," he answered. "I understand."

Hughes didn't say goodbye to the man on the other end. He said nothing. He just disconnected, ending the phone conversation.

He went back to the bar, finished his drink, paid his bill and returned to his room. Slowly he undressed and got into bed. Before he did, he checked himself out in the mirror.

"Not bad for a sixty year old man," he said. "Not bad at all."

And he was correct. He was fit. There was not an ounce of fat on him and he maintained good muscle tone. He exercised regularly and was easily in as good, if not better, shape than most agents in their forties.

He turned off the lights and got into bed. Only the television lit the room. It was his company as he drifted off to sleep.

His mind was full of things as he slept. And as he slept, he dreamt of them and remembered things long since forgotten. He remembered the face of Charley Reed. He remembered it so well that the memory of it woke him. He woke with a start.

"How could I have forgotten?" he asked out loud to the television.

"How could I have forgotten? How stupid of me!" he said once more.

"He was the guard! He was the guard who spoke Spanish. He was the one who talked to Guevara."

All of a sudden John Hughes remembered.

It was the night before they executed him. He and Ed Manion had taken a few hours off to change clothes and get something to eat. Manion was tired and decided to lie down. He went back to check on the prisoner. When he did, he found the Green Beret and the prisoner engaged in a pretty heated conversation in Spanish.

"I didn't know you understood or spoke Spanish," Hughes said to the Staff Sergeant.

"Sir," he answered respectfully. "We all speak any number of foreign languages."

"Yes," Hughes acknowledged. "I guess you do. I must have forgotten."

"Then you've understood what we've been saying?" he asked.

"No, sir," Reed said. "I made it a point not to listen. It would have broken my concentration. I need to concentrate because we expect the Cubans to try to free him. I didn't want to be taken by surprise."

"Good thinking," Hughes said.

Of course, he didn't believe him.

They were talking about some very sensitive information. Guevara told them things they did not know and he told them things that he knew that they did not want him to know.

Hughes suspected, but had no way of knowing, that Guevara and the Green Beret Sergeant were discussing exactly that when he arrived. And when he left, the conversation continued.

In his room in Tidioute, Charley Reed was dreaming. In his dream he was back there in 1967 and he was speaking with Che Guevara.

"You don't like me," he said.

"No," Charley answered.

"It was the little girls," he said to him. "That's the reason."

"Yes," he answered him.

Guevara laughed.

"You dislike me because I had sex with them and then you go and kill them. I wasn't going to kill them. I fed them and I cleaned them and I gave them pleasure. I taught them how to be women. I honored them. You killed them, not me."

Charley didn't answer the man. He ignored him as he continued to taunt him over it.

Then Guevara changed the subject.

"Were you listening to what they were asking me?"

Charley didn't answer him. He really didn't want to talk to the man.

"They're going to kill me," he said. "Even though they said they wouldn't if I cooperated with them, I know they will. They can't let me live. I know too much. I'm too dangerous to them."

He waited for some response from Charley. He upped the ante

when Charley didn't answer him.

"Were you listening when they asked me about the assassination of John Kennedy?"

Guevara laughed.

"They didn't know that I knew."

He laughed again.

"Only Fidel and Raul were supposed to know. They had no idea that I was in the loop, too. Fidel asked me what I thought he should do. I knew it was going to happen a year before they killed him. We set up Oswald to be their fall guy."

Charley had listened when they interrogated him. He listened and was surprised at what he heard. Now, Guevara was telling him exactly what he told them.

"John Kennedy couldn't be trusted not to invade again. He was beefing up Guantanamo Bay to the point that our whole army had to be committed there, leaving the rest of the island without adequate protection. He kept aircraft carrier groups off our shore just as a continued threat. That was when Raul made contact with your Mr. Townsend."

"Why are you telling me this? Am I supposed to be impressed?" Charley asked the man.

"No," Guevara said. "You're not one of them. You're a soldier. You do as you are told and you believe what they tell you to believe. Someone like you should know what they did.

"They call me a terrorist. They call anyone who opposes their oppressive regimes terrorists. They called the Viet Cong terrorists when they are a peoples' army for the liberation of their country. They call everyone terrorists, when it is they who are, in fact, the real terrorists.

"Killing a President, wouldn't you call that a terrorist act?" Guevara asked.

Charley didn't answer.

Guevara waited for an answer, but none came.

"I would," he said. "I would call killing John Kennedy a terrorist act. And it was people within your own government who did the killing. They did the planning and they did the killing.

"Fidel gave them Oswald. Your CIA gave us money and we funded Oswald and put him where he could be implicated. We helped set him up so the real killers could escape detection."

"Why?" Charley finally asked.

"For the guarantee that you would not invade Cuba," he answered. "Your Vice President was more than willing to give us that guarantee. He was more than willing to assume the Presidency, too."

Charley took a deep breath. He was twenty-one years old. He didn't need to know this. He was angry.

"You're saying Lyndon Johnson was part of having the President killed?" he asked.

"Yes," Guevara said. "He was very much a part of it. Besides the generals, who benefited most from him being killed?"

Chained to the wall and sitting on the dirt floor of the brick building, Guevara continued. "I was there in Havana when the deal was made.

"Raul traveled to Toronto and met with your CIA people. They gave him money. He returned and we got in touch with Oswald and brought him to Cuba for training. Everyone looked the other way. He traveled to Mexico City and then to Havana and everyone knew it. He didn't know what we were doing.

"As soon as Kennedy was killed and Johnson took over, he kept his part of the bargain. He cut troop levels in Guantanamo in half immediately and then in half again the following year. He took the carrier groups out of the waters off our shore and he stopped the spy plane flights. We existed, peacefully ignoring one another.

"What do you think?" Guevara asked. "They told me Fidel and Raul gave me up to them? Should I believe them?"

Charley thought about it and then he answered.

"We have been getting very reliable information as to where your people have been. We knew in advance you would be here when we attacked. I don't have any idea where they get their information, but they could have been told by them just as easily as anyone else, if what you say about how they deal with one another is true."

Charley couldn't see him well.

It was dark and the man's bloody and swollen face hurt when he changed his expression. Just the same, he endured the pain and did exactly that and he nodded his head at the same time.

"It makes sense," Guevara said. "I posed a danger to Fidel. He had given up the true feeling of the revolution and he sent me here when I would have much rather been in the Congo. In the Congo I was protected by the people I was fighting with. Here, I am alone with my men. There is no popular support like there was in the Congo. He sent me here to die. He sent me here to be done with me."

Charley recognized the disappointment in the man's voice.

"I'm a victim of the terrorists, also," he said.

He forced a laugh. As he did, he felt the sharp pain of several broken and unattended ribs. He found it hard to breathe.

"May I have water?" he asked.

"You know I'm not allowed to get anywhere near you," Charley answered.

"Yes," Guevara answered.

He didn't press the issue and they didn't speak for several minutes.

Then Charley walked over to a water bucket that was around the side of the building. He took a tin cup sitting next to it and filled it with water. He took it into the building to the man who was sitting in the corner.

"Here," he said. "Here's some water."

"Thank you," Guevara said. "Thank you very much."

"You're welcome," he said.

At midnight he was relieved. He went back to his tent to get some sleep. But as he tried to sleep, he found he couldn't.

He couldn't forget what the man told him about the CIA killing President Kennedy. He couldn't get it out of his head that Lyndon Johnson, the Vice President at that time, was part of it, too.

Was he supposed to believe this man? Was he telling the truth? And why did he pick him to tell it to?

Finally, Charley did fall off to sleep that night, but he didn't sleep very well. He tossed around on the uncomfortable cot and never really fell off to sleep completely. He couldn't get what he'd been told out of his mind.

The next morning he went back to his post. As they led Guevara out of the building, he looked at Charley.

Charley remained expressionless, but Guevara forced a smile. He was being led to his execution and he forced a smile. Charley wondered why.

"Gracias, mi amigo," he said as he passed by.

"De nada," Charley answered.

Charley watched as they blindfolded the man and stood him up against a wall. Guevara wasn't very brave. He was afraid of death and began to weep. He lost control of himself and in fear, wet himself.

Then the rifles exploded and Guevara was thrown back against the wall and then fell to the ground.

Charley woke up as the guns fired on the man and he fell to the ground. He woke feeling as if he was there and it had just happened.

But he wasn't and it hadn't just happened. Thirty-four years had passed. It was thirty-four years ago that he spoke with Che Guevara.

Why was he dreaming about it now?

CHAPTER SIXTY-FOUR

Doug Hauser was playing a hunch. John Hughes wanted all the small hotels, even the fleabags, checked. He took out a map of western Pennsylvania. He looked to the north, south, east and west. Then he calculated from the time the story ran about Reed being seen in Pittsburgh.

"Six forty-five," he said to himself. "An hour to pack up and leave alone makes it seven forty-five."

His reasoning was that if he were with a woman he knew, he would want to keep her safe. Reed knew by now that anyone with him was not safe. He would surely leave her behind and be traveling alone.

"He's fifty-five," he said. "He goes to sleep early. I'll give him two hours of driving before he needed to get off the road and find a place to sleep."

He drew a circle around Pittsburgh centered in the North Hills where the bar was located. The outermost part of the circle was one hundred miles away. Looking at the North Hills of Pittsburgh and even considering Charley Reed was from the South Hills, Hauser dismissed the notion that he would go south or southwest.

"It has to be east back toward New York, or north. What is up north?" he asked himself.

"The mountains are up north. The mountains would be a great place to disappear. There are hundreds of little towns where no one would even give a damn."

He thought about the east briefly.

"Why would he go back to New York? He would easily be identified if he checked into a hotel. No. He wouldn't go back there."

Carefully he plotted several routes north to the mountains. He began in Franklin, Pennsylvania and checked bed and breakfast inns and small motels. He worked his way north to Oil City, then to Tionesta.

Finally around two in the afternoon, he got to the Hotel Tidioute. The girl who answered the phone verified they had an overnight guest who answered the description of the man he was inquiring about. Doug Hauser immediately left for Tidioute.

The government agent was stricken with culture shock the moment he entered the small town on the Allegheny River. And, his condition became acute when he walked into the bar of the one hundred thirty-year old hotel. If anyone ever looked out of place in a suit and tie, Doug Hauser certainly did. Every eye in the place centered on him as he walked up to the end of the bar.

When he introduced himself and showed the woman behind the bar a photograph of Reed, she made a positive identification.

"That's him," she said. "I didn't check him in. Sonny, the owner, did."

"Is he around?" Hauser asked.

"No," she answered.

"Where can I reach him?" he asked.

"You can't," she said. "He's in the woods hunting. He won't be in here until dark."

Doug checked his watch. It was four-thirty and it would be dark in an hour or so. He decided he would stay. Reluctantly, he ordered something to eat.

Just before six Sonny came in. Pam, the woman behind the bar, whispered something to him. Immediately, he turned his attention to the man in the suit.

Sonny was an enormous man. He stood nearly six feet three inches tall and weighed about three hundred pounds. He had a full beard and a full head of hair and huge hands. He walked over to Doug.

"Is there something you need from me?" Sonny asked.

Hauser showed him the picture he showed to the bartender.

"Do you recognize him?"

"Why?" Sonny asked, answering the man's question with a question.

"Do you watch the news?" Hauser asked.

"Do you have identification?" Sonny asked. "Who the fuck are you anyway?"

Hauser took an immediate dislike to the man. He reached into his left pocket and produced identification that said he was with the United States Treasury Department.

"Do you watch the news?" he asked Sonny.

"No," he said.

"Do you recognize this man?" he asked again.

"He stayed here last night. He rented a room from me."

"He's a wanted man," Hauser said.

Sonny immediately corrected him.

"He's not wanted. They just want him to come in for his own protection."

"I thought you said you didn't watch the news," Hauser said.

"I don't," Sonny said glaring at him.

"Then you talked to him," Hauser concluded.

"I didn't say that," Sonny said.

"Then how do you know about him?" he asked.

"Pam told me. She watches the news for me. She tells me what's going on and keeps me posted on anything that she thinks I might be interested in. Beyond that, I don't give a flying fuck."

"Do you know where he went when he left here?" Hauser asked.

Sonny shook his head in a strange way, still glaring at the government agent.

"Is that a yes or a no?" Hauser asked.

"It's a no," he said. "I checked him in, gave him his key, told him where his room was, and told him to park around back. He said thank you and beyond that we didn't have any conversation at all. When I came in this morning, he was gone and the key was in his room."

"He didn't say what he was doing here or where he was headed?"

"No. He didn't say and I didn't ask."

"Is that normal?" he asked.

"Normal?" he laughed. "This is Tidioute, Pennsylvania. Look around. Do you see anyone who resembles normal? The farther north you go the worse it's going to get."

Hauser was frustrated. He had driven up from Pittsburgh and had gotten nothing. He was hours behind Reed and the man he was talking to was uncooperative.

"Thank you for your time," Doug said.

He left and went to his car. He had a parking ticket.

Following a hunch, he continued north to Warren, Pennsylvania. He saw a Holiday Inn and stopped for the night. As he checked in, he took a chance.

"Has my friend Chuck Reed checked in yet?" he asked.

The girl at the desk checked and he watched her face for any changes in her expression, but there was none. She looked and then she looked again.

"No, sir," she said. "I don't show any reservations for him either."

He took his suitcase and laptop computer and went up to his room. He logged on and checked his mail. He had no activity so he took the time to do a report and send it on to Director Hughes using secure communication and encryption. When he was finished, he checked the other hotels in the town. Everything came up negative.

He laid his map out on the bed. Directly north was Jamestown, New York. To the east was Bradford, Pennsylvania and Olean, New York. The town of Kane, Pennsylvania was to the east, also. Going west from Warren was Erie, Pennsylvania. Reed could have gone to any of those locations.

As Hauser thought about it, he decided towns like Erie or even Buffalo were not likely destinations. The fact that Reed chose Tidioute gave him the intuition that he was going to avoid large population centers. Chances were he would go small so he could avoid notoriety and detection.

He folded up his map and went down to have dinner.

John Hughes was still in Pittsburgh when Hauser's communication came through. He smiled at the conclusions his agent in the field was making. He agreed with them completely.

Sonny was sitting at his bar having his fourth beer. He couldn't help but think about the man who was there earlier.

"Treasury Department my ass," Sonny said to Pam. "He was a fucking spook. An FBI agent would have identified himself as FBI. He was after him for his own reasons and it had nothing to do with taking him into protective custody."

Pam agreed.

"I didn't tell him anything. I let you make the decision what you wanted to tell him. I didn't like his looks. I didn't like anything about him."

"Fucking feds," Sonny said.

Sonny got up from his barstool and looked in his address book. He copied down a phone number, took some change out of the cash register, and left the bar. He walked down to the Laundromat and went to the pay phone. He dialed the number for the Rainbow Inn. The operator came on and asked him to deposit seventy-five cents.

"Rainbow Inn," a perky young voice answered.

"Is Buddy there?" he asked.

"Who may I say is calling?" she asked back.

"Tell him it's Sonny."

He heard her lay the phone down. Moments later his friend

picked up the phone.

"My gumba," he said. "How the hell are you?"

"Buddy," he said. "Do you have a stranger up there named Charley?"

"You mean the guy you gave the message about the magazine to?"

"Yeah," Sonny said. "That's him."

"Do you know who he is?" he asked.

"No, not really," Buddy said. "Should I?"

"He's been all over the news," Sonny said. "He's the guy the President was talking about yesterday."

It didn't mean anything to him.

"I don't watch the news unless they break in on the Steeler game with it," Buddy said. "This shit in Afghanistan and the New War is more than I can take."

"I know," Sonny said. "I feel the same God damned way. I'm sick of looking at those assholes on television."

"I'm with you, brother," Buddy said.

"Anyway," Sonny said. "The Feds were here looking for him. Is he there now?"

"Yes," Buddy said.

"Can I talk to him?"

"Sure," he said.

He put the phone down and walked around the bar. Charley was sitting with George Walter talking about hunting and fishing. He tapped him on the shoulder and took him aside.

"My friend Sonny is on the phone for you. Take it on the pay phone over there and when you are done, don't hang up. I want to talk to him again."

Charley walked over to the phone and stopped. He turned to Buddy.

"What's wrong?" he asked.

"I can't talk on the phone. They're looking for me. They can identify my voice."

Buddy got on the phone and explained to Sonny. They spoke for several minutes. When he was through, Buddy laid the phone down and began to speak with Charley. He explained what Sonny told him.

"So what's up?" Buddy asked.

"The guy who was there today would have been from the CIA."

"Why?" Buddy asked.

"The FBI is looking for me just to take me into protective cus-

tody. An FBI agent would have identified himself as one. This guy said
he was with the Treasury Department. He was lying."

Buddy got back on the phone and told Sonny what Charley said.
"He's a fellow vet," Buddy added.

"Yeah," Sonny agreed. "Are you going to take care of him?"

"He asked me if he could camp out on the property. I told him he
could. I told him he could use the old cabin in the back. But my father-
in-law has taken quite a shine to him. He's invited him down to camp
to stay. He's there alone now before the gang gets in for deer hunting
next week."

"Keep him out of sight. Tell him to park that truck of his with the
California plates and leave it parked. If you need anything, give me a
call. Just don't talk on my phone. Leave a message and I'll call you from
the pay phone next door," Sonny advised.

They hung up and Buddy went down to where Charley Reed was
sitting. He sat down next to him and had a drink. He listened as George
told both of them about hunting up in Canada.

While all of this was going on, John Hughes was looking at maps
too.

"Hauser's right," he said to himself. "He's a hundred percent
right.

"Reed grew up in Pittsburgh. His father probably took him up in
those hills camping when he was a boy. With what he's faced with now,
he would go back there. All I need to do is find out where. That's
where we will find Charley Reed."

He wrote back to Hauser and told him to stay on the trail and
keep looking. "I will be in my office," he wrote to him. "Keep me posted several times daily."

The following morning Hughes flew back to Washington.

Doug Hauser went to Jamestown and then to Olean. He checked
hotels, but came up blank each time. He went down to Bradford and
drew a dead end there. He checked with the local police, asking if they
had seen California license plates in the area and that came up negative also. From Bradford he went to Kane and then on down to
Ridgway. Every attempt came up negative.

Finally, he went back to Tidioute. It had been two days since he
was there. He hoped Charley Reed might have returned. It was a dead
end, too. He phoned in and John Hughes called him to Washington.

Meanwhile, the FBI was growing frustrated too. The story lost its national prominence the day after it ran. The bombing in Afghanistan took front seat and with the live coverage there was no room for the story of Charley Reed anymore.

Marty Sporror hoped Charley would come in, but understood why he wouldn't. He didn't trust anyone. He had lost faith in his own government. Considering the number of times it had tried to kill him, he really couldn't blame him one bit.

CHAPTER SIXTY-FIVE

In the meantime, Charley Reed was settling right in. George and he became constant companions.

Charley liked George. The man was seventy-six and a World War II veteran. He'd been in the Navy and served at the end of the war on a hospital ship and evacuated the American prisoners of war from Nagasaki after the second atom bomb was dropped.

He reminded him a bit of his own father, if for nothing else, the way he was always giving him advice. Charley remembered resenting it when his father gave advice. He was young and didn't understand. Now at his age, he welcomed anything that came his way. He realized how badly he had botched things up.

George gave him a bed to sleep in and Charley chipped in for food and booze. They went over to the courthouse and purchased their hunting licenses. Charley didn't want to use his California identification fearing it would expose him, so he claimed he lost his identification and used George's address in Canada. The woman in the County Treasurer's office knew George and was very accommodating.

The news story about Charley was dead.

Sonny called and told Buddy about the agent returning to Tidioute. Buddy told Charley what happened and Charley thanked him.

"Thank you and thank Sonny for me," he said. "You didn't have to do this."

"I know," Buddy said. "You're a fellow vet. We felt like we had to help you out."

"Thanks," Charley said. "You know, I had a very good friend named Buddy."

Buddy laughed.

"What's so funny?" Charley asked.

"Only three people in the world have ever called me Buddy," he said. "My mother, Sonny, and my friend, Edna. Everyone else has always called me Bud. You've been calling me Buddy since you showed up and I have never bothered to say anything."

"Does it bother you?"

"Hell, no. I kind of like it," he said.

"Where's your friend Buddy now?" Buddy asked.

"Dead," Charley said. "He died in a VA Hospital years ago."

"I'm sorry," he said.

Charley shrugged.

"What the hell," he said. "He was wounded in the action that has these assholes looking for me."

"Yeah?" he asked. "Where was that?"

"South America," Charley answered.

"Bolivia?" he asked.

"Yes," Charley said. "How did you know?"

"Ever hear of Night Watch?" Buddy asked.

"No," Charley answered. "What was that?"

"It was a series of flying command posts. C-135's, the military version of the Boeing 707, were in the air on a twenty-four hour a day basis. Five to seven of them were up at any given time and they were in the air all over the world. The idea was that if there was a sneak attack and the President was knocked out or unable to order a retaliatory strike, the three generals on board could.

"There was a hierarchy when we were in the air. One time we were primary, another time we would be fifth in line. It changed all the time and no one was really sure who was on the front line. I used to plot weather maps on one of them."

"Weather maps?"

Buddy laughed.

"Yes, weather maps," he answered. "I plotted weather maps for wherever we had troops or missions. In the summer of 1967, along with a lot of other places, I was plotting weather maps for Bolivia and Chili, too. There was a lot of Air Force activity there.

"We were giving Air Force support to some secret CIA mission. Evidently, it was your mission, Operation Eagle Thrust."

Charley was shocked. Plainly other people did know, but because of so much worldwide activity and the prominence of the Vietnam War, it was dismissed and forgotten.

"You knew the name?" he asked.

"Yes," he answered Charley. "It came across the teletype attached to changing weather conditions. All the secret missions were tagged and we gave weather for all of the areas. We were doing weather for Cambodia and Laos long before anyone knew we were in there."

Charley couldn't believe what he was hearing. Obviously, at one time there was proof. There was proof of everything and it was in a very common place. It was buried in weather reports and plotted maps. He wondered if it still existed.

He asked Buddy, "Do you think any of those still exist?"

"I don't know," he said. "It was thirty years ago. I don't know if the Air Force Bases are still open. Chanute was the training center for the Weather Corps and they closed it down and moved the school to Mississippi, I think. Paper records were probably destroyed rather than moved.

"Scott Air Force Base was the headquarters for Air Weather Services. If they are still there, they might have records.

"And then there was Tinker Air Force Base in Oklahoma. That was where all the teletype transmissions originated. That was where the information about where I was to plot maps for originated. If it's still open, I would guess it would still be in their files."

Buddy thought a moment and shook his head.

"I would say they would have a record of everything, if not there, somewhere else, because they keep records of the weather for climatologic reasons. That information is definitely somewhere."

Charley shook his head. He knew he had to speak with Marie Van Arsdale. He knew he had to, but he also knew he couldn't use the telephone.

While they were talking, John Hughes was meeting with Doug Hauser.

"Years ago a man named Henry Townsend chose me," he said. "He brought me into the inner circle of the Company and because of his trust in me, I was able to do great things in the interest of our nation. He told me I reminded him of himself. "

Doug Hauser listened attentively.

"Doug, you remind me of myself back in those days. He included me in a very secret mission. I was always thankful for that. His trust made my career.

"While my contemporaries were being sent off all over the world and being sacrificed for useless causes, I was kept here at home and worked into a position where I made the decisions about the missions others would carry out. I was the one behind the scenes calling the shots.

"Even though I didn't go all over the world on missions and become assigned to embassies, I still made my bones here at home. I earned everything I ever got and I earned it the hard way. I had to be careful not to get caught. Sometimes that wasn't easy. Sometimes I had to do things I wasn't allowed to do, but it was for the best of the country and the country always came first.

"Do you understand what I am saying to you, Doug?"

"Yes, sir," he said. "The end justifies the action required."

"Exactly!" he said. "Exactly! Sometimes there are things we do that may appear to be against the best interest of the country, but in reality they are for the best."

"Sir?" he asked.

"Sometimes there is a popular politician who can do a lot of harm in the policies and positions he takes. Sometimes that popular politician has to be dealt with. Sometimes he is embarrassed and disgraced. Sometimes he is just eliminated. I was lucky. I was given the privilege of being part of those actions.

"Do you understand?" Hughes asked.

"Yes, sir," Hauser answered.

"Good," Hughes said. "Do you think you would like to be part of something like that? Would you like to participate in the oversight of our nation and the course it is supposed to take?"

"Yes, sir," Hauser answered once more.

"Excellent!" Hughes said. "That is excellent."

The two men went to dinner and discussed several things. Hauser was to become Hughes assistant and take the place of Lou Locante. That meant he had to pick up where Locante left off and oversee something of a very sensitive nature. At the same time he had to be part of a very small group with the mission of eliminating Charley Reed. As they rode together in John Hughes car, he explained it all to Doug Hauser.

Charley Reed was comfortable with Buddy. He liked the man. There wasn't any bullshit with him. It was one way or the other. They had been drinking most of the afternoon and now it was well into the evening. They were talking about Vietnam.

"It all sucked," Buddy said. "We were thrown to the wolves without a thought. It was all because the corporations wanted to make money. It's the same God damned thing today. We're at war so George Bush's rich friends can get richer."

"What about the World Trade Center?" Charley asked. "Do you think they let it happen to get the country behind a war?"

THE FIRST TERRORIST ACT

"Nothing surprises me anymore," he answered. "Hell, some Israeli predicted it was going to happen exactly the way it did as far back as 1989. No one listened to him. No one cared."

"You're right," Charley said. "You are one hundred percent right."

"Christ!" Buddy said. "Look at who is in charge. George Bush was as big a draft dodger as Bill Clinton. Bill Clinton was up front with it all. He just out and out dodged.

"Georgie was different. He was in the Air National Guard or something like that and he never bothered to show up for meetings or summer camp. He was out drinking, doing cocaine and partying his ass off. That was while we were giving up major parts of our lives being in uniform.

"Now he is the commander in chief. Go figure that one out!"

Charley Reed agreed.

"Hell," Buddy continued. "While I was in the service and while you were in the service, the judge in this county was in college protesting the war. He had long hair and was wearing beads. He marched on the Pentagon.

"Now he is the most patriotic son-of-a-bitch going. He is riding around with two American flags on the back of his car supporting the New War. Imagine that, a draft-dodging judge finally becoming patriotic!

"If he's so fucking patriotic now, why didn't he put on a uniform then? What's changed? I really want to know. What the fuck has changed?"

About that time, the bartender came over.

"Uncle Bud," Andrea said. "Watch the language."

"Okay, baby," he said. "I'm sorry."

That only served to temper him for the time being. Charley got him started once more with the next question.

"What about this anthrax business? What do you think about that?"

"Christ," Buddy said. "When it is all said and done, we are going to find out it was manufactured right here in the U.S. of A.

"We'll never find out who really sent the stuff out because if that ever came out, the whole God damn government would come tumbling down.

"They'll pin it on some fall guy when if the truth would be known, it was our own government sending the stuff out to scare the hell out of the American people and keep this war going.

"When you and I were in the service, they had enough of that stuff in Fort Richey, Maryland to kill half the world. They probably manu-factured the AIDS virus there. The right-wingers in the government set it loose to eliminate the fags and it got out of hand. They probably have an antidote ready, but they will never let us know. AIDS, like so many other things, is just one more way for the government to con-trol the masses. That's all this anthrax is. The God damn government, or someone in the government is probably behind it all."

"Uncle Bud," Andrea said again. "Do I have to call Aunt Sherry?"

"No. No," he said. "I'll behave."

The other men at the bar laughed and teased Bud at how his niece could control him with the mention of his wife's name.

"I'm not stupid," he said. "I don't want my ass kicked."

Everyone laughed, including Charley and Buddy.

Meanwhile, Doug Hauser was not laughing. John Hughes had just let him in on information he never in his wildest imagination could believe was true. If John Hughes himself had not told him, he wouldn't believe it.

"This nation is too large," he told Hauser. "How many people are there? Two hundred thirty million? Two hundred fifty million?

"The Constitution and the Bill of Rights were designed for a rural and spread out population. They were set up to insure no one could take a part of this nation and set up their own empire. The founding fathers never envisioned the world we have today with instant communication and technology that makes us so powerful that we pose a danger to ourselves. How could they have imagined that?

"They were smart men for their time. They were even ahead of their time in what they conceived. But, they had no idea of what we have today. Hell, most of the American people have no concept of what we really have at our disposal. We keep most of it hidden from them. It's better they don't even know. They're sheep. And just like sheep, they need to be led and they need to be herded. That's our job."

Charley and Bud kept on drinking. It didn't take long for them to get started again. This time it was the Anti-Terrorism Bill that had been passed into law.

"Fucking lawyers," Buddy said. "They thought it up. Sneak-and-peek warrants that allow secret searches, wiping out the chance to call a lawyer or watch while the police rummage through your things. How do you know they aren't planting things while they are there?

"Hell," he said. "They could break in and plant ten pounds of cocaine and then come back and find it."

He laughed.

"Some democracy!

"They maintain secret databases of suspicious people with no clear guidelines of what names and information are included. Since September 11th they've rounded up and detained indefinitely more than 1,200 people, some on material witness warrants, some on immigration violations such as overstaying a visa, some detained even when an immigration judge has ordered them freed. They don't care. They are making the rules now.

"They have roving wire taps that allow law-enforcement to keep listening to conversations beyond the designated target. And then there are the special military tribunals to try non-citizens suspected of terrorism in secret trials without juries, where the standard for proving guilt falls below beyond a reasonable doubt and where the death sentence requires only a two-thirds vote. And" he said. "There are no appeals.

"What's it all about?" he asked. "They claim it is in the name of fighting terrorism and preserving national security.

"Are you, am I, is America willing to give away its civil liberties for that? It seems to me that some people believe we love security more than we love liberty. Why? Tell me why?"

Andrea wasn't telling her uncle to be quiet this time. The whole bar was listening.

"It's at times like this, times of fear, we tend to place security above everything else. We are quite willing to give the government extraordinary authority. I don't understand why. If the government had done its job, September 11th would never have taken place. It didn't and because it didn't we have to give up our rights.

"It's an old story. With a lot of these bills, they are saying to trust them. Do you trust them? I don't!

"I have trouble with that concept. I really do. Changing the rules right now begins the process of losing constitutional rights. There is no cause or justification for compromising our constitutional rights and principles. There is nothing that happened on September 11th that the American justice system and the Constitution of the United States cannot handle."

Buddy was on a roll and all the men at the bar were listening.

"A lot of people believe we are living through times with unique threats to our society and that we must make sacrifices to protect our national security. Bull shit!

"George Bush has called upon us to go on with our everyday lives and remain vigilant. He wants us to give blood, money, and volunteer efforts to assist our victims; and he wants us to trust and support our military. That's a first! He didn't support it, but he wants us to.

"I don't have a problem with any of it. I really don't. I have a problem when he asks us to accept rules that abridge the very freedoms on which our founding principles are based, no matter how grievous the enemy against whom they might be used.

"The threat to our civil liberties far outweighs the physical threat these rules are designed to contain. They are all bullshit and need to be off the books right away."

For the most part, the men in the bar agreed with him. "What about the military tribunals?" someone asked him.

"Are we afraid of our own system?" he asked back. "Didn't we try Manuel Noriega in an open court? Didn't we try the people who bombed the World Trade Center back in 1993 in an open court of law? We brought them to justice. What's different? Is it because we are at war? How can that make it any different?

"Tell me anything the government could have done any differently before September 11 that these laws would have changed. They had intelligence. They had rumors this was going to happen. They didn't act on it.

"We need to look at what we had and why it was inadequate before we start changing things.

"The Constitution has worked all these years and now we have some people in Washington who say it can't now that we've been attacked. I don't like that. I believe when you do that you are looking to shift the blame from where it belongs.

"I don't believe George Bush has the right to blame the United States Constitution. When he says he needs extraordinary powers, he is doing exactly that. Don't tell me it was our Constitution that made us susceptible to terrorism. I don't believe it and I never will."

Charley stood up and applauded him.

"Well said. Well said, my friend."

Then he joined in.

"I want to know why we didn't detect what was going on and why we couldn't stop fanatics from boarding our airplanes and destroying the World Trade Center and the Pentagon?" he asked.

No one could give him an answer.

"Our government is out of control," Charley said.

Then he turned to Buddy. His voice went down.

"I lost a son in the World Trade Center," he said. "I never knew him."

There were tears in his eyes.

"I never knew my son and he was a fine man. He was a good husband and a father. His widow is pregnant again.

"With all that we have at our disposal, am I supposed to believe we couldn't have stopped it? Or did we know and just let it happen so they could have their New War?"

"I don't know," Buddy said. "I hope it didn't go down that way, but you and I both know what these people are capable of doing."

"Yes, we do," Charley said. "Yes, we do."

Both men sat and stared at their drinks. They didn't talk much after that. The more they thought about what was happening and what had happened, the more they both felt cheated.

Charley thought about the judge with the flags on the back of his car. It was almost comical. But as comical as it might have been, it was equally disgusting. While they were fighting, the judge was setting up his life. He was in law school letting others do their duty to the country while he was safe and preparing to live in the upper ten percent of people in the nation.

While Charley hadn't been homeless or without work, he certainly had the obstacles the war gave him and the judge did not. Yes, he thought to himself, that's the way it is.

"Chuck Ganley and a lot of other fine and good people are dead because someone, somewhere, in some government agency didn't do their job.

"Why couldn't they have stopped them?" Charley asked.

"There was no need to," John Hughes answered Doug Hauser. "It was much like Pearl Harbor. We needed an excuse. If we didn't have an excuse, the American people, the press, the television, all of them would have never tolerated the New War."

"So you let it happen?" he asked.

"Not me," John Hughes said.

"But someone let it happen," Doug insisted.

"Yes," Hughes admitted. "Someone let it happen."

"Who let it happen?" he asked.

John Hughes stared back at Doug with a blank look. It wasn't cold. It was just blank.

"You don't want to know," he said. "Believe me when I tell you. You really don't ever want to know. Not now. Not ever. Forget about it."

CHAPTER SIXTY-SIX

Cindy Ganley couldn't get Charley Reed off her mind. She suffered through Thanksgiving. Tina flew up to Pittsburgh with the girls and Julie came, too. Charley was the main topic of conversation.

"Mom was really upset that I let him stay with us," Tina told Cindy.

"Why?" Cindy asked.

"She didn't want him around the girls or me. She said it was dangerous. Bob even agreed with her and that is a real switch for him."

"She does have a point, Tina," Cindy said. "He told me he wanted to stay longer with yo and the girls, but when the story was going to break about him, he felt it was better if he left. He took a hotel room on the way out of town and paid for it with his credit card just to throw everyone off his trail and draw people away from you."

Julie teased her mother about rekindling an old love affair. Cindy blushed. Tina laughed and teased her a little herself. Tina and the girls stayed through Monday and then flew back to New York.

Cindy was alone again and the time Charley spent with her seemed to consume her waking moments. Even when she slept, she dreamed of him. The days dragged on.

The national news story about him ended as fast as it began. There were much larger things going on in the world. His story was small potatoes and because it was, it made him vulnerable. It also made her vulnerable as well as Tina and Julie. Anyone who was in contact with him was vulnerable. She knew it, but she didn't care. She wanted to see him.

"Where would he have gone?"

She asked herself that same question over and over. She ached for him. She wanted to see him again. She wanted to have him hold her in his arms. She wanted to feel him inside of her. What had been dead was now awake. She wrestled with the new dimension her life had taken and she tried to remember something that would give her a clue.

Cindy thought about what he said when he suddenly announced he was leaving.

"Don't worry," he said. "I have a place in mind that should be safe enough. I can't tell you. It would put you in danger."

He had been living in California all those years. Did he return to California?

She wondered.

"No," she said out loud. "He couldn't risk it. His face was all over the news. He couldn't risk being seen again. He had to have a place he could reach in a day and then drop out of sight."

Then she remembered.

When he was in high school and they first met, there was a major falling out between him and his father over him going away with his dad on the weekends. Once he met her, he didn't want to go anymore. His father didn't like it. Charley would much rather stay at home and see her at the school dances.

At the end of November, right after Thanksgiving, he had to go. It was the beginning of deer season. His father insisted on it and even Charley gave in on that.

"I have to go," she remembered him telling her.

"I've been to every hunting camp with my dad since I was six," he said. "If I don't go this year, it will break his heart."

Cindy remembered she didn't understand. Her dad didn't hunt. He didn't fish. She didn't understand why it was so important to him. What could be so important about shooting a defenseless deer? Why would anyone want to do that?

She pressed the issue with him.

"What am I supposed to do while you are gone?" she asked. "What about the dance. Who will I dance with?"

She knew she hit a nerve with that. She hit a very sensitive nerve. Charley was extremely jealous.

"Dance with whoever you fucking want to!" he said and then he hung up.

The way he exploded scared her at first. She wanted to tell her mother, but she knew if she did then her mother would forbid her to see him again. Instead, she called her friend Jean.

"What did you expect?" Jean asked.

Cindy laughed.

"You're right," she said. "If he didn't act like that, I wouldn't like him."

"Exactly," Jean said.

He went away that weekend because he had to. He was only fifteen. It wasn't as if he had some say in what he did and didn't do. It was that way back then. As she remembered, Cindy smiled. He was sweet.

She didn't go to the dance on Saturday night. She stayed home and babysat her sisters. At nine o'clock the phone rang. It was Charley. She remembered how excited she was when she answered and heard his voice.

It was noisy. She could hear people in the background and she could hear music.

"Where are you?" she asked.

"I'm with my dad in a bar. It's called the Rainbow Inn. I'm sorry for talking to you like that," he said. "I'm sorry I hung up on you."

"I acted like a spoiled brat," she said. "I'm sorry I said that and made you jealous."

"I love you," he said.

"I love you, too," she said back.

"I can't talk long," he told her. "I only have a few dollars. I won them playing poker at camp. Everyone got drunk and I took advantage of them. They wouldn't let me drink, so I fleeced them at poker."

"Good for you," she said. "Have you shot a deer yet?"

"No," he answered. "We don't start hunting until Monday."

"Then why did you have to leave on Friday?" she asked.

"Because my dad said we had to. He wanted to get to camp with the guys and drink and play cards. Today we sighted our rifles. Tomorrow we come back here to watch the Steelers. Monday we hunt."

"When are you coming home?" she asked.

"Wednesday," he answered.

"Where are you, anyway," she asked.

"It's a little town called Marshburg," he said.

"Where is Marshburg?" she asked him.

"It's near Bradford."

As Cindy remembered the conversation that took place forty years ago, she walked to the family room and found the road atlas underneath a stack of old magazines. She opened the book of maps to western Pennsylvania and found Bradford. There was a large green area near it and suddenly she saw Marshburg. It was on the northern edge of the Allegheny National Forest.

Charley had gone back to Marshburg. She knew it as soon as she saw it. Cindy knew where Charley was.

She phoned Julie.

"I don't know how to do this. You know me with computers. Can you find out about Bradford, Pennsylvania for me?"

Julie went to her computer and did a search of Bradford, Pennsylvania. She found Bradford on-line. She clicked on it.

"Okay, Mother, I have Bradford on-line. It is 34 degrees at 5:54 p.m. What do you want to know?"

"Do they have a directory or something like that?" she asked.

"Yes," she said. "What are you looking for?"

"Do they have a listing for the Rainbow Inn?" she asked.

"As a matter a fact, they do," Julie answered. "They are one of the sponsors of the web site."

"What can you tell me about the Rainbow Inn?" she asked.

"There's a picture of it. It looks like a decent place and it says it is 'Catering to the wild spirit of the sophisticate diner.' Do you want me to get more information?" she asked.

"Yes, honey. Please."

A moment passed. Julie began reading the page back to her mother.

"It says: Located in lovely downtown Marshburg, Pennsylvania on Route 59 next to the firehall. Open For Your Dining Pleasure. Catering to the wild spirit of the sophisticated diner! 814-368-9863

"We Have the Best Prime Rib in the World! Forget the plastic chicken and the cold food that you get at other restaurants. Take your choice of the best Prime Rib in Northwestern PA, Louisiana Style Shrimp Scampi, or our famous Burgers and Wings. Seating for parties up to 100.

"We are open Monday - Sunday. Seven days a week. Our Half Pound Sirloin Burgers are the Best around! We offer a Full Menu on Friday and Saturday nights featuring our famous Prime Rib $9.95 and the specials of Chef Sherry. The Rainbow Inn, the friendliest place in the Alleghenies!"

"Thank you, honey," she said. "Thank you very much."

"What's with the Rainbow Inn, Mother?" Julie asked.

"That's where Charley is," she said.

"So what are you going to do?" Julie asked again, already knowing the answer.

"I am going to him," Cindy said.

"Somehow I knew that, Mother. Somehow I just did."

While Cindy Ganley was finding Marshburg on a map, Doug

Hauser turned on his laptop and began to access the Internet. He was interested in what information was out there regarding the September 11th attacks and if there was any scuttlebutt about the U.S. Government having prior knowledge.

It didn't take him long. He pulled up an article about the CIA having foreknowledge of the attacks.

"U.S. and Israeli intelligence agencies received warning signals at least three months ago that Middle Eastern terrorists were planning to hijack commercial aircraft to use as weapons to attack important symbols of American and Israeli culture, according to a story in Germany's daily Frankfurter Allgemeine Zeitung (FAZ).

"The FAZ, quoting unnamed German intelligence sources, said that the Echelon spy network was being used to collect information about the terrorist threats, and that U.K. intelligence services apparently also had advance warning. The FAZ, one of Germany's most respected dailies, said that even as far back as six months ago western and near-east press services were receiving information that such attacks were being planned.

"Within the American intelligence community, the warnings were taken seriously and surveillance intensified, the FAZ said. However, there was disagreement on how such terrorist attacks could be prevented, the newspaper said.

"Echelon is said to be a vast information collection system capable of monitoring all the electronic communications in the world. It is thought to be operated by the U.S., the U.K., Canada, Australia and New Zealand. No government agency has ever confirmed or denied its existence. However, an EU committee that investigated Echelon for more than a year just last week reported its belief that the system does exist.

"The EU committee said that Echelon sucks up electronic transmissions 'like a vacuum cleaner,' using keyword search techniques to sift through enormous amounts of data.

"The FAZ, in its news story, described the system as covering the whole world with 120 satellites. The newspaper also said Israeli intelligence had collected information indicating that Arab terrorist groups planned to hijack planes in Europe to use as weapons to attack targets in Tel Aviv and other coastal cities in Israel.

"Because of increasing concerns of plane hijackings, Israel has tested a new x-ray machine at the Tel Aviv airport, the FAZ said. The machine is capable of detecting all known explosive elements, even if only in small quantities, the newspaper said.

"The FAZ said that German intelligence fears that in coming days planes will be hijacked in Europe and the Near East, and that there is no sure way to protect against it."

As he finished reading that, he found another charging U.S. Government complicity in the attacks.

"Chicago Attorney David Schippers, head of the Clinton impeachment, asserted yesterday on the Alex Jones show that the Justice department had detailed information on 9-11 weeks before the attack was carried out.

"Schippers says that he personally sent information about the impending 9-11 attack to Attorney General Ashcroft asking for an investigation, but Ashcroft refused to do that.

"Schippers got his information from FBI agents who had collected information about the impending attack and all the terrorists subsequently involved.

"The FBI agents sent the information to Schippers after they were explicitly ordered to drop their investigation of signs of the impending attack.

"Given the Government's extremely well documented prior knowledge of and complicity in the first WTC bombing and the OKC bombing, I find this report credible.

"Only the government is benefiting from the fallout of 9-11 as a result of its assumption of drastically increased powers to fight terrorism."

"My God!" he said out loud. "Can this be true?"

Doug accessed the Company computer and looked for information. It was at that point he discovered something known as Project Bojinka. Along with it, was an accompanying e-mail that was intercepted regarding the operation. It was sent out days after September 11th and went to over fifty different people. All of those people, including the author, were placed under electronic surveillance.

"To my Classmates:

"Sometime in January 1995, when Philippine Police authorities captured Ramsey Youssef in Manila, I was asked, because of my affiliation with the NBI, to help decode and decipher the hard drives of the computers found in Youssef's possession. This is where we found most of the evidence of the projects that were being funded by Osama Bin Laden in the Philippines. The first plan was to assassinate Pope John Paul II who was then scheduled to visit the Philippines. The second was Project Bojinka, which called for the hijacking of US bound commercial airliners from the Philippines, Korea, Thailand, Taiwan,

Honking(sic -ed) and Singapore, and then crash them into key structures in the United States. The World Trade Center, the White House, the Pentagon, the Transamerica Tower, and the Sears Tower were among prominent structures that had been identified in the plans that we had decoded.

"A dry-run was even conducted on a Tokyo bound Philippine Airlines flight, which fortunately was aborted by our security personnel.

"It was also from these computers that we found the plans for the first bombing of the World Trade Center in February 1993. This evidence was eventually used to convict Ramsey Youssef, Abdul Hakim Murad and Wali Khan for the WTC bombing.

"Obviously, the original Project Bojinka was modified to give it more significant impact on the USA. By hijacking planes that originated from within the United States instead of Asia, they made sure that AMERICANS would be killed in the hijacking instead of Asians, which obviously would elicit a stronger reaction from the Americans. And transcontinental flights (East Coast to West Coast) would have more fuel for most of the targets, which were on the East Coast. Abdul Hakim Murad admitted that they had been taking flying lessons in the Philippines for Project Bojinka. Obviously, after they were caught and convicted, a new set of terrorists were trained in the United States (Venice, Florida) for the modified Bojinka.

"The Philippines has been having a lot of problems lately because Osama Bin Laden has been funding the activities of the Abu Sayyaf through his brother-in-law, Khalifa Janjalani. The success of these recent terrorist acts in the United States will embolden Commander Robot and Commander Sabaya, both of the Abu Sayyaf, to wreak more havoc in our part of the world. What is strange is that the United States agencies that took possession of the evidence that we gathered, obviously, did not take Project Bojinka seriously. I would have thought that intelligence operatives would have analyzed all the evidence and worked out various scenarios that could have included the modified Bojinka plan. If they had done so, the US would have been prepared for this attack.

"Let us thank God that many of our friends were spared from the horrors of the other day. I have been stuck in Minneapolis for the last two days after attending the reunion of the East Coast Eagles in Washington, DC. I am irritated that I am unable to travel but I am gratified that I am still alive enough to be irritated!"

Finally, Hauser found one more thing. It was intercepted via e-mail also.

"FTW, November 2, 2001 - 1200 PST - On October 31, the French daily Le Figaro dropped a bombshell. While in a Dubai hospital receiving treatment for a chronic kidney infection last July, Osama bin Laden met with a top CIA official - presumably the Chief of Station. The meeting, held in bin Laden's private suite, took place at the American hospital in Dubai at a time when he was a wanted fugitive for the bombings of two U.S. embassies and last year's attack on the U.S.S. Cole. Bin Laden was eligible for execution according to a 2000 intelligence finding issued by President Bill Clinton before leaving office in January. Yet on July 14th he was allowed to leave Dubai on a private jet and there were no Navy fighters waiting to force him down."

Doug Hauser shook his head. He turned off his computer and went to bed. He did not know what to think.

Marty Sporror was still at the office. Charley Reed was old news to everyone except him. He knew now that Reed had no intention of turning to the FBI for help. He realized Reed didn't trust anyone associated with the government. All he could do is hope for a lucky break and find Reed on his own. What he was holding in his hand just might be that lucky break.

On Wednesday, November 21st, a Canadian resident named Charles Reed purchased an out-of-state Pennsylvania hunting license at the McKean County Court House. He gave Whitney, Ontario as his place of residence. At the same time that Reed purchased his license, a George Walter, also from Whitney, Ontario purchased a similar hunting license. After checking with Canadian authorities, it was determined there was a George Walter from Whitney, Ontario; but there was no Charles Reed.

Marty picked up his phone and got the research department's voice mail.

"This is Agent Sporror. I want telephone records, utility records from McKean County, Pennsylvania for George Walter. I want a hard address and location for him in that area. I want them as soon as possible. This is a priority matter. Thank you."

Marty hung up the phone and went home.

On Sunday morning Cindy Ganley woke early and packed.

She didn't know what to take and tried on everything to make sure it fit her. She didn't know how long she would stay or even if she would be able to find him. Not knowing anything for sure, she packed so she could be gone a week.

She squeezed herself into a pair of jeans. She turned and looked at how they made her rear end look.

"Not bad for fifty-four," she said. "Not bad at all."

She picked out a sweater that matched and a light windbreaker. She took her suitcase out to the car and left for the mountains of north-western Pennsylvania.

CHAPTER SIXTY-SEVEN

The men began arriving the Friday after Thanksgiving. First Neil Barnard arrived, then Larry Ely. Rod and Rusty were next. They got in on Saturday. Finally Clayton and his son, Andrew, came in on Sunday. Everyone drank up at the Rainbow and watched the Steeler game.

The next day just before dawn the eight men went out behind George's camp and put on a drive. By night four deer were hanging.

Charley was hunting with a .280 that Buddy loaned him. He had a shot on top of the hill. There was a buck with two doe, but he didn't fire. He just stood there admiring the animals. He didn't care about killing anything. He was just enjoying being out in the woods again and took pleasure from the peacefulness of nature.

They had stuffed cabbage rolls for dinner. Clayton's wife, Joan, made them in advance and sent them down to camp with him. Then they went up to the Rainbow Inn.

That was the routine for the entire week. They got two more deer the rest of the week. Larry Ely shot a huge ten-point buck and Neil got a four-point. Rod saw more deer than anyone, but like Charley, didn't take a shot. Andrew saw and shot a white coyote. He kept it and wanted to get it mounted.

It was a good week. Charley enjoyed everyone, especially Rod and the stories he told. And Rod enjoyed having someone new to tell the same stories to and the week seemed to fly by.

On Sunday everyone left except for George and Charley. They left behind the unused deer tags so the two men could use them if they had the opportunity. Around noon Charley and George walked out of camp to leave for the Rainbow Inn to watch the football game. As they walked out, George looked at Charley's truck.

"Take the front license plate off it," he said.

It dawned on George that anyone driving by could identify the truck. With the front plate off, it looked like every other vehicle from Pennsylvania.

"Right now?" Charley asked.

"Sure," George said. "We're early. Bud will save us seats at the bar."

As George suggested, Charley removed the front license plate and put it under the front seat. As he did, he felt the 9-millimeter pistol. He thought about taking it with him but decided against it. He got into George's van and put on his seatbelt.

Pittsburgh was playing the Minnesota Vikings. It was a close game and Charley was sitting between George and Buddy. In no time at all, he was a Steeler fan again. The three of them were really into the game and when the kicker missed a field goal.

"He's going to cost us the game," Buddy said.

Charley agreed.

For the next three quarters of football, George, Charley, and Buddy were really wrapped up in the game. Charley felt totally at ease with the men. He was watching the television set and didn't see Cindy standing behind him.

She watched him while he was watching the game. While the other men in the bar were watching her, she was watching Charley. George didn't see her and neither did Buddy. They ignored her when the bartender asked her if she wanted anything.

"Canadian Club and coke, please," she said.

Charley didn't hear her. Finally Cindy whispered into Charley's ear.

"How about those Pittsburgh Steelers!"

Charley turned around to see Cindy standing there.

"Cindy, what are you doing here?" he asked her with a surprised look on his face.

"I missed you," she said.

"I missed you, too," he said.

He got up from the bar and kissed her. The men around him started to hoot at him.

"Get a room," Bud said, teasing them and a few other men echoed his sentiments.

George started to complain to Bud about how times had changed.

"Hunting camp is going to hell in a hand basket. There aren't supposed to be women at camp unless they are the old-time variety we keep around to be the camp cook and other things."

"Cool it," Charley laughed.

"How did you find me?" he asked Cindy.

"You called me from here once."

"What?" he asked.

He went back into his memory.

"Wow, that was forty years ago. I'm impressed."

Cindy smiled at him.

"I'm an impressive lady."

Charley gave her his seat. He introduced her to George and Buddy. While they were talking the bar cleared out. The game was over and less than a dozen people remained.

"Where are you staying?" she asked.

"I'm bunking in with George. I've been there a couple of weeks."

"I have a room at the Holiday Inn in Warren," she said to him. "Want to have dinner with me?"

"Sure," he said. "I'll need to change."

"That didn't take long," George chimed in.

"Hey!" Charley said to George smiling.

"You're fine the way you are," she said. "Bring your toothbrush."

Charley smiled and turned back to George.

"It looks like I'm going to be gone awhile," he said. "I'm going to go down to camp and get a few things and will be back tomorrow."

"No problem," he said. "See you when you get back. I have to go up to Northeast and visit with Florence and Guy. Winnie's up there and I have to make my annual appearance. This will work out fine."

Cindy drove him to camp. Charley picked up his clothes and shaving kit. He went out to the truck and took his pistol. It had been on his mind all afternoon and he felt better if he had it handy. He also took the extra ammunition he had purchased for it. He went back into camp and left the keys for the truck on the kitchen table in case George needed to move it. He got back in the car with Cindy and kissed her.

"This is a great surprise," he said.

"For me, too," she said.

As they drove up the hill to the main road and turned right to Warren, the commuter flight from Pittsburgh flew overhead and made the final approach to Bradford Regional Airport. For the most part it was empty. There were only five passengers and two crewmembers. Two of the five passengers were John Hughes and Doug Hauser.

"Where can we stay?" Hughes asked.

"I stayed at the Holiday Inn in Warren," he said.

"How far is that?" Hughes asked.

"About thirty miles."

"Isn't there any place closer?"

"There's a Howard Johnson in Bradford, about ten miles away."

"That's fine," Hughes said.

The two men got off the plane. The pilot thanked them personally for being aboard. He was under the impression they were U.S. Marshals doing routine flight security. They identified themselves as such before they boarded and were cleared to carry weapons.

They rented a car and drove to Bradford and checked into their rooms.

"Where do we start?" Hauser asked his boss.

"We wait," he answered. "We wait until the FBI comes up with the information we want. When they have it, we will have it. Then we move. By the time they get here, the job will be done and we will be on our way."

Doug was beginning to realize exactly how certain elements of the government worked. There was a shadow government within the government and agencies that on the surface that did not collaborate with one another, beneath the surface indeed did.

When Marty Sporror left the office on Friday night and made his request to research, his request, along with the material that prompted the request, was immediately passed on to John Hughes.

Sporror had one mission. Hughes had another.

Doug sat in his room and began to read a document he obtained from breaking into FBI files. As much as he didn't want to believe it, at that particular moment, nothing surprised him.

"In 1985 Oliver North - the only member of the Reagan-Bush years who doesn't appear to have a hand in the current war - sent the Navy and commandos after terrorists on the cruise ship Achille Lauro. In his 1991 autobiography 'Under Fire,' while describing terrorist Abu Abbas, North wrote, 'I used to wonder: how many dead Americans will it take before we do something?' One could look at the number of Americans Osama bin Laden is alleged to have killed before September 11 and ask the same question.

"The story says that, 'Throughout his stay in the hospital, Osama Bin Laden received visits from many family members (There goes the story that he's a black sheep!) and Saudi Arabian Emirate personalities of status. During this time the local representative of the CIA was seen by many people taking the elevator and going to bin Laden's room.

"Several days later the CIA officer bragged to his friends about having visited the Saudi millionaire. From authoritative sources, this

CIA agent visited CIA headquarters on July 15th, the day after bin Laden's departure for Quetta.

"According to various Arab diplomatic sources and French intelligence itself, precise information was communicated to the CIA concerning terrorist attacks aimed at American interests in the world, including its own territory.

"Extremely bothered, they (American intelligence officers in a meeting with French intelligence officers) requested from their French peers exact details about the Algerian activists (connected to bin Laden through Dubai banking institutions), without explaining the exact nature of their inquiry. When asked the question, 'What do you fear in the coming days?' the Americans responded with incomprehensible silence.

"On further investigation, the FBI discovered certain plans that had been put together between the CIA and its 'Islamic friends' over the years. The meeting in Dubai is, so it would seem, consistent with 'a certain American policy.'

"Even though Le Figaro reported that it had confirmed with hospital staff that bin Laden had been there as reported, stories printed on November 1 contained quotes from hospital staff that these reports were untrue. On November 1, as reported by the Ananova press agency, the CIA flatly denied any meeting between any CIA personnel and Osama bin Laden at any time.

"In the most ironic twist of all, FTW has learned that Le Figaro is owned by the Carlyle Group, the American defense contractor which employs George Bush, Sr., and which had as investors - until they sold their stake on October 26 - the bin Laden family."

"Who should I believe?" Doug asked himself.

Doug went on to the next document. It was another he had pilfered from the FBI.

From the looks of things, the FBI was building some kind of case against someone. They were using a document from an Internet magazine called From the Wilderness. It was written by a man named Mike Ruppert. The document read:

"1998 and 2000 - Former President George H.W. Bush travels to Saudi Arabia on behalf of the privately owned Carlyle Group, the 11th largest defense contractor in the U.S. While there he meets privately with the Saudi royal family and the bin Laden family. (Source: Wall Street Journal, Sept. 27, 2001. See also FTW, Vol. IV, No 7 – 'The Best Enemies Money Can Buy.'

"Feb 13, 2001 - UPI Terrorism Correspondent Richard Sale -

while covering a trial of bin Laden's Al Q'aeda followers - reports that the National Security Agency has broken bin Laden's encrypted communications. Even if this indicates that bin Laden changed systems in February it does not mesh with the fact that the government insists that the attacks had been planned for years.

"May 2001 - Secretary of State Colin Powell gives $43 million in aid to the Taliban regime, purportedly to assist hungry farmers who are starving since the destruction of their opium crop in January on orders of the Taliban regime. (Source: The Los Angeles Times, May 22, 2001.)

"May 2001 - Deputy Secretary of State Richard Armitage, a career covert operative and former Navy Seal, travels to India on a publicized tour while CIA Director George Tenet makes a quiet visit to Pakistan to meet with Pakistani leader General Pervez Musharraf. Armitage has long and deep Pakistani intelligence connections and he is the recipient of the highest civil decoration awarded by Pakistan. It would be reasonable to assume that while in Islamabad, Tenet, in what was described as 'an unusually long meeting,' also met with his Pakistani counterpart, Lt. General Mahmud Ahmad, head of the ISI. (Source: The Indian SAPRA news agency, May 22, 2001.)

"July 2001 - Three American officials: Tom Simmons (former U.S. Ambassador to Pakistan), Karl Inderfurth (former Assistant Secretary of State for South Asian affairs) and Lee Coldren (former State Department expert on South Asia) meet with Taliban representatives in Berlin and tell them that the U.S. is planning military strikes against Afghanistan in October. Also present are Russian and German intelligence officers who confirm the threat. (Source: The Guardian, September 22, 2001; the BBC, September 18, 2001.)

"Summer 2001 - According to a Sept. 26 story in Britain's The Guardian, correspondent David Leigh reported that, 'U.S. department of defense official, Dr. Jeffrey Starr, visited Tajikistan in January.' The Guardian's Felicity Lawrence established that US Rangers were also training special troops in Kyrgyzstan. There were unconfirmed reports that Tajik and Uzbek special troops were training in Alaska and Montana.

"Summer 2001 (est.) - Pakistani ISI Chief General Mahmud (see above) orders an aide to wire transfer $100,000 to Mohammed Atta, who was according to the FBI, the lead terrorist in the suicide hijackings. Mahmud recently resigned after the transfer was disclosed in India and confirmed by the FBI. (Source: The Times of India, October 11, 2001.)

"June 2001 - German intelligence, the BND, warns the CIA and Israel that Middle Eastern terrorists are 'planning to hijack commercial aircraft to use as weapons to attack important symbols of American and Israeli culture.' (Source: Frankfurter Allgemeine Zeitung, September 14, 2001.)

"Summer 2001 - An Iranian man phones U.S. law enforcement to warn of an imminent attack on the World Trade Center in the week of September 9th. German police confirm the calls but state that the U.S. Secret Service would not reveal any further information. (Source: German news agency 'online.ie', September 14, 2001.)

"August 2001 - The FBI arrests an Islamic militant linked to bin Laden in Boston. French intelligence sources confirm that the man is a key member of bin Laden's network and the FBI learns that he has been taking flying lessons. At the time of his arrest the man is in possession of technical information on Boeing aircraft and flight manuals. (Source: Reuters, September 13.)

"Summer 2001 - Russian intelligence notifies the CIA that 25 terrorist pilots have been specifically training for suicide missions. This is reported in the Russian press and news stories are translated for FTW by a retired CIA officer.

"July 4-14, 2001 – Osama bin Laden receives treatments for kidney disease at the American hospital in Dubai and meets with a CIA official who returns to CIA headquarters on July 15th. (Source: Le Figaro, October 31, 2001.)

"August 2001 - Russian President Vladimir Putin orders Russian intelligence to warn the U.S. government 'in the strongest possible terms' of imminent attacks on airports and government buildings. (Source: MS-NBC interview with Putin, September 15.)

"August/September, 2001 - The Dow Jones Industrial Average drops nearly 900 points in the three weeks prior to the attack. A major stock market crash is imminent.

"Sept. 3-10, 2001 - MS-NBC reports on September 16 that a caller to a Cayman Islands radio talk show gave several warnings of an imminent attack on the U.S. by bin Laden in the week prior to 9/11.

"September 1-10, 2001 - 25,000 British troops and the largest British Armada since the Falkland Islands War, part of Operation 'Essential Harvest,' are pre-positioned in Oman, the closest point on the Arabian Peninsula to Pakistan. At the same time two U.S. carrier battle groups arrive on station in the Gulf of Arabia just off the Pakistani coast. Also at the same time, some 17,000 U.S. troops join more than 23,000 NATO troops in Egypt for Operation 'Bright Star.'

All of these forces are in place before the first plane hits the World Trade Center. (Sources: The Guardian, CNN, FOX, The Observer, International Law Professor Francis Boyle, the University of Illinois.)

"September 6-7, 2001 - 4,744 put options (a speculation that the stock will go down) are purchased on United Air Lines stock as opposed to only 396 call options (speculation that the stock will go up). This is a dramatic and abnormal increase in sales of put options. Many of the UAL puts are purchased through Deutschebank/AB Brown, a firm managed until 1998 by the current Executive Director of the CIA, A.B. 'Buzzy' Krongard. (Source: The Herzliyya International Policy Institute for Counterterrorism, http://www.ict.org.il/, September 21; The New York Times; The Wall Street Journal.)

"September 10, 2001 - 4,516 put options are purchased on American Airlines as compared to 748 call options. (Source: ICT - above)

"September 6-11, 2001 - No other airlines show any similar trading patterns to those experienced by UAL and American. The put option purchases on both airlines were 600% above normal. This at a time when Reuters (September 10) issues a business report stating, 'Airline stocks may be poised to take off.'

"September 6-10, 2001 - Highly abnormal levels of put options are purchased in Merrill Lynch, Morgan Stanley, AXA Re(insurance) which owns 25% of American Airlines, and Munich Re. All of these companies are directly impacted by the September 11 attacks. (Source: ICT, above; FTW, Vol. IV, No.7, October 18, 2001, http://www.copvicia.com/members/ oct152001.html.)

"It has been documented that the CIA, the Israeli Mossad and many other intelligence agencies monitor stock trading in real time using highly advanced programs that are reported to be descended from Promis software. This is to alert national intelligence services of just such kinds of attacks. Promis was reported, as recently as June, 2001 to be in Osama bin Laden's possession and, as a result of recent stories by FOX, both the FBI and the Justice Department have confirmed its use for U.S. intelligence gathering through at least this summer. This would confirm that CIA had additional advance warning of imminent attacks. (Sources: The Washington Times, June 15, 2001; FOX News, October 16, 2001; FTW, October 26, 2001, - FTW, Vol. IV, No.6, Sept. 18, 2001; - FTW, Vol. 3, No 7, 9/30/00.)

"September 11, 2001 - Gen Mahmud of the ISI (see above), friend of Mohammed Atta, is visiting Washington on behalf of the Taliban. (Source: MS-NBC, Oct. 7.)

"September 11, 2001, For 35 minutes, from 8:15 AM until 9:05 AM, with it widely known within the FAA and the military that four planes have been simultaneously hijacked and taken off course, no one notifies the President of the United States. It is not until 9:30 that any Air Force planes are scrambled to intercept, but by then it is too late. This means that the National Command Authority waited for 75 minutes before scrambling aircraft, even though it was known that four simultaneous hijackings had occurred - an event that has never happened in history. (Sources: CNN, ABC, MS-NBC, The Los Angeles Times, The New York Times.)

"September 13, 2001 - China is admitted to the World Trade Organization quickly, after 15 years of unsuccessful attempts. (Source: The New York Times, Sept. 30, 2001.)

"September 15, 2001 - The New York Times reports that Mayo Shattuck III has resigned, effective immediately, as head of the Alex (A.B.) Brown unit of Deutschebank.

"September 29, 2001 - The San Francisco Chronicle reports that $2.5 million in put options on American Airlines and United Airlines are unclaimed. This is likely the result of the suspension in trading on the NYSE after the attacks which gave the Securities and Exchange Commission time to be waiting when the owners showed up to redeem their put options.

"October 10, 2001 - The Pakistani newspaper The Frontier Post reports that U.S. Ambassador Wendy Chamberlain has paid a call on the Pakistani oil minister. A previously abandoned Unocal pipeline from Turkmenistan, across Afghanistan, to the Pakistani coast, for the purpose of selling oil and gas to China, is now back on the table 'in view of recent geopolitical developments.'

"Mid October 2001 - The Dow Jones Industrial Average, after having suffered a precipitous drop has recovered most of its pre-attack losses. Although still weak, and vulnerable to negative earnings reports, a crash has been averted by a massive infusion of government spending on defense programs, subsidies for 'affected' industries and planned tax cuts for corporations."

Doug couldn't believe what he was reading.

"Who prepared this?" he asked himself out loud.

He checked the source. He found Mike Ruppert on the Internet and he found the website he ran with a subscriber-based newsletter called 'From The Wilderness.'

"How accurate is this guy?" he asked.

Then he started checking. He began referencing the newspapers mentioned. One item after another checked out.

"It's true," he said to himself. "It's really true."

He thought about the conversation he had with John Hughes at dinner. He thought about what he said. He could still hear his words.

"You don't want to know," he said. "Believe me when I tell you. You really don't ever want to know. Not now. Not ever. Forget about it."

They echoed in his head. He couldn't get them out.

"What was he a part of?" he asked himself.

Cindy drove them to Warren and they went straight to her room. She wanted him and she took the initiative.

Even though it was out of character for her, she undressed him and she took their lovemaking in the direction she wanted. Charley didn't complain one bit. He laid back and enjoyed himself. He needed her as much as she needed him. Then it was over.

They lay there in the bed together. They were facing one another and Charley was playing with her breasts.

"Stop," she said. "Haven't you had enough?"

"I don't know," he answered playfully. "You never can tell."

"I can," she said.

She reached down and touched him. He grew hard again. She giggled.

"Come with me," she told him. "Let's take a shower together."

Charley thought the idea was a wonderful one. Cindy ran a hot shower and got in. Charley followed her. She took a washcloth and a bar of soap and began to soap all over his body, paying special attention to his private parts. When she reached them, she gave them a strong lathering and made sure they were especially clean. She had him so hard it excited her to look at him.

"Your turn," she said, handing Charley the washcloth and the soap.

Charley was gentle as he soaped her body. He kissed her neck and ears as his hand with the soapy cloth caressed her breasts and her vagina. He turned her around so she was facing him. His mouth moved down to her breasts. Softly he sucked on each one. Then he moved lower and his tongue reached inside her. She gasped as the warm water beat down on her back.

Both of his hands gripped at her buttocks and pulled her closer to him. His tongue was driving deep inside of her and she could feel herself being driven higher and higher, moving toward another climax.

Then she was there and she clutched his head with both of her hands.

"Oh God!" she cried out. "Oh God! Oh God! Oh God!"

She didn't release her grip on his head. She didn't want it to stop. Finally he stood up and kissed her deeply. She could feel his hardness sticking into her stomach. They got out of the tub and turned off the water. He grabbed a towel and began to dry her. Once he had her nearly dry, he took another for himself and quickly dried off. Then he took her in to the bedroom and on the bed.

He kissed her again and as he did, he forced himself inside of her. She cried out as she felt him enter her. Immediately she had another orgasm. She cried out as he drove himself inside of her. Then she felt him explode. She pulled him close to her and held him. She didn't want to let him go, but slowly he relaxed and then he rolled off her and held her in his arms.

"You're something else," she said to him.

Charley just smiled.

She kissed him and got up to dress and do her hair. Charley watched her as she walked away.

"Nice ass," he said to her.

She stopped and turned to look over her shoulder.

"I said that myself this morning when I put my jeans on. Thank you."

He laughed and stayed in bed while she did what she had to do. Finally she told him to get up and get ready.

"I'm starved," she said. "I don't remember when I have ever been this hungry. Sex must do that to me."

Charley laughed and got dressed. Now that she mentioned it, he was hungry, too. Maybe it was the sex.

He held her hand as they went down to the dining room. They waited to be seated and then he ordered them drinks. He couldn't help being awed by how beautiful she was. But as he sat there, even after the great sex they had just finished, something was missing. He couldn't help himself, but something was not there that he imagined should be. What it was he didn't know. He just knew it wasn't there.

He forced a smile and was as charming as ever. They ate and sat and had cocktails. They made small talk, the kind of talk lovers make. She touched his hand and told him how much she loved him. He picked her hand up and kissed it.

"I love you, too," he said. And for that moment at least, he did mean it.

They went back to the room and made love one more time. Then they both drifted off to sleep.

When Marty Sporror got to the office early Monday morning, the information he requested wasn't there. He made a phone call and wanted to know why. The answer he got wasn't the one he wanted to hear and he exploded at the person on the other end.

"This is a matter of national security," he said. "Get it for me and get it for me now!"

Meanwhile, Doug Hauser continued to wrestle with himself. He had a few simple questions and he couldn't find even a single simple answer.

How could these events have been ignored by the major news media or treated as isolated incidents? Couldn't they see a pattern? Failing that, how could skilled news agencies avoid being outraged, or at least even just a little suspicious? He couldn't quit thinking about all of it.

Doug stayed in his room waiting for the information they needed. John Hughes took the car and drove to Buffalo. He wanted some better weapons and decided to get them from some operatives there.

While all of that was going on, Cindy prevailed on Charley to take her shopping.

"There's a mall in Jamestown and we can have dinner there before coming back."

Charley agreed and he spent most of the day carrying bags around the stores for her.

As the sun was going down, they were going into a fashionable restaurant in the city of Jamestown called the Ironstone.

It was at that moment the phone rang in Doug Hauser's room and John Hughes was getting out of the car in the parking lot of Howard Johnson Motor Lodge in Bradford. Marty Sporror was opening a sealed envelope from the research department. Suddenly the world was smaller for Charley Reed.

Chapter Sixty-eight

When John Hughes knocked on Doug Hauser's door, Hauser had the information they needed to close in on Charley Reed. He had identified the property leased to George Walter on a map that he obtained from the forestry office in Marshburg.

"I went right past this place," he told Hughes.

"Hey," the experienced agent said. "Look at his place. Look at these hills. This is like looking for Osama bin Laden in all of those caves. Anyone with any outdoor experience could easily disappear in the forest and escape detection for months. I don't know what he's like now, but judging from what he did in Annandale last month, I would suspect Charley Reed is still fit enough to go out there and make it. Taking the mild weather we've had into consideration, I would guess he could survive very well."

Hughes looked up at Hauser and smiled. He was a man who seldom smiled. He was as cold and as rough inside as he appeared to be on the outside. A smile for him was very unusual.

"This is it," he said to Hauser. "Do you realize how long I've waited for this?"

Hauser shook his head. Really, he had no idea. He didn't have to ask because Hughes told him.

"He never would have survived 1968 if it wouldn't have been for Lyndon Johnson having an attack of conscience.

"Then in 1973 when Johnson finally died and his moratorium on sanctions died with him, I was on my way to finish the job when we were led to believe he was killed in an automobile accident.

"Congress got involved. That was the worst single thing that ever happened to the intelligence community. That was when this nation started going to hell in a hand basket. It took a Presidential order and an act of Congress to get permission to move on anyone, regardless of how much of a danger they posed to this nation.

"Then fate stepped in. We got a foothold in the Middle East following the Gulf War. We stayed in Saudi Arabia because the King was afraid the princes would overthrow him. Our presence there was a major deterrent. That was when it all started.

"There was the first World Trade Center bombing. The barracks in Dhahran was bombed. Then they bombed our embassies and finally the Cole. In the meantime, there were other attacks that we kept from the American people.

"There was the Egyptian Airlines attack, but the most blatant was TWA Flight 800. They fired two missiles at it and shot it right out of the sky. Imagine their courage to do such a thing!"

Doug Hauser did a double take. Courage? How could that have taken courage? He kept his feelings to himself. He continued listening to his boss.

"We had a warning that it was going to happen. We had a window and we had one of the largest peacetime exercises ever in our own waters going on just to prevent it. But no matter how hard you try, no matter how much military hardware you have, a few dedicated patriots can always succeed."

Once more Doug Hauser was stunned by Hughes choice of words. He was calling terrorists patriots. How could he do that?

"As soon as the missiles were launched, we went in on them, but it was too late for the people on that flight. We tried to take them alive, but they fought back and even fired a missile on one of our destroyers. The captain of the ship took them out with a single shot.

"There were hundreds of eyewitnesses who saw the missiles streaking toward the Boeing 747. They were all questioned and they were all discredited or ignored. That is all of them except for one man. He was on board US Air 217, a domestic flight from Charlotte to Providence. That was Charley Reed. He was using the identity of a friend of his who was killed in Vietnam. His friend worked for us just like Charley Reed did.

"I wanted to move on him right then and there, but Ed Manion wouldn't let me. He seemed to think that if Reed hadn't spoken in all of these years, he never would. And he had a point. Reed had shunned being a part of the TWA 800 thing even though he actually saw the missiles just before they hit the airliner. He knew if he came forward he would be caught.

"Manion wanted to let sleeping dogs lie. I wasn't allowed to go over his head to McMann. McMann was a bloodthirsty son-of-a-bitch and he would have given me the green light.

"But I followed orders just as you do. I left well enough alone and I let Charley Reed have his life. I let him go on living his lie, but it was eating at me how he had been able to elude us. All of those years, when we could have gone after him and finished the job we started way back when, suddenly our hands were tied. Ed Manion told me to put it all away. He wanted me to wait and try to see the big picture."

Suddenly the mention of a big picture brought Doug to life. He had been a listener up until that moment. Now he was a student. He went over to his desk and produced a document.

"Is there any truth to this?" he asked.

He handed him the timeline of events he had gleaned from the FBI taken from the Internet magazine called 'From the Wilderness.' A man named Mike Ruppert wrote it.

Hughes picked it up and looked at it. He looked back at Hauser.

"You've been doing your homework," he said. "You are a good pupil. You're going to do well in the company."

"Is there any truth to it?" he asked again.

"Yes and no," Hughes answered. "On the surface it looks very incriminating. It does because it is.

"Just looking at it, I would say the events chronicled are actual events. George Bush, our former President, and members of the Bin Laden family are close personal friends and they have had financial dealings. Of course, that isn't public knowledge nor will it ever be."

"How can you be sure of that?" he asked Hughes.

"Because for the most part we control what the American people find out."

"I thought so," Hauser said.

"Of course, we do," Hughes boasted. "We have to. We can't have investigative reporters running amuck out there, digging into places they have no right to be.

"Take that Van Arsdale woman, for example. Look at the damage she's done. Operation Eagle Thrust was buried and needed to stay that way. We have key people in key places that benefit greatly by their involvement in our program. They help us keep the news under control. It is very necessary we do it."

"How long has this been going on?" he asked Hughes.

"How long has there been a Central Intelligence Agency?" he asked back and then said, "We've always been doing it. We've had to. We didn't and don't have any alternative."

"So much for the Free Press," Hauser said.

Hughes just laughed.

"My boy," he said. "In 1967 I traveled from Toronto, Canada to Havana, Cuba with my boss and personally met with Fidel Castro and delivered to him five million dollars in U.S. currency. That was at a time when Cuba was the great Satan right along with the Soviet Union.

"What do you think our war on terrorism is all about? Is it about the World Trade Center Towers and the Pentagon? It may be to the President and it may be to some of the people in his cabinet who don't know any better. It may be to our boys fighting in the field, but it isn't to us. No. It isn't to you and me.

"It is about oil and the uniting of the United States of America and Russia in one of the greatest military and economic alliances in the history of the world. It's the beginning of the unification of the world."

He paused and seemed to be trying to choose his words carefully.

"Right here," he said holding up the document Hauser asked him about. "Look at your item twenty-seven. It tells the story.

"October 10, 2001 - The Pakistani newspaper The Frontier Post reports that U.S. Ambassador Wendy Chamberlain has paid a call on the Pakistani oil minister. A previously abandoned Unocal pipeline from Turkmenistan, across Afghanistan, to the Pakistani coast, for the purpose of selling oil and gas to China, is now back on the table 'in view of recent geopolitical developments.'

"Why do you think China has said nothing? They need that oil and the Taliban was standing in the way."

"Did we actually meet with Bin Laden in July?" Hauser asked.

"I can't say we did and I can't say we didn't. I don't know for sure because I wasn't there.

"I do know he was in Dubai. I do know he received treatments for kidney disease and I believe he was in all probability approached to intercede with the Taliban.

"But if you think about it, it was at counter purposes with the Saudi princes who control the price of oil and support him. The oil from Turkmenistan could only hurt them. If he was approached for that purpose, it was a poorly conceived plan. My bet is he was contacted for some other purpose."

"So you don't know for sure."

"No," he admitted. "I don't know that. McMann and Manion did and they are both dead. I would guess the station chief who made contact is dead, too, unless of course, he is the new heir apparent. And the way things work in the Company, that is a distinct possibility."

The two men went down to the bar for a few drinks before dinner. The conversation continued there.

"This is unbelievable," Doug said.

"Welcome to the real world," Hughes told him.

Hughes smiled remembering how naive he had been. He'd been with Henry Townsend when he was told much the same thing.

"You and I are very privileged," Townsend had told him several years ago. "We know things that heads of states don't know. We control the events that happen in the world and we shape history before it happens. Lyndon Johnson was the last President to have direct hands on. After he lost his stomach for it, it was decided the President would no longer be an active player. It was too dangerous.

"John Kennedy nearly wrecked the whole thing. When you think about it," Townsend told him. "John Kennedy was supposed to be the perfect president. He was Joe Kennedy's boy. If there ever was a player, it was old Joe. He was a buddy with the King and he was close to Hitler. Because of what he was able to do, a lot of people made enormous fortunes. He manipulated things for years and when his boy came along, we saw the best opportunity of the entire century.

"We had a cold war and we had us and the Russians at each other's throats for control of the world. It was a perfect situation, but he wanted it all to change. The dumb bastard wanted unilateral nuclear disarmament and he wanted to negotiate a peace between the Soviet Union and us. In return he was going to share technology with them and help them economically. The man who damn near started World War III over the missiles in Cuba was prepared to give the world peace."

Hughes could still remember Henry Townsend shaking his head.

"He had no idea what he was doing. He had no idea the people, the really powerful people he was going to hurt. No one wanted peace. We wanted things exactly the way they were. In an environment like that it was easy to control where things would go. War is the best thing for everyone. That is when you can get things done. We were on the verge of a war and Kennedy was going to change it. He had to go."

Hughes looked back.

Just as Doug Hauser was shocked at the possibility of the CIA having contact with Bin Laden a little over two months before the attacks on the World Trade Center and the Pentagon, Hughes had been equally shocked at what Townsend told him next.

"We killed Kennedy. We had to," said Townsend.

"At first we weren't sure whether we had to kill Johnson along with him. We didn't want to. We didn't want to make it look like some sort of South American military coup. But we had to be sure. We needed to know where Johnson stood.

"We approached him and he surprised the hell out of us. He didn't like the bastard any more than we did.

"Immediately he was our boy. He was ready to take over and give us a free hand and play ball all the way down the line. We had the best of all worlds. We would have our man in the White House and he was going to look the other way while we spun our magic."

John Hughes remembered Henry Townsend's face when he turned and told him about the meeting with Johnson.

"I'll never forget the man's face. It lit up with enthusiasm," Townsend said. "His body became animated and you could see a new life transfused into him. 'At last,' he said. He was absolutely excited.

"He wanted to know how it was going to be done and where it would take place and most of all, when. He couldn't wait. He was a man who really wanted to be President and he didn't care how it happened. It was almost laughable."

Hughes remembered how Henry Townsend got serious when he said that last sentence. He also remembered how he corrected himself, too.

"It was almost laughable, but it wasn't. Even Johnson knew it. He knew it as well as anyone in the room. There was nothing laughable about it. Johnson poured everyone a glass of bourbon. He poured himself a glass of scotch, Cutty Sark. Then he stood up and raised his glass in an unholy toast. It is one I will never forget.

"To the first terrorist act of a new administration, gentlemen. To it and to a new world order!"

"The wheels were set in motion and we carefully put all our ducks in a row. It was a military operation of precise timing and superb execution. We astounded everyone, even ourselves.

"We deceived the nation and we continued the deception with the Warren Commission. A lot of little people made their bones in that deal. Look at what it did for Arlen Specter. His single bullet theory was the largest pile of bullshit ever put on the American public! It was bullshit, but they ate it and they even asked for seconds.

"Everyone got what they wanted and no one was the wiser for it. In a way we looked upon it as saving the world from itself."

John Hughes remembered appreciating the insight Henry Townsend gave him. He didn't have to, but he trusted him enough to do so. In a way, looking back at the last meeting between the two of them, Hughes looked upon it as kind of passing the torch from one generation to another. He always appreciated it. He never had a chance to say it.

Henry Townsend died the next day of a heart attack.

Sitting there at the bar with Doug Hauser, it was more or less the same thing. His career was nearing a close and Hauser's was just beginning to take off. Doug Hauser wasn't even born when John Kennedy was killed. All he knew about it was what he was told in the history books and what he saw in television documentaries.

John Hughes was one of the few men who knew how it really came down. He wondered if he shouldn't pass the story along to his protégé.

He looked at Doug. His perception of the world had certainly changed. He was part of something now and he knew it. John wondered if he had made the proper choice. Henry Townsend certainly had.

"So, what do you think?" he asked Hauser.

"The implications of all of this are totally unbelievable."

"In what way?" Hughes asked him.

"It seems we knew and we did nothing to stop any of it. Even when the planes were first hijacked, for thirty-five minutes, from 8:15 AM until 9:05 AM," he said, quoting almost word for word from the report he obtained, "no one did anything. No one moved, they just watched while it was widely known within the FAA and the military that four planes had been simultaneously hijacked and taken off course. No one bothered or thought to bother to notify the President of the United States."

"What was he going to do?" Hughes asked. "Ask the Pentagon for permission to do something?

"Don't over estimate his power in all of this. Don't make that mistake. His father found out how much power he had in the Gulf War. It was a very rude awakening for him and I am sure it was a rude one for his son when he was flying around the country in Air Force One that day. The President of the United States controls nothing. He does as he is told."

Hughes laughed.

"It was the first time in history four jets were hijacked at exactly the same time. It was supposed to be seven, but two teams lost their nerve and one drew so much attention to themselves the crew wouldn't take off and called the police. They escaped, but we rounded them up. They were a wealth of information until their accidental deaths."

The men finished their drinks and went to the dining room to be seated.

"With any luck we can finish this up tomorrow. We need to before the FBI arrives. If they get here before we are done, that would be unfortunate."

Doug Hauser understood exactly what John Hughes meant by unfortunate.

"Do we have any backup coming or are we it?" he asked.

"We're it," Hughes said. "Don't you think we can handle it?"

"Of course, we can handle it. We know what he looks like. He doesn't know us from a hill of beans. All we have to do is dress to blend in with the rest of them and we'll be okay. I took care of that today. I found a store on Main Street and fitted us with the right clothes."

"Good thinking," Hughes told the other man. "Very good thinking.

"You and I are very privileged."

Then, repeating nearly word for word what was said to him years before, Hughes continued.

"We know things that heads of states don't know. We control the events that happen in the world and we shape history before it happens. Lyndon Johnson was the last President to have direct hands on. You weren't even born when he lost his stomach for it. It was at that time it was decided the President would no longer be an active player. It was too dangerous."

He laughed.

"Look at the presidents. Look at Carter. Look at Reagan. Do you think for one minute any of them even had a clue? George Bush did. He was part of it all at one time. He was smart enough not to try to take it over. When he was told to stop in the Gulf War, he stopped. His generals didn't like it. They weren't part of what was going on. Generals are a necessary evil, just like the President of the United States.

"Bush was smart enough to do as he was told. He knew what would happen if he didn't. He knew very well."

Hughes motioned to the waitress for another drink. When she looked to Doug, he indicated he wanted one, too.

"He knew and he kept his mouth shut.

"Then we had Bill Clinton. What a joke! The world was a safer place because he didn't have a clue," Hughes said. "It really was."

The waitress arrived with their drinks and he stopped talking. As soon as she left, he began again.

"Then we got this new administration. We helped them take power. We knew things and we used things to see that the decision went their way. We looked at it as the lesser of two evils and we count-ed on the fact that since we had been able to work with the father, we would be able to work with the son.

"Then things started to happen. There was almost a real peace in Palestine until they took over. It was as if they consciously set out to undo everything we worked to put in place. It is hard to say how many people they pissed off in the first three months of their administration.

"The first time they listened to us was when they gave the Taliban the forty-three million dollars for farm aid. It was a payoff to keep things under control. That didn't last long.

"Just when we had things pretty well managed and they were about to give in on the pipeline, we reneged on the next payment and the deal was off. We were getting all this flack about human rights and what they were doing to women. Who gave a rat's ass?

"All of a sudden we had this holier-than-thou shit and who knew what was going to come down? My guess is if the station chief visited Bin Laden in July, it was an attempt to bring some order to what was coming down."

"Why didn't we kill Bin Laden right then and there?" Hauser asked.

"We could have, but that would have been dirty pool. He was in Dubai at the invitation of the ruling family. They are our friends and he was their guest. Even we observe proper etiquette."

Hughes chose his next words carefully.

"I did not have first hand knowledge of what was going to hap-pen on September 11th. I was aware of Project Bojinka and I was aware there was a lot of discussion about it in the weeks leading up to September 11th.

"I was in Manion's office one day and he was discussing it with McMann. I was safe enough. They trusted me and spoke freely in front of me. I was under the impression they felt it was going to come down soon. If I was going to date it, I would say I was in the office with them right after Labor Day."

Doug Hauser digested everything his boss was telling him. Then he began to wonder to himself why he was telling him these things. Was he really the man's heir or was he just talking because he knew he was expendable? When all of this was over, was he going to be disposed of like so many already had?

He listened as his boss continued to talk. He listened and he won-dered.

"I believe you asked if we allowed it to happen?"

Doug nodded.

"Of course, we did," he said blankly. "We let it happen so we could justify what we are doing right now."

The two men finished their dinner and went back to the bar. They stayed there watching Monday night football. Then they went back to their rooms. They had a busy day ahead of them.

CHAPTER SIXTY-NINE

Marty Sporror was on a flight to Buffalo, New York the next morning. Finally, he had something concrete. Finally, he had a lead on Charley Reed. Two agents from Erie, Pennsylvania met him at the airport. He placed his bag in the trunk and got into the back of the car. Moments later they were speeding south toward Bradford.

As they were pulling out of the airport parking lot, Hughes and Hauser walked up to the door of George Walter's camp. There was a pickup truck parked outside, but it was the only vehicle around. They didn't give the truck much attention. They focused more on the wooden building. The windows had burglar bars across them and the door was made of thick stout wood. "There's no smoke coming out of the chimney," Hauser noted.

"Yes," Hughes agreed. "No one must have stayed here last night."

"Okay, now what?" Hauser asked.

"Get the number off the license plate of that truck," Hughes said. "Maybe it can tell us something."

Hauser went over to the back of the truck. What he saw told quite a story.

"Look at this," he said, calling over to Hughes.

John Hughes walked over to the back of the pickup truck and there he saw the California license plate.

"Smart," he said. "Real smart. He backs the truck in and puts it in plain sight. The only thing is he takes off the front plate so everyone assumes it's a Pennsylvania vehicle, not one from California. Slick. Real slick."

"Evidently he isn't very far away," Hauser said. "He probably got lucky with some broad last night and hasn't come home yet. We can park up the road and keep an eye on the place."

They found a place just off the road under some pine trees where a spring came out of the hillside. They turned the car around and parked there and watched the entrance to the camp.

Around eleven o'clock a car with three men pulled into the driveway. Hughes and Hauser watched as they got out of the car and walked up to the door of the camp. It was obvious they weren't staying there because they were knocking. It was also obvious they were not hunters either. They were wearing suits.

"FBI," Hughes said to Hauser.

"What does that do to us?" Doug asked.

"Nothing," Hughes said. "Absolutely nothing."

They watched as the men left and returned the way they came. For some reason the FBI agents ignored the pickup truck. They stayed where they were. Hughes just laughed.

"Idiots," he said. "They ignored the pickup. Some crack investigators."

"What time does that beer joint open up?" Hughes asked Hauser.

"Noon," he said.

"We want to be there when the FBI comes in looking for them. We can get all the answers we need without exposing ourselves. We're just two hunters. We look the part. You took care of that."

At noon they were at the Rainbow Inn. They took two barstools at the end of the bar next to the entrance to the kitchen. They ordered two beers and asked for menus. It didn't take long. The three agents came in just before one. They sat and listened as they approached the bartender.

"Is the manager or the owner around?" the first man asked.

"Yes, she is," the bartender said. "Who should I say wants to talk to her?"

He flashed his badge.

"Agent Sporror from the FBI."

The bartender went into the kitchen and moments later returned with another woman.

"Can I help you," she asked.

"Yes, ma'am," he said. "I'm agent Sporror with the FBI. I am looking for Mr. George Walter. Would you know where he is and how I could contact him?"

"He's in Northeast with my mother, visiting her sister. Is there anything I can do for you? I'm his daughter."

"Do you have a phone number or an address? All we want to do is speak with him. He isn't in any trouble of any kind."

While he was talking, the other two agents were looking around the bar. Hughes and Hauser knew they were looking for Reed. When they looked at the two of them, they just looked away.

The woman went back into the kitchen and came out with a piece of paper, handing it to the agent.

"He'll be there until Thursday. Then he's coming back here for the weekend to hunt."

"Thank you," Sporror said.

The three men left the bar.

"Let's go," Hughes said to Hauser.

They paid their bill and left. As the FBI agents pulled out of the parking lot, so did Hughes and Hauser. They followed them as they drove to Warren and then toward Erie. Hughes did the driving and Hauser found the town of Northeast on the map. It was a suburb of Erie.

It took close to an hour and a half to reach Northeast. They followed as the FBI agents turned into a residential area and then parked in front of a house. A van with Ontario license plates was in the driveway. Hughes and Hauser parked two houses away and took the surveillance antenna and recorder out of the trunk. They turned it on and aimed it at the front window. They could hear the doorbell ring.

They listened as Marty Sporror identified himself and asked to speak with George Walter. A woman called for George and they heard him come to the door.

"Yes," he said. "Can I help you?"

Marty showed him his badge and asked if he could come in and ask him a few questions.

"Sure," George said.

They went into the house and Marty began, "Mr. Walter, have you seen this man recently?"

"Yes," George answered.

"When was the last time you saw him?"

"Sunday," he answered.

"Where is he now?"

"I honestly couldn't tell you," George answered.

"Why?" he asked.

"A woman came in the bar. We were watching the football game and she walked up to him like she knew him. He bought her a drink and the next thing I knew, he was thanking me and went back to camp and packed up and left. That was the last I saw of him."

"Is he coming back?"

"I couldn't say."

Listening to the conversation, John Hughes began to laugh.

"Thank you," he said. "Thank you."

"When are you going back to your camp?" Sporror asked.

"Wednesday or Thursday," George answered.

"Are you aware of who this man is?" Sporror asked.

"When he was with me, I wasn't. Now I do. My daughter called me and told me you were on your way to see me. Then my sister-in-law filled me in."

"Mr. Walter," he said. "Even if Mr. Reed doesn't think so, he certainly needs our help. That's all we want to do. He isn't in any trouble. We just want to help him."

"If I see him, I will encourage him to get in touch with you."

Hughes was still laughing as Sporror and the two men got back into their car. They followed the car as it went to the Erie airport and they watched as Sporror boarded a flight to Pittsburgh. They turned around and drove back to Bradford.

"Thursday he'll be back and on Thursday he will be ours."

"Who?" Hauser asked. "That old man?"

"No. Reed. He'll be back on Thursday, too. I'll bet on it and you should, too. Until then we can relax. We're on vacation. We can hang out at the Rainbow Inn and get to know everyone."

Cindy and Charley were relaxing, too. They swam in the indoor pool and spent their evenings in the lounge. Occasionally they went out. Charley was a member of the Moose and one afternoon they went down to the local lodge on Pennsylvania Avenue.

Betty Lou was the bartender. She was a pleasant woman and once he showed his membership card she made them feel welcome.

They met a very handsome older gentleman with a full head of gray hair. His name was Ray Peterson. For some reason they hit it off immediately.

Ray reminded Charley of someone he knew and Charley likewise reminded Ray of someone he knew. In less than an hour they were fast friends and when Ray realized he'd been staying with George and was up at the Rainbow Inn, it just got all that more intense.

"Why I've known George most of my life," Ray said. "And Bud is my good, good friend. You should've brought both of them along with you."

"I like it here," Charley said to Cindy.

"I can see that you do," she said. "I really can."

Charley laughed and continued on with Ray. The conversation drifted to September 11th.

"When it happened," Ray said. "I told George and Bud that this was just the beginning. I told them it would bring all the kooks out of the closet. The kooks would do horrible things so it would be blamed on the people in the Middle East. And it looks like it happened that way, too."

Cindy and Charley listened. They didn't share anything personal with him. They sat and talked and said nothing about themselves.

They stayed there until five. Ray left and Cindy and Charley went back to the Holiday Inn. They took another dip in the pool and then went to the lounge for a few more drinks before having dinner.

As they were sipping their drinks, Cindy got serious.

"I wish you could have known him," she said.

Charley looked back at her. He knew what she was talking about. He didn't say anything.

"He was so much like you. Every time I looked at him he reminded me of you."

Charley knew how painful it had to be for her to talk about Chuck. It was the same way for Tina when she spoke of him, too. He listened in the darkness as Tina cried herself to sleep the first night he was there. He was sorry Cindy was talking about him, but he didn't know what to say to make her stop.

"He was confident like you are. And he looked like you. He stood the same way you stand and he held himself just like you do. Looking at you is like looking at him."

"Does it bother you?" Charley asked.

"No," she said. "When I reach out and touch your arm, it is like reaching out and touching his. It's because he came from you."

She was very serious.

"I'm sorry for what I did," she said. "You deserved better. You really did."

Charley closed his eyes and said nothing. He held his feelings inside.

"Stop," he said. "Don't do this to yourself and don't do it to me. We both deserved better. That was a long time ago. I just wish I could have known him. That would have been nice. That would have been real nice."

He changed the subject.

"Let's go get a table for dinner."

"Fine," she said.

When he ordered a bottle of wine with their meal, Cindy commented on how much they were drinking.

"You have me making up for lost time," she said. "All those years I didn't drink a drop and now it's all we do."

"That and have sex," he said with a grin. "And what's wrong with that?"

"Nothing," she said smiling at him.

"I know," he said to her. "Nothing at all."

She smiled at him and sort of blushed.

"The drinking I can take or leave, but the sex, I like that a lot. I like that a whole lot," she said.

They finished their dinner and went back to the lounge. They had a drink there and then went back to their room and made love again. It was the third time that day.

Charley had been sleeping very well since he went to the mountains. He had slept very well with Cindy. He was totally at ease and was getting all the rest he needed. But that night was different. That night he didn't sleep well at all.

Cindy woke several times to find him tossing and turning. He was talking in his sleep and he was saying things she could understand. He was talking to the men he had served with in Vietnam. And from what she could gather, even though she could only hear his end, it was a two-way conversation.

Charley was very restless.

"No," he said. "You can't ask me to do that. It isn't right. I don't care what he did."

"Of course, I would," he said.

"Okay," he agreed.

"I said okay," he insisted.

Cindy was watching his face. It had a pained look on it. She could tell he didn't like what he was seeing. Then he woke. He woke suddenly and startled. He didn't know where he was.

"It's okay," she said to him. "You were having a bad dream. That's all."

Charley came to his senses. He could see Cindy's face. He knew where he was and who he was with. He shook his head.

"No," he said. "That was no dream."

"What do you mean?" she asked. "I was watching you. You were talking in your sleep. You were dreaming."

"Was I?" he asked.

"I used to think they were dreams. I really did. The only thing is everything I dreamed about always came true. Everything they told me was going to happen actually did. They're here and they are looking out for me.

"We aren't safe anymore. You're going to have to go home tomorrow and I have to help George. They are going to come for him to try and find me. If I'm not there, they are going to kill him."

"But they want to kill you, not him," Cindy said.

"I know."

"What are you going to do?" she asked.

"Kill them first," he said coldly.

And as he said it, Cindy could tell from the tone of his voice he meant it.

CHAPTER SEVENTY

When Charley got up that morning, he dressed for the woods. Cindy questioned him.

"What are you doing," she asked. "It's so early."

"It's time to go back," he said. "It's time for me to go back and it's time for you to go back, too."

She didn't like the suddenness of it all. She pouted. She'd forgotten the way Charley was. She forgot how things could be one way at night and when he woke up the next morning, he knew where he was going and how he was going to get there.

She'd forgotten their last morning together when she was in college and he was going off to war. It was the same way then, also.

They'd made love most of the night. It wasn't the usual sex. It was lovemaking. It wasn't fast with him being done before her and she would be left wondering what it was all about. No, it was true lovemaking.

He had taken his time and cared about her. He truly cared about her and when he was done, she was totally sated and a quivering mass of love for him. Then the next morning he calmly woke up and announced he had to go.

This was nothing more than a replay of that morning in 1966. He did exactly the same thing.

That morning in 1966 he paid the room bill, walked her back to the sorority house and kissed her goodbye. She stood there watching him walk away.

Today he paid the room bill with cash and had her drive him back to Marshburg. She tried to get him to talk to her, but he was preoccupied. She could tell he was ready to face whatever it was he had to. There was a sense of finality in his voice. There was a feeling that he was going to finally deal with old demons and enemies.

When they were just past the Ranger Station, he showed her

where to pull in off the road.

"You can turn around here, babe," he said. "I'm going down over the hill from here and come in on camp from the back in case anyone is watching from the road."

"I want to stay," she said.

"No," he said. His voice was not only firm, it was insistent also. "I don't want them knowing about you. If they come, and I know they will, I don't want to worry about you. You have to be safe and you can't be safe here with me."

Cindy didn't like it at first, but finally accepted what he wanted. She knew he was right and she was glad to have had the time with him she did.

"I love you," she said. "I always have. I wish our lives could have been different."

Charley looked at her.

"So do I," he said. "What happened isn't the life I imagined for you and me when we were kids."

He smiled at her. As he did, she could see tears in the corners of his eyes.

"I was going to be a great right-handed pitcher for the New York Yankees and we were going to be married and live happily ever after. All I ever wanted was you. Even when the war got in the way and I realized I couldn't have that part of my dream, I still held out hope for you. But life is a mother fucker," he said. "It had other plans."

He stopped. He nodded his head and touched her face with his hand.

"When am I going to see you?" she asked

"Soon," he promised. "I'll get my act together up here and I'll come to you. I promise."

He kissed her and got out of the car. She caught a glimpse of a pistol he held in his one hand as he walked away with his bag in the other. She thought about his dream and wondered if it was the way he said.

Did those men really come to him in his sleep? Were they really warning him?

That morning Hughes and Hauser slept in. It hadn't taken them long to fit in at the Rainbow. They got there a little after twelve and stayed well past eight. They met all the locals and bought drinks for everyone there. They became everyone's best friend.

Mark liked them. They were interested in his stories and the problems he had with his ex-wife and how the court system was taking him to the cleaners. It was a side of life the two men didn't see. For a while they forgot who they were.

It was quite a drive down off Marshburg hill back to the Howard Johnson Motor Lodge in Bradford. Hauser wondered how people drove this winding rode every day.

As Hughes woke up with a hang over, he rated the previous day as a success. He was sure Charley Reed would be returning and when he did, he was also sure the locals were comfortable with him.

It took Charley less than a half an hour to make his way down to camp. He looked around and made sure no one was watching before he went in. He put his bag on his bed and took out the .280 and loaded it. He started a fire in the wood stove and made sure they had water. He looked out the windows. He wondered if anyone was watching. When he was sure no one was, he went out behind camp and waited.

He walked across the creek bed and went up the side of the hill, situating himself beneath the enormous hemlock grove that sat above the camp. From his vantage point he could look down on camp and command most of the valley below him. He sat on the side of the hill and he waited.

Charley didn't mind the solitude of the forest. It was peaceful and it gave him a feeling of safety. He sat and listened to the sounds of the birds and the squirrels. He smiled to himself, remembering the squirrels at Walter Reed. That was so long ago and it seemed as if it happened to another person. In the serenity of the setting, he faced the fact it had not. It did happen to him and now was the time for him to face it.

Then he saw some movement. It was below him to his left, up the valley about a hundred fifty yards above camp. He turned his head in that direction and focused on what or who it might be. Then he caught the movement again. It was like a blur of color. It was brown against brown and part of it moved ever so slightly. He focused harder and realized it was a deer.

Then he saw more movement. There was a second deer and then there was a third and finally a fourth and a fifth. There were five deer and they were moving ever so slowly across the valley, west to east, grazing on the small plants as they did. They were totally unaware of his presence.

He stayed seated and slowly raised his rifle. He brought the scope down on the first deer. It was a large doe. A second doe, not as large as the first, but still a respectable size deer, followed her. The next deer had its head down. It wasn't grazing. It was just walking with its head down. He moved the scope to the one behind it.

He made out a set of antlers. He looked at it and realized it was a small buck. It was a four-point, but not a very large deer. It was probably a two-year old at most. Finally, he scoped the fifth one and saw immediately it was another doe, but a very small one.

He went back to the third deer. It still had its head down. Charley was motionless and waited to get a better look. When he did, he had trouble containing himself.

Slowly the deer raised its head. It must have thought it heard something because it looked up and appeared to look right at him. There in the scope was the head of a ten or twelve-point buck staring back at him. He was turned sideways and was totally motionless.

"What a trophy!" Charley said to himself.

He took aim at the deer. He moved the crosshairs of the scope from the head to the neck. He moved down the neck to the area behind the front leg. Did he want to shoot it through the heart or through the neck? He couldn't decide.

The deer didn't move. It stood there as if it saw him and was deciding what or who he was.

Charley moved the crosshairs back to the neck. As he did, he remembered drawing down on men. He remembered doing the same thing to men and at that instant he wondered why it was so important for him to kill a deer.

He took the stock of the rifle out of his shoulder and rested the weapon across his lap. He sat and watched as the five animals crossed the creek bed and climbed the hillside to his left and disappeared into the protection of the grove of hemlock trees.

Twenty minutes later a car pulled into the driveway of camp. There were two men in the car. Charley looked at them through his scope. They were dressed in hunting clothes, but he didn't immediately recognize them. They didn't get out of the car. They turned around and went back up the hill the way they came. He stayed where he was and waited.

George pulled in a little before noon. He waited until George was inside camp and made sure no one was following him before he came down off the hillside and out of the woods to go inside.

"Hello," he said.

"Hello," George said back. "See anything?"

"No," Charley said smiling. "Just two guys in a car who pulled in and turned around about a half an hour ago."

"The FBI was up in Northeast looking for you," George said. "They were at the Rainbow, too. It could have been them."

"When was that?" he asked.

"Tuesday."

"What did they want?" Charley asked.

"You," George answered.

Charley looked down at the floor and shook his head back and forth.

"They said they want to take you into protective custody and keep you safe."

"Right," Charley said.

"I believed them," George said. "They were pretty sincere. I have the guy's card if you want to call him."

"It's not as simple as that, George," he said. "I wish it was, but it isn't."

"I don't know, " George said. "Until you face them, they will always be after you. You can't live like that. You got away with it once, but they won't let you do it again."

"The guys who pulled in were in hunting clothes," Charley said.

"The guys who came to see me were in suits," George said.

"Maybe they were guys just turning around."

"And maybe they weren't," George said. "Maybe they are the ones the FBI wants to protect you from."

"Maybe," Charley said. "Maybe."

While George and Charley were talking, John Hughes and Doug Hauser were talking, also. They were in their car sitting in the parking lot of the Rainbow waiting for it to open.

"Today is just like yesterday," Hughes said. "We're here at the Rainbow Inn and we'll spend the day. We'll make sure they are here and tomorrow morning just before dawn, we'll take them and be on our way."

"Why not today?" Doug asked.

"I want them to settle in and feel comfortable. The FBI was just here. They are going to be on their guard. Reed isn't anyone to take lightly. You have to get the drop on him and take him by surprise or he will get you. I know the kind of training he's had. You never lose that sort of thing. It's with you until the day you die."

George and Charley stayed around camp until a little after three. They went out in the woods until dark in hope of getting a deer. Charley went through the motions for George and went along agreeing some fresh venison would taste great.

But that wasn't the case. They sat in the woods for the better part of two hours and never saw a thing. It was then that they decided to let George's daughter, Sherry, feed them at the bar.

When they walked in, Hughes and Hauser were sitting at the bar on the far side over by the television set and the coyote mount. They didn't notice the two men. They were two of fifteen others who were sitting at the bar and there was nothing that made either of them stand out or appear to be different.

George and Charley sat opposite the two men and ordered a couple of beers.

"Is there a Thursday night football game?" Charley asked Andrea, the bartender.

"I don't know," she answered him.

Sherry came out and gave her dad a hug. Then she looked at Charley.

"Did Dad tell you the FBI was here?"

"Yes," he said.

"We didn't tell them anything."

"Thanks," he said. "I owe you and Bud a lot. You've been great." She smiled at him and went back into the kitchen.

From across the bar John Hughes spoke to them.

"Did you guys do any good?" he asked.

"No," George answered. "How about you?"

"No," Hughes answered. "Haven't had a shot all week."

"There aren't enough people in the woods," George told him. "You need more people to get the deer moving around."

Charley looked at the man across the bar from him. There was something familiar about him, but he couldn't put his finger on it. He dismissed it because he had met so many new people since he first arrived in Marshburg. He looked at the other man and when he didn't recognize him, he let it pass and instead concentrated on the moment and the people around him.

Mark Saporito sat next to him telling him about the buck he shot. Charley listened and sipped his drink. About that time, Bud brought out some venison baked in his own tomatoes and hot peppers.

"Here," he said. "Try this." He gave the three men each a plate and a plastic fork.

Charley tasted it and was taken away by the flavor.

"This is great," he said.

"Do you like hot stuff?" Bud asked.

"Hell, yes!" Charley said.

Bud disappeared into the kitchen. He came back with some tortilla chips and a bowl of salsa.

"If you like hot stuff, you will love my Chula Salsa."

"Chula Salsa?" he asked.

"Yes," Bud said. "I make it for my buddies down at Chula Vista Country Club. Harry, Tony, and Richie love the stuff."

Charlie took a chip and loaded it up with the salsa.

"This is great," he said. "This is really great. You've made a convert out of me."

Bud smiled. Moments later he came back with homemade pickles and hot peppers stuffed with sauerkraut.

"Try these," he said happy to finally have someone who at least made an effort to make it look like he appreciated him.

George laughed and shook his head.

"You've got a friend for life now. He'll feed you more hot stuff than your stomach will be able to take. Believe me when I tell you that."

Charley laughed, too.

"Hey. This is good. I really do like it."

"Here," Bud said. "Try these. Cherries soaked in whiskey." He paused for a moment. "I think they've been soaking for either four or five years. I can't exactly remember."

John Gates laughed.

"Hey, chief. Bring out the Chateau Neuf de Bud 1992."

"No, I'm saving it for Christmas this year," Bud said.

"Oh, God," George groaned.

"What?" Charley asked.

"When he made that my wife got into it one night and she kept everyone up all night talking. Now he's taken the bottles we didn't drink way back when and he's fermented them a second time and claims he has champagne. I'll believe that when I see it!"

Charley laughed, looking around at the guys.

"You seem to have a pretty good time,' he said.

"Yes, we do," George admitted. "Yes, we do.

"That's what having a family is all about Charley," he said. "The silly stupid things we all do make us love one another all that much more. And we have a sense of belonging, too. It's a good feeling."

Charley looked away from George. As he did, he caught the two men across the bar watching him. He didn't hold the stare. He kept his head moving past them and turned to Mark.

Even as he did, he could see them out of the corner of his eye watching him even closer. It was as if they were studying him. As they did, something inside of him was triggered. His internal security mechanisms began to kick into play and he could feel his body tense.

Charley got up off his barstool and walked around the bar to Dave Hall who was sitting next to the younger of the two men. He positioned himself between Dave and the other man and put his arm around Dave's back and shoulder.

"How did you guys do this week?" he asked.

"Two buck and a doe," Dave answered between mouthfuls of Bud's venison.

"Good stuff," Charley said.

"Yes, it is," Dave said back to him.

About that time Bobby Marasco chimed in, "Last week's was better than this."

Charley smiled and as he began to speak, he accidentally bumped into the man sitting next to Dave.

"Excuse me," he said as he felt for a weapon.

Even before he did, he knew what he was going to find. Clearly he felt the holster and the grip of the pistol.

"I'm sorry," he said again to the man.

Doug Hauser shook his head, not realizing what Charley had done.

Charley stayed and chatted with the guys before going back to the other side of the bar. Hauser and Hughes were saying something to one another and then they got up and left. As they did and Hughes turned to give Charley a profile, that same nagging feeling that he knew him came back.

"But where and when," he asked himself.

As they left, Charley followed them out. He stood on the porch and watched as they got into a car and drove toward Bradford. He recognized the car as the one that turned around at camp earlier in the day. As much as he tried, he couldn't remember where he knew the man.

While Charley didn't miss much, neither did John Hughes.

"What was that all about?" Hughes asked Hauser.

"What?" Hauser asked back.

"The thing with Reed."

"He was talking to the guy next to me. He was pretty drunk and bumped into me. This would be a good time to take him."

"No, it wouldn't," Hughes said. "We've been drinking, too. We don't want to move until we are ready and we aren't."

CHAPTER SEVENTY-ONE

John Hughes went to his room and called the front desk.

"This is room 224. I need a five o'clock wake up call and so does room 226."

As soon as he hung up the phone, he went to bed. The alcohol helped him to fall off to sleep in no time.

Doug Hauser went to bed, also. The only thing was he couldn't fall asleep. All he could think about was Charley Reed. Why was it so important that he die? He didn't understand. Anything Reed could have said, he didn't. And even if he did, who would believe him in the first place? It seemed senseless to him, but he had to follow orders. It was his job and his duty.

George and Charley went back to camp. George was pretty drunk and Charley helped him out of the van and into camp. When he got him in, George went straight to bed and was snoring in no time.

Charley had a good buzz, but he knew what he was doing. George had a shotgun, a Winchester Defender, the same kind the police used. Charley loaded it with six rounds and put it behind his bedroom door. He had a bad feeling about the two men from the bar.

He got out of his clothes and put on his sweat pants and a tee shirt. Then he sat in the chair out by the woodstove with his 9-milimeter. In a few minutes he was asleep. Sugar, George's golden retriever, curled up next to the chair and dozed off, too. The only sound in the cabin was the sound of George snoring.

Charley was anxious. He dreamed and he forced himself to wake up. He fell back to sleep and then dreamed again. Once more he made himself wake up. He didn't want to have those dreams. He turned on the television and watched the all night news.

It was filled with stories about the bombing in Afghanistan. There were clips from briefings at the White House and the Pentagon. America was at war. It was at war just like it had been in Vietnam,

THE FIRST TERRORIST ACT

except this time it was different. The nation stood united and wanted this war. The idea of losing American lives didn't bother us this time. We had been attacked. That made all the difference in the world.

As Charley sat there in the darkness, the woman on the news program reminded him what day it was. It was the sixtieth anniversary of Pearl Harbor. December 7, 2001 was sixty years to the date. He wondered what it would be like on September 11, 2061? He wondered what that anniversary would be like.

He thought of his son who died in the attack. Chuck Ganley, his son, who he never knew. He thought about his son and the rest of the people who through no fault of their own became the victims of such an insidious attack. And for what? Why? Why did it have to happen? What was the purpose and how was it we couldn't stop it?

He closed his eyes and tried to sleep, but the question kept coming back at him. It bothered him so much he couldn't fall asleep. He kept asking himself the same thing. He asked it over and over and each time he couldn't find an answer.

"Why couldn't we have stopped it?" he asked. "Are we that stupid we allowed it to happen? Didn't someone tip us off? Don't they always tip us off? And if someone did tip us off, why didn't we act on it?"

He thought about it. He thought about it hard.

"Of course, they knew. They always know."

That was when he got angry.

"Why didn't they stop it? Was it because of Vietnam? Was it that? Did we need something like this to give us the justification to fight a war?"

Charley had a lot of questions. He just didn't have any answers. And the fact he didn't have any answers only served to keep him awake. All he could hear was George snoring away in the other room and the sound of the dog breathing.

The woman on the news kept repeating the same stories. She repeated them to the point he knew them before they came on. Finally at four, he gave in and fell off to sleep.

For a while he did not dream. He was in a deep and restful sleep, but then a voice began speaking to him. It was a familiar voice and he wasn't afraid. For some reason he didn't fight it. He went along and listened.

"Hello, my friend," the voice said.

Charley was squinting, looking into a fog. The shadow of a man was there silhouetted in front of a light that was trying to penetrate the fog.

"You've had a lonely life," he said. "I'm sorry, my friend. I really am."

Charley strained to see the man's face. The fog was too heavy and the light that did penetrate it was in his eyes, preventing him from making out any features that might have been exposed.

"You don't have to let this happen," the man's voice said. "You can stop it."

"Who are you?" Charley asked.

"Stop what?" he asked when he didn't get an answer.

The man didn't speak. He was still there. Charley could see him.

"Who are you?" he asked again.

There was no answer.

Charley wanted to move to the man, but he was frozen where he was. He was unable to move and the lights seemed much brighter.

"Why won't you tell me?" he asked.

As he did, he heard himself. He heard himself speaking and he suddenly realized he was speaking in Spanish. As he realized that, he also realized who he was speaking to. He recognized his voice immediately.

"Ernesto?" he asked.

"Yes," the man said. "It is I."

Charley woke up suddenly.

"John Hughes," he said. "That's who he was! It was John Hughes!"

George was up out in the kitchen. Charley could hear the coffee maker brewing a fresh pot of coffee. George was frying bacon.

"What?" George asked.

"The man in the bar, he was John Hughes! He is Central Intelligence Agency. I remember him."

Charley looked for a clock. The one on the wall said it was six forty-five.

"Is it six forty-five?" he asked.

"It is," George said. "You need to get up and get ready to hunt. Why didn't you go to bed?"

"I couldn't sleep," he answered.

"You were doing a pretty good job of it when I came out. You were talking in your sleep and you were talking in Spanish. What was that all about and what is this about the man in the bar being CIA?"

"Yeah," Charley said. "My dreams are a pain in the ass. I'm at the point I wish I didn't dream. They tell me things I don't want to know."

"Get up," George said. "Get up and hunt. It's Pearl Harbor Day."
Charley smiled.

"What were you doing when Pearl Harbor was attacked?"

"I was in eleventh grade and I think they took us into study hall," George said.

"George," Charley laughed. "Pearl Harbor was on a Sunday. You didn't go to school on Sunday."

"Hell," he said. "How am I supposed to remember that far back?"

As he asked the question, Sugar began barking outside. George went to the door and opened it. And as he did, a man burst through the door, forcing his way into the cabin and knocking him to the floor.

"Stay right where you are," he said to Charley who was still in the chair covered up by a blanket.

Slowly he walked into the center of the room.

"Get up," he ordered George.

Slowly George stood up. He was old and his arthritis made it difficult for him to move. He grabbed on to the edge of the couch and helped himself get to his feet.

"Get over there," he said motioning to the couch on the far wall near the chair in which Charley was sitting.

George limped over to the couch, stumbling as he passed Charley and nearly falling into his lap. As that happened, Doug Hauser walked in behind Hughes.

"Hello, Mr. Hughes," Charley said.

"Mr. Reed," he said. "It's been a long time."

"Yes, it has," Charley said. "Thirty-four years, I think."

Hughes nodded his head.

"Yes. Thirty-four years for sure, and now it all comes to an end here in the middle of nowhere, USA."

Hughes laughed. "You're an interesting man. You really are."

Charley looked at the man's eyes. They were cold and cruel, but he was laughing. It was a contradiction.

He looked at Hauser. His eyes were scared. Charley looked at the way he was holding his pistol. He wasn't the practiced killer Hughes was.

"All these years," Hughes said. "You had the world by the ass. We thought you were dead! You got on the wrong jet and then I had you."

"So why did you wait so long?" Charley asked. "Why didn't you take me then?"

Hughes shook his head.

"Couldn't," he said. "I had to wait. I had to wait until the time was right. With what is going on, no one cares anymore."

He laughed again.

"Who would have thought it? They played right into our hands. Doing what the dumb sons-of-bitches did allowed us to unleash everything we've been waiting and wanting to implement. They did exactly what we wanted them to do."

"You let it happen?" Charley asked.

Hughes laughed that laugh of his and it had a ring of evil to it. It was a dark laugh, one that was mocking and knowing at the same time. He laughed, but he didn't answer the question.

"You did let it happen, didn't you, you cock sucker," Charley said.

Hughes looked at him.

"What difference does it make to you?" he asked.

"All those people and you let them die so you could have justification didn't you?" Charley asked.

"And what if we did?" Hughes asked.

"Nothing ever changes, does it?" Charley asked.

"Not as long as there are patriots like me around it won't," he said.

"Patriot my ass," Charley said. "You and the people like you are cold-blooded murderers who serve themselves and don't give a damn about our country."

"Shut up," Hughes screamed.

As he screamed, two shots were fired in rapid succession. Then two more were fired. Hughes head jerked back and a look of astonishment came to his face. Doug Hauser was thrown back into the door behind him. His face was contorted in pain.

Charley stood up from his chair holding the 9-milimeter pistol. Hughes was still standing. Charley fired again, hitting Hughes in the face. As it passed through his head, it blew out the backside spattering it on Hauser who was sliding down the wall to the floor. Charley fired one more time. That time it was at Hauser and like the last one was a headshot.

He turned to George.

"Are you alright?" he asked.

"Yes," he said. "My god."

"Thanks," Charley said to him.

"What for?" George asked.

"When you stumbled I was able to get the pistol. It was behind me on the chair and you distracted them long enough for me to bring it out and cock it."

"Thank you," George said. "They were going to kill us! I don't know about you, I think I'd like to have a few more hunting seasons."

It was at that moment a voice from outside of the cabin made itself known.

"You, in the cabin. This is the FBI. Come out unarmed with your hands up, everyone of you."

There was a pause. Then the voice spoke again.

"You have ten seconds. Come out now or we will come in shooting."

Charley called out.

"Okay. We're coming out. Don't shoot."

"How many of you are there?" the voice called.

"There are two of us," he answered. "Two men are down. The two of us are coming out."

Charley dropped his pistol on the chair and he helped George up to his feet.

"Come on," he said.

As they walked to the door, he pushed Hauser out of his way with his foot. Then he opened the door and they walked out on the porch with their hands up. Immediately, two agents turned them around, slamming them against the wall and handcuffing both of them.

"Hey," Charley said. "Take it easy. George is an old man and he didn't do anything."

"Shut up," the one agent said and he slammed Charley's head into the wall.

"Hey," George said speaking up for Charley. "You don't have to do that. He was just defending himself. They came to kill us."

"You shut up, too, you old bastard," the other agent said.

"Take it easy, both of you," Sporror told them.

He and another agent walked past them into the cabin. Immediately the man with Sporror came out and began vomiting when he saw the faces and the heads of the two men on the floor.

"God Almighty!" Sporror said. "I didn't need to see that. I could have gone for years without ever seeing something like that."

George and Charley were taken and placed in separate cars. Marty Sporror called for the Pennsylvania State Police for backup. He also called in to the local headquarters and requested a forensic team and a coroner.

"This is a backwoods bum fuck county," he said. "Bring in a first rate one. I don't want some hick screwing this up. We have two federal agents down."

He listened and then he answered.

"No," he said.

"Central Intelligence. You had better notify their duty chief. John Hughes and Douglas Hauser," he told the person on the other end of the phone.

The call to the Pennsylvania State Police produced radio traffic. George Petrisek, a reporter for several local newspapers, was having his morning coffee when it came across the scanner that there was a shooting in a camp near Marshburg and two federal agents were killed. Petrisek wasted no time and started to the area, hoping to scoop everyone else.

When he got to the parking lot of the Rainbow Inn, police vehicles were speeding by with their lights on. He pulled out and followed them as they made a right turn down Route 321 toward Sugar Run. When he saw them pull off into a camp, Petrisek parked on the side of the road, grabbed his camera and walked up the driveway and began to mingle with the crowd of men who were at the scene. They ranged from uniformed State Policemen to local township cops both in and out of uniform.

Four FBI agents wearing jackets indicating who they were, briefed the State Police. They were telling them to preserve the crime scene until their forensic unit and their coroner arrived.

Petrisek didn't have to ask any questions. He listened as one man told the story to another and that man repeated it to two more. He realized the two dead men were federal agents of some kind and it appeared the men in the cars had killed them. No one knew why. All they knew is there were two dead federal agents.

One man speculated they were terrorists there to blow up one of the oil refineries. Another speculated they were terrorists who were going to blow up the Kinzua Dam. Both men agreed that when the agents moved in to stop their illegal and terror-linked activities, the two agents were killed.

A reporter from the local radio station arrived, but was denied access. Police lines were established after Petrisek got in. He looked into two cars and saw George and Charley in the back with their hands handcuffed behind them. Charley's forehead was covered with blood. Petrisek took a quick picture of him and then one of the old man in the other car.

He watched as the two cars with the FBI agents and the two suspects pulled away. He walked out to his car and followed them to see where they were going to take the two men.

Marty was riding in the car with Charley Reed.

"What was that all about?" he asked Charley.

Charley looked out the window and didn't answer.

"You killed two federal agents," he said. "That's a big no no. You know that."

Charley still didn't answer. He knew whatever he said would be twisted. All he could do was sit tight and hope for the best.

George and he were taken to Buffalo. That was the closest U.S. Attorney and it was up to him to make a decision about what was going to be done with them and what charges were going to be placed against them.

George Petrisek, meanwhile, followed the two cars as they made their way across the state line into New York and then up the state toward Buffalo. As he drove, he phoned his wife and began dictating a story for the afternoon Olean Times Herald.

When they arrived at the Federal Court House, the news media was waiting. The news of what happened down near Bradford had made its way north, beating the men. News crews were set up and Petrisek parked and began to mingle with the rest of the media. It was then he met someone from CNN.

In passing, he mentioned he had been at the scene and took twenty or so pictures.

"What?" the reported asked. "Do you have them?"

"Sure do," George said. "I have them here on my digital camera."

The two men went off to a darker area where they could view the pictures.

"These are great," the reporter said.

Then the one of Charley in the back of the car caught his eye. "That's Charley Reed," he said.

"Who?" George Petrisek asked.

"The hero of LAX," he said. "That's who."

"Do you want to be on national television?" the reporter asked.

"Sure," Petrisek said.

"Great," the man said. "You're about to have your fifteen minutes of fame, Mr. Petrisek. Let's get set up. We are scooping everyone else. They think these guys are terrorists. That's a bunch of bunk. The government probably was trying to kill them."

He was on a line to Atlanta telling them what they had. Marie Van Arsdale had been doing all night news and finished at eight. It was ten o'clock Eastern Time and people in the studio began looking for her. She was downstairs eating when they found her and told her come back up to the studio.

The producer decided this was her story and she should anchor the news side. She was to interview the man and the eyewitness in the field. She spoke with the reporter and George Petrisek and at ten-thirty she led off the bottom of the hour.

"Good morning. This is Marie Van Arsdale.

"An early morning gun battle which was initially labeled as a government move on suspected terrorists in rural Marshburg, Pennsylvania, in reality appears to be a government move on the hero of LAX, Charley Reed. Two government agents are dead and Mr. Reed and another unidentified individual are in federal custody in Buffalo, New York."

Following the opening, she broke off to Buffalo and the reporter who interviewed Petrisek. They had taken his pictures to a local computer store and had them printed. During the interview they were able to show the pictures from the scene earlier that morning along with the one verifying it was, in fact, Charley Reed.

When Marie got off the air she went to her producer.

"We need to get him a lawyer. They're going to railroad him. I can feel it in my heart."

"We'll do that," he said. "I want you on the next jet to Buffalo. Get going."

Jerilyn and Bob Holt were having coffee when the story broke. Bob was taking the day off and as soon as Marie Van Arsdale mentioned Charley's name both of them gave her their undivided attention.

"Bob," she said. She didn't have to say another thing.

"Okay," he answered. "I'll do it. I'll do it for you, and I'll do it for Tina and Chuck."

"Thank you," she said.

Bob phoned the airlines. At one-ten that afternoon he boarded a United Airlines flight for Buffalo, New York. Jerilyn was with him.

When they arrived in Buffalo at the Federal Court House, George and Charley were taken to a holding center. An hour later they were fingerprinted, photographed, and booked in as material witnesses to a crime with charges pending.

They were going to run with the story that the two were terrorist suspects so they could cloak the whole thing under the veil of National Security. They were going that route, but when Marie Van Arsdale positively identified Charley Reed from the Petrisek photograph, the FBI had their hands tied.

Immediately, the media began banging on the doors of the Federal Prosecutor and all of his assistants.

Bob Holt was an experienced defense attorney. As soon as he landed, they took a cab to the Federal Court House. He went to receiving and announced himself.

"I am Charles Reed's attorney. I am here to see my client."

They tried to stonewall him, but he wasn't going to hear it. Finally at four forty-five he was taken into an interview room to meet his client. Jerilyn accompanied Bob. He passed her off as his assistant.

"Be careful what you say," he told her. "They passed the new law that allows them to eavesdrop on us. It's an outrage, but they are going to do it."

They sat down at the table and in a few minutes Charley Reed was brought in, his forehead still covered with blood. Charley recognized Jerilyn immediately. He didn't understand what was going on.

"Why hasn't this man been given medical treatment?" Bob demanded.

The guard just shrugged his shoulders.

"Get the handcuffs off of him. And then you get your superior and you get a doctor down here to tend to this man right away. Now get out of here."

Bob looked at Charley after the handcuffs were taken off and extended his hand.

"I'm Bob Holt. I'm going to represent you. I'm also Jerilyn's husband. I'm doing this for her, Chuck and for Tina," he said.

"Thank you," Charley said.

"Hello," he said to Jerilyn. "You look wonderful."

"Be careful what you say," Bob warned him. "They are watching us and listening to everything we say and do. Ashcroft's new law allows them to do it. It's supposed to help fight terrorism, but all it does is take more of our rights away from us. It's bullshit."

"Okay," he said.

"What happened?" Bob asked.

"They forced their way in and were going to kill us."

"Did they say that?"

"Yes," Charley answered.

"Exactly what did he say?"

"He told me my luck had run out. He said I boarded the wrong jet and now my ass was his. He said now he was finally going to finish the job. He said he was going to kill me."

"What jet was he talking about?" he asked.

"A USAir flight I took back in 1996. I saw the missiles that shot down TWA Flight 800."

"Missiles?" Bob asked. "It went down from an explosion in the center fuel tank. It was mechanical failure."

"It was bullshit," Charley said. "TWA Flight 800 was shot down. The CIA knows it and the FBI knows it. They just lied to the American people about it like they lied about so many other things going back as far as the assassination of John Kennedy."

"Jesus Christ Almighty in heaven," Marty Sporror exclaimed as he watched the interview. "How much does this guy really know?" he asked the agent with him.

About that time the supervisor of the guards and a doctor came into the interview room. The doctor looked at his forehead.

"How did this happen?" he asked.

"An FBI agent slammed my head into a wall after I was already handcuffed," Charley said. "Real brave man. I'd like to discuss it with him some time so we can see if he wants to try it again."

"Fuck," Sporror said. "Why did he have to do that?"

The doctor took care of Charley's head wound and left, promising Bob he would look back in on him in an hour or two. The supervisor left with the doctor.

"How is it you shot them?" Bob asked.

"It was them or us. They were going to kill us. I was in a chair sleeping with a blanket over me. I had the pistol in the chair with me. They thought they had the drop on me when I had the drop on them all along."

"You were expecting them?" Bob asked.

"Yes," he said.

"How?"

"I had a dream. In the dream and someone told me they were going to come. I believe in dreams, so I just kept the pistol close. I'm glad I did, otherwise I'd be dead right now."

Bob promised to take care of things for him.

"Don't talk to anyone else," he said. "You'll be fine."

As the lawyer walked out of the interview room, an assistant U.S. Attorney met him. "Can we talk?" he asked.

CHAPTER SEVENTY-TWO

Greg Henry traveled up from Bradford to represent George Walter. While Charley was meeting with his lawyer, the U.S. Attorney met with Mr. Henry and decided there was no reason to hold Mr. Walter. The Federal Agents were not operating with a warrant and there was no case that anyone could point to making him the subject of any investigation. It was obvious to the prosecutor he was the target of an assassination. When they released George, they turned their attention to Charley.

"Mr. Holt," the prosecutor said. "My name is James Villanova. I am the U.S. Attorney in this federal district."

The two men shook hands and then got down to business.

"This is nothing more than a case of self defense," he said. "We are satisfied the agents were operating on their own and they intended to kill Mr. Walter and your client. We have already released Mr. Walter, but your client is a different story."

"How is that?" Bob asked.

"He has made reference to some issues that affect our national security."

"I knew you were eavesdropping on us. Try to use that or anything he said while he was meeting with me and you will have your first test case on a law that is clearly unconstitutional."

"I'm not disagreeing with you on that issue," Villanova said. "If it was me, I would look the other way. Your client has lived for years without ever divulging any state secrets or posing any threat to national security. The FBI wants to detain him for a debriefing."

"Bullshit," Bob said.

"I understand how you feel," he said back to the defense attorney.

"Do you? How about how my client feels?

"He has had agents of this government trying to kill him for over thirty years. And why? No special reason, only because he served his country and did his duty. Now, after he survives an unwarranted attack, actually two unwarranted attacks, the FBI wants to question him for no special reason other than to pick his brain. No way."

Villanova agreed with him personally. But his orders were coming from Washington and they were coming from the highest levels.

"Look," he said. "We can make this as painless as possible. The government will put all of you up at the Marriott. Everything will be first class. We'll provide protection for your client and he can move around within the hotel freely. He can eat, go to the bar, and relax. We'll provide him with clothes. All we want to do is question him tomorrow with you present.

"We, of course, will ask you to sign a national security non disclosure form, which you understand is standard operating procedure.

"The questioning will last no more than four hours a day and you will be compensated by the government for you time and your representation of Mr. Reed. It appears Mr. Reed knows things no one else knows. He can provide us with answers to the many questions we have about this whole episode.

"Really," he said. "We can do that or we can name him as a material witness to the deaths of two agents and hold him indefinitely."

"Let me talk to my client," Bob said. "Can you bring him back?"

"He hasn't left," he said. "I had him detained in the conference room in anticipation of you wanting to discuss this with him."

Marty Sporror didn't understand what was going on. He waited for them to take Charley Reed out of the room, but they didn't. He stayed and watched and saw his attorney walk back into the room. The guard left as soon as he walked in.

"They want to release you," Bob Holt said to Charley Reed.

"Good," he said.

"But they want to question you tomorrow."

"What for?" he asked.

"They want you to bring them up to speed on why the government would want to kill you. They want to know what you know."

"So I have to stay here?"

"No," Bob said. "If you agree, they will move us out to the Marriott where you will have free run of the hotel with all expenses on the government. You can eat, drink, and do what you want as long as you stay in the hotel under their protection. All they want is four hours tomorrow and if need be, four hours the next day."

"Do I have a choice?" he asked.

"No," Bob said. "If you don't agree, they can hold you as a material witness to the deaths of two federal agents."

"Let's go to the Marriott," Charley said.

"What size are you?" Bob asked.

"What?" Charley asked back.

"They are going to pick up some clothes for you. They want your sizes."

Charley gave Bob all the pertinent sizes.

"When can we leave?" he asked.

"Soon," Bob said. "We'll ride together. Jerilyn and I are going to stay at the hotel, too."

He left the room momentarily to tell Jim Villanova that his client agreed.

"We'll have you out of here in a half and hour," he said when he returned. "Sit tight."

"What's going on?" Marty Sporror asked Bob Dunn.

"I don't know," Dunn said. "Does the Bureau want to question him?"

"No," Marty said. "I talked to Washington this afternoon. We wanted him here in protective custody until we could be sure that Hughes and his friend were all that was coming."

"So what's this about?" Dunn asked.

"I don't know," Marty said. "I'm going to find out."

True to his word, Jim Villanova had them on their way to the Marriott in a half and hour. They gave Charley an FBI jacket to wear until he got to his room. Once in his room several changes of clothing were waiting for him. He was in room 545, while Bob and Jerilyn were on another floor in room 622.

Three U.S. Marshals accompanied Charley and he was told they were in the next room. At least one of them would accompany him wherever he went in the hotel. One would be outside his room at all times.

"They're here for your protection," Bob told him.

"From what?" Charley asked.

"I don't know," Bob said. "I suppose it's routine."

Bob asked Charley if he would have dinner with Jerilyn and him. Charley agreed.

"Seven thirty," Bob said. "I'll make reservations and meet you in the main lobby."

Charley showered and cleaned up the gash in his forehead. The hot water felt good and he took his time, allowing the water to beat down on him. Then he dried himself off and dressed. The clothes all fit and were very tasteful, even down to the loafers someone picked out for him.

"These people are efficient," he said.

He turned on the television and immediately he realized he was a major story.

"At this time he is still in custody," the anchor said on the national news.

He went to the phone to call Bob, but couldn't dial out.

"May I help you?" a voice on the other end asked.

"Am I allowed to make outside phone calls?" he asked.

"Our instructions are no," the voice said.

Charley hung up without saying another thing.

"I'm a high-classed prisoner," he said out loud. "They are probably watching me, too."

He walked to the door and opened it. Immediately, a man standing in front of his door turned to ask him what he wanted.

"I'm going to the lounge for a drink," he said.

"Okay," the man said. "Just a moment."

Charley did as he was told while the man radioed to someone else. Immediately, the door of the room next to his opened and another man came out.

"Hello, Mr. Reed," he said. "I'll go with you."

Charley shrugged and walked to the elevator with the man. It was a few minutes before seven when he sat down at the bar.

"Johnnie Walker Black on the rocks," he said to the young woman behind the bar. The man with him asked for a club soda with a lime.

Even though they were sitting together, they didn't speak to one another. Charley had nothing he wanted to say to the man, and it appeared his guard felt the same way. He finished his drink and ordered another. He took a sip from it when Jerilyn walked up to him.

"May I join you?" she asked.

"Sure," he said. "Where's Bob?"

"He'll be along in a few minutes. He had to phone Chicago and New York to check on things. Now that Chuck is gone, he has to pull double duty."

Charley smiled at the mention of Chuck's name.

"You knew him," he said. "You're lucky."

"Lucky," she said. "I nearly lost my mind. I thought he was you."

Charley just shrugged his shoulders.

"He was your spitting image," she said. "His voice even sounded like your voice. He had your mannerisms and walked exactly like you.

It was as if you had come back from the dead."

Charley smiled.

"Why did you do that to everyone?" she asked.

Charley didn't answer.

"Why did you do that to me?"

"I was screwed up," he said. "I was looking to you to make things right. You had your own problems. You couldn't help me. I figured I was better off dead and everyone else would be better for it."

"You were so smart, but you were so stupid, too," she said. "So many people depended on you and so many loved you. How could you think that way?"

"They all were better off without me," he said. "Especially you. Look at the life you have now."

Jerilyn nodded.

"I have a lot," she said. "And I really love Bob. He's a good man."

"He seems like one," he said agreeing with her. "He really does. I'm glad for you."

He took a deep breath and seemed to relax a little.

"It's odd that Tina wound up with my son," he said.

"He was a good man," she said. "He was the way you would have been if you hadn't been caught up in the war. He was someone really worth knowing and being around. He really loved Tina and the girls. She's devastated without him."

Charley sipped the whiskey.

"Thank you for visiting her," Jerilyn said. "It meant a lot to her. When this is all done, she'd like to have you spend more time with them."

"I'd like that, too," he said.

Just then Bob walked up to them. He shook Charley's hand.

"You look good in those clothes," he said.

"Thank you," Charley said. "They bought some nice stuff, even down to the shoes."

Bob joined them for a drink.

"Getting reacquainted?" he asked.

"Kind of," Charley said. "It is a consensus that I am a son-of-a-bitch for doing what I did and I have to agree."

"I didn't say that," Jerilyn said.

"You didn't have to," Charley said. "I was. But on the bright side if I wasn't, I would be dead by now and not sitting here with the two of you."

"You nearly were this morning," Bob said.

"Yes," Charley said soberly.

"Do you know I'm not allowed to make calls on my phone?" he asked Bob.

"Don't worry about it," he said. "I think they just want to keep your whereabouts secret until they debrief you."

Charley accepted the explanation while Bob continued.

"I had a call from Marie Van Arsdale. She's with CNN and is here in Buffalo and wants to interview me. Someone told her I was representing you and now she is hot on my tail."

"She's a ball of fire," Charley said with a smile.

His thoughts quickly went to Alicia. "All of those women are," he said.

"Who's hungry?" Bob asked.

"I haven't eaten all day," Charley said. "I am."

"And so am I," Jerilyn said.

They got up from the bar and went into the dining room where they were seated. The marshal left them alone and sat out in the lobby, waiting for them to finish.

While they were eating, Marty Sporror was trying to find out what was going on.

"Who wanted this?" he asked Jim Villanova.

"It came right out of the Justice Department," he said. "It came from the highest levels. They want to question him about Operation Eagle Thrust."

"They don't have the need to know," Sporror said. "That comes from the President himself."

"I'm just following orders, Marty," he said. "We have him and we are going to question him. A team is on its way here from Washington right now. It's as simple as that."

Marty didn't like it one bit, but at the moment there wasn't anything he could do about it. He decided he would wait until morning and then make an issue of what they were planning to do.

In the meantime, he and Bob Dunn drove out to the Marriott and took two rooms. They were going to keep an eye on everyone. He had a funny feeling about it all.

In Washington Director Hastings of the FBI was on the phone with Thomas Whiteman of the Central Intelligence Agency. Whiteman had recently been reassigned to Langley following a successful posting as Station Chief in Dubai. He returned to the states on

August 31st. He returned to head the anti-terror group within the agency, but with the top-level losses the agency suffered in the recent two months, he moved up and was acting-head, the same job Tom McMann used to hold.

"Yes," Hastings said.

"Yes," he said again.

"I understand," he said to the man on the other end of the phone.

"Yes," he said. "You can count on me."

Whiteman hung up the phone and dialed a number at the Justice Department.

"Okay," he said. "Hastings will go along. His man is in the dark for now. Tomorrow he'll have access to the President and then it will be too late. We either do it now or we never do it."

He listened to the man on the other end of the phone.

"Fine," he said. "They're on their way."

He hung up the phone and made another call. He waited for an answer. Finally someone picked up the phone.

"Go for it," he said.

Then he hung up the phone and sat back in his chair.

By nine o'clock Charley Reed was very tired. He hung in there as best he could, but between the scotch, the wine with dinner, and the meal he ate, he was ready for bed. He asked Bob what time they were supposed to start the next day. Bob told him ten. Charley excused himself and went to the elevators.

Immediately, the marshal stood up and walked with him.

"It must be a boring job sitting around watching me eat and drink."

The marshal didn't answer him. He escorted Charley to his room. There was a different man at the door when he arrived.

Charley said hello to the new man, put his key in the door and opened it.

"Good night," he said to the two men.

Neither acknowledged him. They were talking about orders changing.

He went in and closed the door. He noticed the safety latch on the inside of the door had been removed. He didn't think anything of it. He was sure the marshals had keys and had taken it off so he couldn't keep them out. He also didn't think anything of the loud thump he heard outside his door. He dismissed it as a door slamming.

He turned on the television and turned out the lights. He got out of his clothes, slipped into the new pajamas someone in the U.S. Attorney's Office bought him and got in bed. The men in the next room watched as he finally turned off the television and fell asleep. It was a little before ten o'clock.

The man at the door of Charley's room didn't pay attention to the man and woman who got off the elevator and walked toward him. They opened the door to the room across the hall, room 544, and went in. They looked at him and said hello. He just nodded his head. There was a little activity. Awhile later a man went into room 550 and just before eleven another couple went into room 539.

At eleven o'clock the door to the room next to Charley's opened. A man stuck his head out.

"Come in here," he said.

The marshal at the Charley's door left his post and walked into the room. As he went in, he could see the bodies of three men in the bathtub.

"Here," one of the men said to him. He tossed him a silencer for his pistol.

Carefully and deliberately, he screwed the silencer into place.

"We go in, we whack him, and we are out of here. Understood?"

"Understood," he said.

"No mistakes. We make sure he's dead."

He nodded his head.

"Let's go," the man said.

He turned and walked to the door. He reached for the plastic card in his pocket. It was the key to room 545. Then he opened the door and walked out into the hallway.

He looked up and down. No one was around.

"Okay," he said to the other two men.

They followed him.

Slowly he inserted the key into the door. There was a quiet beep and a light turned green. He heard the lock release. Slowly he pushed on the door. As he did, the door bumped into something. There was something holding the door shut.

"He's blocked the door," he said to the other two men.

"Force the damn thing open!" the man responded.

Then he threw his body into the door and drove it open. Light from the hallway streamed into the room. As he moved in, he tripped over the chair. The other two men were right behind him and with him on the floor, their entry was slowed. They didn't see or hear the door to room 544 open.

"Hold it right there," a man's voice ordered them. "FBI"

The last man into the room turned. He turned with his gun pointed in the direction of the two people who were in the hall. Immediately, Rosemary Povlick fired her .40 caliber automatic, striking him directly in the center of his chest. As she fired, the second man into the room began firing into the bed directly at the form of a man who was sleeping.

Marty Sporror fired at the man hitting him four times. As he did, the man on the floor fired back into the hallway. Rosemary was struck in the shoulder and thrown backward. As she was, she knocked Marty back into the wall. Both of them fell to the floor. When they did, the man rose to his feet and prepared to fire again.

Marty struggled to raise his pistol in defense, but Rosemary's weight had his arm pinned to the floor. He was vulnerable. Then the form of another man came into sight. He lunged out of nowhere and grabbed the man with the gun by his neck and head. Marty heard a snap like the cracking of a bone and then he saw the armed man fall lifelessly to the floor. He strained to see who it was.

There, in his new pajamas was Charley Reed.

Rosemary was bleeding badly. Charley got towels from his room along with a pillow for her head. He covered her with a blanket while Marty called for an ambulance and backup. Within minutes the sounds of sirens could be heard everywhere and shortly after that the hallway was filled with police and emergency paramedics.

Charley grabbed his clothes and took them across the hallway to Marty's room. He dressed and then came back out in time to see them wheel Rosemary away toward the elevator.

"You saved our lives," Marty said.

Charley shrugged.

"Where were you?" he asked.

"On the floor between the bed and the wall wrapped up in the bedspread."

Marty laughed. "You don't trust anyone, do you?"

"If you were me, would you?"

"I guess not," Marty answered.

"What time is it?" Charley asked Marty.

He looked at his watch.

"It's eleven forty-three," he said.

"Pearl Harbor day is just about over," Charley said. "Is it alright if I go to the bar and have a drink? I'm tired of looking at dead bodies."

"Go ahead," Marty said. "I'll come down and join you when I get this wrapped up."

Charley thanked him and walked toward the elevator. Moments later he was sitting at the bar sipping a scotch. Shortly after that Bob Holt joined him.

"Are you okay?" he asked.

"Sure," Charley answered.

"You're lucky," he said.

"I guess," Charley acknowledged. "So much for being tired."

"So drink," Bob told him. "You deserve it."

Charley looked at him and smiled.

"Yes, I do," he said. "I certainly do deserve it."

Jerilyn arrived next. She was genuinely concerned for his safety.

"What are you going to do?" she asked.

"Nothing," he said. "Not a God damn thing. What can I do?"

Marty Sporror came in next.

"Thanks again," he said. "I owe you. If it wasn't for you, he would have killed Rosemary and me."

"How is she?" Charley asked.

"She's lost a lot of blood. You did well there, too. You kept her bleeding under control. She could have bled to death or gone into shock. You knew what you were doing in those first few minutes."

"It comes back to you," Charley said.

"I need to know," Marty asked. "How did you know to block the door with a chair and sleep on the floor? Didn't you trust the marshals?"

Charley thought for a moment before answering.

"What the hell!" he said.

"I trusted them. I went to sleep in the bed. But I had a dream and my buddy Ernesto told me to wake up and protect myself. That's when I put the chair in front of the door and took the bedspread and got on the floor between the wall and the bed after I arranged the pillows to look like I was there in bed."

"Ernesto? Who is Ernesto?" he asked.

Charley smiled.

"You'd think I was nuts if I told you."

He excused himself and went to the rest room.

"Ernesto?" Bob asked out loud.

Jerilyn looked at her husband and then at Marty Sporror.

"Ernesto Che Guevara," she said. "He's haunted him most of his life. He brought Charley a lot of pain. At least now, he's done something constructive."

CHAPTER SEVENTY-THREE

In the days that followed, Charley Reed was whisked from one place to another. The FBI was with him constantly and the wheels of the government began to move in order to put an end to the illegal activities that had taken place.

Thomas Whiteman was found dead. The escalating CIA death toll ended with him. A single shot to the head killed him. It was not self-inflicted. Director Hastings resigned along with several high-ranking directors in the Justice Department.

It was then that Marie Van Arsdale finally caught up with Charley Reed. He was in Pittsburgh at the Greentree Inn with Cindy Ganley.

She wasn't shy. She walked right up to their table and sat down.

"Hi there," she said. "Mind if I join you?"

Charley had enough to drink to say that he did. Marie just ignored him.

He wasn't in the greatest of moods to begin with. He and Cindy were arguing. He told Cindy he wanted to spend Christmas with Tina and the girls.

"What about me?" she asked.

"Come along," he said. "They have a large place. There is plenty of room."

Cindy wasn't thrilled with that idea. She suggested they come to Pittsburgh.

"Cindy," he said. "They're little kids and their mother is pregnant. Did you go away at Christmas with little kids when you were pregnant?"

It was at that point Marie intruded on them.

As irritated as Charley wanted to be, he really couldn't. He sort of liked Marie and if there is one thing one woman can pick up on regarding another woman that is it. It only seemed to aggravate the already tense situation.

"When can I have an interview?" she asked Charley. "You owe me one."

Cindy didn't like the intrusion one bit.

"Give her what she wants now," Cindy said standing up from the table and walking away.

Charley just sat there, watching her walk out of the dining room.

"Did I cause that?" Marie asked.

Charley just looked at her.

"I'm sorry," she said.

"Like hell you are. You aren't sorry one bit."

He took a drink of his whiskey and stood up. "I'll be back," he said.

Charley walked out to the bar, Cindy wasn't there. He walked out front and she wasn't there either. When he went out to the parking lot, he walked outside just in time to see her driving away in her car.

"Great," he said to himself. "That's just great."

He turned around and went back to the table. Marie had ordered herself a drink.

"She left," Marie said matter of factly. "I could have told you that. She didn't like the way you smiled at me. That made her mad."

"I didn't do a damn thing," he said.

"She doesn't see it that way. She saw it as flirting with me. So did I and I kind of like it."

"Cut it out," he said. "I'm old enough to be your father."

"When did that ever stop you?" she asked chidingly.

"You don't know me very well," he said. "This is all a bunch of shit."

"Maybe so, but the lady thinks she has a claim on you."

Charley realized Marie was right. For Cindy to get mad enough to get up from the table and leave him there without any transportation, Marie was one hundred percent correct. He thought back to what was the real source of contention before Marie arrived. It was Tina and the fact he wanted to spend Christmas with her. Cindy didn't like it.

"You can have your interview but not tonight."

"I agree completely," she said. "Not tonight. I'll let you buy me dinner and then you can try to get me to give you a ride home."

"I can take a cab," he said.

"Afraid?" she asked.

"No," he said. "Just smart."

Marie and he didn't have dinner. They drank instead. Charley called a cab about nine and when he got to the door of Cindy's house, all the lights were already out. He let himself in with a key and went to the family room. Cindy was there watching television in the dark. He sat down across from her.

"I'm sorry if I made you angry," he said. "I didn't mean to."

"We don't want the same things," Cindy said.

"How is that?" he asked.

"We're good together. I like it. You just seem to take it for granted and expect it. I don't know how you can do it. I can't. I need you, but you don't need me the same way."

"I like what we have," Charley said.

"But it isn't all you want," Cindy said back. "It's not enough for you."

"What do you mean?" he asked.

"I saw the way you looked at that woman when she sat down with us tonight."

Marie was right, Charley thought.

"And you just want to pick up and go to New York at Christmas and leave me here alone. How do you think that makes me feel? What do I count for? Am I chopped liver?"

"No," Charley said. "I didn't want to leave you. I wanted you to come with me."

"You wanted me to come with you after I said something about it. You were going to go by yourself. You didn't give me a thought."

"I'm sorry if I misunderstood," he said to her. "Julie gave me the impression the two of you were going to Elizabeth's house for Christmas and I didn't want to be in the way or put you in an awkward position. This is Tina's first Christmas alone. I thought I could be of some help. I didn't realize this was going to be a major issue."

"Well, it is," she said. "And so is that woman."

Charley didn't want to fight. He always hated this part of relationships. He hated the stupid fighting. He hated the fighting just for fighting's sake. It was a waste of energy.

"This is dumb," he said. "I'm going to bed."

Charley went upstairs and got ready for bed. Cindy was still downstairs. He got in bed and fell off to sleep. She didn't come up until after midnight.

The next morning she barely spoke to him. He tried to make up, but she wasn't about to. She wanted something from him and he wasn't about to try and find out what it was. Actually, he didn't want to know. He had a good idea what it was and he certainly didn't want to open that door.

"Do you want me to leave?" he asked her that afternoon.

"Yes," she said. "I can see we aren't going anywhere."

Charley nodded his head and packed. He was gone in an hour. He drove away, not knowing exactly what to think. He knew he tried to make something come back with Cindy, but failed.

Like Jerilyn, in the end all she was to him was unfinished business.

While Charley drove back to California, Marie Van Arsdale was looking for her interview. She called Cindy's looking for him. She received a very cold reception and was told that he was gone. No one knew where Charley was until he turned up at his club.

Charley's attorney made Marie Costello manager.   Charley thought she was a good choice, but knew he'd always miss Al. When he went home the house wasn't the same without Alicia. Even when she wasn't there, it was still theirs because she was going to come back eventually. Now he knew she wasn't coming back. This had to be the same feeling Tina had. They both lost.

He phoned her the next day.

"How are you doing, sweetie?" he asked.

"Not good," she said. "I'm so lonely. And now Cindy is mad at me for some reason. I don't even know what I did."

"You didn't do anything," he said. "It's about me, not you."

"Do you still want me to come?" he asked.

"Yes," she said. "I thought Anne Marie was going to come, but now she can't. She's fighting with her boyfriend and it's a big mess. It's Mom all over."

"How are you?" she asked.

"Like you," he said. "All of this has really blown me away. And I hate the holidays. I never had a family and when Alicia was here, we took care of one another and we made it through and enjoyed one another. Now she isn't here and this place kind of sucks."

"You come here and you can enjoy the girls with me. They'll love having their grandpa here. Wait and see. You'll like this Christmas."

"I'll get the next available flight out of here," he said. "I have a car in Washington, D.C. that I have to get eventually. But I'm coming as soon as I can."

"Thank you," she said.

"No," he said back. "Thank you."

He called the airlines and booked a morning flight to JFK. He packed and went to bed, but didn't sleep very well. He was up most of the night and finally gave in and got ready to leave. He called a cab and left for the airport.

He was glad he did leave early. The lines and the security were unbelievable. When they ran his identification, several eyebrows were raised. They asked him to step out of line.

"What now?" he asked.

"Nothing major, sir," the guard said. "The FBI has alerted us to have you contact them, that's all."

It was then that the guard recognized him.

"I'm sorry, sir," the guard said. "I didn't realize who you are."

Charley was taken back at the way the guard came to attention in front of him.

"Thank you," the guard said to him. "It took a lot of courage to stand up to what you did."

At that point Charley was whisked through security, taken to the ticket counter, and personally escorted to his flight. He didn't understand the VIP treatment, but he wasn't about to complain. When he landed at JFK, two FBI agents met him. They got right to the point.

The President wanted to meet Charley Reed. Charley laughed and then he declined.

"I didn't even vote for the guy," Charley said to the two men. "He's been the worst single thing that has ever happened to my stock portfolio. I've lost several hundred thousand because of his idiocy. Why would I want to meet him?"

They accepted what he told them, but they didn't let it end there. He no sooner was at Tina's and hugging the girls when the phone rang. It was Marty Sporror.

Marty Sporror personally prevailed on him.

"Come on, Charley. It's good for the country. It will be good for you, too."

Finally Charley gave in.

"What the hell," he said. "I guess I could do worse things. Just let me have my Christmas first. I need to spend some time here and make a nice Christmas for everyone."

"Okay," Marty said. "I'll call the day after Christmas. I will set this up for that week."

Charley got off the phone shaking his head. "I have to be nuts," he said.

Several days after Christmas Charley Reed went to the White House and met the President of the United States of America. It was then that the President awarded him the Medal of Freedom for saving the life of Senator Young at Los Angeles International Airport. Afterward, the two men chatted privately and Charley changed his mind.

"He's not a bad guy," he told Marty Sporror.

"Neither are you," he said. "Thank you again."

As he did, he handed him a note from Rosemary Povlick who also thanked him.

"You saved my life," she wrote. "I will never forget you. May God bless you and everyone you love. Thank you."

Charley folded the note and shook Marty's hand.

Joanna Reed was sitting at home watching the coverage of her ex-husband being honored by the President. It was Saturday afternoon and she was in the middle of her weekly washing. The cats were laying on the floor near the front door in the sunlight.

Joanna, much against her own will, was caught up in the story about Charley. He had been her husband once and then he chose to leave her. She was not disappointed when he left. In fact, it was more or less a relief. She had been with him nearly seven years. It was never the same after she lost the baby. She thought he blamed her.

It was hard when he first left. She looked back on it and realized it was all only conditioning. She was expected to have a husband and when he left, it made her less than a woman. In those days appearances were everything.

It never made any difference what went on after the doors were closed and the lights went out. She remembered sleeping with most of her clothes on so he could not touch her. She remembered hating him when he did and she remembered hating herself when she wanted him. To her both situations were repugnant. Perhaps the latter was more distasteful to her than anything.

When he died in an automobile accident, she went to the funeral. She saw the casket lowered into the ground. When she returned home, their divorce decree was signed by a judge and waiting in the mailbox. In less than a week it seemed he was out of her life. Then she found out she was pregnant. She knew it was his and she wanted to terminate it. She wanted to, but for some reason she couldn't and she had the baby. As the years went by, she hardly even thought of him. Then it all changed.

He was back.

Charley hadn't tried to contact her. She didn't expect he would.

As she followed stories about him on the television, she knew he had enough trouble and was busy trying to avoid the spotlight.

Marie Van Arsdale ran daily stories about him and the action in Bolivia became a major national scandal. All of Charley's attempts to live a life as someone else ended as a massive failure. Even then Joanna wondered what was in his mind.

Tom was very taken with him. He talked to him on the phone and when he came to Washington to meet the President, Tom went along.

The memory of him was very painful and now it was alive within her once more. There were many questions still unanswered and even though she knew they were better off left so, a part of her still wanted to know. Joanna continued her housework and it was nearly three in the afternoon when the doorbell rang. When she opened the door it was Charley.

"Hello," he said.

"Hello," she answered, surprised by his appearance.

"I figured I owed you an explanation."

"You do?" she asked. "I don't think you owe me anything. You told me everything I needed to know a long time ago. Not only did you tell me, you showed me too."

Charley looked down at the ground. He shuffled his feet and bit his lower lip.

"I understand. I figured I'd try anyway," he said and turned and began to walk away.

Joanna watched his body turn and remembered the all too familiar way he held his shoulders. She looked his body up and down, realizing the years had been good to him. He had managed to stay in decent physical condition. She remembered him as her husband and then suddenly heard herself calling him back.

"Charley!" she called. "Don't leave. I'd like to talk."

He stopped and returned to the front door where she invited him into the house.

"This is a surprise. Please sit down," she said. "I didn't think you'd ever want to see me."

"We're married, aren't we?"

"Actually no," she told him. "The divorce was granted the day before your automobile accident. There wasn't any way for you to know that."

"No, I guess not," he said.

"You never remarried?"

"No," he said.

"Was it because you thought you were married still?"

"No," he said honestly. "I guess maybe there wasn't enough of me left to give to anyone."

"Why?" she asked.

"I guess that's why I'm here," he said.

"What do you mean?"

"I probably want you to know what I've been doing all these years. That is, if you're interested."

Joanna nodded.

"I am," she said. "That's why I called you back."

"Well, I wasn't kidding when I said there probably wasn't enough of me left to give. That wasn't any criticism against you. I'm very serious when I say that. It's just the plain simple truth."

"How's that?" she asked.

"You know I didn't plan that automobile accident bit."

"I know," she said.

"Even before we split up, I was dying. I was drinking, smoking grass, and even doing some coke. I was frustrated with myself and with my life. You were very indifferent toward me and I was very antagonistic toward you. We were husband and wife in name only and I was crazy most of the time."

Joanna nodded her head in agreement.

"You're right," she said. "That's the way I remember it."

"I wanted to die, Joanna. I was going to drive off the bridge into the Pimlico Sound, but I lost my nerve. Life was just a big pain in the ass to me and I wanted to end it."

He paused and looked around the room.

"I knew that," she said. "I didn't know how to help you. You wouldn't let me near you. Then you met Jerilyn."

Charley laughed.

"Jerilyn, that was a good one."

"You were in love with her," Joanna said.

"Yes," he admitted. "I was in love with her. I was in love, but it didn't help me. I was still crazy and the whole thing just made me that much crazier."

He looked at her face and could tell she wanted to know what he had to say.

"I couldn't stay with Jerilyn. I wanted to get back with you, but it seemed every time we got close something would happen."

"It was her," Joanna said. "You couldn't stay away from her."

"Probably so," he said. "I'm sure it seemed that way to you, but I left her, too. I left her so I could try to put things back together. I called and asked if I could come home and you told me no. You were already seeing someone else and had put together a new life without me."

Joanna nodded in agreement.

"I know," he said. "That's when I spent the winter tending bar. I was totally alone then and I really wanted to die."

Joanna sat back in the chair and listened.

"I was guilty. I blamed myself for our marriage not working and I felt like I was a total failure. All around me men my age were going to law school or business school. They were graduating, making the big bucks and I was selling cars or working in a bar."

"You didn't have any patience. I tried to tell you to relax. I wanted you to do different things but you wouldn't listen," she said.

"You're right," Charley agreed. "I never listened to anyone."

"You're different now," Joanna observed.

"Just older and tired," he said.

"Thank you for saving Tommy's life."

"You don't have to thank me," Charley answered her.

"I know," she said. "Thank you anyway. I'm sorry about your friends."

Charley just nodded his head. Joanna could see tears come into his eyes and then watched him turn his head away and wipe them.

"I have changed," Charley said. "I changed the day I realized I was dead."

He paused to wipe his eyes again.

"All of a sudden I was free from everything. I hadn't been doing well with the rejection and I was having problems dealing with my family and even my friends. Everyone was tired of me, including me. I was tired of myself and suddenly, I was dead in an automobile accident."

Charley laughed.

"It's funny. If I hadn't died in the accident, the CIA would have gotten me. By dying, I lived."

Joanna listened as he told her how he made it to Washington, D.C., then Boston, then Buffalo, and how he went to Pittsburgh and saw his own grave.

"I left from Pittsburgh. I dealt some drugs in Buffalo and I had traveling cash. I was in the airport and saw some people I once knew. They walked up to me and asked my name. I told them it was a case of mistaken identity. I even showed them my new driver's license. When the plane took off, I decided I would never come back east again."

"And you didn't'?" she asked.

"I did. I was on a jet when TWA 800 was shot down. It was then that the CIA realized who I really was. That's when it all started again."

"You built a life for yourself out there?" she asked.

"In a manner of speaking," Charley said. "I had a business to occupy my time."

"And Alicia," Joanna reminded him.

"Yes," he said. "I had Alicia. She was more my friend. She listened to my problems and I listened to hers."

"You slept together."

"Of course, we slept together, but I'm not like I used to be," he admitted. "Sex between Alicia and me was kind of an incidental thing. It happened and it was pretty decent, but we weren't like a couple of kids. We were comfortable with one another and we liked each other. That made all the difference in the world. She was a good woman and a good friend. I'm going to miss her."

Joanna watched his mind travel. She knew he was thinking about the others who died.

"I wonder why it all happened now. Sitting here talking to you I feel like none of this could possibly have taken place. It's like I'm in the middle of one of my dreams and I'm waiting to wake up."

"Are you sorry it happened?" she asked.

"Probably," he said.

"Yes," he admitted. "I'm sorry. I wish our marriage could have worked. I wish I would have stayed in college and never gone into the service. I wish I would have done a lot of things, but I didn't and that's that."

Charley sighed and then smiled at her.

"Tom is a fine young man. For some reason, he wants to be around me and know me. I just wanted to see if you and I could be friendly. If it means anything, I'm sorry for everything I've ever done to you."

Joanna smiled.

"And I'm sorry for the way things are in China," she said, repeating a line from an old John Denver song.

"Yes, I am, too," Charley said. "More than anything else, I'm sorry for myself. I'm sorry for everything I've missed and what I haven't been around to give."

Charley rose from the chair.

"Thank you for taking the time to talk to me."

"What are you going to do?" she asked him.

"Go back to the hotel, I guess, and have some dinner."

"I mean beyond that."

"I'm not sure," he said. "The friendly life insurance company has already been in touch with me, demanding to be reimbursed now that I'm alive. I guess I'll sell my business and the house and try to set things straight."

Joanna laughed.

"What's so funny?" he asked.

"You trying to set things straight," she said. "You used to just hit the road."

Charley laughed, too.

"The world has gotten too small. You can't hit the road like you used to be able to do. Bob Walker's gone and I think I'll just let the past rest and maybe it will go away."

"It won't ever go away," she said to him. "It will just become easier for you to live with it."

Charley nodded. He agreed with her.

"Thank you," Charley said. He turned and walked out to his car and drove back to the hotel. He felt at peace with himself. It was a new feeling for him. He enjoyed it.

He walked through the lobby of the Marriott on his way to the elevator when a familiar face appeared.

"Hello," the young woman said to him.

"Hi there," Charley said to Marie Van Arsdale. For once he didn't mind seeing her.

"I've been waiting for you."

"Have you now?" he laughed.

"Have you had dinner?" she asked.

He shook his head. "No."

"I'll buy and you owe me an interview."

Charley laughed. "Okay."

"Where would you like to go?" she asked.

"How about here? They have a nice rooftop dining room and if you pull some strings we can get a table by the window and we can watch the jets landing. They're coming down the river tonight."

"Fine," she said.

They got into the elevator and went up to the dining room. The maitre de recognized both of them and gave them the table they wanted.

"To you," she said toasting him with their first drink.

"Thank you."

"You were impressive with the President today. I was proud of you. The Medal of Freedom, you can put that with your others."

He sipped his drink and smiled.

"I don't have any of them. I gave them all away."

"Are you going to give this one away, too?" she asked.

"I don't know," he said. "Why? Do you want it?"

She laughed.

"You are something else. Where have you been all my life?"

"Is that on or off the record?" he asked.

She just shook her head at that question. Then she smiled at him.

"Off the record," she said. "From here on out everything is off the record. What's the difference? My option is up this week. They aren't renewing it. I'm out of work."

"So what are you going to do?" he asked.

"Probably end up in some place like Harrisburg or Rochester," she laughed.

She sipped her drink.

"What are you going to do with the rest of your life?" she asked.

"I don't know. Maybe I'll play with my grandchildren. Who needs more than that when you are my age?"

"Your age," she said. "Don't try and hand me that. There's nothing wrong with you or your age."

Charley smiled.

"There's that smile that got you in trouble again," she teased.

"What smile?" he asked.

"That one. The one that makes your whole face come alive. The one that makes a woman want to take her clothes off and make love to you."

"You're too much," he said to her.

"What are you going to order?" he asked changing the subject.

They had a nice meal and then they had a few more drinks. She continued to flirt with him, but he didn't take her seriously. Around ten o'clock he thanked her for the meal and the drinks and said goodbye. He took the elevator to his floor, walked down the hall, opened the door and entered the empty room.

Charley walked over to the window and looked out at the city. Below him were trees growing along the bank of the Potomac River. A jet passed overhead as it made its way down the glide path towards Regan National Airport.

He thought of Walker and how they would dine in the restaurant on the top floor and watch the jets pass them in the night, delivering their passengers safely to the nation's capital. Charley watched the jet disappear from sight and missed his friend.

"God damn it!" Walker used to exclaim. "I'm always picking you up or dropping you off at the airport. Why can't you be a normal person and travel by car?"

"That's what you like about me," Charley told him. "I'm not a normal person. Neither are you."

"That's right," Walker said. "We're outlaws. We're Butch Cassidy and the Sundance Kid! We're beautiful motherfuckers and we'll never die old. We'll die young and pretty and all the women will be broken-hearted. In the meantime, we'll drive nice cars, smoke good dope, and drink fine booze. We'll live the good life!"

Charley wondered how much of the good life Bob actually had.

He was dead at fifty-seven. He had been married twice, fathered three the first time and one the second. It seemed he was paying child support from the day Charley first met him. One of the wives was always taking him to court to get more support or back support. He never held a job longer than a year and it seemed he was living his life through movies or other people.

Poor Bob, Charley thought.

He never served during the Vietnam War. He was exempt because of the children. He avoided the danger of the conflict only to die in his own home years later, caught up in something that began when he should have been in the Army.

Charley walked over to the dresser and opened the bottle of Canadian Club. He poured himself three fingers and carried the glass back to the window. Another jet went on by and continued down the river toward the airport.

Raising his glass Charley toasted his friend.

"To you, Bob Walker. I'm going to miss you. I'm going to miss you an awful lot. Goodbye, Sundance."

Charley drank the whiskey in one gulp and walked back to pour more. As he did the phone rang. It was Tina.

"We saw you on television," she said.

"The girls were really excited. Kathy was running around the house saying her grandpa was on television with Elmo. Kimberly was annoyed with her and said the other man wasn't Elmo. He was the President. It was hilarious. I wish you could have seen them."

Charley laughed.

"What are you doing New Years Eve?" she asked.

"Nothing," he said. "I don't even know where I'll be."

"Come here," she said. "I'm so lonely and I miss having you around. I could use the company."

"Okay," he said.

When he hung up the phone he poured the glass of whiskey. He walked back to the window. He looked out into the night and the city he used to call the capital of the world. Once more he raised his glass.

"Bob Walker, my friend. Until we meet again."

Charley went to New York for New Years. He arrived late Sunday morning in time to watch football. The Steelers were on and he began tutoring his granddaughters about the National Football League and even taught them a few new words when the officials blew an obvious call.

The next day he went out and bought some lobster tails and the makings for a Caesar salad. He bought a bottle of non-alcoholic sparkling wine for Tina and a bottle of Canadian Club for himself. After they put the girls to bed, he made them dinner. Then they sat together on the couch and watched the New Year come in. Then the phone began to ring.

First it was Anne Marie. Tina put Charley on the phone and he scolded her for not being with them. Then Jerilyn called and sounded irritated when she realized he was there. Finally, Julie called.

"I miss you," she said.

"How's your mother?" he asked.

"Angry," she told him.

"Oh, well," he answered. "I wish I could make her happy but it doesn't look like I'm going to be able to do that."

"You could if you wanted," she said to him. "You know how she feels about you."

"Do I?" he asked.

"I know I said the past is the past, but at the same time the past is part of me. I tried to say it wasn't, but there were enough people out there reminding me it was. Your mother is one of them.

"I guess it would be nice to believe I could go back and get what I lost, but I know I can't. When your mother chose to marry your father, she ended something and no matter how we might try, once something is over, we can never get it back.

"I'm good for her now because I'm the fantasy she lived when she was unhappy with her decisions. And at the same time, she is good for me because I am getting back what I imagine I lost.

"But it's all only an illusion. In the end it wouldn't work and there is no reason to fight the inevitable.

"All I can say is I'm sorry she's angry, but she should stop thinking about herself and start thinking about someone else for once in her life. If she would have done that way back when, maybe things would have turned out differently."

"Does this mean I'll never see you again?"

"No honey," he answered you. "Your brother was my son. Nothing will ever change that. And you are the aunt to his children who are also my grandchildren. We have them and we have one another. I don't want to be enemies with anyone. I just can't change the past and make it work for the future.

"I don't know what is in my future."

When the phone calls ended, Tina said she was going to bed. Charley kissed her good night and sat up with another drink.

He sat there with the television coverage of the New Year across the country and he wondered what would become of Tina and the girls. He wondered what would become of all the families who had just gone through their first holiday season without husbands and wives, sons and daughters, friends and neighbors. He stood up and walked to the window.

"What evil men live in this world," he said aloud. "What truly evil men. Why?"

It was a question he couldn't answer.

He looked in on his granddaughters. Kathy had kicked off her covers so he covered her up. She opened her eyes and he kissed her. Then he went to bed.

He didn't dream that night. Instead he slept straight through until the girls came bounding in and jumped in bed with him around eight.

As he tickled and wrestled with them, he understood how truly lucky he was. It was the first day of the New Year and he had a chance most men never have. He was content in the fact because he knew that.

Several months later Charley was sitting in the bar of the Holiday Inn South in Rochester, New York. He was talking to a man from Warren, Ohio who was a steel salesman and the bartender, a woman named Amy. Amy recognized him from the television coverage and when he testified before the Senate in March.

Charley's cell phone rang.

"Hello?" he said as he answered the phone.

"Hi!" the woman's voice said. "What are you doing?"

"Having a drink," he said. "How are you?"

"Have another," she told him. "I'm fine now."

"It's a boy! It's a beautiful little boy and I named him Charles, after his father and his grandfather," Tina said.

"When is his grandfather coming to see him?" she asked.

"Soon, honey," he said. "How about his grandmother? Is she coming to see him, too?"

"I would guess so. You're the first one I called. I'll let you know."

"Thanks," he said. He ended the call and took a sip of his drink.

"Who was that?" a woman asked as she walked up to his chair.

Charley turned in his chair.

"You woke up."

"Yes," she said. "Who was that?"

"Tina," he answered. "She had a boy and named him Charles."

"Another Charley," she said. "Do you think the world is ready?"

"I don't know," he answered. "What do you think?"

Marie Van Arsdale kissed him on the cheek.

"Another Charley is fine, as long as I can have mine."

ABOUT THE AUTHOR

Harold Thomas Beck is the author of *Ripe for the Picking, The story of the Kathy Wilson Murder Case*; *Cornplanter Chronicles, A Tale of the Legendary Seneca Chieftan*; and now, *The First Terrorist Act*.

He was born in Pittsburgh, Pennsylvania in 1946. He writes a daily on line column for the *Mountain Laurel Review* at:

http://www.mlrmag.com.

Mr. Beck is a frequent guest on radio and television and appears in many public speaking roles. He is known for his commentaries on politics and life in general.